ROWAN

Book 1 of the Sin & Salvation Series

Jayne Anderson

RLJ & Associates, LLC

Published by RLJ & Associates, LLC

Pittsburgh, Pennsylvania

ISBNs:

Paperpack: 979-8-9922744-0-0

Hardcover: 979-8-9922744-1-7

E-book: 979-8-9922744-2-4

Edited by Rebecca L. Jayne

First Edition: February 2025

Printed in the United States of America.

For my daughter—my greatest adventure, my brightest light, and the reason I dare to dream bigger.

This journey is ours.

J.A.

Contents

The Fallen's

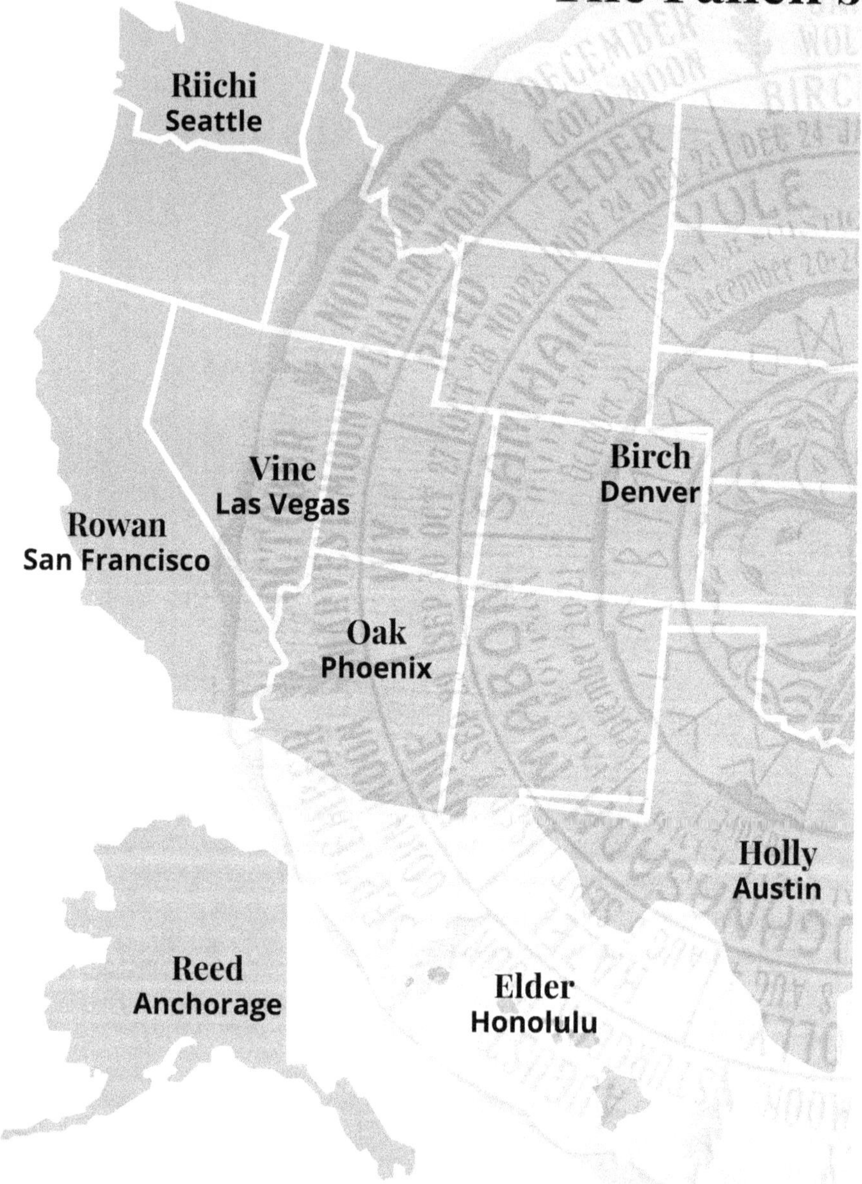

Riichi
Seattle
Vine
Las Vegas
Rowan
San Francisco
Birch
Denver
Oak
Phoenix
Holly
Austin
Reed
Anchorage
Elder
Honolulu

Branches

From their humble origins to their present-day roles as guardians, the Fallen have established themselves across the United States. This map showcases where the Fallen now reside, each location serving as a cornerstone for their mission to protect humanity and preserve hope, much like the branches of a tree extending toward the sky.

Who Are the Fallen?

They are the men and women tucked into the pages of this series.

Dear Reader,

The Fallen are not born as heroes. They are ordinary people from different times and places, plucked from extraordinary circumstances, each carrying the weight of their final moments. *Born under the light of a full moon,* they live lives marked by *kindness, strength, and virtue*—until a single act of *sin* in their last breath seals their fate.

Caught between life and death, they are offered a choice: to let go and embrace the unknown or to *rise again with purpose.* Those who choose to rise are reborn as a Fallen, *tied to a Celtic tree* that mirrors their essence. The tree becomes part of who they are, grounding them in the natural world while reflecting their truest selves.

At their turning, each Fallen meets their *potential soulmate.* Though this meeting is fleeting and fades from memory, *the bond is set.* A connection as powerful as it is elusive, it ties them to the supernatural world and waits patiently for the right moment to bloom. Only when the Fallen are ready—when they *face their deepest fears* and *overcome the shadow of their sin*—does the bond awaken, unlocking *a power that reshapes their destiny.*

The Fallen live to *fight for humanity,* standing as a barrier between darkness and the fragile light of hope. They are guardians, protecting against evils that seek to corrupt and destroy, even as they carry the shadows of their own sins. United by a shared purpose, they prove that even those who fall can rise again, stronger than before.

So, get ready to join them on their journey from *sin to salvation.*

Turn the page, and let the story begin.

Yours truly,
Jayne Anderson

ounty Donegal, Ireland, 1847

C Aidan MacKane stood in a barren field, his gaze sweeping over the desolate countryside. The land was dotted with low, thatched cottages, their silence as heavy as the blight that had ravaged it. No voices called out, no movement stirred—only an oppressive stillness remained. To the west, storm clouds loomed, darkening the horizon and quickening his pulse. The half-tilled soil beneath his boots reminded him how little time he had before the rain came, but he was determined to finish the field. The churning sky seemed almost mocking, a reflection of the weight pressing on his spirit.

County Donegal had been his entire world, filled with the family he cherished. His father, Kane, had shaped him into a man of resilience and duty, while his mother, Shaylee, taught him the strength found in love and tenderness. His fiery brother, Broderick, had always pushed to prove himself, though Aidan knew his worth even when Brody couldn't see it. Gillian, his younger sister, had been the light of their family, adored by all, especially him. And then there was Davina, his wife of five years, carrying their first child—his anchor in an unraveling world. Together, they had been everything to him.

Aidan paused, gripping his shovel as he glanced toward the gathering storm. The air was thick with the scent of rain, but beneath it lay something foul, something unnatural. The acrid stench of death clung to the land, a cruel reminder of what the blight had stolen. He didn't need to see the town to picture the hollowed faces and lifeless bodies, mouths stuffed with grass in a futile attempt to stave off hunger.

The famine had already claimed his family—his parents, his siblings—and now it threatened Davina and their unborn child. He had fought against it, worked himself to the bone, but it was never enough. The land, once vibrant and full of promise, had withered into a graveyard. And Aidan knew, deep in his heart, that no amount of resolve would save what was left.

"Aidan! She's asking for you! Come quickly!" Moira's urgent cry carried up the hill, sharp against the oppressive silence. Aidan's chest tightened at the sound. God bless her—he'd found her half-dead on the roadside weeks ago and brought her home. She had been his mother's dearest friend, and now, with no family left of her own, she'd taken refuge with them. Moira had been tending to Davina while Aidan labored in the fields, clinging to the futile hope of preparing for next year's crops.

Dropping his tools, he sprinted down the muddy slope, his legs trembling under the strain. The earth seemed heavier with every step, as though it, too, bore the weight crushing his heart. When he reached the house, Moira met his gaze. She didn't need to speak; her eyes told him everything. The time had come.

Aidan stepped into the small outshot where Davina lay. Her pale figure rested on a worn feather tick, the rise and fall of her chest shallow and labored. Sweat glistened on her skin, and dark, angry sores streaked her arms the cruel signature of the blight. He grabbed a stool and sat beside her, the air thick and stifling. Without thinking, he smashed his fist through the windowpane. Shards scattered, and fresh air swept in, carrying the scent of rain and earth. Blood trickled from his knuckles, but he barely noticed.

"Aidan," Davina murmured, her tone thin and brittle.

"I'm here, love," he said, leaning closer, his throat dry. "I'm right here." He brushed his hand down her fevered cheek, and she leaned into his touch, her skin burning against his.

"It's so hot…" she whispered, her voice faltering. "Like the fires of hell."

He dipped a cloth into the cool water at his feet and pressed it gently to her forehead. "No, love. You're here, with me. You're safe."

Her lips trembled as she whispered, "The baby. He barely moves."

Aidan's breath hitched, but he forced himself to stay steady. "He's strong," he said softly, though his tone betrayed him. "Like his mother."

Davina's green eyes fluttered open, their light undimmed despite the fever. She smiled faintly. "No," she murmured. "Strong like his father."

"Strong like us both," he replied, his voice cracking as he held her trembling hand in his.

She reached up, her fingers threading weakly through his hair. "Aidan, I love you."

"And I you, my heart and soul," he said, tears streaking his face as he leaned closer. Her hand brushed his cheek, catching his tears, though her own glimmered like emeralds in the dim light.

She drew a shallow breath, her gaze searching his. "Remember me," she whispered. "Aidan…I'm sorry." Her words faded with her final exhale, her hand slipping to her chest. Silence enveloped the room. In one cruel instant, she—and their child—were gone.

Aidan froze, staring at her lifeless body, the seconds stretching into an eternity. Slowly, he bent to press his lips to hers, now cold and still. His hand rested gently on her belly, a futile gesture for the life that would never come. "I will always remember you, my love," he whispered, his speech wavering. The words clung to the air, fragile and raw, as if anything louder might shatter her memory entirely.

Letting go of her hand, Aidan rose unsteadily. The room tilted, a tempest of grief and exhaustion threatening to overwhelm him. He gripped the edge of the stool, forcing himself upright as the dizziness gave way to a hollow, suffocating numbness. Stumbling onto the stoop, he felt like a shadow of himself—cold, empty, a ghost moving through the motions of life.

Moira stood nearby, her hands clasped tightly in prayer, tears streaking her face. When her anguished gaze met his, Aidan gave a faint nod, the confirmation she dreaded. She turned without a word, disappearing into the house. Aidan stayed frozen for a moment, the weight of the evening pressing down as the sky darkened above him.

With heavy steps, he climbed the hill back to the field where his shovel lay. The spade felt unfamiliar in his hands, yet he began to dig, the scrape of metal against soil breaking the silence. The work was meaningless, but he could think of nothing else to do. Thunder rumbled faintly in the distance, and the first drops of rain spattered the earth. Still, Aidan did not stop. He could not stop.

Only when his body betrayed him, when the strength to lift the spade deserted him, did he pause. He stood motionless, staring at the freshly turned soil that seemed to mock his effort. Time slipped into nothingness, the world fading into a void. Then, gently, a hand rested on his shoulder—Moira's. The touch was warm, grounding, and Aidan blinked, dragging himself back to awareness.

The stars had emerged, faint and distant pinpricks against the black sky. The rain had come and gone, unnoticed, leaving the earth damp beneath his boots. The night was quiet, save for the whisper of the wind.

"Aidan, please, you must come inside," Moira urged softly, her plea carrying both tenderness and urgency. She draped a linen blanket over his shoulders, its light weight a fragile barrier against the chill settling into his bones.

"I cannot," he said, his tone frayed with emotion. Grief anchored him, as though the very land beneath his feet refused to let him go. Turning away from her, he began walking up the hill again, compelled by something he couldn't name.

"Where are you going?" she called, her question fractured as it reached him.

"I don't know," he replied, heavy with despair. The silence that followed swallowed them both.

He wandered aimlessly through the dark, clutching the blanket tighter around his shoulders. At last, he stopped beneath the ancient rowan tree, its branches stretching skyward like silent witnesses to his sorrow. This place had been sacred to him and Davina—a refuge where they had laughed, kissed, and dreamed during their courtship. The memories of their younger selves, untainted by hardship, pressed against him now like a distant echo of a life that no longer existed.

Aidan approached the tree, his trembling fingers tracing the faded carving etched into its bark: "D.D. + A.M." enclosed in a heart. Once a symbol of fierce, defiant love, it now stood as a ghostly reminder of all he had lost.

The strength to stand gave out, and Aidan collapsed to his knees. Tilting his head back to the expanse of stars above, he let out a raw, guttural cry—a sound torn from the deepest parts of him. It pierced the still night like the wail of a banshee, reverberating through the emptiness. His grief consumed him, too vast to contain, and he cried until his voice broke, his anguish unraveling in the void.

Everything he had cherished was gone. Davina, their unborn child, his parents and siblings, and the life they had dreamed of together—all claimed by the merciless grip of famine and blight. He had fought to protect them, but it hadn't been enough. He had failed them.

From his pocket, he pulled a knife, the same blade he had once used to carve their dreams into the tree before him. The bitter irony of it struck him—a tool of love and new beginnings, now poised to mark his end. His movements were mechanical as he lifted the blade and drove it into his side.

The pain erupted, sharp and searing, but it was nothing compared to the torment in his heart. The knife slipped from his hand, clattering to the ground as he slumped against the tree's rough trunk. His breaths came shallow and ragged, each one a struggle. Warm blood seeped through his fingers, pooling beneath him—a visceral reminder of the depths of his despair.

Aidan closed his eyes, surrendering to the darkness that crept closer with every labored breath. He waited for release, for the end to come—but it didn't.

Through the haze of pain and fading consciousness, a light pulsed in the distance. At first, he thought it was a hallucination, faint and unsteady. But it grew brighter, steadier, until it cast a gentle glow over the tree and the blood-soaked soil. Within the light, a figure emerged—a woman with flowing blonde hair that shimmered like spun gold, her white gown radiating a brilliance that pushed back the shadows around her. She stood with an otherworldly grace, her presence serene though commanding.

Aidan's breath caught. An angel, surely, sent to deliver him from this shattered world.

"Aidan," she said, her call a melody carried on the wind. Despite the agony tearing through his body, he was transfixed, drawn to the warmth that radiated from her—a light that felt like it could heal the deepest wounds.

But her next statement struck him like a blow. "It is not your time to leave this place."

His brow furrowed, and the fragile hope that had stirred in his chest disappeared. "I do not have the will to go on," he rasped, his speech breaking with grief. "I've lost everything."

"You may lack the will," she replied. Her speech was soothing, carrying a weight that seemed to settle deep in his soul. "But you have the strength. You must go on. You are needed."

"By whom?" he rasped, his anguish spilling out. "There is no one left."

"By Moira," she said gently, her tone unwavering. "By the people of this town, by everyone... by us." She extended her hand, and from the radiant glow behind her, another figure emerged—a younger woman, hesitant as she stepped forward to take Eileen's outstretched hand.

The newcomer was strikingly different. Her dark brown hair framed a face with deep, thoughtful eyes that held a mix of wonder and uncertainty. Unlike the brilliance of Eileen, this woman's presence was quieter, softer. Her clothing clung in a way unfamiliar to him, revealing curves he wasn't accustomed to seeing so plainly, but there was an undeniable light about her—subtle yet potent, radiating from within despite the veil of hesitation that shrouded her.

Aidan turned his weary gaze back to Eileen. "Who are you?" he asked, his voice trembling. "An angel?"

"Not quite," she replied with a kind but enigmatic smile. "My name is Eileen, and this is my daughter." She gestured to the younger woman beside her. "You are needed—by us and by many others. You hold a key to saving lives and fighting the evil that plagues this earth—the same evil that caused the famine."

Aidan let out a bitter, hollow laugh, the sound jagged and raw. "The English caused this famine," he replied with despair and anger.

"No," Eileen said, shaking her head slowly. The golden light surrounding her flickered, stirred by some unseen force. "The evil I speak of is far older than any Englishman. It is ancient, insidious, and relentless. You must help in the war against it—help good prevail over the darkness that haunts us all."

"I cannot," Aidan whispered, his words faint, almost lost to the night. "You are wrong. I have nothing left. I am just a broken man, dying by his own hand, too weak even to wipe the sweat from his brow. How could I help you fight any battle?"

Eileen knelt beside him, her hands warm and steady as they cupped his face. She wiped away the sweat he spoke of with a quiet strength, her touch carrying the kind of calm that felt as though it came from a place beyond mortal understanding. Her gaze held his, unwavering, her expression tender yet resolute. "Yet you must, Aidan. The future depends on you. My daughter will depend on you."

She turned slightly, gesturing with a graceful nod. "Come closer," she urged the younger woman.

The daughter knelt beside him, her presence hesitant and sincere. Aidan turned his head, and his breath caught. Her beauty, so striking, brought a sharp memory of Davina to the forefront of his mind, slicing through him like a blade. Tears welled in his eyes, spilling down his cheeks and into Eileen's steady hands.

"I'm sorry," he whispered, his voice breaking under the weight of his sorrow. "I cannot."

"Please, Aidan," the daughter urged, her tone soft, enchanting, yet tinged with uncertainty. "I don't fully understand all that my mother speaks of, but I trust her. You must trust her, too."

Her deep eyes searched his, and though Aidan couldn't see it, she caught the faint shadow of worry buried beneath her mother's calm exterior. Eileen tried to mask it, but it lingered—a silent, urgent plea woven into her composed expression.

Aidan met the daughter's imploring gaze, her quiet desperation stirring something buried deep within him. Her innocence, tempered by a quiet strength, tugged at the frayed edges of his heart. His hand twitched for a fleeting moment, tempted to reach out and feel the warmth of her skin. But the sharp sting of guilt pierced him, and he recoiled from the impulse.

"How could I help you?" he rasped doubtfully. "You're angels. Surely you're stronger than I."

"No," Eileen replied steadily, though her words carried the weight of absolute truth. "She is still human. You will know her."

His brow furrowed, her words slipping through his grasp. "This is a dream," he murmured, his strength waning as the warmth of his blood seeped into the damp earth. His eyes fluttered shut, his breaths shallow and unsteady.

Firm hands gripped his shoulders, shaking him with surprising force, refusing to let him slip into the void.

"No," Eileen's voice sharpened, her words ringing with urgency. "This is no dream, Aidan—not yours. You are tied to the rowan now—its clarity, its strength, its purpose. You must carry its spirit into the battles to come."

His eyes opened once more, his gaze shifting between Eileen and her daughter. Eileen's golden eyes shimmered with barely restrained desperation, while the younger woman's expression held an uneasy mix of curiosity and fear. Aidan's resolve faltered under their combined stares, but he could not turn away from a woman in need—a lesson his father had etched deeply into him. He released a long, shuddering sigh. "Yes," he whispered.

"Thank you," the daughter breathed, her relief unmistakable. She reached out and placed her hand gently on his shoulder, her touch warm and sincere. "I believe in you."

The moment her hand met his skin, a surge of energy tore through him. White-hot power crackled like lightning in his veins, igniting every nerve. His body seized in shock, his breath stolen by the intensity. A cry of raw agony ripped from his throat, echoing into the night like a storm unleashed. Then, just as suddenly as it began, the energy subsided. Darkness closed in, swallowing him whole. Aidan knew no more.

Chapter One
Awakening Dawn

San Francisco, Present Day

Aislinn jolted awake, sitting up abruptly. Her chest tightened as her heartbeat thundered in her ears, her breathing uneven. *Just a dream,* she reassured herself, forcing deep breaths to slow her pulse. The details lingered faintly, slipping further from her grasp with every passing second, like sand sifting through her fingers. The sharp trill of her alarm jolted her again, its cheery rhythm clashing against the weight of her thoughts. She groaned, reaching over to silence it with a firm slap, before letting her hand fall heavily onto the mattress.

Briefly, she sat there, caught between the dream and the reality of her modest studio apartment. The familiar creak of the old floorboards beneath the bed, the faint whir of traffic outside the window, and the soft hum of her mini-fridge—all markers of normalcy—eased her back into the present. She rubbed her face, her fingertips pressing against her temples as though trying to massage away the remnants of the unsettling imagery.

Swinging her legs over the side of the bed, she planted her bare feet on the cool wooden floor, rooting herself further. Finally, she pushed herself upright, padding to the dresser. She rifled through the drawers, pulling out a clean pair of jeans and a soft gray sweater, before heading toward the bathroom.

At the sink, she splashed cold water on her face, relishing the sharpness that woke her senses. The chill stung her skin, but it also banished some of the fog that clung to her memory. She caught her reflection in the mirror, the edges already misting from the warmth creeping into the small space. Her features looked tired—shadows beneath her gaze gave her a hollowed, weary appearance. *That dream—what was it?* The question gnawed at her, the fragments of it pulling at the edges of her thoughts.

A man was there, she recalled, his piercing blue stare vivid in her memory, filled with sorrow so deep it made her chest ache. *And my mother...* Her face had appeared too, but the details were elusive, like whispers drowned out by the clamor of waking. No matter how hard she tried to grasp at the images, they dissolved, leaving her with only a gnawing unease.

She sighed and turned toward the shower, letting the hot water run until steam filled the room. Stepping under the stream, she closed her eyes, allowing the warmth to envelop her. The water cascaded down her back and shoulders, washing away the remnants of sleep and the frustration clinging to her. *It's just a dream,* she told herself, a mantra she repeated in an effort to convince herself. *Don't let it mess up your day.* But even as she tried to shake it off, the man's sorrowful gaze lingered, a phantom she couldn't quite dispel.

The sharp trill of her phone pierced through the haze, pulling her out of her thoughts. Hastily shutting off the water, she grabbed a towel and wrapped it around herself. Her damp feet squeaked slightly against the floor as she hurried toward the sound, slipping just enough to force her to catch her balance. *What now?* she thought, frustration simmering as she snatched up the device.

"Hello?" she panted into the phone, inhaling raggedly.

"Whoa, am I interrupting something?" came a light, teasing laugh from the other end. It was Johnny, her younger brother, his tone as effortlessly playful as ever.

"No, you moron," she laughed back, rolling her eyes despite herself. "I was in the shower."

"Pity, that," Johnny replied, the grin clear in his tone. "Someone should be getting some."

"Ha, ha," she mocked, though her words were softened by affection. Johnny had always been the joker, using humor to get away with just about anything. She could picture him now: the strong lines of his youthful face framed by a neat fade in his short-cropped brown hair, his dark gaze gleaming with mischief. His tattoos, a mix of bold designs spiraling along his forearms, made him look older than his years, though he still carried an air of cocky, younger-brother charm. Even over the phone, she could feel his grin, the kind that made him equally endearing and infuriating.

"So, how are you? I miss you," she said, her tone softening.

"I miss you, too," he sighed, his usual humor dimming briefly. "And I'm fine. Don't worry."

"Well, somebody has to," she said, her voice dipping. "You don't seem to care about your own well-being. You never should have joined the military."

"Now don't start with that," he groaned, his tone playfully exasperated. "I didn't call to hear a sermon. I just wanted to check in. Besides, someone's gotta protect you and keep you safe, right?"

"And who's going to protect you?" Aislinn asked, her concern slipping back into her voice.

"I've got my boy, Danny, here. He's got my six—not that I need any protection," Johnny joked, his words light but edged with confidence. Aislinn could almost see the grin tugging at the corner of his mouth, the one that always made it hard to tell if he was serious or just trying to rile her up.

"And who's protecting Danny from you?" she shot back, the corners of her lips lifting despite the familiar worry twisting in her chest.

Johnny's laugh was warm and unrestrained, the kind that always managed to lighten the mood. "Now that's the real question, isn't it? But listen, I gotta go. We're heading out soon."

The weight she knew all too well settled over her, pressing into her ribcage like it always did before these calls ended. Johnny only called right before a mission—his version of a goodbye—and Aislinn had learned over time that it would be months before she heard from him again. She forced her voice to stay steady, though her throat felt tight. "Alright, just...be careful," she said softly, the words uttered under her breath.

"Don't worry, big little sis. I always am. Love you."

A small smile tugged at Aislinn's lips, the familiar phrase coaxing a bitter-sweet warmth to her chest. Johnny might have been younger, but he towered over her by nearly a foot, and the "big little sis" joke had stuck from the moment he'd first said it, grinning down at her like a cocky giant. "Love you, too, little big bro."

She paused for a heartbeat after the click on the other end of the line, holding the phone tightly as if it could keep his voice close just a little longer. The faint ache in her chest grew, filling the silence where his humor had been—a silence that always felt heavier after he left.

Aislinn glanced at the clock. Past eight-thirty already. Less than half an hour to open the shop. With a resigned sigh, she headed back to the bathroom to finish getting ready, her footsteps dragging slightly.

Standing in front of the foggy mirror, she grabbed a comb and worked it through her long, dark brown hair with practiced efficiency. She'd long since given up trying to tame it—it seemed to exist in a perpetual state of rebellion, always either frizzy or limp, with no middle ground. Gathering the stubborn strands into a loose bun, she secured it with a hair tie and gave herself a brief once-over. *Why don't I just cut it already?* she wondered, though she knew the answer. Maybe there was something about the challenge, even if it was a losing battle.

Her gaze lingered in the mirror a minute longer, her deep brown eyes meeting her reflection. They looked tired, flat. *Plain,* she thought, the word slipping through her mind like an unwanted visitor. She shook her head and reached for her jeans and favorite baby-doll top, a soft brown fabric accented with a little yellow ribbon stitched near the hem. It was casual but comforting, like armor that didn't try too hard. A quick swipe of blush added a hint of color to her cheeks—just enough to mask the morning's pallor—and she stepped back. *Good enough.*

Descending the stairs into the storeroom of her small coffee shop on Haight Street, Aislinn was greeted by the scent of freshly brewed coffee and buttery pastries. The warm, familiar aroma wrapped around her like a hug, easing the tightness in her chest. For the first time that morning, a genuine smile crept onto her lips. This place, her little corner of the world, always managed to make things feel just a bit brighter.

Takoda and Rain were already there, bustling around behind the counter with the ease of a well-practiced team. Takoda moved with steady precision, her bronzed skin catching the soft morning light as she adjusted the espresso machine. Her wavy brown hair, tousled and full of volume, framed her striking features, and her sharp, almond-shaped gaze carried a mix of focus and warmth. Takoda had always carried an air of quiet strength, a confidence that made her presence calming yet commanding at the same time.

Rain, on the other hand, was a burst of energy by comparison. Her fiery red curls spilled over her shoulders, vibrant and untamed, matching her personality perfectly. She hummed softly to herself as she straightened the pastry display, her delicate features set in an expression of cheerful determination. Rain's dark green gaze sparkled with curiosity, and there was an almost magnetic quality to her, a kind of radiance that made her impossible to ignore.

As Aislinn stepped fully into the shop, the familiar rhythm of her little world wrapped around her, centering her. The last remnants of her dream faded into the background. *This is real. And for now, it's enough.*

"Good morning, sleepyhead," Takoda greeted with a teasing grin, glancing up from her work. "Was wondering when you'd show up. Late night?"

"You wish," Aislinn replied with a smirk, grabbing an apron from the hook near the counter. "I was on the phone with my brother."

"Oh, how is he?" Rain asked, her voice bright with curiosity as she leaned on the counter, her red curls bouncing slightly. Rain hadn't met Johnny in person, but after seeing his photo, she'd fallen head over heels in one of her signature crushes. Rain was like that—falling for someone new every few weeks with a devotion that could rival an epic ballad.

Aislinn rolled her eyes, though her smirk softened. "He's fine. Same as always. Are we ready to open?"

"Yep," they both chimed in unison, their voices blending in perfect sync.

With a nod, Aislinn walked to the front of the store. The morning light spilled in as she flipped the sign to "Yes, We're Open" and unlocked the door. The motion was automatic, a small ritual she'd performed countless times before. No sooner had she turned around than the familiar ring of the bell echoed through the shop. Their first customer of the day had arrived—Howard, a man in his late sixties with kind eyes and a weathered face that hinted at a life of purpose. He helped run a soup kitchen near Fisherman's Wharf, and his visits had become a morning tradition.

"Hey, Howie, you're here early today. The usual?" Aislinn asked, her tone warm as she leaned on the counter.

"Yes, thanks," he replied, his voice raspy from years of smoking unfiltered cigarettes. His weathered face creased into a small smile. "Got a lot of errands today, but I wanted to get the boys their breakfast first."

By "the boys," he meant the homeless veterans who slept near the pier and came to the soup kitchen regularly.

"Coming right up!" Takoda called from the kitchen, her voice carrying easily over the clink of pans.

"I'll grab the coffee," Rain added, already gliding toward the counter with her usual grace, her red curls bouncing with each step.

As Aislinn rang up the order, Takoda appeared from the back carrying a large brown paper bag filled with baked goods, her gaze warm with pride. Rain followed close behind, handing over a thermos of fresh coffee, the aroma rich and comforting.

"I threw in a little something extra for you and the boys," Takoda said, her lips curving into a smile. "I'm trying out a new brownie recipe, so let me know what you think."

"Thanks, child," Howard said, his gruff voice softening as he took the offerings. "I'll be sure to tell you how the boys like them. You ladies have a good day now."

The three women watched him shuffle out the door, the bag of food balanced carefully in one hand and the thermos tucked under his arm.

"He's such a kind soul," Rain said with a dreamy sigh, resting her elbow on the counter. "The world is blessed to have people like him."

"Yeah," Aislinn and Takoda agreed in unison, their tones warm with fondness.

The rest of the day flew by in a flurry of activity, the shop bustling with a steady stream of customers. Between filling orders, chatting with regulars, and sneaking bites of leftover pastries, the hours slipped past unnoticed. It wasn't until after seven that the rush finally slowed, leaving the shop calm as the day wound down.

Aislinn took a seat behind the counter, flipping through the day's sales, her mind already settling into the quiet rhythm of the evening. Across the shop,

Takoda moved efficiently through the kitchen, wiping down countertops and rearranging supplies, while Rain hummed a lilting tune under her breath as she cleaned tables.

Aislinn glanced up from her notebook and smiled softly, taking in the sight of her friends. Takoda's steady presence and quiet strength balanced perfectly against Rain's boundless energy and charm. These women had become her closest friends—her family, really. *I'm not sure what I'd do without them.*

It had been just over six months since Aislinn had arrived in San Francisco, wide-eyed and hopeful. She'd sold her car, packed her modest belongings, and followed her boyfriend of two years across the country, convinced he was "the one." How wrong she had been.

The instant she arrived at his apartment, her dreams came crashing down. A woman answered the door—a woman wearing nothing but an oversized shirt that Aislinn recognized as his. And there he was, standing behind her, looking as if she were the one intruding. The nerve of him to look shocked, even guilty, as though he hadn't orchestrated this betrayal. But it was the casual way he draped his arm around the woman's shoulders that drove the final nail into the coffin. It wasn't an accident. It wasn't a misunderstanding. It was exactly what it looked like.

Humiliated and heartbroken, Aislinn ran from his door, choking back sobs until she collapsed into the backseat of a cab. She didn't even notice where the driver was taking her. The nearest motel would do. That night, she cried herself to sleep in a room that smelled faintly of bleach and regret, the weight of her choices crushing her chest. She had never felt so utterly alone. If it hadn't been for the dream she had that night, she might have booked the first flight back to Pittsburgh the next morning, pride be damned.

In her dream, her mom had visited her, just as she had so many times before. Her presence was warm, comforting, like a patch of sunlight breaking through storm clouds. They didn't speak—her mother rarely did in these dreams—but the comfort she brought was enough.

When Aislinn woke, her pillow still damp with tears, she felt different. A glimmer of resolve had taken root, and with it came a spark of purpose. She took a leap of faith that morning, trading her heartbreak for determination.

Her life's savings became a down payment on a little building in Haight-Ashbury. Within a month, she had opened her coffee shop—a place that felt as much a sanctuary for her as it did for her customers.

Takoda and Rain had walked in together during her first round of interviews, their carefree energy filling the tiny space. Takoda's steady, no-nonsense demeanor balanced perfectly with Rain's effervescent charm, and their dynamic won Aislinn over immediately. Hiring them had been the best decision she'd made since arriving in San Francisco. They weren't just employees; they had become her friends, her anchors in a city that had once felt so foreign.

Aislinn glanced up from the register as the clock inched closer to eight—closing time. The evening lull had settled over the shop, and she could hear the faint echo of the tune Rain had been humming earlier. Takoda and Rain emerged from the back room, now dressed in outfits that screamed they were ready for a night out. Takoda had opted for sleek black jeans and a leather jacket, her dark hair framing her face in loose waves. Rain, as always, went bold—her fiery red curls were styled to perfection, and her emerald-green dress shimmered every time she moved.

Even on a Friday, the shop always closed at eight. Apparently, coffee lost its appeal once the sun went down.

"So, Ash," Takoda began, leaning casually against the counter. "We're heading over to that Irish pub, Donnelly's, tonight. You want to come with?"

Aislinn quickly looked up as she finished counting the cash in the till. "You know I don't go out, guys," she replied, her tone light but firm. "Besides, I've got things to do tonight."

Rain smirked, her blue eyes glinting with mischief. "We-inz girls," she teased, her attempt at mimicking Aislinn's Pittsburgh accent making them both laugh. "What could you possibly have to do that's more important than hanging out with us?"

Aislinn opened her mouth, scrambling for an excuse, but Rain knew her too well. The truth was, she rarely had anything pressing to do after work—just her quiet apartment and maybe a Netflix binge.

I knew it, Takoda's triumphant grin seemed to say, her arms crossing as she tilted her head knowingly. "Another excuse, just like always."

"Come on," Rain whined, stepping closer and resting her chin dramatically on Aislinn's shoulder. "It'll be fun, and you haven't been out with us in ages. Ash, you need some excitement in your life."

"Yeah," Takoda added, her tone more coaxing than teasing this time. "We promise—one drink and you can head home if you want."

"One alcoholic drink," Rain interjected with a pointed look, knowing Aislinn's tendency to order a diet soda whenever they managed to drag her out.

Aislinn sighed, looking between her two friends. Their eagerness was infectious, but so was her hesitation. *Nights out aren't my thing. They never have been.* Still, their hopeful faces made her feel a pang of guilt.

Rain and Takoda doubled down, giving her their most exaggerated puppy-dog eyes. Their expressions were so over-the-top that she couldn't help but smirk despite herself. Letting out an exasperated breath—loud enough to make sure they heard it—she finally caved. "Fine. One drink, and then I'm going home."

"One alcoholic drink," Rain repeated with a triumphant grin before grabbing Aislinn's arm. Takoda grabbed the other, and together they practically dragged her toward the front door like excited children pulling their mom toward the toy aisle.

"Wait, wait!" Aislinn laughed, trying to dig in her heels. "I need to close out the register first!"

The girls groaned dramatically but released her arms.

"Fine, but make it snappy," Rain said, crossing her arms and tapping her foot as if they were on a tight deadline.

"Business before pleasure, Rain," Takoda added with mock wisdom, lifting her chin and folding her arms like some wise elder. The attempt at maturity was so out of character that all three of them dissolved into laughter.

"And while you're at it," Rain teased, leaning against the counter, "let down that hair! You look like a librarian with it all pulled up like that."

Aislinn chuckled, shaking her head as she moved back to the register. "You always say that," she shot back, pulling out the cash drawer and beginning to count the day's earnings.

"I mean it!" Rain called after her, twirling a strand of her fiery curls for emphasis. "How are you supposed to get hit on by a cute bartender if you're channeling Miss Marple?"

Aislinn rolled her eyes but couldn't stop the laugh that escaped. "You're relentless, you know that?"

"It's a gift," Rain replied with a wink, while Takoda smirked and checked the time on her phone.

Rain leaned dramatically against the counter. "That's because it's true! You've got all that gorgeous hair, and you keep it trapped up there like it's in prison. It deserves freedom!"

Aislinn chuckled, snapping the register closed with a satisfying click. "Well, freedom isn't exactly practical when I'm trying to run a business," she replied with a playful smirk, tossing her friends an exasperated look.

Before Rain could fire back, the bell above the door jingled, and a new customer stepped inside, the crisp evening air following close behind. The stranger shook off the chill as Aislinn turned to greet them. Her polite smile faltered slightly as she took in the man's presence. He was tall, his frame cloaked in a long, dark jacket, and his expression unreadable as his sharp gaze rested for a beat too long.

"I'm sorry, but we're closed for the night," Aislinn said, her voice steady despite the faint ripple of unease tightening in her chest. The man's eyes narrowed slightly, his gaze flicking to the counter and then back to her before he nodded and turned to leave.

Something about the interaction stuck with her—an intuition she couldn't quite name.

As the door swung shut behind him, Aislinn shook off the feeling, taking a deep breath to steady herself. *Probably nothing,* she told herself, forcing a small smile as she turned back to her friends. "You two ready to go?"

"Absolutely!" Rain declared, immediately perking up. She grabbed Aislinn's hand with enthusiasm, practically bouncing toward the door. "Let's set your hair free and have some fun!"

Takoda laughed softly, grabbing her jacket from a nearby stool. "We're going to make you regret saying yes, you know."

"Already halfway there," Aislinn muttered, though the corner of her mouth twitched with amusement.

The three women stepped outside into the brisk night air, the faint scent of the city—distant saltwater, car exhaust, and the occasional waft of food from nearby restaurants—filling their senses. A gust of wind swept down the street, tugging at their clothes and hair.

As Aislinn adjusted her scarf, a flicker of movement in the shadows across the way caught her attention. She squinted, her brows knitting together as she spotted a figure slipping behind a dumpster. The glimpse was brief, no more than a shadowy blur, but it was enough to send a chill rippling through her stomach.

She paused briefly, scanning the darkness, but nothing else moved. Shaking it off, she turned back to her friends. "Let's go before I change my mind."

Rain hooked an arm through hers, grinning as if nothing could ruin her night. "That's the spirit!"

"Everything okay?" Takoda asked, glancing back over her shoulder, her brows knitting in concern.

"Yeah, just... I don't know," Aislinn replied, shaking her head as if to clear it. "It just feels like tonight is different somehow."

"Different how?" Rain pressed, her lips curving into a teasing smile. Despite her lighthearted tone, there was a flicker of curiosity in her pale blue eyes.

Before Aislinn could answer, a loud crash shattered the peace of the evening. The sound echoed from the alley beside the café, followed by the unmistakable clatter of boxes spilling across the pavement. The three women froze, the playful atmosphere dissolving as their gazes darted toward the source of the noise.

"Let's go check it out!" Takoda said, her adventurous spirit sparking to life. Her voice was steady, almost excited, as she took a step forward.

Aislinn's heart raced, but not with the same enthusiasm. Her mind replayed the stranger's unsettling gaze, the shadowy figure she'd glimpsed earlier, and the unshakable feeling that tonight wasn't just different—it was wrong. *I don't think this is a good idea...*

"Oh, come on, Ash!" Rain cut in, nudging her lightly with her elbow. "Just a quick peek. What's the worst that could happen?"

Aislinn hesitated, her pulse pounding in her ears. The rational part of her screamed to stay put, to turn around and head for the safety of her apartment. There was something deeper, more primal, pulling her toward the alley. It wasn't curiosity—it felt closer to a compulsion, an unnamed feeling.

She looked at her friends, both waiting expectantly, their excitement practically buzzing in the air. She felt caught between the safety of the familiar and the undeniable lure of the unknown. The night seemed to hum with energy, calling her forward.

With a resigned sigh, she nodded. "Alright. But just a quick look."

Takoda grinned, already leading the way. Rain shot Aislinn a triumphant look as she followed, practically bouncing with excitement. Aislinn trailed behind, her steps slower, more cautious. Whatever was waiting for them beyond the café's comforting walls, she knew deep down, it would change everything.

Chapter Two

The Blue-Haired Biker

Aislinn took a steadying breath, her pulse pounding as the metallic echo of the crash faded into the night's stillness. Takoda's earlier insistence rang in her mind—her friend had been the first to suggest checking out the commotion, her curiosity practically dragging them along. *Alright, just a quick look,* Aislinn relented, unable to resist the magnetic pull of her friends' contagious enthusiasm. The trio darted toward the alley, their footfalls matching the quickening rhythm of Aislinn's racing heartbeat.

As they rounded the corner, the chaos revealed itself like the aftermath of a tiny, sugar-fueled storm. A delivery cart lay overturned, its wooden frame splintered, and its contents—a kaleidoscope of pastry boxes and baked goods—were scattered across the cobblestones. Eclairs glistened like mislaid jewels under the dim alley lights, and the warm, inviting aroma of sugar and butter filled the air, oddly incongruous amid the disarray.

"Oh, this is *horrendous*," Takoda said with a grin, dropping to one knee to retrieve a lone éclair that had rolled into a puddle. "A real tragedy. Look at all this! It's practically begging us to save it!"

Rain's laughter bubbled up like champagne, her hands already rifling through the scattered boxes. "We can't just leave it like this! It's a public service to clean it up!" she declared, her grin wide and mischievous. A spark of shared mischief passed between them, pulling Aislinn in despite the cautious whispers prickling at the edges of her thoughts.

Fine, Aislinn sighed, her lips twitching into a reluctant smile. "But we'll clean it up properly. No excuses if we get caught."

With that, they set to work, their movements a flurry of laughter and energy. Aislinn knelt to gather pastries, the cool cobblestones pressing against her knees as her hands brushed against frosting-smeared surfaces. Flour clung to her fingers like ghostly powder, and soon her blouse bore streaks of sugary evidence.

"Who knew crime scenes could smell this good?" Takoda quipped, stacking a box of slightly squished croissants with exaggerated care.

Rain struck a dramatic pose, holding a half-crushed tart aloft like a trophy. "We're heroes in the pastry underworld," she proclaimed, mock-serious. "Messy, underappreciated, but heroic nonetheless."

Aislinn couldn't help but chuckle, the tension in her chest loosening with each passing second. The three of them worked in chaotic harmony, dodging stray éclairs and licking frosting from their fingers as they restored order to the mess. The cart looked worse for wear, but the mountain of pastry boxes they'd stacked back on top offered a small sense of accomplishment.

"Messy bakers? Try disaster chefs," Aislinn teased, flicking a smudge of flour at Rain, who dodged with a playful yelp.

"Hey! Don't waste the evidence!" Rain shot back, mock-indignant.

Takoda laughed, brandishing a chocolate éclair. "If we go down for this, I'm blaming you two. I was an innocent bystander—just here for the éclairs!"

"Sure, Takoda," Aislinn said, rolling her eyes but unable to suppress her grin.

In the warmth of their camaraderie, the chaotic scene felt less like a mess and more like an adventure—a stolen moment of sweetness and silliness carved out of the ordinary.

As they finished cleaning, Aislinn stepped back to survey the scene, her heart racing from the combination of excitement and nerves. A glimmer of satisfaction flickered in her chest—chaos tamed, at least for now. "We did it. But we're definitely going to need to change before we head out. We're a mess."

"Good idea," Takoda chimed in, brushing powdered sugar from her skirt with little success. Her expression gleamed with anticipation. "Let's head to your place. We've got plenty of time to freshen up before we hit Donnelly's!"

Aislinn hesitated, a flutter of unease breaking through the camaraderie. The rush of the alley continued to buzz in her ears, persistent unease gnawing at the edges of her excitement. "I'm not sure if going out is the best idea tonight," she admitted, her attention darting back to the shadowed corners of the alley as if expecting the darkness to shift.

"Don't be silly, Ash!" Rain said, nudging her elbow with playful insistence. "You can't let a little frosting and flour ruin your night. Besides, you know you want to!" Her grin was a challenge, daring Aislinn to let go of her reservations.

The weight of their shared enthusiasm pressed against Aislinn's reluctance, tipping the balance. Her friends' bright energy was magnetic, impossible to resist. Yet beneath it all, a deeper unease remained, as though the shadows themselves clung too tightly to the night. *Maybe it's nothing,* she thought, shaking it off. "Okay, fine," she said at last, a faint smile tugging at her lips. "Let's get changed."

The trio set off toward Aislinn's apartment, their laughter bubbling into the quiet streets. The night felt alive in a way that sent ripples through Aislinn's thoughts. When they reached her building, her attention flicked to the digital clock in a shop window nearby. 9:30 PM. The glowing numbers seemed oddly significant, like a quiet reminder that time was slipping through their fingers.

Inside the apartment, the girls burst into motion, rifling through closets and drawers in search of outfits that felt right for whatever the night might bring. Aislinn halted for a brief pause in front of the mirror, catching her own reflection. Flour smudges and frosting stains marked her blouse, her tousled hair framed her flushed face, and her wide eyes reflected uncertainty. A nervous energy danced beneath her skin, tangling with a growing anticipation. *Am I ready for this?*

"We'll call a cab around ten, yeah?" Takoda suggested, holding up a shimmery top she'd dug out of Aislinn's wardrobe.

Aislinn nodded, her emotions teetering between excitement and apprehension. "Yeah, sounds good."

Rain emerged from another room, triumphantly modeling a dress she'd borrowed, and struck a silly pose. "Ladies, we're going to look amazing tonight. Just wait—this is going to be epic!"

Aislinn couldn't help but smile at their enthusiasm. She ran her fingers through her hair, trying to smooth the edges of her doubt. Maybe tonight wasn't just about going out—it felt bigger, somehow. Something was pulling her toward the unknown, like an invisible thread winding tighter with each passing moment. She didn't fully understand it, though she couldn't deny its strength.

With a deep breath, she turned back to her friends. "Alright. Let's do this."

At Rain's insistence, Aislinn let her hair down, carefully wielding a curling iron to tame the frizz. Each wave felt like a small concession to her friends' enthusiasm, even as a part of her still yearned for the simplicity of a quiet night at home. As they stepped out the front door, she paused to set the alarm and lock up, the familiar motions fortifying her in a way the night's excitement couldn't.

The cab arrived promptly at ten, and Rain wasted no time giving directions to Donnelly's Pub on Clement Street. Aislinn sighed softly as she slid into the back seat, second thoughts creeping in around the edges of her mind. *I should be curled up on the sofa with a book in hand, not heading into the chaos of a crowded bar.*

When they arrived, the pub was already alive with noise—laughter and conversation mingling with the upbeat chords of a folk-rock band. Aislinn hesitated as she stepped out of the cab, the warm glow of the pub lights failing to ease the unease twisting in her stomach.

Sensing her reluctance, Takoda hooked an arm through Aislinn's and tugged her toward the entrance with an encouraging grin. "Come on, it'll be fun. I promise," she said, her energy as unstoppable as a spring tide.

Resigned, Aislinn let herself be swept along, Rain flanking her other side with equal determination. The pub was packed, the air buzzing with chatter and the smell of beer mingling with faint traces of cologne and perfume. They wove through the crowd until they found three empty stools near the bar, a small victory in the sea of bodies.

Aislinn perched on one stool, her focus drifting to the dance floor. The vibrant scene felt like another world—a world she'd been part of once, though now it seemed foreign. Meanwhile, Rain and Takoda waved down the bartender and ordered drinks, their animated voices blending into the surrounding din.

"Let's go dance!" Rain said suddenly, grabbing for Aislinn's hand with a bright grin.

Aislinn pulled her hand back quickly, shaking her head. "No way. You said a drink, not dancing," she replied, her tone firm, though a hint of panic seeped into her words.

"Oh, come on, it'll—"

"It'll be fun, I know," Aislinn interrupted Takoda, crossing her arms with mock sternness. "Still no."

Rain pouted dramatically but couldn't hold it for long, a mischievous smile slipping through. "Fine," she relented. Then, planting a quick kiss on Aislinn's cheek, she added brightly, "You'll dance later."

Takoda followed suit, pecking Aislinn on the other cheek before dragging Rain toward the dance floor, their laughter trailing behind them.

Aislinn exhaled, watching them disappear into the swirling crowd. *A year ago, I would have been the one leading the charge, coaxing them to let loose and enjoy the music.* Now, she barely recognized the version of herself who had thrived on that energy. Funny how life could shift so much in such a short time.

Her focus wandered, the rhythm of the band fading into the background. The carved wooden beams lining the ceiling caught her attention—subtle patterns etched into their surface, almost like ancient ogham script. The thought lingered only briefly, quickly overtaken by the rising buzz of conversation and clinking glasses around her.

"What'll it be?" the bartender asked, pulling her from her thoughts.

"Diet Coke," she said automatically, the words slipping out before she remembered her promise to Rain to have at least one real drink. Wincing, she amended her plan. *Fine, I'll start with this and have a cocktail after. Two drinks won't hurt me.*

"Here you are," the bartender said as he slid the glass toward her, his lilting Irish accent cutting through the ambient noise like a familiar melody. "Anything else for you tonight?"

"No, thanks," Aislinn replied, finally turning around to face him. "How much do I owe…" The words caught in her throat as her focus traveled upward…and upward.

The bartender was tall—easily over six feet—with a frame that looked more at home on a magazine cover than behind a bar. His bright blue T-shirt clung to his broad shoulders and chest, the vibrant color perfectly matching the striking hue of his irises. They were vivid and piercing, holding a depth that seemed impossible to look away from, like sunlight refracted through a still lake. A slightly crooked yet undeniably charming nose and a dimpled smile added to his rugged appeal, while blue-black hair streaked with cobalt framed his face with an effortlessly rebellious edge.

Her stomach fluttered with an odd sense of déjà vu, though she couldn't place why. Something about those eyes seemed familiar, yet just out of reach, like a fragment of a dream she couldn't quite recall.

When his lips curved into a full smile, revealing perfect teeth and that maddening dimple, her heart gave a traitorous skip. "Like what you see, do ya?" he teased, his Irish lilt wrapping around the words with roguish ease.

Aislinn's brain stalled for a instant. "Yeah," she breathed, the word slipping out before she could stop it. Her cheeks flamed as she realized what she'd said. "I mean no—I mean " She scrambled to recover, flustered under the weight of his amused expression. "Do I know you?"

The flicker of familiarity tugged at her again, though whatever memory she was chasing remained just out of reach.

He chuckled softly, leaning slightly closer as if to study her face. "I don't think so. You'd remember me," he said, his smirk deepening. "And I'd most definitely remember you."

The way he held her attention—intense, curious, and unrelenting—made her stomach tighten. The pub around her seemed to dissolve, the laughter and music fading to a distant hum. Time itself felt suspended under the pull of his presence, like the lull before a storm.

Then, the small exchange splintered.

"Rowan!" A voice cut through the bar's din, clear and sharp. "I need a gin and tonic and an apple martini, stat!"

Startled, Aislinn glanced down the bar to see a petite waitress balancing a tray on her hip. She had dark, wavy hair pulled into a high ponytail and eyes that sparkled with a mischievous glint. A playful smirk curved her lips as she looked between Rowan and Aislinn.

"Or do you want me to make them?" the waitress teased, raising an eyebrow. "You seem a little busy at the moment."

Rowan straightened with a laugh, a low, rich sound that rippled through Aislinn, warming her from the inside out. "I'll be right there," he called to the waitress at the far end of the bar, his attention remaining on Aislinn for a heartbeat longer before he turned to walk away.

As he moved to make the drinks, Aislinn exhaled, realizing she'd been holding her breath. She glanced down at her hands, willing herself to steady, though her thoughts churned in disarray. *There's something about the way he looked at me—like he knows me, or maybe he expects me to know him.*

From her spot at the far end, the waitress flashed Rowan a teasing smile before turning her attention back to her tray. Aislinn didn't hear what she said, though the exchange made her cheeks heat again, her mind tumbling over itself.

Rowan worked quickly, his movements fluid and practiced. He didn't just make drinks; he commanded the bar like an artist with a canvas, each gesture deliberate and mesmerizing. Ice rattled in the shaker, the rhythm aligning with the hum of the music in the background. His hands moved confidently, flipping a bottle mid-air with ease before pouring a perfect stream into a glass.

Aislinn watched, entranced, as he slid two finished drinks onto a tray and handed them off to the waitress with a cheeky wink. In that fleeting second, the way the light played off the cobalt streaks in his hair reminded her of the intricate patterns carved into ancient stone crosses—otherworldly, timeless, and powerful. The comparison stayed with her for a heartbeat, unbidden yet impossible to ignore.

Before she could pull herself together, he was already making his way back to her. The space between them seemed to shrink in an instant, and then he was there again, sliding effortlessly into place as if he'd never left.

"That'll be $2.50," Rowan said, his lilting accent pulling her back to reality.

"Oh, right. Sorry," she fumbled, digging into her pocket for cash. She handed him a five, her fingers brushing his as she passed it over. The warmth of his touch lingered longer than it should have, sending a flutter through her chest.

"Rowan?" she asked hesitantly, tilting her head as if testing the sound of the name. It didn't sit quite right in her mind. "That's an...odd name."

He smirked, pocketing the bill and sliding her change across the counter. "I'm an odd guy," he said, amusement lacing his words.

Aislinn let out a laugh, the sound cutting through the tension. "Well, except for maybe the blue hair, you don't seem that odd. And I didn't mean odd—I meant...unique," she corrected, her cheeks flushing as she stumbled over the words.

Rowan leaned forward slightly, resting his elbows on the bar, closing the small distance between them. His intense expression locked onto hers, his blue irises sharp and unrelenting, as though he could see straight through her. The hum of the bar faded to a distant murmur, the air around them charged with a hidden energy.

"I think I like you," he said, his voice dropping to a low, intimate tone that sent a shiver down her spine.

The words hung between them, electric and magnetic. Aislinn's breath hitched, and she opened her mouth to respond, yet nothing came out. Her thoughts scrambled as her pulse hammered in her chest, leaving her unsure if she was exhilarated or terrified.

Before she could speak, a flurry of motion drew her attention. Rain and Takoda burst back from the dance floor, breathless and giddy, their cheeks flushed with exhilaration.

"Girl, you have to come out and dance," Takoda urged, grabbing Aislinn by the hand. Her energy was infectious, though Aislinn found herself resisting, her thoughts still tangled in Rowan's words and the subtle pull they left behind.

Rain's sharp glance landed on the glass in front of Aislinn, and she pursed her lips in mock disapproval. "Hey, what's this? You promised to have a drink, and all I see is Diet Coke."

Aislinn turned to her friend with an exaggerated pout, clutching the glass like a trophy. "Diet Coke is a drink," she whined playfully, raising it as if to toast her defense.

Rain rolled her eyes and grabbed the glass, sliding it away with a dramatic sigh. "Not the kind of drink we meant. I'm getting you a proper one," she declared, already signaling to Rowan.

Aislinn opened her mouth to protest, yet the words died as Rain effortlessly pulled Rowan's attention back to their side of the bar. His focus flicked briefly to Aislinn, a ghost of a smirk curling his lips, and her breath caught. Whatever had passed between them earlier wasn't over—it was only just beginning.

Rain leaned forward with a dramatic flourish. "Bartender! Get this woman a Long Island iced tea. She's going to have fun tonight if it's the last thing I do."

Aislinn's focus darted back to Rowan, who had now crossed his arms, leaning casually against the back counter with that same infuriatingly charming smile. He gave her a subtle chin tilt. "You got I.D.?"

Her heart inexplicably racing, Aislinn fumbled to hand him her driver's license. As he took it, a jolt of awareness sparked through her, completely unbidden. He glanced at the card quickly, then handed it back with the same quiet confidence.

"Thanks," he said simply, his attention never leaving her face as he began making her drink.

Aislinn watched, fascinated despite herself. His movements were seamless, almost hypnotic, like he was pouring instinctively. He rarely glanced at what he was doing, yet every motion was intentional and precise. *How is he doing that?* she wondered, trying not to stare, though failing miserably.

A few minutes later, Rowan set the drink in front of her, his focus unwavering. He leaned forward slightly, his blue irises capturing hers again, the intensity of his expression making the rest of the bar blur into the background.

"How much?" Rain asked, already fishing in her bag.

Rowan's attention stayed locked on Aislinn, his tone smooth and quiet, wrapping around her like a secret meant only for her. "On the house…Aislinn."

She nearly choked. The way he said her name—soft and measured, like it was precious—sent a ripple through her, leaving her heart pounding against her ribs. She took a quick sip of her drink, trying to steady herself, though the strange pull he seemed to have on her only deepened.

How did he know my name? she thought, certain neither Takoda nor Rain had mentioned it. Then the realization hit her—he must have seen it on her driver's license. Yet something about the way he'd said it gave her pause. Most people butchered her name, turning it into "Ice-lin" or "Ace-lin," but he'd said "Ash-lin," his Irish lilt wrapping around the syllables perfectly, like he'd known it forever.

Her mind raced with questions. *Had he noticed anything else on my license?* The thought sent her heart skittering, her cheeks heating once again. *God, Ash, get it together,* she scolded herself silently, willing the fluttering in her stomach to calm. *You're acting like a schoolgirl with a crush.*

Still, no amount of logic could shake the sensation that Rowan saw her—really saw her—in a way no one else had before. And that unnerved her more than anything.

Before Aislinn could thank him, Rowan gave her a playful raise of his brow and moved on to take another patron's order, leaving her rooted in place, unsure of what had just happened.

"Thank you!" Rain called after him, her tone bright and teasing. Rowan simply waved a hand over his shoulder without looking back, his nonchalance only adding to his charm.

Rain turned to Aislinn, her eyes wide with excitement. "God, Ash, he's hot! And I think he's totally into you!"

"Definitely!" Takoda chimed in, her voice brimming with mischief. "I mean, that blue hair? Plus, did you see the way he was staring at you?"

Aislinn rolled her eyes, her cheeks flushing under their scrutiny. "Whatever, guys—"

"Girls. We-inz girls, Ash," Rain corrected with a grin, earning a snort from Takoda.

Aislinn shot her a look but continued, "As I was saying, whatever. All he did was make me a drink. A really strong one, by the way. I seriously doubt he's developed 'a thing' for me in the five minutes we've been here."

"Fine, if that's how you want to play it," Rain smirked, grabbing Aislinn's drink with one hand and looping her other arm through Aislinn's.

Before Aislinn could protest, Takoda latched onto her other arm with a laugh. "Come on, let's go dance!"

Aislinn groaned theatrically as her two friends dragged her toward the dance floor, relieved to escape the pervasive heat coursing through the room. Whatever had passed between her and Rowan felt like more than just a casual interaction. She wasn't ready to unpack it—not yet.

As her friends spun her onto the dance floor, Aislinn tried to lose herself in the music, her movements hesitant at first. Encouraged by Rain and Takoda's cheers, she finally began to let go.

What was that? Rowan wondered, leaning against the corner of the bar, absently wiping a glass as his focus stayed on Aislinn and her friends on the dance floor. Once she loosened up—no doubt helped by the drink he'd made her—she moved with an effortless grace that was hard to ignore. When she had asked him if they knew each other, he was certain they hadn't met before. And yet, there was something about her—an odd, unplaceable familiarity that tugged at the edges of his memory.

It made it impossible to look away.

He didn't notice Ariel until she sidled up next to him, her voice breaking through his reverie.

"You know, you're going to break that glass if you keep going," she teased, leaning her tray against the bar.

Startled, Rowan jumped slightly, earning a small, satisfied laugh from Ariel. He frowned and handed her the glass, narrowing his eyes. "You shouldn't sneak up on people like that, you little pixie," he muttered, his tone gruff yet not unkind.

Ariel grinned as she slid the glass onto the shelf behind her. "Sorry, couldn't resist."

She'd been pulling him out of his head for two years, ever since the day he'd hired her. Rowan had nicknamed her "little pixie" on her first shift, a moniker that stuck as their working relationship grew into a rare friendship. Ariel liked it—it was a mark of his trust that he didn't give freely.

As she tucked the tray under her arm, Ariel's attention followed Rowan's to the dance floor. A knowing smirk spread across her face when she spotted the reason for his distraction. "She's pretty, isn't she?" she asked casually, her tone light yet probing.

Rowan's posture stiffened, and he snapped his gaze to a random corner of the bar. "Who?"

Ariel rolled her eyes and stepped in front of him. With a playful smirk, she grabbed his chin and turned his head back toward Aislinn. "*Her*," she said matter-of-factly. "The girl you've been staring at for over an hour now. You should ask her out."

Rowan pulled back, shaking his head with a sigh. "Ariel, why do you always insist on trying to set me up with someone? It's called talking to patrons. It's how you figure out what drink they want. Nothing more."

Ariel tilted her head, her expression sharpening as she studied him. "Oh, yeah?" she asked, her words cutting through his thoughts. "Then what's her name? Where does she live? How old is she?"

Rowan stiffened. He had those answers. Scanning IDs was second nature by now, a habit ingrained from years behind the bar. *Too many years*, a small voice in the back of his mind murmured. Still, there was no way he'd give Ariel the satisfaction of knowing that. "I don't know," he lied flatly, his tone devoid of emotion.

Ariel squinted at him, disbelief etched into her face. "Liar. I know you, Rowan. You've been watching her all night."

She gestured toward the dance floor, where Aislinn moved with unassuming but captivating grace. "And that's why you've been wiping the same spot on that glass for five minutes, pretending not to notice how good she looks out there?"

"I wasn't—" Rowan began, but Ariel cut him off with a laugh, leaning casually against the bar.

"Oh, please, Rowan. I've known you long enough to recognize that look. I'm just saying, instead of brooding about it, maybe you should try...you know...*talking* to her. It's not like she's going to bite."

Rowan glanced at Aislinn again, his lips pressing into a thin line. The way she moved, the way her laughter carried across the room—it all felt too familiar. Yet it couldn't be possible. If they'd met before, he would remember.

Unless...

He pushed the thought aside, his jaw tightening.

"Let it go, Ariel," he said quietly, his tone signaling the conversation was over.

Ariel studied him for a flash, her playful smirk fading. She didn't press further, though a flicker of understanding passed across her features as she stepped back, grabbing her tray. "Suit yourself, Rowan," she said lightly, her teasing edge softened. "But don't wait too long. Moments like this don't come around every day."

Rowan didn't reply, his focus returning to the dance floor. The memory tugged at him again, more insistent this time. Aislinn's movements stirred a memory he couldn't place, like the echo of a half-forgotten melody.

He turned away, frowning as he set the glass down. Aislinn wasn't like anyone he'd met before. That much he was certain of.

Ariel sighed, throwing up her hands in mock defeat. "Fine, fine. Just don't come crying to me when someone else asks her out first."

Rowan frowned, her words cutting deeper than he wanted to admit. He stole another glance at Aislinn, the pull of familiarity gnawing at him. *Who are you?* he wondered, the question circling endlessly in his mind, refusing to let him rest.

He let out a frustrated breath, his thoughts drifting, unbidden, to a name he hadn't spoken aloud in years. *Davina.*

There would never be anyone else. Not for him. Not after her.

The name was a shadow in his heart, a wound that never fully healed. Her laughter still echoed faintly in the corners of his mind, soft and melodic, like the chiming of bells on a distant wind. She'd been everything—light, life, and love—until she was gone. And he had been the one who failed to save her.

The ache twisted in his chest, sharp and unrelenting. Rowan turned away, putting an end to the conversation. "Ariel, stop meddling," he said, his tone softer now, carrying the weight of a sadness he couldn't quite hide. "There's no one for me."

Ariel watched him walk away, her chest sinking. She'd heard that before. He always shut her down whenever she brought up the idea of romance, and she knew why. Whatever haunted him had locked Rowan's heart away, leaving him trapped in a prison of guilt and loss.

Still, she couldn't help wanting to see him happy again. He had saved her once, pulling her out of a dark place two years ago, giving her a job when she had nowhere else to go. If it weren't for Rowan, she wasn't sure she'd even be standing here.

Her gaze followed him as he moved to the far end of the bar, shoulders tense, his head slightly bowed as if burdened by the intangible. She wished she could ease that weight, but Rowan didn't let anyone get close enough to try.

Determined, Ariel turned back to the bar and grabbed a shaker. A Long Island iced tea wasn't going to mix itself. She worked quickly, her hands moving with practiced ease, though her mind remained focused on Rowan's guarded expression. *He deserves to be happy,* she thought, tightening the cap on the shaker.

One day, she'd see him laugh again—*really* laugh. And when that day came, she'd be there, ready to help him find that spark of happiness he'd buried so deeply.

Despite her initial hesitation, Aislinn had to admit she was enjoying herself. The band delivered everything Takoda had promised, their lively performance irresistible and infectious. Once she allowed herself to loosen up, she caught herself "getting into the groove," as Rain had teased earlier. The music's pulsing energy blended with the easy camaraderie of her friends, creating a night that was surprisingly fun.

She had just finished her drink when a light tap on her shoulder drew her attention. Turning, Aislinn found herself face-to-face with the waitress she'd noticed earlier. The young woman's smile lit her features as she held out another drink.

"I didn't order this," Aislinn called, raising her voice above the steady rhythm of the music.

"It's from Rowan," the waitress shouted back, her warm smile putting her at ease.

Curious, Aislinn glanced instinctively toward the bar. Rowan, however, didn't appear to notice her; he was entirely focused on serving a lively group of patrons. Her brows knit together. *Why would he send me another drink without so much as a glance in my direction?* Unsure of what else to do, she turned back to the waitress, who still held the glass out with quiet patience. Not wanting to seem ungrateful, Aislinn accepted the drink—a second Long Island iced tea.

"Thanks," she called after her, though the waitress had already disappeared into the crowd, tray balanced expertly in hand.

The hours passed, and Aislinn eventually found herself needing a break. The band had shifted to an upbeat tempo, and the dance floor pulsed with chaotic energy. Though exhilarating, it was beginning to wear her down. Leaning closer to Rain and Takoda, she announced, "I'm going to sit down for a bit." She raised her voice to carry over the rising swell of the music. They both offered to join her, but she waved them off with a small, reassuring smile.

Navigating through the crowd, Aislinn wove her way toward the bar. Relief swept over her when she saw that the stool she'd occupied earlier was still vacant. Sinking into it with a grateful sigh, she gave her aching feet a much-needed rest. She cast a glance toward Rowan, hoping to catch his attention and thank him for the unexpected gesture.

After a few minutes, Rowan approached, leaning casually over the bar in that effortlessly self-assured way of his. "Can I get you anything?" he asked, his words carrying a casual warmth that still felt attentive.

"No, I'm good," she replied with a faint shake of her head. "But thanks for the drink. Both of them. And the Coke earlier, too." She tilted her glass slightly, a small gesture of appreciation.

Rowan's brow lifted, his expression flickering with confusion. "Both of them?" he repeated slowly, glancing toward the far end of the bar where Ariel was stationed. Ariel, caught like a deer in headlights under his sharp gaze, froze for a split second before hastily grabbing her tray and vanishing into the crowd. *That little pixie, Rowan thought, a silent groan echoing in his mind. Of course, she'd meddled.*

Unaware of the exchange between them, Aislinn smiled and took another sip. "These are really good, by the way," she said, holding up her drink. "What's in them?"

Rowan refocused on her, noting the faint glaze softening her expression and the flush warming her cheeks. She smiled cheerfully up at him, but it was clear she was tipsy. Judging by her earlier order, she wasn't much of a drinker, and two Long Island iced teas packed a punch. Without a word, he gently took the half-finished glass from her hand and set it aside.

"There's a lot in them," he said evenly. "But maybe I should get you a soda instead?"

Aislinn blinked at him, his words seeming to reach her from a distance. "You know," she murmured, her head propped in her hand, "that actually sounds really good."

Rowan poured her a diet soda, the fizz bubbling softly as he placed it in front of her. Reaching beneath the bar, he pulled out a small pack of crackers and slid it beside the glass. "Here," he said, his tone practical but kind. "Eat these. They'll help."

"Thanks," she said, sincerity threading through her words as she tore open the package. She nibbled on a cracker, following it with a generous gulp of soda. A relieved sigh escaped her. "Oh, that was exactly what I needed," she admitted with a sheepish chuckle. "Though I probably could've skipped that second drink."

Rowan grimaced, his eyes drifting toward Ariel, who was now weaving through the dance floor with exaggerated enthusiasm. "I didn't offer you the second one," he said, exhaling softly.

Aislinn followed his gaze, her attention landing on the waitress from earlier. Ariel, catching the look, promptly lifted her chin in defiance before stomping off with an exaggerated huff. *She's definitely up to something,* Aislinn thought, amused despite herself.

"Is she your girlfriend?" Aislinn asked, keeping her tone light, though a hint of an emotion she couldn't fully define crept in.

Rowan nearly choked on his drink, the sharp sting of carbonation catching him off guard. He grabbed a napkin, clearing his throat with a grimace. "No," he replied hoarsely, his voice steadying again. "She's more like a kid sister who can't help sticking her nose where it doesn't belong."

Aislinn arched a brow but didn't press the issue. Instead, she traced the rim of her glass with a finger, letting the air settle in silence. The bubbles in her soda rose and popped, each faint hiss a quiet rhythm against the hum of the bar. *A kid sister, huh?* The thought lingered, but she brushed it aside, choosing not to comment further.

The time shattered as Rain and Takoda burst onto the scene, their playful energy cutting through the din of the bar. Rain nudged Aislinn's shoulder lightly, while Takoda flashed a lopsided grin. The jostling sent Aislinn's head spinning, and she steadied herself with a sip of her soda. Rowan leaned back against the counter, arms loosely crossed, observing the trio with faint amusement.

Rain glanced at Rowan and threw him a cheeky wink. "Hey, cutie," she teased, mischief lacing her words.

Rowan chuckled, shaking his head as a small smile curved his lips. "Hey," he replied, his tone steady but light.

Aislinn felt a wave of relief ripple through her. Whatever game Rain was playing, Rowan clearly wasn't taking the bait. Still, a flicker of jealousy crept into her thoughts before she silenced it with a firm mental nudge. *You barely know the guy, Ash.*

Rain, oblivious to the undercurrent of emotions, turned her full attention to Aislinn. "Ash, the band's done here. We're heading downtown to find another place to dance. You in?"

Aislinn sighed, the thought of more dancing making her feet ache pre-emptively. "I don't think so," she said, shaking her head. "I should head home. I'm wiped."

"Aw, come on," Takoda protested, drawing out the words in exaggerated despair. "We were having so much fun!"

"I know, I know," Aislinn replied with a grin. "It's hard to imagine how you two will survive without me, but someone's gotta be responsible enough to open the café tomorrow."

"Whatever, *dude*," Rain said, rolling her eyes as her Pennsylvania slang slipped through. "We're responsible! And besides, we don't open till ten. Want us to call you a cab or something?"

"No, dude, I'm good," Aislinn shot back, waving her hand dismissively. "I think I can manage getting home without a babysitter. I mean, I did make it across the country all by my little-wee-self," she added, dropping her voice into a mock babyish tone that drew a round of snickers.

Behind the bar, Rowan chuckled, the soft sound paired with a smirk that gave away his amusement. Aislinn caught the look, her cheeks warming slightly under his quiet attention. Unable to stop herself, she returned his smile, a flicker of shyness curling at the edges of her expression.

"Fine, whatever," Rain muttered, spinning on her heel. "I'll grab us a cab." With a dismissive wave, she disappeared into the crowd, leaving behind a faint trail of sass.

With Rain gone, Takoda turned back to Aislinn, hands planted firmly on her hips. "You're such a sarcastic drunk," she teased, though the grin softening her words took any sting out of the jab. Her tone shifted as she added, "Are you sure you don't want us to call you a cab? Seriously, it's no trouble."

"No, really. I'm good," Aislinn insisted, her voice calm despite the slight blush staining her cheeks. "I'm just going to finish this soda and head out. Tell Rain I'm sorry if I annoyed her, okay?"

"She'll survive," Takoda said with a quick hug. "Take care of yourself, okay? See you tomorrow."

"See you," Aislinn replied, watching as Takoda disappeared into the sea of bodies, the energy of the bar swirling around her.

She turned back to the bar, finding Rowan still leaning nearby, his arms loosely crossed and an amused smirk curving his lips. He didn't say anything, simply watching her with that calm, unshakable focus of his.

"What?" she asked, suddenly aware of herself under his quiet scrutiny.

"You three are quite the group," he remarked with a low chuckle.

Before Aislinn could reply, a loud call rang out from the far end of the bar. Rowan glanced toward the source, then flashed her an apologetic smile. "Excuse me for a second," he said, his voice warm yet professional as he moved to tend to another customer.

Aislinn watched him go, his steps unhurried but purposeful. Something about the way he carried himself tugged at her memory, stirring a vague and persistent sense of familiarity. Her brow knit as her thoughts wandered. She hadn't been in San Francisco long and rarely strayed far from the café or her apartment. *Where could I have seen him before?* She was certain they hadn't crossed paths at work—Rowan's striking presence was impossible to overlook. Yet the feeling remained, like trying to grasp a shadow just beyond reach.

Her musings broke when a man slid into the seat Takoda had vacated, his presence cutting through her drifting thoughts.

"Hey, gorgeous," he drawled, his grin wide and brimming with self-assurance. "Can I buy you another drink?"

Aislinn blinked, her surprise melting into a bemused eye roll. *Does that line seriously still work on anyone?* she wondered, the cliché nearly laughable.

"No thanks, I'm good," she replied, her tone polite but firm. She cast a brief glance his way, sizing him up. He appeared to be around her age, dressed in faded blue jeans and a snug black t-shirt that hinted at time spent in the gym. He was tall—easily six feet—and leaned toward her with the kind of practiced confidence that felt more rehearsed than genuine. Whatever charm he might have had, though, was ruined by his hair, slicked back with an excess of product, leaving it uncomfortably greasy. Her gaze fixed on his eyes for a beat too long, and a chill crept along her spine. They were unnervingly dark, so much so that distinguishing the pupils from the irises felt impossible. There was something predatory in the way he studied her, as though gauging her reaction rather than truly engaging with her.

"Oh, come on, beautiful. One more drink's not gonna hurt," he coaxed, his voice dropping into what he probably thought was a seductive register. Leaning closer, the faint bitterness of alcohol clung to his breath.

Aislinn stiffened, her unease sharpening into a more visceral edge. Every instinct urged her to create distance. "I really don't want another drink," she said, her words clipped yet civil. "I was just about to leave."

His grin widened as though her refusal were an invitation to press further. "Well, then," he countered smoothly, his tone laced with insistence, "how about I give you a ride home? No need for a pretty girl like you to be out there all alone."

The hair on the back of Aislinn's neck prickled. His persistence had shifted from irritating to unsettling, and she felt the weight of his gaze settle on her like an unwelcome touch. She tightened her grip on her glass, her mind racing. *Where's Rowan? Or Takoda? Or literally anyone right now?*

Rowan's gaze shifted toward Aislinn as he handed a drink to a waiting customer. Her posture held a quality that snagged his attention—the stiffness in her shoulders, the restrained unease in the way she held herself. A man had slid into the seat beside her, leaning far too close, his body language radiating unwelcome intent. Rowan's gut tightened, an instinctive warning flaring within him like a distant alarm. This wasn't just some guy pushing his luck.

The air around the stranger felt off—heavy and charged, like the pause before the upheaval broke. A cold prickle ran through Rowan's chest as the familiar sensation of dark energy settled over him. This wasn't random trouble. It was far worse. His ability to sense evil—a gift, or perhaps a curse, forged over centuries—left no doubt in his mind. The man was Golden Dawn.

Rowan's teeth pressed tightly as the realization struck. The cult had been his enemy for as long as he'd walked this earth, their endless quest for power cloaked in twisted rhetoric. They claimed to purge the world of darkness, yet their actions left only ruin in their wake. Over the centuries, their name had changed—Orphites, Gnostics, Simonians—but their methods remained the same. And now, one of them was sitting far too close to Aislinn, his motives hidden yet undoubtedly malicious.

A cold resolve settled over Rowan, his thoughts sharpening with a protective clarity. *What do they want with her?* The question stirred something deep and unrelenting, a coiling tension in his muscles readying him for action. Without hesitation, he stepped out from behind the bar, his gaze locked onto the man like a predator marking its prey.

"Come on, baby," the man was saying, reaching for Aislinn's hand with an audacious grin. She pulled away sharply, her discomfort plain.

"Really, you should leave," she said, her voice firm but edged with uneasiness.

"Aw, don't be like that." The stranger's voice dropped into a tone that might have been charming in another context, though here it felt as oily as his slicked-back hair. "I'm a nice guy. I'll take you straight home, I promise."

Rowan stepped closer, his voice cutting through the hum of the bar like a knife. "I believe the lady asked you to leave."

The man didn't bother to look up, his lips curling into a sneer. "Mind your own business, bud. Go serve someone else," he said dismissively, his words dripping with disdain.

Aislinn glanced at Rowan, her eyes betraying a trace of uncertainty. His stance had shifted—a quiet intensity, like the calm before chaos. She looked back at the man, sensing the storm brewing between them.

Rowan leaned forward slightly, his voice dropping to a dangerous calm. "Get up, walk out that door, and pray I don't follow. Or I'll make sure you regret stepping foot in here."

The stranger froze, his cocky attitude faltering. For an instant, his eyes narrowed, and his lips pressed thin as though considering his odds. Then he met Rowan's gaze—cold, unwavering, and sharp as a blade. Whatever he saw there made him halt.

"Nice to meet you," the man muttered to Aislinn, the false sweetness in his tone grating. Rising from his seat, he cast one final look at Rowan, his lips pressing into a thin line. He sauntered toward the door, joining a group of others loitering near the exit. Before leaving, he turned back, his gaze locking onto Rowan with a dark promise. He raised two fingers, pointing at his eyes, then at Rowan, the message unmistakable: *I'm watching you.*

Rowan held his ground, the muscles in his jaw flexing, as he watched the group slip out into the night. The air in the room felt heavier now, as though a storm had passed, leaving its weight behind.

When he turned back, Aislinn was staring into her drink, her hands trembling slightly as she fidgeted with the glass. The spark of defiance she'd shown earlier had dimmed, replaced by a fragile uncertainty that tugged at him. A pang of guilt settled in his chest.

"I'm sorry if I scared you," Rowan said, his voice soft now, a stark contrast to the cold command he'd used earlier. His expression eased, the familiar lilt in his voice carrying a quiet gentleness.

Aislinn lifted her head slightly, her voice wavering but steady. "No, you didn't scare me," she said softly. "Thank you." Her fingers tightened around the glass, her gaze flicking up briefly before dropping again.

Rowan reached out, his touch light as he tipped her chin, coaxing her to meet his eyes. "Aislinn, truly, I'm sorry," he repeated, his tone warm and sincere, the steel in his presence dissolving into something softer.

She held his gaze for a second longer before offering a small smile. "No, really, Rowan, it's okay. I'm okay. Thanks to you." Her voice had steadied now, her words carrying an unmistakable note of gratitude.

Rowan let his hand fall back, giving her space but remaining close, his presence a steadying anchor. "If you need anything—anything at all—you let me know," he said, his words firm yet threaded with earnest care.

Aislinn nodded, her smile growing slightly, the warmth in her expression easing some of Rowan's leftover worry. Briefly, the bustling bar around them seemed to blur, leaving only the two of them—a fragile, veiled understanding weaving itself between them.

The sound of his name on her lips stirred an emotion deep within Rowan, a sensation that felt distant yet achingly familiar. It was a feeling he hadn't allowed himself to experience in years—not since... her. A flicker of pain crossed his face, unbidden, and he stepped back, letting his hand fall to his side as if the space could shield him from the memory. *Davina.* The name echoed softly in his mind, bittersweet and sharp, a haunting reminder of what he had lost.

Aislinn caught the shadow that flashed through his eyes, her curiosity stirring. She opened her mouth to ask, but Rowan cleared his throat, the shift in his stance careful as he pushed the moment away. "By the way," he said, a playful smirk tugging at his lips, "I think I agree with your friend—you're definitely a sarcastic drunk."

"I am not drunk," Aislinn shot back, grateful for the change in tone. "Maybe a little tipsy earlier, but I'm completely sober now. And I swear, I'm not a lush." Her smile widened, the tension between them dissipating like morning mist under the sun.

Rowan chuckled softly, leaning his forearms on the bar until their eyes met at the same level. "I don't think you're a lush," he said, his voice carrying an easy warmth. "I think you're a beautiful girl who got dragged out by her friends and actually ended up having a good time." His words hung in the air, soft but strikingly honest. *Did he just call me beautiful?*

Aislinn's cheeks flushed, but this time, she didn't look away. Instead, she held his gaze, her thoughts slipping past her usual filter. "Your eyes are... beautiful," she said softly, the words escaping before she could stop herself. "My mother always said you could see a person's soul through their eyes."

For a heartbeat, the rest of the world seemed to dissolve, leaving only the fragile space between them. A connection sparked—delicate yet undeniable—as though an invisible thread was pulling them closer. But then Rowan straightened, clearing his throat and stepping back, shattering the moment.

"I'm sorry," Aislinn blurted, heat rushing to her cheeks. She cringed inwardly at her own awkwardness. "I didn't mean to embarrass you. Sometimes my mouth just... you know, runs ahead of my brain." *You're such an idiot, Ash.*

Rowan chuckled softly, the sound low and reassuring. "You didn't embarrass me. And... thank you," he said, his voice quieter now, carrying an unmistakable sincerity.

Aislinn felt a flicker of relief but also something deeper—an unfamiliar warmth that left her feeling vulnerable and off-balance. She turned slightly, letting her gaze sweep the room in an effort to steady herself. The bar had mostly emptied, the music long faded, leaving behind a quiet hum of conversation and the faint clinking of glassware.

"I should get going," she said, breaking the silence. "It's late."

Rowan's eyes flicked toward the door before settling back on her. "I'll give you a ride," he offered, his tone casual yet resolute.

"Oh, no. That's really not necessary," she stammered, flustered by the offer. "I'll just catch a cab."

"At this hour? In this neighborhood?" Rowan arched a skeptical eyebrow. "You'd be lucky to find one. And even if you did, it'd cost you twenty bucks." His smirk softened the firmness in his voice. "Besides, I'm free."

Aislinn opened her mouth to protest, but Rowan had already turned toward the other end of the bar. "Ariel! I'm stepping out. I'll be back soon."

Before she could get a word in, Rowan turned back to her, his voice warm yet leaving no room for debate. "Wait here."

And with that, he disappeared into the kitchen, leaving Aislinn staring after him—equal parts bewildered and amused. "What did I just get myself into?" she muttered under her breath, the faintest smile tugging at her lips.

<u>Chapter Four</u>
First Kiss, Last Chance

Rowan strode to his back office, snatching his leather jacket from the hook by the door. Offering to take Aislinn home hadn't been part of the plan—hell, he didn't even know what had made him suggest it. Maybe it was the sharp unease crawling up his spine whenever the Golden Dawn came to mind. Their sudden interest in her didn't add up, and picturing her out there alone made him feel protective. *That's all it is, he told himself. Just a need to keep her safe. Practical. Detached. No deeper meaning.*

That wasn't the whole story, was it? She shadowed his thoughts like an elusive melody, one he couldn't shake no matter how hard he tried. An undeniable pull—raw instinct more than reason—had driven his offer before he'd even thought it through. He couldn't pinpoint what it was about her—maybe the way her presence clung faintly in the air, persistent and impossible to ignore. It didn't make sense yet, but it was enough to keep him on edge. If he hadn't spoken up, she might've walked out that door and vanished, leaving a hollowness he couldn't quite explain.

Rowan shook his head, muttering under his breath. Showing up unannounced at her place, armed with the excuse that he'd memorized her address from her driver's license, was out of the question. Just thinking about it made his shoulders tense. No, this is better. He'd take her home, make sure she got there safely, and leave it at that. Clean. Simple. At least, that's what he kept telling himself, even as the logic felt as thin as the air between them.

He snagged Ariel's jacket from the hook beside his own, letting the soft leather drape over his arm as he strode back to the front of the bar.

Aislinn sat perched at the bar, her fingers idly twisting the straw in her soda as if it might unravel the knots in her stomach. When Rowan emerged, her heart tripped over itself, betraying her calm exterior. The leather jacket clung to him like it belonged there, emphasizing the width of his shoulders and the fluid, unhurried strength in his stride. Another jacket dangled from his hand, his expression steady and impenetrable—a combination that sent a shiver racing through her, equal parts unsettling and magnetic.

She swallowed hard, second thoughts crashing into each other. *Letting a stranger—this stranger—take me home?* What am I thinking? Her dad would flip, and Johnny? He'd probably storm in with all the righteous fury of a younger brother determined to drag her out by the arm.

Still, Rowan had a presence that unraveled her usual caution. Despite the sharpness of his features and the enigmatic air he wore like armor, there was an undeniable solidity to him. Maybe that's why she hadn't bolted.

"You ready?" His voice cut through her spiraling thoughts, low and steady.

He was closer now, close enough that she had to tilt her head to meet his eyes. His gaze held hers, unwavering yet disarming—a quiet weight that made her chest tighten. *Is it nerves? Or... something else?* She couldn't pin it down, and the uncertainty gnawed at her.

All Aislinn could do was nod. Her throat felt tight, her voice too unreliable to risk speaking. Before the awkward silence could stretch, Rowan reached out and took her hand. His grip was steady and warm, an silent reassurance that sent a jolt racing through her—sharp, electrifying, like the first crack of lightning in a storm. Wordlessly, he guided her toward the door, his presence a curious balance of calm authority and restrained intensity that left her pulse unsteady.

They stopped briefly at the counter where Ariel was sorting through a pile of tips, her fingers moving with practiced ease.

"Ariel, I'm borrowing your jacket," Rowan said, holding it up with a glance that left no room for argument.

Ariel's gaze flicked up, darting between Rowan and Aislinn before her lips curved into a sly smile. "Oh, really?" she teased, her voice light with amusement.

Rowan raised a finger before she could push further, his tone firm. "Not a word."

Ariel laughed softly, lifting her hands in mock surrender as her grin widened. "Sure, sure. Whatever you say."

Outside, the night air greeted them with a cool edge, brushing against Aislinn's skin and easing the discomfort simmering just beneath the surface. She exhaled slowly, the rhythmic crunch of their footsteps on the pavement filling the quiet around them.

They walked down the dimly lit street until Rowan stopped in front of a gleaming red motorcycle. The bike seemed alive even as it sat unmoving, its sleek curves catching the faint glow of the streetlights. It radiated raw energy—wild and untamed—that reminded her of Rowan himself, leaving her caught between admiration and unease.

Rowan turned and held out the jacket he'd been carrying—Ariel's. "Here," he said simply.

She hesitated before taking it, her fingers brushing the worn leather. The jacket was oversized, a little rough around the edges, and far bolder than anything she'd normally wear. As she slipped it on, its weight settled over her shoulders like an anchor, pacifying her in the present. The feeling was oddly comforting, even as her mind raced with the sense of standing on the brink of the unknown. *Two paths,* she thought. *One leads back to safety; the other, to him—and everything he might drag me into.*

Rowan swung his leg over the motorcycle with practiced ease, settling into the seat as if the machine were an extension of him. He glanced back, his posture relaxed, yet his presence filled the space with authority. "Come on," he said, his words carrying a quiet certainty.

Aislinn blinked, her gaze fixed on the motorcycle as if it might sprout wings and fly. "You want me to ride that?" she asked, incredulity sharpening her tone.

Rowan paused, one hand adjusting the helmet he'd just grabbed. He glanced at her over his shoulder, a faint smirk tugging at his lips. "Why not?" he replied, a teasing edge coloring his tone as he tossed his hair back and slipped on the helmet. His movements were maddeningly fluid, a casual grace that came from knowing exactly what he was doing—and enjoying every second of watching her second-guess it.

In that sliver of time, Rowan considered the closeness the ride would demand—the feel of someone pressed against him, trusting him completely. It was an subtle intimacy, impossible to avoid on a bike. The thought clung to him longer than it should have, unsettling in its suddenness, before he brushed it aside.

He glanced back at her again, his gaze carrying a subtle challenge, daring her to step into the unknown.

Aislinn stared at the motorcycle like it might spring to life and devour her whole. Her stomach churned, every nerve sparking at the thought of climbing onto that thing. "I think I'm better off calling a cab," she muttered, her words failing to mask the tension tightening her chest.

"Aislinn." Rowan softened his tone, wrapping her name in quiet reassurance that seemed to promise more than just safety on the bike. "It's perfectly safe. I'll go slow, I promise."

A shiver skated down her spine, and she knew it wasn't entirely from the cool night air. The look he gave her—unyielding, like he wouldn't take no for an answer—made her pause. Against her better judgment, she reached for the helmet, her fingers brushing his for the briefest second.

She turned it over in her hands, her grip tightening as she searched for a reason to keep stalling. "What kind of bike is it?" she asked, hoping the question might extinguish her spinning thoughts.

Rowan's expression shifted, his smirk giving way to a flicker of pride. "A fully restored 1951 Harley Panhead," he said, his tone dipping into reverence. He glanced at the bike, regarding it as more than just a machine, as though it were a part of him—an extension of his identity. "She's built for two now," he added more casually, his hand brushing the smooth leather seat he'd replaced.

Aislinn followed his gaze, the knot in her stomach still tight. His pride in the bike was undeniable, and for reasons she couldn't quite explain, that steadied her—if only a little. It was obvious he cared about this machine. If he'd go out of his way to protect anything, it would be his prized possession.

Rowan extended his hand, his expression unreadable. "Do you trust me?"

The weight of the question hung in the cool night air, heavier than she'd anticipated. This wasn't just about the bike—there was more behind his words, an unspoken depth she wasn't ready to name. Her thoughts tangled, fighting to keep up with the quickening beat of her heart. After what felt like an eternity, she slipped the helmet on and placed her hand in his, her pulse surging as she climbed onto the back of the bike.

"If you promise to go slow," she murmured under her breath over her racing thoughts. Then, with a soft grumble, she added, "I must be out of my mind."

Her arms slid around his waist, the motion hesitant, necessary only for balance. She felt him tense briefly before his body relaxed under her touch. The warmth radiating from him caught her off guard, sending a jolt through her that she couldn't quite ignore.

Rowan tilted his head slightly toward her, his amusement clear. "I promise to go slow," he said, a teasing note slipping in before he added, "And for the record, the best people are out of their minds."

The engine roared to life beneath them, vibrating like a living, breathing thing. As they pulled away from the curb, Aislinn's grip around Rowan's waist tightened into an unrelenting vice.

Rowan's chuckle reverberated through his chest, the sound warm and unbothered. He placed a gloved hand over hers, his touch firm, providing quiet reassurance as he gently massaged her arm. The tautness in her grip began to ease, even as her heart raced.

"Both hands on the handlebars, please!" she shouted over the hum of the engine, her tone edged with nerves and exasperation.

His laugh came again, rich and unapologetic.

For the first few blocks, Aislinn kept her eyes squeezed shut, every bump in the road feeding her spiraling thoughts of disaster. As the bike glided with smooth control, the panic began to ebb, replaced by a surprising sense of calm. Rowan kept his promise—not speeding, not weaving recklessly through the streets.

Cautiously, she cracked her eyes open and found herself startled. The empty streets stretched ahead of them, lit by the dim amber glow of streetlights. The world seemed unexpectedly peaceful, the wind brushing her face with a crisp, refreshing edge. It wasn't nearly as terrifying as she'd imagined.

Rowan's hand rested briefly on her arm, a silent reminder that she wasn't alone. Still, she muttered under her breath, "He really needs to keep both hands on the bars."

The thought hit her suddenly. "Do you even know where you're going?" she called out, raising her voice unnecessarily over the hum of the engine.

Rowan's reply came back unhurried. "Nope. And by the way, you don't have to yell. The helmets have mics."

Heat flushed Aislinn's cheeks, embarrassment rushing over her. "Oh, God," she muttered. "I'm so sorry."

His chuckle filtered through the mic, light and easy. "No worries," he said, patting her arm lightly. "So, what's the plan? Are you going to tell me where to go, or should we just cruise around all night?"

She hesitated, biting her lip before finally giving him her address. "Haight Street. Between Cole and Shrader," she said, her tone quieter now, almost shy.

Rowan grinned to himself, sensing the subtle shift as she leaned into him. "Haight it is," he said, his words carrying a teasing lilt as the bike glided smoothly down the road.

As the speed increased, Aislinn instinctively pressed herself closer, her head resting lightly against his back. The wind whipped around them, tugging at her hair. The mingled scents of leather, sandalwood, and a faint trace of mint soothed her in the moment. Rowan felt solid, a steady presence that caught her off guard. A soft sigh escaped her as she let go of the remaining tension she was holding.

"You okay back there?" Rowan asked over the hum of the engine, his concern evident in the gentle tone of his voice.

"I'm fine," she replied quickly, her tone a touch too bright. "Just… yawning."

Rowan hummed, a low sound that hinted he didn't fully believe her but chose not to push. His focus returned to the road, though he remained attuned to her presence.

Through the leather of his jacket, he could feel the faint pressure of her touch—a warmth that spiraled deeper than he anticipated. It hummed with a quiet intensity, sparking emotions he hadn't allowed himself to feel in years. He shook his head, trying to dismiss the thought, but it stayed, impossible to ignore.

She stirred feelings he wasn't sure he could name, let alone embrace.

As they neared her street, an unexpected pang of disappointment tugged at Rowan's chest. He didn't want this to end—not yet.

"Which building?" he asked, keeping his tone level despite the regret creeping in.

"The coffee shop on the left," she replied, her soft sigh echoing the ache he felt. *Is she feeling it too?*

Rowan guided the bike to the curb and switched off the engine. "Shoot," she murmured, the word quietly traveling through the mic. Her reluctance didn't escape him as her hands hovered lightly on his shoulders, holding for just a breath before she slid off the bike.

He removed his helmet, shaking his hair loose and brushing it from his eyes. When Aislinn handed him her helmet and Ariel's jacket, he strapped them both to the rack behind his seat, stealing a glance at her from the corner of his eye. She hadn't moved.

Their eyes met, the silence stretching between them, indefinable thoughts hovering in the cool night air.

"So..." Aislinn finally broke the deep lull, her tone softer than before. "I think it's my turn to offer you a drink. Want to come in for some coffee? I have plenty... unless, of course, you need to—"

Rowan chuckled, cutting her off with a slight shake of his head. "Sure. I've got time."

Stepping off the bike, he hung his helmet on the handlebars and turned back to her, a faint smile playing at the corners of his lips.

She unlocked the door to the shop, the muted chime of the alarm sounding as she disarmed it. Rowan followed her inside, his boots landing quietly on the wooden floors of the inviting space. The scent of roasted coffee hovered in the air, a rich, familiar reminder of the shop's heart and purpose.

"This way," she said, leading him through the shop and into the back, where a narrow staircase wound upward to a small studio apartment.

"Make yourself at home," Aislinn offered as she headed toward the kitchen. "The bathroom's on the left, if you need it."

"Thanks." Rowan glanced around, tugging off his gloves and sliding out of his jacket.

The apartment was compact, infused with a warmth that seemed uniquely hers. It was carefully divided into distinct, thoughtful sections: a cozy living area with a well-loved sofa, a small loveseat, and a modest television; an office nook with a desk and a bookshelf stuffed with novels and journals; and a sleeping area tucked behind folding screens. Every inch radiated personality, as though it had absorbed pieces of her over time.

He draped his jacket over the back of a chair at the small dining table, his gaze drifting over the personal touches—bright throw pillows, framed photos on the shelves, and a few mismatched mugs stacked near the sink.

"This is nice," he said, his tone genuine. "Can I help with anything?"

"No, I've got it," she replied with a quick smile over her shoulder, filling a kettle with water. "It's not much, just... home. I've only been here six months."

She stopped briefly before continuing. "I grew up near Pittsburgh. Ever been?" She glanced at him, curiosity lacing her words. "You've got an accent, though—not from here, right?"

He was struck by her sharpness—most people didn't notice his accent right away. "I've lived here a while, though I was born in Ireland." The admission came easily enough, though it stirred memories he preferred to leave untouched.

"I thought so," she said, a faint smile tugging at her lips. "Your accent fades in and out—it's subtle, but it's still there."

Rowan leaned against the counter, watching as she busied herself with the coffee, her movements quick and mindful. She was nervous—he could see it in the way her gaze flicked away from him and how she filled the silence with steady chatter. He stayed quiet, letting her words flow as his attention wandered: the way her dark brown hair shifted with each movement, the faint gleam of light catching in its waves, and the clean, fresh scent of citrus that surrounded her. It was... distracting.

Without realizing it, Rowan had moved closer, drawn by a pull he couldn't define. When she turned abruptly and found him standing just behind her, she froze, her eyes widening in surprise.

Aislinn startled, stepping back until the counter pressed against her hips. Her gaze locked with his, uncertain yet unwavering.

"I'm sorry," Rowan said softly, his hands bracing the counter on either side of her. He hadn't meant to corner her, and yet, there was no denying the closeness between them now. "I didn't mean to scare you."

"No, it's okay," she replied, her tone shaky as her chest rose and fell with uneven breaths.

They remained motionless, the space between them charged with an energy neither could ignore. Rowan's gaze traced the contours of her face, searching for the slightest hesitation. She didn't pull away. For so long, he'd kept everyone at a distance, walls built so high he hadn't imagined lowering them. With her, those walls seemed to crumble effortlessly, as though she'd found the gaps and slipped through.

"Aislinn..." he murmured, his voice low and unsteady as he leaned in. His lips brushed hers, light and hesitant, a kiss that asked rather than demanded.

Her throat tightened as her pulse thundered in her ears. When he pulled back, her lips tingled, the warmth of his kiss ghosting her skin.

"I've been wanting to do that all night," Rowan admitted, his voice calm, though his pulse raced beneath the surface.

Aislinn smiled, her cheeks flushed, her words quiet yet unyielding. "I've been wanting you to do that all night."

Her confession ignited something deep within him, a spark that flared into a fire he could no longer contain. Rowan cupped her face, his kisses growing bolder, fueled by the passion that had been simmering just beneath the surface. His arms encircled her waist, pulling her firmly against him, their bodies fitting together as though they had always belonged that way.

Her senses blurred—the heat of his touch, the faint taste of mint on his lips, the warmth radiating from where they pressed together. She clung to him, her fingers curling into the fabric of his shirt, savoring each kiss as though it were the only thing tethering her to the moment. The air seemed charged with electricity, crackling with the connection sparking between them.

When they finally broke apart, the world around them felt distant and small, as if only the two of them existed in that space. Their breaths mingled, hearts pounding in a shared rhythm.

Then, a shift. Rowan's expression darkened, his gaze clouding as he abruptly turned away, retreating behind the walls she had just begun to breach.

He cleared his throat, the sound rough and uneven. "I should go," he said, his Irish lilt heavier with the weight of his words. "I need to go."

Confusion flashed across Aislinn's face, her hesitation lasting only a heartbeat before she reached for him. Her fingers were gentle as they cupped his chin, guiding his face back toward hers. His eyes remained firmly shut, his jaw tense beneath her touch.

"Did I do something wrong?" she asked softly, her voice threaded with uncertainty.

Rowan's chest tightened, the ache cutting deeper than he'd expected at her question. The thought that she might blame herself, even for a second, was unbearable. How could this ever be her fault? Of all the fears that haunted him, the idea of making her feel unworthy of their fragile connection was one he hadn't prepared for.

"No, love," he rasped, the endearment slipping out before he could stop it. He brushed the back of his fingers along her cheek, the gesture tender despite the storm raging inside him. "You've done nothing wrong. I just..." He paused, his throat tightening as he struggled to find words that wouldn't shatter them both. "I can't do this right now."

The weight of his feelings cracked through his voice, each word threatening to break him. His eyes stayed tightly shut, as if keeping them closed could hold back the sorrow rising like a tidal wave.

When Rowan finally opened his eyes, the sadness there hit her like a wave, raw and devastating. It was the look of someone barely holding himself together, and for a fleeting instant, Aislinn thought he might crumble under the weight of emotions neither of them dared to name.

His fists clenched at his sides, the tendons flexing as though he was physically restraining himself. She could feel the tension radiating from him, an invisible pull he seemed determined to resist. He wanted to hold her—she could see it in the way looked at her, conflicted—yet something deeper restrained him, as though he knew that giving in might mean losing control entirely.

Her chest tightened, the ache spreading through her with a sharpness that didn't feel entirely her own. The grief in his eyes told her everything she needed to know—this wasn't a simple *"it's not you, it's me"* excuse. It was deeper, more jagged, a pain carved into him by something she couldn't yet understand. What had hurt him so profoundly? What haunted this man who seemed so strong, yet so achingly vulnerable? Aislinn wanted to reach for him, to take his sorrow into her hands and bear the weight of it herself.

"Yeah, okay, um... let me walk you to the door," she said softly, her voice trembling under the heaviness of the realization.

They walked in silence, the air weighted with silent thoughts. Aislinn led him down the narrow stairs and through the dimly lit coffee shop, the faint hum of the cooling equipment the only sound breaking the hush. When they reached the front door, she unlocked it and held it open, waiting for him to step outside and climb onto his bike.

Rowan didn't move.

He stood there, facing her, his expression unreadable. She thought he might speak—his lips parted slightly, as though words hovered just out of reach. Instead, he simply looked at her, his gaze searching. The sadness that remained in his eyes now carried something else—resignation, perhaps, or the quiet weight of acceptance.

Slowly, he reached out, his fingers grazing the side of her face with a tenderness that sent a shiver down her spine. Aislinn leaned into his touch instinctively, her eyes falling shut. It felt natural, as if this fleeting connection was the only certainty they shared, the only thing tethering them to the present.

"I'm sorry, Aislinn," Rowan murmured, his tone low, threaded with emotion.

She opened her eyes, meeting his gaze. The vulnerability etched into his expression was so stark, so raw, that her chest ached for him.

"Don't be," she said softly, her tone warm and certain. "There's nothing to be sorry about."

Rowan hesitated, his lips pursed as if he were physically holding back his thoughts. "Tonight... this wasn't a mistake," he began, his words low and rough-edged. "I just—I need time. There are things I have to work through before..."

He stepped closer, his hands settling lightly on her hips. Anxiety rolled off him, visible in the tight line of his shoulders and the flicker of conflict in his eyes. Aislinn didn't pull away, even as her heart pounded in her chest. She could feel the weight of his turmoil, the depth of whatever war he was fighting within himself.

"When you first walked into the bar," Rowan said, his voice softer now, "you asked if we'd met before. Like there was something between us that you couldn't quite explain."

"Yes," Aislinn said softly, her voice trembling just enough to betray the weight of her words. "That's exactly how it felt. How could you know that?"

He leaned in, his breath brushing her ear as he murmured, "Because I feel it too. Whatever this is—it's real." His tone wavered, as though speaking it aloud made the truth harder to bear.

Before she could answer, he pressed a tender kiss to her temple, the touch lingering just long enough for her to feel the weight of his emotions. As he pulled back, his hands slid slowly down her arms, his fingers giving a light, fleeting squeeze before he let her go.

Rowan's eyes met hers, a blend of sadness and determination reflected in his gaze. "This isn't goodbye," he said, his tone steady despite the emotion threading through it. "I just need to figure things out first. When I do, I'll come back—if you'll have me."

Aislinn's chest tightened at his words. She reached out, her hand resting lightly on his chest, where the strong, rapid beat of his heart pulsed beneath her palm. "Come back," she said softly, her words firm despite the ache growing within her. "I want you to come back."

Rowan nodded, his muscles hardening as though keeping himself together demanded every ounce of strength he had. Without another word, he turned toward the door.

Aislinn followed, her eyes never leaving him as he stepped outside, his silhouette framed by the faint glow of the streetlights. She watched as he mounted his bike, the engine growling to life in the stillness of the night.

"Rowan!" she called, her voice cutting through the quiet.

He froze, his shoulders stiffening before he turned his head slightly, not quite facing her.

"I believe in you," she said, her tone clear and unwavering, the weight of her feelings carried in every word.

The world seemed to hold its breath. His head dipped—a small, controlled acknowledgment—and for a heartbeat, she thought he might turn back. Instead, he tightened his grip on the handlebars and rode into the darkness.

Aislinn stood in the doorway, watching as the bike faded into the night. The ache in her chest was sharp, though beneath it stirred a quiet resolve. He'd said this wasn't goodbye, and she chose to believe him. Whatever storm Rowan was battling, she would be here when he found his way through it.

Yet, as the unmoving quiet of the night wrapped around her, a single thought lingered: *What if the storm is bigger than both of us?*

*R*owan's Week

Aislinn's words loitered in Rowan's mind, an unshakable refrain—*I believe in you.* Simple words, yet they carried a weight that tugged at a place buried deep within him. *Where have I heard them before?* The familiarity scraped at the edges of his memory, elusive and distant, like a shadow slipping just out of reach. His mind churned, restless and fragmented, as he tried to capture the source of the echo. Amid the chaos, one sensation cut through: the kiss.

It should have meant nothing—a spark lost in the noise. Yet it had stirred embers he thought long extinguished, igniting a fire raw and untamed. The intensity of it startled him, unearthing a need he hadn't expected, a yearning he couldn't yet define. *Why now?* The question pierced through the haze, sharp and unanswered.

The motorcycle's engine growled beneath him, its low rhythm steady against the blur of city lights streaking past. The night stretched ahead, an endless void devouring the road and everything in its path. Rowan's chest tightened, his breath caught in the storm of emotions threatening to overtake him. His grip on the handlebars turned rigid, knuckles stark against the darkness as he fought to hold steady.

And then, as if summoned by the chaos within him, her memory surfaced—Davina. She drifted into his mind, a phantom from a life he could scarcely recognize anymore. Her face was blurred now, softened like an old photograph worn by time. The fire he'd once felt for her had long since faded, dulled into a quiet, lingering duty. She was a promise he'd kept out of obligation, not love—a tether to a past that felt impossibly distant. *Am I still holding on to her? Or is she holding on to me?*

The road stretched endlessly, a dark ribbon winding through the night, offering no clarity—only more questions.

But Aislinn wasn't some ghost. She was real—present, undeniable—and the way she had looked at him left a mark he couldn't ignore. Her gaze had been open, vulnerable in a way that unsettled him. The memory of her eyes, the warmth of her lips, clung to him with a pull he couldn't resist, like embers glowing faintly in the dark. *Why her?* The question gnawed at him. *What is it about her that makes me want to reach for something more?* She had awakened a part of him he thought had been buried beneath his grief—fragile, trembling, and terrifying.

Rowan pulled up near Donnelly's, the bike's engine cutting out with a low, resonant rumble. He swung off in one fluid motion, securing it with the ease of habit. Inside, though, his mind refused to settle. Aislinn's kiss, Davina's memory, and the looming threat of the Golden Dawn tangled together in a relentless loop, blurring past and present until he couldn't separate one from the other. Each memory dragged another to the surface, leaving him unsteady, searching for footing he couldn't find.

It wasn't just loyalty to Davina's memory that weighed on him. It wasn't even the guilt hovering like a shadow at the edges of his mind. This was far more dangerous: hope. That insidious spark he'd buried long ago, one he had sworn never to let rekindle. *Hope doesn't get you anywhere—it just leaves you broken.* Yet here it was, creeping in uninvited, stirred to life by someone who refused to let him stay in the darkness he had made his home.

He stayed by the bike for awhile, the crisp night air biting at his skin. The bar loomed ahead, its familiar anonymity offering a fleeting promise of escape. Even that couldn't shield him from the turmoil raging within. Not this time.

Grabbing Ariel's jacket and the spare helmet, he moved toward the entrance, his legs on autopilot while his mind roiled with unanswered questions. As he stepped inside, the stark absence of voices and clinking glasses struck him. The silence pressed in, heavy and unrelenting, wrapping around him like a suffocating shroud.

Each step echoed faintly in the deserted space, amplifying the chaos roaring in his head. The familiarity of the bar felt distorted now, its silence a jarring contrast to the relentless noise within.

"Hey, how'd it—" Ariel started, her tone casual, laced with curiosity. Rowan cut her off with a raised hand and a sharp shake of his head. Words wouldn't come—not now. If he spoke, everything might spill out: the guilt, the yearning, the confusion... and worst of all, the memory of Aislinn's gaze. The way her expression had softened, open and unguarded, refused to let go of him.

I can't talk about it. Not yet. Without a word, he brushed past her, each step feeling heavier than the last.

His room greeted him with the familiar scent of leather and cedar—a familiar constant that hadn't changed. He tossed the helmet and jacket onto the chair before sinking onto the bed, the mattress absorbing the weight pressing down on him. For a passing second, the solid surface beneath him seemed to calm him, offering a fragile steadiness. The chaos inside him, however, refused to relent, dragging the night's events into sharp focus.

The Golden Dawn. Their growing presence gnawed at him, an unrelenting ache he couldn't ignore. *Why here? Why now?* And then there was Aislinn—the heart of it all. *What do they want with her? Why are they watching her so closely?* The questions surged through his mind, sharp and unforgiving. None of them, however, explained the one truth he couldn't escape: the maddening, undeniable need to protect her.

Why does it matter so much? The realization hit raw, unwelcome. *She's strong. She doesn't need me to save her.* Yet every instinct roared otherwise. The idea of her in danger struck a deep, unnameable chord, as though her light—so fierce and defiant against the darkness they fought daily—was a flame he couldn't let be extinguished.

He dragged a hand over his face, the rough motion doing little to calm the turmoil roiling in his head. Exhaustion clung to him—not to his body but to his mind, battered by the unrelenting tide of questions and emotions.

Aislinn's kiss. Davina's memory. The pull he couldn't define. They circled like predators, closing in with a weight that felt as binding as an ancient vow.

Enough. His jaw stiffened as he exhaled sharply through his nose, forcing the whirlwind to recede. Reflection wouldn't untangle the chaos. There were priorities, and this—whatever *this* was—had to wait. The job demanded his full attention.

Rowan snatched up his phone, his grip tightening as if the device were the only thing locking him to reality. His fingers moved swiftly over the screen, tapping out the number before bringing it to his ear. The faint hum of the connecting line steadied his pulse, if only slightly.

"This is Eileen." Her voice came through low, tempered by the kind of calm forged through years of leadership. It wasn't just composure—it was resolve, solid and unyielding, like the foundation of an ancient monument. That steadiness stabilized him, tethering him to purpose when the chaos threatened to pull him under. Without hesitation, he relayed the Golden Dawn's unsettling presence in San Francisco and their apparent focus on Aislinn. Saying their name aloud sent a chill through him, a visceral reminder of their violent history. His gut twisted as the words left his mouth.

"I need answers," he said, his tone clipped and calculated. Despite his effort to contain it, urgency crept in. "We need a meeting—one week."

The silence that followed wasn't empty—it carried weight, like the pause before an oath is sworn. When Eileen finally responded, her voice was firm, unwavering. "Understood. I'll coordinate the others." Then, sharper, exact: "You know what we're up against. Gather as much intel as possible." Her tone carried authority, layered with warning. The Golden Dawn wasn't just a threat—they were a storm on the horizon, waiting to break. Both of them understood the destruction it would bring.

Rowan ended the call, exhaling slowly as Eileen's words settled over him like iron shackles. He rolled his shoulders back, stretching against the tension coiled deep in his muscles. For the first time since leaving Aislinn's, clarity began to push back the fog clouding his mind—a faint light cutting through the chaos. *Stay on task.* The mantra repeated silently, a lifeline he gripped tightly. He couldn't let himself spiral now.

Pushing himself into motion, Rowan headed toward the front bar. Ariel was sprawled at one of the tables, her legs stretched over a chair as she half-watched a grainy black-and-white movie flashing on the wall-mounted TV. A bowl of popcorn rested in her lap, the steady crunch breaking the serenity of the room. It was her usual ritual, one he'd seen countless times—a way to avoid going home, though she never admitted it aloud.

Her gaze flipped to him as he approached, catching the strain etched into his features. Ariel's posture shifted, her relaxed demeanor giving way to a quiet attentiveness. She didn't need words to read him—she could see when something was wrong.

"Ariel, meet me in my office when you're done," Rowan said, his tone even, his focus already racing ahead.

"Sure thing, boss. Gimme ten," she replied, tossing another kernel into her mouth. Her voice remained light and casual, though her gaze sharpened, curiosity flickering in her eyes.

Rowan gave her a brief nod and moved on, leaving explanations behind as he headed toward his office. There was no time for hesitation—he had work to do.

Once inside, he didn't wait for Ariel. The door clicked shut behind him, and he moved with purpose, urgency pressing against him like the weight of an oncoming storm. The phone was already in his hand before he reached his chair, the familiar rhythm of action bringing a tenuous sense of control to the chaos swirling in his mind.

The first call went to Charlie, his long-time contact at the police department. Favors were a currency Rowan never let sit idle, especially when lives were at risk. Years ago, he'd helped Charlie close a few cold cases—murders and disappearances that defied explanation unless you considered truths most refused to believe. Rowan had offered just enough insight, wrapped in plausible explanations, to crack them. Charlie walked away with solved cases; Rowan walked away with a trusted ally.

Tonight, he called in that debt. "I need you to send a couple of patrols past a café in Haight-Ashbury, between Cole and Shrader," Rowan said, his tone precise and firm. "Overnight stakeouts, too. If anything seems out of place, I want to know immediately."

A pause followed, broken only by the scratch of a pen on paper. "You got it," Charlie replied gruffly. "But watch yourself, Rowan. You know how these things can escalate. Don't get in over your head."

"Thanks, Charlie. I'll handle it," Rowan said, ending the call with a curt nod to himself.

His next call went to Ying, the elderly woman who ran a cramped herbal shop tucked into a shadowed corner of Chinatown. To an outsider, her shop appeared to be just another cluttered storefront, its shelves stacked with dried roots and hand-labeled jars. Rowan, however, knew better. Ying was more than a merchant; her influence stretched into every vein of the supernatural underworld, as potent as the secret tea blends she brewed. She knew exactly who to ask, which whispers to follow, and when silence spoke louder than words.

The phone rang twice before Ying answered, her voice as crisp and direct as he remembered. "Rowan. What do you need?"

"Golden Dawn," he replied without preamble. "They've surfaced here. I need you to stay alert and keep watch." Anything you hear—any detail, no matter how small—let me know."

She didn't hesitate. "I'll see what turns up. Be careful, Rowan. They're like weeds—if you see one, there are ten more hiding beneath the surface."

Her warning lingered in his mind, curling like smoke. He knew the truth of it all too well.

"Those vipers have been stirring lately," Ying added, her voice brittle, like leaves crackling underfoot on a dry autumn day. "I'll see what slips through the cracks."

"Thanks, Ying," Rowan replied, his tone steady. He knew she'd follow through—she always did.

The final call went to Howard, a man Rowan relied on more than he liked to admit. Howard spent his days volunteering at Fisherman's Wharf, blending into the churn of tourists and locals. But his past was far darker than the cheerful backdrop of the bay. Years ago, the Golden Dawn had lured him in with promises of power and purpose, only for him to uncover the rot festering beneath their polished facade. What Howard had seen left him broken, his soul scarred in ways time could never heal.

Rowan had crossed paths with Howard not long after he quit the Golden Dawn. Their first meeting had been in a rain-slick alley, Rowan trailing him after sensing the unmistakable shadow of the organization clinging to him. When Howard stopped, Rowan stepped in, cornering him with relentless questions and demands. He still remembered the hollow look in Howard's eyes—haunted yet resigned, the gaze of a man who had walked away from darkness, carrying its weight deep within.

To Rowan's surprise, Howard hadn't resisted. He hadn't lied or tried to escape. Instead, he had stood there, rain dripping from his coat, and quietly shared truths Rowan hadn't been prepared to hear.

Since then, Howard had proven invaluable. Though he'd severed ties with the Golden Dawn, he still knew their patterns, their whispers, and the ominous residue they left behind. Some connections, Rowan had learned, ran deeper than loyalty—deeper than blood.

The phone rang once before Howard answered, his voice roughened by too many cigarettes and nights spent chasing memories he wished he could forget. "Rowan. You've been busy."

"More than I'd like," Rowan admitted, leaning back in his chair. "Golden Dawn activity in the city. I need ears to the ground. Anything you catch—movement, names, even rumors—let me know."

Howard exhaled, the sound heavy with years of weariness. "I'll see what I can dig up. You know how they operate. They don't leave loose ends, and neither do I."

"That's why I'm counting on you," Rowan said, his voice carrying an unspoken note of gratitude. He didn't need to say more; Howard understood the stakes. He always did.

A brief pause followed before Howard spoke again, his tone quieter now. "Watch yourself, Rowan. They don't return to cities like this without a reason."

"I know." Rowan ended the call, his hand lingering on the phone longer than necessary. He had been in this game long enough to know Howard's warnings were never idle.

Rowan let out a slow, deliberate breath, the weight pressing on his shoulders easing—if only slightly—now that the wheels were in motion. Unease simmered beneath his skin, coiled tightly like a spring, but at least he had direction. A purpose. It dulled the cacophony in his head, even if only for a little while.

His gaze shifted to the window, where the glow from the streetlamps stretched jagged shapes across the walls. Outside, the city sprawled beneath a thick shroud of fog, its alleys seeming to breathe with secrets, conspiring to keep the truth hidden. *Doesn't matter,* Rowan thought, his hands balling into fists. *Soon enough, I'll drag those secrets into the light, whether they want to come or not.*

A sharp knock pulled Rowan from his thoughts. The door creaked open a beat later, and Ariel stepped inside, her discerning gaze sweeping over him as though she could see every crack in his armor.

"What's up, Rowan?" she asked, her tone cautious, tinged with humor. "You look like you've been in a fight... with your brain."

Rowan leaned back in his chair, a faint smirk tugging at the corner of his mouth despite himself. "Yeah, well, it's winning," he said dryly. His expression softened as he added in a quieter voice, "About earlier... sorry I was short with you."

Ariel arched an eyebrow, her grin quick and teasing as she placed a hand over her heart with mock dramatics. "You? Short with me? Never. Should I be worried? Is the apocalypse finally here?"

Rowan gave her a pointed look, faint amusement dancing in his eyes, which only made Ariel laugh harder.

She straightened, the playful glint in her gaze fading into genuine curiosity. "Okay, seriously. What's up?"

He hesitated, weighing his words. "I need you to become friends with Aislinn," he said at last. "Keep an eye on her for me."

Ariel's brows shot up, surprise flashing across her face before suspicion settled in. "The brunette from the bar? What's going on, Rowan? Did something happen, or are you just adding 'matchmaker' to your résumé?"

"She had some trouble tonight," Rowan explained, leaning forward slightly, his voice low and cautious. "A guy was bothering her. I want you to keep an eye out, make sure nothing else happens. And don't mention me."

Ariel tilted her head, narrowing her eyes as she leaned back and crossed her arms. "So, let me get this straight. I'm supposed to walk up to this girl, strike up a totally random friendship, and just... casually keep tabs on her? Got it. Should I at least mention that I work for a paranoid biker who's clearly crushing on her?"

Rowan's jaw tightened, his expression darkening. "Ariel."

"Okay, okay!" she said, holding up her hands in mock surrender. "Fine. No mention of you, your creepy stalker tendencies, or the fact that you haven't dated in, like, forever."

He sighed, the tension in his shoulders loosening slightly. "Just don't tell her anything about me that she doesn't need to know."

Ariel's grin returned, sly and full of mischief. "Relax, your secret's safe with me. I'll start tomorrow. Maybe I'll tell her I'm conducting a social experiment on making new friends."

Rowan ran a hand through his hair, muttering under his breath. "Why do I feel like this is going to backfire?"

"Because it probably will," Ariel replied, tossing a piece of popcorn into her mouth. "But hey, what's life without a little chaos?"

He managed a faint smile, shaking his head. "Just don't make it obvious."

"I wouldn't dream of it," Ariel shot back, rising with an exaggerated flourish. As she moved toward the door, she glanced over her shoulder, her expression a mix of amusement and mock seriousness. "And don't stay up all night brooding, okay? You'll get wrinkles."

"Thanks for the concern," Rowan replied, his tone dry, faintly edged with humor.

At the doorway, she paused, one hand resting on the frame. "I'll get the lights on my way out," she said with a genuine grin. "Sleep well, boss." She threw him one last playful smirk before disappearing down the hall.

The soft click of the door closing and the metallic snap of the lock left the room steeped in silence. Rowan leaned back in his chair, exhaling slowly, as though trying to loosen the tension coiled tightly in his chest. The night had been a whirlwind—questions, calls, and plans set into motion. He'd done everything he could for now, but the weight of it remained, pressing down with relentless persistence.

Even so, his mind refused to settle. The Golden Dawn's presence in the city gnawed at him, an insidious ache that wouldn't fade. They never appeared without reason, and he needed to uncover their purpose before it was too late. Yet no matter how hard he tried to focus on their movements, his thoughts kept circling back to Aislinn.

He dragged a hand over his face, the memory of her gaze flashing unbidden in his mind. There had been a spark in her eyes that disarmed him. Trust. Vulnerability. Strength. He hadn't been able to look away then, and now he couldn't stop replaying that moment, searching for meaning. *What is it about you?* The question surfaced again, restless and unresolved.

Shaking his head, Rowan reached for the desk lamp and turned it off, plunging the room into darkness. However, it offered no clarity, only a brief reprieve from the turmoil that refused to quiet. He moved through the shadowed halls, his steps steady while his thoughts churned ceaselessly. Outside, the city sprawled beneath a thick veil of night, its streets wrapped in fog, secrets hovering just out of reach. *Why do you keep pulling me back?* The question landed heavily, louder than the rest.

Finally reaching his bedroom, Rowan paused, letting the silence press against him. Tomorrow would bring its own set of demands—the Golden Dawn, his responsibilities to the Fallen, and undoubtedly more questions about Aislinn. For now, he needed rest. Even if sleep felt like a distant promise, his unanswered questions would stay, circling him like shadows he couldn't escape.

Rowan woke the next morning, determination settling in his chest like stone—unyielding and resolute. His contacts were gathering intel, but waiting had never been his style. He needed to see for himself what the Golden Dawn was planning, to feel the city's pulse under his own hands. The risks didn't matter—not when the stakes were this high.

And then there was Aislinn. The thought of her slipped into his mind uninvited, stubbornly rooting itself in the corners of his awareness. He'd spent half the night replaying glimpses of her: the quiet curve of her smile, the way she tucked a strand of hair behind her ear, the warmth in her gaze that seemed to quiet the chaos in his mind. *Focus,* he reminded himself sharply. *She doesn't need you distracted.* Yet no matter how firmly he tried to push her from his thoughts, she remained—a presence, soft but insistent, glowing faintly at the edges of his consciousness.

After strapping on his gear, Rowan stepped out into the crisp morning air. The chill stung his face, dragging him fully into the present. His mind locked on the task ahead. If the Golden Dawn had taken root in San Francisco, he would tear them out by their foundations.

Even as he moved with purpose, Aislinn's image stayed with him, hovering like a shadow he couldn't shake. He didn't fully understand why she mattered so much—not yet—but one thing burned clear: the Golden Dawn wouldn't touch her. Not while he was standing.

Rowan's first move was to reach out to his informants, knowing he needed every thread of information he could gather. Howard's call came first, jolting him into focus.

"I overheard two guys talking near a café on Haight," Howard said, his voice rough, laced with weariness. "From what I picked up, they're talking about a girl named Aislinn. She owns the place. I'm one of her regulars. They said she's 'the key.'"

Rowan froze, Howard's words sinking into him like lead. *He knows her?* The revelation caught him off guard, but the confirmation struck harder. The Golden Dawn wasn't just watching—they were targeting her. His suspicions were no longer abstract; they were fact.

"If Aislinn is 'the key' to whatever they're planning, I need you to keep her safe, Rowan," Howard continued, his tone grim. "The Golden Dawn's plans won't end well for her, and she's a sweet girl. She doesn't deserve to get caught up in this."

Rowan's grip tightened on the phone, his thoughts racing. The image of her being watched—hunted—twisted deep in his gut. He forced himself to stay composed, though frustration and urgency coiled tightly in his chest like a spring ready to snap.

When the call ended, Rowan sat in silence, Howard's words echoing in his mind. *The key?* Aislinn's life was simple, rooted in calm—a stark contrast to the shadows that consumed his. What could the Golden Dawn possibly want with her? The question gnawed at him, tightening its hold the longer he considered it. She didn't belong in this world of secrets and lies, and the idea of her being dragged into it chilled him.

He forced the surge of anger down, channeling it into action. His next call went to Charlie, who arranged discreet patrols near Aislinn's café. Rowan wanted her neighborhood monitored, every detail accounted for. "Keep it quiet," he instructed. "I don't want anyone catching on."

Finally, he contacted Ying. She was already working her angles, her shop in Chinatown buzzing with whispers from the supernatural underworld. "They're moving carefully," she told him. "But if they're targeting someone, they'll make a mistake. They always do."

Each report fed into Rowan's growing understanding of the Golden Dawn's movements, yet Howard's message persisted, a thorn digging deeper with every passing hour. *Why Aislinn?* He replayed every interaction he'd had with her, searching for a clue, an answer. But nothing surfaced—just the memory of her smile, the gentle cadence of her voice, and the way she'd looked at him, open and unguarded.

And still, the pieces didn't fit. Aislinn was calm, kind, and resilient—a light that cut clean through the shadows of his world. *Maybe that's why they noticed her.* The Golden Dawn thrived on power, on twisting goodness to serve their dark purposes. The thought sent a chill rippling through him. *They won't touch her,* he vowed silently. *Not while I can stop them.*

Determined to uncover their plans, Rowan spent the week descending into the city's shadowed depths. Each night, he prowled through dimly lit bars thick with the stench of spilled beer and despair, abandoned factories where rusted machines loomed like forgotten sentinels, and crumbling buildings steeped in whispered secrets. Beneath the fractured glow of streetlights and shining neon signs, unseen currents twisted and shifted. In these shadows, lives were bartered like cheap goods, far removed from the city's polished veneer.

This was where the Golden Dawn thrived—in the cracks where rules dissolved into nothingness. Rowan moved like a predator, his steps silent as he melted into the gloom, his presence barely a ripple in the oppressive space. He collected fragments of information—murmured names, furtive glances, cryptic symbols scratched into crumbling walls like warnings for those who knew how to read them. The air in these places was thick with a restless energy that thrummed in his bones, ancient and malevolent, like the echoes of curses never lifted.

The Golden Dawn operated like ghosts, slipping in and out of abandoned buildings with unnerving precision. Rowan tracked their movements, unraveling faint threads of their plans, motives buried beneath layers of secrecy. Yet, even as he hunted them, his mind veered back to Aislinn. *What do they want with her?* The question gnawed at him, insistent, tugging at the edges of his focus.

Aislinn, with her quiet strength and unguarded warmth, felt like a world apart from the shadows consuming his reality. She was light in places where despair thrived, a calm presence that defied the darkness. He couldn't stop picturing her—steady and composed, carrying an unspoken resilience that drew him in despite himself. The memory of her laughter, soft and unguarded, stayed on in his mind like a flame cutting through the blackness, easing the weight of the hunt. The idea of someone like her being dragged into this ugliness twisted his gut. *And it's not just duty that draws me to her.* The realization unsettled him, stirring emotions he had long since buried.

One night, his patience finally paid off. He shadowed a pair of Golden Dawn operatives down a narrow alley, the damp air tinged with the metallic tang of rust and decay. Their movements were vigilant, their heads bowed, their steps echoing softly against the slick pavement. Rowan followed from the shadows, his presence a ghostly whisper as he tracked them to a decrepit warehouse on the waterfront. The structure loomed ahead, its jagged silhouette cutting against the faint glow of the city, exuding an aura of abandonment and secrecy.

The warehouse's weathered metal siding was streaked with rust, faint reflections of the bay shimmering across its surface like fragmented glass. The door creaked open, spilling murky yellow light into the night. Rowan pressed himself against the cold brick of a nearby building, his breath controlled, every sense sharpened as he listened. Voices spilled into the night air, low and guttural, their cadence laced with an unnatural edge that set his instincts on high alert.

"...the ritual is set... the girl mustn't be—"

The words hit him like a hammer, freezing him in place. *The girl.* His mind leapt immediately to Aislinn. The connection was undeniable, cutting through his thoughts with brutal clarity. His gut twisted at the implication, dread tightening like a vice around his chest. Her image surged forward—her quiet strength, the warmth in her gaze that steadied him in ways he couldn't explain, the way her presence softened the harsh edges of his chaotic world.

What makes her so important to them? The question thundered through him, relentless and consuming.

Before he could piece it together, a figure stepped out of the warehouse, the dim light carving sharp shadows across his angular features. The man's gaze swept the darkness with a predatory intensity, his posture stiff, as though he could feel the faint ripple of Rowan's presence. Rowan melted deeper into the shadows, every muscle taut, ready to vanish at the first sign of discovery.

The man lingered, head tilting slightly, as if listening for a sound just beyond reach. After a tense heartbeat, he let out a low grunt and slipped back into the warehouse, the door groaning shut behind him. The sound reverberated through the night, heavy and ominous, settling like a weight in Rowan's chest.

Rowan waited a bit longer, his senses razor-sharp and his thoughts racing. The warehouse wasn't just a meeting point—it was a nexus, a convergence of power on the verge of being unleashed. Whatever the Golden Dawn was planning, it was larger and more dangerous than he had feared. And at the center of it, undeniably, was Aislinn.

The realization struck with unrelenting force, dragging a torrent of emotions in its wake—fear, anger, and a fierce, desperate need to protect her. Beneath it all, a deeper emotion stirred, one he refused to name. He couldn't forget the way she'd looked at him that night at the bar, her hesitant smile both grounding and disarming. This wasn't just about keeping her safe—it was *her* that mattered.

No matter how much he told himself to stay away, Rowan found himself drawn to her coffee shop night after night. The brisk San Francisco air clung to him as he melded into the dim cityscape, a silent guardian watching from the shadows. From his vantage point, he could see through the café's windows as Aislinn finished her day—sweeping the floors, wiping down tables, locking the door. Her movements were habitual and steady, her routine so unassuming that it felt almost cruel against the storm closing in around her. She had no idea. The realization coiled tightly in his chest, sharp and unrelenting. The universe had left her in blissful ignorance while danger crept closer with every passing hour.

His unease grew sharper each night. Occasionally, figures idled near the shop—men leaning against lampposts or sitting in idling cars, their attention fixed on the café. Golden Dawn operatives. Rowan recognized the signs instantly—the calculated movements, the sharp stares, the barely restrained tension in their posture. They hadn't made a move yet, but the air around them felt charged, heavy with intent. They were watching. Waiting. Calculating.

The waiting gnawed at him, his instincts screaming to intervene—to walk inside, warn her, pull her away from harm. Yet he held himself back, his legs locked, his pulse pounding with the effort. Not yet. Acting now would only make things worse. She didn't know him well enough to trust him, and even if she did, revealing the truth would only paint a larger target on her back.

Rowan's world wasn't hers—not yet, and not if he could help it. He had seen what happened to people like her when they were dragged into the shadows. It broke them, left scars that never fully healed. The thought of Aislinn looking at him with fear—of seeing the warmth in her gaze replaced by suspicion and wariness—pressed down on him with unbearable weight. As long as she remained unaware, she had a chance to live untouched by the darkness consuming his life.

And yet, every night, he delayed a little longer, his resolve splintering under the strain. Watching her from the edges felt like torment, his emotions trapped between cold logic and an undeniable pull. His chest tightened every time she smiled, the soft curve of her lips stirring feelings he couldn't name but couldn't suppress. He found himself noticing the way she tucked a strand of hair behind her ear as she worked, how her expression softened when she thought no one was looking. She wasn't just kind or composed; she was magnetic, pulling him closer even as he told himself to stay away.

The timing wasn't right. The Golden Dawn was circling, and until Rowan uncovered their plans and found a way to stop them, distance was his only option. For now, all he could do was stand watch, his emotions a tangled knot of frustration and longing as he guarded a woman who had no idea how close danger truly was—or how deeply she had rooted herself in his thoughts.

Ariel had seamlessly worked her way into Aislinn's life, slipping in with a charm and ease Rowan couldn't help but respect. Her laid-back demeanor made her the perfect confidante—someone Aislinn could share coffee and conversation with after hours without hesitation. Each evening, Ariel returned with updates, recounting the harmless details: Aislinn's laughter, her stories about the café, the rhythm of her days.

While Ariel's reassurances soothed Rowan's immediate fears, they did little to quell the frustration gnawing at him. The threat loomed, circling the edges of her life like a predator waiting to strike. Worse, he hated standing on the sidelines, watching Ariel step into the role he wished he could claim—the one who could stand beside Aislinn, protect her, and truly know her beyond the fragments Ariel brought back.

Sometimes, late at night, Rowan caught himself wondering if Aislinn ever mentioned him to Ariel. *Does she think about me?* The question surfaced uninvited, sharpening the memory of her gaze at the bar, the faint blush that had colored her cheeks when their eyes met. He wasn't sure he wanted the answer. If she thought of him, it would only deepen the pull he already felt toward her. If she didn't... the thought of being just another passing stranger in her world stung more than he cared to admit.

As Ariel described Aislinn's laughter, Rowan found himself clinging to every detail: the image of her smile, the sound of her voice, the way she seemed to brighten the spaces around her. He told himself it was about understanding her, about staying ahead of the Golden Dawn's plans. Yet beneath the surface, he knew it was more than that. Aislinn wasn't just someone he felt obligated to protect—she had become someone who mattered, in ways that left him unsettled and exposed in equal measure.

Each night, Rowan returned to his apartment above Donnelly's, his boots thudding against the creaky stairs under the weight of the day. In the dim light of his battered living space, he spread out the notes and reports his contacts had gathered, the table in the corner just holding the disarray of papers. He studied every scrap of information with relentless focus, trying to force the fragmented pieces into a cohesive whole. The picture was forming, but maddening gaps remained. The Golden Dawn's presence in San Francisco wasn't random—of that, he was certain. They were planning something calculated, something vast. And Aislinn was caught at the center.

The realization coiled in his chest, sharp and consuming. Howard's intercepted conversation offered the only concrete clue: *the girl.* That was how they referred to her, stripping away her identity and reducing her to a pawn in their designs. The very notion made his blood burn. *What do they see in her that I don't? Why Aislinn?*

Rowan leaned back in his chair, dragging a hand over his face, his mind chasing answers that refused to surface. He replayed their brief night together, searching for some overlooked clue. But clarity eluded him. Instead, the memories only deepened his turmoil. The softness in her voice when she thanked him, the quiet trust in her eyes as he'd walked her home, the unspoken connection before the kiss—it all endured, embedding itself deep within him. That kiss, sudden and electric, had unraveled a part of him, stirring emotions he thought had been buried for good.

Nothing in her life, nothing in her calm demeanor, hinted at why she'd draw the attention of a group as ruthless as the Golden Dawn. he was balanced, kind, and far removed from the shadows that defined his existence. And yet, she stayed with him, slipping past walls he'd kept fortified for years. It wasn't just her words or actions that haunted him—it was the way she'd looked at him that night. That moment, free of judgment or fear, had left an imprint deeper than he wanted to admit. Trust like hers was rare, and for someone like Rowan, almost impossible to comprehend.

The more Rowan dwelled on her, the harder it became to center his focus. Aislinn wasn't just another thread in the tangled web of lies and shadows he was unraveling. She was real, vibrant, and utterly unprepared for the storm building around her. The thought of her being dragged into this world—her warmth, her light diminished by the cruelty of the Golden Dawn—twisted deep inside him, anger simmering just beneath the surface.

The image of her in their grasp pierced him, leaving him raw in a way he hadn't felt in years. This wasn't just about duty anymore. Somewhere along the way, protecting her had crossed a line he hadn't intended, becoming deeply, unmistakably personal.

As the week dragged on, each tick of the clock seemed to grow louder, the sound drilling into Rowan's mind with relentless precision. Every passing hour felt like a tightening grip, the Golden Dawn's plans inching forward while he scrambled to assemble the fractured pieces of their motives. Frustration burned hotter with every minute of inaction. He was no stranger to uncertainty, to operating in the shadows where answers were scarce. Yet this was different. This wasn't about outmaneuvering an enemy or dismantling a strategy. This was about her. And the stakes had never felt higher.

His gaze fell to the scattered notes on the table, the scribbled words blurring as his thoughts strayed to Aislinn. She didn't deserve this—not the looming threat, not the scrutiny, not the suffocating weight of being called "the key" to something so sinister. The more he struggled to untangle her role in the Golden Dawn's designs, the more deeply he realized she had crawled her way into his world. Protecting her wasn't just another mission. It had become a vow—silent but unyielding—a promise he couldn't break, no matter the cost.

After a long week, the day of the Fallen meeting finally arrived. Rowan spread everything he'd uncovered across the battered table—the Golden Dawn's movements, Howard's grim warning, Ariel's updates. The puzzle pieces were there, scattered before him, yet the full picture remained infuriatingly incomplete. Too many questions hovered unanswered, too many gaps still cloaked in shadow. One truth, however, was undeniable: time was slipping away.

As he prepared for the meeting, his mind drifted back to Aislinn. Keeping his distance had been a trial of will like no other. Every instinct screamed at him to close the gap, to shield her from the tightening noose of danger encircling her life. Yet logic held him in check. Acting now, without fully understanding the Golden Dawn's intentions, would only deepen the risk. The unknowns loomed larger than his need to act.

And yet, she hovered at the edges of his resolve, pulling him back into memories that refused to fade. The hesitant smile she'd given him that night in the bar surfaced again—the way it had softened the storm inside him, steadying him in ways he couldn't explain. Aislinn had left her mark on him, quiet yet indelible, no matter how much he tried to bury it.

A faint smile tugged at his lips as a thought emerged, unbidden: *What if?* What if he could abandon the shadows and stand beside her in a life that felt real? The notion carried a fragile warmth, a fleeting flicker of hope in the suffocating darkness that surrounded him. But the thought dissolved as quickly as it had come, replaced by the cold weight of reality. Time was slipping through his fingers—for her, for him, for whatever the Golden Dawn was orchestrating. And beneath it all, a gnawing fear coiled tightly in his chest: the quiet, insistent dread that he might already be too late.

He inhaled deeply, forcing the thought aside. There was work to be done—answers to find, battles to fight. Yet even as he shifted his focus to the task ahead, the truth clung to him like a shadow. Protecting Aislinn had grown into a far more dangerous influence than duty. It was personal now. And that, more than anything, terrified him.

Chapter Six
Silent Days

Aislinn's Week

Aislinn woke the next morning with a spring in her step, warmth unfurling within her like a treasured secret. Memories of the night before pulsed vividly through her mind, alive with energy, as if the low, rumbling purr of Rowan's motorcycle still vibrated through her ribs. She could almost feel the rhythm coursing under her skin, a visceral echo of a thrill she hadn't expected. At first, apprehension had gripped her, her hands clutching the leather of his jacket like it was a lifeline while she muttered sharp complaints about the "death trap" he insisted was perfectly safe. Then the city had blurred into streaks of light, the world dissolving into motion and wind.

By the time her hair whipped free in the cool night air, fear had unraveled, leaving exhilaration in its place. It felt as though she'd slipped into a world crafted solely for them—woven from the endless road, the crisp night breeze, and Rowan's steady presence ahead of her. *I never imagined I'd love anything so reckless,* she mused, a small smile tugging at her lips.

And then, there was the kiss.

The memory swept through her, drawing her hand to her lips as a rush of warmth spread through her entire being. The heat of his mouth on hers, the sure grip of his hands on her waist—it had been unlike anything she'd known. The world had faded into nothing, leaving only the two of them in a moment so vivid, it hardly seemed real.

Her mind shifted, and the buoyant glow dimmed. A shadow crept into the memory, eroding its clarity. The night hadn't ended as seamlessly as the kiss had promised. Rowan had pulled away, his features clouded by an emotion heavy and unspoken, like a barrier rising between them, solid and unyielding.

What is he hiding? The question settled uneasily in her thoughts, an unwelcome weight pressing against her mind.

Even then, she'd known that whatever haunted him wasn't fleeting. She'd seen it in the way he looked at her—like he wanted to let her in but couldn't. Not yet.

So, she resolved to be patient, to give him the space he needed to confront the shadows clinging to him. Still, beneath her resolve, unease stirred. *What if time isn't enough?*

Shaking off the creeping doubts, Aislinn threw herself into the rhythm of her morning routine. Her hands moved quickly, twisting her hair into a neat bun, the practiced motions helping her focus. By the time she headed downstairs, her steps carried renewed energy.

Rain and Takoda were already busy—Rain arranging small bouquets on the tables, her movements precise, while Takoda restocked the pastry case with calm efficiency.

Aislinn flipped the sign to Yes, We're Open and flashed a grin at her friends.

"Someone's in a good mood today," Takoda teased, her curiosity evident as she glanced up. "Care to share why?"

Aislinn shrugged, keeping her tone light. "Oh, no reason. Just had a good time last night. Thanks for dragging me out."

Rain, ever the sharper observer, tilted her head, a smirk curving her lips as she adjusted a vase on one of the tables. Mischief sparkled in her gaze. "Soo, Ash, how'd you get home last night?"

Aislinn paused for a split second before turning to the coffee maker, pretending it suddenly required her complete focus. "Oh, um. Rowan gave me a ride."

"Rowan? The bartender?" Takoda asked, her eyebrows lifting as she leaned against the counter with a casual air.

"That's the one." Aislinn couldn't fight the grin pulling at her lips, even as she made a valiant effort to stay composed. *Don't give them more than they're asking for,* she reminded herself, but the excitement bubbling inside her was difficult to conceal.

Takoda wasn't one to let a good story slip by. She leaned in slightly, her intrigue almost tangible. "I don't think that grin would be so big if he just dropped you off. What else happened?"

Oh, for the love of— Aislinn tried to suppress the warmth creeping into her cheeks, but the memory of the kiss flared, vivid and intoxicating.

Her face heated, and she ducked her head, pretending to fuss with the coffee machine. "I, uh, invited him in for a coffee... as a thank-you for the ride."

Rain's entire face lit up, excitement radiating from her like a cat spotting an unguarded bowl of cream. "Did he enjoy his coffee?" she asked, her words practically dripping with playful curiosity.

Aislinn's cheeks burned hotter. "He didn't actually... get to drink it."

Rain all but bounced on her toes, her enthusiasm spilling over. "C'mon, Ash, spill it already!"

Takoda leaned farther onto the counter, her grin almost as wide as Rain's. "Yeah, no way he skipped coffee and just walked out. We need details."

Aislinn sighed, resigning herself to the inevitable. Her friends wouldn't let up until they heard everything, and honestly, part of her didn't mind sharing. "Fine. We kissed."

The confession unleashed a chorus of squeals that echoed through the café, Rain and Takoda clapping like they'd orchestrated the incident themselves. Aislinn couldn't help but laugh at their over-the-top reactions, her earlier embarrassment dissolving into warmth.

"And... how was it?" Rain leaned in, her eyes gleaming with uncontainable curiosity.

Before she could stop herself, Aislinn let out a dreamy sigh. "It was... earth-shattering."

Their delighted laughter bubbled through the café like champagne, effervescent and infectious. Aislinn allowed herself to bask in their excitement, her own happiness blooming brighter with every burst of laughter. For a little while, Rowan's distant attitude slipped from her thoughts, replaced by the golden glow of the memory. *Maybe that really was as perfect as it felt,* she thought.

The bell above the door chimed, interrupting their bubble of laughter. Their chatter dwindled as they turned to see who had entered, the café's earlier joy shifting into the subdued hum of activity. Aislinn's bright smile softened as Howard stepped inside.

His movements were slower than usual, cautious, and his gaze flitted around the room, never staying on anyone—or anything—for more than a instant. There was an unease in the way he carried himself that sent a prickle across the back of Aislinn's neck. *What's bothering him?* She instinctively straightened, her focus sharpening.

"Hi, Howard!" she called, infusing her greeting with warmth as she moved toward the counter. Maybe a friendly tone could lighten the weight he seemed to be carrying. "Everything okay?"

Howard glanced up, a small grin tugging at his lips, though it lacked its usual energy. Lines etched his face, and his hand drifted to the back of his neck, rubbing absently, as if working out a knot of tension.

"Oh, I'm fine, thanks," he replied, his tone carrying a distracted edge. "Just one of those mornings, you know? Feels like I've forgotten something important. Getting older does that to you."

"You're sharp as a tack, Howard," Takoda said, her cheerful lilt cutting through the air as she slid the pastry case shut. "Want your regular?"

"Yes, please, thanks," he said, his response slower than usual, his attention elsewhere. His eyes darted toward the door before he added, "The boys are extra hungry today."

Aislinn noticed Rain lift a questioning eyebrow from across the counter, and she responded with a small shrug. Howard was usually steady, even in a rush, *What's different today?* she wondered, her brow furrowing. *What's got him so on edge?*

Even as she prepared his order, the strange pressure remained, curling at the edges of her thoughts like an unanswered question.

As Aislinn rang him up, she couldn't ignore how his attention kept flicking toward the door. His shoulders were rigid, his posture wound tight, as though he were bracing for an attack. Rain and Takoda worked seamlessly through their usual rhythm, assembling his order with practiced ease, while Aislinn's focus stayed locked on Howard, her concern deepening. *What's going on with him?* she wondered again, the unease settling heavier this time.

"So, Aislinn, how've you been?" Howard asked suddenly, his tone casual, though there was a sharpness in his question that made her pause. His focus locked onto her, steady and probing, sending a ripple of unease through her. "Anything unusual happen in, say, the last day or so?"

The question caught her off guard. She froze briefly, trying to piece together what he might mean. "No, not that I'm aware of," she replied slowly, her uncertainty clear. "That'll be $26.50."

Howard handed over the cash, his fingers brushing hers briefly. His touch was cool, almost clammy, and Aislinn's frown deepened. She glanced up, searching his features for clues, but his focus had already shifted elsewhere.

Sensing the nervousness thickening in the room, Takoda stepped in, her lively energy slicing through the heavy air. "I threw in a little extra for the boys. Gotta keep them fed," she said brightly, her tone cutting through the stress like sunlight breaking through a cloud.

Howard's lips curved slightly, but the relief Takoda aimed for didn't quite reach his eyes. "Thank you, ladies," he murmured, his tone quieter now, distant.

As he turned to leave, he stopped at the door. Slowly, he turned back, his gaze fixing on Aislinn with a weight she wasn't used to seeing from him. "Be careful, okay?"

Aislinn blinked, startled by the gravity in his tone. "Yeah, sure, Howard. I will," she said, her words quieter than she meant them to be.

The door swung shut behind him, and the three of them stood in silence, their eyes following him through the glass. He shuffled down the street, his hunched shoulders heavy with an unseen burden.

Rain broke the quiet first. "What was that all about?"

"I don't know," Aislinn murmured, the uneasy feeling twisting in her gut refusing to fade. *Something isn't right,* she thought, her gaze trailing Howard until he disappeared around the corner.

The café seemed to exhale in his absence, but the buoyant energy of their earlier mood didn't return. Instead, a subtle weight settled over the space, like the tension before a storm.

"That was strange," Aislinn said, her eyes flicking back to the door, half-expecting Howard to reappear.

Rain shrugged, the slight crease on her forehead hinting at her haunting thoughts. "He's probably just bored. Or maybe he needs a new hobby."

Aislinn nodded absently, her unease persisting stubbornly. *What's he so worried about?* The question burrowed deeper into her mind, gnawing at her resolve.

Takoda suddenly grabbed Aislinn's hands, her vibrant energy jolting Aislinn back to the present. "Okay, back to business! Tell us what else happened last night. We're dying here," she said, excitement practically radiating from her.

Aislinn chuckled, the sound light and genuine, shaking off the friction coiling in her shoulders. She launched into the story, recounting everything—the creepy guy at the bar who wouldn't take a hint, Rowan stepping in like a knight in shining armor, his firm insistence on taking her home, and, of course, the exhilarating ride on his motorcycle. She painted each event vividly, her words brimming with the same thrill she'd felt the night before.

When she reached the part about the kiss, her tone softened. Warmth crept into her cheeks as she described the way his lips had met hers, sure and deliberate, as if he'd known exactly what he was doing. As she explained how the night had ended, including her choice to give Rowan the space he seemed to need, her voice grew more reflective.

"And you're really okay with that?" Rain asked gently, her gaze steady as she studied Aislinn for any cracks in her calm.

Aislinn considered, her attention drifting to the window as if replaying the memory in her mind, frame by frame. "Yeah," she said finally. "You should've seen his face, Rain. Whatever happened to him before really hurt him. I don't want to add to that. If he needs time, I'll give it to him."

A thoughtful calmness settled over the group. Then Takoda stepped forward and wrapped Aislinn in a supportive hug. "He's clearly into you, Ash. He'll come around, I just know it," she said with unwavering confidence.

Aislinn managed a small, hopeful smile, leaning into the embrace. *I hope you're right,* she thought, continuing to worry despite her friends' reassurance. *I hope he thinks I'm worth coming back for.*

The rest of the day passed in a steady rhythm, the café's familiar hum keeping Aislinn's hands busy and her mind somewhat distracted. Customers wandered in and out, their chatter mingling with the mechanical whir of the coffee grinder and the clink of mugs. Occasionally, a police car cruised by, momentarily catching Aislinn's attention before she dismissed it as nothing out of the ordinary. Howard's strange behavior took root at the edge of her awareness, the unease he'd left behind refusing to fully dissipate. Over the next few days, she continued to notice his distraction—the furrow in his brow hinting at a weight far heavier than simple forgetfulness. *What's going on with him?* she wondered, resolving to keep an eye on him.

Later, just before closing, the door jingled, and Ariel stepped in, shaking drizzle from her jacket. Her springy curls framed her face, and her grin seemed to brighten the entire room.

"Well, look who it is!" Aislinn called, wiping her hands on a towel as she approached the counter.

Ariel's jaw dropped slightly as she glanced around, her surprise obvious. "Oh, hey! Aislinn, right? I didn't know you worked here."

Aislinn's grin widened, pride evident in her tone. "Actually, I own the place."

Ariel blinked, admiration flickering in her gaze. "Really? Wow! This place is amazing. I'm officially jealous."

With a sheepish laugh, Ariel rubbed the back of her neck. "Hey, about last night... sorry if I went a little overboard with that drink. I didn't realize you weren't much of a drinker. I was just trying to, you know, give someone a push. We cool?" She extended her hand, her gesture both tentative and hopeful.

Aislinn clasped Ariel's hand with an easy grin. "No worries. We're good."

Ariel let out an exaggerated sigh of relief. "Good. So, I'm in serious need of a mocha. What else do you have with chocolate? I'm obsessed with chocolate."

Aislinn chuckled, the sound breaking through the remnants of unease from earlier. "Takoda! We've got a chocolate fanatic here. Got anything that'll blow her mind?"

Takoda poked her head out from the kitchen, her face lighting up. "Oh my God, yes! I've got just the thing. Give me a minute."

Turning back to Ariel, Aislinn's grin widened. "Whatever she brings out, it's going to change your life. Guaranteed."

"No doubt," Ariel quipped, leaning casually against the counter.

Overhearing the exchange, Rain bounded over with her usual enthusiasm, practically glowing. "OMG, girl, No Doubt! I love that band! They're iconic!" she exclaimed, her energy spilling out as though she'd found a kindred spirit.

As their chatter continued, Takoda emerged from the kitchen carrying a plate with a slice of cake drizzled in glossy chocolate ganache. The rich, indulgent aroma filled the café, and Ariel's face lit up as she accepted the dessert. She took a bite and groaned with delight, clutching her hands to her chest as though overwhelmed.

"This… is the best thing I've ever tasted!" Ariel exclaimed, her words muffled by cake.

Takoda beamed with pride. "Thank you! I made it myself."

Ariel's eyes widened in mock astonishment. "No way!" she said after swallowing. "If everything here is this good, I might just have to move in!"

Laughter rippled through the café, the atmosphere light and cheerful. Ariel stayed much longer than she'd likely planned, chatting easily with the group as the evening unfolded. The mood remained warm and inviting until it was time for her to leave, with Aislinn insisting the mocha and cake were on the house.

Ariel pulled Aislinn into a quick hug. "Thanks, Aislinn," she said, sincerity coloring her words. Turning to all three of them, she added, "This was seriously the most fun I've had in ages. Let's do this again soon."

"Absolutely," the girls chimed in unison, their laughter trailing after Ariel as they walked her to the door.

They lingered for a brief pause, watching as she strolled down the street, her curls bouncing with each step until the mist swallowed her up.

"I like her," Takoda remarked, breaking the calm that had settled.

"Yeah, me too," Aislinn agreed, her features softening as she turned back to the counter. As she moved to tidy up, her focus snagged on a car parked in the alley across the street. Its shadowy silhouette blended into the gloom, and she was certain it hadn't been there earlier.

A small ripple of unease curled in her stomach, her instincts warning her that the car didn't belong. *It's probably nothing. Just a coincidence,* she told herself, brushing the thought aside as she lowered the blinds and rejoined the others.

The next morning, as Aislinn unlocked the café's door, the sound of Ariel's laughter drifted in, light and carefree. Lifting her head, Aislinn spotted Ariel strolling inside, a pair of oversized sunglasses perched on her nose, looking slightly ridiculous in the foggy, early morning air.

"You again?" Aislinn teased, reaching for the coffee pot. The rich aroma of freshly brewed coffee already filled the space, wrapping it in warmth.

"Yeah, yeah. You can't get rid of me now," Ariel replied with a broad grin, pulling off her sunglasses and settling onto a stool at the counter. Her movements were as casual as if she were in her own living room.

Aislinn shook her head, amusement tugging at her lips. "You're just here for the chocolate, aren't you?"

"Guilty," Ariel admitted, leaning forward and resting her elbows on the counter. "But I also figured you might need some company on this fine, foggy morning."

Aislinn's features softened as an unexpected wave of gratitude swept over her. "Well, you've got perfect timing. We're slow right now." She grabbed two mugs and filled them with steaming coffee. "How do you take it?"

"Black as night," Ariel quipped, a playful sparkle lighting her face as she accepted the mug.

They settled at the counter, sipping their coffee as the conversation flowed easily. Ariel launched into a wild story about a regular at Donnelly's who claimed to be a "psychic to the stars," whose predictions always seemed to involve dubious lottery numbers. Aislinn chuckled, the anxiety she'd carried earlier unraveling with every sip and each over-the-top twist in Ariel's tale.

"You know," Ariel said after a brief pause, her tone turning more reflective, "you're really cool, Aislinn. I don't get why you don't get out more."

The comment caught Aislinn off guard. She blinked, fumbling for a response. "I guess I'm just comfortable here," she said finally, her tone quiet.

Ariel tilted her head slightly, considering her reply. "Yeah, I get that. Sometimes, it's good to shake things up. Life's more fun when you dive in headfirst."

Aislinn offered a small, genuine smile, her gratitude showing. "Maybe I'll try that."

"Good," Ariel replied with a teasing wink. "And you should definitely start with more chocolate."

The easy back-and-forth stayed with Aislinn long after Ariel left. There was an undeniable quality about Ariel's confidence and carefree energy that resonated, stirring a quiet longing deep within her. Ariel made taking risks sound so effortless—just a matter of jumping in. *But is it really that simple?*

Her thoughts, as they often did, wandered to Rowan. The distance between them stretched longer with each passing day, tugging at her heart like an unresolved question. She wondered, not for the first time, if waiting for him to make the next move was a mistake—or if it was time for her to take action.

Maybe Ariel's right, she mused, the idea both unnerving and enticing. *Maybe it's time I take the leap.*

Over the next few days, Aislinn's mind circled Rowan with unrelenting intensity. She had promised herself to give him space, yet as three days crawled by without a single message, her resolve began to falter. The memory of their kiss replayed on a constant loop—the way his lips had claimed hers, how the world around them had seemed to dissolve. It was both a comfort and a torment, a moment she clung to even as doubt began to creep in. *What if I misread everything?* she wondered for what felt like the hundredth time, the distance between them pressing heavier with each passing hour.

"Hey, Earth to Aislinn!" Takoda's lively tone cut through the fog clouding her thoughts, snapping her back to reality. Aislinn blinked, realizing she had been standing motionless by the counter, a towel hanging limply in her hand.

"You've got that faraway look again," Takoda said, her voice light and tinged with curiosity.

"What look?" Aislinn attempted a laugh, but the sound was thin, borrowed, as if it didn't quite belong to her.

"The one that says you've just been kissed and now you're questioning every decision you've ever made," Takoda teased. Her tone remained upbeat, her gaze softening as she searched Aislinn's face for the truth behind her quietness. "Still no word from Rowan?"

Aislinn's eyes flicked to her phone for what felt like the hundredth time, her fingers curling tightly around it as though her grip alone could will it to buzz. She hesitated, then finally spoke, her tone subdued. "No... nothing. I thought he'd at least text me, but now... I don't know." Her gaze dropped to the floor, where the cracks in the old wooden boards seemed to mirror the fractures in her confidence. "What if I misread everything?"

The words hovered in the air, fragile and sharp, and Aislinn immediately regretted saying them aloud. She bit her lip, silently chastising herself for letting the vulnerability slip out.

Rain suddenly burst into the room, her energy sweeping through like a fresh breeze. "You're overthinking it, Ash. You always do this!" she exclaimed, bounding to the counter with her usual exuberance. Her tone carried its trademark cheer, steadying with a layer of reassurance. "Just give him some time. If he feels even half of what you do, he'll reach out. It's only been three days."

Aislinn nodded, trying to hold on to Rain's optimism, but the worry clawing at her refused to ease. The silence from Rowan loomed larger with every passing hour. "What if he doesn't?" she asked, the words slipping free like a dam breaking. She bit her lip again, hating how raw and exposed the question made her feel.

Takoda and Rain exchanged a look, their unspoken communication as clear as if they'd spoken aloud. Rain stepped closer, her usual playful manner shifting to a more thoughtful approach. "Listen, you deserve someone who wants to be with you, Ash. Not someone who leaves you in the dark. You know that, right?"

The words landed gently, wrapping around Aislinn like a warm embrace. She nodded, managing a weak smile, but the doubt crept into her heart stubbornly. *They're right. I deserve someone who won't disappear after a kiss. But what if Rowan isn't the person I thought he was?*

Aislinn exhaled slowly, her emotions pulling her in two directions. She wanted to believe in Rowan—in the man who had kissed her like she was the center of his world. She wanted to trust that he would come back. *Please, Rowan. Prove me right,* she thought desperately, the ache in her ribs settling like a stone.

Two days later, as the lunch rush began to wind down, Aislinn spotted Ariel outside the café, her arms overflowing with shopping bags. She was awkwardly attempting—and failing—to nudge the door open with her elbow.

"Need some help?" Aislinn called, amusement coloring her voice as she hurried to assist.

"Yeah, that would be great," Ariel replied, her tone strained as she juggled the precarious stack of bags. "Thanks. I was doing some very necessary shopping and thought I'd stop by for a snack."

Aislinn held the door open, shaking her head as Ariel stumbled inside and deposited the bags onto a nearby table with a dramatic exhale. "I think you might have a slight shopping addiction," Aislinn teased.

Ariel smirked, mock indignation shining in her expression. "These are all essentials, thank you very much. You never know when you'll need sparkly shoes or... a cat mug." She reached into one of the bags and triumphantly pulled out a ceramic mug adorned with a cartoon cat sporting oversized sunglasses.

Aislinn raised an eyebrow, her skepticism clear. "You don't even have a cat."

"That's not the point, Aislinn," Ariel countered, clutching the mug protectively to her chest as if defending her honor. Mischief twinkled in her eyes as she added, "It's about being prepared."

Aislinn chuckled quietly, settling into the chair opposite Ariel. As they chatted between customers, Ariel's playful energy rippled through the café, easing the worry that had weighed on Aislinn's shoulders all morning.

It wasn't just Ariel's humor—there was an ease to her that felt familiar, as though they'd known each other far longer than they had. Before Aislinn realized it, she was sharing stories she rarely told, even mentioning her family in Pennsylvania and the winding path that had brought her here.

Ariel listened intently, her usual lively behavior muted, offering her with unwavering support. "You've built something amazing here," she said after a thoughtful pause. "That's no small thing."

Aislinn felt a glow of unexpected gratitude, Ariel's words settling into her like a warm embrace. She smiled, her sincerity unmistakable. "Thanks, Ariel. That means a lot."

"Anytime," Ariel replied, her grin brightening again. "And if you ever need a shopping buddy, I'm your girl. I can help you pick out all the cat mugs you don't need."

Aislinn laughed, shaking her head. "I'll keep that in mind."

As Ariel left, waving cheerfully until she disappeared down the street, Aislinn found herself reflecting on how quickly she'd come to treasure Ariel's presence. There was an ease about her—a way of lifting the burden Aislinn had carried, even if only for a little while.

For the rest of the day, Rowan's silence felt less oppressive. Ariel's energy had provided a reprieve from the spiral of endless what-ifs. Yet, as the hours ticked on and evening fell, the ache inside Aislinn began to creep back, sharper than before. Her doubts whispered louder, gnawing relentlessly at her resolve.

Maybe it's time to let go, she thought, her focus drifting to the dim street beyond the window. *Maybe waiting for something that might never happen is worse than facing the truth.*

That evening, the girls gathered at Aislinn's apartment for a much-needed sleepover. Takoda and Rain had suggested it, sensing she could use the company, and Aislinn reluctantly. Ariel arrived just as they were locking up the café, her laughter ringing through the space, bright and melodic.

"Hey, girls! Thanks for including me tonight," Ariel said, leaning casually against the counter, her usual confidence radiating. "It's such a relief to hang out with awesome people instead of drunks and a moody man."

Noticing the flicker of discomfort that crossed Aislinn's face, Ariel quickly backtracked, raising her hands in mock surrender. "I just mean Rowan's usually great—he's just dealing with some things. I'm sure once he sorts it out, you'll hear from him."

Aislinn offered a small, half-hearted smile. "Maybe," she murmured, uncertainty clinging to her like a shadow.

"Or maybe he's just PMS-ing," Rain quipped, her tone light and teasing in an effort to lift the mood. The joke coaxed a faint curve to Aislinn's lips, though it disappeared almost as quickly as it came.

As the group headed upstairs, Aislinn stayed behind to turn off the lights and set the alarm. She hesitated by the door, a sliver of hope tugging at her as she glanced outside, half-expecting Rowan's familiar figure to emerge from the misty evening. Instead, her attention caught on the same unfamiliar car parked across the alley, its dark silhouette merging with the shadows. A chill crept along her spine, her instincts whispering that something about it wasn't right.

It's nothing. Just a parked car, she told herself, shaking off the unease as she locked the door and followed the others upstairs.

The living room had been transformed into a cozy retreat, with fairy lights casting a gentle glow over the space. Takoda and Rain were locked in a playful tug-of-war over a blanket on the couch, while Ariel meticulously adjusted the lights until they were just right. The room buzzed with warmth and laughter, yet Aislinn couldn't shake the sense that the evening's mood would eventually shift.

Takoda nudged her gently as she sank into the pile of pillows. "We can't keep pretending everything's fine. Talk to us."

At Takoda's words, Ariel and Rain paused, their playful banter fading into a more attentive stillness. Their expressions were open and patient, silently encouraging Aislinn to share what was weighing on her.

Aislinn exhaled slowly, her shoulders sinking as the thoughts she'd been avoiding pressed against her. "I just... I feel like I messed up," she admitted in a hushed tone. "Rowan's gone quiet, and I don't know what I did wrong. Should I accept that he's just not interested and move on? Am I making this out to be more than it was?" The words spilled out in a rush, heavy with vulnerability. "Maybe I'm holding onto a wish that's already gone."

Rain spoke first, her steady reply cutting through the uncertainty like a lifeline. "Ash, you're overthinking this. You felt a connection with him, and that's not wrong. But don't let his silence make you doubt yourself." She reached over, giving Aislinn's hand a firm, reassuring squeeze. "You deserve clarity, whether or not he's dealing with his own stuff. This isn't about you doing anything wrong."

Takoda nodded in agreement, her words even and firm. "Sometimes people pull back when they're working through their own issues—it's not always about us. But you can't wait forever, Ash. If Rowan isn't communicating, it's time to take control. Ask him where you stand so you can stop second-guessing."

Ariel, uncharacteristically serious, added softly, "Rowan has his demons, Ash. I've seen them. But if he felt anything real with you, he won't just walk away. Sometimes people get scared when something feels too good." Her expression softened, her gaze steady with encouragement. "Reach out if you want to, but don't lose yourself in the process."

Aislinn exhaled slowly, a sliver of the tension lifting. "I guess I just need to find the courage to reach out—or to let go, huh?"

"Exactly," Takoda replied, her tone resolute yet kind. "And don't let his silence define your worth. You're better than that."

Rain grinned and nudged Aislinn lightly. "And if he doesn't give you the clarity you need, we'll find you someone better—someone who won't vanish after one earth-shattering kiss."

The joke drew a ripple of laughter from the group, and Aislinn couldn't help but join in. For the first time in days, the chill of uncertainty eased, replaced by the warmth of her friends' unwavering support.

When it was time to sleep, the girls settled into their makeshift arrangements. Takoda and Rain sprawled across Aislinn's bed, Ariel stretched out on the couch, and Aislinn curled up on the loveseat, her small frame tucked snugly into the cozy spot. The apartment descended into a tranquil hush, the low murmur of the night wrapping around them like a protective cocoon.

As the faint glow of the fairy lights dimmed and the steady rhythm of her friends' breaths filled the room, Aislinn's thoughts drifted, as they often did, to Rowan. The hollow void left by his absence remained unyielding, but beneath the ache, a flicker of determination sparked. *It's time to stop waiting and figure out what I want,* she resolved, her friends' earlier words steadying her like an unseen hand on her shoulder

Her eyelids grew heavy, and she slipped into a dream so vivid it felt like stepping into another world. She stood in a golden haze, the air around her warm and soothing, as though the space itself welcomed her. Before her stood her mother, Eileen, radiant and serene, her presence dissolving every shadow weighing on Aislinn's heart.

The instant she saw her, Aislinn rushed forward, tears stinging her eyes as she flung herself into her mother's arms. The embrace was achingly familiar, wrapping her in the kind of solace she hadn't felt in years. "Mom, I miss you," she whispered, her voice trembling with emotions she had long kept buried.

"I've missed you too," Eileen replied, her reply melodic and tender. She pulled back slightly, just enough to meet Aislinn's tear-streaked gaze, brushing a stray tear from her cheek with gentle fingers. "You've been carrying something heavy, haven't you? Tell me what's wrong."

Aislinn's chest tightened as the words poured out, unfiltered and raw. She confessed everything—Rowan's silence, the chasm it had opened between them, and the relentless whispers of doubt that she wasn't enough. "I don't understand why he's pulling away," she admitted, her voice breaking. "What if... what if I'm not good enough for him?"

Eileen's arms tightened around her, holding her firm like a strong root in the midst of chaos. "Oh, sweetheart," she said, her response steady and reassuring. "You can't force someone to show up if they're not ready. But that doesn't mean you aren't enough. You have *always* been enough. Never let his silence make you question that."

Aislinn tilted her head up, her vulnerability raw in every word. "But I feel so lost, Mom," she murmured imperceptibly. "Should I let him go?"

Eileen leaned down, pressing a gentle kiss to her forehead, the gesture radiating calm and reassurance. "I know it's hard, honey. Sometimes the best things in life take patience. Rowan might need time to figure things out, but that doesn't mean you should walk away just yet. Trust your instincts. He cares about you—I know he does. Give him a little more time, but don't lose sight of your own strength, no matter what happens. There's power in you that you haven't seen yet, Aislinn."

The tears that spilled down Aislinn's cheeks carried a different weight now—not despair, but release. Her mother's words seeped into her, soothing the tender places where doubt had taken root. She nodded, holding tightly to Eileen's wisdom, letting it mend the fractures within her.

When Aislinn woke, early sunlight filtered through the window, bathing the room in a warm golden glow. She blinked, the dream still vivid in her mind, her mother's words echoing like a melody carried on the gentle morning air.

For the first time in days, the sharp edge of her doubt began to soften. Uncertainty still lingered, but it no longer consumed her. A quiet resolve had taken its place—a decision to trust herself and face whatever lay ahead. Rowan's silence would not define her.

She rose and made her way to the kitchen, pouring herself a steaming mug of coffee. The comforting warmth seeped through her hands as her mother's advice replayed in her thoughts. *If I don't hear from Rowan by the end of the day, I'll reach out,* she resolved, her determination solidifying. *It's time to be brave.*

With renewed purpose, she walked to the window, the sunlight framing her features. A small, confident smile began to form, only to vanish a moment later. Her eyes locked on a figure outside, and the floor beneath her seemed to shift.

Her breath hitched, and the mug slipped from her hands. It hit the floor with a sharp crash, shattering into fragments and sending coffee splattering across the tiles.

The noise jolted Ariel awake. She sat up abruptly, her wild curls framing her face as her eyes darted around the room, searching for the source of the commotion. Her attention landed on Aislinn, who stood frozen by the window, trembling, her fingers gripping the frame as though it were the only thing keeping her upright.

"Ash, what's wrong?" Ariel asked, her voice steady but tinged with alarm as she quickly crossed the room, concern etched into every line of her face.

Aislinn's words came out shaky and barely audible. "I saw someone. The guy from the bar... the creepy one."

Ariel's stomach knotted as her gaze followed Aislinn's to the window. She pulled the curtain aside, peering through the glass. The street below was cloaked in thick fog, the mist curling along the pavement like an ethereal veil. It was empty—eerily so—but the tension radiating from Aislinn was impossible to ignore.

"Aislinn, I don't see anyone," Ariel said gently, though unease crept into her chest. She leaned closer, her instincts sharpening as her eyes swept over the fog-shrouded street, searching for any trace of movement. The unnatural stillness outside mirrored the disquiet swirling inside her.

"I saw him," Aislinn insisted, her voice trembling. Her grip on the window frame tightened, her knuckles stark against her pale skin. "It was him, Ariel. The guy from the bar—I'm sure of it."

Ariel's stomach churned. She didn't doubt Aislinn for a second. The memory of Rowan's grim tone resurfaced—his protective edge whenever he mentioned the man, the way his entire demeanor shifted as if confronting a shadow he couldn't escape. Rowan hadn't just been cautious—he'd been deeply disturbed.

Placing a steadying hand on Aislinn's shoulder, Ariel kept her words calm, even as dread simmered beneath the surface. "Okay. I believe you," she said firmly. "Whoever it was, he's gone now. But don't worry—we'll keep an eye out, and we'll figure this out together. You're not handling this alone."

Aislinn gave a shaky nod, her grip on the window frame easing slightly. The tremor in her breathing slowed, but the shadow of fear still clung to her like a second skin.

Ariel's unease deepened, though she kept her outward expression steady. Her instincts screamed that this wasn't a coincidence. The man's presence felt intentional, calculated, and dangerous—like the prelude to something worse.

The second she had a reprieve, Ariel would send Rowan a 9-1-1 text. Whatever was happening, it wasn't random. And she wasn't about to wait and see how it unfolded.

Chapter Seven

A Protector's Promise

The meeting with the other Fallen loomed, its importance pressing heavily against Rowan's focus. As he approached Salesforce Tower, a flicker of unease stirred within him—worry for Aislinn threading through his thoughts on the mission ahead. The towering structure stood sentinel over the city, its polished exterior catching the faint morning light. Rowan barely glanced at it. What mattered lay within: answers—at least, he hoped.

Crossing the gleaming lobby, he made straight for the elevator. Eileen had, as always, arranged the impossible: a private conference room in one of San Francisco's most exclusive buildings. He didn't dwell on how. Eileen's methods were a puzzle he rarely tried to solve. When the elevator doors slid open, he stepped into the still, empty meeting space, welcoming the brief silence.

The room was sleek and functional, its design speaking more of utility than comfort, yet Rowan dismissed the details. His focus narrowed as he began setting up the slide projector. The photos he'd collected over the past week were meticulously organized, each one a potential key to unlocking the Golden Dawn's movements—a puzzle piece waiting to fall into place.

As the projector powered on, Rowan's phone buzzed in his pocket, shattering his concentration. He snatched it up, Ariel's name flashing across the screen.

A: *Aislinn spotted that guy from the bar. She's freaking out.*

His chest tightened, protectiveness surging like a blade drawn to defend. His reply came fast.

R: *Is she safe?*

A: *Yes.*

R: *Do you need immediate assistance?*

A: *No.*

R: *Why am I only hearing this now?*

A: *It's under control. I didn't want to bother you.*

Rowan's jaw clenched, irritation cutting through his composure. *Aislinn is NOT a bother.* His fingers moved decisively.

A: *I know. I'm sorry...I didn't think.*

R: *Stay with her. Do not let her out of your sight.*

A: *Got it.*

R: *I will be there soon.*

A: *I know.*

Lowering the phone, he gripped it tightly for a moment, the urge to drop everything and go to Aislinn clawing at him. He forced the instinct aside. This meeting was vital. The faster they deciphered the Golden Dawn's plans, the sooner he could secure her safety.

The soft click of the door opening pulled him back to the room. Eileen entered, her movements methodical and fluid, like a current shaping the tides. Her presence shifted the energy of the space, steadying it in a way that defied explanation.

"Do you have enough information to determine the Golden Dawn's plans?" she asked, her tone low yet carrying a weight that silenced distraction.

Rowan met her steady look, "I've gathered significant intel," he said, keeping his tone even. "There are patterns we can use, although we'll need everyone's input to connect the dots."

"Good." She claimed her seat, her posture composed, emanating a restrained authority. "You're leading the discussion."

Her steady focus lingered on him, probing as if she could sift through the layers of his concerns. Rowan didn't need to ask—she was assessing him, her attention unwavering. Eileen never missed subtle shifts in energy, and the tension he carried wouldn't escape her notice.

"Something's happened," she said, her tone softer now but no less resolute. "What is it?"

Rowan hesitated. There wasn't time to explain, not with the weight of the mission pressing down on him. "It's being handled," he said, his reply clipped yet firm. "We can proceed."

Her intent focus remained, as if searching for a crack in his resolve. After a beat, she nodded. "If it's not urgent, we'll continue. I need your full focus, Rowan. No distractions."

"I am," Rowan replied firmly, even as the knot in his chest tightened, twisting with unease.

He straightened, forcing his concentration onto the slides as the other Fallen began to filter in. The low murmur of overlapping conversations and shifting movements grounded him, drawing him back into the meeting. Yet part of him remained tethered to Aislinn.

His fingers pressed against the table's edge, the strain in his grip anchoring him. *The faster we solve this, the faster I can make sure she's safe.*

Oak and Vine entered next, drawing Eileen's attention away from Rowan. Relief washed over him, and he steadied himself with a controlled breath.

Oak gave Rowan a firm nod, his presence unshakable as ever. There was a restrained power to him, a steadfastness that others instinctively leaned on. Coming from Phoenix, Oak carried an earthy strength, as if the desert's resilience had rooted itself in him.

Vine followed with his signature smirk, a flicker of amusement in his eyes. Beneath the confident exterior, Rowan knew Vine's mind was always working, sharp and restless. His bold demeanor carried a touch of Las Vegas' untamed energy, reflecting the city that had shaped him.

Nik, known to most as Elder, entered next, his steps purposeful, his movements as fluid as a slow-moving tide. Stationed in Honolulu but originally from Russia, his presence was steady yet compelling, like an undercurrent that refused to be ignored. Rowan had always respected Nik's ability to weigh calculated risks with unwavering resolve, a balance that few could master.

Holly entered next, her warmth radiating as she greeted Rowan with a quick hug. Her easy smile had a way of softening the atmosphere, bringing a brief sense of comfort to the room. Rowan, however, never underestimated her. Beneath that kindness lay a fierce warrior's resolve, unshakable when it mattered most. She'd traveled from Austin, her unwavering loyalty evident in every meditative step she took.

Riichi, or Hawthorn, followed with his signature precision, each movement thoughtful. Rowan felt a measure of calm settle over him knowing Riichi was here. His sharp, strategic mind often uncovered what others missed, and his focused intensity brought clarity to even the most chaotic situations. Based in Seattle, Riichi embodied calculated poise, a punishing force amidst uncertainty.

Reed was the last to arrive, his presence as cautious as it was subtle. The Alaskan rarely moved without purpose, and Rowan immediately noticed the vigilance in his deep scrutiny as it swept the room, cataloging every detail. How does he always catch everything? Reserved as he was, Reed's calculating nature was impossible to overlook—a mind constantly at work behind his composed exterior.

With everyone present, Eileen rose, the energy in the room shifting as though drawn to her. "This meeting concerns the Golden Dawn's escalating activity in San Francisco. We have reason to believe they're planning a significant attack. Rowan will lead this discussion—this is his city, and no one knows it better."

Rowan stepped forward without hesitation, clicking the remote to display the first image on the projector. A grainy photo appeared, showing the Golden Dawn unloading a large shipment at the pier. "Explosives, gunpowder, and other materials," he began, his tone firm and measured.

The next slide revealed a shadowy exchange in Chinatown. "They've been purchasing herbs commonly used in magical potions," Rowan explained. "Everything they've acquired is being transported to the Old Mount Olympus Mansion in Twin Peaks. Given its secluded location, increased activity, and proximity to key sites, I believe this is their headquarters."

Oak's tone resonated, deep and unwavering. "Have they been seen anywhere else?"

Rowan nodded and flipped to the next slide. "Yes. These are the other locations with significant activity: Stow Lake Boathouse, a warehouse in the Mission District, and the Old Mission Armory on 33rd Street. The number of people entering these buildings is smaller than those leaving. They're clearly mobilizing."

Holly leaned forward, her demeanor sharpening with concentration. "They're preparing for a major move."

That's obvious, Rowan thought, but he simply replied, "It seems that way," his tone firm and controlled.

Reed stepped closer to the projector, his focus narrowing on one of the images. "These figures in the background," he said, pointing to several shadowy outlines, "are magic users. Their faint auras give them away. That explains the need for the herbs."

"What kinds of herbs are they buying?" Elder asked, his arms crossing as he studied the images.

"Cinnamon, ginger, and mugwort," Rowan replied.

"Fire-based potions," Elder noted grimly. "All of those amplify fire magic."

Reed nodded, his tone steady. "That aligns with what we've seen so far. Fire magic is devastating."

Vine, lounging in his chair with practiced ease, finally spoke. "Fire magic, explosives—it's obvious. They're building a massive bomb or planning some kind of catastrophic explosion."

"Agreed," Nik said, his tone calm yet resolute. "The herbs suggest they'll use magic to ignite the device remotely. They won't need to be close."

Eileen's expression darkened, a shadow passing through her composed demeanor as she absorbed their observations. "Given these revelations, does anyone have an idea of their ultimate goal?"

Riichi, silent until now, rose and approached the table. "The Old Mount Olympus Mansion is positioned near major ley lines and the San Andreas fault. It's more than just an ideal meeting place—it's a tactical one. I believe their plan is to trigger an underground explosion powerful enough to cause a 9+ magnitude earthquake. If they succeed, the devastation to San Francisco will be catastrophic."

A heavy silence filled the room as everyone processed his words. Holly was the first to respond, her tone carrying a mix of shock and admiration. "That's a brilliant deduction," she said. "The mansion's proximity to the fault line and ley lines makes perfect sense."

"They're using the earthquake itself as the delivery method," Elder added, his tone grim. "The fire magic will set it all off from a safe distance."

"And the forces they're gathering are for protection," Rowan said. *They'll need significant power to make this happen.*

"Not to mention the arrogance," Reed muttered, pacing as his thoughts churned. "They're gambling with magic and nature, convinced they can control both."

Oak's voice carried the weight of certainty. "We're not just dealing with extremists. These people have nothing to lose. If they're willing to collapse the entire fault line, they clearly don't care about the consequences."

"Or they think they're above them," Vine said, his smirk laced with dry humor. "People like this always assume they'll come out untouched, like gods. Let's hope they're wrong."

Eileen rose, her presence cutting through the discussion with a weight that seemed to settle over the room. "We need to act now. Rowan, continue monitoring all locations. Holly, dig into their magical supply chain—find out what else they're stockpiling. Reed, Oak, focus on the ley lines. Riichi, gather everything you can on attempts to trigger earthquakes with magic. Vine…" She paused, her focus sharpening. "Stay focused."

Vine's grin widened, clearly entertained by her pointed remark. "Always."

Eileen's attention shifted to Rowan, perceptive as always, catching the unease slipping beneath his composed exterior. She didn't need to ask—she understood its source. *Aislinn.* For now, she chose not to press.

For a fleeting second, Rowan's stoic mask faltered, exposing the storm roiling beneath. Reading the tension in the room, Eileen made a decision, her tone softening slightly as she addressed the team.

"Alright, everyone," she announced, her voice resonating with calm purpose. "We've covered a lot, but we're not done yet. Take five—stretch your legs and regroup before we tackle the last of it."

The team dispersed, low conversations sparking in small groups around the room. Eileen moved to confer with Oak, her tone hushed and measured, a power radiating from her as though she drew strength from something unseen. She left Rowan where he sat, his focus drifting elsewhere, pulled toward the one person occupying far more of his mind than he cared to admit.

Aislinn.

His leg bounced, a restless outlet for the energy building inside him. The facts churned relentlessly in his mind. The Golden Dawn was growing reckless—that much was undeniable. Aislinn spotting one of their members this morning only confirmed it. Whatever they were planning, they were closing in.

And Aislinn is at the center of it all.

That realization gripped him harder than he wanted to acknowledge. He could still see her as she'd been the day they met—reserved, introspective, and wholly unaware of how much she mattered. *She doesn't even see it herself,* he thought bitterly. *She doesn't see the strength she carries.*

That was what he admired most about her, even if she couldn't see it. Aislinn's courage was a subtle, unassuming force, the kind too often overlooked. It showed in the way she kept moving forward despite her fears, in the way she faced what should have broken her. And now, the Golden Dawn had turned their attention to her.

Why her? He'd asked himself that question a thousand times. She wasn't a warrior or a mage. She didn't possess ancient knowledge or wield extraordinary power. To everyone else, she was just… Aislinn. Yet the Golden Dawn never targeted anyone without a purpose. Whatever they wanted from her, it couldn't be anything good.

The thought of her in their hands twisted his stomach painfully. What would they do to her? The image forced its way into his mind before he could stop it—Aislinn, terrified and alone, surrounded by people who saw her as nothing more than a pawn.

His fists clenched, his knuckles turning pale. *I won't let that happen. Not to her. Not ever.*

The vibration of his phone jolted him from the spiral. He glanced at the screen—Ariel.

A: *We're good. Nothing new.*

Rowan exhaled, a fragile relief threading through the persistent ache in his chest. He quickly typed a response:

R: *I'll be there soon.*

Moments later, Ariel's reply came—a thumbs-up emoji. The casual response did little to remove his unease. He stared at the screen, the weight of everything pressing harder, before setting the phone down on the table.

Rowan forced himself to remain seated, his fingers gripping the edge of the armrests. The meeting wasn't over. No matter how much he wanted to walk out and head straight for Aislinn, his duty to the team had to come first.

Even as the meeting demanded his focus, so did Aislinn. *What if I'm too late? What if we don't figure this out in time?* The questions circled relentlessly, their answers maddeningly elusive.

Taking a slow, meticulous breath, he worked to steady himself. *There's no room for failure. Not with Aislinn's life on the line.* His jaw tightened as his resolve solidified. *I'll protect her. No matter what it takes.*

For now, he had to finish this meeting.

When they reconvened, Rowan pulled up a picture of Aislinn on the projector. Her face appeared on the screen, and somewhere in the room, a low, appreciative whistle disrupted the scene. Every muscle stiffened instinctively, irritation rising in his chest before he could suppress it.

His attention swept the room, sharp and unwavering, but he didn't bother calling out the culprit. When he glanced briefly at Eileen, he caught her watching him. Her focus was steady, an unspoken force that seemed to pierce through the tension and settle it.

Rowan cleared his throat, forcing the surge of protectiveness aside as he turned back to the screen. "For reasons still unknown, Aislinn Galagher is a person of interest to the Golden Dawn. We intercepted a message where they referred to her as 'the key' to their plans. So far, surveillance of her property has yielded no significant activity. Golden Dawn members have been spotted near her home, but they seem to be tracking her movements rather than making a direct move. However, I received intel today that Aislinn spotted one of them this morning. Nothing's happened since, which means either the one she saw is careless—or they're testing us."

Eileen made a mental note, the glimmer of insight in her expression like the first light of dawn breaking through shadows. No wonder he's been on edge.

Rowan's focus flicked briefly to Aislinn's image on the screen, her familiar features stirring something deep within him. Her smile, the gentleness in her eyes... she doesn't even know she's in danger. He shoved the thought aside, forcing himself back to the task at hand. This wasn't about him or his feelings. The team needed facts, not emotional interference.

Eileen's tone broke through the silence, resonant and deliberate. "Now, what are your assessments regarding Aislinn Galagher?"

At the sound of her name, Rowan's focus returned to her picture. What does the Golden Dawn want with her? Why her? The questions gnawed at him, but he buried them, locking his expression into calm neutrality. This was no time for vulnerability.

Oak spoke first, his tone careful and precise. "Given that they haven't attempted to apprehend her yet, I believe Miss Galagher is not directly tied to their San Francisco operation. Instead, she appears to be a 'key' to a separate plan entirely."

Holly raised her hand slightly before speaking. "Yes, and considering their carelessness this morning and the lack of follow-up activity, I think they're preparing to make a move. They may be trying to intimidate her. Even if Aislinn isn't central to this immediate plot, it would nonetheless be wise for us to keep monitoring her. She's clearly crucial to something larger."

Rowan's chest tightened as Oak's and Holly's words sank in. They're right. She may not be tied to the earthquake plan, but that doesn't mean she's safe. Far from it. Yet, there was a sliver of relief in knowing she wasn't directly linked to the immediate scheme. That gave him a small, precious window to figure things out.

Eileen nodded thoughtfully, her expression carrying a depth that seemed to weigh possibilities beyond what was said. "Rowan, I'd like you to continue your surveillance of Miss Galagher. We need to understand why she's so crucial to their plans. Given their mistake this morning, I also want additional volunteers. Any takers?"

"I volunteer," Riichi said, rising with his usual composed confidence.

"As do I," Nik added, his calm, focused expression locking on Rowan. For a brief flash, Nik's eyes shifted slightly, widening just enough to acknowledge the unease Rowan was struggling to conceal.

"With the three of you sharing this task, we can focus more effectively on the immediate threat of the potential earthquake," Eileen said, her tone steady, yet it carried an undercurrent of assurance that seemed to stabilize the room. Then she turned her full attention to Rowan, her words like a solemn promise. "We will keep Miss Galagher safe."

Rowan gave a subtle nod, though his mind had already drifted far from the room. Aislinn's image remained in his thoughts—her face, her presence, the way she somehow occupied his mind no matter how hard he tried to focus. She doesn't even know the danger she's in, and I can't lose her. Not her. His feelings were complicating everything, clouding his judgment in ways he didn't want to admit.

"Alright then," Eileen concluded, stepping back in front of the group. The room seemed to shift as though her presence itself had realigned its focus. "Rowan, a word. The rest of you are dismissed."

As the others got up and shuffled toward the door, Rowan stayed seated, his eyes fixed on Aislinn's image on the screen. Holly patted his shoulder as she passed, her touch warm with subtle reassurance, though he barely registered it. The room gradually emptied, leaving only him and Eileen behind. The silence that followed pressed over him like a dense fog, heavy and inescapable.

Eileen's focus lingered on him, sharp and perceptive, as though she could see the layers he wasn't ready to unravel. Finally, she walked over and sat beside him, her movements so fluid that he didn't notice her presence until she spoke.

"Do you like her?" she asked, her tone neutral yet piercing, carrying the weight of a question that reached deeper than its phrasing.

The question hit Rowan like a jolt. He stiffened slightly, startled by her directness. "No," he replied too quickly, the denial snapping out like a reflex. His jaw hardened, and after a minute, he sighed, his response softening. "Maybe... I don't know." His gaze shifted from Aislinn's photo, as if looking too long would force him to confront truths he wasn't ready to admit.

Abruptly, he stood and crossed the room, moving toward the window. Pressing his forehead against the cool glass, he let the chill seep into his skin.

The sensation braced him, dulling the chaotic swirl of emotions he couldn't quite explain.

Eileen waited, her presence steady like a calm flame, watching him with the patience of someone who had witnessed this battle before. She didn't push or interrupt, letting the silence stretch, offering him the space to shape his own response.

After a long pause, Rowan finally turned to face her, his expression shadowed with unspoken conflict. "I feel drawn to her," he admitted, his voice quieter now, more honest. "Like I need to protect her, but I don't know why. Maybe it's her... or maybe it's me. I'm still trying to figure it out. And..." He straightened, his shoulders squaring as he fought to regain his composure. "I won't let it interfere with my duties. Whatever I feel, I won't let my emotions compromise the mission. I promise."

Eileen's lips curved into a faint smile, one that carried both understanding and a flicker of amusement, as though she had heard such statements many times before. She didn't respond immediately, instead letting the weight of his declaration settle between them.

Rowan shifted, clearing his throat, his unease evident. "Why did you need me to stay behind?" he asked, seizing the opportunity to steer the conversation elsewhere.

Her expression shifted, the lightness replaced by a solemn gravity. When she spoke, her tone resonated with steady authority and measured. "I wanted to talk to you in private... about Aislinn, actually. I need you to protect her at all costs, even if it means your life."

Rowan's brows furrowed, confusion threading through the determination already etched into his features. "Why is she so important? Why does she need that level of protection?"

Eileen hesitated, the brief pause charged with an intensity that hinted at knowledge far beyond what she was willing to share. When she finally spoke, her voice carried the certainty of someone who saw the shape of things yet to come. "I have my reasons," she said simply, her reply firm and unyielding. "For now, they're mine. Promise me you'll keep her safe."

Rowan didn't even need to think about it. "I promise," he said, the statement carrying quiet conviction. Deep down, he already knew he would protect Aislinn with everything he had. He didn't need this conversation to solidify what was already etched into his being.

Eileen stood, brushing off her skirt with a smooth motion, as if drawing a line under the discussion. But as she reached the doorway, she paused, her presence lingering in a way that felt calculated.

"One more thing, Rowan."

He looked up, curiosity sparking in his otherwise conflicted expression. "What?"

"I hope you do let your emotions get in the way," she said, her tone calm but resolute. "They make you human. And a protector with a heart is far stronger than one without. Don't forget that."

Her gaze lingered on him, imbued with a depth that felt like both a warning and a blessing. She held it just long enough for the weight of her statement to settle before disappearing through the door, leaving an unsettled stillness in her wake.

Rowan stood frozen, her parting words reverberating through him. *Let his emotions get in the way?* The idea cut against everything he'd been taught, everything he believed about control and discipline. *Emotions are a liability,* he thought instinctively, the mantra rising unbidden. Yet Eileen's words stirred a deeper feeling, one he couldn't easily silence.

The weight of the morning's revelations, coupled with Eileen's unexpected parting advice, left him with a singular, undeniable urge. He needed to see Aislinn. *Now.*

Grabbing his jacket, Rowan left the room in a rush, his steps driven by a force he couldn't fully name but couldn't ignore. The weight of everything—Eileen's words, Aislinn's vulnerability, the Golden Dawn's growing threat—pressed against him, propelling him forward.

Taking the stairs two at a time, unwilling to wait for the sluggish elevator, he pulled out his phone and fired off a quick message to Ariel.

R: *OMW.*

Slipping the phone back into his pocket, he pushed through the building's front doors and into the open air. The crispness of it hit him like a jolt, clearing the haze of uncertainty from his mind. He had only one focus now: *Aislinn.*

<u>Chapter Eight</u>
The Weight of Regret

Rowan burst through the building's doors, rain hammering him in relentless waves, plastering his hair to his forehead and drenching him to the bone within seconds. He barely registered the cold. His breath came in quick, uneven gasps, his heart pounding as if it might shatter his ribs. His hands scrambled at the lock on the disc brakes of his bike, slipping against the slick, uncooperative metal. The rain lashed harder, tangling the straps of his helmet and clinging like a second skin. Still, none of it slowed him. His thoughts raced miles ahead, anchored to Aislinn.

From the window above, Eileen observed him, her expression serene yet focused. Her eyes lingered on his hurried movements as he mounted the bike, the engine snarling against the storm's roar. A trace of a smile danced across her lips, so subtle it seemed woven into the rain's rhythm. The tires sprayed arcs of water across the pavement as Rowan disappeared into the downpour.

The streets dissolved into a blur, neon signs smearing across the rain-slicked asphalt like distorted brushstrokes on a dark canvas. Water streaked his visor, turning the lights into flickering, ghostly patterns. The biting wind clawed at his skin, but he hardly felt the sting. Every fiber of his being was drawn tight, his focus unyielding—he had to reach her.

When the café came into view, its light burned like a sanctuary against the chaos of the storm. Relief sparked briefly in his chest, easing the tempest of doubt swirling in his mind. His grip on the handlebars tightened as the engine roared, his turn onto the side street sharper than it should have been. He braked abruptly, cutting the ignition. The sudden stillness pressed in, broken only by the relentless percussion of rain against his helmet.

He paused by his bike, motionless in the pouring rain, as his adrenaline faded, leaving a growing unease in its wake. Tension coiled tight in his chest. *What if I've waited too long?* The question struck harder than any storm. *What if my silence has already destroyed everything?* His fingers dug into the handlebars, as if they could diminish the rising tide of doubt.

Inside the café, Ariel sat near the window, her fingers tapping a quick rhythm on the tabletop. Aislinn, Takoda, and Rain were deep in conversation, their laughter filling the space, but Ariel's attention was elsewhere. Her focus sharpened as Rowan's bike skidded into view through the downpour.

"There he is," she murmured, pushing her chair back and reaching for the umbrella propped against the wall. She glanced at the others with a quick grin. "I'll be back. Ash, I'll bring this back tomorrow."

Before anyone could respond, she slipped out the door, snapping the umbrella open as she stepped into the deluge. Water splashed against her jeans as she jogged toward Rowan.

"You're late!" she called, her voice cutting through the storm with practiced ease.

Rowan glanced up, rain cascading from his hair, his leather jacket molded to his frame. He shook off some of the water, offering her a sheepish look. "The Fallen had a meeting. It ran over."

"Well, Aislinn's been waiting," Ariel shot back, her tone sharper than he expected. She gestured toward the café but caught his arm before he could move.

"Wait," she said, her expression hardening. "You're losing her, Rowan. If you're not ready to give her what she deserves, maybe you should just get back on that bike."

Her statement hit like a blow, and he struggled to deflect it. "What are you talking about?"

"You know exactly what I mean." Her tone softened, though her gaze stayed sharp. "Aislinn deserves more than your silence and halfway attempts. She's giving you another chance you don't deserve. If you mess this up tonight, it's on you."

His stomach churned, her remark cutting deeper than he expected. He didn't argue. The helmet in his hand felt heavier than it should, and Ariel's glare eased just enough to carry a warning.

"Get in there," she said, stepping back and adjusting the umbrella. "Don't mess this up."

Rowan hesitated at the door, the muscles in his jaw flexing subtly as he tried to gather himself. Ariel gave him a firm nudge. "Go. I mean it."

The bell above the café door chimed as Rowan stepped inside, its sound nearly drowned out by the relentless rain outside. Warmth enveloped him, a stark contrast to the storm he'd just escaped, yet it did nothing to loosen the tightness in his chest. His eyes scanned the room and found Aislinn instantly.

She sat at a table in the back with Takoda and Rain across from her. Their conversation halted the moment he entered. The café lights illuminated Aislinn's face, casting shadows beneath her eyes. She appeared composed, but tension clung to the way her hands rested in her lap, her fingers loosely curled. Her expression shifted—surprise, hesitation—before settling into something more guarded, a look that hid her emotions behind an invisible wall.

"Look who I found outside!" Ariel's voice cut through the peace as she stepped in behind Rowan. She gave him a light shove into the room, her tone cheerful yet carrying an unmistakable edge. "Take care of him, okay, Ash? I'm out."

Before anyone could respond, she slipped out, the bell chiming softly again as the door swung shut behind her.

Rowan paused near the entrance, water pooling beneath his boots on the tile floor. The three women at the table turned their attention to him, though his focus remained fixed on Aislinn. She met his eyes directly, her expression steady, but there was a distance he hadn't felt before, a barrier he wasn't sure how to cross.

"Can we talk?" he asked, his voice rougher than he'd intended.

Takoda glanced at Rain before standing, her chair scraping against the floor. The sound echoed in the quiet room. She approached Aislinn, resting a hand lightly on her shoulder and offering a warm, reassuring smile. "Go ahead," she said in a low voice. "We've got things covered here."

Aislinn faltered, her hands gripping the table's edge as she exchanged a brief look with Rain. Rain gave her a small nod, her calm expression edged with curiosity. Aislinn's gaze delayed briefly before shifting back to Rowan.

She exhaled and stood, her chair sliding back with a soft scrape. "Yeah… okay," she said, her tone measured and neutral, without coldness. She smoothed her palms down her sides, the small movement betraying her effort to stay composed, then motioned toward the back of the café. "Let's talk."

Rowan nodded silently and followed as she turned.

The narrow hallway stretched ahead, dimly lit and stagnant, save for the muffled sound of rain beyond the walls. Aislinn's steps were cautious, her arms relaxed at her sides. Her pace carried the air of someone buying time with each movement. Rowan trailed a few feet behind, his own stride slow, his mind churning with the words he needed but couldn't yet form.

The staircase came into view, its wooden steps darkened and worn with age. Aislinn climbed first, her hand grazing the railing. Rowan noticed the tension in her shoulders, the way she moved as if bracing herself for what was to come.

He swallowed hard, the silence between them growing heavier with every step. *I should've called. One message—anything—would've been better than noth-ing. What was I thinking?*

At the top of the stairs, Aislinn slowed. She brushed her fingers along the doorframe before nudging the door open. Without looking back, she stepped inside, leaving it ajar for Rowan.

He paused at the threshold, drawing in a deep breath to steady himself. *She's letting me in. Don't screw this up.*

Rowan stepped through and closed the door firmly behind him. The room's cozy warmth clashed with the lingering chill from the ride, though it did little to ease the knot in his chest. Aislinn crossed the space toward the hallway closet, her movements brisk, her focus locked ahead.

"You're drenched," Aislinn said, pulling out a towel and turning back to him. She tossed it into his hands with a trace of exasperation. "Use this before you soak the floor."

"Thanks," Rowan replied, running the towel over his hair and face. He wasn't sure what kind of reaction he'd expected, and her straightforward practicality unsettled him more than he cared to admit.

Her eyes glossed over him briefly, taking in his dripping jacket, soaked jeans, and the small puddle forming beneath his boots. "You'll freeze if you stay like that," she added, pivoting toward the bathroom. "Wait here."

He watched her retreat, noting the careful control in her movements. Each step seemed measured, her actions purposeful as she worked to stay occupied. She returned quickly, a folded pair of pajama pants in her hands.

"Here." She extended the clothes toward him. "These are my brother's. They're clean, and they should fit. You can change into them, and I'll grab you a shirt."

Rowan took a breath, his words hovering in the air. "You didn't have to—"

"I did," she interrupted, her expression steady. Her fingers tucked a strand of hair behind her ear, a small gesture that revealed vulnerability she couldn't entirely hide. "I don't want you standing around in wet clothes and getting sick." She added softly, "Just... change, okay?"

Her thoughtfulness caught him off guard. Rowan nodded, gripping the pajama pants tightly. "Thank you... for thinking of that," he said, his voice low, edged with unguarded sincerity. He paused, searching for more to say, but instead settled on, "I'll be quick."

Before he could say anything else, Aislinn turned toward her bedroom. "I'll grab you a shirt and socks," she called over her shoulder as she walked away.

Rowan peeled off his soaked clothes, shivering as the cold air nipped at his skin. He slipped into the pajama pants, grateful for their dry warmth, even if they were slightly short. Tossing the wet bundle over a nearby chair, he glanced toward the hallway just as Aislinn returned, a t-shirt and socks in her hands.

"Here," she said, setting them on the table. Her expression softened briefly, her gaze skimming over him before shifting away. "These should help."

"Thank you," Rowan said, pulling the shirt over his head and sliding on the socks. The silence that followed felt heavy, filling the room like an unspoken presence. Before he could think of anything to say, Aislinn stepped toward the kitchen, breaking the moment.

"I'll make some coffee," she said briskly. At the counter, she reached for the coffee pot, her hands moving with practiced ease. Rowan noticed the way her shoulders tensed slightly, as if she were holding her emotions at bay, determined to maintain her composure.

As the coffee brewed, she glanced back at him. "Do you want me to toss your clothes in the dryer?" she asked. "They'll dry faster that way."

Rowan's gaze shifted to the pile of wet clothes. The offer was simple, yet it struck him in a way he hadn't expected. "Yeah," he said after a pause. "That'd be great. Thanks."

Aislinn gave a small nod and crossed the room, gathering the clothes with careful hands. "I'll be back in a minute," she said lightly, disappearing into the hallway.

Left alone, Rowan sank into one of the dining chairs. The dry clothes offered some physical comfort, but his thoughts stayed tangled in everything he hadn't said. When Aislinn returned a few minutes later, she brushed her hands against her jeans and headed for the kitchen without pausing.

"The dryer's running," Aislinn said as she reached for a mug. "It shouldn't take long."

Rowan watched her, noticing how her movements seemed steadier now, more natural. He allowed himself a brief thought, wondering if these small gestures—this simple routine—could be the beginning of bridging the gap between them. *Should I say something? Or let her have this space?*

When he spoke, his expression carried a careful weight. "Aislinn... thanks. Really."

She glanced back briefly, her face hard to read before she turned her attention to the counter. "You don't have to thank me," she murmured. "It's nothing."

It wasn't nothing—not to him. Rowan exhaled, leaning back in his chair as the weight of what remained unsaid pressed heavily on him. The thought hovered, just out of reach, refusing to take shape.

At the counter, Aislinn reached for the coffee pot. Her grip was firm at first, but as her attention drifted, her hand slipped. The pot tilted sharply, and hot liquid splashed across her wrist. She gasped, pulling her hand back quickly. The sudden motion sent the pot crashing to the floor, shattering the quiet in the room.

Before she could react, Rowan was at her side, his hand closing gently around her arm. "Let me see," he said, his tone brooking no argument.

"It's fine," Aislinn said quickly, her words faltering slightly. Rowan was already guiding her to the sink, his movements calm and thoughtful.

"Just let me check," he said, turning on the faucet. He adjusted the water temperature and held her wrist under the cool stream with practiced ease, his attention fixed on the redness of her skin.

The icy water dulled the sting, and Aislinn let out a slow breath. "I didn't expect you to swoop in like that," she said, the barest hint of humor threading through her response.

"Old habits," Rowan replied, completely focused on her wrist. His thumb brushed lightly over her forearm—a gesture so absent it felt natural, grounding her in a way she didn't expect. "Keep it there for a little longer. It'll help."

Aislinn blinked, caught off guard by the quiet care in his actions. The burn's sting eased under the cold water, yet his presence sent a thrill through her chest, a quick fluttering sensation.

"It's just a splash," she said after a brief pause, her tone softening. "Nothing I can't handle."

"That doesn't mean it's not worth treating," Rowan replied. His words were steady, each one deliberate. Satisfied the redness had subsided, he finally let go of her wrist, his actions unhurried, as though reluctant to pull away.

Aislinn grabbed a towel, drying her wrist as she shook her head. "You act like I'm incapable," she teased, her lips curving into a small smile.

"You're not," Rowan countered, the corner of his mouth lifting slightly. "And it's okay to let someone step in once in a while."

She dabbed at her wrist, her attention drifting to the broken coffee pot on the floor. Shards of glass glinted under the light, scattered like a mosaic across the tile. The sight made her stomach knot—a harsh reminder of her momentary distraction.

Rowan followed her gaze before stepping forward. "I'll take care of it," he said, crouching to pick up the larger pieces.

"You don't have to—" Aislinn began, but his glance over his shoulder cut her off.

"I don't want you getting hurt," he said, his words firm as he worked with unhurried precision. He gathered the jagged fragments, each movement careful.

Aislinn paused, uncertain how to respond. The pressure in her chest eased slightly as she watched him. "I'll grab the dustpan," she said, her voice softer now.

Rowan gave a slight nod, not looking up as she stepped away. Returning with the dustpan and broom, she knelt beside him, sweeping the smaller shards into the pan.

"You really didn't have to do this," Aislinn said, her tone light but touched with sincerity. "I could've taken care of it."

Rowan glanced at her briefly, the faintest hint of a smile on his lips. "Maybe," he replied, his words calm, with a trace of warmth beneath them. "You've already had one mishap tonight. No sense tempting another."

Aislinn let out a soft laugh, shaking her head. "It's just a coffee pot, not the end of the world."

"Still," Rowan replied, meeting her gaze briefly, "better to avoid unnecessary casualties."

She chuckled again, the tension in her shoulders easing as they worked. The clink of glass against the dustpan filled the room, replacing the silence. When the last shard was cleared, Aislinn stood, brushing her hands on her jeans and setting the broom aside.

"Thanks," she said, her voice softer now. "For... everything."

Rowan straightened, placing the dustpan on the counter. His attention lingered on her, his expression open and calm. "Anytime," he replied simply, a faint, genuine smile touching his lips.

Aislinn stood motionless under his gaze, not sure of what to say next. Her thoughts tugged her in several directions, none of them staying long enough to settle. "I should probably start another pot of coffee," she said finally, breaking the silence as she turned toward the counter.

Rowan stepped back, giving her space without retreating too far. "You don't have to go through the trouble," he said lightly, his expression holding a teasing edge. "I didn't mean to derail your night."

Aislinn glanced at him over her shoulder, a small, wry smile curving her lips. "You say that like you didn't have a good reason for showing up."

Her remark, casual on the surface, carried a hint of curiosity. Rowan's fingers curled slightly against his thigh before he replied. "I did," he said quietly, his response measured. "But I think you already know that."

Her smile faltered, replaced by a flicker of uncertainty as her eyes stayed locked on his. His response hung between them, fragile but undeniable. For the first time that night, she didn't look away. Instead, she studied him, her breath catching at the raw honesty etched into his expression.

"Why *are* you here, Rowan?" she asked, her words measured, laced with hurt she hadn't intended to show. "Why now, after a week of silence?"

Rowan's shoulders tensed, his gaze firm and focused. "I thought giving you space was the right thing to do," he said, each word measured. "For you, for me. I thought it would help me figure out what I was feeling. It didn't. It only made things worse."

Aislinn folded her arms loosely, frustration pulling at her features. "How does disappearing help anything? All it did was leave me wondering what I did wrong."

Rowan flinched, guilt flashing across his face. "You didn't do anything wrong," he said, his regret evident in every word. "That's on me. I should have called. I should have said something. I was so focused on trying to sort out what I was feeling that I convinced myself silence was easier than facing you—or myself."

"And?" she pressed, her voice softer but unrelenting. "What did you figure out?"

"That I was a coward," Rowan admitted, his gaze dipping before he forced himself to meet hers again. "I was scared of how quickly this... whatever this is... felt important. I didn't want to mess it up or drag you into a situation I wasn't ready to handle. So, I ran. I told myself it was for your sake, but the truth is, I was avoiding everything I didn't want to feel."

Aislinn's posture softened slightly, though the hurt in her expression remained. "You don't get to make that choice for me," she said, her tone steady and resolute. "You don't get to decide what I can or can't handle."

"You're right," Rowan said, nodding faintly. "And I hate that I made you feel like you didn't matter. You do, Aislinn—more than I've been willing to admit, even to myself. I told myself I'd be better off keeping my distance, but all it did was hurt you and make me miserable. I thought I could push the feelings away, but they didn't fade. They only grew."

Her breath caught, her chest tightening at the sincerity in his response. "You really hurt me, Rowan," she admitted, her tone steady despite the ache behind it. "I thought... I thought maybe I imagined everything. That what happened between us didn't mean as much to you as it did to me."

"It did," Rowan said firmly, leaning forward, his hands resting at his sides. "It meant more than I knew how to handle. That's why I left. But I was wrong, Aislinn—about all of it. I thought stepping back would give me clarity, but all it did was make me realize how much I hate being apart from you. How much I care about you."

Aislinn blinked, the emotions he conveyed settling over her. "You can't just disappear whenever things get complicated," she said, her expression calm but carrying strength. "If there's something here—if you care about me—you have to stay. You have to let me in, or it won't work."

Rowan nodded, the weight of her response pressing against him. "I know," he said softly, his sincerity clear in every syllable. "And I promise I won't run again. I don't want to make you feel like that ever again."

He reached for her hands, wrapping hers gently between his own. His touch was warm and reassuring, and Aislinn didn't pull away, though her posture remained rigid. "I don't know what this is yet," Rowan said, his words deliberate but vulnerable. "But I know it's real. And I know I want to figure it out with you."

Aislinn studied him, her expression softening as the raw honesty in his gaze chipped away at her remaining defenses. "I don't have all the answers either," she said, her tone steady despite the emotions swirling inside her. "But I'm willing to try. If you are."

A faint smile curved Rowan's lips, the relief in his expression unmistakable. "I am," he said simply, his confidence unwavering. "For as long as you'll let me."

For the first time that night, Aislinn allowed herself to relax slightly, the weight on her chest lifting just a little. "Then let's see where this takes us," she said, a tentative smile breaking through as she held his gaze.

Rowan exhaled slowly, the tension in his shoulders easing. "Maybe we should sit," he suggested, nodding toward the living room. "Feels like it's been a long day for both of us."

Aislinn nodded, the subtle shift in her expression revealing her relief. "Yeah, that sounds like a good idea," she said, her tone softer now. She turned toward the living room, leading the way with Rowan a step behind.

The lamp in the corner bathed the room in a warm glow, softening the edges of the furniture and filling the space with a calm, inviting atmosphere. Aislinn sank onto the couch, tucking one leg beneath her as she gestured for Rowan to join her. He hesitated briefly, his gaze assessing before he lowered himself onto the cushion beside her.

They sat quietly, the silence between them filled with a fragile sense of possibility, delicate and undefined. Aislinn leaned back against the armrest, her lips curving into a small, reflective smile. "You're different tonight," she said, her voice carrying quiet curiosity. "Not what I expected."

Rowan chuckled, the sound low and introspective, as if weighing her statement. "Maybe I'm just starting to figure out what matters," he said, his response calm, laced with sincerity.

Aislinn leaned forward slightly, her hands settling gently on his shoulders. Her touch was grounding as she said, "Rowan, I've already told you—I believe in you."

The phrase hit him like a physical blow.

I believe in you.

His vision blurred, the air leaving his lungs in an instant. His chest tightened, his muscles locking as his breath hitched. Before he could process—before the impact could fully settle—his knees buckled.

The room tilted, and he slid off the couch, hitting the floor heavily. A strangled sound escaped him, harsh and broken, before whatever had been holding him together snapped entirely.

"Rowan!" Aislinn's voice pierced through the haze, her panic clear, but the darkness surged forward, consuming him with swift, overwhelming force.

Chapter Nine
A Past That Haunts

Aislinn froze as Rowan collapsed, his body folding awkwardly, like a puppet with its strings suddenly cut. She lunged forward, catching him just before his head could hit the floor. "Rowan!" she gasped, her cry shuddering as she eased him onto the carpet. Her hands hovered over his face, brushing a damp strand of his jet-black, blue-streaked hair from his clammy skin. He felt warm, his shallow breathing steady—yet there was a distance in him that made her chest tighten with fear.

What do I do? The thought pounded in her head, relentless. Her shaking hands fumbled for her phone, fingers hovering over the screen. Then she stopped. Instinct told her this wasn't an emergency a doctor could fix. No one could reach wherever he had gone. His face—unnaturally calm—looked like he had drifted to a place far beyond her reach.

"Rowan, wake up," she said, her voice cracking as she shook him gently. When he didn't stir, panic overtook her. She gripped his shoulders tighter, shaking him harder. "You promised me you wouldn't shut me out again," she whispered, tears stinging her eyes. She leaned down, resting her forehead against his, her breathing uneven. "Please... don't leave me like this."

Her hand slid down to grasp his, her hold desperate. She pressed his hand to her chest, as if her heartbeat could somehow guide his back to her. The seconds dragged by, each one heavier than the last. His chest rose beneath her palm, but his unnatural stillness made her instincts scream—she was losing him.

"I'm not letting you go," she said fiercely, her quivering voice firm. "I won't. Do you hear me, Rowan?" Her free hand pressed over his chest, searching for the faint rhythm of his heart. It was there—weak, steady, like a thread she refused to let snap. "Come back to me. Please…"

Rowan was slipping further away, spiraling into a darkness that swallowed everything. Aislinn's touch dimmed, her words fading into the distance. The world dissolved into cold and silence, dragging him into its grip.

The air was damp, sharp with the smell of rain-soaked earth. Ireland—his Ireland—took shape around him. The vivid green hills he remembered were shrouded in gray mist, the land heavy with a sorrow that clung long after the storms passed. Rain lashed against his skin, its icy sting a small distraction from the deeper cold in his chest.

He stood inside the small cottage, its walls dim and shadowed, the paint faded and peeling. The weight of the past bore down on him, pulling him toward a memory he'd buried so deeply it felt like it belonged to someone else.

The bed in the corner creaked under Davina's frail body. Her once-vibrant skin was mottled and pale, dark sores spreading like the blight that had stolen so many others. Rowan's chest tightened as he looked at her, the air refusing to fill his lungs. He had fled this moment—fled her—because staying had felt impossible. The grief wasn't just in her death; it was in the life they had shared, the love he had lost, and everything he hadn't been able to save.

"Aidan," she whispered, her words hardly louder than the faint rustle of leaves outside the windows. The name stabbed at him. *I'm not Aidan anymore.* That man had been lost long before Davina, buried under guilt and years of trying to forget. But here she was, calling for him as if nothing had changed, her love still there in every shallow breath.

He knelt beside her, his hands shaking as he pressed a damp cloth to her forehead. Her green eyes, though dim, held a sliver of warmth he hadn't felt in years. Her thin fingers brushed against his tawny hair, the touch weak but full of the strength she had left.

"Remember me," she murmured, the words fragile as they left her. "Aidan… I'm sorry."

Her entreaty cracked the resolve inside him. He had spent years running from this vision, hiding it behind walls of survival and denial. To remember her meant reopening a wound that had never healed. The grief rose like a wave, pulling him under, drowning him in everything unsaid and undone.

Through the haze of revelation, another voice broke through, sharp and desperate.

"Rowan, please, come back to me!"

Aislinn. Her cry cut through the darkness, shaking and raw, pulling him toward a tangible certainty. He could feel her—the faintest pressure of her hand holding his, refusing to let go.

His body stirred, his fingers twitching as if to grasp hers. His breathing hitched, a shallow gasp breaking through the silence. The storm of Ireland began to blur, its edges softening as her voice grew stronger. She was there—a lifeline calling him back.

Rowan's chest rose more deeply, the fragile rhythm of his heart responding to her. The snapshot of Ireland faded further, its grip loosening as Aislinn's presence pulled him back to the world.

The past refused to release its hold, dragging him deeper into the darkness. The dimness swayed, and suddenly, he was somewhere else—beneath the ancient rowan tree. The air was damp, heavy with the scent of moss and rain-soaked leaves. The rough bark pressed into his back as he slumped against the tree's gnarled trunk, pain radiating through his side. Blood seeped through his shirt, hot against his chilled skin, pooling beneath him as the cold crept into his bones, unrelenting.

This was a place he had sworn to forget, a scene buried under everything he had tried to leave behind. Now it rose before him, vivid and unrelenting, demanding to be faced.

A flicker cut through the gloom, illuminating the grove with an ethereal glow. From it stepped Eileen, her presence calm and unearthly, as it had been that night. Her blonde hair caught the moon's glow, her gaze softening as it landed on him. The echo of her presence filled his mind, steady and firm: "*It is not your time to leave this place.*"

The ache in his chest returned—the void that had swallowed his will to live. The thought crashed over him, dragging him back to the despair that had consumed him as he lay dying. "I do not have the will to go on," he had whispered, his tone soft and strained. "I've lost everything."

Eileen knelt beside him, her movements deliberate, as if one wrong step might shatter him completely. "You have the strength. You must go on. You are needed," she had said, her tone steady, carrying a sorrow he hadn't understood then. Her cool hands brushed his sweat-soaked brow with a tenderness that felt out of place in the chaos.

It wasn't just Eileen. Another figure had stepped forward, her presence gentler yet no less certain. A young woman, her dark hair framing a face he couldn't quite place. Her deep brown eyes had locked onto his, unwavering, piercing through the fog clouding his mind. At the time, her presence had felt like a dream—blurred and fleeting. Now, as the memory sharpened, recognition burned through him. *Aislinn. It had been Aislinn.*

The realization struck him, sending a shudder through his body. *How had I not seen it before?* Even then, some part of him must have known, must have felt the bond that tied them together. The woman he had sworn to protect had stood beside him all along, even as he teetered on the edge of death.

Fragments of that night became clearer, fitting together with an ache that felt physical. Eileen's voice had been low, insistent, urging him to hold on. Her hands pressed firmly over his chest, grounding him as he faltered. And then there was Aislinn's hand, smaller, tentative, resting on his shoulder. Her touch had been steady, and her words had cut through his despair with unexpected strength: *"I believe in you."*

Those four words echoed in his mind, more powerful now than they had been then. At the time, he hadn't realized how much he needed them—how they had tethered him to a glimmer of hope. She had been there. Aislinn had been there at his lowest, before he knew who she was, before she had become the lifeline she was now.

The gloom twisted as pain flared in his chest. Eileen's hand moved over his wound, her voice low, whispering words he hadn't understood at the time—words of power and change. Energy had enveloped him, not soothing but scorching, tearing through him like molten fire. It had dismantled and rebuilt him, piece by fragile piece, until the man who had lain dying beneath the rowan tree was no longer the same. He had been reborn—not as Aidan, but as Rowan. A Fallen.

The transformation had left him gasping, raw and disoriented, his senses overloaded with a clarity that bordered on pain. He had looked up to find Eileen watching him, her gaze calm yet shadowed with sadness. And beside her, Aislinn. Her expression had held compassion and faith, unyielding even in the face of what he had become.

The image seared through him, brighter than the energy that had remade him. Aislinn had been there. She had seen him at his most broken, his weakest, and still, she had believed in him. She had been his support before he even knew her name.

Rowan's body trembled, his fingers twitching as the scene pressed down on him. Aislinn's sob cut through the haze, quaking yet firm. "Rowan, please... I need you to come back to me."

Her cry pierced the darkness, breaking through the despair. He could feel her hand gripping his, steady and unrelenting. It tugged at him, pulling him toward the surface, even as the dream clung to him, heavy and unyielding.

His breathing hitched, a shallow gasp breaking the silence as he fought to bridge the gap between past and present. He wanted to answer her call, to grasp the lifeline she held out to him, yet the pull of the past dragged him down, refusing to let go.

The image distorted again, loosening their hold just enough to thrust Rowan into another flashback. This one felt sharper, more vivid, refusing to blur with time. He was back on his bike, the rumble of the engine vibrating through his chest as Aislinn's arms wrapped around his waist. Her touch, steady through the thick leather of his jacket, sent a current of warmth through him.

It stirred a deep, long-buried emotion within him, a whisper of feeling he hadn't allowed himself to experience in years. Her presence calmed him, yet carried a charge that unsettled him in ways he couldn't name. As they neared her apartment, a knot tightened in his chest, a silent dread of the night ending pressing harder with every turn.

The past bent into a new shape, pulling him into the serenity of her apartment. The yellow glow from the kitchen pushed back the lingering chill of the evening. Aislinn moved across the room quickly, her steps purposeful as she busied herself with the coffee maker. The small, familiar sounds—the clink of a mug, the low hiss of brewing coffee—filled the space, but Rowan's focus was locked on her.

Her dark hair swayed as she moved, catching the dim glow in a way that made his fingers twitch with the urge to reach out. The faint scent of citrus hung in the air, fresh and invigorating. She glanced over her shoulder, offering him a brief, shy smile before returning to her task. That smile ignited a spark within him, awakening a longing he wasn't ready to acknowledge. Instinctively, he stepped closer, drawn to her like gravity pulling him in.

He stopped just behind her, close enough to feel the warmth radiating from her. When she turned to face him, smoothing her hands nervously over her jeans, her eyes lifted to his. For a few heartbeats, neither of them moved, the air between them heavy with thoughts left unsaid. Then, he leaned in.

The first kiss was hesitant, testing the edge of a line neither of them could cross back over. Her lips pressed against his, igniting a fire he had long buried. When she whispered that she'd wanted him to kiss her all night, the quiet confession broke through his walls. The next kiss wasn't careful—it was fierce, insistent, tearing down every barrier he had spent years constructing.

His hands found her waist, fingers pressing into the fabric of her shirt, holding her like she was the only thing tethering him to the world. The noise of the day disappeared, leaving only the warmth of her body against his, the way her hands rested against his chest, and the tacit emotions that burned between them. It was everything—until fear crashed over him like ice water.

It hit hard, cold and suffocating, extinguishing the fire as quickly as it had sparked. Vulnerability surged, dragging the walls back into place with relentless force. He broke the kiss abruptly, stepping back as his pulse hammered with an intensity far heavier than adrenaline.

I can't do this. I'm not ready.

"I need to go," he said, his tone clipped, betraying the chaos inside him. He stepped further away, retreating from the pull of her presence before it could consume him again. Her startled expression caught him, her wide eyes silently asking him to stay, but he forced himself to turn away. Regret clawed at him even as he left her standing there.

Now, trapped in the memory, Rowan saw it all again—the way her lips had softened against his, the small gasp she made when he pulled her close, the trust she had offered so freely. And then, the hollow emptiness that followed when he ran. The truth struck harder than before. He hadn't left to protect her. He had left because he was afraid—afraid of what it meant to need someone again, of the risk that came with letting her in.

If I want to be the man she deserves, I have to stop running. The thought cut through the guilt like a blade. *I have to face her—even if it terrifies me.*

Aislinn's holler broke through the vision, terrified but strong. "Rowan, please… come back to me!" Her cry pierced the darkness, pulling him back to the present.

Her grip tightened on his shoulders, unyielding as if her determination alone could pull him free. He could feel her hands shivering, her fear weaving through the cracks of his unconsciousness. "Please," she whispered, her tone breaking. "Don't leave me. I need you."

A faint crease formed on his brow, a trace of movement breaking through the murkiness. It was small, scarcely there, but it lit a fragile spark of hope in her. Her breath caught, and she leaned closer, her hands cradling his face with care. "That's it," she murmured, her call fierce. "Please, Rowan… don't leave me."

Her touch drew him closer, pulling him toward the surface. The revelation's grip began to loosen, the fear dissolving under her unwavering presence. She was there, keeping him rooted in the present, and this time, he wasn't going to let her go.

The darkness warped one last time, pulling Rowan into a memory that felt both recent and distant. He was seated in the conference room at Salesforce Tower, the hum of the cooling system blending with the muffled murmurs of the Fallen as the scene took shape. The meeting had just ended, leaving the charged tension of their discussion about the Golden Dawn lurking in the air. The others began to file out, their movements fading into the edges of his awareness, while Rowan remained seated, his attention locked on the screen at the front of the room.

Aislinn's image displayed there, her face frozen in a captured frame from the briefing. His leg bounced beneath the table, a restless attempt to release the turmoil tightening in his chest. Holly passed behind him, briefly patting his shoulder in a gesture of comfort that barely registered as the room emptied, leaving him with the heavy quiet that settled around him.

The silence pressed in, amplifying the storm of thoughts swirling in his head. He didn't notice Eileen's approach until she spoke.

"Do you like her?" she asked, the question cutting directly through his haze, free of judgment.

The question hit him sharply, catching him off guard. He straightened, his response spilling out too quickly. "No," he said, the denial rigid and defensive. Yet the truth pressed harder, refusing to be ignored. He exhaled slowly, the tension in his posture easing as he admitted, "Maybe... I don't know."

His gaze dropped from the screen as if looking at her image any longer might force him to confront more than he was ready for. His thoughts twisted, tangled in emotions he hadn't yet unraveled.

Abruptly, Rowan rose and crossed the room. The floor-to-ceiling windows drew him in, the city skyline beyond glittering like distant stars. He pressed his forehead against the glass, letting the chill seep into his skin, offering a small reprieve from the heat building inside him.

Eileen didn't press him. She waited nearby, her silence patient. He could feel her presence behind him, unyielding, though she said nothing.

Finally, he spoke, his voice low and rough with sincerity. "I feel drawn to her," he admitted, glancing at his faint reflection in the glass. "Like I need to protect her, but I don't know why. Maybe it's her... or maybe it's me. I'm still trying to figure it out." He straightened, the unease in his posture replaced by determination. "I won't let it interfere with my duties. Whatever I feel, I won't let my emotions compromise the mission. I promise."

Eileen's lips curved faintly, her expression a mix of understanding and quiet amusement. She didn't reply immediately, letting his admission settle in the air between them.

Rowan shifted under her gaze, clearing his throat as he redirected the conversation. "Why did you need me to stay behind?" he asked, searching for a new focus.

Her expression changed, the ease in her demeanor sharpening. "I wanted to talk to you in private... about Aislinn, actually." She folded her hands, her posture calm, her tone firm. "I need you to protect her at all costs, even if it means your life."

Her words landed heavily, but Rowan didn't flinch. His brow furrowed as he met her gaze, his response steady. "Why is she so important? Why does she need that level of protection?"

Eileen paused, the sharpness in her expression easing slightly. She chose her response with care. "I have my reasons," she said, her tone brooking no argument. "For now, they're mine. Promise me you'll keep her safe."

The reply came without hesitation. "I promise," Rowan said firmly. Protecting Aislinn wasn't just a command—it had already rooted itself deep within him. It didn't feel like an obligation. It felt inevitable, as if it had always been a part of him.

Eileen rose, smoothing her skirt with practiced precision. At the door, she paused and glanced back at him.

"One more thing, Rowan," she said, her voice softer, the meaning cutting deeper.

He turned toward her, curious. "What?"

"I hope you let your emotions get in the way," she said, her tone measured yet piercing. "They make you human. And a protector with a heart is far stronger than one without. Don't forget that."

Now, reliving the memory, Rowan felt the truth of her words strike deeper than they had before. At the time, he had brushed them aside, hiding behind the safety of duty to shield himself from the uncertainty of his feelings. But now, he understood how wrong he had been. His drive to protect Aislinn wasn't just about the mission. It was about her.

Aislinn had become his refuge, the one steady presence in a life that often felt chaotic. Eileen had been right—his emotions didn't weaken him. They gave him strength, pushed him to fight harder, and kept hope alive even when everything else seemed impossible.

If I want to protect her the way she deserves, I can't keep hiding behind fear. I have to be honest—with her and with myself.

Aislinn's voice broke through the haze, fearful but unyielding. "Rowan, please... come back to me!"

Her beckoning shattered the remaining shadows, a lifeline pulling him upward. He could feel her grip on his shoulders, firm and unyielding, her touch pulling him back from the abyss and into the present. The visualizations began to dissolve, their edges fading as her presence grew stronger, brighter. For the first time, he fought to return—not out of duty, but because he needed to be with her.

His breathing quickened, his fingers twitching faintly, and Aislinn's voice cracked with relief. "That's it," she whispered, her hands quivering as she cradled his face. "Come back to me, Rowan. Please."

And this time, he did.

In the present, Rowan's body jerked violently, his chest rising as Aislinn's call cut through the haze, tearing through the fog in his mind. "Rowan, please! I need you!" Her cry echoed within him, ripping through the final threads of darkness holding him down. With a sharp, desperate gasp, he bolted upright, as though breaking the surface of a suffocating ocean.

"AISLINN!"

Her name tore from his throat, raw and frantic, trembling with everything he had just endured. His eyes darted wildly until they found her, and automatically, he reached for her, pulling her into his arms with a desperation that startled even him. His grip was firm, almost as if he feared she might vanish if he let go.

The reality of her presence—the feel of her against him—was a lifeline, pulling him from the void and filling the emptiness with a sense of purpose that had long felt out of reach. His breathing came in sharp bursts as he clung to her, the echoes of his memories fading with every passing second. There was a brief instant where only the warmth of her touch and the rhythm of her heartbeat existed—undeniable proof that she was real, that this was real.

As his senses sharpened, the world around him came back into focus, vivid and unrelenting. The glow from the room illuminated Aislinn's face, pale and streaked with tears. Her wide brown eyes reflected both panic and relief, and her shaking matched the uneven rise and fall of her chest as she fought to steady herself.

Seeing her like this—so vulnerable, so shaken—sent a fresh wave of emotion crashing through Rowan. He pulled her closer, the ache in his chest growing with the need to shield her, to take away the fear he had caused. *I'm here, Aislinn. I won't leave you. Not ever.*

"Aislinn," he rasped, her name faint, his voice hoarse and uneven. Her gaze darted across his face, searching as if needing proof that he was truly awake. Her lower lip trembled, and she shook her head, the words spilling out in a broken rush. "You were—" Her voice cracked. "You wouldn't wake up, and I didn't know what to do."

"Shh, it's okay. I'm here," Rowan murmured, his tone steady despite the raw emotion behind it. He brushed her tears away with his thumbs, his touch gentle, almost timid, as though afraid she might shatter. "You did everything right," he added, his fingers tracing soothing patterns against her skin.

Her nervous hands clung to his arms, her nails biting into his flesh, as though tethering her to a reality she didn't want to lose. "I-I was so scared," she whispered, her voice faltering as the lingering panic spilled over. "I didn't know how to help you."

Rowan's chest tightened at the vulnerability in her voice. He leaned forward, resting his forehead gently against hers, feeling the erratic rhythm of her breaths begin to calm. "You did help me," he said softly, the gratitude in his words impossible to miss. "You brought me back."

Aislinn pulled back just enough to meet his gaze. Her tear-filled eyes reflected everything she had carried to pull him free—fear, determination, and an unyielding resolve. The weight of what she had endured was etched into her expression. The space between them felt fragile, charged with everything unsaid, as if the slightest alteration might unravel the connection holding them together.

Without thinking, Rowan leaned in, his lips brushing hers in the gentlest of kisses. It wasn't hurried or full of passion—it was tender, reverent, a silent promise for both of them. His hand cupped her cheek, his fingers slipping into her hair as if to keep her close. The world around them seemed to fade away, the sounds and movement dissolving into nothingness, leaving only the undeniable pull of their connection, drawing them closer in a way that felt both inevitable and profound.

Then reality surged back, cutting through the fragile calm. The weight of his memories, the truths they had unearthed, and the fear of letting her in too deeply struck him like a tidal wave. He pulled away abruptly, his breath catching as he dropped his gaze to the floor, shame clawing at him.

"I'm sorry," he whispered, his voice strained and raw. "I just... I'm not ready."

The confession hung in the air, heavy with implicit emotion. Rowan couldn't meet her eyes, his chest constricting under the weight of his fear and guilt.

Aislinn's expression wavered, a flash of hurt crossing her features before softening into a quiet gentleness. She swallowed hard, her voice steady despite the ache it carried. "It's okay," she said quietly, her words careful, measured. "I'm here. We'll take this one step at a time."

She rested her head against his chest, her fingers gripping his arm, offering him the calm she had fought so hard to maintain. Rowan exhaled slowly, his arms wrapping around her once more, holding her as though to make up for what he couldn't yet say.

For now, the words between them remained unspoken. In that silence, Rowan knew one thing with certainty—he wasn't going to let her face this alone. Not now. Not ever.

Aislinn eventually lifted her head, worry flickering across her tear-streaked face, the weight of emotions evident in her eyes. "What happened, Rowan?" she asked, her apprehensive question carrying the remnants of panic. "One minute you were fine, and then... you were just gone. I didn't know what to do." Her uncertainty carried a raw vulnerability that pierced straight through him.

Rowan swallowed hard, the weight of her question pressing heavily on him. He owed her honesty, though the truth felt tangled in his memories, impossible to untangle fully. Drawing in a steadying breath, he forced himself to meet her gaze. "I... I've had episodes like that before," he admitted slowly, carefully choosing his explanation. "Sometimes, memories from my past take over, and it feels like I'm being dragged into them. I can't always control when it happens."

It wasn't the full truth, but it wasn't a lie either. It was all he could manage without completely unraveling.

Aislinn's brow furrowed, frustration mingling with concern in her expression. "That's something you could've told me," she said, her statement edged with a mix of hurt and unease. "Instead of avoiding me."

"I know," Rowan replied, his shoulders sagging under the guilt pressing against him. "You're right. I could have—should have—told you." He dragged a hand through his hair, the restless motion betraying the emotions threatening to overwhelm him. "I didn't want to pull you into that part of my life. It's not something I'm proud of."

His response dropped, thick with regret, yet the sincerity behind his admission was unmistakable. Aislinn didn't respond right away, her eyes narrowing slightly as if gauging his honesty. The silence stretched between them, heavy and uncertain, tightening the knot in Rowan's chest.

Sensing her hesitation, he pressed on, each word feeling like shards scraping his skin. "There was someone... a long time ago," he said quietly, his admission spilling out cautiously. "Her name was Davina. I loved her, and I lost her."

He worked to keep his explanation steady, but the admission bore down on him like a crushing tide. He concealed the full depth of that loss—the years of aching loneliness that had followed—but even this small piece of truth felt like reopening an old wound. Saying her name after all this time was like unearthing a grave he had buried deep.

Aislinn's expression softened instantly. The guardedness in her gaze melted away, replaced by tender empathy. "Rowan..." she said gently, her response carrying an understanding that struck him harder than he expected. She stepped closer, her hand reaching out to brush lightly against his arm. "I'm so sorry. I can't imagine how much that must have hurt."

Her words were simple, yet they resonated deeply. He swallowed against the tightness in his throat, his gaze dropping briefly. He hadn't realized how much he needed her to hear him, to truly see him in this moment.

"You don't have to tell me everything," she continued, her steady response calm and measured. "But don't push me away because you're scared. You've been through so much, and I just... I want to be here for you. You don't have to carry this alone."

Her hand rested on his arm, steadying him in a way actions alone couldn't. Rowan exhaled shakily. "Thank you," he murmured, the emotion threading through his response unmistakable. It was all he could manage, but it felt like enough.

Aislinn studied him a while longer, then let her hand fall, her attention sharp and unyielding. "You don't have to push me away," she repeated, her determination cutting through the prolonged tension. "I know it's hard, and I know you're scared, but I need to know you're not going to run when things get tough."

Rowan's throat constricted at her insistence, the unspoken pain behind her statement cutting through him. He could see the glint of vulnerability in her eyes—the fear that he might abandon her like others likely had. The thought of being the one to hurt her made his chest ache fiercely.

"I'm trying," he said softly, his response brimming with sincerity. He reached for her hand, his touch firm yet gentle. "I promise you, I'm trying."

Her gaze held his briefly, searching for the truth in his admission. He could feel the weight of her uncertainty, but beneath it was a faint glimmer of hope. It wasn't everything she wanted, but it was a beginning.

Rowan exhaled slowly, his words dropping to a whisper. "You're right," he said, his gaze steady. "I've been running for a long time. I don't want to run anymore. Not from you."

He tightened his hold on her hand, his grip firm but careful. "I can't promise I won't make mistakes or that I'll have all the answers. I won't push you away. I want to face this... face us."

Aislinn's lips parted slightly, her breathing faltering at his response. The tension between them shifted, loosening as they sat together in silence, the air heavy with meaning. It wasn't resolution, but it was a step—a fragile step toward genuine connection.

The space between them deepened into unspoken understanding. They were stepping into this together, no matter how uncertain it felt. Rowan could feel the tightness in his chest easing, the ache of his past softening. Even as he held Aislinn, the questions gnawing at the edges of his mind refused to fade. The memories from his flashbacks left too many unanswered.

The urge to confront Eileen surged within him. He needed answers—why she had kept so many secrets, why Aislinn seemed to be at the center of it all. But as quickly as the impulse rose, it faded. He had made a promise, and he wouldn't break it. Not now. Not when Aislinn deserved more from him.

He inhaled deeply. "Aislinn... there's someone I need to talk to. I need answers." His gaze swung briefly before locking back onto hers. "Normally, I'd already be out that door, chasing those answers. I'm done running. I'm staying here with you." His statement softened, sincerity threading through every word. "I'm not going anywhere this time."

Aislinn studied him, her brow furrowing slightly before she nodded, relief easing the tension in her features. "Okay," she said quietly.

Rowan gave her hand a gentle squeeze, his response raw as he added, "If it's okay with you... I'd like to stay tonight. Not for anything more. I just... I want to hold you. I need to feel you here with me." His vulnerability wove through every word. "I think... I need that as much as I need to be here for you."

Aislinn hesitated, the weight of his request settling over her. Then, she nodded, her answer barely audible. "Okay... you can stay."

Relief surged through him, easing the turmoil that had clawed at him all evening. He pulled her close, wrapping his arms around her as though to solidify the promise he had made. For the first time in a long while, the restless ache in his chest eased, replaced by a fragile sense of peace. He wasn't running anymore.

Even as he held her, his thoughts circled back to Eileen. The questions nagged at him, gnawing at the edges of his mind and refusing to be ignored. Tomorrow, he would confront her—demand answers, no more evasions. He needed to know why Aislinn was so important, why she had become the center of everything. But tonight, that battle could wait.

What mattered now was keeping his promise. Showing Aislinn—and himself—that he was here to stay.

Chapter Ten
A Heart Unbound

Rowan woke before dawn, pale gray light slipping through Aislinn's bedroom curtains. He lay motionless for a brief while, his attention fixed on the rhythm of her breathing. It was a rare peace, one he hadn't felt in what seemed like years. He reached out, brushing a stray lock of hair from her face. His fingers lingered briefly before he slipped out of bed, careful not to disturb her.

Moving silently to the window, he eased the curtain aside and looked down at the quiet street below. The world appeared motionless, the only movement a jogger crossing at the corner. His gaze swept over the parked cars and shadowed alleyways, searching for anything unusual. No sign of the Golden Dawn since last night—but that didn't mean they weren't lurking. *They're always watching.* The thought coiled tightly in his chest.

His focus sharpened, daring the silent street to reveal its secrets. When nothing stirred, he let the curtain drop with a muted sigh. Turning back, he noticed Aislinn shifting, her fingers clutching the blankets as she began to wake.

"Morning," she murmured, her tone still thick with sleep.

"Morning," Rowan replied, a faint grin tugging at his lips. "Didn't mean to wake you. Thought I'd get a head start on coffee."

Aislinn stretched, her movements unhurried. "Coffee sounds perfect," she said, sitting up and running a hand through her tousled hair. "I've got a busy day at the café."

Rowan moved to the kitchen, his hands working instinctively as he grabbed the mugs and set up the coffee maker. The clink of glass and ceramic broke the silence, adding small sounds to the morning. "You taking any breaks today?" he asked casually.

"Probably this afternoon," she said, padding over to lean against the counter. "Ariel and I talked about meeting up. Takoda and Rain can cover the café while I slip out."

He nodded, pouring the fresh coffee into two mugs. "Good idea. You've earned it."

Aislinn gave him a faint smile, her fingers curling around the warm mug as she accepted it. "What about you? Besides that talk you mentioned, anything else on your plate?"

"Just a few errands. Might stop by the bar to check in," he said with a shrug. "Nothing too exciting."

Her brow lifted slightly, curiosity sparking in her gaze, though she chose not to press him. "Well, don't work too hard," she teased, taking a slow sip of her coffee. "You're not the only one who needs a break now and then."

He let out a soft chuckle. "I'll try," he said, though he already knew the day ahead would be far from restful. His thoughts drifted to the unanswered questions swirling in his mind—questions only Eileen could answer. *I need to know why she made me promise. What is she keeping from me?*

As they descended the stairs together, the old wood creaked beneath their steps. The smell of freshly baked pastries wafted up to meet them, filling the air with warmth and sweetness. At the base of the stairs, Rowan caught sight of Takoda and Rain bustling behind the counter. The two worked in tandem, arranging trays and filling the display case with practiced precision, their movements quick and efficient.

The instant the two women noticed them, Takoda grinned, mischief flashing in her gaze. Rain, ever composed, arched a brow faintly, curiosity flickering behind her calm demeanor. Rowan felt heat rise to his face and quickly looked away, clearing his throat to compose himself.

"Morning," Aislinn greeted them, her words easy and unhurried. She walked beside Rowan toward the door, her steps casual despite the quiet buzz of activity around them.

Rowan paused at the threshold, glancing back at Takoda and Rain. Both were watching, their interest plain even as they pretended to stay busy. Rain leaned in slightly, clearly not wanting to miss anything. Heat rose to his face again, and he cleared his throat, focusing back on Aislinn.

"Well… I'll see you later," he said, his words rougher than he intended. Without giving himself time to reconsider, he leaned down and pressed a brief kiss to her forehead. Straightening, he murmured, "Take care," before stepping outside.

The door had barely clicked shut behind him when muffled chatter burst from within.

"Well, looks like you and Rowan are doing just fine," Takoda said, satisfaction weaving through her comment. "He's adorable when he's flustered."

Rain giggled. "Told you," she said, nudging Takoda. "You were overthinking it. The way he looked at you just now? Yeah, you're good."

Aislinn turned toward them, her reaction a mix of exasperation and amusement. "You know," she said, arching an eyebrow, "if you're going to talk about him, maybe wait until he's out of earshot."

Takoda shrugged, her grin widening. "What can I say? It's not every day you bring a guy downstairs."

Rain smirked, nudging Takoda again. "I'm just saying—he seems like a keeper."

"Alright, enough," Aislinn said, though a grin tugged at her lips. "Pastries aren't going to organize themselves."

The two women sighed dramatically but reluctantly turned back to their tasks. Aislinn didn't miss their glances darting toward the door, as if Rowan might walk back in at any moment. Shaking her head, she let out a laugh, warmth spreading through her chest. *It's going to be one of those days,* she thought, her lips curving despite herself. Their teasing energy, as much as it flustered Rowan, was part of what made the café feel like home.

Outside, Rowan paused as the door clicked shut behind him. Takoda and Rain's muffled chatter filtered through the air, their playful energy unmistakable.

"Well, it looks like—"

"See? I told you—"

The rest of their conversation faded as the door sealed, and a grin tugged at Rowan's lips. *There's something about them,* he thought. Their unguarded, easy energy felt infectious, making him feel lighter. The flicker of amusement dimmed quickly, replaced by the weight of duty. He pulled his phone from his pocket, scrolling to Eileen's number with practiced ease.

When she answered, he didn't wait for pleasantries. "Meet me in the conference room in fifteen minutes," he said, his tone clipped. He ended the call before she could respond, slipping the phone back into his jacket. Agreement wasn't necessary—he knew she'd come. She always did.

Swinging his leg over the motorcycle, Rowan fired up the engine, the deep rumble centering him in the present. The sharp chill of the morning air brushed his face as he maneuvered through sparse traffic. Salesforce Tower loomed in the distance, its glass exterior reflecting the gold of the rising sun. The sight was constant and unyielding, a silent reminder of the responsibilities pressing on him. His grip tightened on the handlebars, his thoughts drifting inward.

Why can't I stop thinking about her?

The question lingered, uninvited and insistent. He knew it wasn't just the Golden Dawn's interest in Aislinn that kept him close. It wasn't even his promise to Eileen, though that carried its own weight. It was something else, unspoken, that tugged at him every time he saw her.

Fifteen minutes later, Rowan stepped into the conference room, his boots echoing against the polished floor. Pale light spilled through the windows, failing to unravel the tension coiled in his chest. Eileen stood by the window, her back to him, composed as always. It was clear she had been anticipating this conversation.

She turned slowly as he entered, her focus unwavering. Rowan didn't wait for an invitation to speak. The frustration he'd been carrying for weeks surged to the surface, spilling out in sharp, biting accusations. "You've been keeping things from me since the beginning," he said, his words slicing through the silence. "A century, Eileen. A century of fighting alongside you, and all I've gotten are riddles."

Her features remained composed, though a flicker passed through her gaze—regret, perhaps, or understanding. "Rowan," she began evenly, "there's more to this than you know."

He let out a dry, humorless laugh, shaking his head. "That's your answer for everything, isn't it? 'There's more to it.'" His frustration deepened, anger threading through his response. "Like when I was newly turned and thought I was dying. You told me not to worry, that God had plans for me. What plans, Eileen? Why didn't you tell me what I was walking into?"

She opened her mouth to respond, but he didn't give her the chance. His frustration spilled over, unchecked. "And the rowan tree," he continued, his voice cracking. "You said it wasn't my dream. You meant it was hers, didn't you? Aislinn's."

Eileen's gaze softened, though she held his. "I did," she admitted, her response calm. "It wasn't the right time for you to know."

He scoffed, disbelief causing a muscle to twitch beneath his temple. "And when you said she needed me? Was that about then, or now? Why couldn't you just be honest with me from the start?"

Her reply was measured, her words deliberate. "Rowan," she asked gently, "why is this so important to you?"

The question struck deeper than he anticipated. Turning away, he paced to the far wall and pressed his palm against the cool surface. He pressed his lips into a thin line as the silence wrapped around him. *Why does it matter? Why can't I let this go?*

The answer clawed its way to the surface, relentless. When he finally spoke, his voice was low and unsteady. "Because... I think I'm falling in love with her." The admission hung in the air, raw and unguarded, like a wound he couldn't hide. Slowly, he slid down the wall, lowering himself to the floor with care, his knees bent, arms draped over them.

"It doesn't make sense," he murmured, his voice soft and difficult to hear. "We've barely spoken, yet every time I see her, I feel it—the pull, like I'm being drawn to her without realizing it. I can't stop myself from watching her, from trying to figure out why she feels so... important." He exhaled shakily, leaning his head back against the wall. "And somehow, she makes me laugh. Even with everything happening, even with all of this—she makes me feel lighter, like there's a reason worth holding onto."

His eyes closed tightly, the weight of his confession bearing down on him. "And that terrifies me," he admitted, his voice trembling. "Because I still carry Davina's memory. Everything we were, everything I lost—it's all still there. I don't know how to let go of that... or if I even can."

The room fell into silence, heavy with his admission. Rowan tapped his head lightly against the wall, the rhythm grounding him as his thoughts spiraled. *What if I can't do this? What if letting Aislinn in means letting Davina go? And what if I fail them both?* The questions churned in his chest, relentless and sharp, refusing to let him breathe.

Eileen's gaze remained intent, her expression softening as she watched him unravel, the tight coil of grief and guilt loosening thread by thread. "It feels like... if I allow myself to love Aislinn, I'm betraying Davina," he confessed, his voice uneven, as though each word carried years of buried pain. "As if moving forward means leaving her—and my family—behind." The urgency of the admission cut deeper with every word.

He leaned his head back against the wall again, the dull thud echoing in the charged silence. "I can't hurt Aislinn," he whispered, his tone breaking. "But I can't betray Davina, either. I keep thinking... if I preserve their memories, if I hold onto them, then I'm honoring them. If I move forward..." His voice faltered, his fists curling against his knees. "What if I forget? What if I let them slip away, like they never existed at all?"

The storm of emotion raged within him, guilt and longing crashing like waves against a fragile shore. He drew in a shuddering breath, his fingers gripping tighter, as if trying to anchor himself to a tangible reality—anything that felt real. "Am I refusing to live because they didn't get to?" he murmured, almost to himself. His words came out in a hushed tone, as if saying them too loudly might make them unbearable. "And if I do live... does that mean I'm leaving them behind for good?"

Eileen moved closer, each step cautious, her words gentle when she spoke. "Rowan," she said quietly, her voice tinged with the weight of centuries of witnessing love and loss. "Loving again isn't a betrayal. It's a testament to the depth of your heart. You're not leaving Davina behind—you're carrying her with you, in everything you do, in the way you choose to live again."

Rowan inhaled sharply, his gaze dropping to the floor as her words pressed against the walls of his grief. They stirred an emotion within him—raw, uncertain. "You make it sound so simple," he murmured, frustration lacing his voice. "But it doesn't feel that way. It feels... impossible."

Eileen's lips curved into a faint, knowing smile, one that carried both reassurance and mystery. "It's never simple," she said softly, "and it's not supposed to be. Some choices shape us, Rowan, and others..." Her voice lowered, almost a whisper. "They free us."

Rowan let her words settle, though his thoughts remained a tangled storm. The conflict within him didn't ease, but there was something in her tone—an unshakable certainty—that gave him pause. Slowly, he lifted his head, meeting her steady gaze. The turmoil in his expression remained, tempered only by a flicker of curiosity.

Eileen had been preparing for this moment ever since Rowan's call. She had seen how grief clung to him, wrapping around him like a second skin, and she knew words alone wouldn't be enough to bring him the closure he needed. There was more he had to face—an obstacle only he could confront to find his way forward.

She reached out, taking his hand with a firm, stabilizing grip. "Come with me," she said, her calm delivery leaving no room for argument.

Rowan paused, confusion furrowing his brow, but he rose to his feet and let her lead him across the hall. They stopped in front of a closed door, one he'd never paid much attention to before. Eileen rested her hand lightly on the doorknob, turning to meet his gaze. "There's someone who's been waiting to speak with you."

He gave her a skeptical glance, his hesitation clear. "What are you talking about?" he asked, his tone dropping low.

Eileen didn't respond. She opened the door and gestured for him to step inside. Rowan's instincts prickled as he scanned her face, but her steady demeanor didn't falter. After a beat, he took a cautious step forward, his boots crossing the threshold. The air inside was cooler, carrying a faint metallic tang, and the flicker of candlelight danced across the room, casting shifting shadows.

At first, all he saw was the dim glow of the candles and the shadows stretching across the walls. Then his vision adjusted, and he noticed the objects meticulously arranged on the central table—bundles of herbs, intricately carved runes, and crystals shimmering faintly in the dancing light. They were Eileen's magick tools, laid out with a purpose he couldn't yet understand.

Unease stirred in his chest. *What is this?*

Turning back toward the door, his mouth opened to question Eileen—but she was gone. The quiet click of the door shutting sent a ripple of tension through him. When he reached for the handle, it refused to budge. She hadn't followed him.

Alone now, Rowan turned back to the room, his gaze drawn to the table. The candlelight caught on the edges of the crystals, making them glimmer like shards of frost. His heartbeat quickened as he took a hesitant step forward, his instincts warning him that this place held more than met the eye.

A subtle shift in the air made him pause. Then he saw it—a figure forming in the flickering light. At first, it was like ripples across still water, faint and indistinct. Then the edges sharpened, unmistakable. His chest tightened.

It was her.

"Davina..." he whispered, the name breaking on his lips.

She stood there, her form faint but achingly familiar. Her eyes—those same deep, warm eyes he had loved so fiercely—locked onto his, filled with quiet understanding. Rowan froze, unable to move, unable to breathe. Time seemed to collapse, pulling him back to the day he had held her, felt her life slip away with every shallow breath.

"Aidan," she said, her melodic voice echoing as it had in life. "It's been a long time."

His body moved instinctively, pulling him closer to her. Emotions crashed over him in a relentless wave. "How is this possible?" he asked, his voice trembling. "Are you... really here?"

"In a way," she replied, her lips curving into a gentle smile. "I'm here because you need to release the pain that's been holding you back."

He shook his head, his fists clenching at his sides. "Release it?" he repeated bitterly. "How can I let go when I've spent the last hundred years carrying the weight of your death? I've tried to atone for it, to make up for not being able to save you, and I don't know how to stop."

Davina stepped closer, her presence serene—a stark contrast to the storm inside him. "Aidan, you don't need to atone for anything," she said, her calm delivery firm. "My death wasn't your fault, and it wasn't something you could control. The world doesn't always make sense—it never has. Holding onto that guilt isn't preserving my memory. It's keeping you trapped in a moment that's already gone."

Her words pierced through the walls he hadn't realized he'd built. "But if I hadn't left—if I'd stayed—"

"Then we both would have died," she said softly, her focus unwavering. "And I wouldn't have wanted that for you. You were always meant to survive, Aidan. To keep going."

His gaze dropped to the floor, his voice not more than a whisper. "I don't know if I can," he admitted. "Every time I think about moving forward, it feels like I'm letting go of you—like I'm leaving you behind."

Her expression softened as she reached out, her translucent hand stopping just shy of his cheek. "You're not leaving me behind," she said gently. "I'm a part of you, just as you're a part of me. What we had—it mattered. But clinging to the past doesn't honor it. You weren't meant to stay in this place forever. You were meant to live."

Her focus sharpened, her words gaining an intensity that made him look up. "You care about her, don't you? Aislinn?"

Rowan's breath hitched. He opened his mouth to answer but faltered, the storm of emotions threatening to overwhelm him. Finally, he gave a small nod, his voice unsteady. "I... think I'm falling in love with her. But it feels like a betrayal. Like I'm letting go of everything we had."

"You're not betraying me, Aidan," Davina said, her warmth enveloping him like a soft glow. "Loving someone else doesn't erase what we shared. It means you're strong enough to let someone see the parts of you you've hidden, even the broken ones. It means you're honoring the life you still have to live."

Her words soothed the ache buried deep in his chest. He closed his eyes, drawing in a shaky breath as the burden he'd carried for so long began to lighten. When he opened them again, her form was already fading, her outline growing fainter with every passing second.

"I'll always be proud of you," she whispered, her tone steady. "And I'll always be with you. But it's time to stop holding on to me so tightly. You can't move forward if you're going to keep clinging to the past. Now, go and live the life you were meant to."

As she disappeared completely, Rowan stood frozen, his chest tight but no longer suffocating. A calmness settled over him, unfamiliar yet welcome—a lightness he hadn't felt in a century. Before he could process what had just happened, the air shifted again. A warm presence emerged behind him, grounding and familiar. Then a voice broke through the quiet, steady and sure.

"Aidan, my boy. What kind of mess have you gotten yourself into now? And look at your hair—it's filthy."

Rowan turned sharply, his breath catching as two familiar figures emerged from the dim glow. His father stood there, broad-shouldered and full of life, his grin warm and teasing, just as he remembered. Beside him, his mother radiated calm pride, the same unwavering presence that had reassured him as a child. They appeared younger than his last memories of them, vibrant and filled with the energy of their happiest days.

"Mam? Da?" Rowan's voice broke, the words catching in his throat. He ran a hand through his hair instinctively, suddenly self-conscious under his father's playful scrutiny.

His father's grin widened. "Aye, Aidan, that hair of yours—it's a complete disaster, I see. Some things never change."

A shaky laugh escaped Rowan, fragile under the weight of his emotions. "I can't believe it's really you," he said, his words trembling. His gaze darted between them, memorizing every detail as though afraid they might vanish at any moment.

"You've come so far, Aidan," his mother said softly, her words filled with love. "We've been watching over you, every step of the way. And we're so proud of the man you've become."

Rowan's throat tightened, his chest swelling with emotions he could barely contain. "I never thought I'd see you again," he whispered, his voice cracking.

"We've always been with you, son," his father said firmly, stepping closer. His hand rested briefly on Rowan's shoulder, though Rowan felt no physical sensation—only the familiar steadiness of his father's presence. "You might not have seen us, but we've been there. Through every battle, every choice, and every moment of doubt, wishing you the courage to keep going."

Rowan swallowed hard, his gaze dropping as guilt pressed heavily on him. "I've made so many mistakes," he murmured. "I've let people down. I've let you down."

His mother shook her head, stepping nearer, her expression glowing with kindness. "No, Aidan," she said gently, her words resolute yet tender. "You've carried the weight of this family on your shoulders for so long, even when it wasn't yours to bear. You've done more for us than we ever could have asked. It's time to forgive yourself."

His father's response cut in, calm and reassuring. "The past is done, Aidan. It's finished. What matters now is the life ahead of you—the future you still have to build."

Rowan lifted his head, meeting their unwavering focus. "What if I fail again?" he asked, his voice raw and uncertain. "What if I'm not strong enough to keep going?"

His mother's expression softened, offering the same reassurance that had calmed him after childhood nightmares. "You are stronger than you realize," she said. "We've seen it, time and time again. And strength doesn't mean never falling—it means standing back up when you do."

His father nodded, his face serious yet filled with warmth. "You've been carrying the past for so long, Aidan. Not just our deaths, but everything—every loss, every regret. You've held it all like a weight you believe you must bear. You don't have to." His voice softened, his words deliberate. "It's alright to let it go."

The words hit Rowan like a wave, crashing over him with undeniable truth. He closed his eyes, drawing in a shaking breath as he tried to absorb them. "I've missed you both so much," he admitted, his voice breaking.

"We've missed you too," his mother said, her tone thick with emotion. "But we've never truly left you. And now, it's time for you to live—not for us, but for yourself."

Her words wrapped around him like a warm embrace, filling the hollowness that had lived in his chest for so long. As their forms began to shimmer and fade, their love lingered, almost tangible, anchoring him in place.

"You're going to be alright, son," his father said, his words echoing faintly as the light around them dimmed. "And we'll always be proud of you."

Rowan reached out instinctively, but their forms dissolved into shadows before his fingers could reach them, leaving him standing alone in the quiet room. The silence pressed against his ears, stark and unyielding. Yet within him, *something* had shifted.

For the first time in a century, Rowan felt lighter, as though the chains that had bound him to his grief had finally been broken. The ache of loss remained, but it no longer suffocated him. Instead, it felt like a part of him—an enduring weight he could carry forward without being consumed by it.

He drew in a deep breath, his chest rising and falling evenly. As he exhaled, a clarity settled over him, calm and unshaken. He wasn't free of his pain, but he was no longer defined by it. And that, he realized, was the beginning of something new.

The door creaked open, and Eileen stepped inside. Her presence carried an intensity that made Rowan pause. The weight in her gaze seemed to shift the very air around them, pressing on his chest. "Are you ready?" she asked, her tone low and resonant with purpose.

Rowan turned to meet her steady eyes, a spark of determination igniting within him. He had spent too long mired in doubt, questioning his role in the grand design that surrounded him. Now, after everything he had experienced, doubt no longer had a place. "Yes," he said simply. "I am."

Eileen inclined her head, a faint, approving smile softening her features. "Some paths are laid out long before we walk them," she said, stepping further into the room. "Yours is one such path, Rowan. And so is Aislinn's. It's no coincidence that you found each other."

Unease stirred in his chest as curiosity flickered across his features. "What do you mean?" he asked cautiously.

"I trusted you with my little girl," Eileen replied, her words imbued with conviction. "Her destiny is tied to yours. From the time you became a Fallen, your lives became intertwined. The connection you feel isn't random—it's a thread woven through your past, present, and future."

His muscles stiffened as frustration sparked alongside intrigue. "Why can't you just tell me what that connection is?" he pressed, his voice rising. "Why all the riddles? Why me?"

Eileen held his gaze, her expression unwavering. "Because there are truths you're not ready to hear," she said protectively. "And because the answers aren't mine to give. Some things, Rowan, you must discover for yourself."

She stepped closer, her presence focusing him even as her words left him unsettled. "I will tell you this," she continued. "Sometimes, it takes stepping into the unknown to discover who you're truly meant to be. Your journey with Aislinn is not just a chance meeting; it's part of a greater design. The choices you make, the paths you follow—they will shape not only your future but hers as well."

Her statement settled over him like an unseen weight, heavier than any sword or shield he had carried into battle. He stood silent, letting the enormity of her implication sink in. There was more at play than he had ever imagined, a purpose that had been set into motion long before he drew his first breath as a Fallen. He wasn't sure if he was ready for what lay ahead, but somewhere deep within, he understood that Eileen's guidance—however veiled—had always led him true.

Eileen studied him, her gaze steady, her features resolute. Then she nodded, a glimmer of pride softening her expression. "Let's make sure you're prepared for what's coming," she said.

As they moved toward the door, Rowan felt an unfamiliar calm settle over him. His fears hadn't disappeared, yet clarity had begun to take their place. For the first time in what felt like ages, the burdens he carried seemed lighter—not removed, but no longer crushing him.

Just as his hand brushed the door handle, Eileen's voice stopped him. "One last thing, Rowan," she said, her tone carrying a gravity that sent a chill up his spine.

He turned toward her, a glint of unease breaking through the calm that had begun to take hold. "What is it?" he asked.

Her gaze darkened, a shadow of apprehension passing across her composed features. "The Golden Dawn isn't the only danger you'll face," she said. "There are forces at work that reach far beyond what we've seen."

Rowan frowned, the weight of her warning rippling through him. "What does that mean?" he asked, his fingers tightening on the door handle.

Eileen's gaze remained unwavering, a rare flicker of uncertainty crossing her otherwise composed demeanor. "There are those who have waited a very long time for you to step into your true role," she said cautiously. "Not all of them wish you well."

Her warning hung heavy in the air, thickening the atmosphere around them. Rowan exhaled slowly, his thoughts churning as he tried to parse her meaning. Whatever lay ahead, it was clear the road was far more perilous than he had imagined.

Eileen stepped closer, her hand brushing lightly against his arm—a rare gesture of comfort. "You're stronger than you think, Rowan," she said, her words softening. "Strength alone won't be enough. Trust the people walking this path with you."

Her statement lingered, layered with meaning she left unspoken. Rowan met her gaze and gave a firm nod, his features grim yet resolute. "I'll do whatever it takes," he said.

Eileen's lips curved into a faint smile, though the shadows in her eyes remained. "I know you will," she replied.

As they stepped out together, the echoes of her warning clung to him, a foreboding presence in the silence, like the first rumble of a distant storm. Rowan's resolve crystallized as he gripped the hilt of his purpose. Whatever forces awaited him, one thing burned with clarity: peace would not come without a fight.

The chill of Eileen's warning clung to Rowan as he walked to his bike, an unwelcome weight that refused to fade. Afternoon sunlight streaked across the city, its warmth casting a deceptive glow over the streets. It hinted at peace, yet Rowan felt the undercurrent of unease beneath it—subtle and insistent, like the distant rumble of a storm. Even the air seemed heavier, as if it braced for an unseen threat.

He paused, resting a hand on the bike's handlebar, his mind straying to Aislinn. The memory of her smile—steady and filled with understanding—had a way of settling him, offering a calm he couldn't find elsewhere. She wasn't just a comfort; she was a constant, a tether to something deeper he couldn't quite define. Not now. Eileen's warning pierced through his thoughts like a sharp wind, biting and unrelenting. The reminder was clear: there could be no distraction—not with so much at stake.

No distractions, he reminded himself, forcing thoughts of Aislinn aside. The Golden Dawn's shadow loomed too large to ignore, and Eileen's cryptic warning only deepened his resolve. His priority had to be ensuring Aislinn's safety—confirming there was no immediate threat to her before he could allow himself to think about anything else. There will be time to see her later, he promised himself. *When I know she's safe. When I can give her more than just half-measures and uncertainty.*

Steeling himself, Rowan swung a leg over the bike and gripped the handlebars with purpose. His path forward was clear, even if it wasn't simple. He needed to act—to gather information and stay ahead of the threat hovering at the edge of his awareness. The unknown was dangerous, and Rowan had never been one to wait for it to strike. Action was his answer to uncertainty, his only defense against the doubt creeping at the edges of his resolve.

Pulling his phone from his pocket, Rowan scrolled to Howard's number. Howard, a former member of the Golden Dawn, had become a vital ally to the Fallen. His decision to break from the organization had been rooted in defiance—an unwillingness to support their destructive and immoral methods. Though his past carried its own shadows, Howard's loyalty had proven unwavering. His insights were indispensable, and Rowan didn't take that trust lightly.

The phone rang twice before Howard answered.

"Rowan," Howard greeted, his tone clipped, carrying the faint weariness of a man who had seen too much. "Figured I'd be hearing from you."

Rowan skipped pleasantries. "Anything new? Have the Golden Dawn been making any moves?"

Howard's sigh crackled through the line. "They're keeping a low profile. No big meetings, no rituals—just the usual low-level activity." He hesitated, and Rowan caught the unease in his words. "Something's off. I can feel it. They're up to no good, Rowan. I just can't pin it down yet."

Rowan's grip tightened on the phone. Silence from the Golden Dawn wasn't reassuring—it was intentional. "If anything changes, call me immediately."

"You'll be the first to know," Howard promised before ending the call.

Sliding the phone back into his pocket, Rowan exhaled slowly. The inactivity surrounding the Golden Dawn felt meditative, like the pause before an eruption. Their calculated absence only deepened his resolve. If they thought they could catch him unprepared, they were wrong.

Rowan refocused, mentally mapping out his next steps. Chinatown came to mind—a place where he could rely on both familiarity and trusted resources. Ying's name surfaced, her sharp instincts and extensive network making her an invaluable ally. The memory of her steadied him as he maneuvered through the city streets, the hum of traffic and the chatter of pedestrians filling the air around him.

When he arrived, Chinatown's lively energy welcomed him like an old friend. Vibrant shopfronts displayed their wares, while the fragrant mix of spices hung in the air, a reminder of the community's resilience. It was a strength that always kept him focused, offering perspective amidst the chaos. Ying's stall sat in its usual corner, its shelves carefully arranged with jars of dried herbs, teas, and roots. Her hands moved deftly through a bundle of ginseng, her focus unbroken even as Rowan approached.

"Rowan," she greeted without looking up, her tone sharp with a trace of amusement. "You look like a man chasing shadows."

A faint smile crossed his face. "Not far off," he admitted. "Have you noticed anything unusual? Larger purchases, new patterns?"

Ying's hands paused briefly before she met his eyes. "The Golden Dawn," she said, her tone measured. "They've been buying in bulk—mostly common herbs. Cinnamon, mugwort, ginger. Nothing rare, but the quantities stand out. They're not exactly subtle about it."

Rowan frowned, pieces of the puzzle clicking into place in his mind. "A large-scale ritual," he said aloud, more to himself than Ying. "Or a diversion."

"Possibly both," she replied dryly, her features sharpening with thought. "I'll keep an ear to the ground. They're careful, but no one's perfect. If they slip, I'll know."

"Thanks, Ying," Rowan said sincerely, offering a quick nod before stepping back into the bustling streets, his mind already racing ahead.

The streets of Chinatown thrummed with life, yet Rowan remained distant from the energy, his mind locked in a relentless cycle of planning and reevaluation. Every step felt like a move in a larger game, the pieces scattered and incomplete. Even as he worked to stay focused, thoughts of Aislinn crept in—her laugh, the way she made the world feel less heavy, how her presence seemed to fill the empty spaces he hadn't realized were there.

Not yet. The reminder steadied him. His focus had to remain on the Golden Dawn and the tangled web they were weaving. Eileen's warning lingered in his mind, a responsibility he couldn't ignore. *I need to make sure she's safe first—to know there's no threat hanging over her.*

For now, vigilance was his only option.

He called Charlie, a young police officer who had quickly become one of the Fallen's most reliable allies. Ever since Rowan had asked him to keep an eye on Aislinn's café, Charlie had exceeded expectations. His patrols were consistent, his stakeouts discreet, and his knack for blending into the background made him an invaluable resource. Rowan respected that Charlie didn't press for answers—he simply got the job done, a rare quality in someone not fully brought into the Fallen's world.

"Hey, Rowan," Charlie greeted when he answered, his easy demeanor tempering Rowan's tension. "I've kept up the patrols like you asked. Nothing unusual happening around the café."

"Good," Rowan replied, shifting his attention to broader concerns. "What about the Golden Dawn? Any sign of their people nearby?"

There was a brief pause before Charlie answered, his tone more serious. "Nothing concrete," he said, hesitation creeping into his response. "But there's been extra foot traffic around the Old Mount Olympus Mansion. Could be nothing—kids sneaking around, urban explorers, that kind of thing. Still, it's more than usual. I figured you'd want to know."

Rowan frowned, already filing the information away. "Thanks for the heads-up. Keep an eye on it, and if the pattern changes, let me know immediately."

"You've got it," Charlie assured him before the call ended.

Rowan slipped the phone back into his pocket, a fraction of the pressure in his chest easing but not fully disappearing. For now, there was no immediate crisis, no imminent threat demanding his attention. The café was secure, and the city calm—for the time being. It was a reprieve, fleeting as it was, and Rowan allowed himself a brief sense of relief.

Inevitably, Aislinn came to mind. Her image surfaced without effort, and this time, he didn't push it away. It wasn't just her face or her laugh that stayed with him—it was the way she made him feel grounded, as though he could glimpse a life beyond the relentless weight of his duties. The thought stirred an unfamiliar question that crept in quietly: *Could there be space for more than just this fight?*

He exhaled sharply, forcing his focus back to the present. The Golden Dawn's plans were still shrouded in secrecy, each unanswered question another thread of danger. He couldn't lose focus—not until he knew she was truly out of harm's reach. *One step at a time,* he reminded himself. Aislinn deserved more than fragments of his attention, more than promises made in the shadow of uncertainty. He needed to ensure she was safe before allowing himself to think beyond this battle.

Redirecting his focus to Charlie's report, Rowan swung a leg over his bike and turned toward the Old Mount Olympus Mansion. The extra foot traffic couldn't be ignored, not when the Fallen had determined just yesterday that the mansion was the Golden Dawn's base of operations. Once a symbol of wealth and grandeur, the estate had fallen into disrepair, its opulence replaced by decay and secrecy. Rowan hadn't had the chance to investigate it himself yet, but with Charlie's tip, it seemed like the ideal time to see what might be hidden within its crumbling walls.

Rowan approached the mansion cautiously, keeping to the shadows as he scanned the area. The estate loomed ahead, its crumbling facade wrapped in ivy that clung like a second skin. Broken windows caught the fading sunlight, their jagged edges stark against the weathered stone. The air around the mansion hung heavy, as if even the wind avoided this place. It wasn't just the physical decay that set him on edge—it was the presence of an unseen force, lurking beneath the surface.

For the next hour, Rowan observed from a distance, his sharp attention tracking every movement. Two maintenance workers emerged from a side entrance, loading crates into a truck. The actions appeared routine, almost mundane, but Rowan refused to dismiss them. A flicker in an upstairs window drew his focus, his pulse quickening as he studied it. A figure, or perhaps two, shifted behind the curtain too quickly for him to make out details.

The oppressive stillness of the mansion unnerved him. It wasn't the kind of silence that came with neglect; it felt calculated, measured. Every detail seemed like part of a larger puzzle he couldn't yet piece together. *They're hiding more than it seems, his instincts warned.*

As the minutes dragged on, Rowan's attention wavered. His thoughts strayed to Aislinn, her smile emerging in his mind—warm and sincere, the kind of expression that had always felt like a balm against the storm. He remembered the way she had looked at him during their last conversation, her gaze steady and unflinching. *She sees me,* he realized, not for the first time, but with more clarity now. *She sees everything I've hidden, even from myself.*

He straightened, exhaling as he turned his focus back to the mansion behind him. Its secrets remained locked away, inscrutable for now, and his surveillance would have to be enough. A flicker of unease remained—an instinctive sense that trouble was brewing—but he reminded himself to take each step as it came. He couldn't let the unknown paralyze him.

Walking back to his bike, his thoughts shifted again, unbidden but sharper now. His recent encounter with Davina and his parents returned to him, their words still echoing. *It wasn't your fault.* They had freed him from the weight of guilt he'd carried for so long, urging him to stop lingering in the shadows of his past and start living. Aislinn had been part of that realization too, even if she didn't know it. She wasn't just comfort—she was the future they wanted for him.

She wasn't a distraction. She was a reminder of what he could have, of what he deserved to fight for. He gripped the handlebars of his bike, the pull to see her growing stronger, like a steady rhythm that guided him forward. *Not yet, but soon,* he thought, the promise carrying the quiet weight of intention. This time, it wasn't about hesitation—it was about ensuring the path ahead was clear enough to move toward her without fear.

The café came into view sooner than Rowan expected, its warm lights spilling onto the sidewalk and creating a soft glow against the cool evening air. The sign on the door read Closed, but shadows moved within, faint silhouettes hinting at the life inside. He parked his bike out front, hesitating longer than he intended. A tightness gripped his chest, the kind that pressed against his resolve. He didn't have anything prepared to say—if the words even existed—but the pull to see her, to take one step toward a possibility he had long denied himself, overpowered his hesitation.

If this is the start of something new, I want it to begin here.

As he approached, his eyes swept the street, instincts sharpening his focus. A parked car with tinted windows caught his attention. Its unmoving presence felt deliberate, sending a ripple of unease through him. It seemed to observe him, its placement too calculated to be mere coincidence. Rowan studied it briefly, committing the detail to memory, before turning toward the door. He couldn't let it slip past unnoticed, but he wouldn't allow it to derail him, either.

The bell above the door gave a light chime as he stepped inside. Warm air enveloped him, carrying the scent of freshly brewed coffee and baked goods. The hum of conversation mixed with the clatter of chairs and the occasional clink of mugs. Aislinn sat at a corner table with Ariel, Takoda, and Rain, laughter still hovering in the air as their evening wound down. Empty cups and crumpled napkins scattered across the table hinted at shared stories and easy companionship.

The scene struck Rowan unexpectedly. It was so ordinary, so unguarded, a stark contrast to the cold vigilance that defined his daily life. For a brief moment, he simply stood there, absorbing it. When Aislinn turned and saw him, her expression shifted, surprise giving way to a gentler look. Her smile lit her face with warmth that seemed to reach him, stirring an ache deep in his chest.

"Rowan," she said, standing to greet him. Her tone held genuine surprise, but her smile lingered. "I wasn't expecting you."

"Hey," he replied, keeping his voice even despite the nervous energy thrumming within him. "Just wanted to check in."

Ariel's eyes darted between them, her grin turning mischievous. "Looks like we should probably clear out," she teased, nudging Takoda and Rain. "See you tomorrow, Aislinn." She stood, motioning for the others to follow, though not without sending Rowan a knowing glance over her shoulder.

Rowan ignored her with practiced ease, his attention fixed on Aislinn. She studied him with an intensity that felt searching, her brow furrowing slightly as if trying to understand what lay beneath the surface. That look always managed to unnerve him and steady him at the same time.

"You okay?" she asked gently, her curiosity evident. "You seem… different."

He hesitated, searching for the right response. "Yeah," he said at last, his tone measured. "Is it all right if we go upstairs?"

Concern flickered briefly across her face, but she nodded. "Of course."

As she turned toward the stairs, Rowan reached out, brushing his fingers against hers in a silent request. "Wait," he murmured, his voice low but firm. "Could you lock up first?"

Aislinn paused, tilting her head slightly before offering him a small smile. She moved to the door, glancing briefly at the parked car outside. Something about it unsettled her—a faint disquiet, like a whisper she couldn't quite decipher. She lowered the blinds, switched off the lights, and set the alarm, each motion methodical, shutting out the world beyond the café.

When she returned, Rowan took her hand again, a quiet reassurance passing between them as they climbed the narrow staircase. The silence between them felt heavy, charged with the weight of unspoken things, but not oppressive. By the time they reached her small apartment, the air seemed to shift around them, creating an almost tangible sense of separation from everything outside.

The door clicked shut behind them, and Rowan turned to face her. For a few heartbeats, he stood motionless, his focus tracing her features as if committing them to memory—the curve of her smile, the way strands of her hair caught the faint glow of the room. The air felt delicate, charged with an unspoken energy that drew him closer, its fragility pulling at him with quiet insistence.

With sudden resolve, he stepped forward, his hand finding the nape of her neck with gentle certainty. Before she could speak, he kissed her.

The kiss wasn't hesitant or cautious. It was raw, unguarded, as though the barriers he had carried for so long had finally given way. His lips moved against hers with intensity, pouring into the connection everything he couldn't say aloud. She didn't pull back. Instead, she leaned into him, her hands threading through his hair as if anchoring him in the present.

Time blurred, the world outside slipping away entirely. Rowan surrendered to her touch, the way she returned his kiss with equal fervor. When her hands tightened against him, pulling him closer, a realization stirred deep within—a part of himself he hadn't known he was ready to share.

Just as the fire between them threatened to consume him, Rowan broke the kiss, resting his forehead against hers. His breath came uneven, his hand lingering at her side as he fought to speak.

"You can't imagine how much I want to keep going," he murmured, his voice low, edged with raw vulnerability. "But there's more I need to tell you first."

Her eyes searched his, her breathing unsteady as concern flickered in her expression. "What is it?" she asked, her voice quiet, laced with worry. "You're starting to scare me."

Rowan drew back slightly, his hands settling on her shoulders, as though maintaining the connection could steady him. "This is important," he said, his words heavier than he intended. The weight of what he needed to say pressed against him, filling the silence. "I can't tell you everything right now, but you need to know this much."

His eyes held hers, watching for any trace of hesitation. Aislinn had always met him with honesty, her clarity often leaving him unsteady, yet this felt different. He didn't know how much she could accept, and the idea of her pulling away, looking at him with doubt, twisted his chest tight. Eileen's warning echoed in his mind, sharp and unrelenting. He couldn't keep her in the dark—not when it might mean putting her in harm's way.

"Can we sit on the couch?" he asked, his voice softening to a near whisper. "I want you to feel comfortable."

Aislinn nodded, her expression unreadable, though a flicker of concern passed over her features. She let him guide her across the room, their hands loosely joined. Rowan waited until she settled on the couch before stepping toward the window. He pulled the curtain aside just enough to peer out, scanning the street below. The muffled hum of the city felt distant, as if it belonged to a different world.

His attention settled on the unmarked car parked across the street, its dark silhouette tucked into the shadowed alley. Rowan pressed his lips into a thin line and raised his hand in a small, practiced thumbs-up. A moment later, a hand emerged from the driver's side, returning the signal before retreating. Relief rippled through him. The officers assigned to watch over Aislinn were in position, their presence a small reassurance against the uncertainty pressing down on him.

Letting the curtain fall back into place, Rowan turned toward the couch, his steps conscious, his thoughts churning. Aislinn watched him closely, her head tilting slightly, a question forming in her features. He sat beside her, leaning forward with his elbows resting lightly on his knees, fingers laced together. The weight of what he needed to say pressed heavily on him, but he forced himself to begin.

"Do you remember the meeting I mentioned earlier?" he asked, glancing at her.

She nodded, concern deepening. "Yes. Did something go wrong?"

"It wasn't that," Rowan replied, shaking his head slowly. "The meeting went fine. It's connected to what I need to tell you." He hesitated, the pause stretching until the silence between them grew heavy. "That meeting was with my boss."

Her brow furrowed, confusion crossing her face. "Your boss?" she asked. "I thought Donnelly's was your only job."

Rowan shifted in his seat, the space between them thickening with anxiety. "Donnelly's is my cover," he said, his tone careful and exact. "It's the job people see, the one I use to explain why I'm in the city. But my real work is with an independent group—something I've never talked about before." Turning slightly, he met her eyes directly, his words carrying the gravity of what he was about to reveal. "We handle dangerous situations and threats most people don't even realize exist."

Aislinn tilted her head again, curiosity softening her features even as unease flickered faintly in her expression. "What kind of threats?" she asked, her voice low, almost hesitant.

"The kind that operate in the shadows," Rowan said, his tone sharpening. "They're involved in things most people wouldn't believe—or wouldn't want to. That man you saw at the bar? He's part of one of those groups. They call themselves the Golden Dawn."

Her eyes widened slightly, her hand moving instinctively to tuck a strand of hair behind her ear. "The creepy guy?" she asked, her voice trembling just enough to reveal her unease. "He was outside the café too..."

Rowan nodded, his shoulders stiffening as he acknowledged her words. "Yes. Ariel told me you saw him near the café. The Golden Dawn is a dangerous organization. They've been on our radar for a long time."

He paused, letting the weight of his words settle in the silence. "The group I'm part of—the Fallen—is different," he continued, his tone softening slightly. "We work to stop people like them, to protect others from the harm they cause."

Aislinn didn't respond immediately, her expression guarded as she processed his words. Rowan resisted the urge to speak again, allowing her the time she needed. When she finally spoke, her tone was calm, though a faint tremor hung beneath her words.

"And you're telling me this because you think I'm in danger?" she asked, her words steady, tinged with unease.

Rowan's jaw tightened, his hands curling briefly into loose fists before he forced himself to relax. "I don't know if you're a target," he admitted, the raw truth cutting through the heavy silence. "But I can't ignore the possibility. That's why I've been watching out for you—why I'm telling you this now. You deserve to know what's out there, even if I can't explain everything yet."

She remained motionless for a moment. Then her hand lifted, settling lightly on his arm. The simple gesture sent a warmth through him, offering a calm reassurance that steadied his thoughts. Her gaze held his, carrying a quiet strength that seemed to reach into the parts of him he often kept guarded.

"Thank you for telling me," she said, her voice calm, carrying a sincerity that cut through his tension. "It means a lot that you're looking out for me."

Her acceptance washed over him, easing a stress he hadn't fully acknowledged. It wasn't just her words—it was the way she looked at him, a confidence that reached him deeply. Rowan swallowed hard, his heart pounding as he leaned closer.

"You don't know what it means for me to hear that," he murmured, his voice rough with emotion. "I don't want to lose you, Aislinn."

The weight of his words lingered, heavy with meaning. Her features softened, understanding settling into her expression that went beyond the danger he described. It wasn't just his confession she heard—it was him, the man beneath the defenses and years of duty. For so long, he had believed those parts of himself untouchable, yet here she was, seeing him as he truly was. It stirred something fierce within him, a longing for the connection he had denied himself for far too long.

Rowan didn't speak. Instead, he shifted closer, his hands resting lightly on her hips as he helped her to her feet. For a breathless pause, they stood together, the air between them charged with an intensity that didn't need words. Then, his lips met hers, the kiss carrying a thoughtful tenderness that spoke of trust and a longing he could no longer hold back. It wasn't rushed or uncertain—it was measured, like crossing an unseen threshold he had been afraid to approach until now.

Her hands moved to his chest, her touch hesitant at first, before sliding up to his shoulders. She responded instinctively, matching the depth of his kiss with her own, leaning into him as though the connection were a tether. The contact between them sent a pulse of warmth through him, reeling him in even as it unraveled buried ache deep inside.

Rowan drew her closer, his hands settling at the curve of her waist. The deliberate motion pulled her against him, letting her feel the unspoken desire simmering beneath his restraint. It wasn't just about passion—it was an unguarded offering of everything he had been too afraid to share. When her fingers tightened against his shoulders, he deepened the kiss, surrendering to the vulnerability that came with trusting her completely.

His heart raced, but not with urgency. It was the weight of being here, with her, in a moment that felt too significant to put into words. As their lips parted, Rowan's forehead rested lightly against hers, his breath uneven as he whispered, "Can I stay? Please."

Her fingers curled into his shirt as she tilted her head back, her expression searching his. "Are you sure?" she asked, her voice soft but edged with vulnerability. "I need to know this isn't just the moment."

"I'm sure," he said, the conviction in his tone leaving no room for doubt. "I want this. I want you."

Her answer was quiet yet firm, her words carrying a sincerity that steadied him in a way he hadn't expected. "Then stay," she said simply, her permission unraveling the restraint he had clung to.

He kissed her again, the intensity building in waves, though never rushed. Each touch of his lips, every motion of his hands against her back, carried a promise of devotion that didn't need to be spoken aloud. He pulled her even closer, erasing any remaining distance between them as the rest of the world seemed to dissolve, leaving only the two of them suspended in this shared moment.

Rowan's hands slipped under her thighs as he lifted her, and her arms wrapped instinctively around his shoulders. She clung to him, her trust evident in the way she relaxed against him as he carried her toward the bedroom. Their kisses softened as they moved, but the reverence in each touch remained unbroken. This wasn't simply about desire—it was about opening themselves to one another in a way neither had dared to before.

When he set her down on the bed, he paused, his attention fixed on her as the dim light highlighted the contours of her face. The moment stretched between them, fragile yet weighted with significance. His hands hovered just above her skin as if to ask permission one last time before he leaned in to kiss her again. This kiss was different—deeper, imbued with every emotion he couldn't say aloud. Devotion, longing, and a quiet hope that she would see all of him and stay.

Every touch became a silent vow. Their connection burned steadily, layered with a depth that seemed to fill the space between them. Rowan's movements were intentional, his focus unwavering. For the first time in what felt like forever, the walls he had built around himself were gone. Vulnerability no longer felt like weakness—it felt like freedom.

The night unfolded with a quiet intimacy that enveloped them, their shared warmth creating a cocoon that seemed to shield them from the world beyond. Rowan held her afterward, her head resting against his chest, her breathing steady and calming. The silence that settled between them wasn't empty—it was rich with understanding, a shared knowledge that they had crossed into territory neither could ever retreat from.

For the first time in years, Rowan felt what he had once believed impossible: peace.

The hours stretched on, though the café below and the city beyond had not disappeared entirely. Outside, the parked car with its tinted windows remained in its shadowed perch. A lone silhouette shifted in the driver's seat, the glow of a phone briefly illuminating their face before fading once more into darkness. Their attention remained fixed on the window of Aislinn's apartment, watchful and unyielding. Rowan may have found a reprieve, but the watcher had not moved on. Silent and patient, they waited, unseen yet ever-present.

Chapter Twelve
Revelations & Ruptures

Aislinn stirred awake, the warmth radiating from Rowan's body pulling her into the peace of the morning. For a few seconds, she lingered, letting the calm settle. Her attention drifted downward, catching on a jagged scar beneath his ribs. Before she could stop herself, her fingers brushed over the uneven skin.

Rowan stiffened, his muscles tightening under her touch. His eyelids fluttered open, heavy with sleep, and he glanced at her hand. A faint flush crept into his cheeks as he pulled the sheet higher, concealing the scar in a motion that felt reflexive.

"Morning," Aislinn said, offering a small smile, as though to soften the delicate unease between them.

"Morning," Rowan replied, his words gravelly from sleep and weighted with an unshakable heaviness.

They lay there in a silence that hung between them—not uncomfortable, but heavy with unspoken truths. Aislinn sensed his thoughts circling beneath his composed exterior. She broke the quiet. "Didn't expect you to stay," she said lightly, her question laced with a teasing edge.

Rowan let out a quiet chuckle, the sound low and uncertain. "Neither did I. But... I'm glad I did."

"Me too." She hesitated, searching his face. "You seemed... distracted yesterday. Like you've been carrying too much."

Rowan exhaled deeply, tipping his head back toward the ceiling. "Yeah. It's just... a lot. Sometimes it feels like I'm drowning, like I can't come up for air."

Aislinn reached for his arm, her fingers curling around it in a gesture of reassurance. "You don't have to do this alone. You can talk to me, Rowan."

His focus shifted to her, and for the briefest instant, his guarded demeanor eased. "I know," he said, his voice dropping into a whisper. "I'm still learning how to let someone in... but you make it easier."

Her grip on his arm firmed. "Good," she said, her resolve clear. "Because I'm not going anywhere."

A faint smile curved his lips as he lifted a hand, brushing a stray strand of hair from her face. "Guess I'll have to get used to that."

Aislinn sat up, stretching her arms toward the ceiling as the first rays of sunlight crept through the curtains. "I'm going to make some coffee," she said, sliding out of bed with easy grace.

Rowan nodded and followed, his movements slower, as though the weight of his thoughts lingered. He raked a hand through his hair, strain visible in every motion.

Aislinn padded to the window, the cool floor a welcome sensation beneath her feet. She reached for the curtain and pulled it aside, welcoming the morning light—until her chest tightened, and she froze. Across the street, shrouded partially in the morning mist, stood a shadowy figure, unmoving. Her stomach clenched, and she whispered, "Rowan."

Rowan was at her side in an instant, his reflexes sharp. "What is it?" he asked, his words calm but edged with urgency.

"There," she murmured, pointing with trembling fingers. "Across the street."

His focus snapped to the figure, his body coiling with tension. Swiftly, he grabbed his jacket and headed for the door, his movements smooth and deliberate.

Aislinn followed, her heart pounding in her chest. "Rowan, wait—what are you doing?"

"I need to know why he's here," Rowan said, his resolve unyielding, determination driving every step.

"You can't," Aislinn said, her voice faltering as panic swelled in her chest. "What if it's dangerous?"

"It'll be fine," he assured her, glancing back as they reached the café below. "This is what I do. If anything happens, I'll call for backup."

Aislinn opened her mouth to argue, but Rowan's unwavering expression left no room for discussion. At the café door, he turned and faced her, his focus unwavering. "Stay here. Lock the door behind me."

She paused at the doorway, frozen, as Rowan approached the figure, his strides purposeful. Just then, Takoda appeared from the opposite direction, her brow furrowed in confusion.

"What's going on?" she called, her attention shifting between Rowan and Aislinn, who hovered near the door.

Before Aislinn could respond, the figure across the street noticed Rowan closing in. In an instant, they bolted, their footsteps pounding against the empty street.

Rowan reacted immediately, his boots hammering against the pavement as he launched into pursuit.

"I'm going after them," Aislinn said, already moving. "Come on, we can't just stand here!"

Takoda hesitated briefly, startled, but quickly followed. The two trailed at a cautious distance, their breathing quickening as they struggled to match Rowan's relentless pace.

As they rounded a corner, a figure vaulted into the street ahead, their long coat flaring like wings caught mid-flight. Each movement was precise, their focus locked with an intensity that held Aislinn's attention for a split second. Tousled dark hair framed their face, giving them a sharp edge that made her chest tighten. *Who is this? Ally or threat?*

"Whoa!" Takoda exclaimed, her surprise breaking the charged atmosphere. "Did you see that?"

"I don't know if he's with Rowan," Aislinn shot back, her words clipped, "but we need to keep moving!"

The fleeing Golden Dawn member darted into a narrow alley, with Rowan and the enigmatic figure in pursuit. Aislinn and Takoda pushed harder, unease prickling at the edges of Aislinn's awareness as the chase drew them deeper into the twisting maze of alleys.

A sudden crackling tore through the air. The Golden Dawn member turned abruptly, hurling a blazing orb of blue fire toward his pursuers. The flames roared down the alley, searing and impossibly bright, the heat tangible even from a distance.

"Rowan!" Aislinn shouted, panic spiking through her as fear gripped her chest.

Rowan reacted instantly, abandoning the pursuit to rush back toward Aislinn and Takoda. In a single, fluid motion, he pressed them both against the nearest wall, his arms forming a shield around them. His breathing came fast, his chest rising and falling rapidly as he braced himself between them and the advancing flames.

"Riichi! Keep going!" Rowan barked, his command sharp and unwavering.

The air shimmered with heat, distorting the alley ahead, but Riichi remained focused. His movements were calculated, his trench coat flowing behind him like a shadow brought to life. Without breaking stride, he reached under the coat and withdrew a gleaming katana. With precision, he swung the blade, slicing through the fireball and scattering blue sparks that sprayed harmlessly across the brick walls.

A new figure stepped out from the shadows moments later—Elder. Each of his steps carried purpose, his posture charged with authority. He raised one hand, conjuring a vivid green flame that pulsed with a force greater than the previous attack. With a flick of his wrist, the flame shot forward, streaking toward the Golden Dawn member with unnerving accuracy.

The fireball struck squarely between the man's shoulders, sending him stumbling before he crumpled to the pavement with a muffled cry. The chase ended as swiftly as it had begun.

Riichi stood over the fallen man, his katana catching the light. His stance remained resolute, his presence radiating composed vigilance.

The air hung heavy, thick with the acrid tang of burnt ozone and the lingering residue of magic. For a single, charged beat, everyone froze, adrenaline coursing like the pounding of a war drum. Rowan's arms stayed firmly around Aislinn and Takoda, his body positioned as a shield against the chaos.

Riichi and Elder emerged, dragging the unconscious Golden Dawn member behind them. Rowan redirected his focus, his features hardening into a mask of resolve as he assessed the scene.

"Elder, take him to Oak," Rowan commanded, his tone clipped. He gestured toward Takoda with a firm tilt of his chin. "Riichi, get her back to the café. Now."

Takoda opened her mouth to argue, but the unyielding look Rowan gave her silenced her. With a reluctant nod, she allowed Riichi to guide her away, casting a worried glance back at Aislinn before disappearing into the distance.

As soon as they were gone, Rowan turned to Aislinn, his restraint unraveling. The anger he had been holding back boiled over, his intensity locking her in place. "I told you to stay at the café!" he shouted, his frustration spilling out in full force. "Do you have any idea how close you were to being killed?"

His pulse roared in his ears, the horrifying image he'd pushed aside during the chase breaking through—Aislinn lying lifeless, blood pooling beneath her. The thought clawed at him, twisting his insides with a relentless grip.

Aislinn glared at him, her own adrenaline fueling her defiance. "And what was I supposed to do, Rowan? Stay there and hope you came back alive? Sit around while you ran headfirst into danger?"

"Yes!" Rowan snapped, his response cracking under the weight of his fear. "I had it under control!"

"No, you didn't!" she fired back, her frustration spilling over. "I saw what was happening! Your 'friend' had a sword, and there were fireballs flying everywhere! Don't stand there and tell me you had that under control!" Her voice rose, disbelief threading through her accusation. "What is going on, Rowan?!"

Her question struck him like a blow, and his anger crumbled, replaced by the crushing reality of the situation. "You don't understand," he said hoarsely, his words almost imperceptible. "It's dangerous... I can't lose you."

Aislinn's breathing quickened as she fought to compose herself. Her tone softened, but her determination remained firm. "Then talk to me, Rowan. Please. You keep shutting me out, and I can't take it anymore. I need to know what's happening."

Rowan stared at her, desperation etched into every line of his face. He opened his mouth, searching for the right explanation to make her understand. Instead, an unexpected question tumbled out. "Aislinn, how old do you think I am?"

She blinked, thrown completely off guard. "What?" Confusion rippled through her as she tried to process the abrupt shift.

"How old am I?" Rowan repeated, his tone sharpened with urgency.

"I don't know… twenty-eight?" she guessed, uncertainty threading through her response.

Rowan exhaled shakily, his hands trembling as he dragged them down his face. When he lowered them, his focus locked on her, his voice lowering. "Aislinn… I'm 205."

Aislinn froze, searching his face for any hint of humor. But there was none—only raw sincerity, stark and unyielding.

"No. No," she whispered, shaking her head as disbelief quivered in her words. "I'm not stupid, Rowan." Her frustration surged, and she shoved him in the chest, forcing him back a step. "You don't have to make things up just to avoid telling me the truth!"

Rowan staggered, more stunned by her reaction than the shove itself. "Aislinn, I'm not lying—"

"Stop!" she snapped, cutting him off. Anger flickered in her expression as she stepped back, shaking her head. "Don't follow me."

"Aislinn—" His voice cracked as he reached for her, but she had already turned away.

She spun back once more, her glare cutting into him with finality. "I said, don't follow me!" And then she was gone, vanishing around the corner and leaving him standing alone in the suffocating silence.

For what felt like an eternity, Rowan stood frozen, his hands trembling as he dragged them through his hair in frustration. His heart thundered, and a storm of emotions churned within him—fear, regret, confusion. *What had just happened? What had he said?*

He leaned back against the wall, tilting his head toward the sky as if it might hold the answers. "Now what?" he muttered, the question muted and fragile against the suffocating air of the alley.

Aislinn's face remained vivid in his mind—the flash of anger, the raw hurt she hadn't been able to hide. Her parting remarks echoed relentlessly, cutting deeper with each repetition. The image of her walking away replayed like a cruel reminder, anchoring him to the spot. His bike was still at the café, but going back now felt... wrong. It would cheapen everything she had said, make her retreat meaningless.

With a frustrated sigh, Rowan pushed off the wall and started walking. His boots crunched against the gravel, the sound jarring in the empty quiet. He didn't know where he was going—only that movement felt better than standing in one place. Maybe if he walked far enough, long enough, he could figure out what to do next.

Back at the café, Aislinn shoved the door open harder than she intended. The lights were off, and the lopsided "Closed" sign hung crookedly in the window. Inside, Takoda and Riichi stood near the counter, speaking in low murmurs, while Rain loitered near the far wall, her attention darting toward the door every few seconds.

The instant Aislinn stepped inside, all three turned to look at her. Without acknowledging them, she strode past, her jaw set, and climbed the stairs with determined steps. Concerned glances followed her, but she ignored them. She needed space—time to think. The weight of everything that had just happened pressed down on her like an oppressive storm cloud.

She reached her room and locked the door behind her with a resolute click. Leaning against the solid wood, she closed her eyes, forcing herself to breathe evenly. The memory of Rowan's revelation, his raw admission, clawed at her composure, refusing to be ignored.

A short while later, the café door swung open again, this time with Ariel's signature burst of energy. Her quick steps carried across the room as she glanced around. The crooked "Closed" sign still dangled in the window, and the pressure in the air made her usual grin falter. Her attention landed on Riichi, standing near the counter with arms crossed while Takoda spoke to him with calm intent.

"Hey, you!" Ariel called, delivering a playful punch to Riichi's arm. "What are you doing here?" Her teasing tone faded as she took in the scene. Rain hovered nearby, her usual ease replaced by unease, and Takoda's furrowed brow spoke volumes.

"What's going on?" Ariel asked, her grin vanishing entirely. "Did I miss something?"

Takoda exchanged a look with Rain before answering. "There was... an incident," she said cautiously. "Rowan and Aislinn had a fight. He left, and she locked herself in her room. Rain and I tried talking to her, but she wouldn't come out."

Ariel's eyebrows shot up in surprise. "Rowan and Ash?" she repeated, disbelief clear in her voice. "What kind of fight would make her lock herself away?" She glanced toward Riichi, curiosity sparking in her expression. "And I'm guessing no one's gotten any answers out of him?"

Takoda sighed, folding her arms. "Nope. He just showed up, said he's here for our safety, and keeps insisting he needs to talk to 'Mr. Rowan.'" Frustration seeped into her tone. "Won't even tell us who he is."

Rain, leaning against the counter, smirked faintly. "The only reason he's still here is because Takoda thinks he's cute."

"What?!" Takoda spun toward Rain, her cheeks flushing a deep red. "That's not true!" Her protest came out higher-pitched than intended.

Rain arched an eyebrow, her grin widening. "Sure, it's not."

Takoda sputtered, her hands flying up as she turned to Riichi, her embarrassment spilling into her words. "I mean—that's not why you're still here!" she stammered. "Not that I think you're, you know, not cute—I just meant—" Her sentence faltered completely, leaving her face burning. "Ugh. Never mind."

Riichi's lips twitched faintly, a hint of amusement breaking through his composed demeanor. He nodded slowly, his calm presence only intensifying Takoda's embarrassment.

Ariel pressed her lips together to stifle a laugh, though her eyes sparkled with mischief. She turned back to Riichi, shaking her head. "Seriously? You couldn't just start with your name?"

Riichi shrugged, unbothered. Ariel rolled her eyes. "This guy is Riichi. He's one of Rowan's closest allies, and yes, he's here to protect you."

Riichi gave a brief, composed nod. Ariel arched an eyebrow at him. "Not so hard, was it? Next time, maybe lead with that." Turning to Takoda and Rain, her smirk softened into reassurance. "All right, I'll take my shot at Aislinn. Wish me luck."

"Good luck," Takoda muttered, her posture relaxing slightly. Rain offered Ariel an encouraging nod.

Ariel headed for the stairs, tossing a glance over her shoulder. "Keep your fingers crossed for me."

Ariel took the stairs two at a time, her steps quick but slowing as she neared the top. She paused outside Aislinn's door, her hand hovering just above the wood before she knocked lightly. "Ash," she called, her tone calm and composed. "It's me. Can I come in?"

The silence pressed heavily against her ears, thick and unrelenting. For a brief second, Ariel worried there wouldn't be a response. Then, the faint click of the lock turning reached her. Ariel eased the door open and stepped inside, closing it quietly behind her. The air felt charged, heavy with the weight of Aislinn's unspoken turmoil.

Aislinn sat at the small dining table, her shoulders slumped. Puffy, red-rimmed eyes and a drawn face made it clear she'd been grappling with thoughts she couldn't escape. Ariel's chest tightened at the sight, a pang of empathy surging within her. On impulse, she crossed the room and wrapped Aislinn in a firm hug, offering support with the gesture.

"Oh, Ash," Ariel murmured, her voice low and steady. "What's going on? What happened?"

Aislinn hesitated, leaning into the embrace briefly before pulling back. Her words came haltingly, her voice faltering. "It's just... everything," she admitted, her hands fidgeting in her lap. She drew in a deep breath and recounted the alley—the fireballs, her fear, and Rowan's protectiveness. But as she reached Rowan's outburst, her words stumbled, and she shook her head, as though trying to shake off the memory. "Then he said something completely insane, and I just... I couldn't handle it."

Ariel tilted her head, her brows furrowing as concern flickered across her features. "What did he say?" she asked, her tone calm but probing.

Aislinn's hands stilled, twisting together as frustration built. Her voice hardened as it spilled out. "He said he's 205," she said sharply. "And it had nothing to do with anything! It felt like he thought I was too stupid to understand what was really going on, so he just threw out the most ridiculous thing he could think of!"

The statement hung between them, strange and heavy. Ariel blinked, her reaction shifting as she brushed her fingers lightly against her chin. She nodded faintly, as if piecing together a puzzle. "I can see why you'd think that was... a lot," she said carefully. "Rowan has a habit of fumbling when he's trying to explain things, especially if he's caught off guard."

Aislinn frowned, the frustration simmering just beneath the surface. "So what was he actually trying to say?" she demanded, urgency threading her words. "Because it didn't make sense. It felt like he was throwing out an absurdity to distract me."

Ariel exhaled slowly, her focus shifting as she chose her next words carefully. "Okay," she began, her tone deliberate, "here's the thing. I promised Rowan I wouldn't share any of his personal secrets, but what you saw out there today? That wasn't exactly a secret. So, I'll tell you this much—but for anything deeper, you'll have to hear it from him."

Aislinn's shoulders tensed, but she nodded, her attention fixed on Ariel with a mix of apprehension and curiosity.

"Rowan wasn't lying," Ariel said gently. "He really is 205. I know it sounds impossible, but it's the truth. He's... different. And he probably thought starting with the wildest fact—the one that's hardest to believe—might help explain the rest. You know, like the fireballs and the guy with the katana." She offered a faint smile, hoping to ease the weight of her revelation.

Aislinn stared, her thoughts whirling as she tried to process Ariel's words. "But... 205? How? What does that even mean?" Her voice cracked with disbelief, her reaction caught between denial and confusion.

"I know it's overwhelming," Ariel admitted, leaning forward slightly. "And I understand why you reacted the way you did. It's not every day someone casually drops that they're over two centuries old. You freaked out—and honestly, I can't blame you." She paused, her voice softening. "But you didn't give him the chance to explain, Ash. You shut him down before he could say more."

Aislinn rubbed her hands nervously, her attention dropping to the table. "I... I guess I didn't give him a chance."

Ariel reached across the table and rested a hand on Aislinn's arm, her touch firm and reassuring. "Look, I'm not saying you were wrong to feel overwhelmed. It's a lot to take in, and Rowan could've handled it better. But if you want answers—and I know you do—you have to give him the opportunity to explain." She gave Aislinn's arm a gentle squeeze and nodded toward the door. "Go find him, Ash. Talk to him."

Aislinn drew in a deep breath, the tension in her shoulders beginning to ease. She nodded, her resolve slowly returning. "Okay," she said, her voice stronger now. "I'll go find him."

Aislinn and Ariel descended the stairs together, the anxiety hanging in the air like a lingering weight. As they reached the bottom, Ariel spread her arms dramatically, her grin breaking the awkward silence. "She lives!" she declared, her energy cutting through the unease in the room.

Aislinn managed a faint smile, though it flickered and faded almost immediately. "I'm sorry for... everything," she said, turning toward Takoda and Rain. "And for not opening the café. I should've—"

Takoda waved her off with a quick motion. "Don't even worry about it," she said. "Life's way more important than a sign on the door."

"Yeah, we've got it handled," Rain added, her reassurance firm. "Take care of what you need to. The café's not going anywhere."

Aislinn felt a swell of gratitude but didn't dwell on their kindness. Her focus shifted to Riichi, who stood near the counter, his composed presence radiating control.

"Do you know where Rowan is?" she asked, her urgency evident.

Riichi's attention moved to her, his behavior composed. "I'm afraid I don't know, Miss Aislinn," he replied evenly.

Aislinn folded her arms, resolve tightening her posture. "I know you can find him. Please, find him."

Riichi inclined his head slightly, acknowledging her request with confidence. He retrieved a sleek phone from his pocket and stepped aside, his low, measured conversation revealing nothing. His calm remained unbroken, and his words were impossible to discern. Aislinn fidgeted, her nerves stretching taut as she strained to hear anything useful.

When Riichi returned, he slipped the phone back into his pocket. "He is at Pier 39," he said with precision.

Without a second thought, Aislinn moved toward the door, her body already deciding her next step.

Riichi's commanding tone halted her in her tracks. "Miss Aislinn," he said, his firm demeanor leaving no room for argument, "I cannot allow you to go alone."

Aislinn turned back to him, frustration edging her response. "Why not?" she demanded, her voice sharper than intended.

"Because," Riichi said, his steady composure unshaken, "if anything happens to you, Mr. Rowan would hold me responsible. I cannot let that happen."

Aislinn exhaled, annoyance giving way to reluctant acceptance. "Fine," she relented, crossing her arms. "What's the plan?"

Riichi dipped his head slightly, his control unbroken. "I will drive you to the pier," he said. "Please wait here while I retrieve my car."

Without waiting for a response, Riichi walked to the door, his movements deliberate. The door clicked softly behind him, the faint sound amplifying the tension in the café.

Takoda let out a low whistle, leaning against the counter. "He's got a way about him, doesn't he?" she mused, casting a knowing look at Rain.

Rain smirked, amusement lighting her features. "Told you—you think he's cute."

Takoda spun toward Rain, her cheeks coloring instantly. "Oh, shut up."

Ariel pressed her lips together, stifling a laugh, and clapped Aislinn on the shoulder. "Looks like you've got your ride. Go sort things out, Ash."

Aislinn nodded, anticipation buzzing in her chest. She glanced once more at the door, determination settling over her. She had questions, and Rowan was going to answer them.

Meanwhile, at the pier, Rowan stood at the water's edge, his hands buried deep in his jacket pockets. The wind off the bay tugged at his hair and clothes, though he hardly registered it. His focus stayed on the smooth stones in his hand, which he sent skipping across the surface one by one until they sank into the depths. Each skipped stone felt like a fragment of his control slipping away, frustration gnawing at him as they disappeared beneath the waves.

He hadn't meant for things to spiral so completely out of control with Aislinn. Her disbelief echoed in his mind, relentless and piercing. *What was I thinking?*

His jaw clenched as the memory resurfaced. Her reaction—hurt flickering across her face, confusion tightening her features—had struck him harder than he'd anticipated. She'd just witnessed fireballs, magic, and chaos, things no rational person could easily process. And instead of offering her clarity, instead of giving her the foundation to trust him, he'd blurted out the one thing guaranteed to make him sound unhinged. *You told her you're 205 like that would explain everything. Brilliant.*

A sharp breath left him, the weight of his failure pressing heavily on his chest. *You handled it all wrong. You should've started slower, eased her into the truth—the magic, the Fallen, everything that mattered.* Instead, fear had twisted his words, warping the truth into a vague and scattered response that was unrelated. The one fact that might have helped her understand had come out stripped of any context. After centuries of guarding secrets, carefully skirting the edges of honesty, the one time he needed to be fully truthful, he'd failed.

Rowan rubbed the back of his neck, his fingers pressing into the tension knotted there. But it wasn't just the magic or his age that had tripped him up. It went deeper than that. *What if, once she knows everything—what I am, what my life really is—she leaves?*

The thought twisted inside him, unrelenting. *She's already walked away once.* The memory—her hurt, her anger, her retreating figure—played in his mind on an endless loop, mocking him with its finality. It left him rooted to the spot, a man who had survived centuries of unimaginable trials, suddenly powerless. *What if she doesn't come back?*

The rhythmic lapping of the water below offered no solace. Its unchanging motion felt indifferent, almost taunting the turmoil in his chest. Rowan stared at the rippling surface, his thoughts tangling into a storm. He'd wanted to follow her, to make her listen, but he knew it would have only driven her further away. *She needed space. That much I understood.* Now, all he could do was wait—a patience he had never truly mastered.

Another stone left his hand, skipping twice before vanishing beneath the surface. He watched the ripples fade, his focus falling to the last stone in his palm. He rolled it between his fingers, its smooth edges comforting him in the smallest way. *I need to make this right... but how?*

A long sigh escaped him as the question circled endlessly, unanswered. The wind tugged at his jacket, the bay stretching endlessly before him as his thoughts remained tethered to the one person he couldn't stop thinking about.

Back at the café, a sleek black car pulled up, its glossy finish gleaming in the sunlight and contrasting with the rustic charm of the building. Aislinn blinked at the sight, the elegance of the car striking her as oddly out of place. Riichi stepped out with deliberate precision, his movements fluid and controlled, as if practiced to perfection. He opened the passenger door, inclining his head in a gesture that was both formal and effortless.

"Miss Aislinn, if you please," he said, his manner calm and measured.

Aislinn hesitated briefly before sliding into the plush leather seat. The door closed behind her with scarcely a sound, and the car hummed to life, its engine almost inaudible. The ride to Pier 39 passed in near silence, broken only by the muted vibration beneath her feet. Aislinn's hands twisted in her lap as her thoughts spiraled, the pressure of everything she'd witnessed pressing against her chest like an unseen weight.

When they arrived, Riichi eased the car to a stop near the water with a smoothness that mirrored his measured movements. Aislinn scanned the pier, spotting Rowan almost immediately. He stood at the edge, his back turned, silhouetted against the shimmering waves. His hand moved in a methodical motion as he tossed a stone into the bay. Even from a distance, his posture reflected the weight pressing on him—a heaviness pulling at every movement.

Riichi stepped out and moved to open her door, but Aislinn shook her head, offering a brief smile. "Thank you. I've got it from here."

Riichi inclined his head in acknowledgment and stepped aside as she climbed out. "I'll wait here," he said evenly.

Aislinn didn't respond. Her attention locked on Rowan as she started toward him, her steps crunching lightly against the gravel. The closer she got, the more her nerves coiled, anticipation mingling with unease. She wasn't sure what to expect—anger, distance, or guarded detachment—but she knew she needed to face him.

Rowan didn't turn as she approached, though his hand paused mid-motion, the stone resting loosely between his fingers. He released it a second later, and it sank immediately, leaving ripples that faded into the water. His breath escaped in a slow exhale, blending with the lapping rhythm of the waves. The tension radiating from him was unmistakable, an undercurrent that refused to dissipate.

"Rowan..." Aislinn began cautiously. She hesitated before continuing, her tone gentler. "I'm sorry. I overreacted. I... I didn't give you a chance to explain."

Rowan turned toward her, relief briefly passing over his face, though uncertainty lingered. For an instant, he hadn't been sure she would come. The fear of losing her, irrational and consuming, had gnawed at him in ways he hadn't expected.

"You don't have to apologize," he said softly. "I didn't handle it well. I... didn't know how to explain what you saw in the alley."

His sentence trailed off, frustration evident in the way his hand swept through his hair. "There's so much I haven't told you. When everything happened so fast, I panicked, and—"

"Ariel already told me," Aislinn interrupted gently. "She explained what happened."

Rowan's brow furrowed slightly, his focus sharpening. "What exactly did she tell you?" he asked cautiously.

"Just about the alley," Aislinn clarified. "She said if I wanted to know more, I'd have to ask you."

Rowan exhaled slowly, some of the tautness in his posture easing. A fleeting sense of gratitude for Ariel crossed his mind, though he wasn't surprised by her restraint. *Good little pixie,* he thought, a faint smirk briefly touching his lips.

Meeting Aislinn's gaze, Rowan took a step closer, his shoulders lowering slightly. "I was worried," he admitted, his voice quieter now, "that after everything you saw… you wouldn't want anything to do with me."

Aislinn's breath hitched at the raw vulnerability in his words, but before she could respond, her attention shifted briefly toward Riichi, who stood waiting by the car. Rowan followed her glance and nodded subtly, his response measured as he said, "Riichi's here to make sure you're safe. If you're okay with it, we could walk back to the café. Just us."

Aislinn considered the suggestion, her attention darting between Rowan and the car before settling on him again. "Yeah, I'd like that," she said simply.

Rowan raised a hand, signaling to Riichi. The man gave a slight nod in response before slipping into the driver's seat. The vehicle rolled away with the same fluidity it had arrived with, leaving the two of them alone by the water.

As the sound of the engine faded into the distance, a soft hush settled over them. Aislinn fell into step beside Rowan as they started walking back. Each crunch of gravel underfoot carried an unspoken weight, the silence between them heavy yet layered with meaning.

Rowan glanced at her briefly, his hands tucked deep into his jacket pockets. His lips parted slightly, as though he were about to speak, but no words came. Instead, the rhythmic lapping of the bay and the sound of their footsteps filled the space, the understanding between them needing no immediate explanation.

"I'm glad you came," Rowan said after a long pause, breaking the tension between them. "I wasn't sure you would."

Aislinn glanced at him, noticing the rare flicker of vulnerability in his expression. "I needed to," she replied, her tone subdued. "I know I ran off, but I came back because I want to understand. I don't know if I can, but… I'm willing to try."

Relief softened Rowan's features, though unease remained. "I'll do my best to explain," he said earnestly. "There's no point in hiding it anymore. Whatever you want to know, just ask."

Aislinn drew in a deep breath, her thoughts swirling with questions she wasn't sure she was ready to hear the answers to. Finally, she began with the one that gnawed at her most. "You said you're 205... How is that even possible?"

Rowan gave a faint nod, as if bracing himself. "I was born in 1819," he began, his voice steady but carrying the weight of deeper truths. "In Ireland. For a long time, I lived what you'd call a normal life—ordinary for the time. Until..." His focus shifted toward the water, where ripples shimmered faintly in the light. When he spoke again, his words came slower, each one carrying the gravity of centuries. "Until I died. Or at least, I was supposed to."

Aislinn's brows knitted together, her breath catching. "Supposed to?"

"I was given a choice," Rowan said, lowering his voice. "A chance to become something... else. And I took it."

"Something else?" she repeated, uncertainty threading her voice. "Like a... supernatural being?"

"In a way," Rowan replied, meeting her gaze. "I became what we call a Fallen. Not an angel, not a demon... but something in between." He paused, choosing his words carefully before continuing, "We're bound to the natural world, to forces older than the stars themselves. We don't age, and we heal quickly, but we can still die."

Aislinn's mind raced, her thoughts piecing together fragments of the impossible. "And the others?" she asked, her tone quieter now. "Like Riichi, the fireballs... all of that?"

"They're part of the supernatural world too," Rowan explained. "There are others like me, each tied to different aspects of nature and magic. And then there are... other things. Creatures forged in shadow, powers drawn from the ley lines that run beneath the earth. Dangers most people couldn't imagine." He glanced at her, his words deliberate. "What you saw in the alley was real, Ash. No illusions, no tricks. It's the kind of thing I've been dealing with for... far longer than I'd care to count."

She swallowed, her voice wavering slightly. "So you... fight these things?"

Rowan nodded. "We fight to protect people. To stop groups like the Golden Dawn—those who twist ancient forces for their own gain. They manipulate magic, distorting it, and they don't care who gets hurt in the process." His jaw tightened briefly, frustration flickering across his features. "The fight feels as old as the stones underfoot—constant, unrelenting."

Aislinn hesitated, her question catching in her throat before she finally asked, "Why are they interested in me?"

Rowan's features darkened, stress deepening the lines on his face. "I don't know exactly," he admitted. "But they've been watching you for a while. That's why I've been so protective—why I didn't want you involved." His voice softened, his focus entirely on her. "I didn't want you to get hurt."

Aislinn stepped closer, her determination cutting through the lingering unease. "I can handle more than you think, Rowan. I just wish you'd trusted me sooner."

He sighed deeply, regret evident in his posture. "I know. I was afraid that knowing would only put you in greater danger. But it seems I never really had a choice."

For a fragment of time, they stood close, the air between them thick with unspoken emotions. "So... what now?" Aislinn asked, her voice barely above a whisper.

"Now," Rowan replied, "we figure out what the Golden Dawn wants with you, and we stop them." He hesitated, then reached for her hand, his touch centering her. "And I promise... no more secrets."

Aislinn squeezed his hand, determination sparking in her expression. "Then we'll face it together," she said, her resolve firm. "Whatever it is, I'm not backing down."

As they approached the café, the empty street carried an eerie hush. The crooked "closed" sign hung in the window, and the café's interior remained dark. A cool breeze stirred, carrying the faint scent of approaching rain. Shadows stretched long and thin across the pavement, brushing against the ground like whispered warnings.

Rowan reached the door first, his hand moving to test the lock. But something caught his attention. A folded piece of paper stuck in the crack fluttered lightly in the breeze, its edges rough and uneven, as though torn in haste. He pulled it free, unfolding it with care as Aislinn stepped closer.

"What is it?" she asked, her voice low, her focus shifting to the paper in his hands.

Rowan scanned the note, his brow furrowing as he read: *I am closer than you think.* Below the message, a twisting symbol sprawled across the page—chaotic and jagged. It didn't match any sigils Rowan recognized, the design deliberately disordered.

"I've never seen this symbol before," he murmured, flipping the paper over as though seeking more clues. The other side was blank.

Aislinn's stomach knotted as she studied the note. "Could it be from the Golden Dawn?" she asked. "Or someone else?" Her unease deepened. "Either way, it's bad."

Rowan's expression hardened, his grip tightening on the paper as he looked at her. The weight of the implied threat pressed on both of them.

Before he could respond, Aislinn reached out, resting a hand on his arm. "Stay," she said, her voice calm despite the fear in her eyes. "For now. I don't want to be alone."

Rowan didn't falter. He saw the vulnerability beneath her determined expression and gave a firm nod. "All right," he said. "I'll stay."

Chapter Thirteen
A Mother's Secrets

The note in Rowan's hand felt like more than just paper and ink, its presence pressing heavily against the fragile threads holding their lives together. His focus shifted to Aislinn beside him, her arms locked around her middle, head tilted downward as if the answers she needed might surface from the ground if she waited long enough. The tension radiating from her filled the space, sharp and suffocating, as if the air itself recoiled from the weight of her turmoil.

She shouldn't carry this alone.

Rowan stepped closer with deliberate intent. "Let's head upstairs," he said, his tone low, his presence meant to soothe her amidst the chaos. He didn't falter this time, his hand brushing lightly over her arm before gesturing for her to follow.

Her nod was small, almost imperceptible, and her steps felt detached, mechanical, as she turned toward the café door. He remained close, an invisible shield at her side, offering a sense of quiet reassurance. At the door, he moved ahead to hold it open, one hand resting on the frame while his other hovered near her elbow, guiding her through without a word.

Inside the apartment above, Aislinn drifted toward the window, her movements distant and sluggish, burdened by thoughts she couldn't bring herself to say aloud. She folded her arms tightly across her chest, her outline rigid against the faint glow spilling in from the street below. Rowan closed the door behind them with a practiced click of the lock, his attention lingering on her. The stiffness in her stance cut into him, leaving a dull ache he couldn't ignore.

I have to fix this. Somehow, I have to help her feel safe again.

Crossing the room, Rowan approached her with calm precision. His hand rested gently on her arm, his thumb brushing against the fabric of her sleeve in a small, supportive gesture. "I'm making a call," he said, keeping his words simple and direct. He shifted slightly, angling himself toward her, trying to meet her lowered gaze, even if she refused to look up. "You don't have to say anything. Just stay close."

Her shoulders dipped, her arms loosening just enough to show she'd drawn a fragment of comfort from his presence. She nodded faintly but didn't turn. Rowan let his hand fall and turned toward the kitchen, sparing her one last glance before pulling his phone from his pocket.

As he dialed, he leaned against the counter, his hand gripping the edge as the gravity of the situation settled over him.

Eileen picked up on the second ring, her voice clipped and direct. "What is it?"

"We found a note," Rowan replied, keeping his tone firm. "It has a symbol I don't recognize. I need you to take a look. I'm bringing Aislinn."

The silence that followed carried a weight of unspoken resistance. When Eileen finally responded, her indecision was clear. "I'm not ready for that."

Rowan's grip on the counter tightened, his knuckles blanching as frustration bubbled beneath the surface. His exhale was deliberate, forcing composure he didn't fully feel. You don't get to hesitate. Not now. She needs you.

"You don't have the luxury of waiting," he said, his voice taking on a sharp edge. "She's already in danger, Eileen. She deserves to know the truth."

"She doesn't—"

"She does," Rowan interrupted, the force in his tone cutting through any excuse she might offer. "She can't stay in the dark anymore. If you won't tell her, I will—but it should come from you."

The pause stretched thin, tension crackling in the silence. Rowan's gaze flicked back to Aislinn. She stood unmoving by the window, her figure framed by the muted glow outside. The sight sent a pang through him, sharp and unrelenting, a reminder of all the ways he had failed to shield her from this.

She deserves more—more than this. More than I've been able to give her.

"She has a right to know," he said, his voice softening with a determined undercurrent. "And we can't protect her if she doesn't understand what she's facing. Do you want me to leave her vulnerable? Because I won't. She's coming with me, whether you're ready or not."

The silence dragged on until finally, Eileen sighed, her resolve bending under the weight of his insistence. "Fine. Bring her."

Rowan ended the call, sliding the phone into his pocket. His hand rested on the counter for a moment as he exhaled, the release slow and deliberate. Nothing about this was simple anymore.

One step at a time. Keep moving forward.

He turned toward Aislinn and stepped closer. "We're leaving soon," he said, his tone calm and resolute.

She didn't meet his eyes, her hand shifting instead, fingers pressing into the curve of her arm as if bracing herself against a tide of emotions. "Okay," she said, the word barely audible.

A single syllable, small but laden with everything unsaid. Rowan watched her carefully, noting the strain in her posture, the way her knuckles whitened as she clung to her composure.

"Aislinn," he said, his voice gentler now as he moved closer. Her head lifted slightly at the sound, her features etched with worry.

"I need to tell you something," Rowan began, his words deliberate, his movements steady. He stopped within arm's reach, lowering himself slightly to meet her line of sight. "It's about my boss."

Her brow furrowed. "Your boss? From the Fallen?"

He nodded, his expression unwavering. "Yes. She's more important than you realize. Her name is Eileen. She's not just part of the Fallen—she's our leader. She's been there for every turning, guiding each of us through it. For all of us, she's been a constant—a figure we rely on for protection and direction."

Aislinn's grip on the edge of the couch tightened, her knuckles pale. "So, she's... like a guardian?"

"In a way," Rowan said, his tone even. "She's kept us safe through her decisions, and we trust her completely. But she's also kept secrets." He paused briefly, then pressed on. "Aislinn, Eileen... she's your mother."

The words landed between them, heavy and unyielding. Aislinn stared at him, her face paling as disbelief washed over her. Slowly, her head began to shake, the motion stiff, almost mechanical.

"No," she whispered. "That's not possible. My mother—she died. I saw her casket. The car accident..."

Her breathing hitched, and she stumbled back a step, gripping the couch for support as memories surged forward, colliding with Rowan's revelation. "Why would she lie to me? Why didn't she come back? Why didn't she tell me she was alive?" Her voice wavered, each question shaking with grief and confusion.

Her knees buckled slightly, and her trembling hands clung to the couch. Rowan's jaw tightened as he stepped closer, his heart twisting at the sight of her unraveling. He moved with purpose, placing a steadying hand on her forearm.

"I'm sorry, Aislinn," he said, his tone quieter now but unwavering. "She thought she was protecting you from the dangers tied to the Fallen, from the Golden Dawn. I know this is too much."

Tears streaked down her face as she gripped the couch harder, her breathing uneven. "She let me think she was dead. All these years... I've been on my own. And she was alive?"

Rowan reached up, brushing a tear from her cheek with deliberate care. "She thought it was the only way to keep you safe. I can't imagine how much this hurts, but she does care. She was still watching over you."

Aislinn shuddered, her sobs quiet but deep, her shoulders trembling as she processed the weight of his words. Rowan wrapped his arms around her, holding her firmly but gently, offering her himself as something solid to lean on.

"I'm here," Rowan murmured, his words carrying quiet intensity. "We'll get through this together." The promise hung between them, steady and unbroken.

The silence stretched, heavy with the rawness of implicit thoughts. Aislinn clung to him for a moment longer before pulling away slightly, her trembling fingers wiping at her cheeks.

"I need to see her," she whispered, her voice uneven but edged with resolve. She met Rowan's gaze, her own distant yet determined. "I need answers."

Rowan gave a slight nod, his movements deliberate. "We'll go now."

Outside, the early afternoon was dim, thick clouds rolling in and softening the sharp lines of the city streets. A light breeze carried the scent of rain, brushing past them as they approached Rowan's bike. Its polished surface gleamed faintly, a sharp contrast to the tension thickening the air between them.

Rowan swung his leg over the bike and held the helmet out to Aislinn. She paused, her fingers hovering above it as her focus drifted elsewhere. After a beat, she took it and slipped it on. Climbing onto the back of the bike, her arms wrapped securely around his waist, her grip conveying both stability and an attempt to maintain control. He felt a tremor in her hold, the subtle quiver betraying her efforts to mask it.

The bike growled to life, and Rowan eased it onto the road. The streets were calm, the sound of the engine steady and familiar beneath them. Aislinn held on tightly, leaning into him as though the closeness could quiet the unrest stirring inside her.

Rowan's attention stayed on the road ahead, even as his thoughts wandered. The Salesforce Tower loomed in the distance, its sleek glass exterior dull against the overcast sky. Inside, Eileen was waiting. There was no avoiding what lay ahead.

He pulled the bike to a halt at the curb outside the building. Cutting the engine, he felt Aislinn shift behind him. She climbed off carefully, her movements deliberate as she regained her footing. Removing the helmet, she let her hair fall loose over her shoulders. Her eyes were fixed on the imposing structure before them, her features taut, a shadow of uncertainty and determination in her stance.

"Are you ready?" Rowan asked, stepping to her side. He reached out briefly, brushing her arm as if to remind her she wasn't alone.

Aislinn didn't respond immediately. Her gaze stayed locked on the building, stress visible in the line of her shoulders and the set of her jaw. With a deep inhale, she gave a small nod. "I need to hear it from her."

Rowan mirrored her nod, his hand resting briefly at her side before they started toward the entrance. The glass doors reflected their approach, the building's stillness towering over them like a silent sentinel.

With each step, the strain between them grew heavier. Rowan noticed how Aislinn's hands curled into fists, her knuckles white, and the subtle stutter in her breathing. On impulse, he reached for her hand, threading his fingers through hers. Her grip was tense, but she didn't pull away.

"I'm here," Rowan murmured, his tone low and sure as they neared the door.

Aislinn squeezed his hand briefly, the motion grounding her as they stepped inside.

The muted click of the door closing behind them echoed in the sleek, polished lobby of the Salesforce Tower. The cool air inside carried an edge of sterility, amplifying the unease that followed them. A receptionist directed them to a private conference room on an upper floor, and as they moved toward the elevator, Aislinn's anxiety grew more pronounced. Her shoulders were set stiffly, and her hands trembled faintly, her control slipping with every step.

Rowan stayed close, his presence calm and steady as if to keep her in the moment without words. He didn't speak, allowing his proximity to speak for itself.

When the elevator doors slid open, Aislinn's stomach tightened. Her breathing grew uneven as her thoughts tangled into a knot. She wanted answers—needed them—but the prospect of facing her mother after everything felt unbearable.

Rowan nudged her forward, the gesture deliberate but unhurried, offering silent encouragement.

"It'll be alright," he murmured, his tone low and firm. "I'm with you."

Ahead, the conference room waited, its glass walls revealing an expansive, brightly lit space. At the far end, Eileen stood motionless, her attention fixed on the city stretching beyond the windows. The approaching confrontation pressed down on Aislinn, heavy and unavoidable.

Rowan released her hand as they neared the door, his expression settling into quiet determination as he prepared to step inside.

Eileen turned to face them, her posture rigid despite the calm facade she projected. Her attention flicked briefly to Rowan before settling on Aislinn. "We need to talk in private," she said, her tone controlled, each syllable deliberate.

Aislinn's stomach churned at the statement. Panic surged through her, and she clung tighter to Rowan's arm, her grip almost desperate. Facing this alone felt unbearable—she needed him to center her.

"No," Aislinn said quickly, her voice sharp as she shook her head. "I want him to stay."

Rowan paused, his focus shifting to Eileen as the tension between them grew heavier. He felt Aislinn's hold, her fingers clutching him like a lifeline, but he understood the deeper truth. She had to face this on her own, even if it hurt to let her.

"Aislinn," he said, turning toward her fully. His hand slid to her arm, strengthening her with a gentle yet firm touch. "I'll be just outside. You've got this."

Her gaze darted between him and her mother, her breathing quickening with each passing second. "I don't want you to go," she whispered, her voice barely audible, trembling under the weight of her fear.

Rowan held her gaze, his expression calm but resolute. "I'll be right there," he promised, his hand brushing lightly over her arm, the motion steadying. "If you need me, I'll come back in. You have it in you to face this."

Aislinn swallowed hard, her tears threatening to spill as she clung to his arm until the last second. Letting go felt like stepping into a void.

Rowan's eyes lingered on Eileen before he stepped away, pressing his lips into a thin line as he forced himself to walk to the door. Leaving Aislinn now felt like betrayal, even though he knew she needed to do this herself. *She's stronger than she realizes,* he told himself, clenching his hands briefly before the door clicked shut behind him, leaving her alone with Eileen.

The room shifted in his absence, the silence thick with emotions that neither mother nor daughter knew how to voice. Eileen exhaled slowly, her expression softening as she stepped closer, faint silver streaks in her hair catching the muted glow filtering in from the window. The light seemed to outline her figure, giving her presence an unearthly calm.

"Aislinn," she began, her words tinged with sorrow that stretched far beyond the moment. "There's so much I need to explain."

Aislinn remained frozen, her pulse thundering in her ears. "You faked your death," she said, her voice shaking with a mix of anger and pain. "You let me believe you were gone. Why?"

Eileen's regret was unmistakable as she responded. "It was the only way to protect you. From the time you were born, you were in danger."

"Danger from what?" Aislinn demanded, her fists clenching tightly at her sides. "From you? From your world?"

"From forces far worse than I could have imagined," Eileen admitted, her voice firm despite the weight of her confession. "The Golden Dawn. The supernatural world I was part of marked you as a target. Staying would have put you at greater risk."

Aislinn shook her head, stepping back as her emotions roared to the surface. "So, you left me? Abandoned me? Do you have any idea what that did to me? I thought you were dead!"

"I know," Eileen said, her voice wavering. "I saw the pain it caused you. It tore me apart every day. But I made the only choice I thought would keep you safe, even if it meant breaking us both."

Aislinn's breathing hitched, her thoughts colliding in an overwhelming rush. "You watched me suffer and didn't do anything? You never stepped in. You didn't even tell me the truth."

"I couldn't," Eileen replied, her tone laden with regret. She moved a step closer, her pace cautious, as though walking a tightrope. "I was being watched, even hunted, by enemies I didn't know existed at the time. But I stayed as close as I could. I tried to guide you in small ways—through your dreams, through what little I could do without drawing attention. It wasn't enough, I know that. But it was all I could risk."

Aislinn's throat constricted as her breathing faltered. "So... those dreams—they weren't just in my head?"

Eileen shook her head gently. "No. I was trying to reach you, trying to be there when I couldn't stand beside you. It was the only way to keep you safe without exposing you to greater danger."

Aislinn's heart raced, her thoughts spinning in chaotic waves. *She's here. It wasn't just my imagination.*

"You've been lying to me my whole life. Why would you even pretend to be human if you knew you couldn't stay?"

Eileen drew a measured breath, her expression shifting as if memories long buried stirred to the surface. "Aislinn, I have been with the Fallen for centuries. The world has changed countless times around me, and I had to change with it."

Aislinn's brow furrowed, suspicion cutting through her confusion. "Centuries?"

"Yes," Eileen answered, her voice quieter now, touched by the passing of those many years. "At times, I would live among humans, blending in to understand the way the world was evolving. During one of those times, I met your father."

Aislinn froze, the air thick in her lungs. "My father?"

Eileen nodded, her words carrying the distant echo of reverence. "He was human, unaware of the world I came from. We fell in love, and for a time, I thought I could have a life with him. And then... you were born."

Aislinn's pulse quickened as her chest constricted. "So, you just left him, too?"

Eileen's shoulders drooped, her regret evident in every line of her posture. "I never wanted to leave either of you. But staying only increased the danger. The Golden Dawn was watching, and by remaining, I made both of you targets."

Aislinn's hands balled into fists, her frustration flaring. "So, you thought faking your death was the answer? That walking away from me would somehow protect me?"

"I did what I thought was right," Eileen said, her voice trembling under the strain of her own pain. "Disappearing was the only way to ensure your safety. I made every choice for you, even knowing it would mean you'd hate me."

Aislinn stepped back, her emotions pulling her apart—anger, grief, disbelief. "I didn't even know you. My whole life, I thought I had no one. Do you have any idea what that does to someone?"

Eileen's regret deepened, her voice quieter but no less weighted. "I loved your father, and I loved you. But staying would have endangered both of you more than I could bear."

Aislinn's breathing hitched as the magnitude of her mother's confession sank in. She had dreamed of this moment, of seeing her mother again. Now, standing before her, she was left grappling with the ache of truths she wasn't ready to accept.

"I don't know if I can forgive you," Aislinn whispered, her tone raw with emotion. "You left me to live a life without you, and for what? To protect me from something I didn't even know existed?"

Eileen took a tentative step closer, her hands trembling slightly. "I know it's impossible to understand. I'm not asking for forgiveness—not yet. But I had to keep you safe, Aislinn. Even if it meant breaking my own heart."

Tears blurred Aislinn's vision as her emotions surged again. "You could have come back. You could have told me the truth. Instead, I mourned you every single day, thinking you were gone forever."

Eileen's response cracked under the weight of sorrow. "I wanted to. Every day, I wanted to come back. But the risk was too great. If they discovered you, if they found out about you... I couldn't live with that. Keeping you safe was all that mattered."

Aislinn wiped at her face, her hands shaking as she fought to steady herself. Anger burned within her, but beneath it, a quiet ache softened in the face of her mother's presence. "I'm still angry. I don't know if that will go away anytime soon. But... I'm also glad you're here."

Her words faltered, hesitant yet heavy with meaning. "At least now... I can hold you. Not just in a dream."

Eileen's eyes glistened, her hands trembling as she hesitated only a moment before wrapping Aislinn in an embrace. "I'm here now," she whispered, the emotion raw in her voice. "And I won't leave you again."

Aislinn held on tightly, years of grief settling into a quiet ache, though no less profound. The pain of her absence lingered, but her mother's arms, warm and solid, offered a fragile sense of comfort. Aislinn tightened her hold, as though letting go might make her mother vanish, and the ache would start all over again.

After a long pause, Aislinn stepped back, wiping her damp cheeks with trembling hands. "I need you to promise me... that you won't leave me again. Not like that."

Eileen lifted her hands, gently cupping Aislinn's face, regret shadowing her features. "I promise. I'll never leave you again."

Aislinn gave a small nod, her emotions raw and tangled, yet the smallest sense of calm began to take hold within her. So much remained unresolved, countless questions clawing at the edges of her mind, yet her mother's presence brought a fragile sense of peace she hadn't known in years.

The door opened behind them, its sound breaking the stillness, and Rowan stepped back into the room. His focus shifted immediately to Aislinn, reading the subtle shifts in her posture and demeanor. Relief moved through him as he caught the softened edges in her expression, though the shadows of sadness remained. *She's holding it together,* he thought, the tightness in his shoulders easing. However, the ever-present protective instinct stirred within him, ready to rise at the slightest sign of distress.

"Everything okay?" Rowan asked, his tone calm, each word deliberate as his attention flicked between Aislinn and Eileen.

Aislinn nodded, her reply cautious. "I think so. There's a lot to figure out, but... we're starting to make sense of it."

Rowan stepped closer, his stance firm with resolve. "We need to talk about the note."

Eileen's regret vanished, replaced by the sharp precision of the Fallen's leader. "The note?"

Rowan reached into his jacket and drew out the folded paper, holding it out toward her. "We found this outside Aislinn's café. The symbol doesn't match anything I've seen before."

Eileen took the note, her hands still as her focus sharpened. The intensity of her concentration settled over her like a tangible force. Aislinn watched the change—the vulnerability from earlier had vanished, replaced by an unsettling composure. The shift left her uneasy in a way she couldn't quite name.

"This isn't from the Golden Dawn," Eileen said after studying it, a crease forming on her brow. "It's old. Ancient. I've encountered markings like this before, but I can't yet pinpoint their origin."

A chill prickled along Aislinn's skin, the unknown pressing heavily against her. "What does it mean?" she asked, her voice barely above a whisper.

Eileen didn't look up from the note, her focus unbroken. "I'll need time to consult my records. This isn't something we can afford to ignore, but I don't have answers yet."

Her stance shifted slightly, and the atmosphere in the room seemed to change as she straightened. Rowan recognized the familiar authority settling over her—the commanding presence of someone accustomed to shouldering immense responsibility.

"For now, we can't lose sight of the Golden Dawn," Eileen said, her tone unwavering. She turned to Rowan, her focus cutting through the space like a blade. "Rowan, I'm relieving you of surveillance duty. Your priority is Aislinn."

Rowan's muscle twitched beneath his temple, his instincts rebelling against the directive. "You want me to focus solely on her?"

"Yes," Eileen replied decisively. "Aislinn's protection takes precedence. Others will handle monitoring the Golden Dawn. She must be our priority."

Rowan glanced toward Aislinn, the enormity of the responsibility pressing down on him. He was used to navigating multiple threats at once, balancing danger as a part of his life, but this felt different. More immediate. More personal. He nodded once, his response measured. "I'll keep her safe. Nothing will happen to her while I'm here."

Aislinn's chest tightened at his words, warmth spreading in its wake. She wasn't used to being at the center of someone's protection, but Rowan's steadfast resolve quieted the fear she had been carrying. The gnawing sense of unease loosened its grip, giving way to the faintest thread of reassurance.

Eileen folded the note carefully, each movement deliberate. "I'll contact you as soon as I uncover anything," she said, her tone composed but tinged with urgency. She slipped the note into her pocket and turned to address them both, her expression unyielding. "Until then, trust no one outside the Fallen."

Rowan's expression hardened, and he inhaled sharply as determination etched across his features. "Understood."

Eileen turned to Aislinn, her features softening. "Take care of each other. And Aislinn... be careful. I need you safe."

Aislinn gave a slow nod, her mind churning with the enormity of everything she'd just learned. It all pressed against her like a crushing tide, unrelenting. Yet Rowan's presence beside her steadied her in a way she couldn't fully explain. For the first time in what felt like forever, she wasn't carrying it alone.

As they stepped out of the tower, the cool evening air greeted them, brushing against their skin and carrying the distant hum of the city below. Aislinn shivered as exhaustion pulled at her like a heavy chain. The emotions and revelations of the day had left her utterly drained, her thoughts sluggish and tangled. Rowan's unwavering presence at her side was the only thing keeping her moving forward.

"You should stay with me tonight," Rowan said, his voice calm as his fingers brushed briefly against her side in a protective gesture. "It's safer."

Aislinn's first instinct was to push back. Independence had been her shield for so long, her defense against vulnerability. But with her mother's words echoing in her mind, she couldn't summon the energy to argue. "Okay," she murmured, her response barely audible.

Rowan glanced at her, his attention lingering on the subtle shift in her demeanor, before giving a small nod. "We'll stop by your place first so you can grab what you need."

The ride through the city passed in a blur, the streets blending into streaks of muted light. Aislinn leaned into Rowan's presence, her thoughts caught in a storm of fragmented revelations. The hum of the engine and the passing streets felt distant, offering no solace against the weight of everything swirling in her mind.

When they reached her apartment, Aislinn stepped inside, her surroundings feeling oddly detached, like they belonged to someone she no longer recognized. She retrieved her phone, her hands trembling slightly as she dialed Takoda. As soon as her friend answered, the emotions she'd been holding back all day surged to the surface.

"Hey, Ash. Everything okay?" Takoda's concern was immediate, her tone carrying a gentle warmth that Aislinn hadn't realized she needed.

Aislinn swallowed hard, the words catching in her throat. "No, not really," she admitted, her voice quiet and unsteady. "I need you to open the café tomorrow. I... I just need some time."

A brief pause followed, filled with an understanding that didn't require explanation. "Of course," Takoda said gently. "Don't worry about anything. Are you sure you're alright?"

"I will be," Aislinn whispered, though the words felt fragile even as she said them. "Thanks, Koda."

She ended the call and set her phone down, turning to find Rowan standing in the doorway. His calm presence filled the room like a steady reassurance, unspoken but undeniable. "You ready?" he asked, his voice even, his focus unwavering.

Aislinn nodded, slipping her bag over her shoulder. Each step back toward his bike felt heavier, as though the weight of the day clung to her limbs. By the time they reached Rowan's place, the burden of everything she'd carried since morning felt suffocating, threatening to pull her under.

Back at Donnelly's, the neon lights buzzed softly, their glow spilling over the bar's weathered surfaces. They were nearing the apartment when Ariel emerged from the back, her teasing grin firmly in place.

"Well, look who's back," she said, her tone light, though her sharp attention flicked between them. "So, I guess you two finally patched things up, huh?"

Aislinn forced a weak smile, her exhaustion evident in the slump of her posture. "Yeah... something like that."

Ariel tilted her head, her playful demeanor softening as she seemed to sense the pressure still lingering between them. "Good. Things felt... off when you two weren't talking. It's nice to see things getting back to normal."

Rowan gave a slight nod, his attention never leaving Aislinn. "We're heading upstairs," he said, gently guiding her toward the door.

"Take care of each other," Ariel called after them, her wink lightening the mood briefly before she disappeared back into the bar.

The second they stepped into Rowan's apartment, Aislinn's legs gave out, and she sank onto the couch. The strain of the day, held together by sheer will, finally collapsed, leaving her trembling as she broke apart. Rowan crossed the room with purpose, wrapping his arms around her in a firm, reassuring embrace.

"I've got you," he murmured, his tone steady, giving her stability in the present.

Aislinn clung to him, the tears she'd held at bay pouring out in unrelenting waves. Everything—the argument, her mother's secrets, the cascade of revelations—consumed her, and she pressed her face against him, letting it all go in the safety of his arms.

"You don't have to carry this by yourself," Rowan said quietly, his hand moving through her hair in a deliberate, calming motion.

Her sobs began to ease, her breathing uneven as she worked to regain control. "I don't even know where to start," she admitted, her voice trembling.

"You don't have to figure it all out tonight," Rowan replied, his grip strong, offering reassurance. "Whatever comes next, we'll face it together."

Aislinn let herself relax into his hold, his warmth drawing her back from the edge. The steady rhythm of his heartbeat beneath her cheek gave her something to hold onto, anchoring her as the storm within her quieted.

"You've endured more than anyone should in one day," Rowan continued, his tone calm, yet carrying an unmistakable conviction. "And you didn't just get through it—you held strong, even when it felt impossible."

A tremor ran through her, the meaning of his words settling over her. She had fought to keep herself together all day, but in his arms, she felt the unfamiliar relief of finally letting go.

Rowan pressed a light kiss to the top of her head, the gesture filled with quiet reassurance. "You're braver than you realize, Aislinn," he said softly.

She lifted her tear-streaked face to look at him, gratitude flickering in her expression. Their eyes met, the silence between them heavy with an unspoken understanding—a connection that neither could deny.

Rowan reached up, brushing his fingers across her cheek to wipe away the last remnants of her tears. His touch carried a tenderness that seemed to melt the edges of her pain. Slowly, he leaned in, his lips meeting hers in a kiss that felt like a promise.

When he pulled back, Aislinn's breathing hitched, the tears threatening to return—not from sadness, but from the relief of no longer facing everything alone. She leaned forward, her forehead brushing lightly against his as she closed her eyes, letting herself savor the quiet comfort of his presence.

"Let's get you some rest," Rowan murmured, his voice low and certain.

Aislinn didn't resist as he scooped her into his arms, his hold protective, as though nothing in the world could touch her now.

After laying her down, Rowan started to step away, but Aislinn's hand shot out, her fingers catching his. "Stay," she whispered, her tone fragile yet filled with unmistakable urgency. "Just tonight."

Relief coursed through Rowan at her request, easing the knot in his stomach that had gripped him since the day began. He had feared she might retreat after everything she'd learned, but her reaching for him was a quiet reassurance he hadn't dared to hope for.

He met her eyes, his expression softening as he nodded. "Of course," he said, his tone carrying a quiet steadiness. He slid into the bed beside her, drawing her into his arms with care. Pressing a kiss to her hair, he whispered, "I'm not going anywhere."

The room fell into a gentle stillness, the only sounds the rhythmic cadence of their breathing. Rowan's presence wrapped around Aislinn like a shield, and the stiffness in her body unraveled bit by bit.

Her eyelids grew heavier, her mind quieting, though remnants of the day continued to flicker at the edges. Rowan's hand rested lightly against her back, his touch holding her to the present.

"There's more we'll have to face," Rowan murmured, almost as if to himself. "But whatever comes, we'll manage it—together."

Aislinn's breathing slowed, her body surrendering to the pull of sleep. Enveloped in the safety of Rowan's arms, she allowed the exhaustion to overtake her, her fears fading as his presence tethered her in the moment.

Chapter Fourteen
Calm Before the Storm

Aislinn woke slowly, light spilling through the curtains in hazy streaks. Rowan's arm rested across her waist, its warmth calming her in a way nothing else could. Behind her, his slow breaths brushed her hair, unhurried and certain. For a breath, the world outside—the Golden Dawn, the Fallen, her mother—faded away.

Rowan shifted, his arm instinctively tightening, as if afraid she might slip from his grasp. "You awake?" he murmured, his voice rough with sleep.

"Mm." She nestled closer, unwilling to let the fragile peace splinter just yet.

His lips brushed her temple. "We should probably get up."

Turning toward him, Aislinn caught the faint shadows beneath his eyes. "Did you sleep at all?"

He managed a faint grin. "Enough."

"Liar." She poked him lightly, a teasing edge in her tone. "You stayed up, didn't you?"

The grin softened into something more real. "I just... wanted to make sure you were okay."

Her chest tightened, a feeling both sharp and soothing. After everything they'd been through, being looked after didn't feel like smothering—it felt steadying, grounding in a way she hadn't known she needed.

Rowan brushed a strand of hair back from her face, his touch lingering. "Let's take the morning off. Golden Gate Park. Lunch after. No missions, no plans. Just us."

Aislinn's lips curved into a small, genuine smile. "That sounds perfect."

For once, Rowan's plan wasn't about survival—it was about living.

Golden Gate Park stretched around them, serene and sunlit, the trees shifting in a gentle breeze. Aislinn let her focus drift, tracing the rustling leaves, the pond glinting in the distance, the lazy hum of life oblivious to the shadows they carried.

Rowan walked beside her, hands in his pockets, his silence not brooding but contemplative, the kind that meant his mind was busy working through thoughts he wasn't ready to share.

She didn't press him. He'd speak when he was ready.

The path curved, leading them to a quiet pond where sunlight scattered across the surface like coins. Rowan slowed, his shoulders rising with a deep breath as he stared at the water.

Aislinn watched him from the corner of her vision, her pulse quickening. She could sense the shift, an invisible line between where they were and what was about to be said.

"I've been thinking," Rowan said finally, his tone quiet but clear, each word careful, as if testing its weight. "About all of this—everything happening around us. I thought I was prepared for anything. Then... there was you."

Aislinn blinked, startled. "Me?"

Rowan glanced at her, the faintest humorless curve to his lips. "Yeah. You." He rubbed the back of his neck, a flicker of vulnerability breaking through. "I'm not good at this—at saying things like this. But ever since that night... I can't stop thinking about you. And it's not because of all the supernatural chaos. It's just... you."

Her heart stumbled over itself. The response tangled in her throat, refusing to come. She didn't need to look at him to know how hard that admission had been.

Rowan's attention returned to the water, his voice quieter now. "I know it's fast, and maybe it's messy. But I'm done trying to push it down. You matter to me, Aislinn. More than I know how to explain."

Warmth bloomed in her chest, sudden and overwhelming. "I feel the same," she said softly, the words slipping out as if they'd been waiting for this moment. "I didn't think someone like you would..." She trailed off, shaking her head. "I didn't expect this either."

"Someone like me?" Rowan turned to her fully, his brows drawing together. "Aislinn, I'm carrying more than my share of wreckage. You'd see that if you knew everything."

Her throat tightened, but her gaze held steady. "You are what matters to me. Not the baggage."

For a second, Rowan didn't say anything, just studied her as though searching for any hint of a lie. Then, slowly, he stepped closer and took her hand, his thumb brushing soft, deliberate circles against her skin. "You really mean that, don't you?"

She swallowed, nodding. "I do."

The corners of his mouth tugged upward into a crooked smile, one that finally reached his eyes. "Looks like we're stuck with each other, then."

Aislinn's smile broke through the tension, warm and unguarded. "Guess so."

They stood there for a while, the time stretching into something solid and real. The world might still be chaos tomorrow, but here and now—with Rowan's hand in hers—it didn't feel impossible to face.

The walk from the park to the café was unhurried, their fingers loosely intertwined as they strolled down the quiet street. The café's outdoor seating offered a cozy respite, the air rich with the scent of fresh coffee and buttery pastries. Aislinn sank into her chair with a soft sigh, the hum of conversation weaving through the atmosphere like background music.

"This feels... normal," she murmured, almost as if speaking the words might shatter the illusion.

Rowan's mouth curved faintly, though his eyes flicked to the street now and then, his vigilance refusing to waver entirely. "Yeah, it does."

The moment barely settled before Rowan straightened, his focus locking onto two figures approaching their table. The man in front had dark, straight hair that framed a strikingly sharp face, his broad shoulders lending him a commanding presence. Beside him, a honey-blonde woman walked with sharp elegance, her features precise and her gaze piercing. Unease rippled through Aislinn as she instinctively sat a little taller.

The man's tone was warm as he stopped at their table. "Mind if we join you?"

Rowan gestured to the empty seats. "Go ahead." His gaze shifted to the man first. "Aislinn, this is Sloane." Then to the woman. "And Caley."

"Nice to meet you," Aislinn said with a polite nod.

Caley's lips quirked with a spark of mischief. "Likewise. Rowan's mentioned you."

Aislinn arched an eyebrow. "Has he?"

"Oh, you know," Caley replied airily, though her gaze held an undercurrent of something sly. "The usual."

As the server arrived to take their orders, Rowan's posture changed—his shoulders tensing ever so slightly, his movements more rigid. The warm ease of the morning dimmed, replaced by a weight that hung between the four of them.

Aislinn picked at the edge of her plate, tension coiling in her chest without clear reason. And then it hit.

The café blurred. The buzz of conversation melted into an empty hum. A face flickered in her mind—handsome at first, then grotesque, its eyes glowing crimson, its grin jagged and cruel. *A demon.*

Her breath snagged, her pulse thudding against her ribs as her grip tightened on the table. *Stay calm. Don't let them see. Not here. Not in front of strangers.*

Rowan's voice cut through the haze. "You okay?"

She forced a weak smile. "I'm fine. Just... dizzy." The words trembled, but she couldn't admit more—not now.

Rowan's scrutiny lingered, his sharp gaze searching hers. Before he could press, she rushed on. "I don't think I'm feeling well. Can we go?"

Sloane, silent until now, glanced between them and cleared his throat. "Rowan, mind if I grab you for a second before you head out?" His tone carried an air of casualness, but his expression suggested otherwise.

Aislinn's stomach twisted. She glanced at Rowan, her forced calm slipping around the edges. "It's fine," she murmured, though unease churned beneath her words.

Rowan hesitated before nodding and following Sloane a few steps away.

Caley leaned in, her tone light and easy. "Don't worry about them," she said, dismissively waving her hand. "Sloane's probably fishing for advice on some surprise he's planning for me. He's annoyingly thoughtful like that." Her disarming smile did little to ease the knot in Aislinn's chest.

Out of earshot, Sloane's demeanor shifted, his voice lowering. "That wasn't just dizziness. I've seen it before—that look. It was a premonition."

Rowan's shoulders stiffened, his jaw tightening. "No. She's human, Oak. There's no way she'd have one." He shook his head, as if willing himself to believe it.

Oak's expression didn't falter. "Powers don't always follow the rules, Rowan. You know that as well as I do. Whatever she saw, it wasn't nothing."

Rowan didn't answer immediately, denial warring with instinct. Finally, he exhaled sharply. "I'll talk to her."

"Good. Don't ignore it. We can't afford to."

When they returned, Caley rose with effortless grace, flashing a bright, practiced grin. "We'll let you two enjoy the rest of your afternoon." She turned to Aislinn with polite warmth. "Feel better soon."

Sloane nodded, his relaxed appearance back in place. "Take care. We'll catch up later."

As they turned to leave, Caley brushed her hand against Rowan's, slipping a folded note into his palm. "From Eileen," she whispered, her tone quiet but pointed.

Aislinn, distracted by the vision still seared into her thoughts, barely noticed. She nodded absently as they left, her mind replaying the grotesque grin and crimson eyes.

Rowan turned back to her, the note forgotten as concern deepened his expression. "Aislinn," he said carefully, "what really happened back there?"

The café's bustling energy now felt stifling, the noise pressing in like a too-tight jacket. She shook her head, scanning her surroundings. "Not here," she whispered. "Can we go somewhere private?"

Rowan didn't hesitate. He stood, pulling out his wallet and tossing enough cash on the table to more than cover the bill. "Let's go."

The firm edge in his tone steadied her, even as her mind raced. She let him guide her back toward the park, silence stretching between them, thick with unanswered questions and the shadow of something darker just beneath the surface.

The path grew quieter as they walked, the distant hum of the city fading into the rush of water beneath the small bridge. Fresh air stirred Aislinn's hair, but it did little to calm the storm swirling inside her. *How do I explain what I saw without sounding ridiculous?* The vision had been so vivid, so unnatural, even she struggled to make sense of it.

Rowan glanced at her often, the furrow in his brow deepening. *She's rattled,* he thought, noting her stiff shoulders and how she avoided meeting his eyes. He wanted to ask, to know, but he wouldn't push her. Not yet.

They reached the waterfall at Strawberry Hill, its low roar filling the space between them. Rowan stopped abruptly, turning to face her. His probing stare left her feeling like there was nowhere left to hide.

"Aislinn," he said quietly, his tone firm but gentle. "I need you to tell me what you saw."

The directness caught her off guard. *How does he know?* For a heartbeat, she thought about brushing it off, pretending it wasn't as bad as it felt. But the way he looked at her—unyielding, certain—left no room for avoidance. They'd promised to face things together. Holding this inside would break that promise.

She swallowed hard, forcing the words out. "It was a man... but his eyes turned red." The memory sent a cold shiver through her. "And his smile—it twisted. Like he enjoyed it."

Rowan's jaw tightened, his focus sharpening. "This wasn't just a demon, was it?"

She shook her head. "No. It was worse. Stronger."

Rowan's mind raced. *An archdemon?* The thought gnawed at him, though part of him resisted. "It could've been an archdemon," he murmured, more to himself than to her. "But no one's seen one in centuries."

"Archdemon?" Aislinn echoed, the unfamiliar word heavy on her tongue.

"They're like rulers," Rowan explained, his voice edged with grim certainty. "Stronger. Smarter. Far more dangerous."

Aislinn's chest tightened. "I don't know what it was," she admitted, her voice trembling. "I didn't want to believe it. I thought if I ignored it—"

"You don't have to go through this alone." Rowan stepped closer, his hand lifting to her cheek. His thumb skimmed her skin, a gentle contrast to the tension simmering between them. "We'll figure it out."

The warmth of his touch steadied her, chasing away the remaining chill of the vision. *I don't know what this means,* she thought, *but I'm not carrying this by myself.*

Rowan exhaled, his expression shifting. Reaching into his jacket, he pulled out the folded note Caley had slipped him earlier. "There's something else."

"What is it?" Aislinn asked, her brows knitting together.

"It's from Eileen. Caley gave it to me at the café."

He handed her the note, their fingers brushing as she took it. The familiar slant of her mother's handwriting sent a ripple of unease through her as she read:

Bring Aislinn to the Fallen meeting tonight. 5 p.m. Salesforce Tower.

Her pulse quickened as she stared at the message. "What does she want with me?"

"I don't know," Rowan admitted, his voice darkening. "But we need to be there."

The urgency of the note, combined with the vision, pulled at her from every direction. But Rowan's solid presence reassured her, his confidence settling her own. *I can do this,* she thought.

"I'm ready," she said, her voice soft but certain.

Before Rowan could slip the note away, Aislinn caught his wrist. He stilled, his gaze meeting hers as her fingers tightened around him. Fear and uncertainty haunted her expression, but beneath it, trust shone through.

Rowan's breath caught at the look she gave him. Without a word, he slipped his arm around her waist, drawing her closer. Aislinn rose onto her toes, closing the distance between them.

Their lips met—tentative at first, as though testing the fragile line between fear and connection. But the hesitation burned away, replaced by a shared urgency that said everything they couldn't. For those stolen moments, the chaos faded to nothing.

When they finally pulled back, Aislinn's heart thundered, but not from fear. Rowan rested his forehead against hers, his voice rough with emotion. "No matter what happens next, we'll handle it."

Aislinn smiled faintly, her eyes still closed. "Together."

The word hung between them, settling like an silent vow.

After a beat, Rowan stepped back, reality creeping in. He glanced at the note, his expression firm. "We should go."

Aislinn nodded, the lingering warmth of his kiss softening the edges of her worry. The fear hadn't vanished, but it had changed—tempered now by quiet resolve.

Rowan slipped the note into his jacket, taking her hand once more. Without another word, they left the waterfall behind, moving back toward the unknown waiting for them.

By the time they reached Salesforce Tower, the sun hung low, casting long shadows across the city like silent sentinels. Rowan's stride quickened as they approached the entrance, every protective instinct humming beneath his calm exterior.

"This is it," he murmured, glancing at her. "Whatever comes, we'll face it."

Aislinn nodded, her resolve hardening. She didn't know what awaited them, but Rowan's presence brought her clarity.

Inside, the sterile elegance of the high-rise swallowed them. The faint hum of elevators and the chill of polished floors pressed in around her, making her feel small. Rowan's occasional brush of her fingers tethered her to the moment, a quiet reassurance.

When the glass doors slid open to the familiar conference room, the view outside seemed distant compared to the tension crowding the space. The Fallen had begun to gather, their presence formidable. *This,* Aislinn realized, *was her true introduction.*

Oak and Holly stepped forward first, their casual personas from lunch replaced with a formal air she hadn't seen before. Oak's calm demeanor stood out, his steady gaze steadying her in turn.

"I think we owe you an explanation," he said, his tone measured. "Sloane and Caley were just aliases. Makes things cleaner out there." He offered a small nod. "I'm Oak."

Holly, though her edges still carried a playful note, nodded in agreement. "And I'm Holly. Oak's the careful one. No more pretending—it's good to see you again, Aislinn."

"Good to see you too," she replied, their shift in manner helping her find her balance.

Next to approach was a man she didn't recognize. He carried himself with sharp confidence, his sandy-blond hair neatly styled, and his assessing look measured.

"Vine," he said, offering a hand with a sly grin. "Welcome to the chaos."

Aislinn shook his hand, startled by the intensity he exuded. "Thanks... I think."

Rowan gave her fingers a brief squeeze, a silent reminder that she wasn't alone.

Another figure followed—Riichi. She recognized him instantly, his movements smooth and precise, his composed features unchanged from their earlier encounter.

"Miss Aislinn," Riichi greeted, bowing his head slightly. His tone was low and formal. "It's an honor to meet you properly. I regret the circumstances of our first encounter."

"Thank you," Aislinn replied, her shoulders relaxing as sincerity softened his precision. "And thank you for helping Takoda that day."

"It was my duty," Riichi said simply, his words as careful as his posture.

Elder approached next, his quiet presence carrying an intensity that needed no embellishment. His unwavering gaze spoke volumes without him uttering a word.

"Nik," he said, extending his hand. "That's my name, though most call me Elder."

Aislinn accepted the handshake, her voice matching his formality. "Nice to meet you, Elder."

He inclined his head slightly, a respectful acknowledgment. His focus flicked to Rowan briefly before moving on, the exchange unspoken but unmistakable.

Lastly, another figure approached—a tall, broad-shouldered man with close-cropped, sandy-brown hair and striking features. His serious expression carried a reserved weight that softened just enough to be approachable.

"Reed," he said, his tone thoughtful, each word carrying purpose. "I'm the quiet one, so don't take it personally."

Aislinn offered a small smile. "I won't."

With introductions complete, the weight of the room seemed to settle on her shoulders. Many eyes remained, observing quietly.

Before the discomfort could deepen, the door opened, and the atmosphere shifted instantly. Eileen stepped inside, commanding attention without effort. Every Fallen turned toward her as she moved to the head of the table, her sharp focus cutting through the room.

She stood tall, her presence radiating a quiet authority. "Before we begin, I have an announcement." Her voice carried a calm strength that silenced the room. "Aislinn is my daughter. From this point forward, she has the right to attend any Fallen meeting she chooses."

A ripple of surprise passed through the group—subtle glances exchanged, curiosity building—but no resistance.

"She will be treated as one of us," Eileen continued, her words measured and firm. "I expect everyone to respect that."

Aislinn straightened, the weight of her mother's words settling over her. Attention lingered on her—some assessing, others intrigued—but none challenged Eileen's decree.

Rowan shifted slightly closer, a movement so subtle it said more than any reassurance could. Aislinn drew in a slow breath, settling herself. Whatever doubts or fears she had, one truth remained: this was where she belonged now.

With the announcement complete, Eileen's demeanor shifted. "Now, to the matter at hand," she said, her tone brisk.

She turned toward Rowan and Aislinn. "A note was delivered to me earlier. The symbol on it belongs to a group of archdemons—archdemons that vanished centuries ago. This suggests their return."

The weight of her words pressed on the room, an unspoken heaviness settling over everyone. Eileen's piercing gaze moved across the group. "If this is true, we need to be ready. The Golden Dawn will pale in comparison to what's coming."

Oak spoke first, his voice calm and calculated. "Preparation alone won't be enough if they return. But the Golden Dawn is still an immediate threat. We take care of them first."

Eileen nodded. "Agreed. Their plan to trigger an earthquake is our top priority. We can't let that happen."

Oak leaned forward, his focus sharp. "I extracted intel from the Golden Dawn member we captured. They're planning to detonate a bomb underground to set off the quake." He paused, letting the weight of the revelation settle. "As for Aislinn, the prisoner said we'd find out soon enough why she's important."

A chill crept along Aislinn's spine, the ominous words gripping her like an unseen force. Beside her, Rowan tensed, his jaw tight, but neither of them spoke.

Eileen's attention flicked briefly to Aislinn before returning to the group. "We suspect this has something to do with the archdemons."

From the edge of the room, Reed broke his silence. "If there's a bomb, we have no choice. We dismantle it before it detonates. A covert mission is our best shot—get in, get out, no mistakes."

Uncrossing his arms, he added, "I'll go. I've done this kind of work before."

Eileen nodded, her focus sharp. "Agreed. This mission must be flawless. We have two days to prepare. One mistake, and the consequences will be catastrophic." Her gaze swept the group. "The magnitude of this earthquake could devastate the entire city. Thousands of lives are at stake."

Riichi inclined his head, his composure unshaken. "I'll join Reed," he said firmly. "Two days will be enough. We'll gather intel, identify weaknesses, and plan every detail."

Reed glanced toward Riichi and gave a brief nod of acknowledgment before turning back to the group. "That makes two of us, but we'll need two more volunteers to make this work."

The room fell into silence, the enormity of the task sinking in. Rowan broke it first. "I'll go."

Aislinn turned to him, worry etched into her expression. *Why does it have to be you?* She didn't need to say it—Rowan caught the question in her eyes. Under the table, his hand found hers, a gentle squeeze meant to reassure.

Eileen's sharp gaze snapped to Rowan, narrowing slightly in silent reminder: *Aislinn is your priority.* Rowan met her stare without flinching, his shoulders squared and resolve unshaken. For a long moment, they held the exchange—Eileen's scrutiny weighing the risk, Rowan's determination answering it.

Finally, Eileen gave a slight nod, a quiet signal of approval. Her expression softened just enough to convey the decision. It was an understanding between leader and ally: the mission demanded someone she could trust, and Rowan was that person.

The silence carried on until Vine leaned forward, a confident smirk tugging at his lips. "Count me in," he said, his tone light, though his eyes carried a spark of resolve. "Can't let you guys have all the fun."

Eileen's words carried a sharp finality. "That makes four—Riichi, Reed, Rowan, and Vine. Two nights. Use every second to prepare. Failure is not an option."

She paused, her tone darkening. "This bomb is only the beginning. The Golden Dawn is our immediate concern, but the archdemons are a far greater threat. Everyone else stays on high alert. This isn't over."

Oak gave a firm nod. "We'll be ready."

From his spot near the edge of the room, Elder spoke for the first time. "No one lets their guard down."

Eileen's gaze cut through the group. "Riichi, Reed, Rowan, and Vine—you meet tomorrow to finalize the plan. Every detail must be accounted for. Surprises are not an option."

Rowan glanced at Aislinn again, her worry tightening the weight in his chest. She didn't speak, but the look in her eyes was impossible to ignore.

As the meeting concluded, Eileen raised a hand, halting Rowan and Aislinn before they could leave. "You two stay behind. We need to talk."

The others filed out, leaving the room heavy with quiet. Eileen turned to face them, her gaze firm but unwavering. "Aislinn, until we know more, you'll stay with Rowan. It's not safe for you to be alone."

Aislinn's chest tightened, unease churning in her stomach. "Mom, I had a premonition today," she said, the admission spilling out before she could stop it.

Eileen's posture stiffened, her eyes narrowing. "What did you see?"

Rowan stepped in, his tone measured but strained. "She saw an archdemon. His face twisted into something monstrous."

For a split second, Eileen's focus wavered. "A premonition…" she murmured, almost to herself, before her composure returned. "It's too soon."

Aislinn frowned, confusion knotting her brow. "Too soon for what? What's happening to me?"

Eileen stepped closer, her voice softening. "Aislinn, there's something you don't know. You're not entirely human."

The words struck like a blow. "What?" Aislinn whispered, her world tilting. "How is that even possible?"

Eileen sighed, regret shadowing her features. "You're my daughter, Aislinn. And I've lived for centuries—longer than you can imagine. The blood that runs through you is part of something far older, far more powerful. I stayed away to protect you, to give you a normal life, but you've always been part of this world."

Aislinn's heart pounded, disbelief clawing at her. "I've never had visions or powers—until today."

"Because your abilities were dormant," Eileen said. "Hidden. Living in the human world kept them asleep, but they're waking now. The premonition you had today is only the beginning."

"The beginning of what?" Aislinn whispered, her fear barely contained.

Eileen cupped Aislinn's face, her touch light but steady. "Of change. It will be hard, but you're stronger than you realize. And you're not alone."

Rowan stepped closer, his hand brushing her arm. "We'll figure this out together," he said, his quiet assurance something Aislinn had come to rely on.

Aislinn's mind reeled, the weight of everything pressing down. "What about the archdemons?" she asked, her voice hushed and faint.

Eileen's gaze darkened. "They aren't supposed to be here yet. Just like your visions weren't supposed to start. There are forces at play we don't understand. This is only the beginning."

The ominous weight of her words lingered as Eileen turned and left the room, her movements deliberate and sure.

Aislinn stood frozen, her pulse thundering in her ears. Slowly, she looked up at Rowan, his presence anchoring her in the chaos. The fear remained, but something else rose alongside it—resolve. Whatever was coming, she wouldn't face it alone.

Chapter Fifteen
The Weight of Fire

T he door to the conference room clicked shut behind Eileen, leaving the air taut with unease, as if the room itself had paused to listen. Aislinn sank back into her chair, the lingering weight of the meeting pressing her down. The space, which moments ago had hummed with purpose and overlapping conversation, now stretched hollow, like an abandoned stage stripped of its actors.

Her fingers grazed the cool, polished table, its smooth grain calming her amidst the swirl of her thoughts. Yet the imprint of Eileen's warning refused to leave, cutting like a shard of glass beneath her skin.

"She's right," Aislinn murmured, her voice barely audible, brittle with tension. "A darkness is coming. Something worse."

Rowan eased into the chair beside her, his movements unhurried. He didn't speak at first, his presence filling the silence. The faint whisper of fabric as he settled was the only sound, and for the shortest time, the quiet seemed to press inward, heavy and unrelenting.

Then his hand brushed hers—brief, intentional. A tether that pulled her back, as if to remind her: *I'm here.*

"It doesn't matter how big it is," Rowan said at last, his voice calm and sure, like a stone sinking steadily through deep water. "We'll find a way."

Aislinn's brow furrowed, frustration flaring to life. "You say that like it's simple. Like we can plan for the unknown."

"We can't plan for it," Rowan admitted. "But we can be ready."

"Ready for what?" She gestured toward the empty chairs, frustration cracking through her composure. "Premonitions, archdemons, my mother—it feels like everything's pulling us apart. None of it makes sense. It's spiraling, Rowan. All of it."

The calm Rowan wore like armor wavered slightly, a tension creeping in at the edges—but she noticed. His focus remained steady.

"Then we hold on to the pieces we can control," he said, his words deliberate.

Aislinn turned to him, startled by the simplicity of the answer. He made it sound tangible, as if she could reach out and grasp it. "How do you do that? How do you act like this isn't—" She hesitated, her hand motioning faintly to the empty room. "—crushing?"

Rowan's gaze dipped, not avoiding hers but searching for the right words to say. For a brief span, the silence stretched, and Aislinn almost regretted the question.

Then he looked up, his eyes clear, with faint shadows hinting at past battles. "Because I've been here before," he said quietly. "In battles where there were no answers. Only chaos. And when that happens, you focus on what's in front of you. One step. One choice."

The words settled between them like steadying hands, quiet and resolute, nudging against the edges of Aislinn's fear. Rowan wasn't offering false promises—no easy assurances. Just a direction. A place to begin.

Aislinn stared at him, her shoulders sagging as her frustration drained away. "What if I don't have your strength?"

"You will," Rowan replied without hesitation. "And until then, I'll share mine."

The stark simplicity of his response caught her off guard, its honesty disarming.

She let out a slow breath, her fingers unfurling from the table as if releasing the panic she had been clutching. Eileen's warning still loomed, sharp and insistent, but Rowan's words pressed against it, solid and unwavering, like a wall she could lean on.

"I don't know if that's enough," she said softly, her voice a thread in the quiet room.

"Then we'll keep moving until it is." Rowan's hand closed over hers again, firm and warm. "This isn't where we stop, Aislinn."

His sincerity cut through the fog in her mind, clearing just enough space for clarity to surface.

For the first time since Eileen's warning, the panic eased its grip, leaving room for a new feeling—one that felt like hope.

Rowan felt the shift beside him, her energy radiating like an unspoken force—intense and impossible to ignore. He knew the storm brewing within her, could sense it in the charged air between them.

"How can you just... agree to this mission?" Aislinn's question broke the silence, trembling with frustration. "After everything Eileen said—after everything we're facing—how can you throw yourself into more danger?"

The words were a blade Rowan had anticipated, but they cut just the same. He met her gaze, his composure sliding into place like armor, even as her frustration pressed beneath it, undeniable and unrelenting.

"This isn't new for me, Aislinn." His tone was quiet, measured, every word deliberate. "It's who I've been for almost two centuries. When there's a threat, I face it. I have to. I won't stand by and do nothing."

The room seemed to hold its breath as he spoke, the tension between them crackling, unyielding. Yet beneath his steady gaze, something flickered, an undercurrent he couldn't quite name.

"That's not enough." Her response came quickly, tight with emotion, her hands curling into fists in her lap. "Things are different now. I'm different. And you're—"

"I know." Rowan's interruption was firm yet gentle, his hand reaching for hers with careful intent. The warmth of his touch halted her words, easing the rigidity in her shoulders. "That's why I'm doing this. I need to stop them before they can get to you."

Her body froze at his admission, but his words sat uneasily within her, like stones pressing into her chest. It wasn't anger—it was fear, raw and ancient, twisting into unrelenting knots.

"You don't get it." Her voice dropped to a threadbare whisper, the fight draining out of her. "I don't want to lose you."

The confession hovered between them, fragile and heavy, filling the space with unspoken truths neither dared to name.

Rowan's shoulders relaxed slightly, the hard lines of his expression softening as he met her gaze—not as the protector or the warrior, but as the man beneath. For a fleeting moment, the walls shielding him slipped, revealing the quiet resolve in his eyes.

"You won't lose me," he said, the certainty in his voice cutting through her fear like sunlight breaking through a storm. He lifted a hand to her cheek, his thumb brushing against her skin in a tender gesture. "This is how I keep you safe."

Aislinn raised her gaze, searching his expression for cracks—for hesitation or doubt—but found none. Rowan's resolve was absolute, as though this decision had been etched into him long before she voiced her fears.

The room felt smaller now, crowded with everything they couldn't bring themselves to say. Her heart raced, her pulse thrumming beneath her skin as a heavy, nameless sensation coiled between them. It wasn't just fear. It was him.

Rowan rose slowly, his movements purposeful as he extended his hand, palm open. "Come on," he said, his tone gentler now. "Let's go back to my place. You need a break, and so do I."

She paused, worry continuing to coil tight in her chest. But when her fingers slid into his, the simple contact eased a turbulent ache inside her.

The streets stretched empty as they walked, the cool air brushing against their skin like a quiet balm. Aislinn's hand stayed in his, Rowan's grip light yet certain, as though the touch tethered them both to something real. The muted hum of the city—distant traffic, the occasional buzz of a streetlamp—faded into the background, leaving the silence to settle between them.

Rowan gave her hand a small, instinctive squeeze, centering them both. The gesture didn't calm the storm in his thoughts or erase the fear in hers, but it was enough for now.

And for now, enough was all they had.

The warmth of the apartment wrapped around them as they stepped inside, yet it couldn't thaw the cold knot twisting in Aislinn's chest. She sank onto the couch, tucking her knees close, folding inward as if trying to shield herself from the weight pressing down on her. The soft glow of the lamps painted the walls in muted light, flickering faintly, like fragile promises. This space should have felt safe. It didn't.

Across the room, Rowan headed toward the kitchen, his footsteps purposeful. He didn't speak, didn't ask how she was—he just moved, losing himself in the rhythm of action to keep his mind from wandering.

Aislinn watched him, her head leaning against the back of the couch. The gentle clink of the kettle settling on the stove broke the silence, its sound oddly soothing against her inner turmoil. Rowan didn't try to fill the quiet or force comfort into the space between them, and somehow, that felt better than empty reassurances. The measured way he moved pulled her from the spiral of her thoughts, just enough to steady her.

As he reached for the tea, Rowan glanced over. His gaze lingered for a heartbeat on how she sat curled into herself. The fire that usually sparked behind her eyes was dim, dulled beneath the weight of Eileen's warning. It twisted something inside him—a tight, unrelenting pull, like a wire stretched to its breaking point. He wanted to fix it. To fix her.

Instead, he made tea. It wasn't enough. It would never be enough. But it was all he could offer.

When he returned, he lowered himself onto the couch beside her and handed her a mug. Their fingers brushed, the touch lasting just long enough to spark a connection neither spoke of.

Aislinn wrapped her hands around the cup, letting its heat seep into her palms. She didn't drink; she only stared into the dark liquid, as though it might hold answers. The silence stretched between them—not oppressive, but heavy with things unsaid. She let herself rest in it.

Rowan held his own mug, though he didn't take a sip. His focus stayed on her—on the way her shoulders curled inward, on the tension etched into her frame. He'd survived centuries of war and countless battles that demanded unyielding strength, but this—seeing Aislinn burdened by fear and uncertainty—felt like a failure he couldn't undo.

"I'm sorry." The words slipped out, softer than he intended, cutting through the quiet like a blade.

Aislinn blinked, his apology drawing her attention. "For what?"

Rowan exhaled, his fingers tracing the edge of the ceramic mug. His gaze hovered somewhere between her and the floor. "For all of this. For pulling you into a world you never asked for. You didn't deserve archdemons, battles, or visions. I hate that I can't protect you from it."

His honesty unsettled her. Rowan was supposed to be solid, unbreakable. Now, his words carried a regret so raw it cut deeper than she expected. She hadn't known how much he carried until now, how much of it he bore alone.

"You didn't pull me into anything," she said softly, the lump in her throat tightening with emotion. "I chose to stay. I chose this path. And I chose you."

Rowan's head lifted, his eyes locking onto hers. She chose him. The weight of those words settled deep, heavier than they should have, because he knew what that choice could cost her. Did she? He wanted to believe she understood, but doubt gnawed at the edges of his resolve.

He set his mug down and reached for her hand. His fingers brushed hers, warm and sure, a touch that broke through the noise in his thoughts. "I just…" He hesitated, searching for words that usually came easily. "I need you to know I'd do anything to keep you safe."

The sincerity in his voice settled over her, anchoring her against the chaos spinning in her mind. Aislinn's pulse quickened, each beat resonating with the weight of his words, the way his touch steadied her in ways she couldn't explain.

"You don't have to do it alone," she whispered, her voice barely audible beneath the faint hum of the kettle cooling in the kitchen.

Rowan froze, as if her words had broken something long buried inside him. His hand trailed gently up her arm, the touch slow and reverent, carrying both hesitation and longing. For so long, he'd kept the world at a distance, afraid to let anyone too close. But here she was, slipping past the cracks in his defenses, leaving him unable to turn her away.

Aislinn leaned into him, closing the distance, as if the warmth of his presence could chase away the cold knot of fear lodged deep within her. The walls they had built—walls of worry, duty, and unsaid feelings—began to crumble.

Rowan tilted his head, his brow brushing hers for a breath before their lips met. The kiss was slow, unhurried, a surrender to everything they had been holding back. It wasn't driven by desperation but by a deeper understanding—a silent promise rooted in trust and need.

Aislinn's fingers curled into the fabric of his shirt, her grip firm, as if pulling him closer might ground them both. The world beyond the apartment faded away, leaving only this—Rowan's presence, his warmth, and the unshakable reassurance that she wasn't alone.

For Rowan, it was a rare, fragile peace. The tenderness of her embrace and the way she leaned into him pulled him from the shadows he had lived in for so long.

The kiss deepened, their movements fluid and deliberate, as Aislinn melted into him, her body yielding to the heat of his embrace. For the first time in days, her thoughts stilled. This moment wasn't about fear. It was about connection—the press of Rowan's lips, the way his hands moved along her back, strong yet reverent, as if she were the most precious thing in the world.

Rowan felt her relax against him, her trust unspoken yet unmistakable in the way she clung to him. It stirred a need within him—not just desire but a yearning for connection, pure and untainted, untouched by the shadows that had once consumed him.

They stumbled back, the couch forgotten as instinct guided them toward the bed. Their lips never parted, urgency building with every caress, every heartbeat. Aislinn gasped softly as his hands explored her, igniting sparks that raced across her skin. She hadn't realized how much she wanted this—wanted him—until now, when nothing remained to hold them apart.

Clothes fell away, scattered without care, until there was nothing left between them but the pull of their connection. Rowan paused, hovering over her, his eyes locking onto hers in a silent question.

Aislinn met his gaze, her hands sliding to his face and drawing him closer. The answer was clear. She was here. She was his.

Their connection deepened, their movements driven by more than urgency—a rhythm born of understanding and need that went beyond the physical. Rowan's hands traced the curves of her body, every gesture speaking emotions he couldn't express aloud. Aislinn arched into him, a soft moan escaping her lips as their bodies moved as one, seamless, as if they had always known this unspoken dance.

Time blurred. The fervor softened, urgency giving way to tenderness. Their movements slowed, each caress and kiss a promise, each brush of his fingers a silent expression of trust. Rowan's fingers tangled in her hair as he held her close, his breath uneven, the stillness around them settling like the calm after a storm.

When it was over, they lay entwined, their shared warmth lingering in the quiet air. Aislinn rested her head on Rowan's chest, her fingers tracing faint patterns along his skin as she listened to the steady rhythm of his heart. The sound was soothing, a steady reminder that he was here—that what they shared was real.

Rowan's hand moved lazily through her hair, his caress gentle and unhurried. The weight of everything—Eileen's warning, the dangers ahead—hovered at the edges of his thoughts, distant and manageable. Here, with Aislinn in his arms, the world beyond the room faded away.

Aislinn closed her eyes, letting the quiet embrace her like a blanket. For once, the silence didn't bring unease. It was full, alive with the shared understanding of what had passed between them—of what they had chosen.

Sleep came gently, the shared warmth drawing them both into its depths. Rowan held her closer, his arms encircling her as a shield against the outside world. For a little while, there was peace—fragile and fleeting, but no less real.

The piercing ring of Aislinn's phone shattered the early morning, a jarring spike of sound that yanked her from sleep. She jolted upright, heart racing, as Rowan reached for the lamp. Its glow spilled across the room, stark and unwelcome against the faint shadows.

His hand rested briefly on her shoulder, grounding her as she fumbled for the phone, her fingers trembling against its smooth surface. Sleep clung to her mind, thick and unyielding.

"Hello?" Her voice rasped, raw and uneven.

"Aislinn!" Takoda's frantic cry burst from the line, charged with panic. "The café—it's on fire!"

The words hit her like a slap of cold water, freezing her in place. "Fire? What are you talking about?"

"It's bad, Aislinn! The whole place is going up. You need to come. Now."

Rowan was already moving, pulling his shirt on in a single practiced motion. His expression darkened at the mention of fire. He didn't need more details; instinct roared to life, sharp and alert, his mind spinning with possibilities. Accident—or an attack?

Aislinn scrambled to her feet, clutching the phone with white-knuckled intensity as her world contracted into a single point of urgency. "We're coming," she said, her voice trembling slightly before she ended the call. Her wide, fearful eyes locked on Rowan. "The café... it's on fire."

Rowan's jaw tightened. He didn't speak. There was no need. He grabbed his keys with grim efficiency and motioned for her to follow. Every movement cut cleanly through her shock, commanding her attention. This wasn't just a fire. It was another piece of her life unraveling.

They were out the door in seconds, the air outside cutting sharply against their skin. Rowan fired up the motorcycle, the engine's low growl breaking the silence of the sleeping city. Aislinn climbed on behind him, her arms wrapping tightly around his waist, her thoughts a tangled blur of disbelief and fear.

The café—her sanctuary, her dream—was burning.

Rowan's grip on the handlebars was ironclad, his focus unwavering as the streets streaked past them in a rush of dark and light. A sense of inevitability churned in his gut. This wasn't random. It couldn't be.

When they turned the final corner, the sight that greeted them hit like a physical blow.

Flames surged skyward, alive and ravenous, painting the night in violent hues of orange and red. Thick smoke spiraled into the sky, heavy and suffocating. The fire wasn't just consuming the building—it was a monster, devouring everything in its reach.

Aislinn slid off the bike, her legs shaky beneath her. Her breath hitched as she took in the inferno. "No..." The word fell from her lips, almost imperceptible, splintered and raw.

The chaos surrounding them seemed distant—firefighters shouting orders, hoses carving arcs of silver against the darkness, the pop and groan of timber collapsing into itself. The café—the one place untouched by the upheaval in her life—was vanishing before her eyes.

"Aislinn!"

Takoda's shout sliced through the haze, sharp as glass. Aislinn turned, her heart lurching at the sight of Takoda and Rain standing near a fire truck, their faces smudged with soot but otherwise unharmed. Relief crashed into her, dizzying and overwhelming, as she ran to them.

They clung to each other, arms wrapped tightly, the kind of embrace that held far more than words ever could. Yet even as Aislinn buried her face in Takoda's shoulder, the devastation hung heavy between them. The café wasn't just a building. It had been their shared dream, their refuge. And now it was ash.

Rowan remained a step back, his piercing gaze cutting across the chaos. The fire was too fast, too intense, as if it had been lying in wait for the smallest spark to ignite it. His instincts, sharpened by centuries of danger, screamed at him to dig deeper.

He turned, striding toward the unmarked police cruiser parked nearby. The officer inside flinched at the sharp rap of Rowan's knuckles against the window.

"What happened?" Rowan's tone was calm, measured, but carried an edge that demanded answers. "You were supposed to be watching the place. Did you notice anything?"

The officer fumbled to lower the window, his face pale in the flickering light of the flames. "It was quiet," he stammered. "Calm. Then—out of nowhere—the fire. The whole place just... went up. It happened so fast."

"And before that?" Rowan pressed, his suspicion growing tighter. "No one out of place? Nothing unusual?"

The officer shook his head, guilt etched into his pinched expression. "No. Nothing. I swear."

Rowan exhaled, his frustration simmering beneath the surface, and turned back toward the blaze. Coincidences weren't real—not in his world. Fires like this didn't just happen.

As he made his way back to Aislinn, his eyes swept the darkness beyond the fire trucks. The shadows stretched long and deep, covering alleyways and rooftops, unnaturally static against the chaos.

"If this was intentional," Rowan muttered, his voice barely above the crackling flames, "they're still here. Watching."

The air around him felt charged, heavy with an unseen presence circling like smoke wrapping its tendrils around his thoughts.

Aislinn trembled, the shock of the café burning rippling through her in waves. Her pulse pounded in her ears as she glanced up at Rowan, standing like an unyielding force amidst the chaos, his attention sharp and unwavering.

A strange awareness stirred within her, like instincts she hadn't known she possessed. Without thinking, her gaze mirrored his, sweeping the dark edges of the scene—the same way she had seen him do so many times. Her breath hitched as her eyes caught movement, scarcely visible beyond the fire's glow.

"Rowan," she whispered, tugging at his sleeve, her voice tight. "There—in the shadows."

Rowan followed her line of sight, his body tensing with a shift so subtle most wouldn't notice. Aislinn did.

He saw the figure immediately. A silhouette lurked, partially hidden in the darkness, watching.

Rowan's arm shot out, stopping Aislinn before she could move. His hand gripped her firmly. "No," he said, his tone low and firm. "It's too dangerous."

Aislinn froze, frustration flashing before she relented. She trusted his judgment, even as it left her unsettled. Rowan was already pulling out his phone, his movements swift and deliberate, his face locked in focus. "Riichi," he muttered, tapping the screen quickly. "Suspect. Four o'clock from the café. Approach from the west."

The minutes that followed stretched endlessly, each second a knot tightening in her chest. Rowan stayed close, his presence a shield, his gaze flickering constantly to the edges of the crowd. His thoughts churned, and the familiar tension of anticipation wound through him. This wasn't an accident. It couldn't be. Whoever was behind this had chosen the café with intent, and the message was clear.

From the corner of her eye, Aislinn spotted Riichi slipping through the smoke, his movements clean and precise. His gaze met Rowan's for a fraction of a second, a silent exchange passing between them before he melted back into the shadows.

Aislinn held her breath, her nerves coiling tighter as Riichi approached the figure, his steps silent and calculated. It seemed he would succeed—but then the figure moved, a faint flicker betraying them. In an instant, they bolted.

Riichi sprang into pursuit, his form vanishing into the night. Aislinn tracked them as long as she could, their shapes twisting and darting in the shifting light, firelight glinting off distant windows.

The seconds dragged into an unbearable eternity. Rowan remained motionless beside her, his focus darting to every corner of the scene, searching for threats hidden in the chaos.

Finally, Riichi reappeared, his steps precise but his irritation evident as he straightened his coat with a brisk motion.

"I almost had them," he reported tightly, his tone clipped. "They slipped into the shadows."

Rowan swore under his breath, his jaw tightening as he turned back to the blaze. "They're toying with us."

He started to say more, turning toward Aislinn, but the look on her face stopped him cold. She'd gone pale, her expression hollowed by a fear he hadn't seen before.

"Aislinn?" Rowan's voice dropped, controlled yet urgent. "What is it?"

Aislinn didn't answer. Her wide eyes lifted past him—upward—fixing on a point beyond the flames. Her pulse quickened, a cold dread settling deep in her chest as the figure on the rooftop came into focus.

High above, silhouetted against the molten glow of the burning café, a man stood at the edge of a rooftop. At first, he seemed no more than a shadow in the smoke, but then—red. His eyes burned with a searing, unnatural light, like embers smoldering in the dark.

Aislinn's breath caught. The man from her premonition.

He smirked, the same cruel, taunting expression she had seen before. Fear rooted her in place as his hand rose, a single finger pressing to his lips. A silent command. Stay quiet.

Her heart pounded, panic threatening to take hold, but Rowan's voice shattered the haze around her. "Aislinn?"

The spell broke. Her voice trembled as she choked out his name. "Rowan." She raised a shaking hand, pointing toward the roof. "There. On the roof."

Rowan's head snapped upward, his focus locking on the figure immediately. His body tensed, coiled with readiness. Riichi stepped closer, his sharp gaze following Rowan's line of sight.

The Archdemon's smirk deepened. His glowing eyes burned brighter as he shook his finger at Aislinn, a mocking reprimand. Tsk, tsk.

Then, with a slow flick of his wrist, the Archdemon snapped his fingers.

"Get down!" Rowan barked, grabbing Aislinn and pulling her to the pavement just as the explosion tore through the air. At the same time, Riichi lunged for Takoda and Rain, his movements swift and instinctive, dragging them down with him as the blast roared to life.

The café erupted in a deafening explosion, the sound tearing into the night with relentless force. A wave of heat surged over them, searing and suffocating, forcing the air from Aislinn's lungs. Splintered debris rained down, scattering across the pavement as flames climbed higher, devouring what little remained of the building.

Aislinn felt Rowan's weight pressing her to the ground, his arms locked protectively around her. His presence anchored her as the chaos roared around them, unrelenting and deafening. Slowly, the noise began to fade, leaving behind an oppressive silence.

Nearby, Takoda and Rain stirred under Riichi's protective hold, brushing ash from their faces as they pushed themselves upright. Ash drifted down like snow, stinging against Aislinn's skin. The acrid stench of smoke filled her lungs as she fought to take a full breath. The world felt heavy and suffocating, the weight of what had just happened pressing down on her.

Rowan pushed himself off her, his movements controlled despite the chaos. His eyes lifted to the rooftop, narrowing as he scanned the darkened edge. The Archdemon was gone.

Rowan's jaw tightened, frustration rippling beneath the surface. "He's playing with us." He turned to Aislinn and gently pulled her to her feet. His hand rested firmly on her arm, grounding her. "This is only the beginning."

Aislinn swayed slightly, the truth of his words hitting her like a stone. The café—her refuge—was gone. The Archdemon had revealed himself, and the danger she had feared was no longer distant. It was here. Real. Unavoidable.

Rowan stayed close, his movements sharp with purpose as his thoughts honed like a blade. Whoever had orchestrated this had made their move.

But Rowan wasn't going to let them win.

Not this time.

Chapter Sixteen
Beneath the Smoke

The flames had been beaten back at last, the last wisps of smoke curling into the pale pre-dawn sky. Rowan lingered, his gaze following the firefighters as they moved across the wreckage, stamping out embers and ensuring the blaze was truly contained. His eyes swept across the rooftops, searching for any trace of the archdemon. Nothing. Not yet.

"We can't stay here," Rowan said, his voice clipped with purpose as he turned to the group. "We're heading to Donnelly's."

He caught Riichi's gaze, the silent understanding passing between them needing no words. They both knew the stakes, the next steps, and the threat that still loomed.

Rowan shifted his attention to Aislinn. Her calm demeanor held, but the weight of the night clung to her. He gave her a sharp nod, a wordless reminder that she'd held firm so far—and he needed her to keep doing so. Then, his focus landed on Takoda and Rain.

"You'll ride with Riichi," he said, his tone measured but leaving no room for debate. "The archdemon saw you. Until we know more, staying close to us is the safest choice."

Takoda blinked at the gravity of his words, then nodded. Rain moved closer to Takoda, her steps small but deliberate, anchoring herself to something tangible amid the chaos.

"Let's move." Rowan turned toward his bike in a decisive pivot, a movement that brooked no hesitation. Aislinn followed without a word, falling into step behind him as Riichi guided Takoda and Rain to his car.

The streets stretched before them, eerily deserted. The hum of engines filled the oppressive silence, their steady rhythm a small comfort against the brittle tension they left behind at the fire. By the time they reached Donnelly's, an uneasy anticipation hung in the air, as though the city itself braced for the unknown.

Inside, the bar greeted them with its familiar scent of worn wood and spilled whiskey, the dim light stretching faint shadows across the room. Rowan locked the door behind them, shutting out the world—at least for now.

"Riichi," Rowan said, his voice firm and direct. "Get Vine and Reed here. And call Eileen. We need her decision on Oak, Holly, and Elder. No texts—I want them on the line."

Riichi nodded immediately, already pulling out his phone. Rowan's gaze shifted to the others. Aislinn stood near Takoda and Rain, her composure intact but clearly carrying the strain of the night. He didn't need to ask—he could see it in the subtle set of her shoulders and the tightness in her jaw.

Rowan approached them, cutting straight to the point. "Are you holding up?"

Takoda answered first, her tone steady despite the flicker of unease in her expression. "Shaken, but we're okay."

Rain nodded, her arms crossed—not out of fear but as if grounding herself in thought. Rowan's attention lingered on her for a moment, noting the quiet strength in her posture, before turning to Aislinn.

"Aislinn, a word?" He motioned toward the far end of the room.

She hesitated, just briefly, before following, leaving Takoda and Rain in the quieter space they seemed to need.

"Where's your head at?" Rowan asked, his tone low enough to keep their conversation private, though it carried enough weight to demand her full attention.

Aislinn pressed her lips together. "I'm managing. It's just…" She exhaled slowly, searching for the right words before shrugging. "A lot."

Rowan nodded once, sharp and deliberate. "It is. But we need to stay sharper. If something's pulling you under, I need to know now."

Her brow furrowed, and she held his gaze for a moment before letting out a slow breath. "I'll manage. I just need a minute."

"That's fine," he replied, his tone matter-of-fact. "But not too long. Takoda and Rain are looking to you for stability, and right now, you're the one they'll follow."

Aislinn glanced back at the girls. Their unease was clear, and a flicker of doubt crossed her features. "I don't even know what to say to them."

"You don't need all the answers. Start with what you do know. Keep them focused on the next step." He paused, weighing his next words carefully. "And call Ariel. She has a way of cutting through the noise."

A faint, genuine smile touched Aislinn's lips. "Yeah, that's smart. I'll do that."

She moved to make the call, leaving Rowan to join Riichi, who was still deep in conversation on his phone. The bar seemed suspended in a restless stillness, like a drawn breath waiting to exhale. Leaning against the edge of a table, Rowan's thoughts churned with contingencies. The archdemon hadn't disappeared—it was out there, waiting. And so were they.

The bar's atmosphere was thick with tension, the kind that hummed in the quiet moments before decisions had to be made. Rowan sat at the table with Aislinn, Takoda, and Rain, making an effort to keep the conversation light, though their thoughts were clearly elsewhere. Takoda's fingers tugged at a loose thread on her sleeve, a restless movement that mirrored the unease in her posture. Across from her, Rain sat with her arms loosely folded, breaking the silence at last.

"I forgot how much this place smells like old wood and beer," she said, wrinkling her nose faintly before glancing at Takoda. "Kind of charming, in that 'we only came here once' kind of way."

A hint of amusement flickered across Takoda's face. "Better than the bonfire smell we left behind," she murmured, her voice soft but tinged with dry humor.

Rain smiled but didn't push further, leaning back into her chair with a quiet ease. Rowan caught the brief exchange and offered Rain a subtle nod of approval, appreciating how she brought Takoda a small moment of relief without forcing it.

Nearby, Riichi stood in silence, his usual stoicism feeling heavier tonight. His gaze occasionally drifted toward Takoda, though he always glanced away the moment her attention shifted in his direction. Rowan noticed but chose not to comment, filing it away for later.

The door creaked open suddenly, and Ariel breezed in with a bright smile that seemed to pull the air in the room toward her. Her energy cut through the somber mood like sunlight breaking through storm clouds, her eyes gleaming as if danger wasn't just outside the door.

"Hey, everyone!" she chirped, giving a playful wave before heading straight to Takoda and Rain. "Looks like I got here just in time. Don't worry—I'll make sure things stay relaxed around here."

Rowan gave her a curt nod, his gratitude apparent despite his brisk demeanor. "Thanks, Ariel. Just keep them company while we handle things in the back."

With a mock salute, Ariel turned her full attention to the girls, launching into lighthearted banter. The shift was almost immediate—Takoda's shoulders eased slightly, and Rain's expression softened as she allowed herself to engage. Aislinn glanced at Rowan, giving him a small, grateful smile before he motioned for her to follow him.

They had barely left the room when the door opened again. Elder stepped in with little fanfare, his movements purposeful yet unassuming. His nod to Rowan was brief before he slipped toward the shadows, his presence folding into the background like a whisper.

Not long after, Oak arrived, his features composed, though his gaze was keen, scanning the room with quiet precision. He exchanged small nods with Riichi and Rowan before heading toward the back.

Minutes ticked by before Holly and Vine entered—separately, but with a synchronicity that felt deliberate. Their expressions were serious, their footsteps unhurried as they made their way to the back without a word. Reed followed, his entrance so unobtrusive that most didn't notice him at all. Rowan did, though, and acknowledged him with a faint nod.

At last, Eileen arrived. Her presence filled the room in a way that defied words, a quiet authority radiating from her as she took in her surroundings.

Her gaze lingered on Rowan briefly before she gestured toward the backroom with a subtle but decisive motion. It was time.

Rowan looked back at Takoda and Rain one last time. Ariel's easy, flowing conversation kept them distracted, her effortless charm carving out a fragile calm in the midst of uncertainty. Aislinn stood beside him, meeting his gaze with a small nod of understanding before the two followed the others into the backroom.

The backroom of Donnelly's hummed with restrained tension as the Fallen gathered around the table. Eileen sat at its head, her piercing gaze sweeping over the group as Rowan and Aislinn took their seats. The devastation of the café hung in the air, unspoken but heavy. Rowan knew they couldn't afford to dwell on it. They had to focus.

"We need to start with what happened at the café tonight," Rowan said, his tone firm, though frustration simmered beneath his composure.

The room's attention locked on him as he continued. "Aislinn and I were asleep when the fire started. Takoda called Aislinn—she and Rain were already at the café when it went up in flames."

Rowan paused briefly, his jaw tightening before he pushed on. "By the time we got there, the fire had consumed the building. The firefighters were battling it, but it was too late. The café is gone."

Riichi, sitting with his usual composed posture, spoke up, his words precise. "When I arrived, I observed a Golden Dawn member near the scene. I attempted pursuit but lost him—he disappeared before I could close in. This wasn't done alone."

Rowan inclined his head in acknowledgment before adding, "Aislinn spotted someone on the rooftop—the archdemon. He was just standing there, watching us, like he was waiting for us to make the first move. When she pointed him out, he snapped his fingers. That's when the explosion happened."

Vine leaned back in his chair, a faint smirk playing at his lips. "They brought the archdemon out just for that? Seems like overkill for a bonfire."

Holly gave him a sidelong glance, her voice calm yet pointed. "It wasn't just fire, Vine. This was personal. If the Golden Dawn was behind it, they wanted to hurt Aislinn—to draw her out or send a message."

Oak, ever measured, chimed in, his words laced with thoughtfulness. "The fire was likely their doing—a distraction, bait, or maybe both. But the archdemon's presence..." He trailed off, his expression darkening. "That's a piece we can't ignore. Are we certain they're working together?"

Elder, who had been quietly observing, leaned forward, his tone deliberate. "That's what we need to determine. If magic was used to start the fire, it points to the Golden Dawn. But the explosion—that was something else entirely. Once the site clears, I'll look for magical residue."

From the shadows, Reed's voice emerged, low and steady. "The archdemon wasn't there for kicks. Whether it's working with the Golden Dawn or not, its presence escalated everything. That fire wasn't just a warning—it was a statement."

Eileen's gaze swept across the room, sharp as the edge of a blade. "So we know the Golden Dawn likely set the fire, and we know the archdemon caused the explosion. But whether they're aligned remains unclear. That's what we need to find out."

Riichi shifted slightly, his tone precise. "The operative wouldn't have vanished so quickly without assistance. Even if the archdemon wasn't aiding them directly, it created enough chaos to cover their escape. Intentional or not, the timing was too convenient."

Vine let out a quiet chuckle, his words edged with a grim humor. "So either they're best friends, or the archdemon's running its own game. Both sound like a bad time."

Oak's expression hardened, his voice resolute. "We need to figure out why this is happening now. If the Golden Dawn wasn't acting alone, the stakes are higher than we anticipated."

Holly nodded, her words calm but unwavering. "They're targeting Aislinn. That much is obvious. Whether it's the Golden Dawn, the archdemon, or both, she's the reason for this attack."

Rowan's fists tightened at his sides. "They're hitting her where it hurts, and they're not going to stop. We need to be ready."

Elder's brow furrowed as his thoughts turned inward. "The boldness of this attack suggests they had a specific objective. Once I confirm whether magic was involved, we'll know if this was purely the Golden Dawn—or if something else is in play."

Eileen leaned back slightly, her presence commanding without effort. "We don't wait for their next move. Whether the Golden Dawn and the archdemon are working together or not, we prepare for the worst. This is escalating faster than we expected."

The room settled into tense stillness after the discussion about the fire, the weight of what had happened lingering in the air. Eileen didn't let the silence stretch too far. She leaned forward, her focus shifting across the group with calculated precision.

"I think we need to move the mission up by a day," she said, her tone firm, carrying an unmistakable urgency. "The sooner we deal with the Golden Dawn, the sooner we can turn our attention to the archdemon. We can't afford divided focus any longer."

The group exchanged uncertain looks, unease rippling through the room as her words settled.

Riichi leaned forward, his posture calm and thoughtful. "We're ready to go sooner if needed. Reed and I have been scouting the Old Mount Olympus Mansion. Their guard rotation is thin, and we've mapped their supply routes. But we'll need precise timing to pull this off."

Vine nodded with a confident grin. "They won't see us coming. We'll get in, grab what we need, and be gone before they even know what hit them."

Eileen shifted her attention to Rowan. "Rowan, I need to know if you're ready after... everything. We still have time to regroup if you need to sit this one out. But I need your answer now."

Rowan tensed, the question hitting a nerve as his thoughts raced. He glanced at Aislinn, sitting beside him—her presence a rare constant amid the chaos. Could he leave her behind after everything they'd endured? The fire, the looming threat of the archdemon—it all pressed against him. His instinct to shield her clashed with the call of duty.

Step aside? After two centuries of fighting the Golden Dawn, it felt unthinkable. This mission could change everything. His role as Aislinn's protector warred with his identity as a warrior.

Aislinn caught his conflicted look and held it, understanding the turmoil within him. She didn't need to hear his thoughts; the weight of his struggle was clear. Rowan had been caught between duty and emotion for too long. After all they had endured, she couldn't be the reason he faltered.

Her pulse quickened as she made her decision. She had to be brave—for him and for herself. Rowan wasn't hers to protect. He was a soldier, and she wouldn't let him waver.

Aislinn gave him the smallest of nods, then spoke with quiet determination. "Recent events won't stop him. Rowan will go."

The room fell silent as her words settled. Eileen's expression softened slightly, her approval evident in the subtle shift of her demeanor. Rowan glanced at Aislinn, admiration surging. She was braver than she knew.

Eileen nodded. "Good. Let's talk strategy." Her focus returned to the group. "Riichi, Reed, Vine, Rowan—you four will infiltrate the mansion. Riichi, how do you propose handling their supply stockpile once you're inside?"

Riichi spoke with measured precision. "Their supplies are scattered across several vaults beneath the mansion. It won't be as simple as grabbing everything at once. We'll need to move in phases, taking what we can while neutralizing their security."

Reed added, his tone low but exact, "Their patrols have increased, but there's a gap right after the shift change. That's our best window. If we hit it just right, we'll catch them off-guard."

Vine cracked his knuckles with a smirk. "I can set off a few 'accidental' alarms on the far side of the compound. Keep them running in circles while you move in."

Rowan frowned, his practical side kicking in. "Even if we slip in unnoticed and grab what we can, we're only four people. How do we manage everything? And what about the earthquake device? If they've started assembling it, we need to shut it down immediately."

Aislinn leaned closer, her words thoughtful. "What about Howard? He's helped you before, hasn't he? Maybe he could... I don't know, help transport the supplies?"

Rowan blinked, the suggestion snapping into place in his mind. Of course. Howard. He turned to her, something easing in his expression. "That's actually a great idea."

Aislinn's lips curved slightly, the tension in her shoulders softening as Rowan straightened, the plan taking shape.

He looked to the group, his focus sharpened. "We know someone who can help. Howard—an old informant of mine. He used to be with the Golden Dawn but left years ago. Now he volunteers at a soup kitchen for veterans. He has contacts there—people he trusts who could move the supplies without drawing attention."

Eileen's interest flickered in her expression. "Howard? The same one who's been tracking the Golden Dawn for you?"

Rowan nodded. "That's him. He's been working to make amends for his past. If anyone can help us discreetly, it's him and the veterans he works with. They're dependable, and Howard's proven himself trustworthy."

Riichi's demeanor remained composed, but a spark of approval lit his features. "An insider with that kind of knowledge could make all the difference. If his team handles the supplies, we can focus entirely on dismantling the device."

Reed nodded firmly. "That'll give us the time we need. The fewer distractions, the better."

Vine leaned back in his chair, his grin widening. "Looks like logistics are covered. I like it."

Eileen inclined her head slightly, satisfaction threading through her tone. "Good work, you two. Rowan, contact Howard. If he can mobilize the veterans, they'll be a major asset."

She turned her focus to Rowan and Aislinn, her words gentler now. "While you're on the mission, I'll monitor the mansion's magical activity and coordinate backup if needed. I'll also make sure Aislinn is protected. The archdemon may strike again while you're gone, and I won't let that happen."

Aislinn looked up, gratitude softening her features. "Thank you," she said, her sincerity clear in every syllable.

Rowan shifted his attention between them, his shoulders easing. He trusted Eileen's abilities and knew Aislinn would be safe, even as the instinct to protect her tugged at him.

He released a slow breath, a sense of clarity settling over him for the first time since the fire. The plan solidified in his mind. He could fulfill his duty to the Fallen while ensuring Aislinn's safety. He glanced at her beside him, reassured by her calm presence and unspoken support, and gave her a brief nod of appreciation.

Eileen addressed the group again, her voice regaining its commanding edge. "You leave tonight. That gives us a few hours to finalize the details. Elder, Holly, I'll need you both on standby in case the archdemon makes a move while we're distracted. Oak, you'll stay here with Aislinn and me."

Oak's calm response broke the momentary lull. "I'll be ready. If the archdemon tries anything, we'll handle it."

Elder nodded thoughtfully. "I'll check the ley lines for disruptions. The mansion is built on a powerful nexus of energy. If the Golden Dawn is drawing from it, we'll cut them off at the source."

Holly's expression tightened with resolve. "I'll coordinate with Elder. We'll keep the area locked down. Whatever happens, we won't let the archdemon take us by surprise."

The room buzzed with purpose, every member focused on their role. Aislinn's heart raced as the reality of Rowan walking into danger settled over her. But instead of fear, she felt a spark of determination. She wasn't a bystander anymore—she was part of this fight.

Eileen's words sliced through the focused hum. "Before we wrap up, we need to address the archdemon. We don't know who he is or what he wants, but his presence at the café proves one thing—this goes beyond the Golden Dawn."

"We need to figure out his endgame," Holly said, her concern evident in her tone. "If he's working with the Golden Dawn, there's a reason."

"We can't afford to face him blind," Elder added. "The more we uncover, the better prepared we'll be."

Eileen nodded. "Elder, Oak, Holly—you're tasked with digging into this. Research everything you can about archdemons. Historical accounts, alliances, rituals—anything that might give us an edge."

"We'll start immediately," Oak said, his tone resolute. "There's plenty in the archives we haven't examined yet."

Eileen turned toward Rowan. "If it's alright with you, they'll work out of Donnelly's while the rest of us finalize the mission plans."

Rowan inclined his head. "That works. Keep things running here."

Eileen rose, signaling the meeting's end. "Everyone has their role. Riichi, Reed, Vine, Rowan—you know what to do. Elder, Oak, Holly, get started on your research."

The group stood, the weight of their tasks clear in their movements. Eileen spoke one last time, her words ringing with conviction. "We move fast, we hit hard, and we stop them before they act again. And we find out what that archdemon is really after."

The meeting concluded, and the team dispersed, each member moving with purpose as they prepared for what lay ahead.

In the bar area, morning light streamed through the windows, casting warm patterns over the worn wooden tables. Ariel, Rain, and Takoda had fallen asleep in the corner, nestled beneath blankets and pillows Ariel had brought down from Rowan's apartment. Even in sleep, Ariel's arm lay protectively over her friends, their rhythmic breathing a soothing contrast to the lingering tension.

At one of the larger tables, Eileen and Oak conjured piles of ancient books and scrolls from their personal collections, each appearing with a faint shimmer of magic. The surface quickly filled with weathered tomes, their bindings cracked and aged by centuries of use.

Oak began sorting the books with meticulous care, his movements deliberate and composed. Holly joined him, already leafing through the first volume with intent focus, while Elder sat nearby, scanning the texts for anything tied to archdemons.

Across the room, Riichi, Reed, and Vine bent over a makeshift map, their conversation low and purposeful as they finalized the mission strategy.

Reed's careful insights balanced Vine's bold energy, while Riichi directed the discussion with a clear and methodical approach.

Rowan crossed the room to join them after finishing his call. "Howard's ready," he said, glancing at the map. "Everything's in place."

Riichi acknowledged him with a short nod. "Good. We've adjusted the plan—Reed and I will cover the lower levels while you and Vine create the distraction."

Vine grinned, flexing his fingers. "I'll give them something to keep busy."

Rowan nodded in agreement. The plan was coming together, and for the first time in hours, a sense of direction cut through the chaos.

At the other table, Eileen sifted through her stack of books, selecting one of the oldest volumes. She carried it to Aislinn, who sat with her hands tense in her lap, her body language betraying the storm of emotions beneath the surface. Eileen placed the book in front of her with calm authority.

"Look at this," she instructed. "It's full of sketches—no photographs, but it's the best chance we have of identifying the archdemon you saw. It's a long shot, but we have to try."

Aislinn nodded, carefully opening the fragile pages. Grotesque drawings of demons filled the book, each one more unnerving than the last. She studied them with unwavering focus, her fingers steady despite the turmoil inside her.

Eileen studied her for a heartbeat, her expression softening as she observed Aislinn. She had endured so much already, and Eileen knew greater challenges lay ahead. Letting her protective instincts take over briefly, she rested a reassuring hand on Aislinn's arm. "How are you holding up?"

Aislinn looked up, her tired smile faint but sincere. "I'm fine... or as fine as I can be. Trying not to overthink everything."

Her gaze drifted across the room, landing briefly on Riichi before she leaned toward Eileen, a hint of amusement creeping into her voice. "I've noticed Riichi keeps glancing at Takoda while she's asleep."

Eileen's lips curved into a knowing smile. "It's not surprising."

Aislinn raised an eyebrow, curiosity sparking. "Not surprising?"

Eileen didn't elaborate, her enigmatic smile remaining as she gestured back to the book. Aislinn let the comment pass, filing it away for later consideration.

She returned her attention to the sketches, her focus intent on each unnerving image until her fingers hesitated mid-turn. Her breath caught as she froze on a face drawn with brutal accuracy—the same face that had stood atop the café.

Her voice wavered in a low whisper. "It's him."

Eileen leaned closer, her features tightening as she studied the page. "Who?"

Aislinn's response was hushed, her words laden with dread. "Lucifer. The archdemon of pride... and the former leader of the underworld."

Eileen's expression hardened instantly. "That's bad. Very bad."

Before they could speak further, Rowan approached, his demeanor grim. "Howard's ready. We're good to go."

Eileen straightened, her focus sharpening. "I need to show this to Oak, Holly, and Elder—immediately. They need to know we're dealing with Lucifer."

She picked up the book, urgency driving her steps as her movements quickened. "This changes everything."

Swiftly, she crossed the room to where the others were gathered. Oak, Holly, and Elder barely glanced up before she set the book in front of them, her determination unwavering.

Rowan watched her go, the weight of Lucifer's name bearing down on him. *The archdemon of pride. Former ruler of the underworld.* His jaw tightened as he forced his focus back to the task at hand. Lucifer's involvement marked a seismic shift, but he trusted Oak, Holly, and Elder to uncover the answers they needed. *They're more than capable.*

For now, Rowan's attention shifted. His eyes lingered on Aislinn, exhaustion etched into every line of her face. *She's been through more than enough already. What she needs now is rest.*

He moved to sit beside her, keeping his tone even and calm. "How are you holding up?"

Aislinn managed a faint smile. "I'm alright. Just... trying to process it all."

Rowan gave a short nod, recognizing the strain behind her words. "It's been a long morning. You need rest." His voice softened as he added, "Why don't I take you upstairs? It's quieter there. You've earned a break."

She hesitated, as if weighing the suggestion, but the weariness in her expression betrayed her. "That sounds perfect."

Rowan rose, extending a hand toward her. Before heading upstairs, he glanced at Eileen, who was deep in conversation with Oak and the others.

"Eileen," Rowan called, waiting for her acknowledgment. "The Fallen can use the bar as long as you need. Ariel won't open it until later tonight."

Eileen looked up briefly and nodded in appreciation before returning to the discussion.

Rowan turned back to Aislinn, his hand still outstretched. "Come on, let's get some rest."

She accepted his hand, letting him guide her away from the tension-filled room. The stairs groaned softly under their feet, and as Rowan pushed open the door to his apartment, the noise from below faded into a distant murmur.

Aislinn let out a slow breath, her shoulders sagging under the weight of everything that had happened. Rowan led her toward the bed, his hand resting gently at the small of her back.

"You need to sleep," he said, his voice low and soothing. *She needs this. More than she realizes.* The warmth in his words steadied her, even as her thoughts churned with the morning's events.

She nodded, though doubt flickered across her features. "I don't know if I can. Not after... all this."

"Lucifer. And then tonight..." Her unfinished thought lingered heavily in the room.

Rowan's jaw tensed briefly, but he pushed the concern aside, sitting beside her so his knee brushed hers. "It's a lot. I know. But right now, you need to rest. You can't carry this all alone."

The familiar refrain in his words wasn't just reassurance—it was a quiet vow. *I'll carry it with you. Always.*

A hint of a smile touched her lips, faint but genuine. "You always say that."

His lips curved in return, and he brushed his thumb lightly over her hand. "Because it's true."

Her gaze dropped, her voice barely audible. "I don't even know how to sleep after all this."

Rowan shifted closer, wrapping an arm around her shoulders and drawing her gently against his chest. "Then don't try to be strong right now. Let me take care of you."

She closed her eyes and leaned into him, the steady rhythm of his heartbeat grounding her. The unease gnawing at the edges of her mind began to fade, softened by his presence.

After a moment, Rowan guided her to lie down, his touch lingering briefly on her arm. "Just rest," he murmured, brushing a strand of hair from her face. "I'll stay right here."

She didn't argue, her exhaustion pulling her under. He settled beside her, draping an arm protectively over her as she sank deeper into the mattress.

The silence stretched between them, unbroken but filled with an unspoken understanding. Rowan's fingers traced absent patterns on her arm, his touch a wordless reassurance. Gradually, her breathing slowed and deepened, her body finally yielding to sleep.

Rowan glanced toward the window. The daylight outside was deceptively calm, masking the storm gathering beyond the horizon. His focus shifted back to Aislinn, her face relaxed in sleep, the tension finally gone.

The weight of what lay ahead pressed heavily on him, more acute now with the knowledge of Lucifer's presence. Tonight's mission would be more dangerous than any before it. The stakes had never been higher.

Protect her. At all costs.

No matter what was coming.

Chapter Seventeen

The Devil's Game

A dusky glow seeped into Rowan's room, coaxing Aislinn awake. She blinked, letting the unfamiliar surroundings sharpen into view. Her head rested against Rowan's chest, rising and falling in a deep rhythm. Beneath the surface calm, an undercurrent of unease remained—a quiet reminder of the night's mission. Nearly six. They'd have to get moving soon.

Aislinn shifted carefully, stealing a moment to study him. His jet-black hair tumbled in loose waves, the vivid blue streaks stark even in the dim light. He'd traded his usual leather jacket for a simple black hoodie, understated yet undeniably striking. The look grounded him, exuding the confidence that made Rowan so unmistakably himself. A smile tugged at her lips. *He really does look good in black.*

Rowan stirred, his eyes cracking open. They met hers, and a fleeting smile softened the weariness etched into his features. Neither spoke; they didn't need to. The weight of the night's significance hovered between them, unspoken but understood. For now, they clung to the fragile calm, a fleeting pause before chaos stirred again.

"We should head downstairs," he murmured, his voice low from sleep, tinged with resolve. Aislinn nodded, though unease still twisted in her chest.

Downstairs, the familiar clink of dishes and muted conversation welcomed them. Ariel, Takoda, and Rain sat gathered at the bar counter. Ariel perched on the edge, legs swinging as she chatted with Takoda. When Aislinn and Rowan entered, Ariel's head swiveled toward them, a grin spreading wide. "Morning, lovebirds—or should I say evening?" Her teasing words danced lightly over the group, though Aislinn caught the serious note beneath her expression.

As they approached, Ariel shot Aislinn a conspiratorial wink. "So, your mom—Eileen—is something else. Just met her this morning, and let's just say we're already planning family holidays." She gave an exaggerated shrug. "Guess that means you're stuck with me."

Aislinn's laugh came easily, the strain in her chest loosening a fraction. Ariel, as always, had a way of finding light in the darkest shadows. Still, the mention of her mom sent a ripple of unease through her. Too much lay unresolved there, too many questions. *Not tonight.*

Ariel tossed a folded note to Rowan. "From Eileen," she said, her demeanor cooling, her words edged with subtle weight. "She says to meet at this address outside the city. 7:30 sharp. Oh, and Takoda and Rain are coming along. I'll catch up after closing the bar."

Rowan caught the note midair and skimmed its contents before tucking it into his pocket. "We should head out," he said, glancing at Aislinn, who nodded, then at the others to confirm their readiness.

As Takoda and Rain moved to gather their things, Ariel leaned casually against the counter, watching Rowan with a thoughtful tilt of her head. "So, Vine," she said lightly, her tone teasing yet curious. "What's his deal?"

Rowan's expression hardened slightly. "Nothing worth your time."

She smirked, shrugging. "If you say so. Just saying, I'm good at reading people."

"Not this time," Rowan said, his tone leaving no room for argument. He turned for the door, muttering under his breath, "This is why I worry about you."

She laughed, her voice trailing after him. "You love me for it!"

Outside, Aislinn lingered, her thoughts drifting until the sight of the car snapped her back to the present. Parked at the curb wasn't Rowan's motorcycle but a sleek, matte-black 1967 Ford Mustang Fastback. Electric blue accents caught the fading sunlight, gleaming like threads of lightning. Her brows lifted, the car's presence unexpected yet fitting—its restrained power a perfect reflection of Rowan himself.

"You have a car?" she asked, surprise breaking through her thoughts.

A flicker of pride crossed Rowan's features. "Sometimes. Needed something that could fit more than just me." Holding the door open for her, he added with a faint smirk, "Not like I can cram all of us onto the bike."

Her lips curved into a small smile. Rowan never failed to surprise her. She slipped into the passenger seat while Takoda and Rain settled in the back, her thoughts wandering to Eileen's note and the unanswered questions waiting beyond the city limits.

Twilight gave way to dusk as they arrived at their destination—a modest two-story house perched on the city's edge. Towering oaks framed its silhouette, their gnarled branches swaying gently in the evening breeze. A white picket fence encircled the property, lending it an air of suburban calm that felt strangely at odds with the weight of their mission.

"It's an Airbnb," Riichi would later explain, having secured it in advance as their temporary base.

Aislinn stepped out, her boots crunching against the gravel drive. The house exuded an unassuming stillness, its quaint exterior hiding the tension simmering beneath the surface. Her nerves buzzed faintly, but she forced herself to focus, exhaling slowly as they prepared to enter.

Inside, Takoda and Rain moved toward the living room, their steps deliberate as they exchanged casual remarks with Aislinn and Rowan. Takoda's easy smile was as much for Aislinn's benefit as her own. "We'll be fine," she said lightly. "Just staying out of the way, letting you guys handle the big stuff." She added with a smirk, "Pretty sure we've had enough excitement for one lifetime."

Rain let out a dry chuckle. "Just another normal night, right?" Her humor was thin, more of a shield than a joke. Aislinn could see it—how both of them were working to reclaim a sense of normalcy. The fire, the truth about the Fallen—it had shaken them, but in their own way, they were piecing themselves back together, even if the cracks still showed.

Rowan rested a hand lightly on Aislinn's back, guiding her toward the stairs. "Come on," he said, his voice low, the words carrying an edge of urgency. "I want to show you something." There was calm in his demeanor, but she caught the tension beneath it—an unspoken reminder of how little time they had before their mission began.

Upstairs, the noise from below faded into faint murmurs. Rowan led her into a small room, its setup purposeful and no-frills. A plain table held a few radio transmitters, and a large map of the city stretched across one wall, marked with notations and colored pins. The space thrummed with quiet intensity.

"You'll be able to hear everything through this," Rowan explained, motioning toward the main radio. "We'll all have mics, so we can stay in contact." His expression tightened slightly. "But I'm not giving you a mic," he added, his tone firm. "I need to keep my focus. You can listen in, but we can't risk any distractions."

Aislinn opened her mouth to argue, but the look in his eyes stopped her. This wasn't about trust—it was about protection. She saw it in the lines of his face, in the set of his jaw. Rowan wasn't leaving room for negotiation, not with so much at stake.

"Your mom will be with you the whole time," he said, his voice softening slightly. "She's fierce when she needs to be." A flicker of a smile crossed his lips. "And a lot of the time when she doesn't."

Aislinn let out a faint laugh, her unease lingering just beneath the surface. "Yeah, I've noticed." Her gaze dropped briefly, the weight of the night pressing in around her. She wanted to tell him to be careful, to say something that mattered, but the words refused to come.

Downstairs, the atmosphere had shifted. The Fallen moved with quiet precision, donning tactical gear and double-checking supplies. Conversations were sparse, replaced by the focused energy of a team locking into place. Eileen stood at the center of the room, her presence commanding yet calm as she reviewed the plan.

"Reed and Riichi," she began, her gaze sharp and unwavering, "you'll handle infiltration. Secure the supplies and, if there's an earthquake device, disarm it."

Reed and Riichi exchanged brief nods, their focus steady.

"Rowan and Vine," Eileen continued, turning toward them, "you're the diversion. Keep their forces split and draw them away from the supply area."

Rowan nodded, his mind already calculating tactics. He and Vine worked well together, and despite the risks ahead, he trusted their coordination. There could be no distractions tonight—not for him, not for anyone.

"Elder," she said, her tone softening, "you'll oversee extraction for the supplies and Howard's team. If necessary, teleport what you can. You'll also be the driver. Howard's team will meet you at Fisherman's Wharf."

Elder inclined his head, his calm demeanor unwavering.

"Holly," Eileen continued, "your priority is protecting Elder while he casts."

Holly straightened, her nod deliberate and sure.

"And Oak," Eileen finished, her gaze settling on him, "you're here with me. You'll keep Takoda and Rain safe and monitor everything from base." Her focus shifted briefly to Aislinn. "I'll keep an eye on her, and we'll both be ready to step in if things change."

The room stilled as the team absorbed their assignments. They had all faced danger before, but tonight carried a deeper weight, something unspoken yet undeniable. It hung in the air, pressing close, mirrored in the quiet resolve etched into each face.

Rowan caught Aislinn's eye, his expression unwavering. "Everything's going to be fine," he said, his voice low, each word steady with certainty. "We've got a strong team. I'll be back before you know it." His hand closed around hers, the warmth grounding her in the present.

Aislinn nodded, though unease churned beneath her calm exterior. *I have to trust him,* she told herself, her gaze drifting to the Fallen as they finalized their preparations. Reed methodically adjusted his gear, his movements precise, every action deliberate. Nearby, Riichi's stance was firm, protective—an unyielding barrier ready to shield those who needed it.

Vine lingered near the door, his sharp gaze sweeping the room, a quiet persistence in his posture that spoke volumes. Elder's presence radiated calm, his quiet composure an anchor amid the growing anxiety, as if he carried the promise of renewal with him. Holly, steady and focused, adjusted her gear, her readiness to guard Elder evident in her determined expression.

Without warning, Aislinn pulled Rowan close, her lips brushing his in a kiss that carried both urgency and promise. It was a wordless plea, a declaration of everything she couldn't bring herself to say. For just a heartbeat, the world narrowed to just the two of them, suspended in this fragile sliver of time before their paths diverged.

A sharp clearing of someone's throat shattered the moment. They broke apart, cheeks flushed, as the room's attention swung their way. Eileen raised an eyebrow, the hint of a smile softening her otherwise composed expression. Takoda gaped openly, while Rain grinned from her perch on the couch, amusement lighting her face like a mischievous cat.

Vine strolled past, smirking as he clapped Rowan on the shoulder. "Nice," he drawled, his tone rich with amusement, before disappearing through the door.

Heat flared in Aislinn's cheeks, but Rowan didn't release her hand. For once, he seemed unconcerned by their audience. His fingers brushed against hers, the faint squeeze speaking volumes, as if he was committing her touch to memory. "I'll be back," he whispered, the promise weighted like an anchor.

As he turned for the door, their fingers held until the last possible second. *I'll be back,* he repeated silently, letting the vow settle over him like armor as he stepped into the night.

One by one, the Fallen filtered out, leaving the house wrapped in a quiet calm. Aislinn stood beside Eileen, her gaze fixed on the door as it clicked shut behind Rowan. The weight of the night settled over her, heavy and cold, creeping in like fog rolling over a silent field.

Eileen's presence beside her felt stabilizing, her composed calm filling the room with a quiet, undeniable strength. She exhaled faintly and turned to Oak, who leaned against the wall, his arms crossed, exuding the steady strength of a tree rooted in wisdom and endurance. Takoda and Rain sat on the couch, exchanging sly glances, their amusement over the unfolding dynamic all too obvious.

"Oak," Eileen said, her tone calm but firm, "you'll stay here and keep an eye on them."

Oak gave a resigned nod, casting the girls a wary glance. They grinned back at him, mischief sparkling in their eyes like twin flames.

"Who's going to protect me from them?" Oak muttered, his voice pitched just loud enough to reach Eileen and Aislinn.

Aislinn's lips twitched into a faint smile, her gaze meeting Eileen's. They exchanged a brief look of mutual understanding, a connection that felt startlingly ordinary. It was a glimpse of what might have been—a fleeting mother-daughter moment in a life that had veered so far from normal.

"Come on," Eileen said gently, breaking the moment as she gestured toward the stairs. "Let's get you set up."

They climbed the narrow staircase in silence, the quiet between them weighted with a shared understanding. There was an unexpected comfort in having Eileen physically beside her, guiding her steps. Their last conversation had been in a dream—ghostly and detached. This felt tangible. Real.

At the top, they entered the small room Rowan had shown her earlier, the radio equipment neatly arranged on the table. Eileen moved with quiet precision, adjusting the setup as she explained the process again, even though Aislinn already knew it. She listened anyway, not for the instructions, but for the cadence of her mother's voice—a sound that felt almost ordinary. For a brief instant, Aislinn let herself imagine a different life, one where her mother had never disappeared, where times like this were the norm.

Eileen's hand lingered on one of the dials, her gaze flicking to Aislinn. Her expression softened, and a playful glimmer lit her eyes. "You and Rowan seem... close," she said. "That kiss was... quite the display."

Heat rushed to Aislinn's face, but she didn't look away. For once, she felt no need to hide. "I think..." She hesitated, her pulse quickening as she gave form to the thought she'd scarcely dared to acknowledge. "I think I'm in love with him."

The words hung in the air, and saying them aloud was both exhilarating and terrifying. She searched Eileen's face, bracing for her reaction.

A gentle smile spread across Eileen's lips, her eyes touched with unmistakable understanding. "It's a good feeling, isn't it? Loving someone like that." Her words carried a warmth only experience could bring.

Aislinn's lips curved into a small smile, and a soft laugh escaped her. "Yeah... it really is." A fragile warmth bloomed in her chest, a small comfort against the weight of the day's looming uncertainties. In the swirl of danger and risk, it felt good to hold onto a sense of stability, something tangible and real.

"It's been a long time since we've talked like this," Aislinn murmured, her voice barely audible. "Since… well, the last time you came to me in a dream."

Eileen's smile deepened, and she reached out to brush a strand of hair from Aislinn's face. "I prefer being here, too. There's something grounding about it. Something I've missed."

They let the silence stretch between them briefly, the weight of their shared history settling over the room. Time lost, words left unsaid, paths never taken—it all lingered in the air. Yet here, in this small room, it felt as if they were finally beginning to bridge the distance.

A sudden crackle from the radio shattered the stillness, yanking them back to the present. Eileen straightened, the warmth in her expression giving way to the sharp focus of a leader. "That's them," she said firmly. "Rowan and Vine are in one vehicle, the others in another."

Aislinn's pulse quickened as the static on the radio grew louder, signaling the mission's beginning. She gripped the edge of the table, swallowing hard against the rising tide of adrenaline.

"You ready?" Eileen asked, her tone calm but carrying a flicker of concern.

Aislinn nodded, even as the anxious flutter in her stomach refused to settle. "Yeah… I'm ready."

The transmitter emitted a faint hum, its persistent buzz the only sound as Aislinn waited, her thoughts spiraling. Rowan was out there. He'd promised to come back, and she had to believe him. The crackling of the radio felt like a fragile lifeline tethering her to the mission unfolding in the shadows.

Riichi's clipped voice broke through the static. "In position near Fisherman's Wharf. Ready for pickup."

Aislinn's heart skipped. The mission was no longer just plans and preparations—it was real now. Howard and his team, human allies in this battle, were waiting. Every second felt heavier with the stakes pressing in.

"Copy that," Rowan responded, his voice steady, controlled. "On our way."

Aislinn closed her eyes, letting Rowan's calm presence center her. She pictured him weaving through the dark streets with the others, a source of quiet strength amidst the chaos. Moments later, his next update crackled through. "Approaching Fisherman's Wharf. All clear."

Her mind shifted to Howard—the familiar café regular, now standing in the shadows, risking his life to protect his city. The stakes seemed to grow heavier with each passing second.

"Howard's team is on board," Rowan said again. "Heading to the compound."

Aislinn's heartbeat quickened, mirroring the urgency pulsing through the mission.

"Proceeding to the Old Mount Olympus Mansion," Riichi added. "No interference so far."

Eileen's calm exterior didn't falter, but Aislinn sensed a subtle shift in her energy—a faint tension that mirrored her own. Both of them knew too much was riding on this.

"Vine, keep lookout as we approach," Rowan instructed. "Report anything unusual."

"Copy that," Vine replied, his usual humor absent, replaced by focused efficiency. They were closing in.

The minutes stretched, each one dragging longer than the last. Aislinn's mind churned with possibilities—an ambush, hidden traps, the earthquake device. Her fingers tightened around the chair's armrests, her nerves coiling tighter with every second.

"We're here," Rowan finally announced. "Arriving at the compound."

Her pulse spiked. She could almost picture the Old Mount Olympus Mansion—its crumbling facade twisted by the Golden Dawn's influence into something darker, more sinister. The thought of them infiltrating such a place felt surreal.

"We're moving in," Riichi reported, his voice clear and deliberate. "Howard's team, follow my lead. Rowan, Vine—prepare the diversion."

"Copy that," Rowan said. "We'll wait for your signal."

Aislinn gripped the chair harder, imagining the team slipping through the mansion's shadowed halls, searching for the supplies while Elder prepared to teleport them to safety. Every second felt razor-edged with risk.

"We're inside the perimeter," Riichi confirmed, his tone measured yet tense. "No sign of an earthquake device. Moving to the supply room."

Aislinn forced a slow exhale, catching Eileen's reassuring nod. *They've got this,* she reminded herself, though anxiety still fluttered in the pit of her stomach.

"Rowan, you're clear to start the diversion," Riichi instructed.

"Copy," Rowan responded evenly. "Vine, let's give them something to think about."

A distant rumble echoed through the radio, unmistakable in its intensity. Aislinn's stomach twisted. It was an explosion—Rowan and Vine's diversion had begun, drawing the Golden Dawn's forces away from the mansion.

"Ooh, did you hear that?" Vine's voice crackled through, his humor slipping back in. "Best sound in the world! Can we do it again, Rowan? Please?"

Eileen sighed, her expression caught between exasperation and resolve. "Focus, Vine."

"Don't worry, Eileen," Vine shot back, his tone light yet steady. "I'm laser-focused. Just... multitasking the fun in."

A few muffled chuckles broke the tension, a brief flicker of levity in the chaos. But it didn't last.

"We've got movement," Rowan's next update came, his voice urgent yet controlled. "They're coming our way. Stay on target."

"We're in the supply room," Riichi confirmed. "No earthquake device. Howard's team is securing what they can. Elder, stand by."

"Preparing the teleportation spell," Elder replied calmly. "Holly, stay close."

Aislinn leaned forward, her heart pounding as she imagined Howard's team loading the supplies as quickly as possible. Each second felt heavier, urgency thrumming in every breath.

"First load's out," Elder confirmed. "Preparing the second."

"Movement's still steady," Rowan added. "They're searching, but Vine and I are keeping them off your trail."

"Good," Riichi said. "Howard's team is moving the last load. Ready for extraction soon."

Aislinn exhaled slowly, her knuckles white as they gripped the edge of her chair. They were so close. *Just a little longer,* she urged herself, clinging to the hope that everything would end safely.

"We've got more incoming from the south," Rowan announced, his voice quickening. "We can't hold them off much longer."

Aislinn's pulse raced as Eileen's gaze flicked to the radio. Her usual calm was still there, but for the first time, Aislinn saw a flicker of unease. *Come on. Finish up...*

"We're done," Riichi confirmed. "Howard's team is moving out with the last load. Elder, teleport the final stockpile."

"Already done," Elder replied. "Final load is out. Howard's team is en route to extraction."

Through the faint static, Aislinn could hear hurried footsteps and clipped commands. It was almost over. The tension began to ease as realization struck—they were pulling back.

"Rowan, Vine," Riichi called, "start the retreat. We're done here."

Rowan's response was swift, his voice carrying both relief and urgency. "Copy. Heading to rendezvous."

The transmitter's low hum filled the room, a constant beneath Aislinn's uneven breaths. Her chest loosened as a wave of relief seeped in. They'd done it. The mission was a success. The Golden Dawn hadn't stopped them.

"They're on their way back," Eileen said, her calm composure unshaken. "It went exactly as planned."

For the briefest instant, Aislinn allowed herself to believe it, letting a flicker of peace settle in. But unease prickled at the edges of her thoughts, coiling beneath her relief. This wasn't over. It felt like the calm before a tempest, the kind that promised a far greater threat.

The radio crackled, pulling her from her thoughts. Rowan's voice came through, steady but laced with exhaustion. "Heading to the meetup now. Won't be long."

Vine's response followed, irreverent as ever. "Took you long enough to catch up. Still distracted from that kiss?"

Aislinn flushed despite herself, a faint laugh slipping free, but the warmth dissolved as sharp static crackled through the radio. The silence that followed was taut, charged with something electric.

"What the—" Vine's startled exclamation snapped out, low and urgent. "Rowan. Ahead."

Aislinn's stomach twisted, her pulse spiking. *Ahead? What's happening?*

Then came Rowan's reply, cold and sharp, a single name cutting through the static: "Lucifer."

Her blood turned to ice. Her grip tightened on the edge of the table, knuckles whitening. *Lucifer.* The name hit her like a hammer, dredging up memories of the café—his cryptic warning, the explosion. He'd been watching, waiting. And now, here he was, standing in front of Rowan and Vine.

"What are you doing here?" Rowan demanded, his voice taut with barely restrained fury.

Lucifer's reply slithered through the transmitter, mocking and lazy. "That's no way to greet an old friend, is it? As for why I'm here... well, that's for me to know and you to find out."

Vine's irritation cut through the tension. "Great. Riddles. Real mature."

Aislinn's heart thundered, her body frozen in place. Her fingers dug into the wood of the table, nails biting deep as she strained to listen.

"What do you want with Aislinn?" Rowan demanded, his fury simmering just beneath the surface.

A long silence followed. Aislinn's breath hitched, her chest tightening as she braced for Lucifer's response.

When he finally spoke, his voice dripped with cruelty, each word a knife. "Ah, Aislinn... She really should have listened when I told her to stay quiet. But she didn't, did she? So I had to teach her a lesson."

The memory of the explosion ripped through her like a physical blow, his words slicing open wounds she hadn't realized were still raw. *He'd caused it.* He'd been watching her all along. Ice spread through her veins, dread rooting her to the spot.

Rowan's next words were edged with suspicion. "Are you working with the Golden Dawn?"

Lucifer's laugh echoed darkly, hollow and sharp. "The Golden Dawn? They're nothing more than my pawns in a larger game."

Vine's sarcasm followed, breaking the eerie quiet. "Another grand plan to 'save the world'?"

Lucifer's tone shifted, soft but menacing. "On the contrary—I'm here to destroy it."

Aislinn's breath caught as Lucifer's mocking challenge grew almost playful. "Enough questions, Rowan. Let's see what Aislinn can do, shall we?"

Panic surged, icy and all-consuming. Her hands trembled, gripping the table as the helplessness closed in. *No. Please, no.*

The radio erupted in violent static, and Vine's panicked shout tore through. "He's got a spear! Rowan, MOVE!"

Her mind filled with the image—Rowan standing defiant, Lucifer's cruel smile taunting him. Her pulse roared in her ears as every muscle in her body strained against her powerlessness.

Lucifer's voice followed, dripping with amusement. "What's wrong, Rowan? You look... distracted."

Her nails carved into the table, her breaths shallow and rapid. *Move. Move!* Her mind screamed the silent plea, willing Rowan to dodge, to fight back, to survive.

Then Rowan's shout broke through—raw and hoarse. "Vine, look out!"

The radio cut to silence. Heavy, unbearable silence.

A sickening thud followed, and then Rowan's scream—a sound so raw it tore through her like shards of glass.

The world tilted as Aislinn shot out of her chair, her own scream breaking free, desperate and trembling. "ROWAN!"

Her body gave out, trembling violently, as Eileen caught her before she collapsed. *No, no, no... this can't be happening!*

Vine's frantic response tore through the static. "He's down! Rowan is down! We need help!"

The door slammed open, Oak storming in, his face hardening at the sight of Aislinn's panic-stricken expression. "What's going on?"

"Man down!" Eileen barked, her voice cutting through the chaos with commanding clarity. "Prepare a room, Oak!"

The radio erupted with overlapping commands and urgent responses. Aislinn clung to Eileen's arms, her breaths uneven, dread wrapping itself around her like a vice.

"Elder!" Riichi's sharp directive came over the static. "Assist now!"

"On it," Elder responded, his words tight with strain. "I can slow the bleeding, but we need to act fast."

Dark spots crept into Aislinn's vision. Her heart raced erratically, each beat twisting in her chest like a blade. *Rowan. I have to see him. Please.*

The walls pressed in, her breaths shallow and fragmented. Her mind screamed his name, panic consuming every thought. *Don't take him. Please don't take him.*

"Breathe, Aislinn," Eileen urged, her voice firm and steady. "Look at me. Breathe."

But the command felt impossible. The room tilted, Rowan's scream echoing over and over in her head. *He can't be… No.*

Eileen's grip firmed on her arms. "Aislinn, focus. I'm right here."

The image of Rowan—helpless, bleeding—refused to leave her mind. She barely registered Riichi's next orders, his voice slicing through her haze.

"Holly, get Howard's team into the truck and drive to their location. Reed and I will meet you."

"I'm on it," Holly replied, her tension palpable.

Aislinn's hands shook violently, her vision blurring as she spiraled deeper into panic. *Rowan. I need him. I need to be with him.*

"Cut the mics!" Riichi's command rang out sharply. "Eileen, we've got this. Shut it down. Now!"

Eileen moved swiftly, flipping the transmitter off with firm precision. The silence hit hard, broken only by Aislinn's ragged, uneven breaths.

Eileen knelt beside her, her hands steady on Aislinn's trembling shoulders. "Stay with me, Aislinn," she said, her voice calm yet resolute. "We're going to help him. But I need you to breathe."

Aislinn fought to steady herself, her breaths shallow and jagged. Her mind clung desperately to one thought, looping through the darkness:

Please don't take him from me.

Aislinn clung to her mother as if letting go would unravel her entirely, her breaths sharp and uneven. She whispered Rowan's name over and over, a fragile lifeline anchoring her to hope. Each time, she poured every ounce of will into it, a silent plea that he'd hear, that he'd know she was waiting—that she needed him to return.

The silence pressed back, unyielding.

Eileen's arms tightened around her daughter, strengthening her as the storm inside Aislinn surged. Her heartbeat hammered, a frantic rhythm of fear and love tangled so tightly it left her gasping for air.

Hurried footsteps cut through the stillness, echoing up the stairs, their clipped urgency unmistakable. The team had returned.

Aislinn's head snapped up, her body tensing. Those sounds could mean only one thing—they were carrying Rowan. He wasn't walking. He wasn't speaking. A crushing weight settled on her chest, making it hard to breathe. Straining against her mother's hold, she begged, desperate to see him. To know.

"Let go," she pleaded, her voice splintering with panic. She pushed against Eileen's arms, her trembling hands frantic. "Mom, I need to see him. Please!"

Eileen's grip remained firm, though worry flickered beneath the surface of her carefully measured expression. "Aislinn," she said, her tone low, steady—but unnervingly controlled. "Let them bring him inside first. You can't be in the way."

"I don't care!" Aislinn choked out, her sobs breaking through in waves. She thrashed now, desperation spilling out in raw, uncontainable force. "I need to see him—let me go!"

Eileen's composure held, but her voice carried a faint tremor. "Listen to me, Aislinn. You need to breathe. For him. He'll need you strong."

The words landed like a jolt, freezing her struggle. For him. Her chest hitched, and the storm inside her faltered for a brief, fragile moment. She shut her eyes, gripping the thought as though it might hold her together. *He needs me calm. He needs me focused.*

The chaos ebbed—slowly, unwillingly—but it ebbed. Aislinn dragged in a breath, each one shaky but deliberate. Her hands trembled as she forced herself to steady, her thoughts narrowing to a single purpose: *Rowan needs me.*

Eileen glanced through the narrow crack in the doorway, her gaze flicking to the far end of the hall where Oak stood, his expression grim and shadowed with unspoken concern. Their eyes met, and Oak gave a single, resolute nod. Whatever they had feared, it wasn't the worst.

Eileen exhaled softly, a barely audible release, before loosening her hold on Aislinn. "Go," she murmured, her voice hushed yet purposeful.

The second her mother's hands released her, Aislinn bolted. Her feet flew down the hall, urgency drowning out everything—her pounding heart, the clawing *what-ifs* swirling in her mind. She had to see him.

She stopped abruptly in the doorway, her breath catching at the sight before her.

The room thrummed with a charged stillness, every movement sharp and purposeful. Rowan lay sprawled on the bed, his shirt torn open to reveal a jagged wound in his shoulder. A spear protruded from it, radiating dark, pulsing magic. The weapon hummed faintly, malevolent energy rippling outward in waves. The skin around the wound was blackened and decaying, jagged veins of corruption snaking across his body like tendrils of poison.

Holly knelt at Rowan's side, her hands slick with blood as she worked frantically to stem the bleeding. Elder hovered nearby, his expression grim, his attention flicking repeatedly to the spear. At the foot of the bed, Vine stood frozen, pale and shaken, his usual composure unraveled.

Aislinn's stomach twisted violently. Her nails dug into her palms as she stood rooted to the spot, unable to move. *This isn't how it was supposed to be. He wasn't supposed to be hurt.*

Rowan stirred faintly, his face ashen, tight with pain. His breaths were shallow, uneven, and a grimace flickered across his features as agony rippled through him. Then, as if sensing her presence, his gaze lifted.

"Aislinn..." he murmured, his tone faint but carrying a fragile relief.

That was all it took. She stumbled forward, dropping to her knees beside the bed. Holly shifted without a word, making space, but Aislinn barely noticed.

Rowan managed the barest hint of a smile, weak and fleeting, as his hand trembled upward to brush her cheek. "I told you I'd be right back," he rasped, his words a fragile echo of his usual warmth. His fingers, trembling and light, traced her skin. "It's going to be okay."

Fresh tears filled her eyes, spilling over as she clung to his hand. It was so like him—offering her comfort, even now, even as pain visibly drained the color from his face. Her heart ached, a sharp collision of love and helplessness threatening to consume her. *He should be the one comforted, not me.*

"I'm sorry," Vine said, his voice breaking, laden with guilt. "Lucifer... he aimed the spear at me. Rowan—he jumped in the way. It should have been me... I'm so sorry."

The apology barely registered. Aislinn's focus had narrowed to Rowan—his shallow breaths, the jagged wound spreading its poison like a living thing through his body.

Her attention dropped to the spear, its malevolent energy radiating in sickly pulses. Twisted veins of corruption snaked outward, carving dark paths along his skin. Her chest tightened, fear coiling inside her like a vice. *This thing is killing him.*

Without thinking, she reached out, her hand trembling as it hovered over the weapon. She had no idea what she could do—whether touching it might heal or harm—but standing idle felt unbearable. Her fingers hesitated, lingering over the jagged spearhead. *What if I make it worse?* The thought gnawed at her, but the alternative—to do nothing—was worse.

As her hand inched closer to the spear, a strange sensation stirred beneath her skin. A faint tingling spread through her fingertips, like brushing against static. Then, faint at first, a glow began to emanate from her palm. It was warm and blue, like Rowan's eyes, pulsing softly, growing brighter with each beat of her heart.

Aislinn froze, her breath catching as the light enveloped her hand. Its warmth seeped into her skin, unfamiliar yet reassuring. She didn't understand it—this wasn't an action she had ever taken before—but it felt natural, as though a part of her she never knew existed had awakened for this moment.

Before anyone could react, the spear shuddered. Its dark magic writhed, resisting her touch, but under the glow of her hand, it began to dissolve, disintegrating into thin wisps of smoke that evaporated into the air.

The room seemed to hold its breath.

Aislinn's gaze snapped to Rowan's shoulder. The jagged wound was healing. The veins of corruption receded, retreating like shadows chased by light. The blackened edges faded, leaving unmarked, healthy skin in their wake. The glow lingered a minute longer before fading, its warmth dissipating as quickly as it had come.

Silence blanketed the room, disbelief hanging heavy in the air. No one moved.

Rowan's breathing steadied, his features softening as the tension melted from his face. He let out a small, uneven sigh, and his lips curved faintly, forming the ghost of a smile. "Looks like I'm not going anywhere," he murmured, his voice rasping but firm despite his exhaustion. His eyelids fluttered shut as unconsciousness pulled him under, leaving his expression peaceful.

Elder was the first to react, moving with measured precision. His fingers pressed against Rowan's wrist, his expression a mix of awe and curiosity as he assessed the injured Fallen. "His vitals are stabilizing," he said, his hand hovering above Rowan's chest. "He's going to be alright."

Aislinn's shoulders sagged as relief surged through her, a tidal wave crashing against the fear that had rooted so deeply inside her. Her body felt weightless and heavy all at once as her head dipped to rest gently against

Rowan's chest. Tears spilled freely now, unrestrained. He was safe. That was all that mattered.

The glow that had encased her hand faded, its warmth disappearing as swiftly as it had come. She didn't dwell on it—the strange power, the unexpected magic. None of it mattered right now. *Rowan was here. He wasn't leaving her.*

From the doorway, Eileen and Oak exchanged a glance, their expressions unreadable but steeped in unspoken understanding. Slowly, Eileen began guiding the others out of the room, her hand briefly resting on Vine's shoulder as he lingered, guilt etched into every line of his face.

"I'll need a full report," she said quietly, her voice carrying a quiet authority. "You were the only one there."

Vine nodded, the motion stiff, mechanical. His gaze lingered on Rowan for a passing second longer before he turned and followed the others.

Eileen closed the door with care, her hand pausing on the knob, fingers tightening as if bracing against an invisible force. She and Oak walked in silence down the hallway, their measured steps doing little to dispel the simmering tension. Lucifer's sudden reappearance after centuries wasn't chance—it was calculated. *Every move is deliberate. He's always several steps ahead.*

By the time they reached the communications room, Eileen paused at the threshold, her fingers brushing the doorframe as she glanced back at Oak. With a small nod, she signaled him to follow.

The hum of the equipment filled the enclosed space, relentless, sharp against the quiet. It clashed with the storm raging in her thoughts. Eileen leaned against the edge of the central table, crossing her arms as her gaze swept over the glowing monitors without truly seeing them. *Lucifer's game has begun—and we're pieces on the board. But why now? Why Aislinn?*

Oak stood across from her, his posture deceptively at ease, though his focus remained razor-sharp as he studied her every move, every nuance. He didn't yet know the full scope of what they faced, but Eileen could see he understood the weight of what lay ahead.

Breaking the silence, her voice emerged low, clipped with urgency. "Lucifer wasn't just here to attack. He's probing for weaknesses—especially theirs. Rowan and Aislinn... he's testing them."

Oak's brow furrowed, his arms falling to his sides. "You think this is about their connection?"

Eileen inclined her head slowly. So much remained unspoken—layers of truth Oak wasn't ready to hear. The intricacies of soulmates, the power their bond could wield. But she had to offer enough to make him understand the threat.

"It's more than that," she said, her words firm yet thoughtful. "Lucifer knows something about Aislinn that we don't. And Rowan's bond with her... it goes deeper than duty. Lucifer sees it, and he's trying to twist it."

A firm knock at the door broke the silence, cutting through the room like a blade. Eileen straightened, her composure snapping into place with precision. "Come in."

The door creaked open, revealing Vine. His usual confidence was stripped away, his shoulders bearing the weight of what he had witnessed. Still, he held himself upright, his expression hardened as he nodded to both Eileen and Oak.

"Vine, step forward," Eileen instructed, gesturing toward the spot across from her. "Tell us what happened."

Vine drew in a deep breath, steadying himself. When he spoke, the usual humor in his tone was gone, replaced by a solemn edge. "We were ambushed. Lucifer appeared out of nowhere—no warning, no sign. One moment, everything was clear, and the next, he was just... there."

Oak's jaw clenched, his attention sharpening as he absorbed Vine's words.

"Rowan tried to get answers," Vine continued, his frustration slipping into his voice. "Asked why Lucifer was so interested in Aislinn. But he didn't even acknowledge the question, like it wasn't worth answering."

Eileen's expression darkened, her lips pressing into a thin line. Lucifer's silence wasn't dismissive—it was calculated. Every move of his was a premeditated piece of a larger strategy.

"Then Rowan asked if he was working with the Golden Dawn," Vine added, his hands curling into fists at his sides. "Lucifer just laughed—called them his 'playthings.' Said they're insignificant to him. He's got his own agenda."

Eileen's fingers tapped lightly on the table, her gaze narrowing as she pieced together the implications. *The Golden Dawn is a distraction. His true goal is far more dangerous.*

Vine hesitated, his expression hardening before a flicker of his usual sarcasm surfaced. "I tried to lighten the mood. Asked if this was one of those 'save the world' schemes, you know, to get him talking." He paused, his voice growing heavier. "Lucifer didn't even blink. Just said, 'On the contrary, I'm here to destroy it.'"

Oak's fists clenched, his stance rigid. He repeated the words under his breath, weighing their meaning. "Destroy it." His tone carried a quiet realization. "Aislinn is part of something much bigger."

Eileen's thoughts raced, fragments of information fitting together in a pattern she couldn't ignore. *Destruction, not domination. He doesn't want control—he wants the end of everything. And somehow, Aislinn and Rowan are at the center of it.*

Vine's voice dropped lower. "Rowan asked again—why Aislinn. Lucifer ignored him at first. Then he said, 'Let's see what Aislinn can do, shall we?'"

Eileen's stomach turned, a chill coiling inside her. *He knew. He's known all along. This wasn't an ambush—it was a test.*

Vine's jaw tightened as he pushed on. "That's when he summoned the spear. He aimed it at Rowan first. Then at the last second, he shifted—and threw it at me."

Oak's expression hardened, fury flashing behind his measured exterior.

"Rowan..." Vine's voice cracked slightly, but he forced the words out. "Rowan jumped in front. He took the hit for me."

A pang rippled through Eileen's chest, though her expression remained calm. *Rowan—always the shield. Always the one to sacrifice. He would never let anyone else take the fall.*

"Before I could draw my sai," Vine continued bitterly, frustration breaking through, "Lucifer vanished. Just... gone. Like he'd never been there."

The room fell into a tense silence, the weight of Vine's recounting hanging in the air. Eileen's thoughts churned, pulling apart the fragments of the encounter. One truth stood above all else: Lucifer wasn't merely toying with the Golden Dawn. He was orchestrating a plan far more dangerous—a scheme with Aislinn inexplicably at its center. *This isn't random. Every move he makes is deliberate, part of a calculated design.*

Oak finally broke the silence, his tone steady, his focus unyielding. "Lucifer isn't just after Aislinn or Rowan. This is bigger than any single confrontation."

Eileen inclined her head, her thoughts clicking into place. *He's not simply testing their strength—it's something deeper. He's trying to break them.* "He's testing them both—Aislinn and Rowan. And it's not just about their strength."

Vine's hands balled into fists, his voice firm with resolve. "I'll make sure Rowan understands what he's up against. He took the hit for me—I owe him that much."

Eileen's gaze softened briefly, and she gave a small nod. "Thank you, Vine."

As he turned to leave, Eileen called out again, her tone steady but threaded with an undertone of empathy. "Vine."

He paused, glancing back, his shoulders rigid.

"Rowan made his choice," she said, her words measured. "You're not responsible for what happened. But we need you focused—completely—for what's coming."

Vine hesitated, the weight of her words settling over him. After a beat, he gave a curt nod before slipping out, leaving a faint unease lingering in the room.

The silence grew heavier, amplifying the weight of what was left unsaid. Eileen stood motionless, her fingers brushing lightly against the edge of the table as she stared at the closed door. Oak, standing nearby, watched her intently, his posture unmoving while his focus remained unyielding. He could sense there was more behind this than Vine's report had revealed.

Eileen turned to Oak, her expression carefully guarded as she weighed her next words. Though Oak was her most trusted confidant, certain truths about the Fallen's history weren't ready to be shared. *Not yet. Not until I know for certain what we're facing.*

"Oak," she began, her tone cautious and precise, "this wasn't just an ambush. Lucifer isn't targeting Aislinn solely because of her abilities—there's something about her bond with Rowan that he's determined to disrupt."

Oak's brow furrowed, his silence urging her to continue.

"For the Fallen," she said slowly, choosing each word carefully, "certain connections can alter the course of redemption. Rowan's bond with Aislinn... it's deeper than duty. And Lucifer knows that—it's exactly what he's trying to exploit."

Oak's jaw tightened, the tension in his stance reflecting the gravity of her words. He understood there was more to the bond than Eileen was sharing, but he trusted her judgment and didn't press her further.

"Whatever Lucifer's ultimate goal is," Eileen continued, the urgency in her voice rising, "it's not about Aislinn's abilities or even the Golden Dawn. It's a threat far greater, one that places both Aislinn and Rowan in serious danger."

Oak straightened, his resolve clear in every line of his stance. "Then we'll protect them. If Lucifer is targeting their bond, we won't give him another chance to exploit it."

Eileen nodded, her thoughts already moving ahead. *We'll have to stay vigilant. Every decision matters now.* "Exactly. We need to keep a close watch on them—no oversights. Especially now."

For a brief span, her expression softened as she looked at Oak. The weight of leadership pressed heavily on her, but her focus remained steady. "None of us saw this coming, but Rowan and Aislinn are in far greater danger than we realized. We need to be prepared for whatever Lucifer's next move might be."

Oak's features hardened with determination. "I'll make sure they're both protected. Whatever it takes."

Eileen met his eyes, her own gaze mirroring the gravity of the moment. "Good. Time isn't on our side. Lucifer could strike again sooner than we expect, and we can't afford to be caught unprepared."

Oak's focus sharpened further, his voice resolute. "We'll be ready."

Eileen gave a small nod. "We'll need every resource we can gather. Thank you, Oak."

They stood in silence for a heartbeat, the weight of their conversation pressing between them. Beneath the pressure, however, Eileen felt a determination settle into place. *Lucifer has made his move. Now it's ours.*

Across the hall, Aislinn sat amidst the quiet, her heart pounding in the suffocating stillness. The chaos of moments ago had faded, leaving a silence so heavy it seemed to press against her from all sides. The world felt different—shifted in a way she couldn't yet grasp.

Kneeling beside Rowan, her fingers hovered uncertainly over his shoulder, the place where her power had surged to heal him. She hesitated, unsure if she should touch him, yet the pull of closeness outweighed her uncertainty. Her pulse raced, the torrent of emotions settling into a knot she couldn't untangle.

Rowan lay motionless, his face pale and drawn, but his breathing was even. She hadn't left his side since collapsing onto him in relief, clinging to the one truth that mattered: he was alive. Now, the cold floor beneath her knees seeped into her body, a sharp reminder of her physical limits. Slowly, cautiously, she shifted onto the bed beside him, curling close. Her fingers brushed his hand, seeking connection, even if he couldn't feel it.

Drawing a shaky breath, her mind replayed the events. Her power—something she hadn't even known she possessed—had risen at the time she needed it most. She had saved him. Somehow, without understanding how, she had saved him. The memory of her hand glowing, the warmth coursing through her as the spear dissolved into nothing, played over and over in her head. *I didn't think. I just... acted.*

Her gaze lingered on his face, pale but peaceful. The rhythm of his breaths settled her, bringing her back to the last conversation she'd had with her mother. That was when she had finally admitted the truth she'd held inside for so long. *I love him.* Saying the words aloud had felt like breaking a dam, but now, with him lying so still beside her, she understood their depth. This wasn't just love—it was a promise, an unshakable resolve to protect him as fiercely as he had always protected her.

As her determination solidified, an icy thought crept in, piercing and unrelenting: *What if I hadn't been able to save him?* The question twisted her stomach, sharp and unforgiving. *What if my powers had failed?* Her fingers tightened around his, the warmth of his skin grounding her, a quiet reassurance that he was still here. But the doubts didn't relent. *What does this power mean—for me? For us? Where did it come from? And what will it demand of me the next time?*

Fear began to coil at the edges of her mind. Could she control it? Or had it been a fleeting spark, one that might fail her when she needed it most? Her chest constricted with another thought, one that struck deeper: *What if this changes things between us?* Her eyes roamed his face, tracing every line, memorizing him. *Will he see me differently? Will I see myself differently?*

The weight of how close she had come to losing him hit her again, stealing the air from her lungs. Tears burned at the corners of her eyes, but she forced them back, refusing to surrender to the fear. Leaning closer, her voice trembled as she whispered, "I love you."

Her words wavered, but the truth didn't. She hadn't been able to say it before, but now, the need to let it out was overpowering. She didn't know if he could hear her, or if she would have another chance, but the words needed to be said.

Her hand shook as she brushed her fingers lightly across his knuckles, tethering herself in the present. For just a heartbeat, she let herself imagine what it would be like when he woke. *Will he understand? Will he share my fears? Or will he reassure me, like he always does, with that quiet strength of his?*

She exhaled slowly, her chest tight with the weight of unspoken emotions. The uncertainties ahead loomed like storm clouds, but one thing remained certain: she couldn't lose him. Not now. Not after realizing how deeply she cared for him.

Closing her eyes, she rested her forehead gently against his arm, letting the faint warmth of his body soothe the lingering fear within her. Whatever came next, she would face it head-on. She didn't know what this new power would mean for their future, but she was ready to learn—ready to embrace it, if that's what it took to keep him safe.

Rowan stirred as if sensing her presence. His eyelids fluttered, the movement slow and unsteady, before they finally opened. His gaze wandered briefly, unfocused, as he took in his surroundings. Then his eyes found hers.

Aislinn sat up, her breath catching as awareness returned to him. She hadn't realized she'd been holding it in. Their eyes met, and relief surged through her, sweeping away the remnants of fear. He was here. He was safe.

Rowan blinked, his features softening as he registered her by his side. Despite the ache that pulsed through his body, her presence soothed something raw and restless deep within him. There was tenderness in her expression, but beyond that, he saw more: relief, vulnerability, and a strength that struck him with quiet force.

He shifted slightly, testing his limits. His body felt weak, but it was enough to remind him that he was alive. Grateful to be alive. Grateful to be here—with her. Aislinn's hand rested lightly over his, keeping him in the moment. For the first time, he let himself feel the truth he had long kept hidden. *I love her.*

It wasn't about duty or an obligation to protect her. It was deeper—a connection he couldn't explain, one that had grown steadily with every quiet moment, every unspoken understanding between them.

"Aislinn…" His voice cracked, hoarse with exhaustion, but her name felt like an anchor, steadying him. He wanted to say more, to tell her everything, but the way she looked at him said he didn't need to. Not yet.

Her fingers brushed his, tentative but unwavering, and she felt something shift within her. She had been so afraid to confront her feelings—afraid that admitting the truth would make it fragile, too real. But now, seeing him awake, feeling the strength of his hand beneath hers, she realized there was nothing to fear. Their bond was unshakable. It had always been there, waiting for her to recognize it.

Her heart swelled, and the weight of everything she hadn't said pressed down on her. She had come so close to losing him before she'd fully embraced what he meant to her. The thought stole her breath. Yet now, as his fingers curled faintly around hers, a quiet resolve settled over her. *I won't let go. Not now. Not ever.*

"You're awake," she murmured, her voice trembling despite her effort to stay calm.

Rowan offered a faint, tired smile. "I told you… I'm not going anywhere." His voice was weak, rough, but the certainty in his words resonated deeply.

Before, it had been a promise to survive. Now, it was more than that—a vow to stay, to face whatever came next by her side.

Her hand closed over his, and she whispered, thick with emotion, "I know. Neither am I."

An unspoken truth lingered between them, fragile yet undeniable. She had already admitted her feelings to herself, but the weight of them felt too immense to put into words. Instead, she shifted closer, resting her head lightly on the pillow beside him. She stayed close enough to feel the warmth of his breath and the gentle rhythm of his chest.

Rowan's eyes remained on her, unblinking. For the first time in years, a profound sense of peace settled over him. He had spent so long searching for redemption, carrying the burden of his past, but with Aislinn, that struggle seemed to dissolve. With her, he had found what he had never allowed himself to hope for: home.

Slowly, his fingers brushed hers, the movement faint but deliberate. His voice, though quiet, carried a certainty that sank deeply into her. "I'm not alone anymore."

Her heart skipped, the words striking with surprising intensity. She lifted her gaze to his, and in his eyes, she saw it: understanding, recognition, and a flicker of emotion—one that mirrored what she felt. They didn't need to speak further. Not now.

Aislinn's lips curved into a small smile, her breath trembling as she let the moment wash over her. She leaned closer, resting her head gently against his chest. The steady beat of his heart soothed the ache lingering in hers.

Rowan's hand moved to her back, the touch light yet certain. It wasn't just a gesture—it was a promise. Whatever lay ahead, they would face it side by side. Their bond, forged through trials and strengthened by trust, was now unbreakable.

For now, they let the stillness surround them, holding onto each other. In the quiet, they both understood what had been unspoken before: the challenges ahead would be inevitable, but they would meet them together.

Lucifer's shadow might loom on the horizon, but united, their light would endure.

The kitchen buzzed with energy as Ariel and Takoda set out the final dishes. Takoda moved with practiced grace, her hands deftly arranging the meal with a precision shaped by love and habit. Cooking was her anchor, a way to center herself amidst the chaos, and today was no exception. The table became a feast for both the senses and the palate—onigiri, tempura shrimp, sushi, stir-fried vegetables, and dango, each dish presented with care as though it belonged in a culinary dream.

Ariel, tasked with slicing oranges, glanced at her plate with a wry grin. Compared to Takoda's edible masterpiece, her contribution seemed almost comical. "Thank God for 24-hour grocery stores," she muttered, rearranging the orange slices. "That list you gave me felt like a blueprint for a covert mission."

Takoda's laugh surfaced as she dried her hands, satisfaction settling over her. "Cooking helps me focus," she said, although the fleeting glance she cast toward Riichi didn't escape notice.

"Uh-huh," Ariel teased, a spark of mischief lighting her features. "I'm guessing this dinner isn't just about thanking everyone for their support, is it?"

Takoda busied herself with the final dish, a small, knowing smile tugging at her lips. Ariel let the subject drop, choosing instead to savor the rare harmony of a shared meal. Watching the group come together after everything they'd endured felt like a balm—necessary, healing. They all needed this, and so did she.

The others began filtering in. Aislinn guided Rowan down the stairs, his arm looped over her shoulder as he leaned into her steadying support. His face was pale, but determination flickered in his expression.

"I'm not staying in bed while everyone else is down here," he'd insisted earlier, his words firm despite the strain in them. Aislinn had tried to argue, concern clear in her features, but eventually relented, helping him into a chair at the table. She stayed close, her presence an unspoken assurance, while his defiance underscored his strength.

With everyone seated, Ariel and Takoda made their final adjustments before Takoda claimed the chair beside Riichi. He had been watching her quietly, his attention carrying an almost reverent air. As she settled, he leaned closer, his tone calm and thoughtful. "Miss Takoda, did you really prepare all of this, or did you buy it?"

Takoda blinked, her surprise quickly giving way to mock indignation. "Buying pre-made? That's practically a crime. Of course, I made it."

Riichi's lips curved faintly, the sincerity in his words catching her off guard. "My apologies," he murmured. "I meant no offense."

Her posture softened, the hint of incredulity replaced by a warm smile. "It'd take more than that to upset me," she said, her amusement evident.

Riichi sampled the food, his reaction immediate as the rich flavors unfolded. It had been years since he'd tasted anything so fresh, so lovingly crafted. "Arigatō," he said, the gratitude slipping out naturally.

Takoda's response was seamless. "Dōitashimashite."

Startled, Riichi choked on his food, and Takoda instinctively reached out, patting his back with genuine concern. "Oh no! Did I overdo the spice?"

From across the table, Rowan chuckled. "I don't think it's the spice," he quipped, earning a round of laughter.

Beside him, Aislinn gave him a light nudge. "Don't tease," she said, concern flashing when Rowan flinched at the contact. "Oh no, are you okay?"

"I'm fine," Rowan assured her quickly, his tone softening as he waved off her worry. The moment shifted, laughter and teasing rippling across the table.

Eileen watched the scene unfold, her features relaxing into serene contentment. Across from Rowan, Reed raised his glass, his presence carrying an effortless warmth. "Good to have you back, Rowan."

The room settled into a steady rhythm, the conversation flowing naturally alongside the laughter. In this rare reprieve, they felt less like warriors and more like family, bound not just by duty but by trust woven deep into their shared experiences.

Ariel leaned back, letting herself bask in the gathering's energy. The closeness filled the room, stirring a raw ache within her. The laughter, the connection—it tugged at a part of her she rarely acknowledged. Before the feeling could take root, she slipped from her chair and quietly stepped outside, hoping no one had noticed.

Yet Aislinn had. She touched Rowan's arm briefly, her focus shifting to Ariel's retreat. "I'll be right back," she murmured, her reassurance firm as she followed her friend.

Ariel perched on the low cement wall just outside the door, her head tipped back toward the midday sky, lids closed as if drawing strength from the sun's warmth. The heat brushed her skin, yet it did little to ease the tight knot coiled within her. The hum of conversation and laughter drifting from inside only deepened the ache she had spent so long suppressing.

Aislinn stepped outside, spotting Ariel immediately. The mask of carefree ease Ariel so often wore had slipped, her posture revealing the turmoil beneath. "Everything okay?" Aislinn asked as she approached, her question casual yet tinged with subtle concern.

Ariel didn't open her eyes, a faint smile tugging at the corner of her mouth. "Yeah, just soaking up some sun. Vitamin D and all that," she quipped, her attempt at humor thin, almost hollow. The words hung in the air, their fragility betraying her effort to deflect.

Aislinn didn't buy it. Crossing her arms, she stepped closer. "Ariel, come on. What's really going on?"

For a long moment, Ariel said nothing, her silence stretching like a barrier. Aislinn wondered if she'd brush her off again. Finally, Ariel exhaled, her focus still on the sky. "It's just... seeing everyone in there, the way they laugh and joke like a real family. It got to me."

Aislinn waited, sensing more beneath the surface.

Ariel straightened, her fingers twisting restlessly in her lap. "My home life was... bad. Constant fights, walking on eggshells, trying to stay invisible. It was survival mode all the time." Her words faltered briefly, but she pushed on, steadier now. "I had to act like nothing could hurt me, like everything was fine—because if I didn't..." She shook her head sharply, as if banishing the memories. "It's stupid. But seeing all of you in there, so close—it's just... hard sometimes."

Aislinn felt her chest tighten. So that's why she always tries so hard to be the life of the party. Lowering herself onto the wall beside Ariel, she let the midday sun settle over them both. "It's not stupid," Aislinn said softly. "And you're not as much of an outsider as you think. Most of the people in that room have been through hell. They lost everything. That's what makes them Fallen."

Ariel blinked, turning toward Aislinn as if hearing this for the first time. "But they have each other. They've built something real."

"They've built it out of their own broken pieces," Aislinn replied, her tone steady. "And you fit right in with them. Your story makes you one of us."

Ariel glanced down, her fingers still fidgeting as she absorbed Aislinn's words. After a moment, a light, almost relieved laugh slipped from her. "Thanks. I guess I needed someone to call me out on my own crap."

Aislinn smiled, nudging her lightly. "Anytime."

The quiet that followed felt easy, unburdened by tension or unspoken thoughts. For the first time in days, Aislinn felt a measure of peace. Helping Ariel like this felt... right. Amid the supernatural chaos overtaking their lives, this was a rare simplicity, a purely human problem—one she could actually fix.

She nudged Ariel's shoulder again. "Sisters?"

Ariel's lips curved into a genuine smile. "Sisters."

They sat a while longer before finally standing and heading back inside. As they reentered, the lively energy of the room wrapped around them. Ariel slipped seamlessly back into her usual role, her quick wit and humor lighting up the space.

Oak caught her eye almost immediately. "Ariel, these are the best oranges I've ever tasted," he declared with exaggerated seriousness, drawing laughter from the table.

Ariel rolled her eyes, shaking her head. "Clearly, you've never had a decent fruit salad, Oak."

Aislinn caught Ariel's look—a fleeting but clear *I'm okay*—and smiled to herself, content knowing she had made a difference. For the first time in a long while, it felt like things were beginning to settle.

After the meal, camaraderie lingered as everyone pitched in to clean up. The clinking of dishes mixed with bursts of laughter as jokes and witty remarks flowed freely. Aislinn moved among the kitchen counters, rinsing plates while Rowan leaned against the counter, his expression thoughtful. He insisted he was fine, but the strain from the mission and the fire was plain to see.

She was about to ask how he was really feeling when Eileen's steady tone rose above the hum of activity. "You know," she began, her demeanor casual yet purposeful, "this might be the perfect time for a shopping trip."

Aislinn blinked. "Shopping?"

Eileen nodded, drying her hands with a dish towel as she stepped closer. "It's been a lot these past few days—missions, fires... everything. Taking a little time for ourselves might help us unwind. And," she added with a knowing glance, "you need to replace some things after the fire, don't you?"

Aislinn hesitated, the reminder of her lost belongings hitting her like a weight she hadn't yet acknowledged. Most of her clothes and essentials had been destroyed. Still, the idea of shopping felt strange, almost frivolous. "I'm not sure," she said, her attention shifting to Rowan as if seeking his opinion. Before he could answer, Eileen turned to Holly.

"Holly, you're coming along, right?" Eileen's suggestion was light yet left no room for debate.

Holly, wiping the counter, glanced up and caught the subtle exchange between Eileen and Rowan. "Of course," she said with a shrug, amusement flickering in her features.

Rowan considered the situation, his focus shifting between them. He didn't like the idea of Aislinn leaving his side, but with Eileen and Holly—both Fallen—he trusted they'd keep her safe. Besides, Eileen had a point: Aislinn needed new things. With a deep breath, he allowed a faint smile. "I think it's a good idea."

Aislinn frowned, caught off guard by his agreement. "You really think so?"

Rowan nodded, crossing his arms. "You could use a break, and you need new clothes. It'll be good for you." His tone softened. "And with Eileen and Holly, you'll be fine."

Aislinn bit her lip, her reluctance evident. Every time she left his side, it felt like disaster wasn't far behind. But with Rowan's approval, she couldn't refuse. "Alright," she said, the hesitation clear in her tone. "Shopping it is."

As the group tidied up, Reed spoke from across the room. "Anyone else notice Vine's been gone most of the day?"

The room paused briefly, glances exchanged. Rowan straightened, dread creeping into his frame. "Where is he?"

Reed shrugged, drying his hands. "He mentioned checking surveillance earlier. Wanted to look at the results from our last mission."

A ripple of unease moved through the group. Rowan's jaw tightened at the mention of surveillance. Vine had carried a heavy load of guilt since the mission, especially after Rowan had taken a hit meant for him. The last thing any of them wanted was for Vine's guilt to push him toward recklessness.

"You think he's alright?" Aislinn asked, her concern shifting to Rowan.

Reed attempted reassurance, but uncertainty laced his response. "He's probably just checking the perimeter. But you know Vine—he doesn't stay still when he feels responsible for something."

Rowan's expression darkened, worry flashing across his features. "We should go find him."

Eileen stepped forward, her approach decisive. "You boys can check on him. The girls and I will head to the shops." Her tone was even, but the authority behind it left no room for argument.

The decision came swiftly. Rowan exchanged a look with Aislinn, their unspoken connection clear. He didn't like being apart from her, but Vine's absence couldn't be ignored.

"Be careful," Aislinn said, her concern evident.

"You too," Rowan replied, his words low as he gave her hand a brief squeeze. Turning to Reed and the others, he said, "Let's find him before he does something reckless."

Aislinn watched as the men prepared to leave, unease twisting in her chest. But Eileen's touch on her arm drew her toward the door, and she forced herself to push the worry aside. *This is supposed to be a break—a chance to breathe. It'll be fine. It has to be.*

The streets thrummed with life as Aislinn walked alongside the women, sunlight glinting off the storefronts. The bustle of the scene offered a welcome contrast to the chaos of recent days, yet the worry lingered at the edges of her thoughts. She glanced at Eileen, who led the group with her usual poise, while Holly, Takoda, Rain, and Ariel followed behind, their chatter light but tinged with an undercurrent of stress.

"Let's focus on getting you what you need," Eileen said, her composed demeanor steadying. "A bit of normalcy will do us all some good."

***

At the same time, Rowan and the other men moved swiftly across the city streets, their strides determined. They had already checked several locations, each turning up empty. Vine had been gone for hours, and no one had heard from him. Concern tightened its grip on Rowan with every step, frustration simmering beneath the surface.

"We'll find him," Reed said, his focus darting to the alley they passed. His words felt more like an attempt to reassure himself than Rowan, and the uncertainty gnawed at Rowan's nerves.

***

Inside the boutique, Aislinn ran her fingers along the fabric of a blouse, the weight of her missing belongings pressing down on her. After the fire, nearly everything she owned had turned to ash. Now, she was here, trying to piece together fragments of what her life used to be. It felt strange—disconnected. Too soon.

Ariel held up a dress with a playful grin. "What about this one? Practical and cute. Total win."

Aislinn forced a small smile, her thoughts drifting back to Vine. Shopping felt hollow, a distraction from larger concerns. But she knew Ariel and the others were trying to help, so she nodded and took the dress. "Sure," she said, her tone lacking conviction. "It works."

***

The men arrived at another site—a rooftop where Vine had often set up surveillance. The view stretched across empty streets, offering no sign of him. Rowan's steps slowed, exhaustion beginning to drag at him. His body was still recovering from the mission, and the relentless search was taking its toll.

"Rowan, you need to rest," Reed said, his tone firm but laced with concern. "We'll keep looking. You're no good to anyone if you collapse."

Rowan hated to admit it, but Reed was right. His legs felt heavier with each step, and the unrelenting ache in his chest warned him he was pushing too far. Letting out a reluctant sigh, he nodded. "Fine. But call me the second you find him."

Riichi gave a sharp nod. "You have my word."

***

Back in the boutique, Holly joined Aislinn as she sorted through the racks. Her presence was calm, steadying. "How are you holding up?" she asked, her tone quiet, careful not to disrupt Aislinn's thoughts.

Aislinn sighed, her hand hovering over the sleeve of a jacket. "I don't know," she admitted. "I feel like I'm just... floating through all of this."

Holly nodded, understanding softening her expression. "That's how it is at first. But you'll find your footing. We all did."

Aislinn met Holly's calm gaze, the quiet reassurance in her words settling into her like a steadying hand. There were no quick solutions, no shortcuts to rebuilding her life. But maybe—just maybe—she could learn to move forward.

***

Rowan parted ways with the others, his thoughts circling back to Aislinn. Her loss weighed on him as much as Vine's absence. The need to protect her gnawed at him, a constant pull he couldn't shake.

His feet carried him to the remains of her café, the charred ruins stark against the skyline. The sight tugged at a deep ache within him, but he didn't stop. Picking his way through the debris, he scanned for anything salvageable—anything to remind her of what she hadn't lost.

***

In the shop, Takoda, Rain, and Ariel slipped into their usual rhythm. Takoda held up a blouse and skirt, giving Aislinn an encouraging look. "How about this combo? Functional and still nice."

Aislinn nodded absently, her thoughts wandering. She felt a flicker of relief seeing Takoda and Rain ease back into themselves, even briefly. They needed this moment of normalcy as much as she did. However, Vine's absence lingered, a shadow at the edges of their lighthearted conversation.

Eileen stepped closer, her tone low yet resolute. "You're doing well," she said. "This—this is part of rebuilding."

Aislinn glanced at her mother, her fingers brushing the fabric in her hands. The unspoken strain between them lingered, but Eileen's words carried a steady assurance. "Thanks," Aislinn replied, her tone softer than she intended. She wasn't sure she believed it yet—but maybe she could.

***

Back at the café, Rowan found what he was looking for. Half-buried under debris in the back, a small, charred box caught his attention. He carefully unearthed it, brushing away the soot. Inside were loose photos and a battered photo album, miraculously spared from the worst of the fire. As he flipped through the pages, relief washed over him. This was what Aislinn needed—a tangible reminder of who she had been before everything fell apart.

He moved to another room, pulling open drawers and sifting through the wreckage of Aislinn's life. Amid the debris, he found a few clothes, including the outfit she'd worn the day they first met. The fabric reeked of smoke, but it was intact, salvageable. Gathering everything in his arms, Rowan stepped out of the café, the weight of what he carried feeling lighter than the burden on his heart.

***

In the store, Ariel darted between racks, tossing playful remarks over her shoulder as she helped Rain pick out accessories. Her energy was infectious, drawing a faint smile from Aislinn as she watched. For a moment, it felt good—almost normal.

"Alright," Ariel declared, spinning to face Aislinn with a triumphant grin. "I think we've done enough damage here. Ready to check out?"

Aislinn nodded, her grip tightening on the shopping bag she carried. The distraction had helped, even if her thoughts still drifted to Vine. "Yeah, let's go."

***

Back at his apartment, Rowan worked methodically. He hand-washed Aislinn's clothes in the sink, scrubbing until the acrid scent of smoke began to lift. He hung them to dry, his thoughts never straying far from her. These small things—photos, clothes—were pieces of her life, fragments of what she had lost. She needed that, a sense of familiarity to keep her centered.

From his closet, Rowan pulled out an old wooden box he had crafted years ago in Ireland. The smooth grain bore faint, intricate carvings. It felt right, using it now. Carefully, he cleaned the loose photos and placed them inside, arranging everything with care. When he finished, he sent her a text: *Can you get dropped off at my place instead of the Airbnb?*

Her response came quickly. *Sure.*

***

As the men continued their search, the streets emptied, the hum of the city fading with the onset of night. Lead after lead ended in the same frustrating emptiness. Vine was still nowhere to be found.

"We'll pick this up tomorrow," Riichi said, his tone measured yet laced with exhaustion.

Reed nodded, his expression distant, betraying the tension lingering beneath the surface. "He's out there. We'll find him."

***

Back in his apartment, Rowan placed the neatly folded clothes in a basket and tucked the wooden box of photos into the closet. His gaze swept the room, finding a faint sense of order in the small space he had prepared for Aislinn. With Chinese takeout on the way, he sank into a chair, hoping tonight might bring a brief reprieve from the chaos swirling around them.

Aislinn stepped into the room just as the delivery arrived. The rich scent of warm food filled the air, but a strange knot tightened in her stomach. She couldn't tell if it stemmed from the weight of the day or the unspoken emotions hanging between them. The atmosphere felt different, heavier, as though this space carried a significance she wasn't ready to confront.

Rowan was setting containers on the table when he glanced up, his smile steady yet faint. For a second, an unreadable flicker crossed his features—a reflection of the unease curling inside her. "Perfect timing," he said.

She tried to return his smile, but her thoughts remained tangled in the grief of all she had lost. They sat together, the stillness broken only by the rustle of takeout bags and the soft click of chopsticks.

"You should stay here," Rowan said, breaking the silence. "At least until you find something more permanent."

Aislinn blinked. "Stay... here?" Doubts swirled in her mind. She couldn't even control her powers—what if she hurt him? What if he discovered she wasn't the person he believed she was?

Sensing her hesitation, Rowan added quickly, "No pressure. I just thought it might make things easier for you."

She studied him, her heart caught between a yearning for comfort and the sharp edge of fear. "What if I'm too much for you? What if I hurt you?"

"You won't," he said, his fingers brushing hers. "And even if you did, I wouldn't go anywhere."

His touch steadied her, and after a pause, she nodded. "Okay. I'll stay."

But even as she spoke, the ache of her losses resurfaced—her café, her home, her sense of normalcy. Pushing her plate aside, her words wavered. "I lost everything. And I feel like no one really understands what that's like."

Rowan's jaw tightened, his gaze hardening. Without a word, he pulled up his shirt, revealing a jagged scar cutting across his torso. "I know more about loss than you think," he said, his tone sharper than she had ever heard. "I've been living with it for almost two hundred years."

Aislinn's breath hitched, her focus drawn to the scar. Hesitantly, she reached out, her fingers brushing its uneven surface. "I... I didn't realize—" Her hand recoiled as her magic stirred, the urge to heal him rising unbidden.

Rowan jerked back, gripping her wrist with startling force. "DON'T!" His tone was sharp, almost panicked.

She froze, her pulse quickening. "I was just trying to help."

"I don't need your help," he said through clenched teeth. "It's not yours to fix."

"Why wouldn't you want to be healed?" she asked, her confusion and hurt spilling out.

"That scar..." Rowan's words trembled, his emotions barely contained. "It's all I have left of them. My past."

Aislinn hesitated, her hand trembling as her gaze lingered on the scar, the jagged line a stark reminder of Rowan's buried pain. The air between them felt charged, heavy with truths that had been held back for too long. And then, unbidden, the memory from her dream surged forward, crashing over her with an almost suffocating clarity.

She was back in that strange, haunting place. A sprawling tree loomed overhead, its twisted branches clawing at a twilight sky streaked with fading hues. The air pressed against her like a tangible weight, saturated with sorrow so deep it seemed to seep into her very being.

Before her stood a man—Rowan, but not. His features bore a haunting shadow, a grief that carved deeper lines into his face than those she had come to know. He was shattered, a figure of anguish held together by fraying threads of resolve.

Nearby, Eileen stood like a sentinel, her presence both commanding and solemn. She spoke to the man—Rowan, though he had called himself Aidan then—her tone low, weighted with meaning Aislinn couldn't hear but felt in the marrow of her bones. Blood dripped from his side, his hand clutching the wound as if it were the only thing keeping him tethered to the world. His spirit hung fractured, barely anchored to the desolate earth beneath his feet.

Aislinn felt bound to the scene, as though caught in its inescapable gravity. The man—Aidan—turned toward her for an instant, his eyes blazing with an anguish so raw it cut straight into her. The force of his pain reached out, pulling her in, threatening to drown her in the depths of his despair.

The memory snapped away like a rubber band, leaving her gasping, her heart pounding as though she were still standing beneath that mournful sky. She blinked, grounding herself in the present, but the name escaped her lips before she could stop it, cutting the air like a blade.

"Aidan..."

Rowan flinched, the name striking him with the force of a blow. His eyes locked onto hers, shock rippling through his features.

Aislinn stepped forward, her voice trembling. "I've seen you before... in a dream. The night before we met. You were standing by a tree. My mom... and I... I was there."

Rowan's jaw tightened, his expression hardening as the truth settled between them, undeniable and heavy. "Yes," he said, his words quiet but laced with a gravity that sent shivers down her spine. "You were there."

Her breath quickened. "How?"

"You crossed into that moment in your dreams. Time... it doesn't flow for us the way it does for others."

"Then why didn't you tell me?" she demanded, her voice cracking.

Rowan exhaled, the sound jagged, his control fraying at the edges. "I didn't realize until the night I blacked out. After everything, I didn't know how to explain it. I didn't want to overwhelm you."

Aislinn's eyes burned with unshed tears, her tone lowering to a whisper. "But you knew I was tied to your death. You knew, and you still kept it from me?"

"It wasn't about you," he said sharply, emotion roughening the edges of his words. "It was me. I didn't want to face it either. My death... it isn't just a moment in time. It's everything I lost. My family. My wife. Our child. I failed them, Aislinn." His words broke, trembling. "I was too proud to ask for help. Too ashamed to live with the guilt. That's why I ended it. That scar..." He touched the jagged mark on his torso, his hand shaking. "It's all I have left of that failure."

Aislinn felt her heart splinter under the weight of his words, his agony pressing down on her like a tidal wave. "Rowan..." she whispered, her tone trembling with raw emotion.

He shook his head, his gaze dropping to the floor as though he couldn't bear to meet hers. "I thought you'd see me differently. That you'd pity me."

"I don't pity you," she said, her voice fierce as she stepped closer. She cupped his face in her hands, forcing him to look at her. "I see you. And you don't have to carry this alone anymore."

His defenses crumbled under her touch, the walls he had spent centuries building collapsing in the face of her unwavering presence. "You're right," he murmured, his voice breaking. "I should've told you. I'm sorry."

Aislinn sighed, her frustration giving way to understanding. "I just wish you'd trusted me. I'm part of your world now, Rowan. No more secrets."

He nodded, the weight of her words sinking into him. "No more secrets."

Their gazes held, a maelstrom of emotions swirling between them. After a long pause, Aislinn nodded, her tone steady and resolute. "This won't break us."

Rowan's breath hitched, his hand brushing her cheek, his thumb tracing the curve of her face. "No, it won't. I won't let it."

She closed her eyes, leaning into him, her voice firm. "Neither will I."

His tone dropped to a whisper, hoarse with emotion. "I don't deserve you. How did I ever find someone like you?"

Her gaze met his, unwavering, her resolve shining through. "You deserve this, Rowan. You deserve us."

***

Back at the Airbnb, the atmosphere shifted the instant Vine stepped through the door. Relief rippled through the group, but it didn't last. One look at Vine's face, and the weight of his expression extinguished any sense of ease. His usual confidence had been replaced by a grim shadow that clung to his every step.

Riichi was the first to stand, his sharp focus already moving to his phone as he quickly texted Rowan: *Vine's back.*

Vine didn't waste a second. "I've been watching the Golden Dawn," he began, his tone steady but grim. "They're regrouping—faster than we expected."

Reed leaned forward, tension coiling in his posture. "How fast?"

"Too fast," Vine said, his brow furrowing deeply. "It's almost like they knew we were coming. They're reorganizing as if we never disrupted them at all."

The group exchanged uneasy glances. Their mission had been meant to cripple the Golden Dawn, but this news shattered those hopes.

Vine's expression darkened further, unease flickering across his features. "That's not the worst of it." His tone dipped, and the room grew still, every set of eyes locked on him. He scanned their faces, his next words deliberate and heavy. "Lucifer was there."

The name landed like a thunderclap, rippling through the room. Oak's shoulders stiffened, Reed's fists tightened, and Holly's expression hardened, her calm veneer replaced by an icy resolve.

"He didn't interfere," Vine continued, his cadence even, though a subtle strain laced his words. "He was just... watching from a distance. But he saw me. I know he saw me."

Elder's gaze sharpened, his tone low. "Saw you?"

Vine nodded, his pitch dropping further, as though the memory left a chill in its wake. "Yeah. He looked right at me—those red irises, that unnerving smile. And then, he vanished."

The room fell into an oppressive silence. Lucifer's presence wasn't just troubling—it was a warning. Everyone there understood the implications: Lucifer wasn't part of the Golden Dawn. He was something far worse.

Riichi's tone cut through the tension, calm but incisive. "Lucifer and the Golden Dawn aren't the same threat," he said, his words measured. "If he's watching, it means he has his own agenda."

Vine's jaw tightened, his hands curling into fists. "He's using the Golden Dawn like pawns. They're just pieces on his board, and he can move them however he wants."

"They're separate threats," Holly said, her arms crossed, her tone clipped. "But we'll have to face them both. Lucifer and the Golden Dawn... neither can be ignored."

"And it's worse than we thought," Vine added, the strain in his tone unmistakable. "Whatever they're planning, it's escalating. We need to be ready."

Reed's expression hardened, his words direct and resolute. "We can't sit around waiting for them to make the first move."

Riichi gave a sharp nod, his tone unwavering. "We regroup. Now. We need to be ready for whatever comes next."

Chapter Twenty
Awakening Forces

Aislinn stirred as morning light filtered through the curtains, brushing the room with muted gold. Disoriented, she blinked, suspended between the lingering pull of sleep and the quiet reality of waking. Then, the warmth of Rowan's arm draped around her waist anchored her, keeping her in the fragile peace of the moment. His breathing was even, his presence a reassuring constant after the storm of raw confessions and truths the night before. Now, wrapped in the calm of dawn, she felt a tentative lightness, as though the weight of the past had eased—if only slightly.

She shifted carefully, hoping not to disturb him, but Rowan stirred anyway, his eyes fluttering open. At first, he simply looked at her, his features softened in a way that always caught her off guard.

"Morning," she murmured, her speech rough with the remnants of sleep.

"Morning," he replied, his response low and unhurried, carrying the faint haze of dreams. He reached out, brushing a strand of hair from her face in a gesture so natural it seemed instinctive. A faint smile played at his lips, muted yet warm.

They were reluctant to stir, neither speaking, as if trying to preserve the brief reprieve the morning offered. But the moment shifted when Rowan sat up, his attention drifting toward the closet. Uncertainty flickered in his movements, subtle yet telling, as though he were weighing an unspoken decision.

"I have something for you," he said, his choice of phrasing deliberate, vulnerability breaking through his guarded demeanor.

"What is it?" she asked, curiosity sharpening her focus as the fog of sleep faded.

Rowan rose from the bed and crossed to the closet, pausing before reaching for a high shelf. His hand faltered at the edge, tension evident in the way his fingers hovered. Is this the right time? What if it only brings more pain? The thought settled heavily, but he pushed it aside, retrieving a small wooden box.

When he turned back, Aislinn's breath hitched at the sight of it. The box, aged but exquisitely crafted, bore intricate carvings that spoke of skill and care. He set it down between them with careful gentleness, the weight of the exchange reflected in the quiet precision of his actions.

"I managed to save a few things from your apartment," he said, his delivery considerate, each syllable carrying an edge of vulnerability. "And I thought... you should have this."

Her fingers traced the box's delicate patterns, her touch skimming over the faintly etched designs that hinted at Irish artistry. "You made this, didn't you?" she asked, wonder threading through her question. The craftsmanship—the knots in the wood, the precise carvings—echoed his heritage in ways he rarely shared.

He nodded, a faint, bittersweet smile tugging at his lips. "A long time ago. Back in Ireland. When I was human." His voice dipped, the memory stirring a hidden emotion to the surface. *I never thought I'd have a reason to keep this. But maybe it can mean something now.*

Aislinn's chest tightened as she lifted the lid. Inside were her photos, each one carefully cleaned and arranged. The gesture—so thoughtful, so selfless—left her momentarily speechless. She ran her fingers over the edges of the box, emotion catching in her throat.

Rowan watched her closely, uncertainty flickering in his features. *Does she understand how much this means? How much I need her to have this?*

"Why?" she asked, her voice uneven as she looked up at him. Her fingers lingered over the photos before meeting his hand. "Why give this to me?"

His focus didn't waver, though a rawness glimmered beneath his composed demeanor. "Because it matters. And... I want you to have something that reminds you not everything is gone."

Her vision blurred, tears welling as his response sank in. This wasn't just a gift—it was a bridge between what had been lost and what might still remain. Without thinking, she leaned forward, wrapping her arms around him. Her words trembled as they spilled out.

"Thank you," she whispered, her gratitude clear in every syllable. She held him tightly, finding solace in the strength he offered so freely.

They stayed that way briefly, the sunlight bathing them in a muted glow—a fleeting reminder that, even in the face of uncertainty, there was still hope.

But the day was already pressing forward.

Rowan shifted slightly, his hand resting lightly at the small of her back. "We need to get ready. The others are waiting."

Aislinn nodded, the weight of the day settling over her once more. The fragile peace of the morning had already begun to slip away. Yesterday had brought answers, but today demanded more. This won't stop. Not until we figure out what Lucifer wants. She pushed the thought aside, forcing herself to focus.

As they dressed and prepared to leave, the calm between them faded into unspoken tension. The future loomed, uncertain and precarious, and although they would face it together, the path ahead felt anything but clear.

They left Rowan's apartment in silence, the city beginning to stir to life around them. As Rowan drove toward the Airbnb where the Fallen had gathered, a heavy silence filled the car, thick with anticipation.

***

Inside the Airbnb, the kitchen buzzed with subdued activity. The Fallen were already assembled, waiting for Rowan and Aislinn to arrive. Eileen stood by the window, arms crossed, her focus fixed on the horizon. Her distant yet resolute demeanor hinted at thoughts she wouldn't share. Oak sat at the table, flipping through the brittle pages of an ancient tome, his brow furrowed as though wrestling with the secrets buried within. Holly and Elder leaned against the counters, their postures composed and purposeful, while Riichi and Reed exchanged low, urgent comments near the doorway.

Vine paced near the fridge, his usual calm replaced by visible agitation. He ran a hand over the back of his neck, muttering under his breath. *Why does it feel like we're always a step behind?* Forcing himself to stop, he crossed his arms, though the rigid set of his shoulders betrayed the frustration simmering beneath the surface.

"Rowan and Aislinn?" Eileen asked, breaking the subdued hum of the room. She turned toward Oak, her calm exterior underscored by subtle urgency.

"They're on their way," Oak murmured without glancing up from the tome. "I'll confirm." He rose and stepped into the hallway, pulling out his phone.

Eileen's focus lingered on the doorway before shifting to Holly. "And Takoda and Rain? They're safe here, right?"

"Yes," Eileen replied, her assurance firm. "They stay. The wards on this house will protect them, and we can't risk exposing them further. Lucifer saw them at the café fire—that makes them targets. They've been through enough."

Moments later, Takoda and Rain appeared in the doorway, their light steps drawing attention. Takoda's steady poise belied the exhaustion etched into her features, while Rain blinked groggily, still rubbing at her eyes.

"You're leaving again, aren't you?" Takoda asked, her words measured, frustration laced in her tone.

Eileen stepped closer, resting a hand on Takoda's shoulder in a gesture meant to reassure. "Yes, but you'll stay here. This is the safest place for you. The Fallen will ensure nothing happens to either of you. You've done enough." Her response softened. "We'll keep you updated as soon as we know more."

Takoda pressed her lips into a thin line, concern flashing briefly in her features. *They're protecting us, but it doesn't feel like enough. How can I just stand by while they face this?* The thought gnawed at her, but after a pause, she gave a reluctant nod. "Fine. Just don't shut us out."

Rain's hesitant question came quietly. "We'll be safe here?"

Eileen met her eyes directly, her conviction unwavering. "Yes. You've done nothing to bring this upon yourselves. We won't let anything happen to you. Rest now. You're safe."

The two women exchanged a glance before retreating toward the bedrooms. As they disappeared, Oak reentered the room, tucking his phone into his pocket.

"Rowan and Aislinn are on their way," he said, his reply clipped. "They'll be here soon."

The group instinctively gathered closer, the energy in the room shifting as the weight of their purpose settled over them. Eileen stepped forward, her presence commanding, the air around her carrying an intangible gravity.

"We need to determine why Lucifer is targeting Aislinn," she began, her delivery measured. "Time isn't on our side, and Vine's findings confirm that Lucifer has already positioned himself as a threat. If we're going to stop him, we need to understand his motives."

Holly tilted her head, skepticism flickering in her features. "Why Aislinn and not you, Eileen? You share the same bloodline, the same powers. Why isn't he coming after you?"

Eileen's composure remained intact, though her jaw tightened slightly before she replied. "It's not that simple. My abilities are too stable. I've spent centuries mastering them—Lucifer knows he can't manipulate me. Aislinn, on the other hand, is different. Her powers are raw, unrefined. That's what makes her dangerous to him—and to us."

And he knows better than to come after me directly. The unspoken truth lingered in her thoughts, a burden she carried silently. *They can't know what I really am. Not yet.*

Vine shifted his stance, locking his arms tightly across his chest. "So, he's after her because she hasn't learned to control her powers yet?"

Oak flipped a page in the tome, his finger tapping a marked passage. "It's more than that. According to these texts, Lucifer needs a Conduit of Prophecy to regain control over the archdemons. Aislinn's premonitions and healing abilities put her in his sights. But there's another layer we hadn't considered."

He looked toward Eileen, who gave him a solemn nod.

Oak continued, his voice low. "It's the bond between Aislinn and Rowan. That connection is amplifying her abilities."

The front door swung open, and Rowan and Aislinn stepped inside. Their gazes swept across the room, absorbing the heavy atmosphere that cloaked the Fallen. Rowan's posture tensed, a ripple of unease radiating from him, while Aislinn stayed close, a knot of anxiety twisting in her chest.

"Sorry we're late," Rowan said as they approached the group. Aislinn sank into a chair at the table, her movements careful, while Rowan remained standing nearby, his stance instinctively protective.

"What's going on?" Aislinn asked, her voice measured, though her fidgeting hands betrayed her unease.

Oak gestured to the book spread open on the table, its ancient pages worn thin with time. "We've been trying to figure out why Lucifer is targeting you, Aislinn."

Her pulse quickened as her gaze flicked to Rowan for reassurance. His shoulders tensed, but he gave a subtle nod, silently urging her to focus on Oak. "Okay," she said, though her voice wavered. "Why me?"

Eileen stepped forward, her words carrying an unusual gentleness. "Your powers are just beginning to emerge—your premonitions, your healing. But you're my daughter, and your lineage means those abilities are only the beginning. As you grow, so will your powers, in ways even I can't fully predict. Lucifer knows this, and he's coming for you because of it. Your abilities are raw and untrained, which makes you vulnerable to him."

Aislinn frowned, uncertainty clouding her features. "If that's true, then why me and not you? You're stronger—"

"It's not that simple," Eileen said quickly, her response sharp but even. "My abilities are stable, refined through centuries of control. Lucifer can't use me for his ritual. But you... your powers are still forming. That leaves you exposed. He believes he can manipulate them to serve his purpose. And your bond with Rowan is amplifying those powers."

Aislinn turned sharply toward Rowan, her heartbeat hammering in her chest. "Our bond?"

Oak nodded, his expression grim. "Yes. The connection between you two is significant. It's enhancing your abilities in ways we're only beginning to understand. Lucifer isn't just after you because of your powers—he's drawn to the bond you share with Rowan. He believes it holds the key to unlocking power beyond even what Eileen possesses."

Rowan's expression darkened, his hand instinctively finding Aislinn's shoulder. "So this is my fault?" he asked, frustration crackling in his tone. *Why does it feel like I'm only making this worse?*

Eileen stepped closer, her gaze steady. "No, Rowan. Lucifer would have gone after Aislinn regardless. Her powers are growing because of her heritage—he would have targeted her no matter what. But the bond between you two makes her abilities more potent, more threatening in his eyes. That's why he wants both of you. This isn't your fault."

Rowan exhaled sharply, guilt flickering across his face. "But I am making her a bigger target," he argued, his frustration bubbling to the surface. "How am I not supposed to blame myself for that?"

"You're making her stronger," Eileen countered, her voice softening as she stepped nearer. "The bond isn't just a vulnerability—it's a source of strength. It's giving Aislinn access to powers even I don't fully understand. Lucifer wants to exploit it, but it's also something we can use against him."

Aislinn reached for Rowan's hand, her grip firm despite the storm of unease swirling inside her. "We'll figure it out," she said, her tone quiet but steady.

Rowan's muscle twitched at his temple, his protective instincts sharpening. "So what's the plan? What do we do next?"

Eileen straightened, her expression resolute. "We don't have a choice but to bring Aislinn into this fully. She's no longer someone we can protect from the sidelines. She has to be part of the fight."

Rowan's response came instantly, his words edged with defiance. "She's not ready! She's untrained—"

"She's already involved, Rowan," Eileen said firmly, cutting him off. "Whether we like it or not, Aislinn is at the center of this. Lucifer won't stop coming for her, and leaving her unprepared is more dangerous than training her for what's ahead."

Aislinn swallowed hard, the weight of the conversation pressing down on her. *Can I really do this? What if I can't?*

Rowan crouched beside her, his voice low but unwavering. "You don't have to do this alone."

Eileen's demeanor softened, just enough for her words to land. "No one is asking you to face this alone, Aislinn. We're all here to help. But you can't avoid what's happening anymore."

Aislinn's hands clenched in her lap, apprehension rippling through her as fear and determination battled within. Eileen was right—there was no more running from this. She had to confront it, not just for herself but for everyone relying on her.

"I'll help," Aislinn said, her voice low but firm. "I want to help. I need to understand what's happening to me."

Rowan's grip on her shoulder steadied her, and after a minute, he nodded. Reluctance still showed in his expression, but his resolve was clear. "Then I'm with you. Wherever this leads."

Eileen turned to Oak. "You'll help Aislinn learn to control her powers. We need her ready as soon as possible."

Then, addressing the rest of the group, she continued, "Riichi, Reed, and Vine—focus on the Golden Dawn. They're desperate, and we need to stay ahead of their moves. Elder, Holly, and I will focus on deciphering Lucifer's ritual and identifying how their plans intersect."

Oak nodded, the weight of responsibility evident in his stance. He faced Aislinn, his tone steady and measured. "We'll start immediately. It won't be easy, but you'll get through this."

Aislinn exhaled slowly, the enormity of her situation settling over her. She was no longer just someone to protect—she was a target. And she needed to be ready for whatever lay ahead.

Vine stepped forward, his words sharp and focused. "Since the last mission, I've uncovered more about the Golden Dawn's movements. They've abandoned large-scale attacks—like the earthquake we stopped—and redirected all their efforts toward Aislinn."

Rowan frowned, skepticism crossing his face. "You figured all that out in one day?"

A faint smirk tugged at Vine's lips. "I'm good at what I do."

The hint of humor quickly faded as he continued, "The Golden Dawn is desperate. Their rituals are failing, and they're convinced Aislinn is their answer. Capturing her has become their top priority."

Riichi stepped forward, his tone calm yet decisive. "If they're concentrating everything on Aislinn, their strategy becomes more predictable. We can anticipate their moves, but their desperation will make them even more dangerous."

Reed crossed his arms, his expression grim. "Predictable doesn't mean safe. Desperation breeds recklessness, and reckless actions put all of us in danger."

Aislinn's pulse quickened, her gaze darting to Rowan. "But why? They don't even know what I can do."

"They don't need to," Vine said. "They've pieced together fragments of ancient magic. They believe you're the key to unlocking forces they can't access—forces that could grant them unimaginable power."

Eileen's brow furrowed, her tone weighted with urgency. "That recklessness makes them dangerous enough, but their unpredictability makes them even more of a threat. If they succeed, the consequences could be catastrophic—not just for you, Aislinn, but for the balance between realms."

Rowan straightened, his protective instincts sharpening. "Then we make sure they never get close to her."

Elder's calm, firm tone broke through the tension. "Do we know what their next move might be? Are we expecting an ambush, or could this be an attempt to mislead us?"

Vine's expression tightened. "It's hard to pin down. They've been scattering false leads to throw us off. But one thing's clear—they're preparing for a major move."

Riichi exchanged a glance with Reed before speaking again. "We'll need to stay coordinated. If they're spreading misinformation, they're trying to divide us. We won't let that happen."

Eileen nodded, her approval evident in the subtle shift of her expression. "Good. Stay on top of their movements. Report back the moment you find anything."

Vine gave a curt nod. "Understood. They won't catch us off guard."

Oak turned back to Aislinn, his voice steady. "The more control you gain over your powers, the harder it'll be for them to use you. We'll begin your training now."

Rowan's tone carried sharp resolve. "They won't get near her. Not while I'm here."

Eileen stepped closer to Aislinn, her expression softening just slightly. "We'll protect you, but you can't rely on us alone. This is about getting you ready. You're not on the sidelines anymore."

Aislinn squared her shoulders, a newfound determination settling over her. "Then let's get started. I want to be ready."

Eileen surveyed the group, her tone shifting. "Take a short break now, then start your tasks. We'll reconvene in two days to assess our progress and adjust as needed."

The tension in the room began to dissipate as the group dispersed. Aislinn gave a small nod, grateful for the brief reprieve even as the weight of her role loomed over her.

Rowan met her gaze, and without speaking, the two of them stepped outside into the wooded area behind the Airbnb. The crisp scent of pine mingled with damp earth, and the towering trees stretched skyward, their branches interwoven like ancient guardians of the forest. Shadows blanketed the earth, creating a sense of isolation as they ventured deeper, searching for a brief reprieve from the chaos.

The weight of the earlier conversations hung heavy between them, pressing down with each step. Neither broke the silence, allowing the rustling leaves and distant bird calls to fill the space. The forest offered solace, its stillness a stark contrast to the turmoil that followed them, though it couldn't erase the reality of what lay ahead.

Rowan walked slightly ahead, his movements measured, his shoulders taut with tension. Aislinn followed, her attention fixed on him, noting the weight he carried in the set of his posture. Since Vine's revelations about Lucifer and the Golden Dawn, a change had settled over him. He had grown more reserved, his guarded manner revealing the strain he refused to release.

They reached a small clearing, and Rowan stopped abruptly. He shoved his hands into his pockets, staring at the ground as though trying to untangle the thoughts clouding his mind. Aislinn slowed beside him, her gaze searching his face for a glimpse of what lay beneath his silence.

"They're both after you now," Rowan said at last, his words strained. "Lucifer and the Golden Dawn. I knew it already, but hearing it laid out like that... it feels different. It's real in a way I wasn't ready for."

Aislinn's chest tightened. Rowan had always been the one she could lean on, the protector who shouldered the impossible. Now, she could see how deeply the weight of protecting her was cutting into him.

He exhaled sharply, his hands curling into fists at his sides. "I don't know if I can do this," he admitted, his voice faltering under the weight of the confession. "I don't know if I'm strong enough to protect you from all of it." His jaw clenched, and he turned his head away. "I've failed before. My family... I couldn't save them. And Davina..." He shook his head, bitterness threading through his words. "What if I can't keep you safe either?"

The rawness of his admission struck Aislinn deeply. She hadn't realized the extent of his guilt, how much it ate away at him in silence. He carried so much, far more than he let anyone see, and now all of it stood laid bare before her.

She stepped closer, her hand brushing his arm in a small attempt to anchor him. "Rowan, you've never failed me," she said, her voice even as emotion welled in her chest. "You've done more than anyone else ever could. I'm still here because of you."

He shook his head, her reassurance seeming to slide past him. "You don't understand," he said, his hands clenching at his sides. "Every time I care about someone, every time I think I can protect them... I lose them. My family. Davina. What if—" He broke off, his shoulders stiffening, and the next sentence rushed out before he could stop it. "What if I lose you too? I can't—" He stopped abruptly, clamping his mouth shut, his hands trembling at his sides.

Aislinn hesitated, her heart aching for him. The depth of his pain, the unspoken fears he carried—it made her want to reach for him in ways she hadn't fully understood before. "Rowan," she said, stepping directly in front of him, her voice steady. "You can't control everything. None of us can. But you don't have to do this alone. I'm not going anywhere, and I won't let you carry this by yourself."

Rowan's eyes lifted to hers, his gaze shadowed with uncertainty. His lips parted slightly, but instead of speaking, he exhaled, his breath uneven as he lowered his head. "Watching you," he said after a pause, his voice raw. "Your strength, your determination... it's why I love you."

Aislinn froze, her pulse quickening as his confession settled in the air between them. It caught her off guard—not just the words, but the unfiltered way they escaped, as though he hadn't meant to say them aloud.

Rowan's expression shifted, as though he hadn't intended to let the words escape. He ran a hand through his hair, his movements tense and restless. "I didn't mean to... I didn't want to scare you," he stammered. "I think I'm just... beginning to—"

Her chest tightened again, though now it carried warmth rather than unease. "You didn't scare me," she said, resting her hand lightly on his arm. She hesitated, her lips curving into the faintest smile. "I think... I'm starting to feel the same."

Rowan blinked, his expression shifting from panic to a cautious relief. "You are?"

She nodded, her smile growing just slightly. "It's new, but it's there."

The rigid line of his shoulders eased, though his doubt remained as if afraid to believe. They stood in the clearing, neither rushing to fill the quiet, the growing connection between them becoming more profound with each passing moment.

Rowan reached out, his hand brushing her cheek with deliberate care. She leaned into his touch, her eyes closing briefly, and when their lips met, the kiss was slow and purposeful. It carried no urgency, only a deep acknowledgment of the fragile connection they were beginning to explore.

Aislinn's fingers curled into the fabric of his shirt as she kissed him back, warmth wrapping around them like a shield against the outside world. When they finally pulled apart, their foreheads rested together, the cool air mingling between them.

Rowan's voice carried a steadiness born of resolve. "I don't know what's coming, but... I'll do whatever it takes."

Aislinn rested her hand over his heart, her gaze unwavering. "We'll figure it out. One step at a time."

The forest enveloped them, its ancient stillness offering a fleeting peace. For now, Aislinn clung to the calm, Rowan's kiss lingering in her mind like a promise she wouldn't soon forget. The looming threats and chaos felt distant here, held at bay by the fragile sanctuary they had found in each other.

But then, a hum stirred deep within her—a low, insistent vibration that felt alive. She stepped back instinctively as the sensation crawled beneath her skin, sharp and unrelenting. Her chest tightened as her heartbeat quickened, and a prickling heat spread through her fingertips, growing stronger with each passing second. Whatever this was, it wasn't stopping. It was building, clawing its way to the surface.

"Rowan…" she whispered, the trembling edge of panic slipping into her words. "Something's wrong."

He moved closer immediately, concern drawing sharp lines across his expression. "What's happening?"

"I don't—" She broke off, squeezing her eyes shut as the pressure inside her surged, relentless and consuming. It wasn't contained within her—it was her, spreading and intensifying with every breath. Heat pulsed under her skin, rushing to her hands, where it burned and trembled. "I can't stop it," she gasped, fear tightening her chest as the energy threatened to tear loose.

Rowan placed his hands firmly on her shoulders, steady and deliberate. "Aislinn, listen to me. Breathe. You're in control."

But control was slipping further and further from her grasp. The energy roared, burning brighter and hotter as faint ribbons of light began to coil from her trembling fingers. She stumbled back, her throat constricting as desperation rose. "I—I can't," she choked. "It's too much!"

The air around them responded as though the forest itself had sensed her instability. Leaves whipped into a frenzied spiral as the wind surged, branches groaning under the sudden pressure. Aislinn glanced at her glowing hands, dread twisting in her chest. "I don't want to hurt you," she cried out. "I don't know how to stop this!"

"You won't hurt me," Rowan said as he stepped closer, his movements cautious and unwavering even as the glow around her hands flared erratically. "I trust you."

Her panic swelled as the energy reached its breaking point. A cry tore from her lips as light burst forth, a wave of force erupting from her hands. The blast struck the trees behind Rowan with a deafening crack, splitting bark and sending leaves cascading in fiery spirals. The earth shuddered beneath their feet, the energy dissipating in a storm of heat and scorched wood.

Rowan turned briefly to assess the damage, but his focus returned to her immediately. "Aislinn," he said, his gaze steady as he closed the distance between them. "Look at me."

Her breaths came in quick, ragged bursts as her eyes met his, the fear she couldn't hide etched plainly on her face. "I—I can't do this," she whispered, her voice trembling. "I don't know how to make it stop."

Ignoring the danger, Rowan cupped her face with both hands, his grip grounding her as he leaned closer. "You can," he said, conviction clear in his steady gaze. "You're stronger than this. Focus on me."

The calm in his words steadied her. Aislinn closed her eyes, her breathing shaky as she forced herself to focus on the warmth of his hands anchoring her. Slowly, the storm within her began to fade. The glow dimmed, the searing heat receding to a faint warmth beneath her skin. When she opened her eyes, her hands no longer trembled, and the light had vanished.

Her shoulders sagged as exhaustion swept through her. She stared at her hands, now still and calm, but the memory of the eruption lingered. "I don't know how to control it," she murmured. "What if this happens again? What if next time, I can't stop it?"

Rowan's hands remained on her cheeks, his touch reassuring. "You'll learn," he said firmly. "You're not doing this alone. Oak will help. Eileen will help. And I'll be here. Always."

Aislinn looked up at him, the fear in her chest easing slightly under the steadiness in his gaze. She swallowed hard, nodding. "Okay," she whispered. "But I'm still scared."

"I know," Rowan said, his hands dropping to his sides. "It's okay to be scared. You'll get there. I believe in you."

She drew in a deep breath, the cool forest air soothing her frayed nerves. The wind had stilled, the leaves settling as though the woods themselves had exhaled with her. Yet the hum beneath her skin remained—a faint, persistent reminder that the storm hadn't disappeared entirely. It was still there, waiting.

Aislinn glanced at Rowan, warmth flickering through her remaining doubts. His unwavering presence centered her, giving her a reason to keep trying. She wasn't sure she could ever fully master what was inside her, wasn't sure she'd ever be ready for the challenges ahead.

But as the forest wrapped them in its calm, the danger receded, if only for now. And in this fleeting reprieve, the weight of what still loomed between them was left unspoken yet undeniable.

Chapter Twenty-One
Edge of Control

The woods behind the Airbnb carried the sharp scent of charred bark and scorched earth, the aftermath of the blast still clinging to the air. Aislinn's pulse raced, the energy beneath her skin thrumming with restless unease. The destruction behind Rowan—a jagged scar splitting the trees—was a stark reminder of how close she had come to losing control.

She wrapped her arms around herself, as though trying to cage whatever threatened to break free. "I don't know how to handle this, Rowan," she murmured, frustration lacing her words. "It's like something inside me is waiting to explode. What if I can't stop it next time?" The unspoken fear—the image of Rowan caught in the blast—was too vivid, too raw.

Rowan stepped toward her, his movements careful, deliberate, as if rushing might shatter the fragile balance she clung to. "I know it's scary," he said evenly. "But this isn't about holding it back forever. Oak can help you understand it—what it means, how to use it. That's what you need to focus on."

Her hands curled into fists, her fear twisting into frustration. She wasn't sure what angered her more—losing control or hating how much she needed to admit Rowan was right. The thought of asking for help made her stomach twist—it wasn't something she surrendered to easily.

"I just—" She faltered, searching for the right words. "I've always figured things out on my own. But this... this feels different." Her voice dropped, hardly discernible. "I don't know if I'm strong enough."

Rowan's focus remained steady, unwavering. "You don't have to prove you're strong enough to handle this alone. You're not supposed to. This is about figuring out what this power can do and making it yours." He stepped closer, his hand hovering near hers. "That's why Oak's here. He knows what you're dealing with because he's been through it. And I'll help you with the rest—how to live with it, how to make it work for you."

She glanced down at their hands, her fingers brushing his. The energy beneath her skin churned wildly, unrelenting. "What if it's too dangerous? What if I can't stop it, even with Oak's help?" Her voice wavered, the fear coiling tighter.

Rowan's grip firmed, anchoring her. "Then we work through it, step by step. You don't need all the answers today, Ash. Start small—just take the next step. Oak will teach you how to channel it, and I'll make sure you never face this alone. But you've got to start."

Doubt lingered in her mind, but deep down she knew he was right. She had to confront this, no matter how terrifying it felt. If she didn't, it wouldn't just hurt her—it would hurt the people she cared about most. And Rowan understood that without her saying it aloud.

"Okay," she whispered, her voice firmer now, as if giving shape to her decision lent her strength. "I'll talk to Oak."

Relief flickered across Rowan's face, though he kept his expression composed. His thumb grazed her knuckles, a small gesture, yet settling. "We'll start today. If you can trust Oak and take this one step at a time, you'll see how much stronger you are than you think."

Aislinn nodded, tentative but resolute, some of the weight on her shoulders lifting. She wasn't convinced—not yet—but Rowan's presence made her fear a little easier to bear. She glanced back at the scorched trees, the destruction that had seemed so uncontrollable just minutes earlier, and exhaled slowly.

"I just need to find my center," she murmured, more to herself than to him.

"You will," Rowan assured her. "And you'll grow stronger. This is just the beginning."

Her lips curved into a hesitant smile, though unease still simmered beneath the surface. The storm inside her hadn't vanished, but it had calmed. The energy beneath her skin still thrummed, but with Rowan's steadying hand in hers, it didn't feel as overwhelming.

As they turned back toward the house, the woods seemed to hold their breath. The calm was fragile, like the pause before a storm. Their steps fell into rhythm as they moved, traces of her earlier outburst lingering in the air. Rowan's constant presence kept her focused, silently bracing her for what lay ahead.

When they reached the porch of the Airbnb, Oak sat in the shade beneath the eaves, carving a piece of wood with practiced precision. As they approached, his focus shifted, a knowing look settling on his features as if he had anticipated this exact conversation.

Without a word, he motioned for them to come closer, his composed presence bringing Aislinn a sense of ease she hadn't realized she craved.

"We need to talk," Rowan said, his low, direct words cutting through the humid air as they stepped onto the porch. There was no preamble—this wasn't the time for it.

Oak set his carving aside and straightened, his gaze moving steadily to meet Rowan's. "I figured as much," he replied, his response weighted with understanding, making it clear he already had some idea of what was coming. He patted the bench beside him in invitation. "Come on, sit. Let's hear what happened."

Rowan and Aislinn exchanged a glance before sitting down. The bench groaned faintly beneath their combined weight, the cool wood beneath her stark against the residual heat still coursing through her skin. Her pulse pounded in her ears as she worked to steady her breathing, fighting to regain her composure.

Rowan's knee grazed hers, a small, supportive gesture that helped her untangle her racing thoughts. She clasped her hands tightly in her lap, struggling to find the right place to start.

"It happened again," Aislinn said finally, her strained voice carrying the echoes of fear. "Another... power. This one was different. Stronger." She paused, glancing at her hands, almost expecting to see the glow of the energy that had overwhelmed her. "It was destructive. I couldn't control it."

Oak leaned forward, his elbows resting on his knees, his posture signaling attentiveness. "Take me through it," he said, his tone even, patient. "How did this power surface?"

Aislinn's focus shifted to Rowan. His slight nod encouraged her, his unspoken support urging her onward.

Her face flushed as she began, her voice quiet. "It happened right after..." She hesitated, her hands fidgeting as the admission caught in her throat. "We were kissing," she finally admitted, her voice just a murmur, the embarrassment heating her skin.

For a time, silence stretched between them. A flicker of surprise passed across Oak's features before his usual calm demeanor returned. He leaned back slightly, his gaze moving between them with a spark of understanding.

"I see," he said, his voice carrying a hint of comprehension. "That explains why you came to me instead of Eileen."

Rowan cleared his throat, a wry smile tugging at his lips. "Yeah," he said, the faint humor in his tone breaking some of the tension. "We figured telling her might... complicate things."

Oak chuckled lowly, the sound free of judgment. "It would," he agreed, his response matter-of-fact. "But I will need to consult her at some point."

Aislinn's stomach twisted at the mention of her mother. She had expected this, but the idea of Eileen knowing how personal the trigger had been made her uncomfortable. "Does she really need to know... everything?"

Oak met her gaze steadily. "No," he said. "Not unless you want her to. But she'll need some understanding of how your emotions connect to your abilities. It might help us figure out why this is happening and how to manage it."

The constriction in Aislinn's chest eased slightly at his reassurance, though unease lingered. She felt Rowan's hand graze hers again, anchoring her. She wasn't facing this alone, and that realization kept her from retreating into her doubts.

"I don't know how much more I can take," she admitted, her voice soft, like a breeze. "Every time I think I'm starting to handle it, another blow comes. I feel like I'm losing control."

Oak nodded, his expression calm yet serious. "That's why we'll take this step by step," he said. "Your emotions are more tied to your powers than I think you've realized. The stronger the emotion, the stronger the reaction.

That's where we'll focus—on finding balance. This is as much about understanding yourself as it is about your abilities."

Aislinn flushed, his explanation striking a chord deep within her. It wasn't just her emotions—it was Rowan, and feelings she hadn't fully acknowledged yet. That vulnerability made her shift uncomfortably in her seat.

"I'm afraid of what I could do to someone," she admitted, her voice trembling slightly.

Oak's gaze softened further, his composed demeanor steady. "You won't," he said. "That's the purpose of training. You're not expected to have control over a power that's only just beginning to surface. Now that we understand the connection, we can work on it."

She nodded slowly, her thoughts still spinning, but no longer chaotic. The weight pressing on her chest lifted incrementally. She wasn't sure she believed Oak entirely, but his conviction offered her a glimmer of hope. With Rowan beside her and Oak guiding her, a way forward began to take shape—one small step at a time.

"Let's begin," Oak said, his steady reassurance held her firm. "Close your eyes, and don't think about controlling the power. Just let it surface. Trust yourself."

Aislinn swallowed hard and obeyed, shutting her eyes and working to block out the world around her. The subtle hum of energy under her skin was constant, a persistent reminder of what she carried. Her heart raced faster, anticipation knotting with anxiety. The last time she had released it, she had almost lost control. What if it happened again?

You can do this, she told herself, holding on to Rowan's earlier encouragement. His presence nearby felt like a lifeline, helping her edge the fear aside, even if only briefly.

Slowly, she reached inward for the energy waiting beneath the surface, the faint pulse hovering just out of reach. It responded almost immediately, a tingling wave climbing her arms and gathering at her fingertips. Her hands twitched on their own as the hum intensified, growing louder, as though the power itself yearned to break free.

"Good," Oak said, his guidance unwavering. "Don't force it. Just observe. Let yourself feel the connection."

Her forehead creased as the power climbed, warmth blooming within her like a slow-building flame. She recognized the familiar strands of her abilities—the healing energy's gentle thrum, the flicker of premonitions skimming the edges of her awareness. And then, there was the kinetic force—the raw, untamed energy that always seemed a step away from tearing through her entirely.

Her breathing hitched as the memory of the trees exploding behind Rowan resurfaced. Fear surged, and with it, the energy swelled uncontrollably. A faint glow began to spread over her hands, growing brighter with every passing moment.

"It's slipping," she whispered, panic closing her throat as the power threatened to spiral beyond her grasp.

Oak stepped closer, his voice calm yet firm. "You don't need to control it yet. Let it flow, but stay grounded. Remember—this is about managing your emotions, not the power. Start with your breathing."

Aislinn tried to inhale deeply, but her chest constricted, her pulse erratic. The fear of losing control gripped her like a vise. Her thoughts spun back to Rowan—to how close she had come to hurting him—and the pressure mounted. She could feel his focus on her, his quiet support both a comfort and a weight as she fought the rising panic.

"Aislinn, focus," Oak said, his words cutting cleanly through her chaotic thoughts. "You have support. Trust the connection, and stay present in this moment."

Her hands trembled as the glow intensified, but she listened this time. She centered on her breathing, letting each inhale and exhale slow the frantic rhythm of her heart. Gradually, the energy shifted. It still pulsed within her, vibrant and alive, but it no longer clawed to escape. It remained just as powerful, just as intense, yet it began to align with her breathing instead of resisting her.

And then she felt it—an almost imperceptible sensation linking her to Rowan. It wasn't just emotional; it was a presence, a pulse of energy stretching outward to connect with him. Her power seemed to recognize him, reach for him, as if it instinctively knew he was essential to her balance.

Rowan felt it too. The air between them buzzed faintly, charged with an unseen current brushing against his skin like static electricity. The bond wasn't overwhelming, but it was undeniable. Her energy stirred something deep within him, quiet yet profound, weaving them closer together.

Aislinn's breathing hitched as the connection deepened. For the first time, the power inside her didn't feel oppressive. It felt... aligned.

"Good," Oak said, approval evident in his tone. "You're doing it. You're starting to understand."

Aislinn exhaled unevenly, the glow in her hands fading to dim embers. The energy coiled inside her, potent but no longer volatile. It no longer felt on the brink of breaking loose.

Her eyes opened gradually, meeting Oak's composed gaze. "I... I did it," she said, disbelief threading her words.

Oak nodded, a small smile lifting the corners of his mouth. "You did. But remember, this is only the beginning. Control isn't about suppression—it's about understanding the connection between you, your power, and those around you."

Her focus shifted to Rowan, who had stepped closer. The bond she had felt—the tether of energy drawing them together—still lingered. She wondered if he had felt it too.

Their eyes met, and Rowan's expression softened. A silent understanding passed between them before he spoke, his words precise. "I felt it. Your power... it reached for me. Like it recognized me."

Aislinn's stomach tightened at his statement, her mind racing. She had felt it too, that inexplicable connection, but hearing Rowan confirm it made it real. Whatever this bond was, it ran deeper than she had imagined.

Oak observed them silently, his brow furrowing as if trying to piece together a puzzle. After a long pause, he spoke with careful precision. "I've never encountered anything like this before—two people sharing a connection through one person's powers. It's unusual, to say the least."

He glanced between them, his expression difficult to read. "It might be tied to the nature of your abilities, Aislinn. Or it could be more complex. I'll need to consult Eileen, discreetly."

Aislinn's stomach tightened at the mention of her mother, but Oak quickly added, "Don't worry. I'll only share what's necessary. But we need to understand this bond."

She nodded, a mix of relief and curiosity surfacing. The idea that her powers could create such a link with Rowan was both comforting and unsettling. What did it mean for her abilities—or for them?

Oak stepped back, his gaze shifting to the darkening sky as the sun dipped lower. "That's enough for today. We'll continue tomorrow. Patience is key. This isn't something you can rush."

Aislinn released a slow breath, the strain of the day's training pressing down on her. There was much to learn, so much to master, yet for the first time, it didn't feel insurmountable. She glanced at Rowan, who met her eyes with a composed, reassuring nod. And for the first time, a flicker of hope replaced the doubt within her.

As they returned to the house, Aislinn's thoughts began to settle. The storm inside her hadn't disappeared, but it no longer felt unmanageable. Rowan walked beside her, and with Oak's advice echoing in her mind, a tentative sense of hope began to take root. A path forward was emerging, even if it remained uncertain.

When they stepped into the Airbnb, the warm evening glow filtered through the windows, softening the edges of the room. Takoda and Rain were tidying up in the kitchen, the faint clinking of dishes breaking the quiet. Takoda noticed them first, her smile radiating a welcoming warmth that lightened the atmosphere.

"There you are," she said, her concern evident. "How did it go?"

Aislinn offered a small nod, masking her exhaustion beneath a composed exterior. "It went... well," she replied, her hesitation revealing the effort the session had taken. "There's still a long way to go."

Takoda set the dish towel on the counter and approached, her gaze steady as she took in Aislinn's expression. "Progress is progress," she said, giving Aislinn's arm a reassuring pat. "The important thing is, you started. Keep at it."

Rain leaned around the corner, her playful grin cutting through the weight of the conversation. "And don't forget to keep an eye on each other," she teased, her remark laced with good-natured humor.

Aislinn let out a soft laugh, the tension in her shoulders easing just a little. She returned Rain's grin, thankful for the brief levity.

Rowan exchanged a few polite words with Takoda and Rain before guiding Aislinn toward the door. His motorcycle waited outside, parked in the glow of the setting sun. The crisp evening air greeted them, mingling with the distant sounds of the city and the subtle rhythm of the woods around them.

He handed Aislinn her helmet, his concern reflected in his eyes. "You all right?" he asked, his voice low.

Aislinn nodded as she accepted the helmet, slipping it on and swinging her leg over the bike. She wrapped her arms around Rowan's waist, resting her cheek against his back as the engine roared to life. The vibration coursed through her, grounding her as they pulled away from the house and onto the winding road.

The ride was soothing in its simplicity. The rhythmic vibration of the bike and the rush of wind against her skin created a rare sense of tranquility, giving her the space to process the day. Yet her thoughts circled back to the energy she had felt—the way it surged when Rowan's presence steadied her, as if their connection had somehow shaped it.

By the time they reached Rowan's apartment, the city lights shimmered against the streets, casting long streaks of brightness over the asphalt. Rowan parked and turned to help her off the bike, his hand resting briefly on her back as she regained her balance.

Inside, the familiar atmosphere of his apartment enveloped her. The glow from the lamps and the quiet comfort of the room made it feel like a refuge after the intensity of the day. Aislinn sank onto the couch, exhaling deeply as Rowan joined her, sitting close but leaving enough space for her to unwind.

The silence stretched between them, easy yet weighted by unspoken reflections. Aislinn ran her fingers through her hair, the tension of the day unraveling slowly, even as lingering questions nudged at the edges of her mind.

"You seemed more in control by the end," Rowan said at last, breaking the quiet. "You're figuring it out. Oak was right—you're stronger than you give yourself credit for."

Aislinn's lips curved faintly, exhaustion softening the gesture. "It doesn't feel like that. It feels like there's so much I don't understand—about my powers, about whatever's happening with us."

Rowan leaned back, his brow knit in thought. "That connection earlier... Did you feel it too? Like your energy reached out to me?"

Aislinn's chest tightened. "I did. It was like... when I started to lose control, I felt you there. Like your energy stabilized mine, keeping it from unraveling." Her voice dropped lower. "I don't know what that means."

Rowan's expression turned thoughtful as he considered her statement. "It felt that way to me, too. At first, I wasn't sure if it was real, but the longer it went on, the more certain I became. It wasn't just you holding it together—it felt like your power drew mine in, creating... balance."

Aislinn's heart clenched at his observation. "Do you think it's because of my powers? Or is it something else entirely?"

Rowan shrugged lightly. "Maybe it's connected to your abilities, or maybe it's about us—how we interact. I don't know. But whatever it is, it didn't feel wrong. If anything, it felt like we're stronger together. Like your power amplifies a strength in me, and mine keeps you centered. Does that make sense?"

She nodded slowly, her thoughts racing. "It does. But what if that link puts you in danger? What if I lose control and you're the one who gets hurt?"

Rowan rested his hand on the couch between them. "If that's the risk, then we'll face it together. This isn't something to fear—it's an opportunity to understand."

Aislinn hesitated, her voice barely above a whisper. "I'm afraid of what could happen, Rowan. I don't want to hurt you."

He shifted closer, his hand finally covering hers. "You're not going to hurt me. And even if you did, it wouldn't change anything. I'm not walking away from this, Aislinn."

Her grip on his hand tightened slightly, a fragile reassurance threading into her doubt. "I don't know if I believe in myself the way you do," she murmured.

Rowan's eyes held hers with steady resolve. "Then let me believe enough for both of us."

The sincerity in his statement struck a chord deep within her, and the tightness in her chest eased. The bond between them, whatever it was, felt unshakable in that moment.

"Thank you," she murmured, the weight of gratitude clear in her voice. "For trusting me. For staying."

Rowan's lips curved into a small, steady smile. "I'm not going anywhere."

The questions hadn't vanished, and the challenges ahead remained, but the crushing doubt had loosened its grip. Aislinn leaned back slightly, letting a rare calm settle over her. The storm inside her had eased, its force tempered by Rowan's unwavering presence.

The hum of the city outside blended with the quiet of the apartment. Aislinn leaned her head back against the couch, exhaustion finally catching up to her. Tomorrow would bring new challenges, but tonight, she allowed herself to rest in the peace of the present.

Rowan sat beside her, his presence a reassuring anchor. She didn't feel the need to fill the quiet; his nearness was grounding. Whatever came next, they would face it together.

The pale light of dawn began to seep through the blinds as Rowan's phone buzzed on the table. He blinked awake, shielding his eyes from the glow of the screen.

Oak:

Meet me at the field I found, just east of the Airbnb. Today's session needs more space. See you there.

Rowan exhaled, running a hand over the back of his neck. He glanced at Aislinn, still curled up on the couch where they had drifted off the night before. The notification caused her to stir slightly, but she didn't wake. For a few heartbeats, he watched her, her features softened in sleep despite the burdens she carried.

Leaning down, he gently brushed a strand of hair away from her face. "Ash," he said quietly. "Time to get up."

Aislinn's eyes fluttered open, groggy at first, sharpening quickly as the weight of the day ahead returned. "Already?" she murmured, rubbing at her temples.

"Yeah," Rowan replied, his voice low. "Oak's got plans. Says we'll need more space today."

Aislinn pushed herself upright, the familiar hum of energy flickering under her skin. Yesterday had pushed her limits, but today... *today will take me further.* She could feel it.

They grabbed their gear and headed outside. The morning air carried a crisp chill, sharp with the scent of dew as Rowan started his motorcycle. Aislinn climbed onto the seat behind him, wrapping her arms around his waist as they sped toward the field Oak had mentioned.

As they crested a hill, the space came into view—a vast stretch of land edged by scattered trees. Oak stood near a cluster of boulders, silhouetted by the pale glow of morning. He waved them over as Rowan parked the bike at the edge of the field.

"Morning," Oak greeted, his gaze sweeping the open expanse as if appraising it. "We'll need this space today. You ready?"

Aislinn nodded, drawing in a deep breath to steady herself. "As ready as I can be."

Oak's lips twitched in approval as he motioned toward the targets he'd set up—wooden posts, their rough surfaces marked with faint rings for aiming. "Today's about testing your boundaries," he said, leading them closer. "We've started building control, but now we need to see how far you can push yourself without losing it. This is about knowing your limits and finding your strength."

Aislinn's heart quickened at his words, but she locked her focus on the task ahead. The hum of energy beneath her skin felt steadier than the day before, though its wildness remained. She glanced at Rowan, whose slight nod infused her with quiet confidence.

Oak stepped back, giving her space. "Start simple," he instructed. "Aim for the post and release a burst of energy. Don't hold back, but stay present. Stay connected to the energy."

Aislinn closed her eyes briefly, drawing her focus inward. When she opened them again, her hands glowed faintly, the pulsing light matching the rhythm of her heartbeat. She inhaled deeply and released the energy in a controlled burst. The blast struck the target dead center, splintering the wooden post and scattering fragments across the ground. The surrounding area remained untouched.

"Good," Oak said, his approval evident despite his measured tone. "Again. And this time, give it more."

Aislinn nodded, narrowing her focus as she summoned the energy. The glow in her hands flared brighter as she unleashed another burst, this time with more force. The blast shattered the post at its base, sending it crashing backward. Briefly, the energy wavered, teetering on the edge of instability. She clenched her focus, pulling it back under control before it could slip away.

Oak crossed his arms, nodding. "Better. Now, let's try something different." He turned to Rowan, his focus sharpening. "Step in."

Rowan tilted his head slightly, noticing the shift in Oak's demeanor. "What's the plan?"

Oak gestured to the remaining target. "Yesterday, you both experienced a connection. I want to test how deep it runs. Aislinn, aim for that post again, but this time, Rowan will visualize how he would physically strike it. Don't share what you're imagining. Let's see if this bond extends beyond conversation."

Aislinn hesitated, her stomach twisting with unease. "You think I can... sense what he's thinking?"

Oak nodded, curiosity flickering in his expression. "It's possible. If Rowan's energy is influencing yours, this bond could be more intricate than we realized."

Rowan didn't falter. "What do I need to do?"

Oak motioned for him to move closer to Aislinn. "Focus on the target. Picture yourself attacking it—how you'd move, the force behind the strike. Don't overanalyze it. Just concentrate and let's see what happens."

Rowan glanced briefly at Aislinn before locking his focus on the post. He adjusted his stance, his attention sharpening as he envisioned the motion and power of his strike.

Aislinn closed her eyes, exhaling slowly to steady herself. The energy within her stirred, rising in response. This time, she reached outward, seeking the subtle thread she had felt yesterday. Rowan's presence resonated like a steady drumbeat, grounding her in its rhythm. *Trust it,* she told herself, leaning into the connection.

The hum of her power deepened, aligning with an external force. A flicker of movement passed through her mind—an image vivid and sharp. It wasn't hers, yet it felt familiar. She could see Rowan's imagined strike, feel its intent and precision as if it were her own.

When she opened her eyes, her hands glowed brighter, the energy within them focused and honed. Her body moved without conscious thought, reacting instinctively to Rowan's intent. She lunged forward, the energy crackling outward as she struck the post. The force splintered it cleanly in half, the impact shaking the ground beneath her feet.

She stumbled back, her breathing unsteady, staring at the shattered target. "Did I just...?"

"You mirrored me," Rowan said, stepping closer, awe lacing his voice. "Every movement—it was exactly what I pictured."

Aislinn's pulse quickened as the realization sank in. She hadn't just imagined Rowan's strike—she had felt it, and her energy had responded as if it were her own.

Oak stepped forward, his expression contemplative as he studied them. "This confirms what I suspected," he said, his tone deliberate. "Your bond isn't just emotional—it's physical. Rowan's strength is feeding into your power, merging with it."

Aislinn blinked, questions spinning in her mind. "But why? Why would that happen?"

Oak folded his arms, his gaze steady. "It's the nature of your magic. Your abilities are responding to connection—drawing strength from it. But this bond with Rowan... it's unique. I'll need to discuss this with Eileen. It changes everything. You're not just mastering your own power, Aislinn. You're learning to channel his as well."

Rowan's jaw tightened as he stepped forward, determination hardening his expression. "Then let's test it," he said firmly. "If this bond is real, we need to understand what it means—and what it can do."

Oak studied him for a minute, weighing his response. "Alright," he said finally. "But we'll take it step by step. This isn't just about testing—it's about finding the boundaries. If this bond is as strong as it seems, precision will matter as much as strength."

The hours blurred into a series of tests and challenges. Oak pushed them relentlessly, each exercise designed to explore the connection between Aislinn and Rowan. Every time Rowan visualized a movement—a strike, a defense, a leap—Aislinn's magic responded, translating his intent into action.

At first, the connection was clumsy, as if moving within someone else's skin. But with each attempt, the bond grew smoother, their energy synchronizing. By late afternoon, exhaustion weighed on Aislinn like a second skin. Her hands trembled, and her breaths came in shallow bursts, but for the first time, the power inside her didn't feel wild. It thrummed with purpose, moving in harmony with her intent.

The three of them gathered near the rocks to rest, the sun casting long shadows across the field. Oak leaned against a stone, his expression thoughtful. "You've made real progress today," he said, his tone steady but edged with caution. "But understand this—this is just the beginning. Your powers are growing, but so is the threat. Lucifer and the Golden Dawn aren't waiting. They're making moves, and we're running out of time."

Aislinn nodded, her muscles aching but her resolve solid. "I'll be ready," she said, the quiet conviction in her voice surprising even herself.

Rowan placed a hand on her shoulder, the weight of his touch grounding her. "We both will."

As the sun dipped below the horizon, streaking the sky in crimson and indigo, Oak's gaze shifted toward the encroaching night, unease flickering in his expression.

"We'll stop here for today," he said after a long pause, his voice quieter now, burdened by unspoken thoughts.

Rowan frowned. "What is it?"

Oak hesitated, his eyes narrowing as they fixed on the horizon. "There's more coming," he said finally, his words heavy with warning. "Lucifer is moving faster than we anticipated. And we're not ready for this."

A chill crept down Aislinn's spine, Oak's words settling like a weight on her chest. Whatever storm loomed ahead wasn't just approaching—it was on their doorstep. She glanced at Rowan, whose expression mirrored her unease.

But Oak wasn't finished. His voice dropped lower, laced with a foreboding that seemed to chill the air around them. "And it's not just Lucifer," he said, his gaze distant. "There's something worse. Something ancient, circling at the edges of this fight."

The gravity of his words pressed down on them. Aislinn's heart raced as she stared at him. "What do you mean, worse?"

Oak's expression darkened, as if he were trying to discern an obscured truth. "I don't know yet," he admitted. "But it's coming."

The air shifted, colder now, the hum of energy in Aislinn's veins faltering for an instant. She didn't need more details to grasp the severity of Oak's warning. Whatever lay ahead was bigger than anything she had faced before.

As they stood in the fading light, Oak's final words lingered in the air, a stark reminder that the fight wasn't just beginning.

It had already arrived.

By the time Aislinn and Rowan returned to the apartment, the evening sky had deepened into a rich indigo, the last traces of daylight giving way to the quiet glow of city lights. The hum of traffic faded into a distant murmur, drowned by the lingering echoes of their grueling training with Oak. Rowan closed the door behind them, his movements deliberate, the clink of his keys on the table breaking the stillness. Fatigue hung between them like a weight, their silence filled with questions neither had yet voiced.

Aislinn dropped onto the couch, the cushions a welcome relief after the day's intensity. "That was... exhausting," she murmured, her voice cutting through the quiet that had followed them home.

Rowan leaned against the doorway, his face reflective. "Oak didn't hold back."

She looked up at him, the churn of her thoughts reflected in her eyes. "That connection between us—it's stronger than I expected. When I mirrored your movements... it felt like I could sense your intentions, almost as if they were my own."

Rowan crossed the room and sat beside her, his brow furrowed. "It wasn't one-sided. I felt it too—like I was pulling energy from you. Not just strength, but... a link I can't explain."

Aislinn hesitated, her forehead creasing as she turned the idea over. "Do you think our bond flows both ways? Could you be channeling my magic the way I tap into your strength?"

Rowan's gaze grew distant, his features clouded. "I felt a surge—sharp, like pure adrenaline—but it wasn't just physical. I thought it was the intensity of training, but now I'm not sure."

"It's deeper than that," she said, the certainty in her tone cutting through the room. "If I'm drawing from your physical abilities, maybe you're accessing my magic."

He rubbed the back of his neck, the implications settling over him like a heavy cloak. "If that's true, we need to understand it—fast. This bond could be a powerful advantage or a dangerous vulnerability, depending on how much control we have."

Aislinn reached out, her fingers brushing his arm with quiet steadiness. "I trust you, Rowan. If we're careful, if we approach this consciously, we'll figure it out."

His eyes met hers, and briefly, his concern softened into a quiet vulnerability. "I just don't want you to get hurt. Not because of this, not because of me."

Her voice gentled, though her resolve shone through. "We've faced too much to falter now. Whatever's coming, we'll meet it head-on."

Rowan exhaled slowly, running a hand through his hair. "Oak seemed... uneasy today. Like he knows more than he's telling us."

Aislinn's countenance darkened. "Lucifer and the Golden Dawn are moving faster than we anticipated. But it's more than just their schemes. There's an older force at play, a presence lurking at the edges of all this."

Rowan's jaw tightened, his focus sharpening. "If Oak's worried, we can't afford to let our guard down."

She nodded, her determination hardening. "This isn't just about us. If this bond really is as significant as it feels, we need to understand it and find a way to use it."

Rowan leaned back, the tension in his posture easing only slightly. "Do we bring Oak into this now? Tell him what we've figured out?"

"Not yet," she said after a moment, her tone cautious. "Let's confirm it first—test the limits before we bring anyone else into it."

He studied her, then nodded, a faint smile breaking through the seriousness of his appearance. "Fair. But promise me you'll be careful."

Her lips curved into a small, knowing smile. "Only if you promise the same."

A quiet laugh escaped him, low and warm. "Deal."

The weight of the day lingered between them, but the questions that had clouded their path forward began to clear. Whatever this bond might mean, they would face it together.

Aislinn stifled a yawn, the edges of exhaustion creeping into her voice. "We should get some rest."

Rowan stood, offering her a hand. "Agreed. Tomorrow isn't going to be any easier."

As they moved toward the bedroom, Aislinn glanced at him, her expression turning introspective. "Do you ever think about why all of this is happening to us?"

"More than I'd like to admit," Rowan replied, his voice steady. "But maybe it's not about why—it's about what we do with it."

Her lips curved into a quiet, contemplative smile. "That's... surprisingly wise."

The familiar routine of settling in for the night brought a fleeting sense of normalcy, though the unspoken tension lingered like a shadow. As Aislinn closed her eyes, unease flickered at the edges of her thoughts—a foreboding presence that felt ancient and inescapable. It wasn't just another challenge ahead. It was a force poised to test them in ways they couldn't yet fathom.

With Rowan beside her, a fragile sense of reassurance steadied the edges of Aislinn's uncertainty. Even so, sleep evaded her, her mind circling around the bond they had uncovered—potent, enigmatic, and unlike anything she had ever imagined. Whatever lay ahead, they would face it together.

Eventually, exhaustion pulled her under, though her rest was far from peaceful. Even in unconsciousness, the pull of their connection remained—a thread that refused to sever.

When Aislinn blinked awake, she found herself standing in a place that felt alien, yet deeply tied to Rowan. The air around her thrummed with a charged intensity, heavy and electric. Distantly, the sound of clashing steel and shouted cries reached her, blending into the acrid tang of smoke that clung to the atmosphere. Her senses flared to life. *This isn't real—this isn't my dream. It's Rowan's.*

She turned, her surroundings slowly coming into focus. A battlefield sprawled before her, chaos unraveling in every direction. The ground was strewn with shattered debris and ash, while figures clashed violently in the haze. Their movements blurred, indistinct, like shadows caught between worlds. And then, she saw him.

Rowan stood in the midst of the chaos, his blade a gleaming arc as it carved through the enemies pressing toward him. He moved with deliberate precision, each strike calculated and powerful. But as Aislinn stepped closer, the weight on his shoulders became clear—his movements carried a heaviness she hadn't noticed before, his strikes slower, less fluid. His exhaustion was evident in the tightening of his posture and the faint hesitation in his attacks.

"I can't lose her," Rowan murmured, his voice raw, breaking through the cacophony. His words were filled with an anguish that cut through Aislinn. "I can't let her fall."

Aislinn froze, the weight of his words settling over her like a shroud. *This is his fear—his deepest fear.* She followed his frantic focus, her stomach twisting when she saw herself in the distance. Her other self fought against an onslaught of enemies, her movements labored and strained. Every time Rowan turned to fend off another foe, his attention darted back to her, his anxiety palpable.

He was fighting for her, yet his doubt was unmistakable—doubt in his ability to protect her, to shield her from the forces bearing down on them. She could feel it emanating from him, a gnawing panic that threatened to consume his every movement. *He doesn't trust himself to keep me safe.*

"No," Rowan muttered again, his blade tearing through another enemy. His voice cracked with desperation. "Not again."

The battlefield blurred around her, the smoke folding into itself as the chaos softened. When the haze lifted, she was no longer a distant observer. She stood closer to Rowan now, her presence solid beside him, though the version of herself still fighting remained in the distance. The figure beside Rowan shimmered faintly, bathed in a pale, otherworldly glow.

Rowan's focus shifted to her glowing form. His tension eased, if only slightly, as though her presence alone gave him strength. His hand reached out toward her, his movements uncertain, his brow furrowed with worry. He didn't speak, but his face said more than words could.

Aislinn felt his emotions radiating from him—protectiveness, guilt, and a deep, unshakable need to ensure her safety. It wasn't a confession of love, but it was raw and vulnerable, exposing the weight he carried for her. The glow surrounding her projection brightened, and for a fleeting moment, she thought she felt his trust in her reach across the bond between them.

The shadows surged again, snapping Rowan's attention back to the battlefield. But a shift had occurred. The hesitation in his movements was gone, replaced by a quiet determination. He adjusted his stance, his grip on the sword firm as he faced the encroaching wave of enemies. His strikes grew sharper, fueled by an unspoken belief that steadied him.

"She's stronger than they realize," Rowan murmured, his tone resolute. "Stronger than even she knows."

He moved with renewed purpose, no longer fighting to shield her but fighting as though he trusted her to stand beside him. Each strike was precise, fueled not by fear but by confidence—in himself and in her.

Aislinn stood rooted to the spot, her chest tightening as she watched the change in him. His faith in her wasn't just in her ability to fight; it was in who she was. The Rowan she saw now wasn't driven by fear—he was driven by trust, by belief.

The battlefield around her began to dissolve, the shadows melting into mist as the dream unraveled. Rowan's form blurred, but his words lingered, steady and unshaken.

"She's ready," he said softly, the conviction in his tone echoing in her mind. "She doesn't need me to save her—she never has."

Then the dream collapsed, and Aislinn woke with a start. Her chest heaved as the dim light of the apartment came into focus. Her heart raced, her thoughts tumbling over what she had seen. This wasn't just a dream. She had stepped into Rowan's mind—seen his fears, felt his quiet faith in her, and glimpsed the profound way their bond had begun to shape him.

Turning toward him, she found Rowan still asleep beside her, his brow faintly creased. Even in rest, emotions seemed to cling to him—concern shadowed his features, steady resolve in his posture, and an enduring sense of care that felt as unyielding as the earth beneath her feet. He carried a quiet strength, one that he believed she shared.

She hadn't fully grasped the depth of his faith in her until now. After stepping into his dream, it became clear—he didn't view her as someone fragile to shield but as an equal to stand beside him. That understanding stirred a resolve deep within her, an ember catching flame.

Carefully, she slipped out of bed, each movement cautious to avoid disturbing him. As she paced the room, her thoughts tangled and re-formed. This new ability—dream-walking—was unlike anything she had ever encountered. She couldn't keep this from Rowan. They'd made that mistake before, and she refused to repeat it.

Behind her, Rowan stirred. His eyes blinked open, adjusting to the faint light filtering in from the window. When his focus found hers, a quiet understanding passed between them, unspoken but undeniable. The day ahead would demand more from them than the last.

"We should get moving soon," he murmured, his tone still thick with sleep. "The meeting isn't far off."

Aislinn hesitated, her determination solidifying. "Before we go, there's something I need to tell you."

Rowan shifted upright, his expression sharpening. "What is it? Did anything happen?"

She drew in a breath, steadying herself. "I think I've unlocked another ability. Last night... I wasn't just dreaming. I was inside your dream."

His features shifted, confusion giving way to clarity. "You were in my dream?"

"Dream-walking," she said, her voice steady despite the weight of her admission. "I saw everything—your fears, how much you care, and the way you... believe in me, even when I struggle to believe in myself."

Rowan studied her intently, the edges of his face growing tender. "You saw all of that?"

She nodded, stepping closer to him. "I didn't mean to intrude—it just happened. But what I saw..." Her words faltered, the memory lingering. "It was overwhelming, Rowan. Your trust in me... I've never felt anything like it."

He released a slow breath, his gaze turning inward as he absorbed her revelation. "I didn't sense you there, but if this is true, this isn't just another ability. Dream-walking is rare, Ash. It's significant."

"I couldn't keep it to myself," she said, her voice dropping lower. "You deserved to know."

Rowan reached for her hand, his grip firm but gentle. "Thank you for telling me. And, for what it's worth, everything you saw in that dream—I meant it. Every word. I trust you, Ash. I always have."

Her throat tightened at the weight of his conviction. "I just don't want this to change anything between us."

"It won't," he said, his tone resolute. "If anything, it makes us stronger. This bond, these abilities—they're more than Lucifer could ever prepare for. We're not the same people we were when all of this started."

Aislinn exhaled slowly, relief washing over her like a cool breeze. She nodded, a small but determined smile finding its way to her lips. "Then we'll figure it out together."

Rowan stretched, rolling the stiffness from his shoulders as he stood. "Let's take the car today. The bike's quicker, but we've been too visible lately."

She agreed without hesitation. The threat of the Golden Dawn pressed too closely to risk being reckless. As they stepped into the sharp morning air, a renewed clarity settled over her. Whatever waited ahead, she knew they were ready—not simply because they faced it side by side, but because they had learned to trust in the strength they brought out in each other.

As morning light filtered into the Airbnb, Aislinn and Rowan entered to find the Fallen already gathered, their faces tense with the weight of the situation. The low murmur of conversations faded as Eileen stepped forward, her presence commanding attention with a quiet authority that seemed to radiate from her. It was the kind of presence that demanded focus, as though light itself bent toward her words.

"We've uncovered critical information," Eileen began, her tone measured but carrying a sharp edge of urgency. "Lucifer's plan still centers on Aislinn, but we believe he's waiting for something specific—an element beyond her powers alone."

Unease stirred in Aislinn's chest, coiling like a serpent. Though she had come to terms with her role, hearing her name tied so directly to Lucifer's plan sent a shiver down her spine. Her gaze flicked to Rowan, his steady presence grounding her, though it did little to quiet the knot of anxiety tightening in her stomach.

Near the window, Oak stood with his arms crossed, his stance solid as an oak itself. His voice was low, measured. "Lucifer is watching closely. He knows your abilities are still developing, Aislinn, but we believe he's waiting for more than their full emergence. Your connection with Rowan—it's part of what he's after."

Rowan's features hardened, his jaw tightening as he stepped forward. "He's waiting for us? What could our bond have to do with his plan?"

Eileen folded her arms, her attitude thoughtful yet intense. "We don't have all the answers yet, but your connection is amplifying Aislinn's magic. That bond may be an essential component of whatever ritual Lucifer is planning."

Aislinn's pulse quickened, her voice trembling slightly as she asked, "Why? Why would our bond be so important to him?"

Oak exchanged a grim look with Eileen before speaking again. "Lucifer's motives aren't always straightforward, but it's clear that your bond is more than a source of strength. He may see it as a way to manipulate or channel your powers—a thread he can twist to his advantage."

Rowan's gaze sharpened, resolve flashing in his eyes. "If he thinks our bond is the key, we can use that against him. There has to be a way to turn it into a force he can't control."

His words lingered in the room like an unspoken challenge. The Fallen exchanged brief glances, their silence heavy with possibility, until Oak nodded slowly, his tone thoughtful. "You might be onto something. If Lucifer expects to use your bond, but you two take control of it—strengthen it on your own terms—you could turn the tables."

Eileen stepped closer, her steady presence filling the room. "If you deepen your connection, you might be able to transform the bond into more than just a link. Together, your magic and Rowan's physical strength could merge into a force Lucifer could never predict."

Rowan glanced at Aislinn, his protective instincts clear in the way his shoulders squared. "But that means complete synchronization," he said, his tone firm. "It's not enough for her to master her magic or for me to focus on strength. We'll need to align—completely."

Aislinn frowned, the weight of the suggestion settling heavily on her. "But if Lucifer is waiting for this bond to grow stronger, wouldn't that just make it easier for him to exploit us?"

From the edge of the room, Elder finally spoke, his calm demeanor cutting cleanly through the tension. "It's a possibility. But if you control the bond together, if you shape it into a unified whole, you might create a barrier—an unbreakable shield that only the two of you can command."

Rowan's expression shifted as realization dawned. "A shield," he echoed, his voice steady and clear. "Built from both of us. If I focus on protecting Aislinn and she channels her magic, we could create a barrier Lucifer won't be able to penetrate."

Oak nodded, his tone tinged with approval. "Your bond is already enhancing her abilities. If you learn to harness it fully, you could refine that enhancement into something Lucifer can't touch. It's about balance and working as one."

Aislinn turned to Rowan, her thoughts racing. "So, we'd need to combine my magic and your strength into a single, unified force?"

Eileen's face grew more tender, though her words carried a steady weight. "Exactly. Lucifer is waiting for this bond to expose a vulnerability, but if you develop it intentionally, it could become your greatest weapon."

Rowan's jaw tightened as he looked at Aislinn, determination etched into every line of his features. "We'll make it work, Ash. If we figure out how to align completely, we can ensure this connection becomes a weapon Lucifer can never use against us."

Riichi, ever the tactician, stepped forward, his mood thoughtful yet precise. "Synchronizing at that level will be anything but simple. It will take relentless effort and time. But if you succeed, it won't just protect you—it could completely derail Lucifer's plan."

Aislinn's pulse quickened, the weight of the challenge settling over her like a heavy mantle. Yet, beneath the pressure, a spark of determination ignited. "So this bond isn't just a liability. If we master it, we could turn the tables on him."

Elder, who had remained silent until now, spoke with calm, deliberate precision. "It's more than a tool for defense. If you fully control it, your bond could become impenetrable. The key is transforming it into a force that only the two of you can wield—something Lucifer cannot corrupt."

Oak crossed his arms, his stance unyielding, his words carrying the weight of measured thought. "We've already seen how it amplifies Aislinn's magic. The next step is refining it—shaping it into an advantage that can't be exploited. That level of mastery would make it untouchable."

Rowan placed a steady hand on Aislinn's shoulder, his focus locked on her, his tone unwavering. "Then that's exactly what we'll do. We'll make this bond work for us—not him."

Aislinn exhaled slowly, anchoring herself against the enormity of what lay ahead. "If it means taking back control, then it's worth every ounce of effort."

The group nodded collectively, the atmosphere shifting from hesitant uncertainty to steely resolve. Rowan's quiet determination and Aislinn's growing confidence rippled through the room, a shared purpose solidifying. Their bond, once a vulnerability, would now become their weapon.

Riichi cleared his throat, redirecting the discussion. "While Lucifer waits for this bond to evolve, the Golden Dawn hasn't paused their efforts. They're still trying to capture Aislinn, but their tactics are shifting. They've started smaller rituals—test runs. They're desperate to tap into her abilities without direct contact."

Vine, his posture tense but composed, spoke next. "We've intercepted signs of them gathering fragments of old magic—artifacts, broken spells, pieces of ancient power. They think Aislinn is the key to breaking the barriers between realms. They don't fully understand her yet, but they're close. We can't let them get any closer."

Aislinn's chest tightened, a chill running along her spine. "If they succeed, what happens? What are they trying to do with this rift?"

Elder's expression darkened, his words purposeful and unyielding. "The Golden Dawn believes they can summon forces greater than Lucifer—ancient demons or worse. They think it will give them the power to overthrow him, but their ambitions don't end there. They want dominion over all realms. If they shatter those barriers, they'll unleash chaos they think they can control—but they won't."

Rowan clenched his fists, his frustration a quiet storm radiating from him. "If they capture Aislinn, they'll use her to open the rift, and that chaos will hand Lucifer the perfect opportunity to finish whatever ritual he's planning."

Eileen's gaze hardened, her presence a sharp, steadying force. "Exactly. The Golden Dawn's recklessness is dangerous on its own, but if they succeed, Lucifer will use the chaos as a doorway to complete his plan. We cannot let it get that far."

Holly, her arms crossed and her tone cutting, broke the tension. "We need to stop them before they try to take Aislinn again. Sitting back and waiting for their next move puts us at a disadvantage—and that's exactly what they want. We need to act first."

Oak inclined his head, his gaze distant but resolute. "She's right. Staying reactive keeps us on their timeline. It's time we seize the initiative."

Riichi stepped forward, his stance as measured as his words. "From what we've tracked, the Golden Dawn is preparing for something significant. Their leadership is growing impatient, and we suspect they're planning a full-scale attempt to take Aislinn soon. If we disrupt their plans now—eliminate key figures or sabotage their rituals—it could delay them significantly."

Vine, his features sharp with intent, added, "We've pinpointed a potential target—a gathering they're organizing. If we act decisively, we can strike before they're ready. Take out their leadership, dismantle their infrastructure, and cripple their efforts before they make their move. Without Aislinn, their plan collapses."

The room fell into a charged silence, the weight of Vine's proposal settling over the Fallen like an unseen force. Aislinn felt the tension press down on her, heavy and stifling, but deep within, a certainty stirred—a quiet voice telling her this wasn't the right path.

Her gaze instinctively found Rowan's. The bond between them flared to life, the connection crackling with unspoken clarity. Without exchanging a single word, they both understood—Vine's plan was reckless. Aislinn's intuition and Rowan's protectiveness aligned, an unbreakable current passing between them. They couldn't follow this course of action.

Rowan's grip on her hand tightened, his voice cutting through the room with unmistakable conviction. "That won't work."

Aislinn immediately followed, her focus still locked on Rowan. "They're expecting us to attack. If we move now, we'll be walking straight into a trap. It's exactly what they're waiting for."

The room fell silent again, the weight of their unified objection hanging heavily. Eileen's sharp gaze narrowed on them, her look shifting as though she were seeing them in an entirely new light.

Rowan continued, his tone measured but firm, each word considered. "They've set this up to bait us into acting recklessly. If we attack the gathering, they'll use it against us—they'll be ready."

Aislinn stepped in seamlessly, her certainty anchoring the moment. "An attack doesn't just disrupt their plans—it accelerates them. They're expecting it, and it will play right into their hands."

Rowan nodded, the intensity in his countenance unwavering as he turned to the others. "We need to approach this differently. Study their preparations, find the core of the ritual, and dismantle it from within."

"We can take out the components holding their magic together," Aislinn added, her grip on Rowan's hand tightening. "If we do that, their entire plan collapses without risking a direct confrontation."

The Fallen exchanged uncertain glances, the charged atmosphere palpable. Rowan and Aislinn's synchronized insight left a visible impression on the group. Eileen's expression turned contemplative, her voice deliberate. "Sabotaging the ritual before it starts... it's bold. But it may be the only way to stop them without playing into their hands."

Oak broke the silence, his voice steady. "It's a clever approach. No direct assault means no chance for them to counter. I didn't expect you two to work this... seamlessly."

Riichi, his face unreadable, let out a soft chuckle, his dark eyes glinting with restrained approval. "If you can keep reading each other like that, you'll give us an advantage they won't see coming."

Vine, his earlier confidence tempered but still present, tilted his head thoughtfully. "It's risky, but it tracks. Taking the ritual apart at its foundation would leave them with nothing."

Aislinn felt the energy in the room shift. Where there had been doubt, respect now lingered, acknowledgment of the power Rowan and Aislinn had begun to uncover. Rowan gave her hand a subtle squeeze, his words low but meant only for her. "We're on the right path."

She nodded, her voice quiet but filled with resolve. "We'll make this work."

Vine spoke again, his tone grounded. "We'll need precise details. What spells, what artifacts—they're the linchpins. If we miss even one, they'll recover."

Elder, his arms folded and his gaze steady, added, "If we dismantle their setup, they won't have the means to use Aislinn's power. Without the ritual, their strategy falls apart."

Rowan's posture shifted, protective yet calm, as he addressed the group. "Our focus will be on strengthening the bond. If we can anticipate their moves, we'll stay ahead of them—and stop them from catching us off guard."

Aislinn felt Rowan's hand warm against hers, their connection thrumming between them. She met his gaze, her determination solidified. "We'll be ready."

Eileen's sharp gaze swept the room, her words crisp and decisive. "Here's the plan. Riichi, Reed, and Vine—you'll track the ritual's exact time and location. No more guesses. I want confirmation by tonight."

Vine's confidence returned in full as he gave a firm nod. "We're close. I'll have the details soon."

Eileen turned to Oak, her tone more measured. "Keep working with Aislinn and Rowan. If this bond really is as important as it seems, it could be our strongest weapon. Elder, Holly, and I will focus on identifying how to dismantle the ritual safely. We'll also monitor Lucifer's movements to ensure he doesn't act independently. Once we have everything in place, we strike before they know what hit them."

The tension in the room eased slightly, replaced with a renewed sense of purpose. Aislinn glanced at Rowan, her resolve steady. Whatever came next, they would face it together—only now, they had a clear path forward.

The room pulsed with a quiet determination, a simmering energy coursing through the group. As the Fallen began to disperse, Rowan leaned close to Aislinn. "We should talk to Eileen now. She'll want to know about last night."

Aislinn nodded, her heart tightening as they approached Eileen, who lingered near the table. "Mom, can we have a word in private?" she asked.

Eileen turned to face them, her sharp focus relaxing slightly. "Of course. Let's step outside."

They followed her to a quiet corner of the porch, the hum of voices from inside fading into the background. Eileen crossed her arms, her gaze shifting between them. "What's on your mind?"

Aislinn hesitated for only a moment before speaking. "Last night... I unlocked a new ability. I think it's dream-walking."

Eileen's eyebrows lifted slightly, her interest clearly piqued. "Dream-walking? That's rare. Tell me everything."

Rowan spoke up, his tone steady. "She was in my dream. She saw everything—my fears, my thoughts. She even felt... the bond between us."

Eileen's mood grew reflective, her sharp gaze locking on Aislinn. "Dream-walking is no small thing, but it's also not a fully developed ability. It takes time to strengthen, and it often reveals itself slowly. For now, it's important to focus on Lucifer and the Golden Dawn. But if you experience it again, I want to know immediately."

Aislinn nodded, her voice firm. "We will."

Eileen's features relaxed, her commanding presence easing for the briefest instant. "You're doing well. Both of you. This bond—it's more powerful than even I realized. Keep working on it, and keep me updated."

Rowan's hand found Aislinn's briefly before they turned to rejoin the others. Her thoughts churned, but a sense of clarity settled within her. They had direction, and for now, that was enough.

Outside, the wind stirred, its restless whisper carrying the promise of a storm. They would strike first, but as Aislinn's eyes lingered on Rowan, a faint unease crept in. The Golden Dawn's desperation made them unpredictable, but it was Lucifer's far-reaching schemes that cast the larger shadow—unfolding in ways none of them could yet grasp.

Though they had taken their first steps to counter one threat, Aislinn knew this was only the beginning. With two enemies moving unseen, the true battle was still on the horizon.

Chapter Twenty-Three

Bound By Light

The early morning air stung Aislinn's cheeks, crisp and biting with enough chill to wake her senses as she followed Rowan into the open field near the Airbnb. Oak was already there, standing beneath a cluster of trees like a sentinel, arms folded, his sharp eyes scanning the horizon for unseen threats.

There was no room for chatter, no pretense of ease. Today demanded focus. Rowan's body stiffened, brimming with controlled energy. Aislinn felt the unspoken tension between them—a shared understanding that they were about to be pushed to their limits.

They both understood why this mattered: the Golden Dawn was closing in, and Lucifer's arrival loomed ever closer. There was no time to waste. If they couldn't fight as one, everything they cared about would be lost.

Oak acknowledged their approach with a nod, his expression unreadable. He let the moment stretch before breaking the stillness.

"Before we start, you need to understand what this training is about," Oak began, his tone controlled and purposeful. "This isn't just about fighting. It's about building your connection—learning to move and think as one. Rowan, you've spent centuries honing your skills. Aislinn, you're new to this, and that's not a weakness—it's an advantage."

Aislinn's brow furrowed, doubt constricting her chest. *An advantage? I can barely control my powers, and now they expect me to train like part of a seamless unit?*

As if sensing her thoughts, Oak stepped closer, gesturing between her and Rowan. "The two of you share a bond. It's emotional, yes, but it's also deeper. You can't see it fully yet, but it's there. That bond will be your greatest strength. It will amplify your abilities if you learn to recognize it, trust it, and lean into it."

Rowan stood with arms crossed, his focus locked on Oak. Aislinn glanced at him, wondering how he interpreted all of this. *He'd endured so much—how am I supposed to match his experience?*

Oak continued, his voice unwavering. "There are three things we're focusing on: coordination, tactical integration, and mental resilience. But before any of that, you need to feel the connection between you. That's where it all begins."

Aislinn's pulse quickened as Oak's words sank in. She'd felt that connection before—in brief flashes during earlier training and most vividly during the Fallen meeting, when they seemed to speak as if their thoughts aligned perfectly. A powerful thread bound them, just below the surface. But now, under pressure? It felt like an entirely different challenge.

Oak raised his hand, and a series of targets materialized in the air, hovering like phantom adversaries. His expression stayed calm, yet his eyes were sharp and commanding as they shifted between the two. "We'll start with coordination. Your movements need to align—timing, communication—it all starts here."

Rowan's posture stiffened, his attention narrowing on the targets. *I've faced horrors Aislinn could barely fathom, but this is different. I need her just as much as she needs me.*

Oak turned to Aislinn, softening his tone without losing its edge "You'll struggle at first. That's expected. But if you trust this bond, you'll see how your abilities—his strength, your intuition—can flow together. That's what we'll build on."

Aislinn swallowed against the dryness in her mouth. She wanted to trust this connection, but how could she when her own powers felt so elusive? She glanced at Rowan, and their eyes met. His blue-streaked hair glinted in the morning sun, and beneath his calm exterior, she caught a flicker of reassurance meant for her. He nodded, a small gesture that carried undeniable weight. *Whatever it took, we will make this work.*

Oak stepped back, his face giving nothing away as he allowed them space. "We're starting simple. Rowan, let your instincts guide you, but don't overcompensate. You're not just leading—you're working with her. Aislinn, don't second-guess yourself. Trust your instincts. Hesitation will only hold you back."

Aislinn inhaled deeply, pushing her doubts aside. She had to do this. The enormity of the task pressed on her, but Rowan's steady presence comforted her, even as the path ahead seemed daunting.

"Close your eyes," Oak instructed, his voice cutting through the morning stillness.

Aislinn hesitated, startled, but Rowan obeyed immediately, his eyes closing without question. She followed his lead, her nerves sparking under her skin.

"Feel the space around you," Oak continued. "Not just physically—emotionally, mentally. Focus on the connection between you. Rowan, reach for Aislinn's aura. Aislinn, do the same. It's subtle, almost imperceptible, but it's there."

She tried, but all she could register was the sharp cold on her skin and the fluttering anxiety in her chest. *How am I supposed to find something so intangible?*

"Stop overthinking," Oak snapped, his tone cutting into her thoughts. "Let go of your expectations. Just feel."

Aislinn exhaled slowly, forcing herself to relax. She let her awareness center on Rowan, on the quiet strength he seemed to emanate. Gradually, a change stirred. It started faintly, like the touch of a breeze, but it was there—a fragile thread of power connecting them. Her heart skipped.

Rowan felt it too. He exhaled slowly, letting the faint connection tug at his senses. He didn't question it; instead, he leaned into it, allowing it to root him. This was more than just physical coordination—it was a foundation they had to trust if they wanted to move as one.

"Now," Oak said, his tone softening, "use that connection. Move together."

Rowan moved first, a blur of precision and speed that nearly threw Aislinn off balance. She scrambled to follow, sending out a kinetic blast aimed at one of the targets. It veered wide, missing by inches. Frustration prickled under her skin.

"Not fast enough," Oak barked, his tone cutting through the tension. "Again!"

Aislinn clenched her fists, irritation bubbling as she tried to match Rowan's pace. Her second blast hit closer to the mark, but their movements still felt out of sync. Rowan struck the targets with practiced precision while she fumbled to align her attacks.

"You're hesitating," Rowan muttered as he sidestepped a mock enemy Oak conjured out of nowhere.

"I'm trying," Aislinn shot back, heat rushing to her cheeks. The sharpness in her voice didn't faze Rowan; he recognized the tension in her brow, the stubborn set of her jaw. She was second-guessing herself, wrestling with what didn't need to be controlled. He could sense the raw power thrumming just beneath her surface, locked away by her fear of losing control.

Let it go, Rowan thought, studying her. "Stop forcing it," he said aloud, his tone firm but measured. "You're trying too hard. Trust your instincts. We'll move together."

Oak, ever watchful, paced a slow circle around them. "This isn't about domination. It's about connection. You don't need to lead or follow—react to each other. Complement, don't compete."

Rowan glanced at Aislinn, noting the frustration simmering in her expression. She was so focused on keeping up that she wasn't allowing herself to find their rhythm. He needed to guide her without stepping on her confidence. Pushing too hard would only make things worse.

"Aislinn," he said, softening his tone. "Don't anticipate every move. Feel the flow between us. React when it's time, and let me do the same."

Easier said than done, she thought, forcing herself to take a calming breath. The frustration swirling inside her threatened to take over, but she fought to push it back. She focused on Rowan, watching his movements and trying to attune herself to the energy threading between them. She had felt glimpses of their potential before—brief flashes of harmony—but those moments had been fleeting. She needed to find that again.

Rowan could feel it—Aislinn was getting closer. The bond between them was strengthening, but it still wasn't right. Not yet. He adjusted his pace, deliberately holding back just enough to let her catch up. She needed space to find her rhythm and push through the frustration that radiated from her like a low hum in the air. And she was fighting through it. *Good,* he thought. *She's learning.*

"Timing!" Oak's voice cut through the air, sharp and unrelenting. "Close, but not close enough. Synchronize! Stop working against the connection and start trusting it."

Aislinn's thoughts spiraled. *How am I supposed to synchronize when I can barely manage my own powers?* Her eyes shifted toward Rowan, noting the way his body moved with effortless accuracy, every motion controlled and exact. Emotionally, they were connected—there was no doubt about that. But fighting together? That felt like an entirely different mountain to climb.

Her frustration surged, and with it, her powers flared unexpectedly. A blast of energy erupted from her palms, slamming into one of the targets with enough force to disintegrate it into mist. Pride sparked briefly in her chest, but it quickly faded with the realization that her shot had gone wide. Again.

Rowan turned to her, his breathing steady despite the intensity of the session. He saw the strain in her stance, the hardness in her posture. "You're caught in your own head," he said, a hint of dry humor in his tone. "Feel it. Don't think it to death."

Aislinn scowled, though her annoyance barely masked the exhaustion threatening to drag her down. "Easy for you to say," she snapped, her tone sharp. "You've had centuries to get this right."

Rowan's expression softened, though his resolve stayed firm. "And you'll get there," he replied. "We're not doing this alone. Lean on me when you need to. Let's find our rhythm."

They tried again. And again. For every misstep, there was a small victory—a perfectly timed strike, a synchronized motion. It wasn't flawless, not by a long shot, but it was progress. Rowan could feel Aislinn beginning to trust the bond between them, her kinetic blasts growing more accurate and focused. He adjusted his movements to meet hers, each step drawing them closer to a rhythm that resembled cohesion. The frustration hadn't vanished entirely, but she was channeling it now, sharpening it into focus.

Finally, Oak called a halt. The sun hung low in the sky, casting long shadows across the field. "Better," he said, his tone neutral, his expression giving nothing away. "But it's still not sufficient. When it's time to face Lucifer, this won't cut it."

Aislinn's chest constricted, her breath catching at the mention of Lucifer's name. The pressure of what was coming pressed down on them like a storm cloud. Rowan felt it too—a tension settling in his gut. There was so much ground to cover, but today had been a step forward. And that was something.

The vibration of their phones shattered the stillness. Rowan pulled his from his pocket, his expression hardening as he read the message:

Meet back at the Airbnb. ASAP.

—Eileen.

He glanced at Aislinn. Despite the exhaustion etched into her flushed face and trembling hands, her expression held firm, her posture unyielding. She met his eyes briefly, the silent exchange reflecting her determination, before they both turned to follow Oak. The older Fallen was already striding toward the path, his movements brisk and purposeful. "No time to waste," Oak muttered, slipping his phone into his pocket as he quickened his pace.

Aislinn swiped a hand across her brow, brushing away the sweat as adrenaline fueled her aching muscles. Rowan moved to her side, his steady presence centering her. He gave her a subtle nod—not encouragement, but acknowledgment of her efforts. She had fought hard today, and he had noticed.

Their steps fell in sync as they made their way back, the importance of Eileen's message heavy in the air between them. Conversation felt impossible, tension building with each stride. By the time the Airbnb came into view, the last light of the setting sun stretched across the horizon in vivid streaks of orange and gold, casting the house in a fleeting, fiery glow as the shadows of the encroaching night began to creep closer.

Inside, the air carried a palpable charge, thick with anticipation and unspoken urgency. Eileen stood just beyond the entrance, her gaze sweeping over them like a blade honed for precision. Though her expression remained calm, her presence radiated authority, commanding the room without a single word. With a simple gesture toward the kitchen, she set them all into motion.

"Takoda, Rain, stay here," Eileen instructed, her tone sharp yet measured, carrying the significance of unchallenged authority. "This won't take long."

Takoda nodded slightly, her gaze lingering on Aislinn as if silently checking on her. Rain, however, tried to ease the tension with a fleeting grin. "We'll hold down the fort," she said softly, though the usual lightness in her tone was edged with a seriousness she rarely showed.

Aislinn returned the smile faintly, though the immensity of the coming revelations pressed heavily on her shoulders. As Rowan's hand brushed against her lower back in a brief, grounding gesture, she drew in a measured breath, steeling herself. Whatever Vine had uncovered, it wouldn't be good.

The door to the kitchen closed behind them, sealing off the rest of the house. Eileen moved to the head of the long table with deliberate steps, her presence sharp and resolute, like a storm gathering just before the first crack of lightning. The Fallen were already gathered: Vine, Riichi, and Reed sat at the table, their postures tense, their focus unyielding. Holly and Elder leaned casually against the counter, but their keen eyes betrayed their readiness.

Breaking the silence, Eileen's voice carried through the room with cutting precision. "Vine has uncovered intel on the Golden Dawn's next move. It's worse than we expected."

The enormity of her words settled heavily before she motioned toward Vine. Straightening in his seat, Vine clasped his hands together on the table, his expression somber yet focused. "We've confirmed the time and location," he began. "In two days, the Golden Dawn will gather at an abandoned warehouse in the Mission District to perform a major ritual. They've kept it quiet, but we've intercepted the details."

Rowan's thoughts raced as soon as the ritual was mentioned. Calculations of risk and danger flooded his mind, most of them centering on Aislinn. His protective instincts surged, but he kept his expression neutral, forcing himself to stay focused.

"This ritual is part of their larger plan for power," Vine continued, his voice steady but tinged with urgency. "And as we feared, Aislinn is central to it.

They're not making a move on her yet, but they're laying the groundwork. We've confirmed enough to know this is a critical step in their preparations."

Aislinn's chest tightened as his words sank in, the intensity of them pressing like a stone against her ribs. She glanced at Rowan, who stood rigid beside her. The tension emanating from him was palpable, his clenched fists a silent reflection of his unspoken resolve.

Eileen's voice cut cleanly through the atmosphere, leaving no room for hesitation. "We don't have time to wait. If the Golden Dawn is gathering in two days, we act tomorrow night. We'll sabotage the ritual before they can complete it."

Riichi and Reed exchanged a brief glance before Riichi spoke, his voice calm yet edged with urgency. "We've studied their movements. The ritual requires specific items and incantations. It's dark magic—powerful enough to attract attention. If we act quickly, we'll have a narrow window to strike before they notice."

Reed added, his words precise, "Disruption isn't enough. We need to dismantle it completely. If anything is left behind, they'll regroup and retaliate with more force. This is high-risk."

Rowan's chest tightened further at the phrase *high-risk*. The thought of Aislinn's involvement magnified the danger in his mind, each worst-case scenario flashing vividly. However, he kept his silence—this wasn't the time to voice his concerns.

Eileen's gaze swept across the room, sharp and assessing. "Everyone has a role. Riichi, Reed, and Vine—you'll lead the charge to dismantle the ritual. You know the location, and your familiarity will be an asset."

Vine nodded firmly. "Consider it done."

"Elder, Holly, and Oak," Eileen continued, "you'll secure the perimeter. Make sure no one gets the drop on us. If the Golden Dawn has stationed guards, neutralize them swiftly."

Holly gave a slight grin, though the seriousness in her gaze didn't waver. "Understood," she said. Elder offered a curt nod, his calm exterior masking the precision and intensity he brought to every mission.

Finally, Eileen turned to Rowan and Aislinn. Aislinn's pulse quickened, her anticipation knotting into a heavy weight. Beside her, Rowan remained still, his expression unreadable but his body taut with a quiet strain.

"Rowan, you'll stay with Aislinn," Eileen said, her tone leaving no room for argument. "Provide cover and support. Aislinn, your abilities could be critical if things go sideways—healing, yes, but more if necessary. Rowan's experience will guide you."

Aislinn swallowed hard, the pressure of her assignment settling like a weight against her chest. She glanced at Rowan, who said nothing, his silence speaking volumes. The clench of his jaw and the rigid line of his shoulders betrayed his true feelings—he hated this, but there was no room for protest.

Eileen's gaze rested briefly on Rowan, as though silently acknowledging the unease she noticed, before she turned back to the group. "I'll lead the distraction. While Riichi, Reed, and Vine dismantle the ritual, Oak and I will draw their attention elsewhere. The Golden Dawn's focus will be on us, giving you the time to act swiftly and leave without being detected."

Rowan's fists tightened at his sides, his protectiveness warring with his sense of duty. Aislinn could feel the strain radiating from him, but there was no time to address it. The mission was clear, and their path set.

Eileen's final words carried through the room, sharp and unwavering. "We move tomorrow night. Rest while you can. Once this starts, there's no turning back."

For a moment, silence reigned, each of the Fallen absorbing their roles and the risks ahead. Aislinn stole a glance at Rowan. His expression remained a careful mask, but the tightness in his posture said enough. They would have to talk later—about the mission, about her role—but for now, nothing more could be said.

The scrape of chairs and quiet murmurs broke the stillness as the meeting dissolved. Aislinn remained rooted in place as the enormity of what lay ahead pressed down on her, growing heavier with each second.

Rowan was already moving, his expression a mask of control as he gave Eileen a curt nod. Without speaking, he reached for Aislinn's arm, his touch firm but careful, guiding her toward the door. The gravity of the moment pressed between them, the silence growing thick and oppressive, twisting her stomach in a tangle of uncertainty.

They stepped outside into the crisp evening air, where the cool breeze carried the faint scent of pine and distant rain. But the chill did little to ease the tension coiling between them. The mission loomed over them, unspoken yet undeniable, and neither broke the silence as they walked to Rowan's car. Aislinn glanced at him, searching his face for a crack in his composure, a hint of what lay behind his stoic demeanor. But his eyes stayed fixed ahead, his shoulders squared, his movements rigid with barely restrained emotion.

When they reached the car, he unlocked it without a word or even a glance her way. Sliding into the passenger seat, Aislinn tried to steady her racing thoughts, but the quiet inside the car wrapped around her like a vice, each second of silence stretching taut. She made a few tentative attempts at conversation—questions about the mission, remarks about the evening, even an observation when they stopped briefly to grab takeout for dinner—but Rowan's replies were clipped, his focus locked on the road. His knuckles whitened as they gripped the steering wheel, and with every passing mile, the distance between them seemed to grow, a canyon opening that neither dared to cross.

Her discomfort deepened, and doubt began to gnaw at her resolve. *Why won't he talk to me? Does he think I can't handle this?* The questions clawed at her, growing louder with each passing moment. The enormity of them settled in her chest, heavy and unrelenting, until by the time they reached Rowan's apartment, the silence had become suffocating.

Inside, the quiet lingered like a heavy fog, thick and unyielding. They sat at the table, the untouched takeout sitting between them, an afterthought in the charged atmosphere. Rowan pushed his food around the plate, his expression distant, his thoughts clearly tangled elsewhere. Aislinn's patience frayed, the frustration bubbling beneath her surface until it finally snapped.

She slammed her fork down, the sharp clang shattering the silence. "Alright, Rowan. What the hell is going on?"

He didn't answer immediately, his grip tightening around the fork before he set it aside with deliberate care. When he looked at her, his dark eyes were raw, conflicted—brimming with emotions he could no longer contain.

Whatever was eating at him had been simmering all night, and now it threatened to boil over.

With a quiet, hoarse voice, he finally spoke. "I don't want you to go on the mission," he admitted, the magnitude of his words landing heavy in the room.

"What?" Aislinn shot to her feet, her heart hammering in her chest. "What do you mean you don't want me to go? You think I'm not strong enough?"

"No—" Rowan stood abruptly, running a hand through his hair in a frustrated gesture. His movements were sharp, his tone taut with restrained emotion. "It's not that."

"Then what is it?" Her voice rose, cutting through the room. "If it's not about me being strong enough, then what? You don't trust me? You think I'll screw it up?"

Rowan's eyes flashed, his control slipping like a taut rope fraying under strain. "It's about me, Aislinn!" he shouted, his voice cracking with the force of his confession. "It's about the fact that I can't protect you. That I'm terrified something's going to happen to you, and I won't be able to stop it."

The raw honesty of his words hit her like a blow, and her anger faltered. "You... you think you'll fail?" she asked, her voice softer now, disbelief woven into her tone.

"Yes!" Rowan's voice broke as he stepped closer, the intensity of his emotions spilling over. "Yes, I'm scared. I'm scared out of my mind that disaster will strike, and it'll destroy me. Don't you get that?" His breathing grew uneven, his fists clenching at his sides. "I've seen too much, Aislinn. I know what's out there, what we're up against. And the thought of losing you—" His voice trembled, faltering as his emotions overwhelmed him. "I love you, Aislinn. I love you, and I can't lose you. I won't survive it."

Aislinn froze, his confession crashing into her with the force of a tidal wave. He loved her? The words hung suspended in the air between them, reverberating through her mind, shifting the ground beneath her. He loves me.

"You... you love me?" she whispered, her voice trembling as her anger melted into a fragile, unsteady emotion.

Rowan's chest heaved, his breaths uneven as he nodded. "Yes," he said, his tone softer now but still charged with intensity. "I'm in love with you, and that's why I can't let you do this. If something happens to you..." His words faltered, weighted by a fear he could no longer hide.

Aislinn took a shaky step toward him, her emotions surging in the wake of his confession, colliding and intertwining in ways she couldn't yet untangle. "Rowan," she murmured, her voice soft yet steady with the truth welling up inside her. "I love you too."

His eyes widened, the tension visibly unraveling from his body. In an instant, he closed the space between them, pulling her into his arms as though she were the only thing tethering him to the world. She clung to him, her heart pounding in time with his, the vulnerability and unspoken truths between them forming an unbreakable bond.

The significance of Rowan's admission seemed to fill the room, saturating the space between them with a profound and undeniable truth. Aislinn's heart raced as his arms tightened around her, his grip grounding her in the moment's fragile intensity. His gaze, raw and open, mirrored the storm of emotions within her—the hope, the fear, the shift that had irrevocably changed everything between them.

"I love you," Aislinn whispered again, her voice barely audible above the relentless thrum of her heartbeat. Rowan's breath hitched, his forehead resting gently against hers as though anchoring himself to the enormity of what they shared. The world outside fell away, leaving only the two of them suspended in this singular moment.

"And I love you," Rowan replied, his tone unwavering, his words carrying the depth of an unbreakable vow.

When their lips met, it felt like the spark of a wildfire—hesitant at first, then growing into a blaze that was fierce and consuming, driven by the emotions they had kept buried for so long. It wasn't just a kiss; it was the release of every hidden yearning, every unspoken need, every fragile hope laid bare. Rowan's hands cupped her face with a reverence that sent a current of warmth through her, his touch both steadying and electric.

The air around them seemed alive, vibrating with an invisible force that thrummed in time with their connection. It felt as though the universe itself had paused, holding its breath to honor the gravity of what was forming between them.

As they moved toward the bed, an almost tangible pull seemed to draw them closer, the space between them charged with a magnetic energy. Rowan's gaze never left hers, his emotions stripped bare in a way that stole her breath. "You're everything," he murmured, his voice rough with unguarded emotion. "This—us—is where I'm meant to be. Together."

Her pulse quickened, his words igniting a fire within her, fierce and unrelenting. She pressed his hand against her chest, letting him feel the steady thunder of her heartbeat. "I feel it too," she said, her voice trembling but sure. "I need you, Rowan. Completely."

Rowan's breath shuddered as he closed his eyes briefly, her confession unspooling a long-buried emotion deep inside him. When he looked at her again, his gaze burned with a mix of love and raw intensity that left her rooted. Without hesitation, he wrapped her in his arms, his embrace conveying safety, devotion, and an all-encompassing love. "Let me show you," he whispered, his lips brushing hers with a tenderness that sent warmth spiraling through her. "Let me show you what you mean to me."

Their next kiss was slow and deliberate, steeped in the boundless love they had both been afraid to admit. It carried no urgency, only the profound truth of their connection—a merging of devotion, hope, and unrelenting need. Rowan's hands moved over her with care, each touch reverent, each caress an unspoken promise. What they shared wasn't just physical—it was alive, crackling with an intensity that seemed to defy the boundaries of the world around them.

Aislinn responded instinctively, her fingers tangling in his hair as she leaned into him, not to claim him but to meet him in the shared intensity of the moment. The emotion between them was tangible, almost sentient, guiding them in perfect harmony. Their love wasn't confined—it spilled over, vast and uncontainable, as though it could light the entire world.

The room began to shift, the air vibrating with a pulsing energy that seemed to emanate from within them. It started as a faint hum, delicate yet undeniable, before building into a crescendo of light and warmth. Aislinn gasped as a surge of power coursed through her veins, her skin shimmering with iridescent streaks of blue. She stared at her hands, awestruck by the flowing energy moving like liquid starlight across her skin, alive and ever-shifting. Her breath hitched as she looked up at Rowan.

He glowed as well, his entire being bathed in a golden brilliance that pulsed like the steady rhythm of a heartbeat. Light and shadow danced across the walls, casting their connection into vivid relief. His glowing eyes met hers, filled with wonder, awe, and a depth of emotion that seemed to transcend the physical.

The light between them intensified, waves of ethereal energy pulsing outward in perfect harmony with their hearts. It wasn't just light; it was a force, alive and untamed, cocooning them in a protective aura. Rowan's glowing hands rose to cradle her face, he moved close to her ear as the energy around them pulsed and flared. His whisper was hoarse, breaking the charged silence. "Do you feel that? It's... us."

Aislinn's chest rose and fell, her breathing uneven as she nodded. "It's more than us. It's everything. It's—" She faltered as another surge of light flared around them, brighter and hotter, filling the room with its brilliance. The energy seemed to carry a life of its own, untamed and alive, coursing through their bodies like fire. The power was ancient, wild, as though it had waited for them all along.

Their movements became effortless, guided by an instinct neither fully understood but both embraced. Each touch felt charged, electric, carrying a depth that defied words. Every glance between them ignited a profound spark, a sense of something eternal. It was no longer just love or desire—it was the merging of their very souls, a unity so complete it transcended anything they had ever known.

Rowan's grip on her waist tightened, his voice thick with emotion as he whispered, "You are the best thing that has ever happened to me. No battle, no victory—nothing comes close to this. To you."

Aislinn's heart swelled, her emotions cresting like a wave she could no longer contain. Tears glistened in her eyes as she cupped his face, her fingers brushing against the edge of his jaw as though anchoring herself in the truth of his words. "You are everything I didn't know I needed," she said, her voice raw with certainty. "And I will never let this go. I will never let you go."

The energy around them surged in response, a luminous wave of light that encircled them in waves of heat and brilliance. It wasn't merely a glow; it was alive, flowing between them like a sacred river, unyielding and eternal. They weren't just together—they were one, bound by a force, timeless and unbreakable. Rowan kissed her again, his tenderness igniting a warmth that seemed to echo the energy around them, flowing through them with a boundless force. Their connection was infinite, undeniable, a force that transcended the physical world.

As the power around them ebbed, its intensity softening into a gentle rhythm, they lay entwined in its warmth. The light remained, shifting in soft, radiant waves that painted the walls with patterns like celestial constellations. Their breaths slowed, their hearts beating in unison, the rhythm of their connection as natural as breathing.

Rowan's voice broke the quiet, soft but resolute. "This is ours, Aislinn," he said, drawing her closer. "No one can take it. No one can touch what we've created."

Her hand pressed to his chest, her fingers resting over the steady beat of his heart. "It's more than ours," she whispered, awe threading through her words. "It's who we are now. Together."

The challenges ahead still lingered, but they seemed like distant shadows against the brightness of their bond. The light between them pulsed gently, not just an aura but a living testament to the love and strength they now shared—an enduring presence, boundless and infinite.

The night stretched on, the light casting delicate shadows that danced across the walls. They lay facing each other, fingers intertwined, their gazes holding a tenderness that spoke of love too profound for words. In each look was the immensity of endless devotion, unburdened by fear or doubt. For the first time, there was only certainty—a certainty that filled the space between them like an unspoken promise.

Whatever this was, it wasn't fleeting. It was infinite. It was theirs.

Across the city, perched on the edge of a towering skyscraper, Lucifer watched. The city lights stretched beneath him in a restless expanse, shimmering like a fractured sea of fire. But his attention was fixed on a single, distant window—the one leading to Rowan's apartment.

Faint pulses of blue light flickered in the darkness, steady and unrelenting, a beacon that pierced through the shadows. A slow, sinister grin spread across Lucifer's face, his eyes gleaming with dark amusement and cruel intent.

"Ah," he murmured, his voice a silken rasp, the word drawn out like a blade sliding from its sheath. "So, it begins."

His hands moved deliberately, fingertips tapping together in a slow rhythm as though savoring the thought. The air around him seemed to still, heavy with his presence, as his grin widened into something predatory. The shadows at his feet curled and writhed as though alive, responding to his energy, eager to obey.

"It's time to play," he whispered, his voice low and cutting, like steel scraping against stone. The promise of chaos hung in the air, sharp and suffocating.

Lucifer turned his gaze back to the distant light, his smile twisting into a sinister sneer. The game had begun, and he was ready to make his move.

Chapter Twenty-Four
Shadows of the Eclipse

Aislinn stirred, cocooned in the warmth lingering from the night before. She kept her eyes closed, savoring the weight of Rowan's arm resting across her waist and the steady rise and fall of his breathing against her back. His lips grazed the nape of her neck, drawing a quiet laugh from her. She turned to face him, their legs tangling beneath the sheets, and her breath caught as their eyes met. He kissed her—a slow, intimate kiss that held everything unspoken between them.

When they parted, Aislinn brushed her thumb along his cheek. "Morning," she murmured.

"Morning," he replied, his voice low and rough with sleep. "Did you sleep well?"

"Better than well," she said, nestling closer. "Last night was... magical."

A shadow of thought crossed his face, and his features turned thoughtful. "That blue glow... it wasn't just power," he said, his voice intent. "It felt like every part of us—everything we are—came together in that moment. Like it was always meant to happen."

Aislinn's thoughts drifted to the overwhelming sensation as she replied, "I think it was. It wasn't just energy or magic—it felt alive, like it's tied to us... together."

Rowan's fingers combed absently through her hair, his focus distant. "It wasn't just physical. It felt limitless, as though it reached into a depth I've never felt before—something beyond words." His brow furrowed, tension rippling through him. "Maybe it's part of what we're meant to face... with Lucifer."

The name shattered the fragile cocoon around them, pulling them back to reality. Aislinn propped herself up on her elbow, her fingertips trailing lightly along Rowan's arm. "You know I'm going with you tonight," she said firmly, her resolve leaving no room for argument.

Rowan exhaled, the weight of hesitation evident. "Aislinn, you don't have to—"

"I do," she cut in, her gaze steady. "We're stronger together. Whatever happened last night—it means something."

"I know," he admitted, his hand tightening around hers. "But if anything happens to you—" His voice faltered, the words too heavy to finish.

Aislinn leaned closer, her forehead pressing gently to his before she kissed him. "Nothing will happen," she whispered, her conviction unwavering. "But you have to trust me. I need to be there."

Rowan closed his eyes briefly, tension flickering across his features before he relented. "Alright. But if things go wrong, you fall back. Let me handle it."

"I promise," Aislinn whispered, though the thought of retreat unsettled her. She knew he needed the reassurance. "Only if there's no other choice."

Rowan's lips curved into a faint smile, easing the knot of worry between them. "You never make things easy, do you?"

She grinned, brushing a kiss against his lips. "Would you want me to?"

"Not at all," he admitted, pulling her closer. "I wouldn't."

They remained in the comfort of each other, a deeper bond weaving silently between them in the aftermath of all they had shared. Aislinn pressed her palm against his chest, warmth radiating back through her, as though their very beings had intertwined.

"I love you," she whispered, the words flowing effortlessly.

Rowan's expression softened, his reply unguarded and sure. "I love you too." The admission tethered them, grounding them before the storm that loomed ahead.

Eventually, Rowan exhaled, breaking the silence. "We should get moving," he said, though neither made an effort to leave the sanctuary of their embrace just yet.

Aislinn groaned, tracing idle patterns along his arm. "Can't we stay here? Just a little longer? Pretend the rest of the world doesn't exist?"

"I wish we could." Rowan kissed her forehead, his voice lighter. "But if I'm letting you come on this mission, we need to prepare. We have to be ready."

With a reluctant sigh, Aislinn sat up, stretching. "Fine. Saving the world doesn't wait."

"Not for long, anyway." Rowan grinned, pulling her upright beside him. "But we've got this."

Dressed and ready, Rowan and Aislinn walked up the hill toward the open field near the Fallen's Airbnb. The crisp morning air carried the earthy scent of pine, cool and invigorating against their skin. For a fleeting breath, everything felt almost normal. Rowan's hand in hers was warm, a steady reassurance against the uncertainty ahead. They shared a brief look, a silent acknowledgment of the bond between them, stronger now than ever.

Ahead, Oak stood waiting, his composed manner unwavering. Today, he wasn't alone. Beside him stood Elder, the team's most skilled magic user. Taller and more imposing, Elder radiated calm authority, his relaxed stance hinting at the restrained power beneath.

As they approached, Aislinn caught a subtle exchange between Oak and Elder. No words passed, yet there was an unmistakable understanding in their posture. Rowan's grip tightened briefly, pulling her attention back.

"Think we should mention the blue glow? What happened last night?" Rowan asked, a playful smirk tugging at his lips. "We could tell Oak... or just see what happens."

Aislinn grinned, a thrill of excitement sparking in her chest. "Let's keep it to ourselves," she said lightly. "See if it happens again."

The allure of exploring this newfound power together was irresistible. Whatever it was, it felt like it belonged to them alone, at least for now.

"Good morning," Oak greeted, his measured voice steady. "You two look well-rested." His gaze lingered on them for a heartbeat longer than usual before continuing, "I've brought Elder to assist with your training. His expertise in magic will challenge and push your progress."

Elder gave a small nod, his deep baritone cutting through the still air. "I'll be testing your bond," he said, assessing them with an intensity that demanded attention. "Magic isn't just about strength—it's about trust."

Rowan nodded, resolve settling in his posture. Aislinn felt her own determination rising to match his. Whatever awaited them tonight, they would stand side by side to meet it.

The training began like before, with Oak guiding them through drills designed to sharpen their coordination. The field was hushed, save for the occasional hum of magic cutting the air. Their communication had improved, but small missteps still broke their flow—hesitations, competing instincts.

"Focus," Oak called from across the field. "Trust each other's instincts. Don't think—just move."

Aislinn tried to let go, to trust the connection instead of analyzing every step. Yet the clash of their thoughts tripped them up. Sweat trickled down her temple as she noticed Rowan's strain mirrored her own. Still, they couldn't falter—not now.

Without warning, Oak signaled to Elder. A flash of green erupted from Elder's hand—a crackling orb of magic streaking toward Rowan. He didn't see it, but Aislinn did. Her chest tightened as instinct surged.

Rowan!

The cry tore through her mind, raw and commanding. Rowan turned sharply, as though hearing her directly. At the same instant, her hands shot up, unleashing a vivid blue light that solidified into a shimmering shield behind him. The green energy slammed into it, shattering harmlessly.

Rowan spun back to her, surprise lighting his face as the blue glow faded into a faint haze. Then, as though their bond had truly awakened, the luminescence returned, flickering around them like a living presence.

Aislinn met his gaze, and for the first time, there was no need to speak. Moving as one, they glided through Oak's next set of obstacles. Rowan guided her away from danger with unerring precision, while she unleashed bursts of blue energy, each strike precise and devastating. They were no longer two individuals but halves of the same whole, their movements perfectly synchronized.

By the time the final target fell, the glow had dissipated, leaving behind an electric undercurrent. Hand in hand, they returned to Oak and Elder, the shared exhilaration between them unspoken.

"How was that?" Rowan asked, a note of satisfaction evident in his voice.

Oak and Elder exchanged looks, their reactions tinged with a hint of awe. "What was that?" Oak finally asked, shaking his head as though struggling to grasp it. "It was... radiant."

Aislinn's lips curved into a faint smile. "We were hoping you could tell us."

Elder's sharp gaze held steady, his words considered. "It was like a surge—your auras blending into something entirely new. I've never seen anything like it."

Oak crossed his arms, his expression turning thoughtful. "A radiant s urge..." he murmured, the name settling naturally. "I'll need to research this—whatever it is, it's unique."

Rowan glanced at Aislinn, a flicker of understanding passing between them. Neither spoke, content to let the mystery linger a little longer.

Oak clapped his hands, shattering the reflective atmosphere. "There's more work to do. Now that we've seen what you're capable of, training will get more intense."

And it did. Elder tested their limits, casting faster spells and channeling stronger magic. The obstacles became increasingly intricate, yet even without the glow of Radiant Surge, Rowan and Aislinn moved with growing certainty. Mistakes persisted, but each stumble seemed to fortify their foundation, forging a bond that was unbreakable. Their connection sharpened, evolving into seamless synchronization.

By early afternoon, Oak signaled the end of the session. "You've made remarkable progress," he said, a rare note of approval weaving into his usually calm demeanor. "You're ready for tonight."

Elder inclined his head, his approval subtle but evident. "You've earned this."

As they descended the hill toward the Airbnb, the weight of that looming task, however, was a quiet assurance—a sense that whatever challenges lay ahead, they were prepared to meet them head-on.

The warmth of the midday sun followed them down the path—until it vanished. Aislinn slowed, her steps faltering as she glanced upward. The sky's golden hue had dulled, its brilliance replaced by an unsettling dimness.

This wasn't a coastal marine layer or a sudden weather shift. The change felt... wrong.

"Is it just me, or did things suddenly turn strange?" Rowan's grip on her hand tightened, his focus shifting outward.

Aislinn's attention stayed fixed above. "No," she murmured, her voice low and wary. "It's not just you."

The sun, so steady minutes earlier, now seemed partially eclipsed by a shadow that defied explanation. There had been no forecast, no warning. A faint unease unfurled in her chest, gnawing at the edges of her thoughts.

Rowan studied her as they walked, catching the way her pace slowed and her concentration remained anchored on the sky. "You feel it too," he said, his words measured, his concern unmistakable.

Aislinn's chest tightened, the unnatural dimness pressing into her thoughts like a heavy fog. "Something feels off," she replied softly.

She tried to summon a small smile, but it flickered and disappeared. "Maybe it's nothing," she added, though even she didn't believe it.

By the time they reached the Airbnb, an uneasy silence lingered between them. Inside, the rest of the team had already gathered, their attention riveted to the television. The flickering screen painted uneven shadows across the room as a news report repeated on loop. An anchor spoke of an unexpected partial solar eclipse, showing bewildered locals shielding their eyes as the daylight faded across the city. Theories filled the airwaves, but none of them offered clarity.

Oak entered a moment later, his purposeful stride drawing the team's attention. He scanned the room and stopped at Eileen, seated near the back. Her hands gripped the armrests of her chair, her rigid posture betraying the storm brewing beneath her calm exterior. The weight of her presence seemed to deepen the tension in the room.

Oak moved to her side and placed a hand on her shoulder. She looked up, their unspoken exchange filled with meaning. A few seconds later, she nodded, rising to join him. Together, they stepped out onto the porch, their silent departure brimming with intent.

Rowan's eyes narrowed as he watched Oak and Eileen step outside, unease twisting inside him. He turned to Aislinn, leaning closer. "This isn't random," he muttered. "Do you think it's tied to tonight?"

Aislinn's attention shifted to the window, where the muted sky loomed over the landscape like a smothering weight. The pressure in her chest coiled tighter, impossible to ignore. "It has to be," she murmured, almost to herself. "But I can't see how."

Rowan slid his hand into hers, his grip firm as he led her toward the others gathered by the television. He sank into a chair, pulling her into his lap, his hold grounding and protective. Aislinn leaned into him without hesitation, letting the warmth of his embrace ease the knot of unease tightening within her. His arm wrapped securely around her waist, steady and strong, while she rested her head against him, focusing on the soothing rhythm of his heartbeat.

The droning news broadcast filled the room, a relentless stream of speculation and incomplete answers. Neither Rowan nor Aislinn could ignore the certainty settling over them—this wasn't natural. It wasn't coincidence. It was deliberate. A signal. A warning. And as the oppressive restlessness spread through the room, it was clear they weren't the only ones who felt it.

Outside on the porch, Oak stood beside Eileen, both staring up at the partially obscured sun. The eerie dimness cast fractured shadows across the ground, their jagged edges shifting unnaturally. The silence between them carried weight, an unspoken understanding hanging in the air. Finally, Oak broke it.

"This isn't normal, is it?" His voice was measured, though they both knew the answer already.

Eileen shook her head, her attention dropping to the warped patterns etched into the earth. "No," she replied, her words quiet but certain. "It's supernatural."

Oak's focus followed hers, his expression hardening as he studied the distorted shadows. Their sharp edges twisted subtly, forming shapes that sent a chill through him. "Do you see that?" he asked, lowering his voice.

Eileen's breath caught as the fragments aligned into an unmistakable pattern. "It's the same symbol," she whispered, her pulse quickening. "The one Rowan and Aislinn found."

Oak's expression hardened, realization settling over him. "You're sure?"

"I'm sure," Eileen confirmed, her tone clipped. The puzzle pieces clicked together with alarming clarity. The eclipse, the symbol—it all pointed in one direction. "This is from Lucifer."

Oak exhaled slowly, his composure faltering for an instant before he steeled himself. "He's making his move, isn't he?"

"Yes." Eileen's focus shifted back to the twisted shadows, her voice firm with resolve. "Something's changed. He's ready."

A tense quiet stretched between them, the weight of her words heavy with meaning. Oak straightened, his tone sharpened with urgency. "There's more. During training, Rowan and Aislinn... they triggered a Radiant Surge."

Eileen's head snapped toward him, her sharp focus locking onto his face. "A Radiant Surge?"

Oak nodded, his mouth set in a straight line. "They moved like they'd been doing it for years. It wasn't just strength—it was like they were in complete harmony."

Eileen's chest tightened, a mix of apprehension and resolve settling over her. "They're Soulbound."

Oak frowned, confusion flickering across his features. "Soulbound? What does that mean?"

Eileen's expression grew serious, her tone unwavering. "Don't tell any-one—not Rowan, not Aislinn, and definitely not the others. They have to realize it themselves."

Oak hesitated but gave a curt nod. "What does it mean?" he pressed.

Eileen exhaled, her explanation careful. "When two people fall deeply in love, they unlock abilities that go beyond what they could ever achieve alone. But it only works when they're together—it's extremely rare, and it comes with incredible risk. Lucifer knows they're Soulbound. The eclipse—it's his signal."

Oak's shoulders squared, the gravity of her words sinking in. "We're not ready to face him like this. We need reinforcements."

Eileen's jaw set, her resolve unshaken. "Agreed. Get the rest of the Fallen here within two days. We'll need everyone ready. We don't know when he'll strike."

Oak gave a sharp nod and disappeared into the house to make the calls. Eileen remained on the porch, her focus fixed on the jagged symbol imprinted in the shadows. Whatever it meant, this was only the beginning. Lucifer was moving, and failure wasn't an option.

Eileen stepped into the living room, her movements measured, her composure unshaken despite the urgency radiating from her presence. The group turned toward her—Rowan, Aislinn, and Elder seated, while Vine, Holly, Riichi, and Reed remained near the back. Takoda and Rain hovered by the doorway, their unease palpable, bracing for what was to come.

"The eclipse isn't natural," Eileen began, her voice cutting cleanly through the room. "It's a signal from Lucifer."

The silence that followed was thick, every syllable settling like a weight over the group. Rowan's hand tightened on Aislinn's, pulling her closer as his jaw set with fierce determination.

"What kind of signal?" Rowan asked, his words steady but edged with concern.

Eileen gestured toward the TV, where the footage of the eclipse repeated endlessly. "Lucifer's been lying low, but this changes everything. The eclipse proves he's ready to act."

Rain folded her arms, her features hardening. "So he's close."

Eileen nodded. "Yes. For your safety, I'm giving you the option: stay or leave. No one will judge you if you decide to go—this is dangerous, and no one is obligated to face it. But if you stay, you have to be ready."

Takoda stepped forward, her resolve clear in the way she held herself. "We're staying."

Rain nodded immediately, her voice steady. "We're not going anywhere."

Eileen acknowledged them with a small nod, a flicker of approval crossing her face before she turned back to the group. Before she could continue, Aislinn froze. Her body stiffened, her gaze losing focus as her surroundings faded into swirling shadows. Darkness twisted and shifted, forming the sigil she and Rowan had discovered outside the café. A low, mocking voice echoed in her mind, smooth and chilling.

I'm coming. I'm ready to play.

The vision shattered abruptly, leaving her breathless. She inhaled deeply, forcing herself to regain control as her surroundings came back into focus. The weight of the group's stares pressed in on her as she spoke, her voice firm despite the urgency running beneath it. "He's coming. He's... ready to play."

The atmosphere grew heavier as her words settled, the implications tightening like a vice around everyone present.

Rowan leaned closer, his hand resting firmly on her back. "What did you see?"

"I felt him," Aislinn replied, her tone calm but unwavering. "I saw shadows forming the sigil from the café. He sent a message. He said he's coming, and he's ready."

A ripple of unease passed through the group, their focus narrowing as the gravity of her revelation sank in.

Eileen's expression hardened, her response brisk. "Then we don't have much time. Oak is contacting the rest of the Fallen. They'll arrive within two days. Until then, no one can be alone—especially not Rowan and Aislinn."

She turned to Riichi, her instructions sharp. "Find us a larger Airbnb. Rowan and Aislinn will stay with the group. They'll be safer here."

Riichi nodded without hesitation, already pulling out his phone. "I'll handle it."

Aislinn glanced at Rowan, curiosity breaking through the tension. "There's more of you?"

Rowan's lips curved faintly, and his hand brushed lightly against her back. "There's always more."

Vine stepped forward, his attention fixed on Eileen. "Reinforcements are coming, but what do we do until then?"

Eileen straightened, her resolve unshaken. "We stay on task. Tonight, we take down the Golden Dawn. Lucifer's warning only underscores the importance of this mission. Once they're handled, we prepare for him."

Oak entered the room, nodding to Eileen. "The others are on their way."

Eileen's gaze swept over the group, her tone steady but resolute. "We have two days to regroup. Tonight, we deal with the Golden Dawn."

Aislinn exhaled as the enormity of the situation settled over her. The stakes had never been higher, but Rowan's arm around her grounded her. Whatever came next, she knew they wouldn't face it alone.

The room seemed to hum with the weight of their discussion, silence creeping in as everyone processed the gravity of the moment. It was Takoda who finally broke it, clearing her throat as though gathering her courage.

"I, uh, just wanted to say…" Takoda began hesitantly, her voice faltering. The group's attention shifted toward her—not heavy or stifling, but patient and expectant. She cast a quick glance at Rain, who offered an encouraging smile. "We're really grateful for everything you've done for us. Since the fire… keeping us safe, letting us stay here…"

Her fingers fidgeted slightly, but no one interrupted. She drew a steadying breath and continued, "We wanted to thank you by making you all a meal before the mission. Maybe stir-fry or fish tacos?" Her eyes scanned the room, uncertain. "I don't know if eating before a mission is normal for you, so I figured I'd ask."

Rain jumped in effortlessly, her warm tone easing the hesitation in the air. "It's the least we can do. Besides, you've gotta eat, right?"

Aislinn smiled, her words gentle. "Takoda's an amazing cook."

Eileen gave a slight nod, her expression calm yet approving. "That's thoughtful of you. Thank you."

Takoda's shoulders relaxed as her face brightened. "Great! I'll make stir-fry." Without another word, she headed for the kitchen, Rain trailing close behind.

Rowan leaned closer to Aislinn, amusement flickering in his features. "Another Asian dish?" he teased in a low murmur.

Aislinn shot him a mock-stern look. "Be nice, Rowan," she said, her voice playful. "What's gotten into you?"

He grinned, pulling her effortlessly into his lap and drawing a soft laugh from her. "You," he said simply. "You make me happy."

Her mock irritation melted into a tender smile as she leaned in, brushing a kiss across his lips. "You make me happy too," she murmured, a warm glow spreading through her chest.

In the kitchen, Takoda and Rain wasted no time, the steady clatter of pans and utensils breaking the quiet. Minutes later, Rain slipped out to begin setting the table. As she placed silverware in neat arrangements, Riichi entered, his typically composed character tinged with unease, his movements rigid.

"Miss Takoda," he began, his voice unusually formal. "May I assist you with the preparation?"

Takoda glanced over her shoulder mid-chop, startled by his sudden offer. "I've got it under control, but—"

"I insist," Riichi interrupted, his tone unwavering. "It would be my honor."

Her brows lifted slightly at his uncharacteristic tone, but she gave him a small smile. "Alright, you can help with the vegetables."

They fell into an unspoken rhythm, the rhythmic sound of knives against cutting boards filling the space. When Takoda nicked her finger, the dynamic shifted. She winced, a sharp gasp escaping her lips, but before she could react, Riichi moved with startling speed. In one fluid motion, he lifted her gently by the waist and carried her to the sink, guiding her hand under the cool stream of water. His touch was careful yet precise as he cleaned the cut and applied a bandage.

Takoda blinked, startled not just by the swiftness of his response but by the gentleness in his movements. From the doorway, Rain peeked back into the kitchen, her grin widening as she watched. With a sly smile, she slipped away, muttering, "I'll be right back."

Neither Takoda nor Riichi noticed. Their eyes met briefly, the air between them charged with an unspoken tension.

Riichi cleared his throat, his tone softer than usual. "You'll be fine," he said, his words calm and deliberate. "It's just a small cut, and we caught it quickly."

Takoda smiled, her voice light. "Thanks. You didn't have to go through all that."

Riichi glanced away, his composure wavering for a moment before he straightened. "My apologies if I overstepped, Miss Takoda."

She let out a soft laugh, shaking her head. "You don't have to be so formal with me. You're not like this with the others."

For the briefest instant, Riichi's features softened, his reserved behavior giving way to something more vulnerable. But just as quickly, he straightened, his usual restraint snapping back into place. "I... I apologize," he stammered, faint color rising to his cheeks. "I didn't mean to offend."

"You didn't," Takoda reassured him, her smile widening slightly. "I actually like it when you're more... relaxed."

Riichi's blush deepened, and he stepped back, retreating slightly. "I think I should go," he said awkwardly.

"You don't have to," Takoda said gently, her tone inviting. "I didn't mean to embarrass you."

"You didn't," Riichi replied quickly, but before she could say more, he gave a hasty, stiff bow and exited the kitchen, the door swinging shut behind him.

Moments later, Rain reappeared, her grin bright and full of mischief. "What was that about?" she teased, setting a dish on the counter.

Takoda stared at the door for a beat, a thoughtful smile tugging at her lips. "I'm... not sure," she admitted softly.

The brief exchange between Takoda and Riichi faded as the sounds of cooking filled the kitchen again. Soon, the inviting aroma of stir-fried chicken and vegetables spread through the space. When the meal was ready, Takoda served generous portions of tender chicken, vibrant vegetables, and fluffy rice—a simple yet comforting meal. The group gathered around the table, and Aislinn smiled as Ariel, whom she had invited earlier, slipped in and took a seat.

Ariel, usually brimming with sharp humor, seemed gentler in that moment. "Ah, stir-fry. You really know how to make a girl feel welcome," she said, her tone light but sincere.

Rain grinned from across the table. "Gotta keep everyone fueled up for what's ahead."

As they ate, the atmosphere softened, the earlier unease melting away as the Fallen murmured quiet thanks to Takoda and Rain for the thoughtful gesture.

"You were right, Aislinn," Holly said, her voice warm with gratitude. "Takoda's an incredible cook. I can't wait for the others to meet her."

"The others?" Rain asked, curiosity flickering in her expression.

Holly nodded, her face lighting up. "Ivy, Willow, and Hazel. You'll love them."

Ariel, who had been listening silently, added with a small smile, "Seems like this family of yours just keeps growing."

Riichi, ever composed, spoke up next. "I've arranged for a larger Airbnb. We'll move tomorrow."

Rain let out a low whistle. "Sounds like it's about to get cozy."

As the meal wound down, Ariel's attention shifted to Vine, seated beside her. His quiet demeanor caught her interest—self-assured, yet with a restrained energy that hinted at more beneath the surface. She hadn't spoken to him before, but whispers about him from the others had piqued her curiosity.

The faint trace of his cologne—clean, with a hint of spice—lingered in the air, pulling her focus. Acting on impulse, she leaned slightly toward him, her words casual but edged with curiosity. "So, you're Vine. I've heard a lot about you."

Vine's attention shifted to hers, a faint smirk tugging at his lips. "All good things, I hope."

Ariel tilted her head, feigning thoughtfulness. "That depends. Does arrogant, annoyingly clever, and maybe a little too smooth count as good?"

He chuckled softly, leaning back in his chair. "Depends on who you ask. But I'd say that sounds accurate."

Her lips curved into a sly smile. "At least you're honest."

His eyebrow lifted slightly, his smirk deepening. "And you must be Ariel. The one who keeps everyone on their toes."

Her grin widened. "Only when they deserve it. What about you? Do you?"

"Guess you'll have to stick around and find out," Vine replied, his voice carrying an undercurrent of amusement.

Their brief conversation went unnoticed by most of the group, but an unspoken spark lingered as Ariel leaned back, her expression unreadable. Vine's gaze held hers for a second longer before he returned to his plate, the corner of his mouth twitching with quiet humor.

As the meal concluded, a pensive calm settled over the table. The Fallen exchanged glances, and one by one, subtle nods passed between them. Elder rose first, his deep voice breaking the silence.

"We have something for you, Aislinn," Elder began. "Each of us has prepared a token for you before the mission." He stepped forward, presenting her with a small, intricately enchanted bracelet. "This holds protective magic. It can act as a shield when you need it." His focus remained steady as he added, "My life for yours."

Aislinn accepted the bracelet with quiet gratitude, the significance of the gesture clear in her expression.

Vine approached next, his typical smirk softened as he handed her a pair of sleek, fingerless leather gloves. "Versace, of course," he quipped with a wink. "They'll protect your hands without interfering with your magic. Plus, you'll look damn good while kicking ass." His tone shifted, sincerity threading through his words as he added, "My life for yours."

Aislinn smiled, shaking her head slightly at his humor, but the sentiment behind his offering wasn't lost on her.

Riichi followed, offering her a modernized kunai, the blade gleaming as it caught the light. "This weapon is from my homeland. Stay vigilant—it will serve you well." His voice carried a rare warmth as he added, "My life for yours."

As she accepted the blade, her fingers brushed his briefly. For just a heartbeat, his usual reserve gave way to a hint of unspoken care.

Holly stepped forward with a Sgian Dubh, carefully placing it into Aislinn's hands. "In Scotland, we keep these close. Small but effective. You'll know when the time comes to use it." Her smile brightened as she said, "My life for yours."

Oak approached next, presenting her with a small, silver Cornicello pendant. "An Italian symbol of protection," he explained. "I made it myself. Keep it close." His voice carried steady resolve as he pledged, "My life for yours."

Reed handed her a tactical vest, his approach as practical as ever. "Lightweight and durable. It won't slow you down, and it's designed to deflect harmful magic." He gave her a firm nod. "My life for yours."

Finally, Eileen stepped forward, her presence radiating calm strength. She held out an intricately crafted pin engraved with protective symbols. "This has been in our family for generations. It's enchanted to shield you when danger strikes." Pinning it carefully to Aislinn's jacket, she spoke with quiet conviction. "My life for yours."

As Eileen kissed her daughter's forehead, Aislinn felt the full weight of the moment settle within her. These weren't just gifts—they were vows, tangible expressions of the bond they all shared.

Ariel, who had remained respectfully quiet throughout the exchange, now smiled warmly. "Looks like you've got quite the squad," she said, her voice tinged with admiration.

Aislinn drew a deep breath, overwhelmed by the care imbued in each token. These weren't just tools for survival—they were promises, reminders of the family she had found among the Fallen. Each pledge of "My life for yours" echoed in her heart.

From his seat, Rowan watched silently as the moment unfolded, the gravity of it settling over him in unexpected ways. He hadn't known about this plan, and seeing the others pledge their lives for Aislinn stirred an emotion deep within him. For so long, the fear of failing to protect those he loved had weighed on him like an unrelenting shadow. But now, seeing the collective commitment to her safety, a quiet sense of reassurance began to take root.

She wasn't a burden—she was his equal, his partner. As he glanced around the room, the realization struck him: they weren't just fighting for her. They were fighting with her.

When the final gift was given, Aislinn met Rowan's gaze. No words were spoken, but the understanding between them was clear—she was one of them now.

Eileen rose, her calm voice cutting through the meditative quiet. "It's time to prepare."

The group stood together, a shared sense of resolve settling over them. The road ahead loomed heavy with challenges, but so too did the strength of their unity.

Aislinn looked to Rowan, the connection between them unshakable. No words passed, but the promise was there, silent and steadfast. Whatever came next, they would face it as one.

Far beyond the warmth of the house, shrouded in the shadows of the unknown, Lucifer stirred. His time to strike had not yet come. Tonight was for observing, for learning.

He would dissect their every move—uncovering their strengths, exploiting their weaknesses, and finding the fractures they had yet to notice. Each decision they made tonight would inch him closer to his goal, unraveling their defenses thread by thread.

The Fallen, oblivious to the storm brewing on the horizon, couldn't see the web tightening around them. The game had already begun.

And soon, he would make his move.

Chapter Twenty-Five
Radiance In the Dark

The air inside the Airbnb vibrated with a tension so tangible it could have been woven into the fabric of the room. Aislinn perched at the edge of the worn couch, her fingers tracing the smooth pendant Oak had given her earlier. The metal was cool under her touch, strengthening her like a tree's roots stretching deep into the earth. The clock crept closer to their mission, each tick a reminder that no charm could shield her from what lay ahead. Elder's bracelet rested snugly against her wrist, and her mother's pin lay over her heart, the silver catching faint light as if warding off unseen shadows. These weren't trinkets—they were quiet vows of protection, faith, and a fragile hope against the unknown.

Across from her, Rowan inspected his gear with methodical precision. His jaw set firm, his movements deliberate, revealing just how heavily the night's weight pressed upon him. Yet when his eyes lifted to hers, the sharp edges of his intensity softened, his concern slipping through like a whispered reassurance.

"Everything in place?" His question, spoken calmly, carried more than the query itself—a steady promise of support.

She nodded, her grip tightening on the pendant as though its solidity could still her racing thoughts. "Yeah, I'm ready." She spoke with strength, even confidence, though unease twisted deep within her. This wasn't a drill. No plan or preparation could fully shield her from the uncertainty waiting beyond the door.

The room buzzed with focused energy as the team moved with silent efficiency. By the window, Riichi polished his katana, the blade catching slivers of light like a streak of dawn breaking through shadow. Vine and Reed adjusted their commlinks, their hushed conversation dissolving into the ambient friction. Elder and Holly stood close, exchanging murmured reassurances. Though their voices didn't reach, the clasp of their hands and their calm demeanor conveyed everything unspoken.

Eileen stood at the center, her presence commanding without effort, like an ancient force pulling the room's gravity toward her. The map sprawled before her became a battlefield in miniature as her fingers skimmed over its worn surface. "We disrupt the ritual, dismantle the altar, and get out before the Golden Dawn realizes what's happening," she said, her tone resonating with a calm authority that silenced any doubts. "Oak and I will draw attention to the mansion. The rest of you know your roles. Trust each other. Trust the plan."

Rowan shifted beside Aislinn, his presence a constant anchor in the growing storm of her nerves. As he secured his commlink, his hand brushed hers, the brief contact enough to draw her focus. "Stick to the plan," he murmured, his words meant only for her. "If it goes sideways, you fall back. That's non-negotiable."

Her stomach twisted, the thought of retreating gnawing at her resolve. "I'm not planning on it," she said, forcing a faint, determined smile.

His lips quirked, a rare flicker of amusement that softened the strain hardening his features. "That's what worries me." He didn't elaborate, but the look he gave her—a depth of concern that words couldn't hold—spoke volumes. His worry wasn't for the mission. It was for her.

Eileen's clipped command cut through the moment. "We move out in five minutes."

Aislinn exhaled, her gaze darting to the others. Every movement seemed intentional, yet beneath their practiced efficiency, she could sense the implicit gravity threading through the room. This wasn't training or theory. It was real, and there would be no turning back once they stepped into the night.

Rowan spoke again, quieter this time yet firm. "Don't waste energy thinking you have to prove anything. You're here because you're ready, not because you're flawless."

The statement hit deeper than she expected, breaking through the shell of her doubts. Her grip on the pendant loosened as she looked up, her reply softer now. "I don't want to let anyone down."

His expression shifted—no pity, no condescension, just an unwavering understanding that steadied her. "You won't. Focus on what's ahead. That's enough."

A knot within her untangled—not entirely, but enough for her breath to even. "You'd better take your own advice," she said, a faint edge of humor slipping through her gratitude.

The corner of his mouth lifted in a ghost of a smile. "I will. Let's get this done."

It wasn't perfect reassurance, but it didn't need to be. What lingered between them was a quiet resolve, born not of promises but of a bond forged through trust and shared purpose.

***

The Mission District streets were cloaked in an unnatural hush, the usual city hum replaced by an eerie void. The faint whistle of wind weaving through narrow alleyways and the distant rumble of traffic only sharpened the oppressive silence. Ahead, the warehouse loomed like a forgotten sentinel, its jagged windows reflecting shards of moonlight. The structure betrayed no hint of the ritual within, its darkened facade hiding secrets steeped in shadows.

Aislinn kept close to Rowan, her steps purposeful, though her senses prickled with the magnitude of the night. The air carried a charged expectancy, pressing around her like a storm waiting to break. Oak's pendant lay warm against her skin, its subtle pulse of magic keeping her present. The protective charm was a whisper of reassurance, though it couldn't dispel the unease coiled in her chest.

A faint crackle on the commlink shattered the stillness before Vine's message followed. "Eileen and Oak have engaged. Distraction's in full swing at the mansion. The Golden Dawn's preoccupied—they won't be heading this way anytime soon."

Rowan gave a curt nod, his gaze fixed on the warehouse's shadowed outline. "Good. We move fast and stay unseen. If they think the ritual is untouched, they'll keep their focus on the mansion."

The churn of nerves twisted tighter in Aislinn's stomach, but she pushed the feeling aside, redirecting her thoughts to the plan. The chaos unfolding at Old Mount Olympus Mansion, crafted with Eileen's unyielding precision and Oak's formidable strength, was their chance to strike. Every moment the distraction held mattered.

The team dissolved into motion, slipping into the dim light like wraiths blending with the night. Riichi, Reed, and Vine moved toward the warehouse entrance, their movements fluid as they vanished into the shadows to dismantle the altar.

"Perimeter secured," Holly's calm voice filtered through the commlink, crisp and controlled. "Elder and I are in position on the south side."

Aislinn's senses sparked as a ripple of magic flickered through the air, faint yet unmistakable. It carried an ominous resonance, like the distant rumble of thunder before a storm. The energy wasn't passive—it seemed to move, alive and probing, its invisible threads brushing against her awareness with a disquieting persistence. The magic felt wrong, its presence heavier than air, laced with a cold malice that seeped into her skin and settled deep in her chest.

She followed Rowan, her steps measured but her heart beating faster. They moved toward the rear of the warehouse, cloaked in darkness yet acutely aware of the unseen forces waiting within. The magic bristled, its charged edges pressing against her as if testing her resolve. It was no longer just an awareness—it felt like the air itself pushed back against them, warning them to turn away.

Minutes dragged, stretching longer with every breath. Rowan stood beside her, his posture composed but humming with readiness. His eyes scanned the shadowed structure, unyielding as if daring the darkness to move. His hand hovered near his weapon, each motion purposeful, carrying the burden of battles fought and survived.

"They're banking on the mansion being enough to hold everyone's attention," Rowan murmured, his voice low, barely a ripple against the stillness. "They won't see this coming."

Aislinn nodded, feeling the press of protective charms against her. Oak's pendant, Elder's bracelet, and her mother's pin each hummed faintly with latent power, their magic a quiet reminder of the safeguards woven around her. However, the tightness in her chest remained, fed by the intensity of the mission and the gnawing doubt that shadowed her thoughts. Her first field mission as one of the Fallen—it felt like standing at the edge of an uncharted abyss. Could she meet the expectations set for her?

Her gaze shifted to Rowan. His calm presence steadied her in ways she hadn't anticipated. There was no hesitation in him, no crack in his focus. He moved with the confidence of someone who had weathered storms and emerged stronger. Watching him gave her a sense of stability, even as it underscored her own inexperience.

"Stop second-guessing yourself," Rowan said, cutting cleanly through the tangle of her thoughts. His tone wasn't harsh, but it carried a weight that demanded she listen. "You wouldn't be here if you weren't ready. Trust yourself."

The statement rooted itself within her, pushing aside the doubt that had taken hold. It wasn't gentle reassurance—it was truth, plain and unadorned. She let that truth anchor her, as solid as the earth beneath her feet.

She inclined her head, her grip easing on the pendant as it slipped back to rest against her chest. "Understood."

A flicker of a smile ghosted across Rowan's face. "Good."

The air grew heavier, charged with an intensity that made every breath feel deliberate. Aislinn flexed her fingers, her focus shifting from fear to resolve. Elder's bracelet was cool against her skin, its presence a tether as her determination crystallized. The task ahead was daunting, but she refused to let it break her.

"We're inside," Riichi's message crackled through the commlink. "Starting to dismantle the altar now."

Inside the warehouse, Riichi, Vine, and Reed moved with the precision of master craftsmen dismantling a dangerous puzzle. The altar sprawled across the concrete, larger and more intricate than any of them had expected. Symbols etched into the floor glowed faintly, their angular designs radiating a sinister energy that pulsed in time with the low flicker of nearby candles. The warped light danced over dark artifacts arranged with meticulous intent, their presence exuding an oppressive, unnatural force.

"There's a ward here," Riichi said, his words clipped with tension as his hands hovered over the altar's surface. "We didn't account for this."

Outside, Aislinn felt the shift in the air like a ripple passing through her. The invisible pressure settled over her shoulders, a volatile energy that buzzed against her senses, making her skin prickle. She exchanged a brief look with Rowan, who nodded once—a silent decision passed between them.

"We go now," Rowan said, already moving toward the warehouse's rear entrance. His steps were quiet yet purposeful, carrying the responsibility of urgency. Aislinn followed, her heartbeat quickening as the magic surrounding the building grew heavier, its chaotic hum clawing at the edges of her awareness. Every movement felt careful, the path ahead charged with the knowledge that any misstep could unravel their mission.

They were just steps away from the entrance when the earth shook beneath them.

An unseen force erupted from within the warehouse, tearing through the earth with the intensity of a tremor. Aislinn stumbled, her balance faltering as the vibration surged up through her boots. She reached out instinctively, her hand grasping at nothing. Before she could fall, Rowan's arm caught her, steady and unyielding, pulling her upright as the earth beneath them trembled.

And then the explosion came.

A blinding flash erupted from the warehouse doors, cutting through the darkness with a brilliance that burned her retinas. The sound followed an instant later, a deafening roar of unleashed energy that crashed over them like a wave. The force was wild and merciless, tearing at everything in its path. Aislinn's protective charms activated instantly, flaring with light as their combined energy deflected the worst of the blast.

Her mind didn't linger on herself—her thoughts turned to Rowan in an instant.

Fear surged through her like a lightning strike, swift and unrelenting. Without hesitation, she yanked the pendant from around her neck, the chain snapping in her grip. Acting purely on instinct, she threw her arms around him, the pendant's magic blazing outward in a radiant shield. The barrier enveloped them, shimmering with power as it absorbed the chaos raging around them.

Rowan moved with practiced swiftness, pulling her closer as they crouched low together. The air howled with the force of the explosion, the ground beneath them threatening to give way, but the protective shield held firm, crackling with energy as it blocked the destruction.

When the roaring subsided, the stillness that followed was unnerving. Aislinn's ears buzzed, her head spinning as the shield's glow dimmed to nothing. Her arms stayed locked around Rowan, her body trembling as adrenaline coursed through her. The pendant lay in her palm, warm but dim. It had done its job, shielding them both from harm.

Rowan exhaled, his question carrying a faint rasp from exertion. "Are you hurt?" he asked, urgency evident in his words.

"I'm okay," she said, though her voice shook as she unclenched her fingers from the broken chain. Her gaze darted to him, her relief mingled with lingering panic. "What about you?"

"Unscathed," he replied, his focus slicing cleanly through the chaos. He straightened, his fingers briefly grazing hers as he shifted his stance.

Aislinn glanced at the pendant in her hand, its faint warmth a testament to the strength it had provided. The narrow line they had walked between survival and disaster left her shaken. *We barely made it.*

Rowan's gaze shifted back to the warehouse, his expression hardened as his attention locked on the building's jagged outline. "That ward wasn't just strong—it was designed to stop anyone from interfering," he muttered. "At least it's gone now."

He pressed a finger to the commlink at his ear, his tone firm but edged with worry. "Riichi, report. Are you all right?"

There was a pause before Riichi's voice came through, calm yet clipped. "We're fine. Reed got us out before the worst of it, and Vine threw up a shield to handle the rest."

Rowan exhaled, relief breaking through the tension gripping his features. He nodded once, though no further explanation came—none was needed. For now, it was enough to know they had survived.

The air shifted abruptly, carrying a suffocating heaviness that clung to Aislinn's skin. She inhaled sharply, her senses firing as the undercurrent of energy from the explosion thickened, darkened, as if an unseen force crept into the space it left behind.

Eileen and Oak emerged from the haze, their movements fluid yet charged with purpose. The grim set of their features spoke of success at the mansion, though their focus had already pivoted.

Eileen froze mid-step, her posture rigid as her gaze swept the surrounding void with sharp precision. "Lucifer's here," she said, the faint sound scarcely breaking the heavy silence.

A chill settled deep in Aislinn's core. She didn't need to see him to know the truth in Eileen's words. The air itself had shifted, pressed down by an invasive presence. The feeling was impossible to ignore—a calculated attention that pricked at her awareness like talons grazing too close. He was near, observing, his presence coiling like smoke at the edges of her mind.

Rowan's hand brushed hers, the touch brief yet grounding. The small gesture carried an unspoken assurance that steadied her nerves, allowing her to draw strength where fear had begun to take root. She clenched her fingers, forcing her resolve to take hold even as the sensation of being watched stayed behind.

Lucifer's approach wasn't an attack. It was a predator's patience—a calculated circling, assessing their defenses, seeking the cracks he could exploit. His intent hung in the air like a hunter's snare, his attention suffocating and precise.

Eileen's message filtered through the commlink, measured and clear. "He's watching. Not moving. Observing. He's analyzing everything."

Aislinn's heartbeat drummed louder, her pulse erratic as the realization clawed at her thoughts. Lucifer was reading them, dissecting their strengths and weaknesses, gathering knowledge for an unseen purpose.

"Block him. Now," Eileen commanded, her tone cold and resolute.

Rowan inclined his head toward Aislinn, urging her forward without hesitation. Eileen's gaze locked on her as she continued, "Aislinn, Elder—set the barrier. Follow my lead."

The oppressive force of Lucifer's presence pressed harder as Aislinn moved. It probed at the edges of her mind, a predator testing the fence for weak points. There was no time to falter. They couldn't let him break through.

Elder stood ready, his energy flowing like a steady stream. Aislinn closed her eyes and reached inward, calling on the spark of magic she knew would answer. The power within her rose, a flicker of heat that surged forward and intertwined with Elder's strength. Together, their magic merged, building into a force greater than either of them alone.

Eileen's power joined the weave, folding into theirs with effortless precision. The combined magic stretched outward, weaving a dome that encased the warehouse. The air around them shimmered, rippling with the barrier's glow as it solidified, creating a boundary that resisted the invasive weight pressing against it.

Lucifer's response was immediate. The pressure on the shield surged, relentless and calculating. Aislinn gritted her teeth as the strain bore down on her, an invisible weight constricting her breath. Elder's presence anchored her, a centering force against the mounting assault, while Eileen's energy reinforced the edges of the barrier.

"We hold," Elder said, his tone as firm as a foundation.

Aislinn pushed harder, pouring more of her magic into the shield as Lucifer's influence pressed against them with renewed force. The barrier wavered but did not break. Eileen's magic bolstered its structure, and with their combined effort, the shield pushed back against the attack. The oppressive presence began to wane, its claws retracting as the boundary held firm.

When the pressure finally eased, Aislinn's muscles trembled from exertion. She opened her eyes, her body tingling with exhaustion as the glow of the barrier began to fade. It had worked—they had held him back.

"He knows we're here," Eileen said, her gaze hard and unyielding. "We don't have time to waste."

Inside the warehouse, Riichi's voice crackled over the commlink, frustration lacing his words. "We need backup. There's another ward—stronger than the others. We can't break it."

Aislinn turned to Rowan, their hands instinctively clasping as though drawn together by an unseen force. The bond between them ignited, and Radiant Surge flared to life. A soft blue glow enveloped their joined hands, rippling outward in steady waves, a visual testament to their unity.

The others turned, their attention caught by the glow. Even Eileen paused, her usual calm giving way to faint surprise as the light spread around Rowan and Aislinn.

The energy pulsed in rhythm with their steps as they moved forward, their connection amplifying the powers already within them. Rowan's strength steadied her, a force she could rely on completely, while her kinetic energy responded effortlessly, as though guided by the bond between them. "Let's end this," Rowan said, his tone resolute.

The faint glow followed them like a whisper of power as they stepped into the warehouse. The air grew heavier with each step, charged with the ward's chaotic energy. Sparks crackled around the altar, and jagged tendrils of dark magic lashed out, violently resisting Riichi, Vine, and Reed's attempts to dismantle it.

As Rowan and Aislinn crossed the threshold, the oppressive energy seemed to hesitate, as though recognizing the combined force they carried. The glow around their joined hands intensified, pressing back against the writhing darkness.

Riichi turned sharply, relief softening the tension in his features. "Finally," he muttered, though his tone carried the barest hint of awe.

"That's new," Eileen's message came through the commlink, measured but intrigued.

The ward surged violently, its unstable energy flaring in defiance. Rowan advanced first, his grip on Aislinn's hand tightening as he shattered the outer defenses with brute strength. Aislinn followed immediately, her kinetic energy weaving into the fractures he created, widening and unraveling the threads of dark magic that clung to the altar like chains. Their movements were fluid and instinctive, their connection guiding each strike.

"We're almost through," Rowan said, his calm resolve evident as he tore another layer of the ward apart.

The ward faltered, its defenses breaking under their combined assault. Aislinn funneled her energy into the remaining fragments, dismantling the final strands of magic with cautious precision. As the last piece unraveled, she raised a shimmering shield around the group, bracing for the inevitable backlash.

The ward collapsed in an explosion of chaotic energy. A shockwave rippled outward, but Aislinn's shield held firm, absorbing the impact. The air settled, and the oppressive darkness that had filled the warehouse began to dissipate.

"Ward's down," Riichi's relief came through the commlink. "We're clearing the rest now."

Aislinn exhaled, her pulse racing as the blue glow of Radiant Surge dimmed to a faint flicker before fading entirely. Her hand remained clasped tightly in Rowan's, and for a moment, the significance of what they had accomplished settled over her.

"We did it," Rowan said, his grip reassuring as his gaze met hers. The certainty in his words steadied her.

The faint pulse of energy beneath their connection lingered, like an echo of the bond they'd called upon. Aislinn marveled at the power they'd wielded—not new, but amplified through their synchronization. It left her awed and uneasy in equal measure, a reminder of the strength they could achieve together and the responsibility it carried.

The commlink crackled again. "The altar's fully dismantled. We're clear," came Reed's message.

Relief rippled through the group like a tide receding. The altar was destroyed, the ritual thwarted. The warehouse, once thick with dark magic, now stood lighter, though faint traces of corruption still clung to the air, bitter and acrid like smoke.

Rowan exhaled and released Aislinn's hand with careful intention, his fingers hovering briefly before falling to his side. Though his shoulders eased, the sharpness in his gaze didn't waver, scanning their surroundings with measured vigilance. The faint hum of dissipating magic hung in the air, a reminder of what they had just endured.

As they stepped out of the warehouse, Eileen approached with calm authority, her measured strides carrying an unspoken weight. Her expression was carefully composed, her sharp gaze moving over the group in silent assessment. Yet, as her eyes moved to each member, a flicker of pride softened the rigid lines of her face.

"Well done," she said, her calm authority evident. Her attention shifted to Aislinn, the intensity of her appraisal unwavering. "You handled yourself well tonight. Your first mission—and it won't be your last."

Aislinn's chest tightened, a surge of pride welling inside her. She hadn't realized how much Eileen's acknowledgment would mean, but it settled within her like a securing force. Gratitude flickered across her face, and she gave a small nod in response.

The rest of the group began to gather, their exhaustion evident yet mingled with quiet accomplishment. Riichi, Vine, and Reed exchanged brief glances, their silent camaraderie speaking to the trust forged during the mission. The altar was destroyed, and the Golden Dawn's plans had been disrupted—for now.

"We'll monitor them tomorrow," Riichi said, a pragmatic edge sharpening his statement as he turned to Eileen. "If they regroup, we'll know."

Eileen inclined her head, her piercing gaze sweeping over the team once more. "We've bought time. Don't mistake it for victory. The Dawn won't let this slide."

With those words, the team began their retreat, moving away from the warehouse and toward the waiting vehicle. Rowan's hand rested lightly at the small of Aislinn's back, his presence supportive as the adrenaline coursing through her began to fade.

The drive through San Francisco's darkened streets passed in silence, the engine's low rumble the only sound. The air inside the vehicle remained heavy, each member of the team lost in their own thoughts. Aislinn leaned against the seat, fragments of the night replaying in her mind—the barrier's glow, the fractured ward, the suffocating presence of Lucifer. Her breathing began to slow, a small relief, only to catch again when the car jerked to a sudden stop.

Her eyes snapped open, and her heart leapt as the headlights illuminated a figure standing motionless in the road ahead. Lucifer.

He radiated quiet menace, his presence oppressive even from a distance. The fragile calm inside the vehicle shattered as tension clawed its way back into the air, sharp and suffocating. Rowan's hand closed over hers, firm and stabilizing, though her attention was riveted on the figure before them.

Lucifer didn't move. His expression held an eerie calm, but a slow smile crept across his face as he raised a hand in a mocking gesture of acknowledgment. When he spoke, an unsettling calm lingered in the air, his smooth cadence slicing through the silence. "Well played."

His eyes tarried on Aislinn, his sharp gaze assessing her with unnerving precision before sliding over the rest of the team. "The score is tied."

The words hit her like a blow. The fire at the café, the destruction—it had been him. The Golden Dawn had set the stage, but Lucifer had ensured the devastation was absolute. He had been there, orchestrating it all, and now he stood before them to make sure they knew it.

Rowan's jaw clenched, his features hardening as the reminder of their unfinished battle settled heavily in the air. Tonight's hard-fought success suddenly felt tarnished by the magnitude of what lay ahead.

Lucifer's smile widened, the edge of mockery sharpening his tone. "And thank you for sharing." He tapped his temple with a deliberate motion, the gesture steeped in false amusement. "That barrier... impressive. Now I know exactly what you're capable of."

Aislinn's stomach dropped. The barrier had been necessary to block him out, but in doing so, they had revealed too much. The satisfaction radiating from him made it clear—he had gained an important insight.

Lucifer took a step back, his amusement chilling in its subtlety. "I'll allow this one," he said, his tone laced with mock generosity. "But don't get comfortable. I never play fair."

And then he was gone, dissolving into the shadows as though he had never been there.

For a long moment, no one spoke. The silence in the car was oppressive, the earlier relief obliterated by the charged apprehension left in Lucifer's wake.

Eileen finally shattered the stillness, her firm command slicing through the haze of unease. "He's testing us. We didn't have a choice, and he knows it. Don't let him unsettle you. This was still a win."

The vehicle resumed its journey, the low hum of the engine filling the silence. Inside, the enormity of the encounter hung heavy and unspoken in the air. Aislinn turned toward the window, her thoughts spiraling as Lucifer's parting words echoed in her mind, a grim reminder that tonight's victory was only the beginning of a larger battle.

She inhaled deeply, forcing the tension from her chest. *Not tonight.* She wouldn't let his taunts overshadow what they'd accomplished. Her gaze drifted to Rowan, his hand still resting over hers. The quiet strength in the gesture settled her frayed nerves, igniting a small, steady resolve within her. Whatever came next, they would face it together.

When they arrived at the Airbnb, the atmosphere inside reflected the aftermath of the mission. As the group stepped into the dimly lit space, Takoda and Rain looked up from the sofa. Their expressions brightened with relief at the sight of everyone returning, but the faint unease in their eyes betrayed how closely they had been bracing for the worst.

"How'd it go?" Takoda asked, her gaze sweeping over the group, silently cataloging their well-being.

Aislinn hesitated, glancing briefly at Rowan before stepping further into the room. Eileen, ever direct, answered in her usual concise manner. "Mission was a success. The altar is dismantled, and the ritual has been disrupted. Now we wait to see if it's enough to destabilize the Golden Dawn."

Relief rippled through the room as Takoda and Rain exchanged glances, their shoulders easing as the tension dissipated slightly. For the shortest time, the impact of the night seemed to lift.

No one mentioned Lucifer. His presence remained a shadow in Aislinn's mind, too fresh to speak of yet. There was no need to burden the team further—not tonight.

"We took care of a few things while you were out," Rain said softly, her tone careful. "Packed up the communications room and started organizing some of the others' things."

Rowan's lips tilted into a faint but genuine smile. "Thank you. That helps more than you know."

Takoda nodded, her gaze shifting to Aislinn. "We just wanted to make things easier for everyone."

The sincerity in her voice stirred an unfamiliar feeling in Aislinn, a quiet warmth spreading through her that she wasn't entirely used to. The sense of belonging, of being part of a purpose that truly mattered, pressed against her thoughts. It wasn't about survival anymore; it was about contributing, about showing up for others the way they had for her. She gave a small nod of gratitude, unable to find the words to express the feeling fully.

After a few more brief exchanges, Rowan turned to her, his request softened. "We should head to my place," he said. "Get our things together before meeting everyone tomorrow."

Aislinn nodded, exhaustion beginning to settle into her limbs as the adrenaline ebbed. Eileen had made it clear that the team needed to stay together for safety, but the thought of a more peaceful space with Rowan offered the solace she needed. A chance to step away from the seriousness of the mission, to breathe, and to begin piecing her thoughts together in the calming presence of someone who understood.

***

Rowan's apartment welcomed them like a sanctuary, its stillness a sharp contrast to the chaos they had left behind. The soft glow from a single lamp painted the room in golden hues, its warmth wrapping Aislinn in a soothing reassurance. As the door clicked shut behind them, she exhaled deeply, the tension coiled within her finally beginning to loosen.

Rowan turned to her immediately, his expression open yet searching. "Are you okay?"

Aislinn managed a faint smile, though her thoughts still churned with remnants of the night. "I think so. Just... trying to take it all in." She stepped closer, the weight on her shoulders easing by degrees. "It was... a lot."

He nodded, his reliable presence a constant she hadn't realized how much she relied on. "It always is. But we came through it."

Her gaze lingered on him, and for the first time since the mission, her mind slowed enough to reflect on all they had accomplished. A sense of pride rose within her, warm and unfamiliar. "I'm proud of us," she said softly, the words carrying a quiet strength. Her eyes searched his. "Especially you. The way you handled everything—it felt like, no matter what happened, you'd make sure we were okay."

Rowan raised an eyebrow, the corner of his mouth quirking into a faint smile. "Me?"

"Yes, you." Her grin turned playful as warmth crept into her cheeks. "Watching you tonight—how in control you were, how precise—it was..." She hesitated, her blush deepening. "It was kind of... sexy."

His grin widened, amusement flickering in his eyes. "Sexy, huh?"

"What can I say?" she teased, her smile growing. "Strength and confidence look good on you."

Rowan's chuckle rumbled low and deep as he stepped closer, his arms slipping around her. "Good to know I have my moments."

As she rested her head against his chest, his warmth seeped into her, soothing the remaining adrenaline still coursing through her veins. The steady rhythm of his heartbeat stilled her racing thoughts, grounding her in a way nothing else could. "You did more than impress me," she murmured. "You made me feel safe. Even when it felt like everything might fall apart, I knew you wouldn't let anything happen to me."

Rowan's arms tightened subtly around her, his voice a gentle rumble. "That's all I wanted—to keep you safe."

Aislinn tilted her head to meet his gaze, her chest aching at the raw sincerity reflected in his features. "You always do," she whispered, emotion thickening her breath. "When I'm with you, I don't feel like I have to face anything alone."

The strain of the night seemed to melt away, replaced by the quiet solace they found in each other. The dangers, the chaos, even Lucifer's haunting presence—all of it receded into the background. Lost in the now, surrounded by the warmth of Rowan's apartment, they existed in a space that felt untouched by the outside world.

After a pause, Rowan exhaled, his expression shifting to one of quiet thoughtfulness. "There's something I've been meaning to give you," he said, stepping toward a small shelf by the wall.

Aislinn watched as he returned, a carefully stacked bundle in his hands. Her breath hitched when she recognized it: a photo album, folded fabric, and the outfit she had worn the night they first met.

"You… kept these?" she asked, her voice barely audible.

Rowan nodded, his gaze tender. "You knew I went back to the café after the fire while you were out. I gave you the photos already, but I couldn't leave these behind."

Her fingers brushed the fabric, her throat tightening as a flood of memories rushed back. "I didn't think anything could be saved," she murmured, emotion thickening each word. "And you… you kept it?"

Rowan's hand lingered over the outfit, his touch reverent. "I couldn't let it go," he said quietly. His eyes lowered briefly before meeting hers again. "That night changed everything for me. I don't know why, but it felt like something I had to hold on to."

Aislinn's chest swelled with gratitude, the significance of his gesture overwhelming her. "I thought it was all gone," she whispered, her voice breaking. "But you… you saved it."

"I wasn't going to let that happen," he said simply, his tone soft but resolute. "I even cleaned it myself. I wanted it to be just as it was—not because of the fire, but because of what it means."

Emotion surged within her, too vast to name. "Thank you," she said, her breath trembling. "I don't even know how to tell you how much this means to me."

Rowan smiled, his expression unguarded and warm. "You don't have to. I just wanted you to have it."

Without hesitation, Aislinn closed the space between them, pressing her lips to his. The kiss carried everything she couldn't put into words—gratitude, love, and a profound sense of belonging. Rowan kissed her back with equal intensity, his hands framing her face, anchoring them both in the here and now.

The world outside fell away, the dangers and burdens of the night fading into the distance. Here, in Rowan's arms, surrounded by the serene refuge of his apartment, nothing else mattered.

Time blurred as they stayed close, their touches growing softer but no less meaningful. When the intensity ebbed, Aislinn rested her head against his chest, his heartbeat a soothing rhythm that eased her toward stillness.

"I don't know how to explain it," she murmured, her voice thick with emotion. "I love you so much it scares me."

Rowan's hand moved gently through her hair, his tone low and filled with understanding. "I know. I feel the same way."

Speech felt unnecessary. What they shared, immersed in the present, surpassed language, a connection unbroken by the shadows loitering beyond. In his embrace, Aislinn found a peace she hadn't known in years.

As sleep tugged at her, a flicker of unease stirred at the edge of her mind—not fear, but a steady certainty that challenges loomed ahead, ready to test everything they had built. She tightened her fingers around Rowan's, her resolve solidifying: *Whatever comes, they would meet it head-on as one.*

Outside, the city remained silent, its depths hiding forces that waited for dawn, ready to move unseen and unrelenting.

Chapter Twenty-Six

The Coming Storm

The first light of dawn barely brushed the horizon, leaving the Old Mount Olympus Mansion cloaked in shadow. Reed crouched low, pressing himself against the damp earth, his focus fixed on the darkened windows. The mansion loomed in an unnatural silence, a stillness that prickled at his instincts. They'd expected a sign by now—a reaction, a ripple of fallout from last night's sabotage.

"Nothing yet," Riichi's words filtered through their link, measured but tinged with unease.

Their strike had been exact, dismantling the altar in the Mission District warehouse—a keystone to the Golden Dawn's plans. Without it, capturing Aislinn and tearing open a rift between worlds should have been impossible. Yet here they were, hours later, with the mansion untouched. The silence was no coincidence.

"They should be scrambling," Vine muttered. "This doesn't feel right."

Reed tightened his jaw. The destruction of the altar should've sent shockwaves through the Golden Dawn's ranks, yet the mansion stood unmoved. *Something's wrong.*

"We'll wait a little longer," Riichi said. "If nothing changes, we regroup."

Reed scanned the windows again, his sharp gaze catching a faint flicker deep within the house. He stilled, every muscle taut. A figure moved briefly past the shadows.

"There," he murmured through the link. "Someone's inside."

The air around them thickened, heavy with an unseen force that pressed against their senses. Reed exchanged a glance with Vine, who crouched nearby. Gone was his usual air of smug ease—now replaced with unshaken focus. They all felt it: a dark anticipation coiling in the air, not of a mere response but an impending threat far worse.

"Stay sharp," Riichi said, his tone clipped, resolute. "This isn't over."

The shift came like a whisper of warning.

Reed felt it first—the sudden drop in temperature, the way the world seemed to draw inward. His muscles coiled instinctively. *It's close.*

"I'm 'walking,'" he said through the link, low and certain. He didn't wait for acknowledgment. Closing his eyes, he reached for the shadows that gathered around him. They answered instantly, cold and alive, wrapping around him like an old ally. The air chilled as he let them consume him, his form dissolving into darkness until only the faintest ripple hinted at his presence.

Reed didn't just move through the shadows; he became part of them. His awareness expanded, the physical world fading into muted outlines and whispers. The void cradled him, a dark expanse he navigated with instinct and ease.

As the mansion loomed closer, the oppressive energy sharpened. The shadows pressed warnings against his thoughts, their cold grip urging caution. This wasn't the Golden Dawn's typical presence. It was ancient. Vast. Consuming.

Lucifer.

The name surfaced unbidden, a weight that settled heavily in his chest. No confirmation was needed. The raw, suffocating power emanating from the mansion left no room for doubt.

Reed drifted closer, every sense honed. Through the cracked window, the figure came into view—a silhouette cloaked in living darkness, the air around him twisting unnaturally. He didn't simply stand in the space; he controlled it, bent it, as if the mansion itself yielded to his presence.

Reed forced his breathing steady, his pulse slowing as he crept toward a broken window. Every step was a whisper against the earth, his movements fluid and soundless. The air seemed to pull back from the mansion, carrying an unnatural chill that bit into his skin.

A glance over his shoulder revealed Riichi and Vine, their outlines blurred by the fog that thickened the air. Raising two fingers, he signaled his next move—advancing, taking position. No words passed between them; the weight of Lucifer's presence made speaking impossible. From this point on, there could be no mistakes. Everything depended on precision and silence.

Closer now, Reed caught the faint hum of voices drifting from within the mansion. His breath froze as he strained to hear. One voice rose above the others—Lucifer's. It wasn't loud, yet it filled the space, resonant and commanding. The kind of presence that didn't demand attention; it was attention. Reed's pulse quickened, though his focus remained unbroken. He pressed against the cold stone wall, letting the shadows wrap around him like a second skin.

The voices sharpened as Reed edged closer, every movement blending seamlessly with the void. He didn't need to see Lucifer to feel him. The air around the mansion pulsed faintly, a ripple of energy pulling everything toward its source. Reed's senses heightened as he locked onto the words.

"You've failed," Lucifer said, his tone calm, slicing through the stagnant air. "Your failure is an opportunity—for me."

Reed tensed, his hands bracing against the cool, uneven stone. *Opportunity.* Lucifer wasn't here to clean up a mess—he was here to take control. Reed held his position, every muscle taut as he listened.

"With me," Lucifer continued, his words cutting through the quiet, "you will do more than just capture the girl. You will bring both her and Rowan to me. Their bond holds the power we need. Once I have it, I will regain what was taken from me. I will rise, and you will follow."

Reed's pulse thundered in his ears. *Rowan, too?* It wasn't just Aislinn. Lucifer needed them both. Their bond wasn't just important—it was the crux of his plan. A chill prickled down his spine. *This isn't a typical mission—this is far more dangerous.*

"The source of their combined strength must be harvested," Lucifer continued, his words deliberate, each one cutting like a blade. "Once I have it, I will perform the ritual here, at the heart of the Golden Dawn—one week from today. We will strip their bond, and with it, I will reclaim what was lost to me."

One week. The weight of the deadline hit Reed like a blow, but he forced himself to remain perfectly still. The ritual wasn't just a threat; it was a declaration. Lucifer wasn't aiding the Golden Dawn—he was consuming them, pulling every resource into his grasp to guarantee success.

"Their bond must be severed," Lucifer said, his words final, carrying a force that pressed outward even through the walls. "Only then will the power reveal itself. And with it, I will rise to my full strength."

Reed's jaw locked. *Severed.* Lucifer didn't just want to destroy them; he wanted to fracture their connection, extract its power, and use it to restore himself. Aislinn and Rowan weren't just players in his plan—they were the foundation.

Lucifer's voice hardened, an edge of warning threading through his command. "You follow me now. One week. If you fail again, you won't live to regret it."

The command radiated through the air, a weight Reed couldn't shake. *One week. Rowan and Aislinn's bond was the keystone of Lucifer's return to power.* Whatever force tied them together, he intended to rip it apart—and with it, reclaim what had been taken from him.

Through the com-link, Riichi's whisper broke the silence. "Rowan, too..."

Reed's teeth clenched. They'd always known Aislinn was vital, but Rowan's connection to her—their bond—was the true target. Whatever power was buried within it, Lucifer was determined to claim it.

"We need to move," Vine murmured, his voice tight with urgency. "One week isn't enough."

Reed gave a slight nod, his body locked with tension. Moving too quickly would give him away. Inch by inch, he began his retreat, slipping deeper into the shadows, the cold void cocooning him. The pull of the darkness made him weightless, his steps silent as he drifted back, every movement measured and exact. The shadows carried him, their chill smudging the lines between his form and the void.

As he neared the others, movement flickered inside the mansion. A figure stepped toward the cracked window, and Reed froze, flattening himself against the stone. The silhouette paused, its energy radiating fear and subservience—an extension of Lucifer's will. The figure lingered for a instant before retreating into the mansion's depths.

Reed exhaled slowly, his body easing back into motion. He continued his retreat until he reached Riichi and Vine, their outlines emerging from the mist as the shadows released him. They waited in silence until they had moved far enough from the mansion to speak.

"He's after both of them," Reed said, his tone measured. "Rowan and Aislinn. Their bond is the key. He's going to break it and use the power it holds."

Vine exhaled sharply, raking a hand through his hair. "It's worse than we thought. We've been focused on Aislinn, but Rowan's tied to this too—he's part of the equation. Lucifer's not just stepping in; he's taking over."

Reed nodded, his expression grim. "The ritual happens in one week, at the mansion. If he succeeds, we lose everything. He's not leaving room for failure this time."

Riichi's gaze hardened, his voice firm with determination. "Then neither can we. The Fallen need to know—every one of us. This fight isn't just about stopping Lucifer anymore. It's about protecting them. Both of them."

Without another word, they disappeared into the mist, their movements precise and swift. The countdown had begun. Lucifer wasn't just another adversary—they were up against the full force of his will. And at the center of it all stood Rowan and Aislinn, their bond the only thing keeping Lucifer from regaining his power.

***

The early morning light filtered gently through the blinds in Rowan's apartment, casting faint lines across the floor. Aislinn stirred first, stretching as the weight of the day settled on her. Today, they'd leave the quiet refuge of Rowan's place and rejoin the rest of the Fallen. It was the safest decision—there was no real alternative—but the thought of leaving this small sanctuary tugged at her.

Beside her, Rowan lay unmoving, one arm draped lazily over his face. He'd been awake for a while, his thoughts racing ahead to the challenges that awaited them. The apartment had offered a fragile sense of calm, a brief pause in the chaos. Staying wasn't an option—not with the danger tightening around them.

"Time to go," Aislinn murmured, more to herself than to him.

Rowan stirred, lowering his arm and giving her a tired smile. "Yeah. Time to go."

They'd packed the night before, their bags waiting neatly by the door. Rowan sat up slowly, running a hand through his hair. His gaze drifted across the room, a flicker of reluctance crossing his expression. Leaving felt like shutting the door on a part of himself he wasn't ready to let go of. Even so, staying wouldn't keep her safe.

"I always thought moving in together would feel a little different," he said, his smirk faint but genuine.

Aislinn's lips curved in response. "Yeah, me too."

The moment was brief, but it lightened the heaviness between them. They both understood what this meant—not just leaving the apartment, but stepping deeper into the storm building around them. Their time here had been a fleeting chance to simply be themselves. That time was over.

"It's not easy," Rowan admitted, his voice quieter now. "But being with the team gives us a better chance. This is the right move."

Aislinn nodded, her fingers grazing the edge of the blanket absently. "I know. It's just... we're giving up more than a place. It felt like ours, in a way. Now it won't just be us anymore."

Rowan stood and moved to the window, the city stretching out before him in muted morning light. "Yeah. I feel it too." His words carried a steadier edge now, less weighed down. "We'll make it work."

Aislinn rose and joined him, her hand brushing his briefly. The small gesture carried an unspoken reassurance. "We always do."

They moved quickly after that, falling into a practiced rhythm. When everything was ready, Rowan grabbed the car keys—choosing the car over his bike for the extra space and discretion. The streets felt different now, their once-familiar paths charged with a quiet menace. Bags loaded in the trunk, they settled into the car. The silence between them wasn't strained but filled with an understanding neither needed to put into words.

The drive to the Airbnb, where the rest of the Fallen waited, was subdued but comfortable. Rowan's focus remained on the road, while Aislinn stared out the window, her thoughts wandering. They'd been apart from the others long enough. Now it was time to regroup and face what lay ahead.

The house came into view, tucked into a quieter corner of the city. It wasn't as grand as the mansion they'd soon call home, but it had served its purpose. Rowan parked along the curb, keeping the car out of view, and they stepped out with their bags in tow.

Inside, the house was alive with movement. Boxes shifted, doors opened and closed, and voices echoed from every direction. Takoda and Rain stood chatting near the front with Oak, Holly, and Ariel, who had stopped by to help with the move. Ariel waved as they entered. "About time you two showed up!"

Rowan rolled his eyes, a smirk playing at his lips. "We had to double-check we weren't leaving anything behind. You know how it is."

Ariel handed a box to Oak with a laugh. "Good thing I'm here to keep things moving."

Aislinn and Rowan dropped their bags in the hallway, the hum of conversation and the shuffle of belongings surrounding them. Before they could join in, the front door opened again. Riichi, Reed, and Vine entered, their expressions sharp, their energy vibrating with urgency.

They made their way straight to Eileen, who had been overseeing the move, and Reed motioned her aside.

"We need to talk," Reed said quietly, his words purposeful.

Eileen's focus flicked across their faces, her composure shifting ever so slightly. She met Riichi's eyes before nodding. "What is it?"

"Lucifer," Reed replied, his voice lowered. "We've got new information. It changes everything."

Eileen's jaw tightened as she glanced toward the rest of the Fallen. The house bustled with activity—boxes scraping against the floor, conversations blending together, everyone focused on packing and preparing to leave. "Not now," she said, her words firm and steady. "We're in the middle of a move. If you tell them now, it'll only cause chaos."

Reed's hands flexed at his sides. "This can't wait. They need to know."

"They will," Eileen replied, her quiet authority unyielding. "The information isn't going to change in the next few hours, and we need their focus to stay on getting out of here safely."

Riichi stepped forward, arms crossed, his urgency clear. "You don't understand. This shifts everything."

"I *do* understand," Eileen said, her resolve unwavering. "Right now, the priority is getting everyone out of here. Let them finish the move first. If we throw this at them now, it could derail everything. We'll regroup at the new location, and you can share it then."

Vine opened his mouth to argue but stopped, exhaling sharply, his shoulders easing slightly. He knew she was right. They couldn't risk distracting the team while they were still vulnerable.

"Fine," Reed muttered, his reluctance clear. "As soon as we're settled."

Eileen nodded, her steady gaze holding his. "As soon as we're settled."

Vine released a sharp breath as Eileen walked away, irritation curling tighter in his chest. Reed and Riichi left without another word, their focus already shifting to the next task. Vine stayed behind, arms folded, his eyes drifting over the room with a detached air. Boxes shifted, doors creaked open and closed, and voices merged into the backdrop of activity. He didn't move. *Why rush? They'll get it done eventually.*

"Wow," a voice broke through the hum, light and unmistakably teasing. "Look at you, standing there like royalty while the rest of us actually get things done."

He turned his head lazily to find Ariel approaching, a duffel bag slung over her shoulder. Her grin was easy, the kind that dared a response. "Observing is an essential skill," Vine replied smoothly. "Something not everyone seems to appreciate."

Ariel stopped a few feet away, shifting the bag with exaggerated flair. "Oh, I appreciate it," she said breezily. "I just figured the all-powerful Vine might actually do something instead of perfecting the art of looking unimpressed."

His lips twitched, the closest thing to a smile she'd get from him. "I'm sure someone like you has that covered. No need to complicate things."

She tilted her head, clearly unimpressed. "Right. Wouldn't want to risk breaking a sweat. Maybe I should ask Eileen to find you a throne so you can really settle into the role."

Vine let out a faint huff, part amusement, part annoyance. "If you think I need a throne to prove my value, you're more delusional than I thought."

Ariel's grin widened, her tone mock-serious. "Not delusional—just persistent. But hey, keep standing there. If nothing else, you make great scenery."

She gave him a quick nod and walked off, the duffel bouncing lightly against her side. Vine watched her retreat, his gaze narrowing slightly as his thoughts shifted. *Persistent, indeed. Doesn't know when to stop. Still... not entirely insufferable.*

Ariel reached the van she was loading and glanced back briefly, catching him still rooted in place. She shook her head with a knowing smile. *Full of himself, obviously. But there's something there. He'll crack eventually, and I want a front-row seat.*

By late morning, the Fallen had packed what little they'd brought and prepared to leave. Bags were loaded into their vehicles with quiet precision, each movement purposeful to avoid drawing unwanted attention. The old Airbnb had served its purpose, but it was time to move on.

The drive out of the city passed in subdued silence. The events of the past day lingered heavily, yet the hush inside the vehicles felt like a necessary reprieve. No one spoke—it seemed as though breaking the stillness would shatter the fragile calm. The road stretched ahead, carrying them toward their next refuge.

The new Airbnb emerged on the outskirts of San Francisco, a sprawling mansion shrouded by towering trees and bordered by a wrought iron fence. Its weathered stone exterior bore the marks of time, exuding a sense of permanence and quiet resilience. The estate extended far beyond what the dense forest revealed, offering the Fallen the solitude they needed to regroup and prepare. It felt secure, hidden from both prying eyes and the threats pursuing them.

The iron gates creaked as they swung open, revealing a wide courtyard enclosed by the mansion's commanding walls and the wilderness beyond. The space felt expansive yet sheltered, providing a sense of freedom within a protective boundary. Rowan parked the car, his gaze sweeping over the property with methodical care. "This'll work," he said under his breath, his tone steady.

Aislinn climbed out beside him, her eyes tracing the contours of the estate. The grandeur of the place struck her immediately, its seclusion a welcome contrast to the constant exposure they'd faced. "It feels... right," she murmured, her voice carrying a trace of cautious optimism. *This could be a place to find our footing again.*

One by one, the others arrived, stepping out of their vehicles and surveying the mansion with muted interest. Eileen joined them, her discerning gaze assessing the estate and its surroundings. "Take a few hours to settle in," she instructed, her composure even and unyielding. "We'll meet later to plan our next steps."

The group dispersed, each retreating into their own reflections as they adjusted to the new environment. Outside, the gentle rustling of leaves mingled with faint conversation. Takoda and Rain's animated chatter rose above the quiet, their excitement over the pool breaking through the heavier mood—a small reminder of simpler, lighter moments.

Inside, the mansion's vast halls carried a different energy. The stillness of the space magnified every soft sound, from the muted thud of footsteps to the occasional groan of the floorboards. Each room stood empty, untouched, waiting to be filled with purpose. The corridors stretched long and shadowed, inviting exploration but also introspection.

When the group reconvened in the mansion's conference room, a charged silence filled the space. Afternoon light spilled across the tall windows, casting a muted glow over the long, polished table at the center of the room. Each seat filled with cautious movements, the air heavy with anticipation. Rowan and Aislinn sat near one end, their expressions a mix of apprehension and determination, while the others settled into place, quiet but attentive.

Eileen entered last, her composed presence drawing their attention without a sound. She moved to the head of the table, her sharp gaze sweeping over the group, absorbing the tension radiating throughout the room. This house, with its still halls and protective walls, offered a fragile reprieve. They all understood it wouldn't last. What waited beyond these walls would demand every ounce of their strength.

Her statement cut through the silence, steady and direct. "We're safe here for now. Things have shifted. Reed, Riichi, Vine—tell them what you found."

Reed leaned forward, his expression grim as he prepared to share what they'd uncovered. "We went to the Golden Dawn's headquarters to see if last night's sabotage slowed them down. To see if we had the upper hand." He paused, the severity of what came next settling heavily on his features. "What we found was worse. Lucifer showed up. He's leading the Golden Dawn now."

The room froze, the revelation hitting like a physical blow. Rowan's shoulders stiffened, his hands curling into fists beneath the table. Beside him, Aislinn's fingers pressed into the edge of the wood, her knuckles turning white.

"Lucifer?" The question broke the quiet, disbelief sharpening its edges. "He doesn't lead anyone. Since when does he align himself with a group?"

Reed's jaw tightened as he gave a short nod. "That's what we assumed. He's using their desperation to take control and make his move."

Before anyone could respond, Vine spoke, his tone measured and deliberate. "There's more. We thought Lucifer was after Aislinn alone, but we were wrong. He's after Rowan, too."

The statement landed like a blow, reverberating in the room. All eyes shifted to Rowan. His chest tightened, his pulse pounding as the reality sank in. *Why me?* The question churned, unrelenting. *Lucifer targeting Aislinn made sense—her importance to them is undeniable. But me?* His fists curled tighter beneath the table, his entire body rigid as frustration burned beneath the surface. *What makes me a target? What does he see that I don't?* The questions gnawed at him, but even his anger couldn't smother the chill creeping through his thoughts.

Aislinn's voice broke the tension, quiet but steady enough to carry. "What?" Her breath hitched as Vine's words echoed in her mind. *Rowan, too?* Her gaze darted to him, her stomach knotting at the implication. The danger had always loomed large, but now it felt closer, sharper, more immediate. Rowan wasn't just her partner in this fight—he was part of the target. She straightened, her fingers releasing the edge of the table as she forced herself to push back against the rising fear. *Lucifer's sights are on both of us now. Whatever this means, we'll deal with it together.*

Vine continued, his tone steady, though his message carried a darker edge. "Lucifer plans to use your bond. He wants to sever it, take the power it holds, and use it to restore what he's lost."

Aislinn's hands trembled slightly before she stilled them, lifting her gaze to meet Vine's. "Our bond? What does that even mean?" Her voice carried a defiant edge, though her thoughts spiraled. *How could something between us hold that kind of power?* Their connection had always felt private, an unvoiced but potent bond. Now it was being twisted into a weapon, a target their enemy sought to destroy. A sharp ache stirred in her chest, but she forced it back. *Lucifer doesn't get to decide what it means. He doesn't get to take this from us.*

Holly spoke next, her composure firm but tinged with concern. "Lucifer isn't after just any power. If your bond is critical to his plan, then it's not just significant—it's essential."

Elder leaned back in his chair, his expression grim, his words carrying a cautionary weight. "If that's true, this fight isn't like anything we've faced before. It changes everything."

Rowan's response was immediate, his tone sharp with frustration. "So what now? Are we supposed to sit here and wait for him to come to us?" His fists clenched harder as his resolve surged. *No. This isn't on Lucifer. This is our fight, our bond. He doesn't get to dictate what happens to us.*

Eileen raised a hand, her calm command cutting through the rising tension. "If Lucifer is targeting both of you, our priority has to be keeping you safe. Protecting you ensures we stay ahead of him." Her piercing gaze moved between Rowan and Aislinn. "We can't let him get to either of you."

Rowan shoved his chair back, the screech of wood against the floor shattering the quiet. "No. We're not going to sit back and hide while everyone else fights."

Aislinn rose beside him, her voice firm. "Rowan's right. Hiding won't solve anything. We need to go after him. Take the offensive."

The room hung heavy with the weight of the decision, each statement pressing harder against the air. Eileen met their resolve with measured restraint. "Going on the offensive means putting yourselves directly in Lucifer's path. He's already targeting both of you. If we make the wrong move, we could hand him exactly what he's waiting for."

Rowan's response came swift and unyielding. "Hiding gives him that advantage. If we stay back, we're giving him time to prepare. If we act now, we can force him to react to us instead."

Aislinn's stance didn't waver as she added, her resolve firm, "We're not powerless. If Lucifer is focused on us, we can turn it against him. Waiting only lets him dictate the terms, and that's not a risk we're willing to take."

Reed leaned back in his chair, arms folded tightly, his skepticism etched into his features. "It's a risk no matter what. You and Aislinn are his targets. Moving now might push you straight into his hands."

Eileen's expression hardened, concern etched across her face. "Rowan, you're one of our strongest fighters. If we lose you, the entire plan falls apart. Keeping both of you protected is how we protect everyone."

Rowan's frustration simmered just beneath the surface, his fists curling as he leaned forward. "So what's the plan? Lock us away while everyone else fights? That's not going to happen. We're not just chess pieces to be shifted around. Our lives—our choices—belong to us. Sitting back guarantees we lose the chance to end this on our terms."

The force of his declaration silenced the room. Aislinn placed a steady hand on his arm, her gaze unwavering as she addressed the group. "He's right. This is our fight too. If we let Lucifer control the battlefield, we've already lost."

Vine exchanged a glance with Riichi before speaking, his tone measured. "The longer we wait, the more time Lucifer has to consolidate power. Moving now, while he's still pulling the Golden Dawn together, might catch him off guard."

Elder frowned, his piercing gaze resting on Rowan and Aislinn. "But if you act now, you'll be stepping straight into the danger he's setting up. It's what he's counting on."

Rowan's jaw tightened as he shook his head. "The real danger is waiting. If we give him more time, he'll only get stronger. Holding back doesn't make us safer—it makes us weaker."

Oak nodded slowly, the weight of Rowan's argument settling over him. "It's dangerous, but Rowan's right. Letting Lucifer gain the upper hand puts us all at greater risk. Striking now might be our only chance to disrupt his plans."

Holly tapped her fingers against the table, her words measured. "Safe isn't part of the equation anymore. It never was. Moving first could give us the only edge we'll get."

Eileen's command cut through the discussion, firm yet composed. "We can't act without a plan. If we move blindly, we'll lose before the fight begins. Rowan, Aislinn—if you're out there, exposed, Lucifer will do whatever it takes to capture you. If we fail, everything falls apart."

Rowan's voice rose, carrying the sharp edge of his frustration. "Doing nothing is the real failure. Waiting lets him call the shots. We have to take control of this—not let Lucifer decide how it ends."

The room fell silent again, the impact of his words lingering. Eileen studied Rowan for a long moment before sighing, her expression softening just enough to show her understanding. After a pause, she nodded. "It's bold, but you're right. The longer we wait, the more time he has to strengthen his position. If we do this, it has to be planned. Every step must count."

Rowan met her gaze, his stance resolute. "We're not asking for protection. We're asking to fight. This is our fight, and we won't let Lucifer control the outcome."

Aislinn's voice followed, quieter but just as firm. "This isn't just about us. It's about all of us. We're ready, and we're not backing down."

Eileen's gaze swept the room, her eyes locking on each of them, searching for hesitation. Finding none, she gave a decisive nod. "Then it's settled. We take the offensive."

Her attention returned to Rowan and Aislinn, her resolve unwavering. "You'll be at the center of this whether we like it or not. But we'll find a way to turn his focus on you into a weapon against him."

The decision made, the tension in the room shifted—no less urgent, but with a sharper sense of purpose. Rowan felt his determination solidify, the fire within him burning brighter. This was their fight, and they wouldn't wait any longer.

Aislinn caught his gaze, her conviction mirroring his. Together, they would face what came next.

Eileen stood, signaling the end of the meeting. "We have one week. When the others arrive, we'll finalize the plan. Every moment matters."

The group dispersed, their movements purposeful, the urgency of the situation driving them forward. Rowan lingered for a second, his thoughts racing. *A week.* The word felt fragile, barely enough to brace against the storm bearing down on them. *Lucifer won't wait.*

His gaze shifted toward Aislinn, and he exhaled slowly. Their calm had been fleeting, replaced now by urgency. The storm wasn't on the horizon anymore—it was here, pressing closer with every second.

There was no turning back now.

Chapter Twenty-Seven
Gathering Strength

The morning light filtered through the curtains in soft, golden streaks as Aislinn lay curled against Rowan. His arm rested lazily over her waist, his fingers tracing slow, thoughtful patterns along her back. The rhythmic motion lulled her into a serene stillness, one she wished she could hold onto. In his embrace, it was easy to forget the demands waiting for them beyond the quiet sanctuary of their room. Yet time was slipping away, and they both knew it.

Rowan's words, roughened with sleep, broke the fragile silence. "Busy day ahead," he murmured, his hand pausing mid-stroke. "New recruits. Training. Strategy meetings. It's going to be a long one."

Aislinn shifted, rolling onto her back to face him. His gaze met hers, and though he said nothing, the unease in his expression betrayed the thoughts he hadn't yet voiced. The burden of their shared decision hung between them, unspoken but ever-present.

"You're sure about this?" he asked, his tone quiet but edged with concern. "Taking the fight to Lucifer?"

She held his gaze, letting the moment settle. His outward calm couldn't quite mask the unease coiled beneath the surface. She could feel it as acutely as her own resolve.

"I'm sure," she said, her words firm. "Hiding was never an option. We have to stop him, and this is the only way." Her hand found his, fingers threading together in an unspoken promise. "And I'm with you. Every step."

The faintest flicker of relief softened his expression, and he offered a small smile before leaning down to press a kiss to her forehead. "Then we fight. Together."

Before the intimacy of the morning could stretch further, a sharp knock shattered the calm. Takoda's voice rang through the door, brimming with playful mischief. "Hey, Rowan! You've had Aislinn long enough. She was ours first!"

Rain's laughter followed, light and teasing. "Better share her, or we're coming in."

Rowan groaned, burying his face in the crook of Aislinn's neck. "Ambushed," he muttered, his lips brushing her skin in a way that sent a wave of warmth through her. She couldn't help the soft laugh that escaped her. "You're lucky I like them."

Aislinn nudged him, her amusement mirrored in the sparkle of her eyes. "They're not wrong. I was theirs first."

With a resigned sigh, Rowan let her go as she slid out of bed and reached for a nearby sweater. His gaze lingered, his smile faint but genuine. "Alright," he called toward the door, "come in before you break something."

The door burst open, and Takoda bounded in, pulling Aislinn into a tight embrace before she could take another step. Rain followed, grinning with barely concealed mischief. "We've got plans," she declared, leveling a mock scolding look at Rowan. "And they don't involve you hogging her all morning."

Aislinn's laughter bubbled up, light and unguarded, the tension of earlier experiences dissolving in their presence. It was times like this—full of camaraderie and irreverent banter—that reminded her there was more to life than the shadow of the battles ahead.

Takoda grabbed her hand, tugging her toward the door. "Come on! Let's give you the grand tour of this ridiculous mansion before Fallen duties steal you away. I've almost gotten lost twice already."

The trio wandered through the mansion's winding halls, Takoda and Rain trading jokes at the sheer absurdity of the decor. Rain gestured dramatically toward yet another chandelier, shaking her head. "How many chandeliers does one place need? Are they trying to blind us?"

Aislinn's laugh rang gently as her fingertips skimmed the smooth walls, but her amusement faltered when Rain suddenly stopped in front of a bookshelf, her head tilting slightly as though drawn by an intriguing presence.

"What's this?" Rain murmured, her hand hovering over a cluster of books. Without hesitation, she pressed one. A low creak echoed faintly through the hall as the bookshelf slid aside, revealing a narrow, dimly lit passage.

Aislinn's eyes widened, excitement bubbling in her chest. "A secret passage?"

"No way," Takoda whispered, leaning closer, her expression bright with curiosity. "We *have* to see where it leads."

Without another word, they slipped inside, their footsteps soft against the worn stone as they climbed a hidden staircase. The passage smelled faintly of earth and aged wood, and the air carried a lingering sense of something ancient, like the quiet echo of history pressed into its walls. It opened into a small circular room perched high above the mansion. Narrow, arched windows—reminiscent of an old Celtic tower—framed sweeping views of the grounds below. Sunlight streamed in with a warm, almost enchanted glow, catching the intricate carvings etched into the wood-paneled walls—knots and spirals woven in delicate patterns, a quiet nod to the mansion's past. The room felt cozy and secluded, as if it had been waiting for them to uncover its secrets.

Aislinn's thoughts spun with possibilities. *This could be perfect.* She could already picture it—a private retreat for her and Rowan, away from the relentless weight of their responsibilities. Inspiration sparked, and she turned to Takoda and Rain with a grin that spread wide and bright.

"I think I know how to make this place special. I want to surprise Rowan, but I'll need your help."

Takoda's grin mirrored hers. "Say no more. We're in."

Rain nodded, her excitement contagious. "We can keep it secret, set it up just the way you want."

Relief and gratitude warmed Aislinn's smile. "Thank you. This will mean a lot to him... to us."

As they descended the hidden staircase, their whispered plans filled the narrow space. The faint sound of their steps blended with the soft scrape of stone. When the bookshelf slid shut behind them, their liveliness still buzzed with excitement. Yet the moment didn't last—Rowan's words drifted down the hall, pulling Aislinn sharply back to the present.

"Aislinn?" His call carried an unmistakable urgency. "The other Fallen are here. Training starts soon."

Aislinn exchanged a quick glance with Takoda and Rain, their silent understanding sealing the secret. "I'll be there," she called back, her reply even and firm. Turning to her friends, she added in a lower tone, "You know what to do."

Takoda hugged her tightly. "Don't worry. We've got this."

Rain winked. "Leave the decorating to us. You just focus on kicking Fallen ass."

Aislinn smiled, her gratitude evident. With one last look at the hidden passage, she stepped away to join Rowan. The playful lightness of the morning faded, replaced by the heavy reality of what lay ahead. Side by side, they left the library, her thoughts shifting from the plans they'd just made to the challenges waiting outside.

Aislinn followed Rowan through the mansion's maze-like halls, her heartbeat quickening as they stepped into the expansive courtyard. Fallen had already begun to gather, their low conversations weaving across the open air. Though sunlight spilled generously over the stone pathways, its warmth did little to ease the tension rippling beneath the surface—a shared understanding that today's training was more than routine drills. This was preparation for the real fight.

The group of Fallen grew as Oak stepped into the center, his calm authority tangible. He raised a hand, and the murmurs faded instantly. Without speaking, the sheer gravity of his presence commanded their attention.

"Today, we focus on harnessing our strengths and learning how they complement one another in battle," Oak began, his words smooth and resolute. "We'll split into teams. Each team will demonstrate their abilities, and we'll discuss how they can be used strategically in the field."

Aislinn's stomach fluttered as she glanced at Rowan. Excitement and uncertainty warred within her. She had spent countless hours honing her abilities, but standing among warriors who had centuries of experience, she felt like an amateur trying to wield a sword too heavy for her hands. *What if I'm not ready? What if I hold them back?*

Rowan must have noticed her hesitation because he brushed his fingers lightly against hers, anchoring her spiraling thoughts with a reassuring touch. "You'll be fine," he murmured, his words a quiet promise. The certainty in his tone brought her focus back, reminding her she wasn't in this alone.

Oak's steady voice broke through her inner doubts. "First team: Reed, Hazel, Holly... and Aislinn."

Her stomach lurched. *First?* She wasn't ready to be the center of attention, not yet. A rush of nerves prickled at her skin, but Holly's playful wink pulled her back from the edge.

"No sweat," Holly said, her words light and confident. "We've got this."

Hazel offered a reassuring smile, the calm in her expression settling Aislinn's pulse. Reed was already moving forward, his quiet composure evident in the purposeful way he stepped into place. Aislinn exhaled, her resolve strengthening as she joined them, though the weight of the group's collective gaze pressed heavily on her shoulders.

Holly gestured toward Reed. "Our shadow master starts things off."

Reed stepped forward without hesitation, shadows rippling like ink around his feet. In one fluid motion, they swallowed him whole. Aislinn blinked in astonishment as he reappeared several feet away, the shadows dissipating as if he had bent time and space to his will.

"Whoa," she whispered, awe threading through her words.

Hazel followed, lifting her hands with practiced grace. The water from the nearby fountain rose in swirling arcs, forming intricate patterns. But it was more than manipulation—there was a deeply connected, almost symbiotic quality to the way she moved with the water, as though she were calling on its essence rather than commanding it.

Then it was Holly's turn. A mischievous grin tugged at her lips as the courtyard shimmered and blurred. Aislinn blinked, suddenly surrounded by a misty forest, the vivid trees and shifting fog so real she could almost feel the damp air. Just as quickly as it had appeared, the illusion dissolved, leaving her breathless.

And then it was her turn.

Taking a calming breath, Aislinn stepped forward and summoned the energy she had worked so hard to control. With a sharp motion, she unleashed a kinetic blast that sent leaves and dust scattering in a wide arc. It wasn't as powerful or accurate as she'd hoped, but it was enough to show progress. Drawing on that focus again, she conjured a translucent shield, its faint shimmer trembling under her concentration before solidifying.

Oak's approving nod steadied her. "Reed, practice shadow walking with Aislinn next time. In battle, she'll need to move with you seamlessly."

Reed inclined his head slightly, a flicker of humor in his otherwise serious expression. "Let's try it now," he said, his words calm but edged with teasing. "Stay close—but not too close. Don't want to make Rowan mad."

Aislinn managed a small laugh, her tension easing. "Got it," she said, stepping closer.

As shadows coiled around them, the world dimmed, and in an instant, they reappeared on the other side of the courtyard. The sensation was dizzying yet exhilarating, and as the darkness faded, she let out a measured breath, feeling more stable.

Reed glanced at her, his lips curving in the faintest of smiles. "You did fine. No angry Rowan in sight."

She exhaled again, a flicker of accomplishment warming her chest. *Maybe I'm not as far behind as I thought.*

Oak stepped forward once more, addressing the group. "Suggestions on how these abilities can be used in combat?"

"Reed's shadow walking can get us out of tight spots—ideal for sneaking or quick escapes," Vine offered.

Riichi nodded. "He could bypass sentries and traps, clearing the way for the rest of us. If he scouts ahead, we'll know exactly what we're up against before we engage. Catching them off guard could turn the tide."

"Hazel's water control could slow enemies or create barriers," Willow added.

Elder folded his arms, his expression pensive. "Her water barriers can hold a line if we're outnumbered. She could buy us time to regroup or press forward."

Ivy grinned, leaning back slightly. "Holly's illusions will keep them off balance—perfect for confusion while we strike."

Vine chimed in. "Or she could make them see each other as enemies. Turn the whole fight into chaos. It'd be one hell of a distraction."

Oak nodded thoughtfully as the Fallen exchanged ideas, though he made no assignments yet. It was clear these strategies would be revisited in the meeting to come.

As the suggestions flowed, Aislinn felt her confidence begin to take root. The Fallen weren't just observing her; they were guiding her, helping her carve out a place within the team. She wasn't merely catching up—she belonged here.

Elder's calm voice cut through her thoughts. "Aislinn's kinetic blasts could disrupt enemy formations. If they advance, she can scatter them, giving us time to regroup or push forward."

Riichi, arms folded in his usual contemplative stance, added, "She could also serve as a secondary defense. If Reed's scouting, her shields could protect him from surprise attacks. It's not just about offense—it's about holding the line when it matters most."

Oak stayed silent, his focus intense as he absorbed the feedback. Aislinn could feel the weight of his attention, assessing not only her performance but how she might fit into the team's larger strategy.

When the discussion wrapped up, Aislinn drifted back to Rowan's side, her mind racing with what she'd witnessed. As she reached him, his hand found hers, squeezing gently. "You're doing great," he said, his words low, meant only for her. "This is just the beginning."

"I had no idea Reed could do that," she murmured. "And Hazel... it's like she connects with the water on some deeper level, almost like it's alive."

Rowan chuckled softly, the sound steadying her. "They've had centuries to perfect their abilities. You're catching on faster than you think. It gets easier with time."

She hesitated, curiosity gnawing at her. "But if they've had these abilities for so long, why didn't any of you use them before? I mean... it feels like you could have taken down threats easily."

Rowan's demeanor shifted, his smile fading as he glanced around to ensure no one was listening. "It's not that simple," he said, his voice low. "We've always had to stay hidden. Using our abilities openly could have exposed us—and drawn attention we couldn't afford. The Golden Dawn, other enemies... they've been watching, waiting for an excuse to move against us."

He paused, his expression softening as his gaze returned to hers. "And we didn't always know what we were dealing with. Sometimes it's safer to hold your cards close until you're certain of what's coming. But things are different now. We can't afford to hold back anymore."

The weight of his explanation settled over her, but Aislinn's curiosity lingered. Her brow furrowed as her thoughts shifted back to their names. "And your names? They're... unusual, aren't they? Holly, Hazel, Reed... Rowan. They sound like they belong together somehow. Why trees?"

Rowan exhaled, his focus drifting briefly to the others before settling back on her. "Eileen gave us those names during our turning. They're not just names—they're tied to the Celtic tree calendar."

Aislinn tilted her head, intrigued. "The Celtic tree calendar?"

"It's an ancient system," Rowan explained, his words measured and deliberate. "Each tree represents certain qualities—strengths, weaknesses, potential. Eileen chose names tied to the trees because they reflect who we are or who we could become."

He gestured subtly toward Holly, who was talking animatedly with Hazel. "Take Holly, for example. Her tree represents perseverance and protection. It fits her perfectly. She's relentless, always stepping in to shield others or turn the tide when things seem hopeless."

His attention shifted to Hazel, who was laughing lightly at something Holly had said. "Hazel's tree stands for wisdom and creativity. Her connection to the water—it's not just a power. It's like she can feel its essence, drawing on it with an understanding most of us can't even begin to grasp."

Finally, Rowan nodded toward Reed, who stood apart, his posture calm and composed. "And Reed—his tree represents harmony and adaptability. He's the one who links us, whether it's by scouting ahead or creating paths where there were none. He's quiet, but he's always the one holding the team together when it matters most."

Aislinn listened intently, her gaze shifting from one Fallen to the next. The deeper meaning behind their names added a new layer to how she saw them—not just as warriors but as intricate threads in a larger tapestry, deeply interconnected. "So, their names aren't just names. They're a part of them."

Rowan nodded, a faint smile tugging at his lips. "Exactly. The trees remind us of who we are and what we're meant to bring to the team. Each of us has a role to play, and together, we're stronger—like a forest."

Aislinn's chest tightened at the thought. She glanced at Rowan, curiosity sparking again. "What about you? What does the rowan tree represent?"

Rowan hesitated, his expression briefly guarded. Then, with a slow breath, he answered, "The rowan tree is the protector. It stands for resilience, strength, and connection. My job is to keep everyone safe, no matter what. Sometimes I wonder if the tree lives up to its name more than I do."

Aislinn frowned, ready to argue, but the warmth in Rowan's gaze held her back. Instead, she reached out, her hand brushing his briefly. "You're doing more than you realize," she said softly. "I think you live up to it just fine."

Rowan's smile returned, faint but genuine. "Thanks. That means more than you know."

Her thoughts shifted as the next team—Vine, Elder, and Ash—stepped forward. Still buzzing from her own demonstration, Aislinn turned her attention to the trio, curiosity sparking once more.

Vine moved first, extending his hands as arcs of electricity crackled between his fingers. The current leapt toward a stone pillar, striking it with a deafening crack and shattering part of its surface.

"Vine's electricity can dismantle defenses in seconds," Alder remarked.

Birch nodded thoughtfully. "He could weaponize it further. Wet surfaces or conductive materials would amplify the damage, making him a nightmare on the battlefield."

Rowan leaned closer to Aislinn, a subtle smile lifting his expression. "Vine's Celtic tree symbolizes resilience and renewal. He's like the pulse of the team, steady and relentless. His power can be devastating, but it's also restorative. It reflects who he is—even if he doesn't like admitting it."

Aislinn glanced at Vine, who stood with a composed confidence that seemed at odds with the raw power he had just displayed. The subtle vulnerability Rowan hinted at made her wonder what more lay beneath his polished surface.

Next, Elder closed his eyes, and the earth beneath them began to rumble. Massive chunks of rock rose into the air, hovering briefly before slamming back down with enough force to send tremors through the courtyard. Aislinn's breath caught at the sheer magnitude of his power.

"Elder's terrain control could trap enemies or strengthen our defenses," Riichi observed, his analytical tone cutting through the murmurs of awe.

Ivy leaned forward, her expression thoughtful. "It's not just defense. He could force enemies into choke points, disrupt their formations, or even create unstable terrain to throw them off balance. They wouldn't know how to advance."

Rowan gestured subtly toward Elder, his words measured. "Elder's Celtic tree represents transition and endings. His power shifts the battlefield, forcing change on anyone who stands in his way. If there's a fight that needs finishing, he's the one to end it."

Aislinn watched Elder with a mixture of awe and unease. His calm, deliberate movements mirrored the gravity of his power, and she couldn't help but feel there was an air of finality about the way he stood, unshaken by the rumbling earth.

Ash stepped forward last, a grin lighting his face as his body shimmered and transformed. In seconds, he became a sleek panther, his movements fluid and predatory as he darted across the courtyard. Leaping over Elder's rubble with ease, he landed silently on the other side, his tail flicking once before he turned back toward the group.

Rowan smirked faintly. "Ash loves to show off."

"Ash's shapeshifting is perfect for stealth," Holly added, her smile bright. "He could slip in and out without anyone noticing."

Elder's voice rumbled with approval. "He'd be invaluable for reconnaissance—scouting ahead in a form no one would suspect."

Rowan leaned slightly toward Aislinn, his voice softening. "Ash's Celtic tree symbolizes strength and transformation. He's a fighter, sure, but his real strength lies in how he adapts. Whatever the team needs, he finds a way to become it."

Aislinn's gaze lingered on Ash as he shifted back to his human form, his grin still firmly in place. The idea of transformation stayed with her—more than just changing shapes, it was a way of thinking, a way of fighting.

As the demonstration ended, Oak raised a hand, and the Fallen began brainstorming strategies.

Holly was the first to speak. "Combine Vine's electricity with Elder's earth, and we could electrify reshaped ground. It'd trap anyone who tries to cross."

"That's dangerous," Alder agreed, his brow furrowing. "And devastatingly effective. No one would expect it."

Willow added, "Ash could scout ahead, drawing their attention while we set the trap. Once they're disoriented, we strike from the shadows—Reed, Holly, Aislinn. All of us hitting from different angles."

The vitality among the group shifted, their determination sharpening as they envisioned how their combined abilities could turn the tide in battle. Aislinn felt the subtle shift too—the possibilities were endless, and for the first time, she could see how she truly fit into their intricate plans.

When it was Rowan's turn, Aislinn's pulse quickened. She had seen his strength before, but something about this felt different. He wasn't holding back today.

Oak motioned for Willow, Birch, and Alder to step forward, followed by three more Fallen. A charged hush fell over the courtyard as everyone recognized this wasn't a routine sparring session. Rowan, known for his unmatched power, was about to face six opponents.

Rowan rolled his shoulders, stepping into the center of the courtyard. Gone was the easygoing demeanor Aislinn had come to know. In its place was a sharp intensity that sent a shiver through her. He looked fierce, resolute, unstoppable.

"Begin," Oak commanded, his tone calm yet firm.

Willow struck first, a blast of energy hurtling toward Rowan. With a twist of his arm, he deflected it effortlessly, redirecting the force away. Alder lunged next, aiming for Rowan's side, but Rowan ducked low, landing a swift, calculated blow to Alder's ribs, sending him stumbling back.

Birch charged, his sheer strength driving him forward, but Rowan sidestepped with precision, delivering a perfectly placed kick to Birch's knee.

The larger man collapsed with a grunt, leaving Rowan to face the remaining three.

They attacked simultaneously, their movements coordinated, but Rowan moved like liquid. Aislinn could barely track him as he weaved between strikes, countering with flawless accuracy. Within minutes, all three were on the ground, defeated. Rowan stood at the center, barely winded, his breathing even.

The courtyard fell silent, the air thick with awe.

Ivy broke the stillness, her analysis sharp. "Rowan's speed and precision make him almost impossible to predict. On the frontlines, he'd keep enemies off balance, anticipating their moves before they even act."

Vine added, "Willow's energy manipulation could shield Rowan and the frontliners from magical attacks. She'd be a critical defense."

Reed nodded. "Pair her with Birch. His endurance boosts would keep Rowan going. Together, they'd last through the toughest battles."

Birch grinned as he flexed his arms, recovered and clearly unbothered by his earlier fall. "Yeah, I'll keep the frontliners going strong. Rowan won't break, and neither will I."

Riichi's agreement was subtle but firm. "Birch's stamina in long fights will be critical. Rowan's strength paired with Birch's support means we can push harder, longer."

Oak raised a hand, signaling for Rowan to remain in the center while the six Fallen regrouped. "Now, Rowan—take on all six at once."

Aislinn's heart leapt as the six Fallen formed a loose circle around him, their determination sharpening. This wasn't just a test of Rowan's skill—it was a demonstration of what he was truly capable of.

Rowan adjusted his stance, rolling his shoulders once more. "Don't hold back," he called, his voice steady. "I won't."

Oak gave the signal, and the courtyard erupted into motion. Willow and Birch moved first, Birch charging head-on while Willow's energy blast arced toward Rowan. He twisted to avoid Birch's attack, redirecting the magical blast into the earth with one swift motion. Alder came next, his powerful strike aimed for Rowan's midsection, but Rowan ducked low, using Alder's momentum against him to send him sprawling.

The others attacked in rapid succession. Riichi's katana glinted as he swung with precision, but Rowan deflected the blade with his sword before pivoting to avoid Reed, who emerged from the shadows with startling speed. Ivy, standing off to the side, waved her hand, and the space between her and Rowan rippled unnaturally, forcing Rowan to adjust his footing. Without hesitation, he used the unstable terrain to his advantage, launching himself into the air and flipping over Birch's massive frame. He landed behind him with a sharp kick that sent Birch stumbling forward into Alder.

Willow's magic flared again, and Rowan spun, his blade slicing through the energy before it could reach him. In an instant, he turned on Reed, catching him by the wrist and twisting him to the ground with surprising ease. Riichi and Ivy moved in tandem, Riichi's strikes perfectly synchronized with Ivy's attempts to distort Rowan's surroundings. But Rowan anticipated their rhythm, parrying Riichi's blows while sidestepping Ivy's shifting battlefield with almost impossible speed.

It didn't take long before all six were on the ground, some groaning, others catching their breath. Rowan stood at the center, his sword lowered but his stance still ready for action. His breathing remained even as he surveyed the group.

A charged silence settled over the courtyard before Oak spoke, his words deliberate. "That is why Rowan leads."

The Fallen nodded, murmurs of agreement rippling through the group. Aislinn's heart thundered in her chest, her awe mirrored in the wide-eyed reactions of the others.

Rowan returned to Aislinn's side, his intensity fading as he reached her. Her heart was still pounding from what she'd just seen.

"Impressed?" he teased, a flicker of pride in his expression.

She nodded, still trying to process it all. "Six of them, and it looked like you barely broke a sweat."

He chuckled, running a hand through his hair. "It's all about discipline. Although, I'll admit, having you here is a little distracting."

Aislinn raised an eyebrow, crossing her arms. "So, I'm a distraction?"

Rowan leaned in slightly, his demeanor steady yet carrying a quiet intensity. "You were, at first. But not anymore." His eyes met hers directly, unwavering. "The bond changes everything. Instead of pulling me off balance, you center me."

A warmth spread through her as she held his gaze. The connection between them wasn't just personal—it was becoming a cornerstone of how they fought, how they'd face what lay ahead.

As the exchange lingered, Aislinn glanced at the others and then back at Rowan, curiosity sparking again. "Willow, Birch, Alder..." she began. "Their abilities are incredible. Do their names reflect them, too?"

Rowan nodded, his tone contemplative as he followed her gaze. "Willow's Celtic tree symbolizes flexibility and resilience. Her power isn't just about striking with energy—it's about bending without breaking, finding ways to protect and attack no matter the situation. She's our safeguard."

He motioned toward Birch, who was shaking off the earlier fight with an easy grin. "Birch represents renewal and strength. He holds the frontlines, keeps us going when the fight drags on. His stamina—it's more than just physical. It's a kind of steady endurance."

Finally, Rowan gestured subtly toward Alder. "Alder's tree stands for determination and strength. He's all force and drive—when we need to break through a wall, literal or metaphorical, he's the one we call. His power can shatter defenses."

Aislinn glanced between them, her mind turning over Rowan's words. Each of them had a role, a purpose, tied to their name and abilities. The connection felt profound, and it gave her a deeper sense of what it meant to be part of this team.

Willow turned to Birch, her determination evident. "If we combine our support, we can keep Rowan and Alder fighting longer. I'll handle magical energy, and you take care of physical endurance."

Birch nodded, resolve sparking in his gaze. "Sounds like a plan. I'll keep an eye on Rowan and the others. If anyone starts to falter, I'll make sure they're back in the fight."

The Fallen were evolving, their individual abilities weaving into a cohesive unit. This wasn't just training—it was preparation for war, and the stakes grew clearer with every demonstration. Aislinn could feel it in the air: every move, every strategy, was a step closer to the battlefield ahead.

As the group regrouped after Rowan's display, Oak stepped forward, his commanding presence drawing everyone's attention. He motioned for Ivy and Riichi to join him, the tension in the courtyard sharpening. This trio, known for their seamless coordination, was about to show why they were among the most formidable of the Fallen.

"We'll keep this straightforward," Oak said, his words measured. "Barriers, bending, and reflection. Watch closely."

Ivy began. With a single wave of her hand, reality itself seemed to ripple. The earth twisted into unnatural angles, objects stretching and folding as though space itself had been unraveled. Aislinn blinked, temporarily disoriented, before Ivy snapped reality back into clarity with a knowing smirk.

"Ivy warps reality," Rowan murmured to Aislinn. "She can manipulate the battlefield however we need."

Willow nodded. "If we need to escape or move quickly, Ivy's the one to count on."

Birch folded his arms, his gaze sharp. "She could turn the ground into a maze—force the enemy to second-guess every step."

Rowan added, "Ivy's Celtic tree symbolizes growth and determination. She's relentless, always finding a way to turn the battlefield to her advantage. Even when things seem impossible, she keeps going until there's a way out."

Aislinn watched Ivy with growing admiration, noting the way she carried herself—calm yet entirely in control, her abilities bending the world itself to her will.

Next, Oak raised his hands, summoning a shimmering, translucent barrier around himself, Ivy, and Riichi. The barrier pulsed subtly, its magic dense and unyielding.

"Oak's barriers are unbeatable for defense," Reed said. "They'll hold the line no matter what's coming."

Elder added, "If we're overwhelmed, Oak's barriers will give us the time we need to regroup."

Rowan leaned in again. "Oak's Celtic tree represents strength, endurance, and wisdom. He's the foundation of this team—unshakable and steady. When the rest of us falter, he holds the line, no matter the cost."

Aislinn's eyes followed Oak's imposing figure, and she couldn't help but feel a quiet sense of security in his presence. It wasn't just his strength—it was the way he carried it, like an unspoken promise to the others.

Then, all eyes shifted to Riichi as he stepped forward, katana gleaming in his hand. He moved with an effortless grace, every step deliberate, every shift in weight perfectly balanced. His strikes were fluid, exact, and impossibly fast—each one an exercise in both control and power.

When his blade met Oak's barrier, the impact rebounded with a crackling surge of power, but Riichi didn't falter. Instead, he spun with liquid smoothness, dodging his own reflected blow as though he had anticipated it long before it happened. His counterstrike was so swift it left a ripple in the air, his katana slicing through the space with pinpoint accuracy.

Rowan leaned closer to Aislinn, his words laced with pride. "He was a Samurai before he became Fallen. Every movement, every strike—centuries of discipline in action. He's the most skilled fighter I've ever known."

Aislinn watched, captivated, her breath catching as she took in Riichi's movements. They weren't just skilled—they were mesmerizing, like a master artist painting with his blade. His strikes weren't reactive; they were preemptive, as if he could read the barrier's magical signature before it even shifted. Every motion was purposeful, no energy wasted, no hesitation.

It was a dance of lethal beauty, a display of centuries of training distilled into perfection. He struck again, the rebound narrowly missing him, but he was already shifting, countering the next movement with an elegance that seemed almost otherworldly.

"Riichi's precision is terrifying," Vine remarked, his usual lightheartedness replaced by quiet respect. "He doesn't just react—he knows what's coming before it happens."

Holly leaned in slightly, her words reflective. "He'd be perfect to guide Reed and Vine through enemy territory. No one would see them coming."

Elder nodded in agreement. "Pair Riichi with Reed, and they could neutralize threats before the rest of us are even in position."

Rowan spoke again, his tone calm and steady. "Riichi's Celtic tree, the Hawthorn, symbolizes balance and protection. Every movement he makes is deliberate, calculated. He doesn't just fight—he creates order out of chaos. That's why he's so deadly."

Aislinn's pulse quickened as she listened. Each of them carried more than power—they carried purpose, an intricate thread woven into the fabric of the Fallen.

As Riichi concluded, Oak lowered the barrier, the power fading into the still air. The courtyard was silent, the weight of the demonstration lingering like an unspoken challenge.

Ash broke the quiet first, his words thoughtful. "Oak's fortifications and Riichi's ability to reflect and predict—that's an impenetrable defense."

Birch glanced toward Ivy, an idea sparking in his expression. "And if things fall apart, Ivy could warp the field, give us an escape route, or shift the enemy's path entirely."

Oak's gaze swept over the group, his words steady and firm. "Strength, control, adaptability—these are what will win us this fight. Alone, each of you is powerful. Together, you're a force nothing can break."

Rowan leaned toward Aislinn, his tone intimate, meant only for her. "This is why we train like this. Alone, we're strong, but together..." He paused, his words resonating with certainty. "We're something far greater."

Aislinn nodded, her heart pounding with new understanding. This wasn't just about mastering their powers—it was about trust. Trust in each other, trust in the bond that tied them all together, and trust in the strength they shared as a team. *Together, they would be unshakable.*

Oak stepped forward, his commanding presence stilling the courtyard. "For the final demonstration, Rowan and Aislinn, step forward." With a motion of his hand, glowing targets appeared in a wide arc around the center of the courtyard. "Let's see Radiant Surge in action. Elder, step in as well and throw magic bursts their way. I want to see how they protect each other—not just strike."

Every eye turned toward them. Aislinn froze under the weight of their attention, her nerves threatening to overwhelm her. This wasn't just about strength—it was about their bond. Her hands trembled slightly, but Rowan leaned closer, his words grounding. "We've got this," he murmured. "Just focus on us. It's you and me, nothing else."

She swallowed her nerves, took a steadying breath, and extended her hand toward Rowan. His fingers closed around hers, warm and reassuring. The connection sparked immediately, the bond humming to life. The air around them shimmered subtly as their joined forces began to build. A pulse of blue light radiated from their hands, faint at first but quickly intensifying, spreading outward like ripples in water. It enveloped them in a radiant, vibrant glow, their magic merging into a single, unified force.

With a shared nod, they stepped forward together. Every movement was perfectly synchronized, each action feeding off the other as though guided by the energy flowing between them. Rowan lunged at the first glowing target, and Aislinn followed effortlessly, anticipating his moves as though they were her own. His strikes were sharp and deliberate, her shields rising instinctively to deflect incoming threats. The targets dissolved one by one under their combined assault, their seamless coordination creating an almost hypnotic rhythm.

Then Elder raised his hands, sending bursts of magic crackling toward them. Aislinn tightened her grip on Rowan's hand, casting a shimmering shield of blue magic. The magic slammed into it, rippling outward harmlessly. Rowan didn't falter, guarding her flank as they advanced to strike down another target. Their roles shifted effortlessly—Rowan striking with precision, Aislinn shielding with impeccable timing, each covering the other as though they were two parts of the same entity.

The power of Radiant Surge pulsed stronger with every action, its glow illuminating the courtyard. Aislinn could feel the bond deepening with every step, every shared breath. Offense and defense flowed together as one, their connection more than a tactic—it was a force.

As the final target vanished under Rowan's blade, Elder hurled one last burst of magic toward them. Aislinn reacted instantly, her shield flaring brighter than ever as it absorbed the impact. The magic dissipated into the air with a soft hum, leaving the courtyard silent as they came to a halt.

Standing side by side, their breathing steady, the glow of Radiant Surge lingered faintly around them. The bond's energy thrummed strong and unbroken.

The Fallen stared, the significance of the performance settling heavily over the group.

Oak's voice broke the silence, his words calm but approving. "Well done. Comments?"

Vine was the first to speak, his tone reflective. "Their bond amplifies their abilities. If they fight like that, Rowan will be nearly unstoppable with Aislinn protecting him."

Riichi crossed his arms, his focus unwavering. "It's more than power—it's precision. The enemy won't see two fighters; they'll see one, perfectly in sync."

Reed nodded. "With that kind of coordination, they can overwhelm anyone who tries to come between them. It's not just strength—it's how they move."

Aislinn glanced at Rowan, her pulse still racing. His steady smile brought a wave of calm over her, keeping her in the present.

Holly broke the silence with a teasing grin. "Not bad for someone just getting started," she said lightly. "A few more rounds, and you'll be showing Rowan how it's done."

Aislinn smiled, appreciating the levity. What had started as a demonstration had grown into a deeper understanding—a reminder of what the Fallen shared as a team. It wasn't just about fighting—it was about protecting one another and moving as one.

Oak scanned the courtyard before dismissing the group. "That concludes today's session. Take the afternoon to rest. We need everyone at their best for tonight's meeting."

As the Fallen began to disperse, Rowan turned to Aislinn, his expression softening. "You did amazing. I knew you would."

She smiled, the lingering hum of Radiant Surge still pulsing faintly between them. "I couldn't have done it without you."

He chuckled, leaning in slightly. "Good thing you won't have to."

They remained on the training field as the others filed back toward the mansion, the glow of their bond fading gradually into the warm hues of the late afternoon. Aislinn glanced toward Rowan, her mind still spinning from the demonstration as they finally began to walk back toward the mansion.

"That went better than I thought," Rowan said, his words tinged with amusement. "I think we impressed a few people."

She nodded, her lips curving upward. "We were in sync out there. It felt like we've been training together forever."

Rowan met her gaze, his words steady and sure. "It's not just training—it's the bond. And this is just the beginning."

Their path was interrupted as Eileen stepped into view, her presence commanding, her eyes flicking between them. "I need both of you to follow me," she said, her tone clipped with urgency.

Rowan stiffened beside Aislinn, his posture sharpening. "What's going on?"

Eileen didn't answer immediately, instead gesturing toward the side entrance. "There's something we need to discuss. Privately."

A knot of unease tightened in Aislinn's chest as she glanced at Rowan, her pulse quickening as they followed Eileen through the mansion's dimly lit halls. The weight of her stride and the tension in her words left no room for doubt—something was wrong.

At the office door, Eileen paused, her hand resting briefly on the handle before pushing it open. "This won't be easy to hear," she said, locking eyes with Aislinn. "But you need to know... before it's too late."

The door clicked shut behind them, the sound heavy with foreboding. Whatever awaited them in that room felt like the beginning of something that would change everything.

The soft clicking of Eileen's heels echoed faintly in the hall, each step carrying an muted tension. Aislinn walked beside Rowan, her heart pounding beneath her composed exterior. As they approached the heavy wooden door to the office, a tangible sense of foreboding seemed to thicken the air around them.

Eileen paused, her hand resting on the doorknob. Her gaze settled on Aislinn, her features grave, the veiled hush between them laden with unspoken meaning. "What I'm about to say won't be easy. However, with Lucifer rising, there's no more time to delay." Her glance shifted briefly to Rowan before she turned the handle and pushed the door open.

The door closed behind them with a muffled thud, the sound final, as though sealing them into the moment. The dimly lit office carried a weighted hush, the only sound the crackle of a fire in the corner. Eileen moved to the round table in the center of the room, her posture rigid as she clasped her hands together. Rowan and Aislinn took the chairs across from her, the closeness of the space amplifying the charged undercurrent between them.

"I've been holding something back," Eileen began, her words low, carefully measured. "Something I should have told you earlier, although I hoped there would be time."

Rowan shifted imperceptibly beside Aislinn, tension radiating from him. "What is it?"

Eileen's expression softened for a fleeting second. "Before I explain, I need to ask—how do you feel about each other?"

The question seemed to freeze the room. Aislinn's pulse quickened, yet she glanced at Rowan, needing no reply. His solid presence offered all the reassurance she needed.

"I love her," Rowan said firmly, his declaration leaving no room for doubt. His hand brushed lightly against Aislinn's under the table, a subtle act of comfort. "We've admitted it."

Aislinn felt warmth rise to her cheeks, yet she nodded. Their connection had taken them both by surprise, its depth and intensity building far faster than either could have anticipated.

Eileen exhaled softly and leaned back in her chair, her countenance shifting to something heavier. The firelight caught the edge of her features, casting faint shadows that seemed to deepen her presence. "Then my suspicions are confirmed," she said, her tone deliberate. "You two are Soulbound."

Aislinn blinked, the word hitting her like a sudden chill. "Soulbound?" she repeated, the term foreign and unsettling. She felt Rowan tense, his hand brushing hers as if anchoring them both.

Eileen nodded, her voice calm but carrying the resonance of authority. "It's a bond far deeper than love," she explained. "It's extraordinarily rare. Your souls are linked in every possible way—emotionally, spiritually, even physically. It will strengthen both of you." She paused, her features darkening. "But there's a cost."

Aislinn's stomach tightened as her mother's words took on a sharper edge. "If one of you dies," Eileen continued, the faintest hesitation breaking her controlled demeanor, "the other will too."

The fire's crackle filled the heavy silence, far too loud against the oppressive stillness. Aislinn sat frozen, her mind spinning as Rowan abruptly stood, his movements abrupt and charged with frustration.

"Why didn't you tell us this sooner?" he demanded, the frustration in his tone unrestrained as his hands clenched at his sides. "We should have known."

Eileen held her ground, though a flicker of regret softened her features. "I wasn't certain," she admitted, quieter now. "And the stakes are enormous. If Lucifer or the Golden Dawn discover this... they will weaponize it against you." She rose, leaning forward just enough to underscore her urgency.

"This must stay a secret. No one can know—not even the Fallen. They don't understand what this bond truly entails."

Rowan's thoughts churned, her statement landing like blows. *Soulbound.* The protector in me wants to focus only on the strength this bond gives us, but I can't. *The cost is too great. Protector—that's who I've always been.* Yet protecting Aislinn now wasn't just about shielding her from harm; it meant surviving himself. *How do I protect her when everything is tied to keeping us both alive?* The question clawed at him, leaving a cold, relentless fear in its wake.

Aislinn remained seated, her thoughts colliding as she tried to process the revelation. The knowledge that their lives were so deeply entwined felt like both a gift and a curse. Her fingers tightened instinctively around Rowan's, as though holding on to him could keep the looming threat at bay. *How can we fight now, knowing this? How can we face what lies ahead with this shadow over us?*

Rowan's frustration softened as he looked at her, his expression raw yet centering. "We'll keep it secret," he said, his statement low but resolute. He turned back to Eileen. "On my honor."

Aislinn nodded, her stomach churning with equal parts dread and resolve. "We won't tell anyone," she said, her words steadier than the storm of emotions swirling inside her.

Eileen's features softened, the leader's mantle slipping briefly to reveal the concerned mother beneath. She sighed, quieter now. "I don't want to lose you—either of you," she said gently. "Maybe it's time to reconsider."

Rowan tensed beside Aislinn, but Eileen pressed on, the worry in her gaze unmistakable. "With the Soulbound connection, it's too dangerous. You could hide, lay low until this is over. Let the Fallen face Lucifer. There's no need for you to risk everything."

Aislinn's chest tightened at the raw concern in her mother's plea. She understood it—felt it echoing within her—yet retreat wasn't an option. Not now. She reached across the table, her hand finding Eileen's. Her thumb brushed lightly over her mother's knuckles, a wordless reassurance. *I know you're scared, Mom. I'm scared too. But we can't run.*

Rowan's jaw set with determination as he spoke, his conviction unshaken. "Hiding won't save us. It won't stop Lucifer or the Golden Dawn. If we back down now, they'll come for us anyway. I won't let them dictate our fate."

Eileen's lips pressed into a thin line as she looked between them, her fingers tightening around Aislinn's. "You're not just fighting for yourselves anymore," she said, her voice steady yet laden with emotion. "You're fighting for each other's lives now. You have to understand how much is at stake."

Aislinn nodded, fear and determination swirling within her chest. "We do, Mom. And that's why we have to fight—united. We won't let them take control of us."

Rowan reached for Aislinn's hand, his grip firm and filled with steady determination. Turning to Eileen, he softened his demeanor, though it remained resolute. "We'll be careful. But we're not running."

Eileen's gaze shimmered with unsaid fears as she looked at them. Her fingers lingered on Aislinn's, reluctant to let go. Finally, she nodded, but the tension in her features didn't ease. "Then be careful," she whispered, her statement trembling faintly. "Both of you. I've lost too much already."

Aislinn stood, leaning down to wrap her arms around her mother in a fierce embrace. "We'll get through this," she whispered, even as the pressure of her own fear weighed on her. *I promise.*

As they turned to leave, Eileen's parting statement clung to the air like a shadow. "Stay vigilant. Time is running out."

Once outside the office, Rowan drew Aislinn close, his lips brushing her forehead in a silent vow. Bound now in every way that mattered, they would meet whatever came next—on their terms.

Even as the unease lingered between them, life in the mansion continued, a reminder that lightness could still flicker amidst the darkness. As Rowan and Aislinn retreated to their room to process the revelations, Takoda and Rain were busy with plans of their own, taking shape within the library's hushed depths.

Down in the mansion's library, Takoda and Rain slipped inside, their arms loaded with decorations for the secret room they were setting up for Aislinn and Rowan. The library was grand, almost cathedral-like, with towering shelves that vanished into the dim heights above. A serene calm filled the space, a contrast to the mischievous glint in Rain's eyes as she tiptoed forward.

Before they could reach the hidden entrance behind the bookshelf, Rain froze mid-step, her attention locking onto Elder seated at a table near the far wall. He was engrossed in a thick, ancient tome, his sharp features illuminated faintly by the glow of a nearby lamp.

Rain nudged Takoda, her whisper quick and urgent. "Uh-oh."

Takoda glanced over, her eyebrows arching in question. "What?"

"Just act normal," Rain muttered, crouching slightly to drop her pile of streamers behind a nearby table. Takoda followed her lead, though the faint thud of the decorations hitting the floor made her wince.

Without lifting his head, Elder's measured voice drifted across the room. "What exactly are you two doing?"

Rain straightened immediately, her face breaking into an overly bright smile. "Oh, nothing, Nik. Just hanging out," she said breezily, shrugging as she nudged a stray banner out of view with her foot. "What are you doing?"

Elder's focus shifted slightly at the sound of his real name, his face unreadable except for the faint flicker of surprise in his features. Closing the book with deliberate care, he set it aside. "Reading," he replied, his tone as dry as ever. "Isn't that what one does in a library?" His attention dipped briefly to the half-hidden decorations, a faint smirk tugging at the corners of his lips. "Or are you planning something else?"

Rain tilted her head, unfazed. "Planning? Us? Never," she said with mock innocence, nudging the last visible streamer under the table with exaggerated casualness. "We're just taking a break, exploring a little. You should try it sometime, Nik."

She paused, letting her gaze sweep over him before adding, "You're what—25? Not 95. Just because you're named after a tree doesn't mean you're ancient. Maybe hit the pool or check out the game room instead of being holed up reading all day."

Rain's teasing was light, but beneath it was a quiet understanding. Most people defaulted to calling him Elder, a name that seemed to reinforce the distance he kept from others. Yet Rain chose to call him Nik, the name he preferred—a small act of respect that acknowledged him not as a figure shrouded in mystery, but as a peer, one of them.

Elder rose with thoughtful ease, his movements smooth, his expression giving nothing away. His attention skimmed briefly to the pile of decorations before returning to hers, though he didn't press the matter. "Clearly, you're trying to get rid of me," he remarked, his tone laced with faint amusement. He nodded slightly. "I'll save you the trouble."

Rain blinked, momentarily caught off guard by how easily he dismissed them. "Wait, Nik, where are you going?"

Elder paused at the doorway, glancing back with a faint smirk. "To the game room, apparently. Since you seem so insistent I take a break."

And with that, he disappeared into the hallway, leaving Takoda and Rain biting back laughter.

"Wow," Takoda whispered, shaking her head. "How do you do that?"

Rain grinned, brushing her hands off with exaggerated flair, as though she'd just pulled off a masterful heist. "Guess I'm just that good."

As they returned to their task, Rain's thoughts flicked briefly toward the doorway Elder had exited. *Let's see how long it takes him to find that game room.* She shrugged it off, though a spark of amusement lingered at how effortlessly he'd played along with her teasing.

Turning to Takoda, her grin grew sly. "Let's see how long it takes him to find that game room."

Takoda chuckled softly, shaking her head as they resumed their work. The atmosphere between them stayed light and carefree.

Down the hall, Elder's pace slowed just a fraction, the faintest trace of a smile playing across his lips. Rain's energy was sharp and unapologetic—unlike most who tiptoed around him. Few people cared to challenge him; fewer still treated him like the young man he truly was. It was a refreshing change, one that stirred a hint of curiosity he hadn't expected. *For now, though, there's a game room to investigate—assuming it even exists.*

As the sun dipped below the horizon, the mansion glowed with the warmth of twilight, golden light casting shifting shadows along the hallways. The transition from day to night signaled the beginning of the meeting. One by one, the Fallen gathered in the conference room, their steps purposeful. The scrape of chairs and the faint rustle of fabric were the only sounds as they settled around the large table, the fading sunlight yielding to the muted glow of the room's lamps.

The magnitude of the coming mission hung in the air, an understood pressure that settled over them. While the Fallen had faced countless threats before, the alliance between Lucifer and the Golden Dawn raised the stakes to an unprecedented level. Every decision made tonight carried the burden of the world's fate.

Eileen stood at the head of the table, her presence steady and commanding as she surveyed the room. The firelight caught the edge of her features, lending her an aura of quiet authority. "We all know why we're here," she began, her voice clear and firm. "Lucifer's forces are amassing strength. If we don't act now, we lose our advantage. This is our moment to strike—before they're fully prepared."

A charged stillness followed, the room holding onto her statement as it took root. Rowan sat beside Aislinn, his posture seemingly relaxed, yet his attention was razor-sharp, locked entirely on the discussion. Anticipation coursed through him—a familiar energy forged by years on the frontlines. Yet this time, his thoughts strayed to Aislinn. She would be at his side, and the thought fueled both his determination and a flicker of unease.

Aislinn sat upright, her features composed, her focus steadfast as she absorbed Eileen's every word. The burden of responsibility pressed on her shoulders, but her resolve held firm. Her mind dissected the plan, analyzing each phase with precision. Rowan's presence beside her strengthened her, a stabilizing force in the storm of her thoughts. They had faced danger before and would face it again—united.

"Lucifer's alliance with the Golden Dawn is a direct response to our last strike," Eileen continued, her voice steady and deliberate as she gestured to the map spread before them. "They see us as a threat, and they're already moving to counter us. That's why we need to act decisively—strike first, while they're still organizing."

She pointed to several key locations on the map, drawing their attention to the stronghold's vulnerabilities. "This mission will unfold in phases. Each phase is designed to dismantle their defenses and create openings for a decisive strike."

Rowan's concentration intensified, his thoughts narrowing on Eileen's explanation. The looming battle was no surprise—he already understood where he fit into the plan. His role was clear, as was Aislinn's, and the thought of fighting alongside her only deepened his resolve. He glanced at her briefly, catching the fire of determination in her expression. *Whatever lies ahead, we'll face it together.*

"Phase One will be led by Reed, Vine, and Riichi," Eileen announced, her finger tracing the stronghold's outer defenses on the map. "Your mission is to infiltrate the stronghold, disable their security systems, and create the entry points we need."

Reed gave a single nod, his usual stoicism unshaken, the importance of his role reflected in his stillness. Riichi and Vine exchanged a brief glance, their focus sharpening as they acknowledged the seriousness of their task. Both understood there was no room for error in this phase. Together, they embodied harmony, resilience, and precision—the adaptability needed to navigate unseen threats and outmaneuver the enemy.

"Phase Two," Eileen continued, shifting her attention to Oak, Elder, and Hazel. "You'll secure the perimeter. No one enters or exits without your authorization. We need to control their movements from the outside."

Oak leaned back slightly in his chair, a confident smirk tugging at the corner of his mouth. "Understood," he said, his words tinged with ease, though his sharp attention revealed his readiness. Elder, in contrast, maintained a composed, measured focus, his gaze locked on the map as though already visualizing the execution of the strategy. Hazel gave a firm nod, her poised demeanor reflecting the precision and discipline she brought to every mission. Their combined strengths—Oak's unyielding endurance, Elder's mastery of transitions, and Hazel's inventive problem-solving—formed a near-impenetrable shield, ensuring no gaps in their defense.

Eileen's tone sharpened as her attention moved to the next group. "Phase Three will be our main assault." Her eyes landed on Rowan, Ash, Holly, and Alder. "Rowan, you'll lead the charge. Ash, Holly, and Alder will join you on the front lines. Your goal is to keep their forces engaged and distracted while the infiltration team executes their task."

Rowan straightened in his chair, the importance of his assignment settling naturally on his shoulders. The front lines were where he belonged, and he had expected nothing less. Ash cracked his knuckles, the sound cutting through the charged atmosphere, his eagerness for the fight evident in his grin. Holly folded her arms, her calm posture masking the storm of strategy turning in her mind. Alder gave a subtle nod, his jaw tightening as he absorbed the gravity of their role. This team embodied strength, adaptability, and persistence—traits rooted in their Celtic identities that would guide them through the chaos of battle.

Eileen's gaze shifted briefly to the map before returning to the group. "Vine and Riichi will join you after they complete Phase One. Their expertise will strengthen the main assault, reinforcing your efforts to keep the enemy forces occupied. Coordination between the teams will be critical."

Aislinn exhaled softly as she listened, her faith in Rowan and the rest of the team unwavering. While her heart ached at the risks they all faced, she carried no doubt about their ability to succeed. The energy in the room shifted, rising like a noiseless tide as the magnitude of their shared purpose settled over them.

"Phase Four will be support and emergency extraction," Eileen said, her focus shifting to Ivy, Birch, Willow, and Aislinn. "This phase is our contingency. If anything goes wrong, we need to be able to pull everyone back swiftly."

Ivy nodded, her unerring concentration sharpening. Birch leaned back slightly, his grounded presence radiating calm strength, while Willow's composed expression revealed her readiness to adapt. Together, their roles would depend on Ivy's ingenuity, Birch's steadfastness, and Willow's flexibility—traits deeply tied to their Celtic roots, enabling them to respond under pressure.

Eileen's tone grew more deliberate as she added, "Reed will join this team after completing Phase One. His sole purpose will be to stay with Aislinn, protecting her and ensuring her safe arrival at Rowan's side when the time comes for Phase Five."

Reed gave a brief nod, his calm demeanor unshaken as he absorbed the full scope of his added responsibilities. The extraction phase carried unique pressures, requiring seamless precision amidst the chaos. With Ivy's ability to manipulate the battlefield, Birch's unyielding endurance, and Willow's quick adaptability, the team embodied the qualities needed to face unforeseen threats—and to safeguard Aislinn above all else.

Eileen's voice softened as she addressed the final phase. "Phase Five," she said, her attention shifting to Rowan and Aislinn, "is when your combined power will be critical. The Radiant Surge will give us the edge to break through Lucifer's defenses."

Rowan felt the familiar burden of responsibility settle over him at the mention of their Soulbound ability. The others didn't know the full depth of their bond, but what they did know was enough: the Radiant Surge had the potential to shift the tide of battle. His hand flexed lightly against the table—not out of fear, but out of readiness. He trusted Aislinn completely, just as he trusted himself.

Aislinn felt the same gravity pressing down, but she didn't falter. She and Rowan had faced countless dangers before, and their bond had only grown stronger. The Radiant Surge was their ace, and when the time came, they would wield it. She met Rowan's gaze, a quiet understanding passing between them. *We're ready.*

Eileen's next statement carried a note of warning as she added, "The timing must be exact. If we move too early or too late, we risk everything."

The room fell into a profound silence, her words settling like an unseen weight over them. Each member of the Fallen sat absorbed in the scope of the plan, their roles and responsibilities etched clearly in their minds. Rowan glanced at Aislinn once more, her calm expression mirroring his resolve. Together, they would see this through—just as they always had.

As Eileen shifted her stance, preparing to speak again, her voice softened further. The silence deepened, each member leaning in as they sensed the gravity of what was to come—a truth that carried both significance and difficulty.

"There's one more aspect we need to discuss," Eileen began, her voice measured. Her attention lingered on Rowan and Aislinn. "You won't be fighting together during the initial phases."

Rowan's head snapped up, his entire body tensing. His hands, which had rested on the table moments before, curled into fists so tight his knuckles whitened. His pulse thundered in his ears as Eileen's statement settled over him. *Separate?* It was the one scenario he hadn't prepared for. Across from him, Aislinn turned toward Eileen, her breath catching.

"To ensure both of your safety," Eileen continued, her unwavering gaze locking onto Rowan's, unyielding. "Aislinn will join the support and extraction team. Reed will complete his infiltration duties in Phase One, and after that, his sole mission will be to stay by her side. He will protect her and, when the time is right, shadow-walk her to you for the Radiant Surge."

Rowan felt the words hit like a blow to the chest. His protective instincts flared, drowning out reason. He couldn't sit still, couldn't stay silent. Fear—raw and visceral—ripped through him, dredging up memories he had worked so hard to bury. Faces of those he'd lost, of those he had failed to save, flashed through his mind in sharp, painful fragments. The thought of Aislinn joining them was unbearable, and that fear morphed into anger, hot and consuming.

"You're asking me to leave her behind when Lucifer's after both of us?" Rowan's outburst rose, louder than he intended, edged with desperation. His chair scraped harshly against the floor as he shoved it back and stood, his look a storm of fury and fear. "How am I supposed to fight knowing she's not with me? That I can't protect her?"

Aislinn's chest tightened at his declaration, the depth of his emotions radiating off him. She wanted to stand with him, to protest just as fiercely, but her mind was at war. *He's right... and yet Eileen isn't wrong.* The logic of the plan was sound, but her heart rebelled against it. The unspoken truth hung heavily between them—that if one of them fell, the other would follow. Only she, Rowan, and Eileen truly grasped the full magnitude of that reality.

Eileen met his blazing stare steadily, her voice calm but firm. "I understand how hard this is for you, Rowan," she said, her tone carrying the depth of her knowledge. "But keeping you together from the start makes you both too easy a target. Lucifer wants you both, and separating you makes it harder for him to strike. Reed will be with her. She won't be left unprotected."

Rowan stood rigid, his chest heaving as emotions clashed within him. He wanted to argue, to shout until the plan unraveled, but he couldn't. Memories of Davina, his family, and every person he hadn't been able to save surged forward, tightening his throat. Losing Aislinn would break him, and the mere thought of not being there to prevent it clawed at him like a fresh wound.

Riichi, who had been silently observing, leaned forward, breaking the tense atmosphere. As Rowan's closest friend, he understood better than most what this stirred inside him. He knew the pain of Rowan's losses, the lingering guilt of failing to protect those he loved. His calm, empathetic response broke through the tension.

"The goal is to keep them off balance," Riichi said, his measured tone deliberate. His focus shifted between Rowan and Eileen. "If you and Aislinn are together from the start, you'll give Lucifer exactly what he wants—a clear target. He'll come for you both immediately."

The words landed like a blow. Rowan clenched his jaw, the logic undeniable, though it twisted like a blade in his chest. Riichi wasn't just speaking tactics—he was reminding Rowan of what was at stake, of the lives depending on their success.

Rowan gritted his teeth, trembling with the effort to suppress the storm inside him. His mind understood the strategy, but his heart railed against it. For the first time in years, he felt utterly powerless.

Elder's deep statement interrupted the stillness. "I know you want to protect her, Rowan," he said, his usual composure softened with understanding. "But sometimes protecting someone means trusting others to do their part. Reed will be with her. You're both stronger together, but if we lose you too soon, there won't be anyone left to stop Lucifer."

Reed, silent until now, finally spoke. His voice was calm, resolute. "I'll make sure she's safe until the Radiant Surge," he said, his focus shifting between Rowan and Aislinn. "You can count on me, Rowan. I'll shadow-walk her to you when the time comes, and if anyone tries to come after her, I'll get her out of there."

Rowan's fists tightened further, the strain visible in every line of his frame. He trusted Reed—he had to—but the thought of Aislinn being out of his sight, beyond his reach, while Lucifer's forces hunted them both sent cold dread coursing through him. When he finally spoke, his words cracked, raw with emotion. "If anything happens to her—"

"It won't," Reed interrupted, his resolve steady and unshakable—his Celtic harmony evident in his calm presence. He stood fully, turning to face Rowan directly. His gaze carried a steadfast conviction that resonated with more power than the statement itself. "My life for hers."

Before Rowan could respond, Vine rose from his seat, the usual glint of mischief absent from his eyes. His easygoing demeanor was replaced by a rare solemnity, his unflinching loyalty to the team and to Aislinn reflected in his stance. Vine's declaration was almost unrecognizable as he repeated it with unwavering determination. "My life for hers."

Riichi was next. Rowan's closest friend, the one who had walked beside him through pain and loss, stood with his usual calm. Rowan saw the precision in the way Riichi spoke and stood—every action careful, every word carrying significance. He didn't need to say more than the vow itself; the depth of his understanding spoke louder than anything else. Meeting Rowan's eyes, Riichi's response was quiet but steady. "My life for hers." His subtle nod carried the significance of a reminder: *You're not alone in this fight. You never have been.*

Elder rose next, his movements methodical, his presence as composed and unshakable as ever. The connection to transitions and endings echoed in the way he leaned forward, his deep voice carrying the vow forward. "My life for hers." The conviction behind his words felt timeless, carrying the enormity of oaths sworn across lifetimes.

Oak, usually brimming with bravado, pushed back his chair with a confidence that felt tempered, more grounded. His strength and endurance were evident in his stance as he locked eyes with Rowan, a silent respect passing between them. His delivery was firm, with none of his usual flair but all the intensity of his resolve. "My life for hers."

The room fell silent for a breath before Holly stood, her smaller frame almost dwarfed by those around her. Yet her steady determination carried perseverance and protection unfaltering. "My life for hers." She glanced briefly at Aislinn, her loyalty clear without the need for further explanation.

Ash stood next, his usual cocky demeanor subdued. He cracked his knuckles, the familiar sound oddly comforting. His strength and adaptability burned in his expression, unwavering and resolute. "My life for hers," he said simply, no bravado, just truth.

Alder followed, his calm and steady presence a counterpoint to Ash's energy. His determination shone in his unflinching tone, each word a steady force. "My life for hers."

Birch and Ivy rose almost simultaneously, their movements in sync despite their contrasting tones. Birch's quiet endurance and Ivy's relentless determination reflected their inner resolve in every motion. Birch's reply was soft, anchoring. "My life for hers." Ivy's was sharper, tinged with urgency, but no less heartfelt. "My life for hers."

Hazel took her time, rising deliberately as her measured eyes met Rowan's. Her wisdom softened her tone, but the conviction beneath it was unshakable. "My life for hers."

Finally, Willow stood, her graceful movements purposeful as always. Her resilience and flexibility were evident in her firm voice. "My life for hers."

The room stilled again, every eye turning to Rowan. Yet it wasn't over.

Eileen, who had remained seated in observation, rose from her place at the head of the table. Her calm strength carried the burden of all that she had endured. When she spoke, her statement was quieter but imbued with deep authority. "My life for hers."

Rowan felt the weight of their words press against him, but instead of suffocating, it steadied him. Each vow, each promise, reminded him of the unity in this room—the unbreakable bond they shared. The storm of emotions that had threatened to drown him moments before began to settle, replaced by a clarity he hadn't felt since the plan began.

Aislinn felt Rowan's hand brush hers again under the table, the subtle touch grounding her. She turned to him, catching his gaze, and in that instant, she knew he felt it too. *This is our family. Together, we'll make it through.*

Rowan's hands, once clenched tightly into fists, slowly relaxed. He glanced at Aislinn, the unspoken connection between them strengthening further.

We've carried so much, just us two—but now, we're not alone. They weren't just fighting for each other anymore. They had an army behind them.

Eileen's final statement, softer now but no less commanding, broke the silence. "We are a team," she said firmly. "And we will fight as one. Rowan, you're not alone in this."

For the first time since the meeting had started, Rowan felt a sliver of peace settle over him. It wasn't much, but it was enough. He gave a single, slow nod to the rest of the Fallen, a silent acknowledgment of their vow. It was his way of saying what he couldn't bring himself to voice aloud: gratitude. He wasn't just Aislinn's shield. They all were.

As the meeting resumed, the plan unfolded, though the atmosphere had shifted. The risks ahead lingered like a shadow, but the collective resolve of the team now underpinned every detail. Rowan felt it—the shared determination that bound them all. They would protect Aislinn. They would protect each other.

Eileen's cadence remained measured as she finalized the details, the tension in the room deepening with every word. Each piece of the plan had fallen into place, every role defined with precision, yet the enormity of the mission loomed over the table like a storm cloud. Reed's task was clear: after Phase One, he would stay with Aislinn, shadow-walking her to Rowan when the time came for the Radiant Surge. But even the most carefully crafted plans couldn't eliminate the unknowns of what lay ahead.

"You all know your roles," Eileen said, her gaze sweeping across the room. "There's no room for error. Adaptability is key, and the timing of Rowan and Aislinn's reunion is crucial. We can't afford delays."

Rowan sat in silence, the enormity of the plan pressing against him. Yet the earlier fear, the suffocating tension, had eased slightly in the wake of the team's vow. Still, the thought of being apart from Aislinn gnawed at him, an ache he couldn't ignore. He forced himself to trust Reed, to trust the others. *I have no choice.* But the unease lingered, sharp and unrelenting, like a blade poised to strike.

Across the table, Aislinn kept her appearance composed, though turmoil churned beneath her calm exterior. She trusted the team. She trusted Reed. But the idea of waiting—of relying on someone else to bring her to

Rowan—left her restless. A knot tightened in her chest, each what if spiraling into darker possibilities. *What if something goes wrong? What if I'm too late?* She buried the thoughts, knowing now wasn't the time to waver. Everyone was counting on them to remain steady.

Eileen's steady rhythm broke the silence, her tone laced with a solemnity that couldn't be ignored. "We're as ready as we can be," she said, softening slightly. "But not everything is predictable. Be prepared for anything. And watch each other's backs."

Rowan met Aislinn's gaze, their eyes locking in a long, unbroken moment. It was as if the room around them dissolved, leaving only the two of them in the stillness. They couldn't speak the fears clawing at them, couldn't give shape to the truth they both knew: one wrong move could mean losing each other forever. But in that shared look, there was a promise. *We'll fight. We'll survive. And we'll find our way back to each other—no matter what.*

Eileen drew a deep breath, her gaze lingering briefly on Rowan and Aislinn, as though sensing their unspoken exchange. When she spoke again, her tone carried a cryptic edge. "This is just the beginning. Lucifer is more dangerous than any of us know. Even I can't see all that's coming."

The room seemed to darken, the atmosphere shifting with a subtle yet undeniable unease. Outside, the wind howled against the windows, rattling them in their frames. The storm that had hovered on the horizon was closing in now, its presence seeping into the mansion's sturdy walls.

Eileen's firm cadence broke through the tension. "We're as prepared as we can be, but nothing about this fight is guaranteed. Trust in each other. Lean on the bonds you've forged—those will be your greatest strength."

The Fallen nodded, their expressions resolute. The weight of her statement settled heavily over them, a solemn acknowledgment of what lay ahead. Slowly, they rose from their seats, their movements purposeful as they prepared to disperse. No one spoke; there was nothing more to say. Each step carried the shared understanding that this might be the last time they were all together like this.

Rowan stood, his hand brushing against Aislinn's as they turned to leave. Her fingers curled briefly around his, anchoring him to the stark reality of what lay ahead. The Fallen weren't just warriors; they were roots in the same forest, each drawing strength from the other. Together, they had the resilience to weather any storm, their unity as enduring as the trees that symbolized their names. Whatever chaos awaited, Rowan knew one thing: they would stand strong, no matter what came for them.

As they stepped into the hallway, the first crack of thunder rumbled low and distant, a harbinger of the storm's arrival. The wind lashed harder against the windows, its eerie wail carrying through the mansion's corridors. The air felt heavier now, charged with the enormity of what was about to unfold.

The storm wasn't just brewing—it was here.

And the battle was only beginning.

As they walked down the corridor, their footsteps whispered along the stone walls, the sound a muted rhythm in the still air. Neither had spoken since leaving the meeting, unease drifting between them like a shadow at dusk. Rowan's hand brushed Aislinn's, a quiet gesture of reassurance, though she could feel the gravity of his thoughts, unrelenting and heavy as carved granite.

Down the hall, Aislinn noticed Takoda and Rain waiting near the library entrance. Rain flashed a sly thumbs-up, her cheeky grin as bright as ever, while Takoda greeted them with a warm nod, her excitement gleaming in her features. It was ready.

"I'm not quite ready to head back to our room yet," Aislinn said, nudging Rowan lightly. "There's something I want to show you."

A flicker of curiosity softened his expression, and he nodded. "Lead the way."

She guided him toward the library, her pulse quickening as they reached the hidden bookshelf. Sliding her hand along the dusty spines, she found the lever, its cool metal centering her like the roots of an ancient oak. With a soft click, the shelf shifted, revealing a spiral staircase curling upward into shadow.

"We found this earlier," Aislinn explained as they ascended. "Takoda, Rain, and I went exploring and stumbled on it. I thought it'd be perfect for us—a little escape." She glanced back, her grin shy but hopeful. "They helped me decorate it while we were at training and the meeting."

Rowan's lips tugged into an amused smirk. "A hidden room, huh? Find anything else lurking in this place?"

Aislinn chuckled, her fingers brushing the cool, timeworn stone of the railing. "Not like this. Though it does make you wonder, doesn't it? What else might be tucked away in a place like this?" She paused, looking back at him, her face softening with care. "I thought we could use a surprise. Just for us."

At the top of the staircase, they stepped into a circular room aglow with the warm light of lanterns. Narrow slits in the walls allowed streaks of twilight to filter in, painting the space in dusky hues of violet and amber. The room felt timeless, a sanctuary cradled within the castle's ancient bones—a place where the burdens of the world might loosen their hold, if only for a while.

Rain and Takoda had transformed the space with thoughtful care. Rich crimson and gold drapes softened the bare stone, their folds adding warmth and elegance, while plush cushions in jewel tones scattered across the floor created an inviting retreat. In the center of the room, a small picnic awaited—a delicate spread of fresh fruit, neatly arranged sandwiches, and intricately crafted sweets, unmistakably Takoda's touch.

Aislinn's chest tightened with gratitude as she took it all in. "They really outdid themselves," she murmured, turning to Rowan. "What do you think?"

Rowan's gaze swept the room, his features easing into a look of tenderness. "It's perfect," he said, his voice steady but sincere. "You did this for us?"

She shook her head with a faint smile. "It was Takoda and Rain. They wanted to give us a place to breathe."

Their eyes met, and briefly, an understanding passed between them, fragile yet profound. This space, however fleeting, felt like a shield against the relentless storm beyond its walls.

"We should talk about the battle," Aislinn said, breaking the silence. Her voice softened as she turned to face him. "I know you're worried."

Rowan exhaled slowly, his nostrils flaring slightly as he stepped closer. "You know I am," he admitted, his tone rough, the strain evident. "I don't like the idea of us being separated."

Aislinn nodded, sensing the storm within him. *He's always carried so much.* "I'll be with the support and extraction team. Reed will stay with me the whole time. If anything happens, he can shadow-walk me to you in an instant."

His brow furrowed, and his hands settled on her shoulders, his grip firm and balancing. "And what if something happens before that? What if I'm too far, or—" He stopped himself, shaking his head as though willing the thought away. "I can't protect you if I'm not there."

She placed her hand over his, her touch steady. "You're not alone in this. The Fallen have their vows, and keeping us apart is part of the strategy. If Lucifer or the Golden Dawn captures one of us, they won't have us both. It's safer."

His grip firmed on her shoulders, his protective instincts clashing with the cold logic of her reasoning. *He hates being helpless. Yet he knows this is right.*

"You know Reed is capable," Aislinn continued, her tone calm yet firm. "He can shadow-walk me anywhere in an instant. And I'll sense if anything goes wrong, Rowan. If you need me, I'll find a way to get to you. I'm not defenseless."

Rowan exhaled again, his hold easing as some of the strain left his stance. "I trust Reed. And I trust you." His features softened slightly, though traces of concern remained. "It doesn't make it easier. I'll still be worried."

Aislinn offered a faint smile, her fingers slipping down to clasp his hand. "I know. But we both have our roles to play, and I'll be safe. I'll make sure of it."

His thumb brushed over her knuckles, an absent motion that tethered him. "You better," he murmured, the worry not entirely lifted. "Or I'll have Reed shadow-walk me straight to you."

A laugh escaped her, genuine and bright. "I'll hold you to that."

For a heartbeat, the room seemed to draw inward, not with tension but with an intimacy that focused everything on them. The lanterns cast a golden glow that softened the edges of the space, blurring the line between this sanctuary and the uncertainty beyond. Despite everything, their connection stood unshaken—a quiet understanding that, no matter what, they would find their way back to each other.

Rowan's concern eased further, though it still lingered beneath the surface. "You'll be able to shield me, too, right? When the time comes for Radiant Surge?"

"Yes," Aislinn said, her reply measured despite the flicker of doubt stirring inside her. "I'll shield and heal you when it matters most. I've practiced enough to feel it—if you need me, I'll know. We'll make it through this."

He studied her briefly, intent on committing her to memory. Not from fear, but from a need to center himself in the certainty of her presence. Then he leaned forward, their foreheads touching. The action was deliberate, an unspoken assurance that no worry or doubt could fracture what they shared.

"I love you," he murmured, the words low but unwavering.

Aislinn's lips curved, the familiar confession sparking a resolve within her. It wasn't the first time he'd said it, yet in this pause, the vow felt like a thread binding them together no matter what lay ahead. "I love you too," she replied, her certainty unwavering.

They remained like that for a beat longer, holding the world outside at bay. When Rowan lifted his head, his lips brushed hers in a kiss that wasn't hurried or fleeting. It lingered, keeping them both in the present, a reminder of the strength they would need for what awaited.

Aislinn shifted, her hand slipping into his as she guided him toward the cushions scattered across the floor. The room's warmth enveloped them, wrapping the scene in a sense of ease. Settling beside him, she rested her palm on his chest, over the rhythmic pulse of his heartbeat.

"We're Soulbound," she said, her pacing measured. "That means we're tied together in every way. If anything happens to you..." Her breath caught, the rest of the sentence sticking in her throat.

Rowan covered her hand with his, his fingers curling firmly around hers. "If one of us dies, the other does too," he finished. Saying it aloud again didn't ease the burden of it, but it sharpened their focus.

Aislinn swallowed, her grip on his hand tightening. "It's not just the battle that scares me. It's how much we're risking—everything we've built, everything we could still have. If anything goes wrong..." She exhaled, centering herself. "It feels like too much to lose."

Rowan didn't let go, his focus steadfast. "It is a lot. That's why we fight for it, Aislinn. We don't have a choice—not if we want that future."

She nodded, his statement sinking into her like an unshakable truth. "I'm afraid of what we might lose," she admitted, her whisper barely audible. "But I'm also afraid of what we could gain."

Rowan tilted his head slightly, curiosity lighting his countenance. "What do you mean?"

Her response came slowly, hesitant as she tried to shape the storm of emotions within her. "I want to have a future with you, but that means surviving this. And I'm scared—not just of the battle, but of how much I want that future. It makes everything feel..."

"Riskier," Rowan finished for her, understanding evident in the way he regarded her. "It feels like the stakes are higher now, doesn't it?"

She bobbed her head, the enormity of their bond and the battle ahead pressing down on them as they sat in silence. The room, for all its comfort, couldn't hold back the encroaching shadows stretching in from the world beyond.

Rowan exhaled, breaking the pause. "We need to practice," he said, his resolve clear. "Radiant Surge isn't a skill we can afford to get wrong out there."

Aislinn nodded, her thoughts drifting back to the challenges of their bond. "What about the blue glow? It'll make us easy targets."

Rowan rubbed the back of his neck, his brow furrowing in thought. "That's why we need to practice. If we can control it—dim it—we'll be able to use it without giving ourselves away."

They rose together, the atmosphere in the room shifting to a sense of purpose. Rowan extended his hand, and Aislinn took it, the familiar pulse of their combined power sparking to life. The blue shimmer of their magic began to swirl, flowing around them in fluid, rhythmic waves.

"It's still too bright," Aislinn observed, concentrating as the light spilled across the walls, casting shifting shadows that seemed to breathe with the flickering lantern flames.

Rowan's jaw tightened as he focused. "We need to secure it—focus it inward, like you've been doing with your kinetic blasts. It's about precision, not force."

They tried again, channeling the magic through the bond that connected them. The glow softened, its edges dimming slightly, but it still sputtered, unstable. The energy resisted fully aligning, as if it carried a will of its own.

Aislinn paused abruptly, an almost imperceptible change in the atmosphere catching her attention. It wasn't their magic—it was an unfamiliar presence entirely. She turned toward the windows, her pulse quickening.

"That's not us," she murmured, nervousness lacing her words.

Rowan followed her line of sight, his movements deliberate as they approached the slitted windows. Below, in the courtyard, Elder walked away, his back to them, one hand raised in a brief, understated wave. A faint shimmer rippled across the windows, a protective barrier now enclosing the room. Their magic dimmed further, veiled by the enchantment.

"He... put up a barrier," Rowan muttered, surprise threading through his tone.

Aislinn's attention stayed on the retreating figure, curiosity stirring as she watched Elder vanish into the deepening shadows. Relief mingled with intrigue. Elder's reserved nature had always made him more of an observer than an active participant, but this subtle gesture hinted at depths rarely seen.

Rowan's brow creased, recognition flashing in his eyes. "It's a ward," he murmured, his voice thoughtful as he moved closer to the window. "Celtic magic. Protective, ancient. Elder used to talk about them—charms meant to shield places of power or block unwanted attention."

Aislinn glanced at Rowan, her surprise evident. "You've seen him do this before?"

"Once or twice," Rowan admitted, his attention fixed on the shimmer clinging to the window's edges. "But never without saying anything. That's... new."

They exchanged a glance, an understanding passing between them. Whatever Elder's reasons, his actions left no doubt—he had their backs. Rowan's lips twitched. "Guess we don't have to worry about being seen."

Aislinn's smile was soft, her response measured. "We should keep practicing."

Rowan inclined his head, a flicker of gratitude passing between them without the need for words. "Fair point."

They turned back to their magic, focusing again on dimming the glow. Each attempt brought incremental progress—the brightness softened from glaring blue to a gentle shimmer—but the instability remained, the energy vibrating just beyond their control. Rowan's guidance was deliberate as he walked her through the process, his persistence giving her focus.

"Let it settle here," he said, his hand brushing hers. "Feel the bond and let it guide the flow. Don't force it—align with it."

Aislinn closed her eyes briefly, centering herself. The energy surged between them, vibrant and alive, before easing into a calmer rhythm. The glow dimmed further, faint but still imperfect. It was progress, though not mastery.

Rowan's lips quirked in a small grin, a light chuckle escaping him. "Not bad for tonight."

Aislinn tilted her head, amusement softening her features. "Not bad," she agreed, "but not enough."

He stepped closer, his hand slipping to her waist as he drew her into a gentle embrace. His fingers brushed the back of her neck, offering reassurance as he rested his chin against her hair. "We'll get it right," he said, his statement firm. "We always do."

The glow shimmered around them, but Aislinn couldn't ignore the instability beneath its surface. The energy felt stretched, as if the burden it carried was too great to fully contain. *It has to work,* she thought, unease curling in her chest.

"I just hope we're ready," she murmured, the words slipping out unbidden.

Rowan's arms tightened, the strength of his presence calming her. For an instant, the room held its fragile peace, their shared determination settling like an unspoken promise.

Aislinn's attention drifted over the space, taking in the cushions and blankets Takoda and Rain had carefully arranged. The lanterns cast a warm light that felt timeless, like the glow of hearth fires in old tales—a reminder of safety found in small, sacred places.

"We could stay here tonight," she suggested, her fingers brushing Rowan's arm. "It feels like a place meant for rest. We don't have to go back."

Rowan's features softened as he took in the room, his posture easing as he nodded. "That sounds perfect," he said simply.

They settled into the cushions, the stress of the day unraveling as they lay together. Aislinn nestled into Rowan's arms, the rhythm of his breathing calming the frayed edges of her thoughts.

In the soft glow of the lanterns, they drifted off. The room, protected by Elder's ward and the comfort of their bond, became a haven untouched by the chaos outside. For a little while, the battle waiting beyond its walls seemed distant, the sanctuary holding them in a peace they both knew wouldn't last.

***

The sky remained dense with night as Reed, Riichi, Vine, and Alder slipped from the mansion, their movements as fluid as shadows gliding across the courtyard. The chill of the early morning clung to them, sharp and biting, the gravity of their mission understood without the need for conversation.

Reed led the group, his footsteps inaudible on the damp earth as they moved through the fading darkness toward the Old Mount Olympus Mansion—the Golden Dawn's stronghold. His years of shadow-walking had honed his instincts, making him the ideal guide for a mission like this. Riichi followed close behind, his movements precise, his attention sweeping the forest for any sign of danger.

At the rear, Vine and Alder remained attuned to the threads of magic weaving through the air. Alder, his awareness unusually heightened, scanned the atmosphere for the pull of a vision. Though nothing stirred yet, a tension prickled at the edges of his consciousness—a warning he couldn't yet define.

The mansion loomed ahead, a hulking silhouette barely visible through the mist and skeletal trees. The silence here pressed heavily, as though the land itself recoiled from what it had witnessed. It was an atmosphere thick with the residue of dark rituals. Each step closer deepened the unease in the air.

They stopped at the forest's edge, crouching low behind a tangle of gnarled shrubs. Reed raised his hand, signaling them to halt. They froze, breaths shallow as they assessed the scene.

Even from this distance, the preparations were unmistakable. A massive stone altar dominated the courtyard, its surface etched with glowing sigils. Half-formed magical wards shimmered weakly around it, crackling with energy—a trap for the unwary. The atmosphere buzzed with a dark anticipation that made the hair on Alder's neck stand on end.

"The altar's already assembled," Alder murmured, his voice barely audible. "They're moving faster than we expected."

Reed's expression darkened as his sharp attention took in the scene. He motioned for them to advance, and they crept closer, each step deliberate. The wards and sentries scattered around the perimeter became clearer with every inch gained. The Golden Dawn wasn't just preparing for battle—they were preparing for a far more sinister purpose.

"They're setting traps," Riichi whispered, his certainty unwavering. His focus shifted to the sigils glowing on the ground, their patterns intricate and dangerous. "Magical ones. They're designed to ensnare anyone who gets too close."

Vine's usual ease had hardened, his concentration unbroken. "We don't have five days," he muttered grimly. "Three at best. Lucifer's accelerating everything."

At Vine's words, Alder's hand twitched, his gaze fixed on the altar. A pressure coiled within him, a silent trigger of an impending revelation. His prophetic gift stirred faintly—not yet a vision, but an unease rippling through him like distant thunder.

"Three days," Alder said finally, his certainty cutting through the strain. "That's all we have."

Reed's lips pursed at the revelation. Three days. It wasn't enough. Lucifer's arrival had pushed everything forward, forcing their carefully laid plans to shift.

"We need to get back," Reed said, his words clipped but calm. "Warn the others."

Before they could retreat, Alder froze, his entire body locking as an unseen force swept over him. His fingers gripped the nearest tree, knuckles white as his breathing faltered. The vision took hold of him without warning, pulling him into its depths.

"Alder?" Riichi whispered urgently, his hand reaching to steady him.

But Alder didn't respond. His stare went vacant, his mind consumed by the images flashing before him. He saw fire and darkness—an altar bathed in crimson light. A figure stood over it, chanting in a language that felt both ancient and wrong, its resonance twisting through the air like a dirge. The ritual unfolded with brutal clarity, yet there was an undercurrent—a presence lurking just beyond the edges of the vision. It was darker, hungrier. Its form eluded him, but its malice was undeniable.

When the vision finally released him, Alder staggered, his breath ragged, his color drained. "We have to move," he rasped, his words strained but urgent. "It's worse than we thought. Lucifer... he's already begun the preparations. If we wait any longer, it won't just be the ritual. There's more—something I couldn't see clearly. But it's dangerous."

Reed exchanged a grim look with Riichi and Vine, the decision passing between them unspoken. There was no time to waste.

"Let's go," Reed ordered. Without delay, they turned and melted back into the forest, their steps swift and careful. The urgency in their movements mirrored the dread coiling at the edges of their thoughts.

Alder remained silent as they ran, the density of his vision pressing hard on him. The images still burned in his mind—the altar, the shadows, the overwhelming sense of doom. They had come seeking answers, and now they had them—but it was far worse than they had feared.

The Fallen would have to act, and soon.

***

Back at the Fallen mansion, the kitchen felt like a world apart from the tense mission Reed and the others had undertaken. Morning crept in gradually, pale hues of dawn softening the misty estate outside. Inside, the warmth of the kitchen stood in contrast, alive with the hum of activity and the comforting scent of freshly baked croissants.

Takoda moved with ease, her hands following the practiced rhythm of preparing breakfast. The golden-brown croissants glistened as she pulled them from the oven, their buttery aroma mingling with the sweetness of fruit Rain was slicing beside her. The colorful spread on the counter—a mix of berries, melons, and citrus—offered a cheerful reprieve from the tension coursing through the mansion.

Cooking brought Takoda a rare sense of peace, a reminder of mornings spent working in Aislinn's café before the fire that had changed everything. Back then, the scent of bread and pastries had filled the air as she prepared the day's offerings, her hands busy while Aislinn greeted customers with a welcoming grin. Now, in the midst of training and preparing for the battle ahead, cooking was one of the few ways she felt she could make a difference.

"This is going to be amazing," Rain said, her upbeat tone cutting through the air as she handed Takoda a bowl of freshly cut strawberries. "Think they'll appreciate it?"

Takoda's lips twitched in a small grin as she arranged the croissants on a large tray. "Reed will. He's not picky—as long as it's food, he'll eat it."

Rain chuckled, though a flicker of unease crossed her face. Takoda caught the shift, the kind of worry they all carried. Yet here, surrounded by the comfort of warm food and familiar tasks, it was easier to push those feelings aside.

"They've been working hard in training," Rain said in the next breath. "I wonder if they're as nervous as we are."

Takoda paused, her hand hovering over the tray. "Probably," she admitted softly, her tone reflective. "But this... it helps. Doing anything, even something small. It feels like it matters."

Rain nodded, her gaze drifting to the window as the mist began to thin, revealing glimpses of the garden outside. "Yeah. Keeping busy makes it easier."

The sound of light footsteps drew their attention as Aislinn entered the kitchen, her hair tousled from sleep and her appearance noticeably more relaxed than it had been the night before. She inhaled deeply, her smile brightening as she took in the spread before her. "You two have outdone yourselves," she said, her lips curving into a playful smile. "Is this all for the Fallen, or can I sneak a bite?"

Takoda laughed lightly, waving her off. "Help yourself. It's grab-and-go this morning. We figured they'd want a quick bite to eat before training."

Aislinn plucked a croissant from the tray, breaking off a piece and popping it into her mouth. "I swear, if it weren't for you two, I'd starve."

"Or survive on burnt toast and coffee," Rain teased, nudging her playfully.

Aislinn smirked, but as she slid onto a stool at the counter, her expression grew thoughtful. "How are you two holding up?" she asked, her question gentle yet direct. "With all this training and everything coming?"

Takoda exchanged a glance with Rain before answering. "We're managing," she said, her voice light despite the weight behind her words. "This helps, you know. Cooking, keeping busy—it keeps my mind from wandering."

Rain nodded in agreement. "Same here. I feel better when I'm doing something useful."

Aislinn's smile widened as her gaze shifted between them. "You've both been keeping busy," she said, a teasing glint sparking in her eyes as she added, "Speaking of staying productive... you and Riichi, huh?"

Takoda nearly dropped the tray of croissants, her cheeks flushing deep pink as her eyes widened. "What? No. Absolutely not."

Rain burst into laughter, leaning against the counter with a grin. "Come on, T. I saw you two in the kitchen that one time. There's definitely something going on."

Takoda shot her a glare, though the warmth creeping up her neck betrayed her. "He was just helping me cut vegetables. I slipped and cut my finger, and he bandaged it. That's all."

"Uh-huh, sure," Aislinn teased, her grin widening. "I've seen him sneaking glances at you more than once. He doesn't look at anyone else like that."

Takoda rolled her eyes, though her pulse quickened at the thought. The teasing wasn't entirely unwelcome, but she wasn't about to admit that aloud. *You're imagining things,* she told herself, turning her attention back to the tray. "Riichi is just... helpful."

Rain snorted, her grin widening. "Yeah, helpful. Is that what we're calling it now?"

Takoda threw her a look but couldn't help the small smile tugging at her lips. "I just find him... interesting," she admitted, her voice quieter. "The way he talks so formally with me and Rain yet is so casual with the others. It's... different."

Aislinn exchanged a knowing glance with Rain before leaning forward on the counter. "Sounds like more than just 'helpful' to me."

Takoda shook her head, though her heart felt lighter in the company of her friends. Despite the teasing, their banter brought comfort—a brief escape from the looming threat that hung over them all.

They fell into an easy rhythm, the kitchen filled with the hum of activity and the welcoming scent of freshly made breakfast. Between grins and playful remarks, the tension of the outside world eased for a little while. But beneath it all, the knowledge of what lay ahead lingered—a reminder that these moments of peace wouldn't last forever.

Near the entrance, the morning mist clung to the courtyard as Rowan stepped outside, the cool air biting against his skin. The mansion seemed more subdued than usual, the quiet broken only by the rustling of leaves and distant bird calls. As he surveyed the property, his focus shifted to a familiar group—Riichi, Vine, Alder, and Reed—returning from their early morning scouting mission.

Rowan's attention settled on Riichi, his closest friend among the Fallen, whose precise movements carried an ease unaffected by the responsibility of their task. Raising a hand, Rowan signaled him over. The others continued toward the mansion, but Riichi broke away and approached, his composed demeanor carrying a subtle trace of knowing.

"How'd it go?" Rowan asked, his attempt at a casual tone undercut by the pressure weighing on his mind.

"Fast-moving," Riichi replied, his delivery precise. "We got what we needed." His gaze paused on Rowan briefly, the corners of his mouth tightening. "How's Aislinn?"

Rowan leaned back against the stone wall, exhaling through his nose. "You know how it is," he admitted, a wry grin tugging at his lips. "I'm trying to keep her safe, but it's hard to shake the feeling that I have to protect her from everything."

Riichi's behavior shifted, his usual reserve softening as a rare warmth threaded through his tone. "You're not the only one who wants to protect her. We all do. You don't have to carry this alone."

Rowan inclined his head, but the burden of responsibility clung to him. Tapping his fingers absently against the wall, he allowed a teasing smirk to surface. "By the way," he said, his tone lightening, "I couldn't help noticing you've been spending a lot of time around Takoda lately."

Riichi raised a single brow, his composure unshaken. "It's not what you think," he said smoothly. "Since the café fire, I've felt responsible for her. That's all."

Rowan gave him a skeptical look, his grin widening. "Responsible, huh? Funny, I've seen the way you look at her. Looks more like interest than duty to me."

Riichi hesitated, just long enough for Rowan to notice, before replying, his voice quieter. "She's... intriguing. She's an excellent cook. And she speaks Japanese."

Rowan chuckled, crossing his arms. "Good food and your native language? Sounds like you're smitten."

Riichi glanced away, though faint amusement flickered across his features. "It's not that simple," he said, his voice dipping. "There's a uniqueness about her."

Rowan clapped a hand on his shoulder, a familiar gesture that spoke of their bond. "I get it," he said, sincerity lacing his words. "But don't hide behind 'responsibility.' Maybe it's time to stop overthinking and do something about it."

Riichi's smirk returned briefly, though his expression soon grew serious. "Maybe. But we've got bigger problems to deal with right now."

The teasing dropped away as Rowan straightened, noting the shift in Riichi's demeanor. "What kind of problems?"

Riichi's gaze didn't waver, his delivery deliberate. "Lucifer's influence—it's stronger than we expected," he said, each word chosen carefully. "We'll need to act faster than planned."

Rowan frowned, the impact of the statement sinking into him. "Anything I need to know now?"

"Not yet," Riichi replied, his tone measured. "Just be ready. Things are going to escalate."

Rowan nodded sharply, his jaw tightening. "Understood."

Riichi glanced toward the mansion, his posture taut. "I need to speak with Eileen. We'll figure out the next steps."

As he turned to leave, Rowan called after him, unable to resist one last jab. "Hey, if Takoda makes another special dish for you, don't forget to save me a plate."

Riichi didn't break stride, but Rowan caught the faintest trace of amusement in his parting response. "We'll see."

Remaining in the courtyard after Riichi disappeared, Rowan breathed in the crisp morning air. The shadows of their conversation lingered, but a small grin crept onto his face. Even with Lucifer's threat looming, moments like these—fragments of friendship and possibility—still found a way to push back the darkness.

Inside the mansion, a charged intensity permeated the air. Eileen stood near the entrance of the main hall, her keen attention scanning the room as she waited for the scouting party to return. The others, scattered throughout the mansion, remained absorbed in their tasks, their focus unrelenting as the battle drew closer with every passing hour.

The heavy oak doors groaned open, and Reed, Vine, and Alder stepped inside. Eileen immediately registered the gravity in their postures, her awareness narrowing as she absorbed the tension radiating from them. They exchanged a brief glance but paused, waiting. A short time later, Riichi entered, his composed manner intact, though the rigidity in his stance carried an unmistakable urgency. Eileen noticed it instantly.

Without speaking, she motioned for them to follow her into a smaller room off the main hall. The space, reserved for private discussions, felt insulated from the rest of the mansion, the walls absorbing the unease that deepened with every revelation.

Once the door closed behind them, Eileen's gaze swept over each of them, sharp and expectant. "What did you find?"

Reed stepped forward, his delivery firm and unwavering. "Lucifer's influence is accelerating. The altar for the ritual is already in place, and they've started setting up magical traps around the perimeter." He paused, his words deliberate. "We don't have five days like we thought. We have three."

Eileen's eyes narrowed, though her composure remained steady. "Three days," she repeated, her cadence measured as the significance of the situation settled over her. "And the traps?"

Riichi stepped in seamlessly, his tone calm but edged with worry. "They've woven wards into the ground, designed to ensnare anyone who approaches. It's not just preparation—they're fortifying. If we're not careful, we'll walk straight into it."

Vine leaned back slightly, crossing his arms. "They're expecting us. If we delay, they'll only grow stronger."

Alder, who had remained silent near the back, stepped forward, unease evident in the tightness of his frame. "There's more," he said quietly. "I had a vision while we were scouting. It wasn't clear, but I saw a shadow—an entity beyond the ritual. It's powerful, dangerous. If it enters the picture, we might not be ready for it."

Eileen's focus shifted to Alder, her attention sharpening. She trusted his visions implicitly, knowing they often revealed fragments of a greater truth. Her fingers tapped lightly against her side as she processed his words. "Lucifer is pushing his plans forward because he's confident—too confident."

A muscle in Reed's temple twitched as he added, "We'll need to adapt. Strike sooner. Hit harder."

Eileen nodded, her expression darkening as she reached a decision. "I'll tell the others at the start of today's training. They need to understand what we're up against before we move forward."

As the group turned to leave, Riichi lingered, his instincts deeply rooted in his Celtic heritage. His attention caught Eileen's. "It feels like one of us is going to fall," he said quietly, the words stark and unrelenting. There was no attempt to temper the gravity of his statement—just a cold, undeniable truth that settled heavily between them.

Eileen's composure didn't waver, though her focus locked on his for a second longer. "Then we catch them," she said simply, her tone firm and unshaken.

Riichi gave a small nod, the intensity of the moment passing unspoken between them, before turning and following the others out of the room. Each carried the burden of what they had learned. Eileen paused briefly, her mind already mapping out the next steps.

Outside, the mansion rested under a cool morning haze, the mist clinging to the garden paths and softening the hard edges of the stone walls. The air felt charged, electric with the weight of looming decisions. Eileen stepped into the stillness, her focus unwavering as the pale light of dawn filtered through the mist. The time they had left was slipping away, and with it, the certainty of what lay ahead. Whatever came next would push them all in ways they had yet to imagine.

Takoda and Rain moved deliberately along the table near the mansion's back entrance, setting out trays of food with a practiced care that reflected the stress of the morning. Freshly cut fruit glistened under the dim light spilling through the windows, arranged beside rows of golden croissants and muffins, their warmth still clinging to the air. Bottled juices stood in orderly lines, their rich hues offering a soft contrast to the subdued atmosphere. This breakfast was more than a meal—it was a small gesture, a fragile comfort before the storm.

The Fallen began to gather, nodding in greeting and murmuring muted thanks as they reached for the food. A few lighthearted remarks broke through the solemnity, drawing tentative smiles that felt almost out of place amidst the gravity of the day. These fleeting instances of ease clung stubbornly to what little normalcy remained.

Vine reached for a croissant, a subtle smirk tugging at his lips as he tore off a piece. "Nothing like carbs to get you battle-ready," he quipped, his remark edged with wry humor, though a trace of unspoken sincerity flickered beneath it. He popped the piece into his mouth, the brief shift in his demeanor revealing a genuine appreciation that hadn't quite faded. The comment earned a few chuckles, a brief reprieve from the heaviness pressing down on them all.

Rowan caught Aislinn's eye as they approached, a shared understanding passing between them. It was a recognition of the resolve it took to create this stability, to offer a sense of balance while the world tilted on its axis. Turning to Takoda and Rain, Rowan spoke with appreciation that eased the chill in the air. "Thank you, both of you. This... it's more than breakfast. It's a reminder."

Rain's lips curved into a small smile as she met his face. "We just want to make sure you're ready for whatever's coming," she replied, keeping her delivery calm even as a trace of concern crossed her features. Beneath the simplicity of her reply, there was a deeper meaning—as if this small act of care was her way of wrapping them all a silent promise of home, of a reason worth fighting for.

Takoda rested a hand on Rowan's shoulder, her grip light but assured. "Think about what's ahead—with the Golden Dawn and Lucifer," she said, her words firm, meeting his gaze briefly. "Rain and I will make sure everything here is handled."

A brief pause followed, the impact of her words resonating with quiet support and readiness. With subtle nods, the Fallen gathered their breakfasts and began moving toward the training area. The lightness of those brief exchanges remained, but with each step, their movements grew more purposeful, their resolve sharpening with every stride. The morning shadows stretched long and thin across the courtyard, a muted reminder of the challenges looming just beyond reach.

The Fallen stood assembled on the training grounds, clustered in teams, shoulders squared, stances firm. Low murmurs rippled through the group as final words were exchanged, eyes scanning the horizon or meeting briefly in reassurance. The air felt heavier, charged with a tension that had taken root since first light. Today's training was no longer just practice—it was preparation for the final battle with Lucifer.

At the edge of the courtyard, Eileen emerged, her presence cutting through the low hum of conversation. She moved with an authority that silenced the murmurs as the Fallen turned toward her instinctively. Her assessment swept over the group, as if measuring the strength each carried beneath the surface.

"We're short on time," she began, her voice firm but carrying an urgency that couldn't be ignored. "Our window is tighter than expected. The Golden Dawn and Lucifer plan to begin their ritual in three days—not five. This means we move out tomorrow night."

A ripple of unease coursed through the group, their expressions tightening as the gravity of her words settled. *Tomorrow.* The enormity of that realization pressed down on Rowan, his heartbeat quickening in response to the urgency. His gaze shifted to Aislinn, catching the steely resolve mirrored in her eyes. *We've prepared for this, but the stakes have never felt so immediate.*

Eileen's attention landed on Rowan briefly, a hint of silent trust passing between them before her gaze moved across the rest of the group. Her voice remained calm, each word measured. "We need to make this day count. After training, we'll begin fortifying the mansion property to prepare for any ambush or retaliation." She paused, letting her words sink in. "This isn't just about being ready anymore. It's about surviving."

The weight of her declaration settled heavily over the group, each member absorbing the shift in their mission. Rowan's mind raced with questions, calculations, and potential scenarios, the urgency knotting tighter in his chest. Around him, the others wore the same intensity, a collective understanding that this was no longer about readiness—it was about endurance.

Oak stepped forward, breaking the rigidity with a sharp clap of his hands. The sound sliced through the heavy air, pulling everyone's focus back to the task at hand. "Alright, you heard her. Let's make it count. Team One, with me." His words carried a crisp confidence, a rallying call that steadied the group.

As the teams fell into formation, Rowan felt a renewed sense of determination take hold of him. This wasn't routine anymore. This training was intentional, tailored to the roles they would play in the mission's carefully structured phases. Each deed was preparation for what they would soon face.

The training space buzzed with fierce determination. Every Fallen moved through the drills with heightened concentration, their exercises designed to reflect the critical moments they would face in battle. Mistakes here meant vulnerabilities later. They adapted swiftly, recalibrating their movements and refining their techniques, every action exact and purposeful. Each motion carried depth—a silent oath to themselves and one another to be ready for the fight to come.

Reed, Vine, and Riichi moved seamlessly into position for Phase One preparation: infiltration and sabotage. Reed led the way through a mock obstacle course mimicking the Golden Dawn's defenses, his form melting into shadow as he navigated traps and sensors with near-invisible precision. "Watch for the sensor here," he murmured, his voice no more than a whisper. This was his strength, honed through countless missions. Yet a thought lingered in the back of his mind: *This time, the stakes are higher than ever.*

Vine followed closely, his steps cautious as arcs of electricity flickered between his fingers. He scanned the mock defenses, sparks flaring as he reached out to disable an "alarm." Each calculated burst of power severed the simulated systems with ease. *These practice alarms will never match the real thing,* he thought briefly before dismissing the doubt. *Trust your training.* Years of discipline had brought him here, and he clung to that certainty now.

As Vine signaled him forward, Riichi stepped into position, katana in hand. His gaze swept over the course, every subtle shift scrutinized as he assessed potential threats. For Riichi, this wasn't practice—it was duty. Each phantom enemy he encountered, every trap he anticipated, became another scenario to conquer. Catching the uncertainty in Vine's posture, he moved closer, his presence steadying. With a sharp nod, he gestured for the team to advance, a silent promise: *Whatever comes, I'll be ready.*

When they finished the course, Reed, Vine, and Riichi crossed the yard to rejoin the Frontline Assault team. Rowan caught their approach out of the corner of his eye and gave a brief nod before refocusing on his target dummy. His strikes landed with unyielding precision, every blow a reflection of his commitment to Phase Three: offense and support. Each motion carried meaning, a controlled strength radiating outward as he honed his edge. *This isn't just practice; it's a promise—to Aislinn, to the team, and to myself.*

Nearby, Ash shifted seamlessly between forms, alternating between his predator shape and his human self as he tested Rowan's reflexes. His actions were sharp and unpredictable, keeping Rowan on edge. "Keep up, Rowan!" he taunted, his tone carrying a playful edge, his concentration fixed as he studied Rowan's every move.

Rowan smirked, though his focus remained unbroken. "Watch and learn, Ash." He sidestepped the next lunge with a swift pivot, his blade slicing through the air as Ash twisted into his next form, evading the strike by a narrow margin. Their rivalry was unspoken but ever-present, each pushing the other to sharpen their skills. For Rowan, Ash's relentless challenges were fuel, a reminder to anticipate, to act instead of react. *This is how you prepare for chaos,* Rowan reminded himself, each act solidifying his resolve for the battle ahead.

Holly moved through her drills with unrelenting determination, her hand lifting to conjure a series of illusions that came to life across the field. Phantoms darted and twisted around the team, slipping in and out of sight, each crafted with meticulous detail. Rowan and Ash shifted instinctively, recalibrating their movements as Holly's creations layered confusion into their drills. The illusions forced them to adapt, sharpening their reactions and keeping them in the present moment.

For Holly, these illusions weren't mere fabrications—they were her contribution to Phase Three. Each impression mirrored the chaos they would face in battle, where misdirection would be crucial to creating an opening. Her narrowed eyes reflected her determination, every endeavor unhurried as she refined her craft. *We'll be ready to throw them off balance—every step will count.*

Vine joined the drill, positioning himself just beyond Holly's illusions. His electrokinesis sparked to life as arcs of energy crackled toward the phantoms. One by one, the illusions dissolved as the current struck them, bursts of light breaking the stillness. Timing and precision were critical, and Vine allowed himself a fleeting surge of satisfaction with each dismantled illusion. *The Golden Dawn's defenses won't fall this easily,* the thought surfaced briefly, but he shoved it aside. There was no space for doubt. His role in Phase Three required flawless execution—disabling traps and systems with absolute accuracy.

Across the field, Riichi moved with fluid discipline, his katana slicing through Holly's illusions with swift, calculated strikes. Every step carried intention, his reflexes sharpened as though each phantom was a tangible threat. For Riichi, this was more than practice—it was preparation. He treated every drill as if it were the mission itself, ensuring his path was clear while covering his team. *We'll dismantle their defenses piece by piece,* he thought. *Nothing will break through.*

As the illusions dissipated, the team paused, their breathing settling as they exchanged quick, understanding glances. This wasn't about perfection—it was about synchronization. Each strike, each flash of illusion, and every burst of energy brought them closer to becoming the unified force they needed to be.

Oak and Elder worked steadily along the outer perimeter, their efforts practiced and efficient. Oak raised his hand, commanding the earth to respond as unseen barriers threaded themselves through the stakes they had planted. His face remained composed, though the set of his jaw hinted at the burden he carried. This wasn't just a defense—it was a line he had vowed to hold, an unyielding threshold.

Kneeling nearby, Elder pressed one hand firmly into the soil, the other shaping the earth with careful precision. Hidden traps emerged—subtle pits and hollows designed to blend seamlessly into the terrain. "One more here," he murmured, his tone measured as his focus deepened. His mind mapped out every potential scenario, anticipating where reinforcements might try to break through. *They won't get past us without paying the price,* he resolved, each trap a quiet testament to his determination to protect the Fallen.

Hazel stood just beyond them, her hands weaving gracefully as she directed a shimmering wave of water from a nearby barrel. The liquid coiled and layered itself over Oak's barrier, forming a translucent shield. Her movements were careful, each sweep of her hand adding strength to their defenses. Hazel's eyes met Oak's briefly, a flicker of shared resolve passing between them. This wasn't just a shield—it was a promise that the line they drew here would not falter. Without a word, they turned back to their work, the silent understanding between them reinforcing the integrity of their barrier.

Farther down the grounds, Birch and Willow practiced the transfer of energy that would be crucial during battle. Birch hefted weighted sandbags, absorbing the strain as he channeled energy into himself before passing it to Willow. Her hands glowed faintly as she redirected the energy back to him in steady pulses, her focus unwavering. Willow's thoughts moved quickly, preparing herself for the chaotic forces they would face. This was her role—to anchor and stabilize, ensuring the team could endure even the most volatile moments.

Aislinn stood a few paces away, her shoulders squared, her hands raised as her kinetic shield shimmered into existence. The translucent barrier pulsed faintly, suspended between her and the imagined threats of the training contraption. She drew a deep breath, centering herself in the rhythm of her magic as it expanded outward, solidifying into a protective field. It wasn't enough to deflect attacks—she had to become the shield itself, unyielding against any force.

Small projectiles launched from the contraption, arcing toward her. Each one struck the shield with a sharp impact, the sound reverberating briefly before the objects bounced back. Aislinn absorbed each collision, bracing and recalibrating. *This shield will hold,* she told herself, her confidence growing with every deflection. These drills were more than exercises—they were foundations, each one a promise that she would stand unbroken when it mattered most.

Reed moved with silent precision, slipping through shadows as he sent small stones flying toward Aislinn from unpredictable angles. She adjusted instinctively, shifting the shield's angle with each strike. His actions were intentional, his aim was designed to push her limits, forcing her to refine her skills. This wasn't just training—it was preparation for her role in Phase Four. Aislinn knew her shield wouldn't simply protect her—it would safeguard all of them. *There can be no cracks, no hesitation.*

Each stone glanced off the shield with perfect clarity, each successful block reinforcing the quiet resolve within her. Aislinn rooted her focus, her heart steadying as she envisioned Rowan on the other side of her shield. She reached for that image, letting it tether her and strengthen her resolve. *This isn't just defense—it's a promise,* she thought, *a vow that no harm will reach him, or any of the Fallen, without going through me first.*

Lowering the shield briefly, she allowed it to dissolve back into her, the magic settling like coiled energy, ready to spring into action. Her resolve deepened, the gravity of her commitment strengthening her. *When the time comes, I will be their wall—the line between survival and defeat—and I will stand firm.*

Rowan caught Aislinn's eyes and gave a brief nod, signaling it was time to practice Radiant Surge. They moved into position, standing across from each other. For an instant, the rhythmic sounds of drills and footsteps on the training area faded into the background. All that remained was the charged stillness between them—a connection alive with trust and weighted by the enormity of what they were about to summon.

Rowan's features softened as he met her eyes, a hint of a smile breaking his otherwise serious demeanor. "Ready for this?" he asked, keeping his tone low, meant only for her. Beneath the question lay an assurance—a reminder of their shared strength, of his unwavering trust in her. Whatever they faced, they would rise to the challenge, bound by a connection no force could sever.

Aislinn nodded, steadying her breath as she stepped forward, reaching for Rowan's extended hand. The instant their palms touched, power surged to life within her, sparking like a current threading through them. Their connection locked instantly, weaving their auras and focus into a single, unified force. The familiar glow began to build, expanding outward in waves, casting a radiant light across the grounds.

Yet they both understood it couldn't remain so conspicuous. In battle, such brilliance would make them targets. Rowan's gaze held hers, his silent expression clear: Pull it back. Together, they concentrated, reining in the energy. The glow softened, retreating until it became an ethereal halo emanating strength and control.

The power coursing through them was fierce, yet now it felt contained, balanced—like a river flowing within its banks. Rowan felt the intensity of Radiant Surge weaving through him, amplified by Aislinn's unwavering focus, their energies merging seamlessly. Together, they directed the surge toward the target. Rowan focused on destroying it, and Aislinn sent out a pulsing wave of magic, striking with precision and obliterating the target without any blinding flare.

A silent contemplation settled over the estate as the other Fallen absorbed what they had just witnessed. The impact of the event rippled outward, a silent testament to what Radiant Surge represented. This ability was more than a weapon—it was hope, forged through trust and tempered by discipline. As the teams returned to their drills, a shared understanding deepened among the Fallen.

The day pressed on, and Takoda made her way toward the grounds, balancing a tray of water bottles with practiced ease. Moving between the groups, she offered quiet words of encouragement to each Fallen as they paused to hydrate. Her presence was a small but constant reminder of home, of something familiar and centering. With every bottle she handed out, Takoda could see the resolve in their expressions, the intensity of their focus sharpening as they prepared for the battle tomorrow night.

When she reached Riichi, he straightened slightly, accepting a water bottle from her with a respectful nod. "Thank you, Miss Takoda," he said, his voice low, carrying a subtle formality that felt almost out of place. His eyes met hers, and for a heartbeat, a quiet acknowledgment lingered between them, neither willing to break the connection too soon.

Takoda felt a faint warmth rise to her cheeks despite herself, though she kept her expression composed. Offering him a soft smile, she replied, "You're welcome, Riichi." Her tone was light, almost casual, but the unspoken tension in the distance dividing them was impossible to ignore. There was an intensity in his eyes that left her searching for the right response, yet none seemed to suit the instant.

For Riichi, that brief eye contact stirred an emotion he hadn't allowed himself to explore—a connection he had felt before but continually set aside. His life was defined by loyalty, duty, and readiness, leaving little room for distractions. Allowing anything beyond those responsibilities felt like a risk he couldn't afford. Yet, standing there, the warmth in her eyes pulled at a part of him he had long kept buried, leaving a faint, unshakable impression.

He held her gaze for a beat longer before giving a slight nod, a quiet signal of appreciation, and then turned back to his drills with the same precision and dedication he always brought. Takoda watched him briefly, her thoughts fixed on their exchange, a spark of warmth breaking through the demands of the day.

With a balancing breath, she resumed her rounds, moving to the next group with steps that felt just a touch lighter. The subtle connection they shared remained unsaid, but it lingered nonetheless, like a quiet thread tying them together amidst the burden of everything else.

As the last of the training drills came to an end, Oak stepped forward, his commanding presence cutting through the hum of activity. He raised a hand, signaling for the team's attention. "That's enough for now," he announced, the urgency in his command leaving no room for hesitation. "We're moving on to fortifying the property. Be prepared for anything—we need every line of defense ready and waiting."

The group dispersed quickly, each Fallen moving with purpose, no motion wasted. Near the mansion's perimeter, Elder and Alder took the lead, their focus trained on casting protective wards. Elder knelt, his hands moving with calm accuracy as energy flowed into the earth. He murmured incantations under his breath, anchoring the wards deeply into the soil. Beside him, Alder's brow furrowed in concentration, his hands glowing faintly as he reinforced the wards. Prophetic layers wove into Alder's work, subtle cues designed to detect even the faintest disturbances—anything that might threaten their defenses. Together, their efforts created a protective barrier, a line of defense ready to conquer what came.

A few paces away, Reed, Vine, and a handful of others worked methodically on physical defenses. Each undertaking carried the steady rhythm of organization, their actions decisive as they fortified the outer edges of the estate. Concealing traps beneath leaves and debris, they focused on small but effective measures to slow any unexpected attackers. Reed moved through the shadows, his sharp gaze sweeping the terrain for the best vantage points. "Lookout posts up there," he suggested, nodding toward a small rise that offered a clear view of the grounds.

Vine took his cue, securing weapon caches nearby. A faint smirk touched his lips as he double-checked each stash, the trace of satisfaction visible in his precise movements. "If they make it through the first line, they'll have a surprise waiting for them here," he muttered, the remark half to himself as he tightened the last strap on a concealed supply bag.

At the outer boundary, Rowan and Aislinn worked alongside Elder to strengthen the defenses. Rowan's focus was unwavering, his tone brisk and efficient as he exchanged ideas with Elder. Together, they mapped out the intersections where magical and physical defenses would merge, ensuring no gap was left exposed. Nearby, Aislinn raised her hand, summoning a shield that shimmered into place beside one of Elder's wards. The translucent barrier seemed to pulse faintly, its energy bolstering the protective magic Elder had tethered into the earth. The quiet intensity of the task weighed on her, a reminder that this was more than just precaution—it was their promise to protect this place.

"Good," Elder murmured, nodding to both of them, his words measured but edged with respect. "If they come, they'll find us ready."

As they finished securing the area, Aislinn glanced toward the mansion entrance and spotted Takoda and Rain making their way to Holly and moved to join them. Holly stood near the edge of the tree line, her hands faintly glowing as she wove illusionary protection charms into the surrounding forest. The shimmering veils of magic blended seamlessly with the natural terrain, creating layers of hidden defenses. She looked up as Aislinn, Takoda, and Rain approached, her expression curious.

"Thought we could use a little break later," Aislinn suggested, a small, knowing smile playing at her lips. "Join us for some baking in the kitchen?" Her voice was light, a welcome contrast to the day's intensity, her warmth cutting through the heaviness. "Bring the others, too—Hazel, Ivy, Willow."

Holly's features shifted, her usual intensity easing into a rare smile. "Baking sounds like exactly what we need. I'll make sure everyone knows." Gratitude threaded through her reply, as if the idea of even a brief reprieve felt like a lifeline amidst the demands of their work. With a brief nod to each of them, she turned back to her warding efforts, her attention renewed but now tinged with anticipation.

The grounds were nearly fortified. A quiet intensity settled over the mansion as every line of defense found its place, each Fallen carrying the shared significance of what was to come. Commitment thrummed in the air, binding them together in readiness.

As the others finished their tasks, Rowan caught Aislinn's eye, a silent question passing between them. Without a word, they made their way toward the mansion, slipping quietly inside in search of a brief reprieve. Their steps carried them to their secret spot, the room hidden behind the old bookshelf—a sanctuary where they could steal a few precious minutes of calm before everything changed.

Inside the peaceful refuge of their hidden room, Rowan and Aislinn slipped into a brief pause of tranquility. The weight of the day's preparations faded just slightly as they left the bustle of the mansion behind. A faint light filtered through the edges of the bookshelf, casting a warm glow that softened the lines of the space, creating a sense of shelter from the uncertainties waiting outside.

Rowan leaned casually against the wall, his arms crossed, though his awareness remained fixed on Aislinn with a mixture of intent and distraction. "You know," he began, his voice easy but edged with something deeper, "I've noticed you've been spending a lot of time with Takoda and Rain since we got here." His eyebrow arched just a fraction, a teasing smile teetering at the corners of his lips. "I'd almost think you're getting sick of me."

Aislinn laughed, closing the small distance between them, amusement clear in her features. "Getting sick of you?" she repeated, the humor shifting into a deeper sincerity. "Trust me, that's not happening." She paused, her demeanor changing as she considered how to continue. "I just... missed spending time with them. It feels good to have everyone together, even if it's because of the dangers ahead. And honestly... there's a part of me that's scared I might not get another chance to be with them if—" She stopped, gathering herself before continuing, refusing to let the fear take over.

Rowan's features shifted, the teasing fading as concern became evident. He reached for her hand, his fingers wrapping around hers in a firm hold. "Hey," he murmured. "I don't know exactly what's coming, but I do know one thing—I trust you. Whatever happens, I know you'll find your way through it."

His words carried quiet conviction, a promise that felt stronger than the uncertainty looming ahead. Aislinn felt the tension ease slightly, her heart steadying at the warmth in his expression and the way his hand clasped hers, as if he wasn't just holding her hand but her fears, too.

She placed her other hand on his arm, her gaze unwavering as a small, reassuring smile lifted her lips. "You don't have to worry about me getting sick of you. I'm madly in love with you, Rowan. That's not going to change."

A small smile tugged at his lips, his hold on her hand relaxing as he exhaled slowly. "Good," he said, the meaning in his reply clear. "Because I don't know what I'd do without you." His reply settled between them, carrying both his love and his deep need to keep her safe.

After a pause, Aislinn gave his arm a gentle squeeze and stepped back, her smile softening. "I'm going to spend some more time with Takoda and Rain," she said, her tone light. "We could all use a little normalcy before things get more intense." Tilting her head, she added with a playful glint in her eyes, "And you? Maybe you should find Riichi or the others. I think it'd be good for all of us."

Rowan nodded, a flash of gratitude passing over his face, though the seriousness in his gaze didn't waver. "Yeah," he agreed, his voice quieter now. "Maybe I will." His hand rested on hers briefly before he released it, a final exchange of reassurance before she turned to go.

For a beat, they stood in comfortable silence, sharing a breath of unspoken understanding. Then, with a last glance, they returned to the tasks awaiting them, each carrying a renewed sense of purpose and a quiet vow to see the other through whatever lay ahead.

After her time with Rowan, Aislinn made her way to the kitchen, where laughter and the scent of freshly baked cookies greeted her. The room was filled with a cozy warmth as she joined Takoda, Rain, Holly, Ivy, Hazel, and Willow. Each of them had rolled up their sleeves, working together on a fresh batch of cookies. The sweet aroma of flour and melted butter mingled with their conversation, a soothing sound that offered a reprieve from the demands of the day. Bowls and measuring spoons clattered softly as they gathered ingredients, their rhythm of mixing and stirring settling into a comforting cadence.

The sound of the front door opening carried into the kitchen, followed by Ariel's familiar voice. "Starting the party without me? Rude." She stepped inside, brushing off her jacket with a teasing grin. "I come to see how you all are doing only to find I'm missing cookie duty."

"You're right on time," Holly said, tossing Ariel an apron. "Grab some dough and make yourself useful."

Ariel tied the apron around her waist, moving to the counter with an easy air. "Cookies are the one thing I'll show up for on time," she quipped, picking up a rolling pin. Her attention swept over the group, lingering for a beat on the tray of freshly shaped cookies.

As they worked, Takoda nudged Holly with a playful glint in her eye. "All right, now that we're all here, you have to spill—what are the Fallen men really like when they're not all stoic and intense?"

Rain leaned in, her grin widening as she dusted flour over the dough. "Yeah, give us the good stuff. What's it like when they're not in warrior mode? We want details."

Holly exchanged a knowing glance with Ivy, a hint of warmth touching her features as she leaned back against the counter. "Well, since you asked, let's start with Rowan." She cast a teasing look at Aislinn, her voice carrying a playful edge. "Before you came along, he was all business. Serious, intent, kept to himself—classic warrior type. But even then, he always had this protective streak, especially with us Fallen."

Ivy nodded, her hands deftly shaping the dough into neat rounds. "Rowan's always been the first to jump in if any of us needed help, no hesitation. He didn't say much, but you knew he cared. Now, though?" She grinned at Aislinn. "Let's just say he smiles more often these days."

Aislinn felt her cheeks warm under their gazes, a quiet smile of her own forming as she shaped another piece of dough. She glanced down, hiding the flicker of pride that rose at their words.

"That's for sure," Ariel added, rolling out a piece of dough with practiced precision. "When I first met Rowan, I thought he was part statue. He didn't even crack a joke—not one. I don't know how you did it, Aislinn, but you've managed to make him human." Her teasing comment shifted, her smile holding as she glanced at Aislinn. "He's better for it. We all see it."

Aislinn looked up, meeting Ariel's eyes, and for a second, no words were needed. She nodded slightly, the warmth in her chest spreading as she returned her focus to the dough.

Takoda glanced at the group, curiosity brightening her features. "And what about Riichi?" Her brow furrowed slightly as she rolled dough between her palms. "He's so formal—always calling me 'Miss Takoda.' Is he like that with the Fallen?"

Ariel raised an eyebrow and replied, "Riichi? Formality is his armor. If he's calling you 'Miss Takoda,' it probably means you make him nervous."

Willow laughed, scooping more dough onto a baking sheet. "That's true. He's comfortable with the Fallen, but around others? He gets stiff as a board. If he's formal with you, Takoda, it means you've gotten under his skin."

Takoda let out a soft laugh, though the thought lingered in her mind. *What about me makes him uncomfortable?* she wondered, the question playing in her thoughts as she worked. The idea that she could unsettle someone as composed as Riichi sparked a quiet thrill she couldn't quite explain.

The conversation flowed as they worked, shifting to the others in the group. Rain leaned against the counter, shaping dough into balls. "And what's the deal with Elder? Or Nik, rather," she added, glancing at Hazel. "He acts like some ancient sage who's seen it all, but he's still got enough fight in him to keep up with the rest of us. Why doesn't he hang out more instead of acting like the grumpy old man in the corner?"

Hazel shrugged, her eyes glinting with humor. "That's Nik for you. He's always been an old soul—carries himself like he's got the weight of the world on his shoulders. But he's sharp. Reads people better than anyone I've ever met." She caught Rain's gaze, her smile hinting at something quieter. "Seems like you've picked up on that."

Rain blinked, a faint blush warming her cheeks as she returned her focus to the dough. "I guess," she murmured, though the corners of her lips twitched upward.

The attention turned to Vine, and Ariel glanced at the tray of cookies with a small smile. "So, what's Vine's deal?" she asked, her tone light but edged with curiosity. "He doesn't exactly strike me as the open-book type."

Holly rolled her eyes, letting out a mock sigh. "Vine is… well, exactly what he seems. Confident, arrogant, and fully aware of how charming he is." She shook her head, her exasperation softened by a playful smile. "And he uses it. We call it his 'Vegas charm.' Completely insufferable sometimes, but he means well."

Ariel's smile lingered, her expression briefly distant before she picked up another piece of dough. "Sounds about right," she murmured, though the faintest flicker of something unreadable passed across her expression.

As the group continued their work, laughter and stories filled the kitchen, the air light with camaraderie. For Aislinn, the comfort of the exchange felt stabilizing, a respite from the burden of what lay ahead. But as she glanced around the room, a bittersweet note touched her heart. This gathering, this laughter—it all felt precious. *How many more moments like this will we have?* The thought remained, but she shook it off, choosing to focus on the sound of her friends' voices.

They slid the tray of cookies into the oven, tidying up as Aislinn glanced out the window. Dark clouds gathered on the horizon, a distant rumble echoing—a storm's warning growl. The laughter softened, a shared glance passing among them as they each felt the shift.

The first raindrops tapped against the glass. Aislinn felt a chill creep through her, but she steadied herself, anchoring her heart in the resolve she'd carried all day. This is only the beginning, she thought. *Whatever lies ahead, I'll carry this warmth with me. It's as much a shield as any magic I can summon.*

Chapter Thirty-One
Breaking the Line

Ⓣhe Fallen's mansion was cloaked in dimness, the deepening twilight casting elongated patterns across the grand entrance hall. The reticence that filled the room was dense, heavy with the magnitude of what lay ahead. The tall windows stood dark, the fading light outside barely outlining their frames. It felt as though the walls themselves braced for a storm, the usual sense of sanctuary replaced by an ominous tension.

Rowan stood by one of the massive pillars in the hall, his attention fixed on the windows, where the faint remnants of daylight clung to the glass, casting an eerie glimmer. He couldn't shake the feeling that something was wrong—the unnatural chill creeping through the stone, the oppressive silence pressing down on them. It was as though Lucifer's presence lingered even here, casting a pall over what had once been their haven. He clenched his jaw, his thoughts turning over the risks they were about to take—all for Aislinn, all for this final mission.

From the corner of his eye, Rowan noticed Aislinn approaching, her steps quiet on the polished floor. Her face was composed, her gaze drifting around the hall as though she were absorbing every detail, the familiar surroundings cast in a new, foreboding light. When she looked up and met his eyes, a hint of warmth softened her expression, a silent understanding passing between them. At that instant, the significance of what lay ahead seemed to intensify, as though they both sensed the danger waiting for them.

Rowan reached out, his fingers brushing hers. She didn't pull away, and they stood together, drawing strength from the contact as the oppressive air weighed on them. He leaned closer, his murmur soft but firm. "Whatever happens out there, stay close. We're in this together."

Aislinn's hand tightened in his, her expression flickering with uncertainty. "Rowan… I can't stop thinking… what if not everyone makes it back?" Her voice wavered, her vulnerability breaking through the composure she had worked so hard to maintain.

He held her hand firmly, his gaze locked with hers. "We've faced worse," he said, his assurance steady and unshakable. "We're not the same people we were at the start of this. You're stronger than you realize, Aislinn. And so are the Fallen. We're all fighting together, and we'll bring everyone home."

Around them, the Fallen began gathering in small groups, their expressions resolute. Rowan held Aislinn's gaze, his own unwavering with the promise that he would be by her side, no matter what awaited them beyond the mansion's doors.

Aislinn took a slow breath, courage coming back into her features. She nodded, releasing his hand as she stepped back, her attention shifting to the others, each one readying themselves in their own quiet way.

The silence deepened, every Fallen member sensing the charged anticipation in the air. They each drew a calming breath, bracing for the call that would signal their first steps into the darkness.

Across the hall, Takoda stood near the back of the group, her attention lingering on Riichi as he meticulously adjusted the straps on his katana, his expression as unreadable as ever. She could almost hear her friends' teasing from the night before about his formality, his way of keeping everyone at a distance. She knew it was more than respect—it was a shield, a way to protect himself from the world. Yet an unfamiliar pull tugged at her now, a feeling that demanded acknowledgment, even if only for a second.

"Riichi…" she began, her voice quieter than usual as she stepped closer, hesitating. "Please… be careful."

He straightened at her address, his hand resting on his sword as his features shifted subtly. With a small nod, he replied, "I appreciate your concern, Miss Takoda. I'll proceed with utmost caution." He kept his attention ahead, his usual restraint hiding whatever lay beneath.

She couldn't leave it at that. She held her attention on him, a rare vulnerability breaking into her remark. "We both know you'll do more than that." A small, unguarded smile formed as she added, "Just... promise me you'll come back."

For the first time, his full attention shifted to her. He paused, her statement settling heavily between them. A flicker of surprise crossed his features—an unexpected depth that was neither hidden nor overstated, yet impossible to ignore. "I give you my word," he said, his usual edge easing. For a breath, it seemed he wanted to say more, but he turned back to his preparations, leaving any further thoughts unsaid.

Takoda exhaled, her fingers curling around the small pendant in her pocket. It wasn't much—just a tiny anchor in the storm of what they were about to face—but it steadied her. Her attention lingered on Riichi as he moved toward the others, and she couldn't shake the sense that this promise, like so many others, might come at too great a cost.

The Fallen began to cluster into one group as they completed their preparations, their readiness evident in the deliberate precision of their movements. Eileen stood at the forefront, her presence a pillar of determination and purpose. Her sweeping attention brought clarity to each of them, her voice resonating with a calm authority that settled even the most frayed nerves. There was an intangible strength about her, a presence that steadied the team as if she carried a piece of ancient wisdom meant only for moments like this.

"As we go into this, remember what makes us strong," she began, her rare, almost maternal warmth softening the steel of her demeanor. "Together, we've faced dangers that could have broken us. Yet here we are, standing as one—ready to protect each other and the world beyond these walls." Her statement rippled through the group, centering them, reminding them they were not just warriors—they were family, united by loyalty and determination. Her words seemed to reach beyond the surface, stirring a deeper resolve in each of them, as though she drew from an unseen well of strength.

One by one, she looked at each member, offering a brief recognition that felt personal and profound.

"Elder," she said, her tone measured, "your roots run deep, the foundation that holds us firm. Your resilience carries us forward."

Elder returned a firm nod, his stance unyielding. He absorbed her acknowledgment, knowing his role extended beyond combat—it was about enveloping the group in strength and protection.

She turned to Vine, who met her with measured intensity. "And you, like the vine that binds and weaves, your insight and adaptability keep us connected. Stay sharp."

Vine nodded, the faintest flicker of a smile softening his otherwise stoic expression. The importance of her statement wasn't lost on him—it carried both trust and responsibility.

As Eileen's attention shifted to Riichi, her expression gentled, a rare glimmer of trust shining through. "Riichi, you are the hawthorn—precise and steadfast. Your clarity guides us, guiding us through the storm and shielding us from harm."

Riichi inclined his head slightly, his hand resting lightly on the hilt of his katana. Her recognition settled deeply, though a shadow briefly crossed his expression—a quiet acknowledgment of the risks ahead, a reality they all understood but rarely voiced.

Lastly, Eileen addressed Reed, who lingered slightly apart, his features unreadable. "Reed, you bend without breaking. Your vigilance and instincts are our silent guard."

Reed briefly glanced toward her, and though his face betrayed little, the subtle incline of his head carried a wordless acknowledgment.

Eileen stepped back, her gaze sweeping over the group as her voice softened further. "We are family, and that's why we fight—not just for ourselves, but for everyone who deserves freedom from this darkness." At that instant, she seemed more than their leader, embodying a force that went beyond the physical—a presence that reminded them why they stood together.

A palpable unity filled the room, each of them balanced by her statement, ready to face the unknown.

The Fallen moved with persistence, each member checking weapons, adjusting armor, or securing charms and amulets. Their preparation carried an almost sacred rhythm as they settled into their roles, their thoughts narrowing on the battle ahead.

Rowan tightened the strap of his armor, his thoughts drifting to Aislinn. So much had changed since he'd met her. He wasn't just fighting for duty anymore but for love—a choice he never expected to make again. This moment felt like the culmination of every step he'd taken, a decision he would repeat a thousand times if it meant protecting Aislinn and the family they'd built together.

Across the room, Aislinn steadied herself. The pull of her powers, still unfamiliar, weighed heavily on her. Yet today, she resolved to embrace her role fully—to fight not only for herself but for Rowan and the family she'd found among the Fallen. Her silent vow was clear: she would protect those who had shown her this new world, no matter the cost.

Takoda exhaled slowly, her gaze lingering on Riichi. She wasn't a fighter, but she would do everything possible to support the team from the sidelines. His parting words echoed in her mind, leaving an ache in her chest. For him, she would hold firm, clinging to hope for his safe return. Still, unease stirred within her, an unsettling sense that this battle carried stakes far greater than any they'd faced before.

Eileen raised her hand, and the room froze as every Fallen turned to her. Her statement rang out, stable and commanding. "This isn't just a battle—it's a stand against everything the evil has taken from the world. We fight to restore what should never have been lost."

With her final declaration, the group moved into formation. One by one, each team slipped into the shadows, vanishing as they took their positions. The enormity of the moment hung in the air, every step a descent into the unknown, their resolve unwavering as they prepared to face the inevitable confrontation.

Rowan paused briefly, catching Aislinn's eye. In that glance, they exchanged promises and fears they didn't need to say aloud. With a subtle nod, they parted, stepping into their respective roles.

At the edge of the hall, Takoda watched them go, her fingers curling around the small pendant again. She closed her eyes, releasing a silent prayer—a wish for the safe return of the family she had come to love.

***

The Fallen gathered just inside the gates of the Golden Dawn's territory—a bleak expanse bordered by rusted metal and looming structures that seemed to watch in silent vigilance. The lingering night clung heavily to the air, amplifying every sound and intensifying the unease rippling through the team. Eileen stood at the forefront, her presence unwavering as her gaze swept over each member. With a subtle lift of her hand, she set them into motion, her silent gesture commanding their full attention.

Reed moved first, vanishing into the shadows with a practiced grace that rendered him nearly undetectable. His shadow-walking wove him seamlessly into the dark, his actions effortless and precise as he slipped between realms. Every step was careful. Clearing the first line of defenses without a sound, he reappeared briefly, signaling Vine and Riichi to follow.

Vine advanced, faint sparks crackling at his fingertips as his electrokinesis sprang to life. Tiny surges of static snaked toward the cameras Reed had marked, silencing their lenses in controlled bursts. One by one, the lights dimmed and extinguished, opening the path ahead. Determination emanated from him, his energy disciplined yet charged, propelling their mission forward with silent conviction.

"Advance carefully," Eileen's calm instruction came over the comms, her tone steadying even as they ventured deeper into enemy territory. Her presence, even from afar, felt like an unshakable anchor, a quiet strength that seemed to reach beyond the moment, rooting the team against the mounting tension.

At the rear, Riichi tracked the guards' activities with unflinching accuracy, his instincts honed to an exacting edge. His hand signaled Reed and Vine with calculated accuracy, each gesture ensuring their approach remained undetected. He read the patrols as if following a map etched into the darkness, adjusting their route with the practiced intent of a hawthorn's thorn—precise and protective. Every motion shielded his team, his vigilance unyielding.

The group moved like specters, slipping through the defenses with seamless coordination. The air around them thickened with apprehension, the unknown pressing closer with each step. Suddenly, Reed halted, his heightened awareness catching the faint glow of a magical sensor—a trap lying in wait. One misstep would summon the enemy in force.

Without pause, Vine stepped forward, his expression resolute. Energy coiled at his fingertips, and with a decisive motion, an EMP rippled outward, extinguishing the sensor's dim glow. The pulse dissipated soundlessly, neutralizing the danger. Reed acknowledged him with a brief nod, their silent exchange speaking of mutual trust, before they moved on, bypassing the trap with accuracy.

"Time is short," Riichi's clipped command came over the comms, his urgency driving them onward. Their pace quickened, every step measured, each action a calculated move in the delicate cadence of survival.

Reaching the designated safe zone, Reed raised his hand in the all-clear signal. Moments later, Eileen's directive came over the comms, her composed tone threaded with a quiet urgency. "Well done. Regroup for Phase 3."

Reed, Vine, and Riichi melted back into the shadows, their movements perfectly synchronized, years of trust transforming their actions into a seamless progression. With calm determination, they pushed further into enemy territory, the confrontation drawing closer with every step.

Eileen's voice returned, clear and resolute as she directed the next stage. Gesturing toward the perimeter, her attention fixed on Oak, Elder, and Hazel. "Hold this line. Nothing gets through." There was an undeniable authority in her words, one that seemed to carry the knowledge of something timeless. Her unshakable certainty sliced through the charged air like a blade, stabilizing the team's resolve. The trio nodded in unison, moving into position with the kind of determination that reflected the gravity of her command. Their defenses solidified, bracing for the inevitable assault.

Oak stepped forward, his hands surging with energy as he steadied himself, channeling the force radiating from within. His fortification powers flared, each controlled exhale fueling the dense, nearly impenetrable walls rising around the perimeter's weakest points. Stone and earth obeyed his will, surging upward with relentless care as he sealed every potential breach.

The oak's ancient resilience coursed through him, each barrier a testament to his unwavering resolve, a silent promise to shield the Fallen at all costs.

Eileen's directive came through the comms, breaking into his concentration. "Stay vigilant, Oak. They'll be watching for weak spots."

"Understood," he replied, his words rough with determination. His eyes swept over the perimeter, scrutinizing every wall and corner with meticulous care. These barriers weren't just stone—they embodied his vow to protect, a stalwart defense against the advancing darkness.

Alongside him, Elder worked with methodical intensity, his fingers skimming the ground as he summoned the earth's power to create traps and obstructions. Roots twisted and rocks jutted upward under his direction, forming concealed snares and defensive barriers. The terrain shifted like a living ally, reshaping itself into strategic formations designed to confuse and entrap intruders. With a quick flick of his wrist, a tangle of dense roots erupted, lying silently in wait for an unwary step. The protective essence of the elder tree seemed to echo in every intentional shift of the earth beneath his touch.

Nearby, Hazel knelt, her senses attuned to the energy rippling across the battlefield. Every faint tremor and magical disturbance resonated within her like whispers carried on unseen currents. "Oak, reinforce the eastern wall," she said, her tone urgent and clear. "There's a weak point—they'll exploit it if we don't act fast." Her fingertips grazed the earth as if drawing strength from it, her powers ready to summon shimmering water shields at a moment's notice. The fluidity of the hazel tree infused her efforts, her vigilance unwavering as she scanned for emerging threats.

Their coordination was seamless, each Fallen weaving their unique abilities into the defense, crafting an invisible barrier teeming with protective energy. Even with their efforts, the unpredictability of the enemy loomed large. A sudden surge of magic pulsed from the west—a jarring spike of energy that sent a ripple of warning through the air.

Oak turned toward the disturbance, his jaw tightening. Promptly, he extended his powers once more, summoning another barrier that erupted upward with crackling force. The unyielding spirit of his namesake tree rooted him, his focus resolute. "They've detected us," he muttered to Elder, irritation simmering beneath his determination.

From the distance, shadowed figures began to emerge, their movements purposeful as dark energy crackled around them. Elder's gaze narrowed, and his voice dropped, sharp and focused. "The Golden Dawn isn't just adjusting their tactics—they're preparing for a full confrontation. We need to hold this position."

Elder's expression hardened as he bent to the ground, his movements swift and precise. "We'll make them regret it," he said, a faint smirk tugging at his lips. His hands reshaped the terrain with practiced efficiency, transforming the earth into a labyrinth of jagged ridges and impassable obstacles. The land became a fortress under his touch, each barrier a challenge to any who dared cross. Every shift carried an unspoken defiance, a statement that no inch would be yielded.

Hazel's attention remained fixed on the defenses, her quick instincts catching another potential breach. Her pulse quickened as she raised her hands, summoning a translucent wall of water that materialized instantly. The rippling barrier surged into place, sealing the gap while deflecting any immediate threats. Her concentration never wavered, the fluid nature of her magic flowing seamlessly into the defense. "Gap secured," she reported, her pledge calm but tinged with vigilance, her senses scanning for the next vulnerability.

Together, Oak, Elder, and Hazel created an unassailable line, their abilities interwoven to repel every attempt at breaching their defenses. Their combined efforts forged a barrier as formidable as it was unyielding. For a fleeting instant, the chaos subsided, leaving a heavy calm to settle over the battlefield—a brief but welcome pause.

Eileen's command came over the comms once more, clear and weighted with approval. "Excellent work. Hold your positions. Phase 3 begins now."

At Eileen's directive, they held their location, every sense heightened and braced for the next move. The tension thickened around them, taut as a bowstring ready to snap at the first sign of the enemy's advance.

Eileen's orders crackled over the comms, measured yet charged with tenacity. Her words carried an almost imperceptible control, like the quiet pulse of an archaic force guiding them forward. Rowan adjusted his grip on his weapon and glanced toward Ash, Alder, and Holly. "We're here to draw their attention, not tidy up. Keep it chaotic and keep moving," he instructed, his half-smile edged with a dangerous confidence. They were the diversion—a tempest designed to fracture the enemy's cohesion and create an opening for the next phase.

As enemies began to break through the barriers and emerge from inside the mansion, Rowan surged forward, a whirlwind of exactness and ferocity forged through centuries of conflict. His blade sliced the air with unrelenting accuracy, every strike demanding attention. The fluid rhythm of his assault forced the guards' focus entirely, creating a perfect cover for Alder and Holly to maneuver into their positions, unnoticed amid the chaos.

Ash's form rippled, his towering, monstrous silhouette exuding raw, primal menace. In an instant, he shifted again, becoming a sleek predator that moved with blinding speed. His strikes shattered the guards' defenses, their shouts morphing into cries of panic as they scrambled to recover, only to fall under his next attack. His shapeshifting was a force of nature—unpredictable and devastating.

Behind Rowan, Alder's faintly glowing eyes reflected the lucidity of his prophetic awareness, each vision sharpening his actions in real time. Guided by these flashes of insight, he called out with unerring precision. "Rowan—strike left. Now step back." Every decree kept Rowan ahead of the guards' counterattacks, his movements seamlessly avoiding their attempts to land a blow, leaving them disoriented and vulnerable.

Holly murmured her incantations, her quiet spells unraveling into vivid illusions that danced across the battlefield. Ethereal figures of the Fallen materialized, weaving in and out of sight like wraths, their actions haunting and unhurried. The guards faltered, their ranks fracturing as they struggled to distinguish reality from deception. Holly's conjured phantoms turned the field into a maze of confusion, their presence dismantling any cohesion among the enemy.

From deep within the Golden Dawn's ranks, an officer emerged, his commanding presence cutting through the turmoil like a knife. His piercing gaze zeroed in on Rowan, and with each cautious step, he forced the guards to regroup behind him. Holly's illusions wavered briefly as she shifted her focus, adapting to counter his calculated resolve.

Alder's warning broke through the comms, his instructions urgent and clipped. "Rowan, west flank—high-ranking officer incoming. Prepare yourself."

From her position in the safety zone, Aislinn watched the unfolding scene with staunch attention, her hands poised to summon a shield if needed. Every movement of the Golden Dawn officer was scrutinized, her readiness fueled by a fierce determination to protect Rowan and the others. The energy of her magic simmered just beneath the surface, waiting for the moment she'd need to act.

Rowan pivoted, his attention locking onto the advancing officer. Holly acted instantly, conjuring a cluster of identical Rowans, each one mirroring his every move with flawless accuracy. The officer hesitated, his frustration mounting as his attention splintered, unable to distinguish the real target among the shifting duplicates.

Vine, Riichi, and Ash worked in unison to shield Alder and Holly from the advancing Golden Dawn soldiers. Vine's sai crackled with electricity as he struck with precision, paralyzing enemies and giving Holly time to sustain her illusions. Riichi's katana moved with lethal grace, cutting down anyone who got too close, while Ash, in his massive wolf form, tore through the ranks with raw power, scattering the opposition. Together, they formed an impenetrable defense, ensuring Alder could guide Rowan while Holly kept the officer disoriented.

The officer faltered, his steps slowing as the illusions kept him off balance. Rowan seized the opportunity, steadying his stance with unyielding determination. He drew on the resilience of the rowan tree—a timeless symbol of courage and protection—to root himself, bracing for the inevitable clash. Alder's timely guidance focused him, while Holly's illusions continued to shift, maintaining the officer's confusion and keeping him on the defensive.

With the Golden Dawn forces fractured and floundering, Rowan's command came through the comms, firm and decisive. "Position secure. Hold here until Phase 4 begins."

Eileen's response followed without delay. "Status confirmed. Stand by—Phase 4 is ready to commence. Stay alert. Every move we make depends on your vigilance."

Her directives carried an undeniable weight, resonating with a calm assurance that strengthened even the most uncertain hearts. There was something about her words that seemed to align each Fallen with a greater purpose, a presence that quietly reinforced their tenacity as they moved flawlessly into their roles.

Birch closed his eyes, drawing deeply from his reserves, his breaths controlled and methodical as he summoned his energy. With a slow exhale, he extended an invisible thread of connection, linking himself to Rowan, Ash, Alder, Holly, Riichi and Vine—the frontline fighters. Each pulse of energy bolstered their endurance, sharpening their clarity and reinforcing their determination. Though removed from direct combat, Birch's concentration remained unbroken, his energy flowing unrelentingly into sustaining the team. The resilience of the birch tree—a symbol of renewal—seemed to course through every line he forged.

Beside him, Willow lifted her hands, drawing ambient magic from the air and channeling it toward Birch. The energy flowed into him, amplifying his already formidable endurance, his stance solidifying like the roots of a mighty tree. Her movements mirrored the pliancy of her namesake, the magic weaving seamlessly to bolster his strength. She glanced at Birch and said quietly but with certainty, "You're reinforced for now. Let me know if you feel a strain—I'll boost it again."

Birch gave a slight nod in acknowledgment, his recognition almost a whisper. "Understood." His attention remained fixed on channeling energy to the frontline, every pulse an anchor to keep the team grounded and resilient.

Nearby, Ivy stood poised, her posture exuding latent strength as the air around her seemed to hum with readiness, waiting for her command. Her gaze darted toward Aislinn. "Stay close. If Rowan needs you, I'll help Reed get you there in seconds," she said, her oath carrying the same unwavering conviction as the ivy she embodied, her presence rooted in certainty.

Aislinn nodded briskly, her senses tuned to the shifting battlefield. Every nerve felt taut, her premonitions faintly buzzing as if awaiting the precise moment to act. Closing her eyes briefly, she reached out with her magic, connecting to the essence of each frontliner. The threads of their energy hummed against her awareness, forming an intricate network she could tap into at a moment's notice. This bond allowed her to remain poised, ready to throw a protective shield around any of them the instant danger struck. She lingered near Eileen, drawing strength from the calm presence of her leader and mother. Eileen rested a hand gently on Aislinn's shoulder, the touch a silent but powerful reminder of her purpose.

Just as the group settled into place, a surge of dark magic swept through the air, thick and oppressive, pressing down on them like a suffocating weight. The shockwave carried the malevolent signature of a powerful Golden Dawn member, threading through their defenses and threatening to destabilize their protective barriers.

Eileen's command cut through the mounting pressure, tenacious and measured. "Hold your positions. Reinforce where needed."

Willow's hands moved swiftly, layering additional energy into shields to surround Aislinn. "You're covered," she assured, her tone cool yet definite as the shimmering barriers absorbed and deflected the invasive force.

Birch took the opportunity to refresh Rowan's stamina, intensified the flow of energy through their connection. Each pulse fortified Rowan's vigor, an unbroken rhythm of support carrying the enduring essence of the birch tree. His presence remained constant—a silent promise to sustain the team against the rising storm.

Eileen's leadership remained calculated, her comments binding the team together as they pushed back against the dark magic pressing down on them. Her guidance acted as an unseen force, bolstering their unity and strengthening them against the opposition.

Gradually, the oppressive energy began to dissipate, the air lightening as the tension eased. Eileen's declaration came again, transparent and direct. "Phase 4 secure. Status check." One by one, the team responded, their voices steady, their readiness undiminished.

Turning to Birch, Willow, and Ivy, Eileen gave a small nod of acknowledgment. "Maintain your positions. We're holding firm." Though her words were simple, they carried a quiet certainty that seemed to resonate on a deeper level, maintaining those around her.

Birch continued channeling energy into the link, his connection flowing like a current into Rowan's team. Willow kept her shields intact, her stance relaxing slightly but her vigilance unbroken. Ivy remained alert, her energy simmering beneath the surface, prepared to act at a moment's notice.

As Phase 4 concluded, Reed shifted closer to Aislinn. Eileen's next mandate came over the comms, her orders measured and purposeful. "Stay vigilant. Complications will come, but they're manageable. Rowan, adjust your team before advancing. Riichi, remain outside to provide combat support."

She paused briefly, issuing her final commands. "Birch, Ivy—join Riichi on perimeter defense. Vine, Rowan, Holly, Ash, and Alder, continue as the entry team." Her words seemed to carry more than strategy.

Rowan gave a firm nod, exchanging brief looks with his team. Riichi pulled back to the perimeter, taking position as Birch and Ivy moved forward to join him. Together, they reinforced the outer line, braced for any threat that might breach their defenses. Rowan led the entry team deeper into the Golden Dawn's lair, Vine, Holly, Ash, and Alder forming a cohesive unit around him as they advanced with care into the menacing corridors.

The hallways inside the headquarters seemed to constrict as Rowan's group pushed forward, the oppressive chill of the air seeping into every step. The narrow passages carried an eerie stillness, each action drawing them further into a labyrinth laced with unseen wards and deadly traps. Rowan's grip on his weapon tightened as he scanned the dim path ahead, every muscle coiled with anticipation.

Beside him, Ash and Vine moved in perfect tempo, their forms blending into the dimness, their steps silent on the stone floor. Alder took the lead, his movements fluid and thoughtful, guided by an almost instinctive awareness of their surroundings. Holly trailed behind, her hands hovering near her sides, ready to conjure illusions at the first sign of danger, her presence an unspoken safeguard.

Each step heightened the tension, the crushing silence amplifying the significance of their task. Outside, the hush of the battlefield broke like a shattered mirror, the clash of steel and the pounding of boots echoing across the area.

Golden Dawn reinforcements surged into the fray, their weapons glinting under the faint light. With the Fallen's position already exposed, the enemy pressed forward in greater numbers, their advance marked by a relentless, lethal intent.

Riichi moved like a blade given life, his katana flashing in precise arcs that dismantled the guards with surgical efficiency. Each strike carried a fluidity that turned every opening into a decisive blow. His mastery was unyielding, a relentless force that tore through the enemy ranks in an instant.

Nearby, Ivy barreled forward, her Amazonian strength carving through the opposition. Wielding her dual blades with effortless command, she shattered armor and shields, her strikes rippling with a power that sent guards crashing to the ground. She was a living bulwark, an immovable force that refused to give an inch.

At her side, Birch's relentless energy was a force of nature. His chakram sliced through the air, cutting down opponents and dismantling their defenses before returning to his hand. Each throw struck with devastating accuracy, while his swift, unyielding movements turned the guards' aggression against them. A guard staggered back, only to be brought down by the return arc of Birch's weapon. He fought with unshakable resilience, embodying the steadfast endurance of the birch tree.

Elder and Hazel joined the defense, their powers blending seamlessly with the others'. Elder pressed his hands into the earth, summoning roots and jagged rocks that erupted to form barriers and traps. "Shift right! Ivy, hold the left!" he called, his words exact as he manipulated the terrain with practiced ease.

Above, Hazel lifted her hands, pulling moisture from the air to craft shimmering water barriers. Her shields absorbed strikes before transforming into razor-sharp jets that struck with unerring accuracy. "Perimeter holding," she reported, her voice calm but edged with vigilance as she bolstered the line around Riichi, Ivy, and Birch.

With the added support, the Fallen's formation solidified, their combined efforts forming an indomitable wall. Riichi's precise strikes carved through the advancing guards, Ivy's raw power held their position, and Birch's un-yielding endurance absorbed the assault. Elder's geomancy and Hazel's water shields closed every gap, their coordination forming a seamless defense that pushed back the tide.

The guards hesitated, their momentum faltering under the relentless strength of the Fallen. Their hesitation was brief, however, as another wave surged forward, driving the battle into renewed chaos. Bracing for the fresh assault, the Fallen stood firm, their weapons flashing in the pale light as they prepared to meet the next charge.

Inside the lair, Rowan's team advanced with deliberate care. The quiet hung heavy, broken only by the faint sound of their steps echoing against the stone. Without warning, a ripple of dark energy surged through the corridor, setting off a trap. Barriers of glowing, hardened smoke erupted from the floor, cutting across their path and isolating them from one another.

Rowan pivoted sharply, his gaze darting across the room as the barriers erased sightlines. Muffled shouts from Ash and Vine barely reached him before dissolving into an oppressive silence. Holly extended her hand, her fingers brushing against the shimmering surface of the obstruction as her breath caught in her throat. Rowan's instructions came through the comms, urgent yet measured.

"Hold position. Ash, Vine, Alder—take alternate paths. We'll regroup."

Static crackled over the comms, fracturing his words before the connection failed entirely. Every attempt to reestablish contact dissolved into an unsettling quiet, Rowan's voice lost in the rising interference.

Outside, the silence struck Aislinn like a physical blow. She clutched her earpiece, calling Rowan's name repeatedly, each unanswered plea tightening the weight in her chest. Her breaths came fast and shallow, panic swelling as her vision blurred at the edges. Her hand trembled, knuckles white around the mic, desperation threading through her every attempt. "Rowan... Rowan, please answer me..."

The lack of communication stretched endlessly, every second dragging into an eternity. Each heartbeat pounded louder in her ears, the air around her feeling thin, insufficient, as fear clawed its way to the surface. Her pulse raced, threatening to overwhelm her completely.

A firm hand rested gently on her shoulder, settling her. Reed removed her mic with measured care, setting it aside as her breathing faltered. His voice, low and considerate, broke through the rising panic. "Aislinn, breathe. Look at me," he said, his calm presence cutting through the storm. "Rowan's out there, and he knows what he's doing. Stay with me for now."

Her breathing hitched, but Reed's steady gaze drew her back, his words creating a tether she could cling to. "Inhale with me—slowly. Now let it out," he murmured, his tone firm yet soothing as he matched his own breaths to hers. Aislinn latched onto the pace, each step a small move away from the edge of panic.

Then, a warmth spread through her thoughts—a familiar presence, gentle yet steady, that softened the sharp edges of her fear. Eileen's tone entered her mind like a quiet melody. "Aislinn, my love," she murmured, her presence enveloping and reassuring. "You're safe, Rowan's safe. Breathe deeply with me… just like before. Let's find our calm together."

Aislinn's heart still raced, but Eileen's presence wrapped around her like a comforting embrace, steadying her. The sensation of her mother's touch filled her mind, a beacon cutting through the chaos. "I'm here with you, sweetheart. Deep breaths—slow and steady," Eileen whispered, her tone unwavering. "Rowan's fine. You're fine. Let the fear go, darling. I've got you." Her words carried more than comfort—they seemed to instill strength, as if drawn from a source far greater than the moment.

Gradually, Aislinn's breathing slowed, her pulse easing as the panic began to recede. "That's it," Eileen continued, her comforts carrying the unshakable love of a mother. "You are stronger than this. You've got this, my love."

The crackle of the comms broke the stillness as Rowan's voice emerged, faint at first but clearing quickly as the interference faded. "Holly and I cleared the disruption. Vine's disarming a ward, and we've located a few major Golden Dawn leaders ahead. Be ready—this isn't over."

Relief flooded Aislinn as she gripped the earpiece tightly, her breathing evening out. Rowan's tone softened, a thread of concern weaving into his words. "Aislinn, are you all right? Sorry about the silence. I didn't mean to worry you."

Eileen's presence remained in her mind, a soothing reminder of safety. Yet, as Rowan spoke again, his concern evident, Aislinn hesitated. She searched for an answer, but the connection between her thoughts and her ability to respond felt distant, her earlier panic slowly losing its grip.

Eileen's voice nudged her forward, quiet but insistent. "Aislinn, darling, speak to him," she urged gently. "He needs to know you're okay. Don't leave him carrying this."

Aislinn inhaled deeply, her trembling hand reaching for the mic Reed held out to her. He passed it back without hesitation, his expression calm and steady as he watched her. Summoning her resolve, she spoke into the comm, her determination clear in every syllable. "I'm here, Rowan. Just... stay safe. I'll be here," she said, the strength of her promise evident.

A faint chuckle traveled back over the comms, Rowan's relief palpable. "Good. Stay with us, Aislinn. We're going to see this through together."

Aislinn drew in another slow breath, her resolve firming. Reed's hand stayed lightly on her shoulder, a reassuring presence, as Eileen's warmth began to recede from her thoughts. But before it fully faded, her mother left her with a final reminder, her message calm yet unwavering. "Stay strong, my heart. Whatever comes, you are ready."

The sentiment settled deep within Aislinn, bringing her back further. Even as Eileen's presence withdrew, the love she left behind lingered—a quiet reassurance that filled her with renewed strength.

Eileen knelt on the cool earth nearby, her eyes closed as she let the tension of the moment dissipate. Slowly, she opened her eyes, taking in the surroundings as they sharpened into focus. Her gaze landed on Aislinn, whose breathing had steadied, her shoulders no longer trembling. Their eyes met, and a silent understanding passed between them—a bond forged long before this night, strengthened through shared love and trust.

A hint of a smile curved Eileen's lips, pride and affection evident in her demeanor. Aislinn returned it, her gratitude shining in her eyes. For an instant, the battlefield faded into the background, leaving only the connection between mother and daughter—a reminder of the light that would carry them through the darkness ahead.

But the pause broke as a shift rippled through the air. A dense, unnatural stillness blanketed the field, heavy and foreboding. Eileen's expression hardened, her attention turning outward as she tilted her head, sensing the threat lurking beyond sight.

A low hum vibrated in the distance, deep and resonant, like the warning growl of thunder. The ground beneath them pulsed faintly, each beat a dark, rhythmic warning. Aislinn glanced toward her mother, the question clear in her wide eyes, but Eileen's focus remained fixed, her posture tense as she scanned the horizon.

"Stay close, Aislinn," Eileen murmured, her tone a quiet warning edged with steel. "This calm... it's the edge of the storm."

In the far distance, barely visible but undeniable, a sinister glow flickered. The faint pulse of Lucifer's dark energy pressed against the air, oppressive and brimming with malice—a harbinger of a force unlike any they had faced before.

Aislinn swallowed hard, the remnants of her mother's warmth steadying her even as a chill ran through her veins. The encroaching darkness wasn't just nearing—it was bearing down on them, merciless, unrelenting, and unstoppable.

Chapter Thirty-Two
The Final Surge

The battlefield roared with the clash of steel and the volatile hum of magic, the Fallen locked in a desperate struggle against the advancing Golden Dawn. Riichi moved through the chaos, his katana flashing like liquid silver as he dismantled his enemies with lethal precision. His strikes flowed unbroken, but his attention kept darting to the horizon, where the ominous glow marking Lucifer's presence pulsed with a sinister rhythm.

At the rear of the field, Aislinn stood close to Eileen, her breathing uneven as she fought to calm the residual panic gripping her chest. Reed remained unwavering beside her, his posture a silent promise to intercept anything that threatened her. Eileen's focus sharpened as the oppressive pressure thickened around them, her composed exterior masking the urgency clawing at her from within. A subtle glimmer of an eternal essence seemed to ripple in her presence, almost as though the very air around her acknowledged a concealed ability.

A crushing silence swept across the battlefield, suffocating its sounds until even the clash of swords seemed to crumble into nothingness. The malevolent power radiating from Lucifer crept like invisible tendrils across the field, freezing Golden Dawn fighters in mid-motion. It pressed down on the Fallen with relentless intensity, growing heavier with every second, as though the earth itself sought to drag them into the abyss.

Reed moved, instinctively stepping in front of Aislinn as Lucifer advanced. His body remained taut with vigilance, his focus locked on the figure moving toward them with unhurried steps. One by one, every combatant—Fallen and Golden Dawn alike—turned toward Lucifer, their movements frozen under the suffocating influence emanating from him. He strode forward, his pace measured, his gaze sweeping the field as though evaluating each life in turn before dismissing it entirely.

Inside the mansion, Rowan stopped mid-step, every instinct screaming in warning. The pulse of malevolence pressed into him like a vice, unmistakable and vile. He didn't need confirmation, but it came anyway—Eileen's calm yet warning-laced message crackled through the comm. *"Lucifer is here."*

The statement ignited a spark in Rowan, and he bolted. His boots thundered against the hardwood floors as he sprinted across the building, every sense locked onto the field beyond. By the time he reached the door, his lungs burned with urgency. He shoved it open and stepped into the cool night air just as Lucifer neared the center of the battlefield, his presence obliterating everything else.

"How quaint, this little resistance," Lucifer said, his mockery cutting into the stillness. His words carried calculated disdain, and his steps were slow and deliberate. His attention finally fell on Riichi, a twisted smile spreading across his face like a fresh wound. "But there are bigger games to play tonight."

Then, without warning, Lucifer moved. A blur of motion and speed, he closed the distance between himself and Riichi in an instant. Rowan shouted a warning, his voice fueled by urgency, but it came too late.

Riichi reacted with the sharp instincts of a seasoned warrior, his katana slicing upward in a flawless arc to intercept the strike. But Lucifer's abilities defied comprehension. The impact shattered the blade as though it were glass, sending shards flying. The resulting shockwave of magic rippled outward, hurling Riichi backward with devastating force. Blood painted the air in crimson streaks before his body hit the ground with a bone-jarring thud. He lay crumpled, his form unnervingly lifeless.

The battlefield froze in collective paralysis. The Fallen stood rooted in place, the crushing weight of Lucifer's power suffocating the space around them. Eileen's fists clenched at her sides as she forced herself to stay composed. The faintest shimmer of light seemed to flicker near her—a subtle reminder of a force far greater than the immediate chaos. She refused to give Lucifer the satisfaction of a reaction.

Rowan, however, wasn't as controlled. Rage ignited within him, hot and immediate, his chest heaving as he took a step forward. His hand gripped his sword tightly, fury carved into his every feature. "Bastard!" The word ripped from him, guttural and raw, tearing over the heavy atmosphere.

Lucifer stood motionless above Riichi's broken form, his grin widening as though Rowan's anger was exactly what he'd wanted. "I'll be waiting for you... at the altar," he said, his tone dripping with cold amusement. "It's time we finish this little game." His attention halted on Rowan, the malice in his eyes razor-sharp and unrelenting.

With one last mocking laugh, Lucifer gave a slight, exaggerated bow. "Let's play, shall we?" In a blink, he vanished into the encroaching darkness, leaving behind the cloying remnants of his presence—a dread that hung over the battlefield like a gathering storm.

Eileen's breath caught as Lucifer vanished, leaving the battlefield cloaked in an suffocating silence. Her attention returned to Riichi's broken form, his katana shattered and his body motionless. Abruptly, she activated her power, a ripple of shimmering energy radiating outward and freezing time itself. The chaos halted, fighters locked mid-motion as though caught within a suspended heartbeat.

Her combat attire changed with a delicate shimmer, transforming into flowing white robes that exuded a luminous radiance against the frozen battlefield. She crossed the field with deliberate, swift strides, her focus entirely on Riichi. His earlier words echoed in her mind, unyielding and haunting. *"It feels like one of us is going to fall."*

A thought struck her—a Hawthorn, Riichi's Celtic tree. Resilient and enduring, it withstood storms but could still break under the fiercest blows. *You've stood strong for all of us, she thought. Now it's my turn to catch you.*

Eileen knelt beside him, her hands hovering over his wounds, her expression a mix of sorrow and fierce determination. Blood pooled beneath him, its dark sheen testing her resolve. Slowly, she tilted her face upward, her voice breaking the silence in a near-whisper. "Forgive me... I couldn't stand aside this time."

Her fingers pressed gently to his chest, her power flowing into him in a radiant stream of vitality. The light around her hands brightened as she worked swiftly, knitting his wounds closed from within. With a single motion, she drew Riichi closer, an ephemeral gentleness crossing her features. Then, with a measured exhale, she touched his shoulder, and they disappeared from the battlefield, reappearing beside Aislinn as the frozen world held its eerie stillness.

Eileen stood beside Aislinn and rested a steadying hand on her daughter's shoulder. Her touch shimmered subtly, a ripple of energy flowing into Aislinn as she released her from the frozen condition. The stasis around them remained unbroken, but Aislinn jolted as her senses reignited, the scene crashing into her with brutal clarity.

Her mother stood before her, dressed in ethereal robes that radiated gently amid the frozen turmoil. Eileen's face reflected fierce resolve mixed with an aching tenderness, but it was Riichi who drew Aislinn's attention. His pallor was ghostly, his unnatural immobility unsettling, with blood staining his chest and pooling beneath him.

"Mom... what's going on?" Aislinn's voice trembled, her thoughts racing to piece together the surreal scene. "And why are you... like this?"

Eileen's response held a measured control and undeniable determination. "Aislinn, there's no time. I need your help to heal him," she said, her features briefly marked by a passing vulnerability. "His injuries are severe."

Aislinn's gaze darted from Riichi's wounded form to her mother's face, emotion rising within her like a tidal wave. Gripping Eileen's arm, she blurted, "You've had this ability all along? Then why didn't you stop this? Why let any of this happen?"

Eileen met her daughter's eyes, sorrow swirling alongside a profound resolve—rigid and definite. "Breaking certain rules carries a cost, Aislinn," she said, her manner laced with restraint. "He..." She hesitated, the thought catching as though it burned. "He would be disappointed if I interfered so directly."

Aislinn's frustration broke free, pouring out unchecked. "But you're already interfering to save Riichi! Isn't that breaking the rules? Why does it matter now? Why Riichi?"

Eileen's lips tightened, her features unreadable at first before she sighed, the burden she carried evident in the way her shoulders sagged. "It's too close now," she murmured, almost to herself. Her focus turned to Riichi, her words carrying a rare gentleness as though speaking to more than just her daughter. "Riichi's time is near. He's on the verge of something greater, and we need to make sure he gets there." A trace of conflict crossed her face as she added, "I only hope this act will be forgiven."

Gently but firmly, Eileen guided Aislinn's hands to Riichi's wounds. "This isn't the time for questions. He needs you now—focus, and we'll give him a chance."

Aislinn felt stable reassurance flow through her mother's touch. Pushing aside her frustration, she closed her eyes, concentrating on Riichi. Their skills intertwined, a force both soothing and overwhelming as it coursed within her. Under their combined effort, she felt his pulse grow stronger, his breathing beginning to steady.

After murmuring a final blessing over Riichi's brow, Eileen placed a hand on his shoulder, her touch firm yet tender. In a flash of brilliance, they vanished from the battlefield and reappeared within the Fallen's mansion. The warmth of the familiar space was jarring compared to the chaos they had left behind. Immediately, Eileen called out, her command ringing with clarity, "Takoda! Rain!"

In moments, the two appeared from the kitchen, concern etched into their faces as they took in the scene—Riichi, unconscious and wounded, supported by Eileen. Takoda's steps faltered as her eyes locked onto him, her breath catching audibly. "No... no, this can't be happening," she whispered, her words breaking as she rushed forward. Her hand trembled as she reached out, fingers brushing his shoulder before curling into a fist, her knuckles whitening with strain.

Rain, though equally shaken, recovered quickly. Her jaw tightened as she stepped beside Takoda, offering support with a secure hold on her arm. Eileen remained composed as she addressed them, her order firm but leaving no room for debate. "Take care of him. Keep him safe, and don't let him die," she ordered, each syllable landing with obvious authority.

Takoda's tear-filled gaze lifted to Eileen. "I won't let anything happen to him," she vowed, her voice trembling yet certain.

Rain's brow furrowed as she glanced at Eileen. "We'll do everything we can," she said, her attention drawn to Riichi, worry visible in her posture.

Eileen's composure didn't waver, but her presence deepened, carrying an almost otherworldly weight. "There is something else," she said, her words careful. "You must not speak of what you've seen tonight—how I brought him here, or the nature of my presence. To anyone. Not now, not ever."

Takoda blinked, her lips parting as if to protest, but the force of Eileen's command silenced her. She swallowed hard, her trembling hands cradling Riichi's arm. "I promise," she whispered, her breath thick with emotion.

Rain hesitated, glancing at Eileen's shimmering robes before meeting her steady stare. "I promise," she echoed, her manner calm despite the unasked questions reflecting in her eyes.

Satisfied, Eileen's features softened. She cast a final look over Riichi, concern flashing briefly before she straightened. Her presence seemed to fade as her hands lowered to her sides.

In a flash, she was gone.

***

The battlefield remained frozen as Eileen reappeared among the Fallen, her glowing robes replaced by combat gear. She stood tall, her features steely and unyielding. The warmth from earlier had vanished, replaced by an authoritative presence that brooked no argument.

Aislinn, seeing her mother's return, felt a rush of emotion. She took a step forward, ready to demand answers, her seething anger bubbling to the surface. But Eileen raised a hand, stopping her mid-step. The gesture was swift, allowing no room for protest.

"The fight isn't over, Aislinn," she said, her tone unflinching. "Concentrate. I can't hold this time freeze much longer."

Aislinn's irritation churned within her, but the power of Eileen's directive rooted her in place. In that instant, she saw not just her mother but the stubborn leader of the Fallen—a figure who bore the burden of their world on her shoulders. Forcing herself to nod, Aislinn let the tension dissipate, fortifying herself. *For now, I'm a soldier.*

Eileen lowered her hand, and time snapped back into motion in an instant. The battlefield erupted into chaos as battle cries and the clash of weapons roared to life. Golden Dawn guards surged forward with renewed ferocity, their attacks swift and brutal.

Eileen's words came through the commlink, evident and determined amid the storm of combat. "Everyone, stand firm. Riichi has been taken to safety. He will recover," she said, her directive imbued with an influence that secured the Fallen in the chaos. "Phase 5 is a go."

Aislinn's gaze swept over the battlefield until it locked with Rowan's. His expression was taut with strain but unshaken, and she felt a current of resolve flow through her, as though drawn from his steadfast composure. Eileen's tone altered minutely, carrying both an order and a warning. "Rowan, Aislinn—activate Radiant Surge. We need everything you both can give."

The impact of the order struck with distinctive lucidity. Radiant Surge—a technique they had barely mastered, demanding perfect alignment between her abilities and Rowan's. She cast a brief glance at him, her pulse racing, but his solid nod reassured her. *We can do this.*

His response came through the commlink, sure and direct. "Aislinn. Let's show them what we're made of."

She inhaled deeply, centering herself as the oppressive atmosphere around her seemed to thrum with Lucifer's ever-present influence. The stakes had never felt higher.

Suddenly, shadows twisted around her, and before she could react, Reed appeared at her side. His hand gripped hers with firm urgency, and the world blurred as his shadow-walk pulled her seamlessly through the fray, reappearing beside Rowan in a heartbeat. A feeble, knowing grin tugged at his lips as he turned to Rowan. "See?" he said casually, his comment edged with purpose. "I told you I'd keep her safe. Now it's your turn."

Reed's hand remained briefly on Aislinn's shoulder, a supportive, reassuring squeeze before he vanished back into the night as quickly as he had come. For a second, his absence felt like an ache, but Rowan's presence fortified her once more. Their stares met, and the fierce determination burning in his face calmed her completely.

Rowan's concentration remained locked on her, his look carrying a silent promise. The crushing intensity of the battle pressed around them, but instead of breaking, it seemed to forge an implicit bond. Together, they stepped closer, reaching out in perfect accord. The second their hands met, warmth flowed through them, growing stronger with each heartbeat as their powers began to fuse, intertwining seamlessly.

A brilliant glow began to bloom, emanating from their clasped hands. The brightness grew gradually, intensifying with every passing second until it lit the battlefield around them. It wasn't just illumination—it was the embodiment of their unity, a visible symbol of their combined forces growing into something far greater. The tyrannical energy that had loomed over the field seemed to falter, retreating in the face of their connection.

The shine from Radiant Surge rippled outward in rhythmic waves, a declaration of their shared abilities. Across the battlefield, the Fallen paused, their attention instinctively drawn to the gleam as though compelled by its significance. Rowan and Aislinn stood secure, their hands clasped and their bond exuding an unshakable potency.

Radiant Surge didn't scatter enemies or break barriers—it didn't need to. It was a beacon, a message to both allies and foes that Rowan and Aislinn were in perfect harmony, their strength united as one. The energy resonating between them pulsed with certainty, a silent but distinctive promise that this fight was far from over.

Rowan and Aislinn pressed forward, their movements measured and adamant as they cleared a path for their teammates. Behind them, Vine, Ash, Alder, and Holly kept close, their attention razor-sharp and their tenacity unwavering. Together, the group advanced deeper into enemy territory, unified by purpose and determination.

With Radiant Surge casting a pale luminescence around them, Rowan and Aislinn moved in seamless synchrony, their bond palpable. The glow emanating from their connection pushed back the stifling dimness clinging to the corridor's walls. The air felt dense, almost suffocating, but the relentless stride of the Fallen carved through it with conviction.

The first wave of guards emerged from hidden alcoves, their weapons flashing as they attacked with ferocity. Rowan lunged forward, his blade slicing in the air with deadly accuracy, each strike honed by centuries of combat. Beside him, Aislinn extended her hand, releasing a burst of energy that hurled the nearest attacker backward.

Holly stepped into the fray, her fingers creating intricate shapes that shimmered and shifted in the air. The illusions danced like mirages, their unearthly forms baffling the guards and throwing their attacks into disarray. In that brief moment, Ash surged ahead, his body rippling as he transformed into a massive wolf. With a guttural snarl, he brought one disoriented guard down before pivoting to another, his movements swift and lethal.

Vine's sai flashed as he intercepted a guard's strike, twisting the weapon from his opponent's grasp before delivering a fastidious blow that left the attacker crumpling to the floor. Nearby, Alder stepped in, his sword slicing through the turmoil with measured efficiency as he deflected an attack meant for Rowan before countering with a decisive thrust.

A second wave of guards charged at them, but Aislinn raised both hands, unleashing a shockwave that rippled through the corridor, throwing the attackers off balance. Rowan pressed forward, his blade a blur as he dispatched the staggering foes with unerring accuracy. Vine moved at his side, cutting down another with calculated efficiency, while Ash, now a sleek panther, leapt onto a third, his claws tearing through armor with ease.

Holly's illusions altered again, morphing into spectral figures that seemed to rise from the very walls. The guards hesitated, fear taking hold as the apparitions closed in. Alder took full advantage of their hesitation, his strikes careful and unrelenting as he cut through their ranks like a seasoned warrior.

Rowan dropped low, sweeping a guard off his feet with an abrupt strike. Aislinn vaulted over him, unleashing a forceful blast that sent another attacker sprawling. The team moved as one—every step, every action executed with flawless coordination. The guards fell one by one, their defenses collapsing under the combined strength of the Fallen.

As they approached the end of the corridor, a Golden Dawn mage stepped out of the gloom. His guttural incantations filled the air, summoning a swirling vortex of magic that pulsed and writhed like a living entity. Aislinn's countenance hardened, her focus narrowing as she reached for Rowan's hand. Unflinchingly, he clasped it, and their energies merged into a unified might.

The resulting surge of power erupted forward, a blinding arc of vividness that tore through the mage's spell and illuminated the corridor. The magic shattered as if struck by the first light of dawn breaking through dark clouds.

The mage staggered, his concentration fractured. Rowan released Aislinn's hand briefly and stepped forward, delivering a final blow with meticulousness. His blade struck cleanly, and the mage collapsed to the floor, motionless.

With the path now clear, Rowan and Aislinn exchanged a glance of shared purpose. Together, they approached the heavy double doors that marked the altar room. Each grasped a handle, and with synchronized muscle, they pushed the doors open.

Inside, shadows writhed and coiled like living things, pooling thickly around the massive stone altar at the room's center. The air thrummed feebly, laden with malice as the darkness shifted, coalescing into a familiar figure.

Lucifer stood tall, his presence exuding dominance, his facade curling into a smug, predatory grin. His gleaming eyes carried a calculated mockery, as though he were sizing them up, savoring the moment.

"Ah, you finally arrived," he drawled, his words dripping with venomous delight. "I was beginning to think I might die of boredom waiting for you."

Rowan and Aislinn held their stance, their resolve unshaken as they faced him head-on. The room seemed to pause, heavy with dread and anticipation, as the final confrontation loomed.

As Rowan and Aislinn stepped forward, Lucifer's twisted smile deepened, his expression alight with cold pleasure. He remained motionless, hands clasped loosely behind his back, his posture radiating a maddening lack of urgency.

"You've come all this way," he began, his words silken yet barbed with mockery. "And for what, exactly? Do you truly believe you can challenge me?" His attention shifted to Aislinn, a calculating gleam flickering in his gaze. "A mere mortal, clutching at borrowed strength? Tell me, girl, do you really think you can stand against forces that existed before you even understood what strength was?"

Aislinn's jaw tightened, frustration sparking in her, but she held onto her bearings. Beside her, Rowan's steady presence acted as a stabilizing force, his unshaken resolve bolstering her own. The faint hum of Radiant Surge rippled between them, a rhythm like a drumbeat of war, steadying her thoughts and fortifying her focus.

Lucifer chuckled, shifting his piercing gaze to Rowan with an edge of menace. "And you, Fallen hero... how far will loyalty carry you? Are you truly ready to throw everything away for a futile cause?" He took a slow step forward, his voice dropping to a low murmur that reverberated through the chamber with a chilling weight. "You're tied to a power you can't even grasp."

Rowan remained silent, his grip tightening on his weapon as he adjusted his stance with subtle exactness. Aislinn inhaled deeply, forcing her composure to hold as Lucifer's taunts clawed at her control. When her eyes met Rowan's, a silent knowledge passed between them—a bond forged through trust and determination, defying the darkness before them. They had chosen their path, and it led directly through him.

Side by side, they advanced, their combined energy radiating outward in waves, each step cutting through the suffocating gloom like sunlight piercing a tempest. Lucifer stood unmoving, his confidence unbroken, his bearing steeped in disdain.

The shadows around the altar erupted to life, writhing and coiling into massive tendrils that lashed out with predatory intent. Rowan and Aislinn dove apart, narrowly avoiding the black appendages as they struck the ground with bone-jarring force. The room descended into chaos, the shadows moving with an unnatural will of their own.

Aislinn thrust her hands forward, unleashing a blast of concentrated might that tore through the nearest tendrils, scattering them in a searing burst. Rowan followed close behind, his blade arcing through the air in precise, relentless strokes as he cut down the next wave of shadowy attacks.

Lucifer tilted his head slightly, faint amusement playing across his features. With a twist of his wrist, new tendrils surged from the surrounding dimness, replacing those destroyed. Their sinuous movements carried an unnerving fluidity as they coiled toward the pair. One wrapped tightly around Rowan's weapon, wrenching it from his grip.

Rowan twisted sharply, reclaiming his blade in a fluid motion, though the effort left him exposed. Aislinn reacted instantly, stepping forward to unleash a burst of kinetic power that obliterated the tendrils encircling him, clearing his path. Together, they pressed on, their movements perfectly aligned, their bond strengthening with every step.

Meanwhile, Vine, Ash, Alder, and Holly concentrated on the altar itself, their determination driving them through the turmoil. Holly extended her hands, contriving illusions that shimmered and shifted like ethereal lanterns. The spectral forms confused the shadowed sentinels defending the altar, their attacks faltering against the ghostly apparitions.

Alder's sword struck with purpose, each swing calculated and vigorous as he chipped away at the cursed stone. Sparks flew with every impact, cracks spreading steadily across the altar as his strikes gained momentum.

Ash shifted effortlessly into the form of a massive boar, his tusks driving deep into the altar's supports. The raw force of his charge sent tremors through the structure, fissures spidering outward as debris crumbled to the floor.

Vine darted through the chaos with deadly precision, his sais slicing cleanly through shadowy tendrils. With a deft flip of his wrists, arcs of electricity sparked between his weapons, crackling with energy before surging outward. The currents struck both the altar and its defenders, disrupting the evil magic saturating the room. The shadows recoiled, granting the team temporary openings to continue their assault.

The altar pulsed with a resistance that felt almost alive, its malevolent power palpable. But the team's determination never faltered. Each fracture in the stone felt like progress, a step closer to breaking Lucifer's hold.

The chamber throbbed with opposing energies —Rowan and Aislinn's luminous energy clashing against the consuming darkness commanded by Lucifer, while their teammates dismantled the altar piece by piece. Each strike, each movement pushed the battle toward its climax, the pressure rising with every second as the final confrontation drew closer.

Lucifer's mocking voice echoed through the chamber, sharp and resonant, untouched by effort. "Is that the best you can do?" he taunted, the shadows surrounding him surging and twisting, transforming him into his true monstrous form that loomed over Rowan and Aislinn. His grin widened as he watched their struggle, the shadows bending to his will as though it were an extension of himself. "You should've stayed in the light."

"Impressive," Lucifer drawled, sidestepping their attacks with a grace so effortless it bordered on contempt. "But futile." With a flick of his hand, he conjured a dense mass of corrupt power that slammed into them like a storm surge, sending both skidding across the stone floor.

Rowan barely recovered before Lucifer's onslaught resumed. The demon's strikes came fast and unrelenting, each one aimed with precision to disman-tle Rowan's defenses. The clash of blade against magic reverberated through the chamber, each impact forcing Rowan closer to his limits. Aislinn moved swiftly to support him, sending bursts of crackling energy across the room in an effort to disrupt Lucifer's relentless assault. But Lucifer weaved through the onslaught with unnerving agility, his foul magic absorbing her strikes with the ease of dry earth soaking in rain.

Abruptly, Lucifer's focus shifted, his cold stare locking onto Aislinn. With a sharp motion, he unleashed a crushing wave of power in her direction. She threw up her hands, deflecting the attack just in time, but the impact rattled her, forcing her back a step.

Rowan surged forward, closing the gap with renewed determination. His blade sliced with precision, but Lucifer countered with brutal efficiency, delivering a blast that shattered Rowan's guard and sent him reeling.

Aislinn's pulse raced as she pushed through the consequence of mounting exhaustion, determination fueling her every movement. Her hands flared with brilliant light as she gathered her strength and unleashed it in a searing wave that crashed into Lucifer. For a fragment of time, the shadows around him faltered, quivering as though disturbed. Rowan seized the opportunity, his strikes swift and deliberate, each blow exploiting the narrow opening.

The respite was brief. Lucifer's smirk returned, his command over the surrounding darkness tightening as the shadows coiled around him once more, dense and impenetrable. His posture straightened, his presence ex-panding, the atmosphere around him growing heavier with menace. "Is that the best you can do?" he asked again, his tone dripping with disdain. With a sweeping gesture, he unleashed a colossal wave of revolting energy. The crushing potency sent Rowan and Aislinn hurtling backward, their shared energy shaking as they struggled to stay upright.

Lucifer chuckled softly, the sound a sinister echo rippling through the chamber. "You are but children playing with fire. But by all means... keep trying. I find it amusing."

Rowan and Aislinn exchanged a brief glance, their breaths labored, the toll of the battle evident in their postures. Yet the spark in their eyes remained undimmed. Together, they braced themselves, their determination as adamant as steel. The importance of their mission pressed down on them, the air around them thrumming with the restlessness of an impending final clash against the darkest force they had ever faced.

Then, without warning, a pulse of warmth coursed through their bodies, steady and comforting, like a current threading into their cores. The heaviness of their exhaustion lifted, their burdens momentarily lightened.

Birch's voice came through the commlink, calm yet carrying a quiet strength. "You're not done yet. Draw on it—take what you need."

The reassurance in Birch's words resonated in Rowan's chest, the renewed energy settling into his limbs and softening the ache in his muscles. His breathing evened out as he gave a small nod. "Birch... you've got good timing."

Aislinn felt the fatigue recede, her strength returning like water flowing into a parched riverbed. Straightening her posture, she summoned her resolve anew. In her thoughts, she offered a silent thank-you to Birch, a quiet prayer of gratitude. Fortified not only by their shared bond but also by the steadfast support of their allies, she turned her attention to Rowan.

Their eyes met, and in that final, wordless exchange, they drew deeply on the renewed energy coursing through them. Their resolve solidified, their connection unshaken. Together, they prepared to face the malevolence again, unrelenting in their fight.

Reinvigorated, Rowan and Aislinn stepped forward in perfect harmony, each stride carrying the vigor of their team like an unbroken thread binding them together. Their movements were fluid, synchronized, as though the connection between them echoed an ancient rhythm—unwavering and eternal.

The relentless clash continued, and Aislinn's thoughts raced, searching for a way to shift the tide. Lucifer's presence loomed, harsh and overwhelming, each strike of his aimed not only at their bodies but at their very will. His attacks sought to unravel their steadfastness, to crush their spirit. Then, a fragment of memory emerged: Eileen's words from long ago. *"Together, not as two separate forces."*

The realization hit Aislinn like a flare in the night. She and Rowan couldn't rely on brute strength alone to defeat Lucifer. Their power lay in unity—in the bond flowing between them like ancient rivers, intertwining them into a singular force to stand against the overwhelming evil.

"Rowan, wait." Her voice cut through the chaos, sound and determined. She reached for him, her hand finding his. Rowan paused immediately, sensing the shift in her. With confidence, he nodded, his fingers lacing with hers. Together, they rooted themselves, channeling their energy as one.

The glow around their hands flared brighter, spreading outward in a steady, protective radiance that encircled them both. This wasn't the fleeting bursts of energy they had relied on before but a constant, solid shield—a beacon of their unity, as unyielding and sacred as the light of Brigid, pushing back the encroaching darkness.

The chamber brightened as their glow intensified, driving away the shadowed tendrils clinging to the corners like cobwebs. Lucifer's composed façade cracked, a hint of irritation flashing across his features as he took an involuntary step back. With a sharp gesture, he unleashed a massive torrent of phantoms, their twisting forms surging toward them. The wave slammed into their barrier, but instead of breaking it, the darkness was absorbed, dissipating into nothing against the radiant energy surrounding them. The light expanded further, chasing away the remnants of evils, leaving no place for them to linger.

"Enough!" Lucifer bellowed, his voice a thunderous roar filled with fury. Raising both hands, he summoned every ounce of his dark power. The air around him writhed violently, trembling under the immensity of pure malice as he condensed the energy into a swirling vortex. With a guttural cry, he hurled the full force of his strength at them in one devastating strike.

Rowan and Aislinn refused to back down, unshaken. Their combined energy surged, Radiant Surge blazing brighter than ever before. In flawless unison, they funneled their power, Rowan's super-human strength and Aislinn's kinetic energy, into a single, concentrated blast, unleashing it to meet Lucifer's attack head-on.

The collision of light and darkness rocked the chamber to its foundations, the resulting explosion blinding and deafening as it rippled outward. Their unity absorbed and deflected Lucifer's strike, shattering his assault and sending shockwaves through the room.

When the brilliance faded, silence blanketed the chamber. Dust hung thick in the air, and the faint hum of dissipating energy lingered in the stillness. Lucifer was gone—his suffocating presence, which had moments ago dominated the room, had vanished. This was not a victory of destruction, but of retreat. Their strength, their unity, had forced him back. But both Rowan and Aislinn knew this reprieve was temporary. Lucifer would return. For now, though, they had prevailed.

Drained but triumphant, Rowan and Aislinn paused to catch their breath. Their heavy exhalations filled the quiet space as they turned to each other, exhaustion mingling with the profound significance of what they had achieved. For just a heartbeat, their bond felt unshakable—a shield that had not only saved them but their team.

Behind them, Vine, Ash, Alder, and Holly remained hard at work dismantling the altar. Alder's blade struck with relentless determination, splintering the crumbling foundation. Ash, in the form of a colossal boar, drove his tusks into the supports, sending fresh tremors through the structure as fissures spread and debris tumbled to the floor.

Holly's shimmering illusions flickered like will-o'-the-wisps, confounding the last of the ghostly sentinels, drawing them away from the altar's defenses.

Vine crouched near the base, his sharp eyes scanning a cluster of glowing runes etched into the stone. The intricate patterns pulsed faintly, their endless spirals designed to defy logic and resist comprehension. His expression darkened as understanding dawned. "Wait—there's a bomb here," he said, his voice tight with alarm.

Promptly, Vine raised his hand, arcs of electricity sparking between his fingers as he attempted to disrupt the mechanism. The cursed runes resisted fiercely, their magic reinforcing the device's defenses. Frustrated, Vine stepped back, urgency bleeding into his tone. "It's no good! We've got two minutes! Move!"

The impact of his statement hit the team like a shockwave, and they sprang into motion. Rowan reacted first, his directive cutting through the turmoil with clear intent. "Everyone, get out—now! Spread the message to clear the area!"

Abandoning the altar, the group sprinted through the dim corridors with purpose. With Radiant Surge still active, Rowan and Aislinn led the charge, their combined energy forming a protective barrier that deflected debris and shielded them from remaining shadows as they carved a path to safety.

Bursting through the building's entrance, they were met with the chaos of the battlefield. The clash of steel and cries of combatants still echoed across the field, Fallen warriors and Golden Dawn fighters locked in desperate battle.

Rowan's command carried over the tumult, cutting through the noise with unrelenting authority. "Everyone, fall back—get out of the blast zone!"

Even as Rowan and Aislinn pressed onward, the fleeting passage of time weighed heavily around them. The battlefield, though quieter now, bore the unmistakable marks of chaos. Fallen warriors stood battered but unyielding, their resilience undiminished, while the scattered injuries across their allies served as a stark reminder that the fight was not yet behind them.

A shared determination flared between Rowan and Aislinn, fierce and unyielding. Aislinn's grip on Rowan's hand tightened, her features sharp with purpose. "Rowan," she began, her voice steady but urgent. "We need to combine our powers—not just to protect them, but to heal the Fallen, all of them, at once. If we amplify my healing ability through our connection, I can destroy the Golden Dawn with a kinetic blast while restoring our team."

Rowan's gaze locked with hers, grounding her in his quiet resolve. "You're sure?" he asked, though the flicker of faith in his eyes spoke volumes.

Her grip on his hand tightened further. "I know it'll work," she said, her conviction unwavering.

Rowan gave a single nod. "Together," he agreed, the word a quiet pledge.

The Radiant Surge around them flared brighter, its glow intensifying as they raised their clasped hands. Drawing deeply from their bond, they allowed their energies to merge completely, forming a singular force. Aislinn's voice, low but brimming with determination, cut through the charged air. "For all of us."

From their joined hands, a brilliant light erupted, sweeping across the battlefield in a radiant wave. The energy surged outward like an unstoppable tide, carrying with it a warmth ancient and unyielding, imbued with the strength of an eternal force. Wherever the wave traveled, it transformed. Fallen warriors felt their wounds mend, the crushing burden of exhaustion lifting as renewed vitality coursed through them. The Golden Dawn fighters faltered, their weapons slipping from numb fingers as the light extinguished their fury and swept away the shadows clinging to the field.

When the glow receded, a profound calm settled over the battlefield. The Fallen stood revitalized, their astonishment evident as they examined healed injuries and unmarred armor. Scattered among them, the Golden Dawn fighters lay motionless, their chaotic fervor silenced. The transformation was complete.

At the heart of it all, Rowan and Aislinn remained, their hands still clasped. Their unity had been the source of the radiant wave. Though exhaustion shadowed their features, it was tempered by the quiet triumph glimmering in their expressions.

"We did it," Aislinn whispered, her voice a mix of relief and the lingering impact of victory.

But the instance was fleeting. Vine's urgent shout shattered the quiet. "Thirty seconds left! We have to shield ourselves—there's no time to get clear!"

The warning struck like a thunderclap, jolting Rowan and Aislinn into motion. Their hands tightened together, their gazes locking in silent understanding. On impulse, they raised their clasped hands toward the sky, channeling their combined energy with a force born of desperation and instinct.

A blinding surge of blue light shot upward, unfurling rapidly into a protective dome above them. The shimmering barrier formed with breathtaking speed, its surface alive with intricate spirals and interwoven patterns—symbols of eternity and ancient protection. The crystalline dome sparkled with refracted hues, its shifting colors gleaming like fragments of a living star.

Eileen's breath caught as she stepped forward, her expression softening with awe. Her whisper, though faint, carried the weight of reverence. "The Shield of Ages," she murmured, her voice trembling. It was a force she hadn't seen invoked since the earliest days—a power reserved for bonds forged in pure intent and moments of dire need.

The shield descended slowly, its radiant surface locking into place around the Fallen just as the countdown reached zero.

The explosion erupted with a deafening roar, the ground buckling beneath them. Waves of fire and debris slammed against the shimmering barrier in unrelenting torrents, the impact reverberating across the battlefield. The dome absorbed the onslaught, glowing brighter with each collision as its intricate designs pulsed with ancient strength.

Within the shield, the Fallen remained untouched, their sanctuary holding firm as chaos raged beyond. The earth shook violently, and the air grew heavy with uncertainty, but the protective barrier did not falter. It stood unyielding—a testament to the bond that had summoned it.

As the echoes of the blast faded into silence, a sacred calm enveloped the battlefield. The Shield of Ages shimmered once more, its blue light fragmenting into countless shards that ascended like pieces of starlight, vanishing into the ether. The smoldering ruins of the mansion lay in stark contrast, a sobering reminder of the devastation narrowly avoided.

At the heart of it all, Rowan and Aislinn stood together, their hands still clasped. Their shoulders rose and fell with the strain of exertion, the glow of their unity gradually fading but leaving behind an undeniable influence. Drained yet resolute, they turned toward Eileen, who stood watching with an expression softened by pride and profound relief.

Rowan inclined his head toward her, his voice quiet but steady. "Let's go home."

Rowan and Aislinn moved quietly across the battlefield, their steps heavy with exhaustion yet purposeful. The chaos had subsided, leaving behind only faint echoes of its fury. Around them, the other Fallen lingered, finishing their final tasks and steadying themselves amidst the aftermath. Rowan and Aislinn didn't look back; their part was finished. Together, they walked toward the waiting vehicles, retreating from the devastation they had endured.

As they neared the vehicle, Aislinn slowed, her gaze drifting back across the field. The wreckage spoke of destruction, but the resolve of their allies was unmistakable as they moved among the remnants of battle. Some knelt to aid the wounded, while others stood in reflective silence, their faces marked by the magnitude of survival. Aislinn's voice broke softly, tinged with hesitation. "Shouldn't we tell them what happened to Lucifer?"

Rowan followed her line of sight, watching as their friends regrouped, piecing themselves back together after the storm. He exhaled deeply, a quiet sense of finality settling over him. "They'll figure it out. They don't need us for that, Aislinn. We did what we came here to do." His response was calm, steady, carrying both reassurance and quiet conviction.

He reached for her, pulling her into an embrace that was firm and comforting. The intensity of the battle mingled with the relief of its conclusion, anchoring them in the present. "We did our part," he murmured.

In his arms, Aislinn closed her eyes, letting the tension seep from her body as she leaned into him. The even rhythm of his breathing quieted the storm lingering in her thoughts. "Yeah," she whispered, the enormity of their victory settling over her. "We did."

They stayed like that for a while longer, finding solace in the shared understanding of what they had overcome. It wasn't just the end of a fight—it was a bond renewed, strengthened by the crucible of their struggle. Whatever came next, they would face it together.

Rowan released her gently, his hand brushing hers as he opened the vehicle door. They climbed inside, the quiet interior offering a haven from the battlefield behind them. Silence wrapped around them, soft and comforting, as the chaos outside began to fade. Rowan leaned back, his eyes closing briefly, the stiffness in his shoulders gradually loosening. Beside him, Aislinn sat in stillness, her gaze wandering back to the field.

In the distance, the other Fallen continued their work, their movements slower now as they began clearing the battlefield. They worked methodically, erasing signs of the conflict to ensure nothing would draw the attention of the general public. Some offered hands to help others rise, a few exchanged words of quiet resolve, and others focused on removing debris and concealing the aftermath, their faces reflecting both weariness and resilience. Aislinn watched them, her heart stirring with the shared bond that had solidified between them all.

Rowan reached for her hand, his fingers threading through hers. "We'll wait for them," he said softly, a note of pride coloring his voice. "They'll be ready soon."

Aislinn nodded, leaning back with a gentle sigh. Their hands remained clasped, the simple connection balancing them amid the aftermath. Outside, the remaining Fallen began to gather, slowly making their way toward the vehicles. Each step was a testament to their resilience, but also the strength of unity—a force that had guided them through the darkness.

Inside the vehicle, the peacefulness deepened, drawing them into its embrace. Weariness crept over them, heavy and inescapable. Rowan shifted slightly, his fingers tightening around Aislinn's as his head rested back against the seat. Aislinn followed suit, sinking into the comforting silence, her breathing soft and measured. Their hands stayed intertwined, even as sleep claimed them, the bond between them unbroken.

By the time the rest of the Fallen reached the vehicles, Rowan and Aislinn remained motionless, their features softened in peaceful repose. The sight stirred quiet respect among their comrades, each one recognizing the toll the battle had taken and the sacrifices Rowan and Aislinn had made.

Vine paused at the door, casting a glance toward them before speaking softly to the others. "They've earned it. Let them rest." His tone held an unexpected gentleness, tempered by the exhaustion etched into his own face.

One by one, the Fallen settled into the vehicles, their movements deliberate and subdued. The battlefield behind them showed no visible signs of battle, meticulously cleared to conceal the chaos that had unfolded, yet the unity forged in the fires of their struggle remained unbreakable.

As the convoy rumbled to life and began the journey home, the Fallen carried more than victory with them. They carried hope, tempered by resilience and fortified by the bonds they had forged. And as the world outside dimmed, peace wrapped itself around them. Rowan and Aislinn slept on, their part in the battle complete—for now.

A rare solidity enveloped the mansion, as if the walls themselves absorbed the lingering heaviness of the night's struggles. In the dim glow of Takoda's room, Riichi lay motionless on her bed, his shallow breaths barely perceptible. Takoda stood over him, her usual composure faltering as her eyes traced the bruises and torn skin marring his body. Eileen's parting reminder echoed in her mind, sharp and unyielding: *Take care of him.*

Her fingers hovered just above his injuries, trembling. Seeing him like this fractured a part of her deep inside, yet she shoved the ache aside. *Keep it together, Takoda. He needs you.*

"Come on, Riichi," she whispered, gripping his hand tighter. "You're not leaving us." The plea steadied her, forming a fragile shield against the fear clawing at her resolve.

The soft shuffle of footsteps behind her signaled Rain's arrival. She entered with determined purpose, carrying the supplies they'd need. Rain's eyes flicked to Takoda, her calm presence steadying the charged atmosphere in the room. "You've done everything possible," she said firmly, pulling Takoda back to the present.

Rain moved with precise care, her actions deliberate and assured. Together, they fell into a rhythm, the silence between them broken only by the muted sounds of their work. Rain's focus stayed locked on her tasks, while Takoda's attention never wavered from Riichi, her tenacity dragging her forward, inch by inch.

After a time, Rain rested a hand on Takoda's shoulder. "Take a moment. Step outside."

"No." Takoda shook her head sharply. "I'm not leaving him." The quiet intensity of her refusal brooked no argument. Rain inclined her head and stayed beside her, her hand returning to Takoda's arm now and then—a silent assurance that she wasn't alone.

The minutes stretched on, shadows shifting like restless sentinels across the walls. The air felt taut, balanced on the edge of hope and despair. Riichi's breathing remained faint yet even, his battered face resolute despite its delicate resilience.

The distant rumble of engines broke through the tense silence. Rain's hand hovered briefly on Takoda's shoulder before she stepped back. "They're back. I'll go meet them."

Takoda gave a slight nod, her attention fixed on Riichi. Rain slipped from the room without a sound, leaving Takoda at his side. Whether together or apart, their shared determination held firm, waiting for him to find his way back.

The mansion's vibrant energy had dimmed, replaced by a solemn tranquility that settled in the air after the battle. Fallen members moved softly through the space, exchanging nods and clasping shoulders—each gesture an unspoken acknowledgment of shared survival. As Rowan stepped inside, his eyes instinctively sought Rain's. The stiffness in his shoulders eased, giving way to a fleeting sense of relief.

Low murmurs rippled through the group, heavy with concern for Riichi. Rain stepped forward, her composure steady, though her hands clasped together as if preparing herself. "Riichi's injuries are serious, but he's stable. Takoda and I stopped the bleeding, and he's resting now. We'll make sure he has everything he needs."

Her statement settled over the room, offering reassurance, though unease continued to flicker in their eyes. Rowan approached her and rested a hand on her shoulder, his gratitude clear in the gesture. "You've done everything you can. Riichi is lucky to have you and Takoda looking after him."

Aislinn joined them, her faint smile carrying a reassuring steadiness. "He'll recover. And so will we." Her remark held an understated strength, a reminder of what they had endured together that lightened the strain pressing down on Rain's mind.

Rowan let his gaze drift across the room, taking in the fatigue etched into every face. Turning back to Rain, his voice softened. "You're the heart of this group. Check in with everyone—it'll help pull them together."

Rain's lips curved in a small, tired smile as she gave a faint nod. "You're right. We all need that." She took a slow, thoughtful breath and began moving through the room, stopping briefly with each person. A touch on a shoulder, a shared smile, a few hushed exchanges—every interaction felt intentional, threading the group back together.

Gradually, the Fallen gravitated toward the main room, their footsteps light against the worn floorboards. Clusters formed naturally, drawn together by shared camaraderie. Low laughter rose here and there, genuine yet subdued, mingling with soft conversations. Some sat in reflective silence, their eyes distant, while others spoke in murmurs, piecing together fragments of the night. The mansion seemed to exhale, its calm no longer heavy with sorrow but contemplative, as if holding their shared resilience.

Aislinn hung back near the edge of the room, her arms loosely crossed. She observed how they leaned into one another—each connection an anchor, a quiet reminder of the trust they had forged. Her focus eventually found Rowan across the room, standing among a small group. While he didn't speak, his presence radiated calm, a subtle strength that steadied those around him. When he looked up and caught her eye, a brief smile passed between them. For the first time that night, the heaviness in her chest began to lift. This is where I'm meant to be, she reflected, the certainty settling within her as an unshakable truth.

Rain moved to the center of the room, her steps measured as she scanned the gathered faces. When she spoke, her statement rose above the soft hum with warm resolve. "We're all here," she said. "And together, we'll be ready for whatever comes."

The words resonated, drawing nods and murmurs of agreement. The stiffness in their postures altered, replaced by a steady determination that seemed to knit them closer. While the scars of the night lingered like shadows, the space felt lighter, as though hope had begun to take root.

In the entrance hall, muted conversations blended with the soft scrape of boots and occasional echoes of weary laughter. The Fallen drifted through in loose groups, exchanging nods and brief touches that conveyed more than words could. Aislinn stayed close to Rowan, his calm company strengthening her as the room's tension unraveled bit by bit. Her eyes moved across the scene, drawn to the subtle gestures—hands clasped in comfort, fleeting smiles exchanged in silence. With every small act of connection, the strain of the night seemed to ease, leaving behind a fragile but growing sense of relief.

She turned to Rowan, ready to ask his perspective on the night's events, when Eileen approached with measured steps. "Aislinn," Eileen said, her calm demeanor threaded with urgency. "Could we speak in private?"

Aislinn glanced at Rowan, catching the slight nod he gave—a silent reassurance. Decisively, she followed Eileen down the dim hallway. The soft murmur of voices from the main room faded behind them, replaced by a silence that pressed heavily on her senses. Each step seemed to carry unspoken gravity, the air taut with uncertainty that constricted Aislinn's chest.

At the end of the corridor, Eileen opened the door to her office and gestured for Aislinn to enter. The warm glow of the room's golden light softened the harsh edges of the night's chaos, casting the space in a sense of sanctuary. Aislinn eased into the chair opposite her mother, drawn by the serenity Eileen radiated. There was a complexity layered in her gaze—depths that hinted at truths waiting to surface.

Eileen broke the silence, her delivery measured and precise. "Tonight, you witnessed powers few ever see," she began, her phrasing careful. "It wasn't something I planned to reveal, but sometimes circumstances leave no room for hesitation. I imagine it must have been overwhelming."

Aislinn met her mother's steady eyes, feeling questions swirl within her, though she kept them contained. For the first time, she saw her mother's role in a way she hadn't fully grasped before—a responsibility that stretched far beyond what she had imagined. The realization stirred a profound sensation deep within her, a silent reckoning.

Leaning forward, Aislinn allowed her urgency to surface. "I need to understand," she said, her voice firm. "These abilities... they're far beyond what I imagined. What else haven't you told me?"

Eileen reached across the desk, her hand resting lightly over Aislinn's. The touch carried a grounding reassurance, as if tethering Aislinn to an eternal force. "You deserve answers," she said, her words clear yet resolute. "But this must stay between us. The others don't need to bear this."

Aislinn nodded, the trust in her mother's statement settling over her like a mantle, keeping her in the moment. Eileen drew a confident breath before continuing. "What you witnessed tonight is not merely a skill I've refined. These abilities were entrusted to me by a force far beyond anything we can fully comprehend. They carry a responsibility—a promise to use them only when there is no other choice."

As her mother spoke, Aislinn listened intently, absorbing the significance of what she was hearing. These powers were not simple tools; they were bound by sacred rules, their use governed by a purpose she was only beginning to grasp.

"There are boundaries I must honor," Eileen continued, her gaze unwavering. "Though I lead the Fallen, I answer to someone far greater. His wisdom and authority surpass anything I could ever hope to understand. These powers are not mine to claim—they are granted, but only under strict conditions. Should they ever be misused, they will be taken back."

The revelation settled deeply within Aislinn, sparking a sharper curiosity she couldn't ignore. "Who is this force?" she asked, her voice calm but tinged with urgency. "The one you answer to?"

Eileen's expression softened, a flicker of reverence crossing her features. "In time, you may come to know Him," she said, her tone carrying the weight of a deeply personal truth. "But for now, understand this: He acts with purpose, intervening only when necessary. I serve His will, and it is a path that demands careful choices."

Her gaze softened further, and for a second, Aislinn glimpsed a vulnerability beneath her mother's composed strength. "These powers," Eileen said quietly, "come at a cost. Every time I use them—whether bending time or moving through space—it demands something in return. It takes a part of me."

Aislinn's muscles in her jaw flexed, her mother's statement striking deeper than she expected. "A part of you?" she asked, the concern in her question unmistakable. "What does it take, exactly?"

Eileen's gaze drifted, her reply quieter now. "Pieces that aren't easily named—strength, time, will. It's not always the same, but every use leaves a part of me behind. These abilities are not without their price—it's a truth I confront every day."

The room seemed to pause, the air charged with layered truths. Aislinn's jaw clenched as she absorbed the enormity of her mother's sacrifice. "You've carried this burden," she said, her drive firm. "How long? How long have you been paying this price?"

Eileen's focus sharpened, her calm resolve steadfast. "Long enough to understand the gravity of every choice," she replied. "But this isn't just about me, Aislinn. There is a spark within you, too." Her gaze shifted, conviction threading through her words. "I sensed it tonight—your potential is far greater than you realize. These powers are not mine alone to bear. But understand this: they will demand much from you."

Aislinn shook her head, the events of the night cascading through her mind. "If this is what it takes, how can I be ready for that? How can I make choices like the ones you've had to make?"

Eileen leaned forward, her expression firm. "You will be ready because you won't face it alone. I'll guide you. These abilities must be embraced gradually, with care. Power can be a burden, but I will help you carry it."

Aislinn's hands tightened in her lap, her mind racing, but she forced herself to meet Eileen's eyes. "I want to understand," she said. "I don't want to be blind to this anymore. If there's something in me, I need to know what it means."

Eileen's gaze softened, though her tone remained balanced. "You'll learn, step by step. But what you've seen tonight must stay between us. The others wouldn't understand, and some truths must remain protected. Silence isn't about fear—it's about wisdom. This secret is as much a shield as it is a burden."

The trust in her mother's statement settled over Aislinn, binding her to the responsibility of the truth. "I won't say anything," she promised. "Not to Rain, not to Takoda—no one. I understand why this has to stay between us."

Eileen leaned closer, her whisper carrying a quiet intensity. "I will shield you from what I can and teach you to carry the rest," she said. "My greatest purpose has always been to protect you."

Emotion swelled in Aislinn's chest, raw and undeniable. "I see that now," she said, her breath trembling slightly. "But I don't want you to carry all of this alone. You've already given so much." Her resolve firmed, conviction threading through her statement. "Whatever comes next, I'll be ready. Just promise me you'll let me help."

A faint smile touched Eileen's lips, though her expression remained serious. "There are mysteries we are not meant to solve—only to trust. One day, you may understand. Until then, know this: you are held by a force far greater than my power, my leadership, or even my love. That is where my strength comes from."

As her mother's statement settled over her, Aislinn felt a profound peacefulness take hold. The night's revelations had unveiled forces far beyond her comprehension, but they had also illuminated the depth of Eileen's sacrifices. Rising from her seat, she carried with her a newfound sense of purpose and responsibility, rooted in the enduring strength of her mother's love and her own growing affection.

***

As Aislinn followed Eileen down the hallway, Rowan veered in the opposite direction, heading toward Riichi's room. The low murmur of conversation from the main room faded with each step, replaced by the faint creak of the old floorboards beneath his boots. When he reached the door, he paused, hand resting briefly on the frame before stepping inside.

The room was dimly lit, the faint scent of salves lingering in the air. Riichi lay unmoving on the bed, his chest rising and falling in a sturdy rhythm, his face marked by the night's battle—bruises, cuts, and a stillness far removed from his usual energy. Takoda sat beside him, her chair pulled close, one hand resting on the edge of the mattress. Her focus stayed fixed on Riichi, her composure solid but shadowed with exhaustion.

She looked up as Rowan approached, straightening slightly. "He's stable," she said softly. "The bleeding's stopped, and his breathing is even."

Rowan nodded, stepping closer and glancing at Riichi. Relief flickered through him at seeing his closest friend alive, even in this state. "Thank you," he said sincerely, his voice low. "For staying with him, for everything you've done. It means a lot."

Takoda shook her head, brushing the gratitude aside. "I just did what anyone would've done."

"Not everyone would have stayed by his side," Rowan replied, his tone light but pointed. "That's not nothing, Takoda."

She looked away, her fingers grazing the edge of the mattress. "It's... I just didn't want him to be alone," she murmured.

Rowan studied her for a brief span, noticing the way she sat just close enough to suggest concern, without revealing anything deeper. "You know," he said casually, "Riichi's stubborn as hell. He'd probably complain about being fussed over when he wakes up, but..." He glanced back at Riichi's face, a faint smile tugging at his lips. "I think even he'd appreciate you being here. Even if he doesn't say it."

Takoda let out a soft laugh, though she quickly stifled it. "He'll definitely complain," she said, her voice lighter. "He doesn't strike me as the type to take being looked after very well."

"You're not wrong," Rowan said with a chuckle. "That doesn't mean he doesn't notice when someone cares enough to stick around."

Takoda glanced at Rowan, uncertainty crossing her face. "I'm just doing what I can," she said quietly.

"And that's enough," Rowan said, his tone calm and sincere. He placed a hand on her shoulder briefly, a small gesture of reassurance. "If he gives you grief, let me know—I'll remind him he owes you."

Her lips quirked into the faintest smile, though her attention stayed on Riichi. "Thanks, Rowan."

With one last look at Riichi, Rowan turned to leave, pausing at the door. "You're good for him, Takoda," he said, his conviction evident, carrying a depth that stayed with her. "Whether he realizes it or not."

He didn't wait for a response, stepping out into the hallway and letting the door close quietly behind him. Relief settled over him as he walked back toward the main room. Knowing Takoda was there with Riichi eased some of the stress he'd carried since the battle. If anyone could get through to him, Rowan was sure it was her.

***

As Aislinn closed the door to her mother's office, the gravity of their conversation settled heavily within her. Pausing in the dim hallway, she drew a steadying breath, her thoughts turning to Rain. After everything they'd endured—the battle, Riichi's injuries—she knew her friend could use someone to check in, even if only for a few minutes of reassurance.

She found Rain in the sitting room, where several Fallen remained in subdued conversations, their murmurs low yet tinged with relief. Rain stood near the room's edge, her posture seemingly at ease, though the distant look in her eyes betrayed the thoughts persisting to tangle her mind in the night's events.

Aislinn approached with a faint smile. "Rain," she said gently. "I just wanted to check in. It's been a hard night for all of us."

Rain's features softened, a tired smile brushing her lips. "Hasn't it for everyone?" she replied, her voice quiet with exhaustion. She exhaled slowly, her shoulders loosening slightly. "I keep telling myself it's over, that we made it through. But Riichi..." Her words trailed off, worry briefly clouding her face.

Aislinn nodded, her tone warm yet concerned. "Takoda hasn't left his side since they brought him in. I'm on my way to check on her now. Have you noticed how she's holding up?"

Rain's brow furrowed, her focus sharpening. "She's steady, but you can see the strain. She hasn't taken a break—not even for a second."

Aislinn's expression held a mix of admiration and concern evident. "She's always been that way—completely unwavering. I'll remind her to take a minute for herself. Even Takoda needs to rest."

After a brief pause, Aislinn's behavior changed, a serious edge creeping into her request. "Rain, about my mother... I need you to keep tonight between us. What she did—everything you remember—is not what Eileen wants shared."

Rain frowned slightly, confusion flickering in her face. "What are you talking about? She drove Riichi back here, and we helped her get him out of the car. Why would that need to stay quiet?"

Aislinn blinked, the realization hitting her like a jolt. *She doesn't even have a driver's license.* "Exactly that," she said quickly, keeping her tone light but firm. "Eileen doesn't drive—she doesn't have a license. If anyone asks, it could lead to awkward questions, and she'd rather avoid the attention."

Rain's countenance eased slightly, though her brow remained faintly knit. "I guess that makes sense," she said slowly. "Still, it's strange..."

"It is," Aislinn agreed softly, steering the conversation toward reassurance. "But that's why it's better to keep it quiet. Let's focus on helping everyone get through the next few days."

"Alright," Rain agreed. "If she wants to keep it a secret, I'm not going to argue."

The turmoil in Aislinn's head eased as relief began to settle over her. "Thank you, Rain. I knew I could count on you." Her lips curved into a small smile. "And maybe take a moment for yourself. A walk in the courtyard might help clear your head—it's been a long night."

Rain considered her words, a hint of gratitude relaxing her muscles. "You're right. Some fresh air might help." She nodded, offering a faint smile. Aislinn gave her shoulder a light squeeze, a small gesture of reassurance.

As Rain made her way toward the courtyard, Aislinn watched her go, a faint calm taking root. The resilience of her friends was a reminder of the strength they had built together—a bond shaped by trials and fortified through trust. After a final glance around the room, Aislinn turned toward Takoda's room, her determination firm as she prepared to offer her friend the support she needed to carry on.

***

The courtyard lay bathed in the silvery glow of moonlight, shadows stretching long across the stone path. Elder stood near the ivy-covered wall, his posture relaxed, though his gaze seemed far away, as if sorting through fragmented memories of the night's battle. Rain spotted him from across the courtyard, her steps light as she approached, noting the faint weariness clinging to his otherwise composed demeanor.

She stopped a few paces away, crossing her arms with a playful smile. "Hey, Nik. Glad to see you're still in one piece," she said, her attitude breezy, as though the brutality of the night had already been left behind.

Elder looked up, his distant focus moving to her. He nodded once, the faintest curve of a smile touching his lips. "Thanks," he replied, his words carrying a thread of exhaustion. For him, that single word conveyed more than enough.

Rain studied him briefly, her playful behavior softening as she caught the unspoken strain in his stance. He shifted slightly, letting his hands fall to his sides as his attention drifted across the moonlit garden. The silence between them was unhurried, a shared pause in the wake of chaos. Then, to her surprise, Elder turned back to her, his manner unusually direct. "I think I'd like to see that game room you mentioned. Right now, it sounds like exactly what I need."

Her eyebrows lifted, a grin spreading across her face. "Nik wants to relax? Someone write this down—we've got a historic moment here." She laughed, her voice light and teasing, as if nudging him further from his usual stoicism. "Careful, or I might start thinking you're finally showing your age—or maybe a few centuries younger."

A faint spark lit his eyes, and while he didn't laugh, his features softened—a rare break in his usual reserve. "Lead the way," he said, his tone calm, carrying a subtle note of amusement.

Rain's grin widened, and she motioned him forward with a playful wave. "Come on, then. Let's see if I can take you down a notch or two." She turned and began walking toward the mansion, Elder falling into step beside her.

The quiet between them wasn't strained or expectant, but easy—a reprieve from the night's lingering tension.

Crossing the threshold into the house, distant murmurs replaced the serenity of the courtyard. The creak of the wooden floorboards underfoot and the inviting atmosphere of the mansion contrasted with the cool air outside. Rain led the way down the hallway toward the game room, her pace casual yet purposeful.

"Didn't think you'd actually take me up on this," she said with a teasing lilt as they neared the door. "But I'll admit, it's nice to see you unwind a little."

Elder shrugged, the corners of his lips lifting slightly. "Even I can appreciate a good distraction," he replied, his face carrying a rare lightness. The response caught her off guard, and for an instant, she simply smiled, savoring the unexpected ease of his company.

Reaching the game room, Rain opened the door with a small flourish, throwing him a mischievous look over her shoulder. "Prepare to lose," she said, her words brimming with mock confidence.

Elder's behavior changed again, that rare, almost-hidden smile reappearing as he followed her inside. Together, they stepped into the room, leaving behind the night's heaviness, finding a momentary escape in the simplicity of shared companionship.

***

The stillness of the room enveloped Aislinn as she stepped inside, her footsteps soft against the worn floorboards. Takoda sat beside Riichi, her hand resting lightly near his, her shoulders drawn tight under the strain of the night. Her focus stayed on his face, though a trace of uncertainty in her gaze hinted at emotions she hadn't yet untangled.

Aislinn approached carefully, sensing the exhaustion etched into her friend's posture. Placing a gentle hand on Takoda's shoulder, she spoke in a low voice. "You've stayed by his side through everything, Takoda," she murmured, her words filled with reassurance. "Riichi's strong. If anyone can fight through this, it's him."

Takoda's eyes shifted toward her, a quiet emotion flickering in her face. After a long, measured breath, she spoke, hesitant and raw. "I... I don't even know why I'm here, Aislinn," she admitted, her voice trembling slightly. "I just... feel like I need to be, and I can't explain it."

Aislinn studied her friend in silence, sensing the vulnerability that echoed a feeling she recognized. Memories stirred—times when she, too, had felt an unexplainable pull toward Rowan, a connection she hadn't fully understood at first. The idea surfaced briefly, but she set it aside. This wasn't the time to push or speculate. Instead, she focused on offering the solid reassurance Takoda needed.

Takoda turned back to Riichi, the worry etched in the lines of her forehead softening as she watched him. Aislinn's eyes narrowed with determination. She knelt beside Takoda, resting her hand lightly over her friend's. "Takoda," she said gently, her tone calm and steady, "I can try something... something that might help."

Takoda's brows furrowed, confusion mingling with cautious hope as she gave a small nod. Aislinn didn't wait for further permission. She leaned forward, placing her hands over Riichi's injuries. Takoda's breath caught as a faint, warm glow began to spread from Aislinn's hands, bathing Riichi in a soft blue light.

Realization washed over Takoda like a wave—Aislinn was healing him. Awe filled her as she watched, her breath caught between disbelief and fragile hope. The radiance swept gracefully over Riichi's battered body, mending bruises and torn skin with an otherworldly energy that exuded a profound presence.

When Aislinn finally withdrew her hands, a subtle change filled the room. Riichi's breathing had grown steadier, his features easing, as though he had found a minute of peace even in unconsciousness. Though still motionless, the faint improvement was enough to kindle hope between them.

Takoda spoke, her wonder evident. "Thank you, Aislinn," she whispered, emotion clear in her demeanor. "I... I didn't know you could do that." Each syllable carried the significance of witnessing a sacred event, her awe unmistakable.

Aislinn met her gaze with a small, reassuring smile. She reached for Takoda's hand and gave it a gentle squeeze. "I'm just glad I could help," she said, her words warm and steady.

For a heartbeat, they sat together in silence, the air in the room feeling lighter now. Takoda let out a soft sigh, her voice barely above a whisper. "I don't even know what I'm feeling," she admitted, her eyes drifting back to Riichi. "But I know I don't want to lose him. He's been there through everything, somehow. Even when I wasn't looking."

Aislinn's grip on her hand tightened slightly, her tone carrying quiet assurance. "We're all with you in this, Takoda," she said. "You're not alone, and Riichi knows how much he matters to you. He'll come back—I believe that."

Takoda leaned back slightly, her shoulders loosening as a small, grateful smile curved her lips. "Thank you, Aislinn. For being here… and for him."

Aislinn returned the smile, the warmth of their shared bond settling over her. Together, they kept their vigil, the atmosphere of the room no longer heavy but filled with calm resolve. As they sat side by side, their companionship carried them, a silent promise shared between friends.

***

Rowan sat alone in a secluded part of the mansion, his mind tangled in the night's events, questions haunting like unshakable shadows. The quietness around him felt oppressive, pressing inward as he replayed the choices and battles they'd faced. The last he'd seen of Aislinn, she had gone to speak with Eileen, yet the thought of her lingered, settling him even as uncertainty gnawed at him.

After a minute, he pulled out his phone, the intensity of the night urging him to reach out to the one person who could bring some lightness back into the mansion. He sent a text to Ariel: *Mission's over, and everyone's safe. Close the bar early tonight and come over—the others could use your bubbliness right about now.*

As the message delivered, a faint relief seeped into his chest. Ariel had a way of lifting spirits, and he knew her energy would be a welcome distraction after everything. Just as he pocketed his phone, the soft tread of footsteps drew his attention. Looking up, he saw Eileen step into the room, her face calm yet carrying a gravity that immediately captured his focus.

She paused, closing the door behind her with deliberate care, before turning to face him. Rowan straightened instinctively, his gaze sharpening as concern rippled through him. "Aislinn?" he asked, his words edged with restrained worry. "Where is she?"

"She's fine," Eileen assured him, her delivery measured, touched with warmth. "She's checking on Rain and Takoda. She'll join you again soon."

Rowan exhaled slowly, relief easing the tension in his shoulders, though he didn't miss the intensity still visible in Eileen's eyes. It was clear she hadn't come to offer reassurance alone. She crossed the room and settled into a chair across from him, her movements composed, her presence commanding his full attention, as though the very air shifted to acknowledge her authority.

When she spoke, her message carried both gentleness and significance. "Rowan," she began, "it's time for you to make a choice."

Her statement landed heavily, stirring a knot of apprehension in his stomach. He met her gaze, questions swirling, yet he remained silent, sensing the weight of what she was about to say.

"There are two paths before you," she continued, her tone cautious yet compassionate. "You can remain as you are—a Fallen, unbound—and allow Aislinn to live free from the supernatural dangers that surround us."

The meaning behind her statement struck him with force, the depth of the decision becoming painfully clear. He listened as she pressed on.

"Or," she said, her voice softening, "you can choose to become her Soulmate. This bond would tie your lives together completely and irreversibly. If one of you falls, so does the other. It means sharing the dangers we face—our enemies, the risks, and the uncertainty—but it also means sharing a connection that transcends everything else."

Each word cut through him, amplifying the internal conflict already brewing. He hadn't anticipated how deeply this choice would challenge him, or the implications it carried for both of them. His instinct to protect Aislinn clashed with the yearning to fully embrace the bond they had been building.

"What if I'm only bringing her into a life she's not meant for?" he murmured, his question barely audible. The question wasn't for Eileen as much as it was for himself. Guilt and doubt clung to the edges of his tone, his desire to shield Aislinn warring with the pull of his heart.

Eileen's expression eased, her statement carrying an undeniable determination. "This choice isn't only about you, Rowan," she said with care. "It's about Aislinn—and what you believe is best for her. Think of the life she could have, free from the dangers we face."

He looked away, her words carving through his turmoil. The image of Aislinn living in peace, untouched by the threats he had grown accustomed to, was a vision he couldn't easily dismiss. Yet before it could settle fully, Eileen continued, her voice calm but resolute, as though she spoke with the wisdom of something far beyond this time.

"But also consider this," she said. "Aislinn has proven her strength over and over. She has chosen to stand by you, even when she didn't have to. Sometimes love isn't about shielding someone from every risk—it's about trusting them to decide for themselves. It's about standing together, no matter the uncertainty."

Her words stirred emotions deep within him, pulling at memories of Aislinn's resilience and the quiet courage she carried. He thought of her emerging powers, the steadfast loyalty she showed through every challenge, and the way she stayed—not out of obligation, but out of unwavering choice. A realization began to take hold: perhaps Aislinn was already bound to this life in ways neither of them had fully acknowledged.

A flicker of resolve began to form in his chest. Rowan raised his eyes, his tone steady as he spoke. "I know she deserves peace," he said softly, "but I also know I can't imagine a life without her."

Eileen's attitude shifted, a faint smile touching her lips as she saw the clarity in his steadfastness. "Whatever you decide," she said gently, "let it come from love. Aislinn's happiness and safety matter most. Trust yourself to make the choice she'd want."

Her statement hovered in the space between them, resonating with profound wisdom, as if imbued with a sacred truth only she could carry. Rising, she gave him a final, encouraging nod before leaving the room, her steps fading into the mansion's stillness.

Left alone, Rowan remained seated, Eileen's guidance looping through his mind as doubt and longing twisted within him. The enormity of the decision pressed down, each path before him marked by sacrifice. Aislinn's strength, her devotion, and the bond they shared pulled at his heart, yet so did the instinct to shield her from the dangers he faced daily.

Running a hand through his hair, Rowan let his gaze fall to the floor, the conflict churning inside him. Could he truly bring her into a life so fraught with risk, knowing her safety would be forever tied to his? And yet, the thought of stepping away from the connection they had built felt just as impossible.

In the silence that followed, no answer came—only the awareness of the choice before him. Love, he realized, wasn't just about shielding someone; it was trust, vulnerability, and the willingness to share both burdens and joy. Even knowing this, clarity remained elusive.

For now, all he could do was sit with the enormity of the decision, the echo of Eileen's wisdom and the memory of Aislinn's steadfast presence balancing him as he wrestled with the question that would shape both their lives.

***

Rowan moved to the courtyard after his conversation with Eileen, the crisp night air brushing against his face as he sought a reprieve from the tangle of his emotions. The chill bit into him just enough to ground him, while the air around him seemed to echo the turmoil within. He closed his eyes for a second, letting the calm settle over him, hoping for some clarity.

The sound of familiar footsteps broke through his solitude. "You look like you've been through the wringer, Rowan," Ariel said, her teasing lilt cutting through the silence. A grin tugged at her lips as she stopped in front of him. "Mind if I sit?"

He looked up, her presence already beginning to loosen some of the tension in his chest. A faint smile softened his features. "Go ahead," he said, gesturing to the spot beside him. He'd texted her earlier, knowing the spark of life she brought could lighten even a night like this.

Ariel dropped onto the bench beside him, her eyes sweeping the courtyard with casual interest. "So… this is the Fallen mansion," she remarked with a wry smile. "Not bad. Though, I'll admit, closing up Donnelly's early for a late-night call wasn't exactly on my to-do list."

Rowan smirked, her easy attitude cutting through the heaviness clouding his mind. "Not exactly a typical night for me either," he replied, leaning back slightly. "Figured we could all use some of your energy tonight."

She grinned, nudging his shoulder playfully. "I've been telling you for years, this place needs more of me. Glad you're finally catching on." Her grin softened after a beat, her gaze searching his face. "Seriously, though—are you okay?"

Rowan hesitated, the question slipping past the guard he'd been holding. "It's been… a lot," he admitted, his tone carrying the weight of his doubts. "Aislinn's changed everything. I never thought I'd let anyone in again, let alone become Soulbound. It's overwhelming. And I'm still not sure I can give her the life she deserves."

Ariel studied him, the humor fading from her face as her reply turned thoughtful. "You care about her," she said gently. "That much is obvious. But you're carrying around all this guilt like it's some kind of badge of honor. Maybe it's time to let some of that go."

Her words struck a chord, and Rowan exhaled slowly, his gaze lifting to the stars above. "I've spent so long trying to protect myself from this—feeling this way again," he said, his voice quieter now. "But with Aislinn, it's different. She makes me want to be better. She's worth every risk, every uncertainty. I just don't know if bringing her into this life is fair to her."

Ariel leaned back, her demeanor warm yet firm. "Let me ask you something—do you really think she's not already in it? Aislinn's tougher than you give her credit for, Rowan. She's not standing beside you because she has to. She's there because she chooses to be."

Rowan let her words linger, memories of Aislinn's quiet strength threading through his mind. "She is incredible," he admitted softly. "And I know she's capable of more than I ever thought possible. But asking her to live this life—tied to the same risks and dangers—it feels like too much."

Ariel tilted her head, a knowing smile curving her lips. "You're not asking her. You're giving her the choice to share it with you. That's a big difference."

Her statement settled over him with quiet force, and Rowan felt some of the turmoil within him begin to shift. "I never thought I'd feel this way again," he said, his voice steady. "But Aislinn... she's worth it. She's worth everything."

Ariel's grin returned, bright and mischievous but tempered by warmth. "She's lucky to have you, Rowan. And you're lucky to have her. That's not a bad deal."

Rowan smiled, the weight on his shoulders lifting just a little. "Thanks, Ariel."

She stood, stretching dramatically. "Alright, enough with the serious stuff. You've got some serious 'happily-ever-after' energy going on, and I'm here for it." She shot him a playful look. "Next time, I'm bringing popcorn for the drama."

Rowan chuckled, shaking his head. "I'll hold you to that."

She gave him one last wink before strolling off, her footsteps light as she disappeared back inside the mansion. Her presence remained like a spark of warmth, a reminder of the support and camaraderie he had beyond the chaos.

Left alone, Rowan looked out over the courtyard, the night's stillness now less oppressive. Ariel's words blended with Eileen's earlier guidance, weaving a clearer perspective through the haze of his emotions. He could still feel the pull of his instincts warring within him, the battle between love and protection unresolved. Yet, for the first time, a quieter truth began to emerge: Aislinn wasn't someone to be sheltered from the world—they were meant to face it together.

As the night deepened, Rowan remained in calm reflection, the decision ahead still daunting but no longer insurmountable. Amid the uncertainty, one constant anchored him: his love for Aislinn, a force powerful enough to guide him toward whatever came next.

T he courtyard lay shrouded in stillness, the late evening air carrying a distant chill as the mansion's shadow stretched over the stone path. By the garden wall, Rowan stood motionless, his silhouette caught in the interplay of dim light and encroaching darkness. Aislinn spotted him, her steps careful, the hush of her approach almost imperceptible.

"Rowan?" she murmured, her voice laced with both question and invitation.

He turned toward her, his countenance flashing between apprehension and resolve, and nodded without speaking. Together, they slipped into motion, their paths aligning as they wove through the mansion's muted halls. The faint echo of their footsteps faded as Rowan led her to the hidden door. With practiced ease, he pressed the latch, and the door surrendered with a quiet creak, revealing the secret room that had become their sanctuary.

Inside, the silence deepened, wrapping around them like a fragile cocoon. The soft click of the door's closure seemed to seal the world away. Here, in this secluded refuge, the burdens they carried felt momentarily suspended. Aislinn studied him closely as they settled into the room, noting the subtle signs of unrest—the flex of his fingers before they stilled on his knees, the muffled sigh that slipped past his lips, almost too muted to catch.

Rowan inhaled deeply, steadying himself before lifting his eyes to meet hers. In his expression, a raw honesty reflected the magnitude of a decision that had taken root in his mind.

"Aislinn, Eileen left me with a choice." His tone carried a solemn gravity, as though speaking too loudly might fracture the delicate calm. "It's not just about us... it's about what I could end up pulling you into."

Her unwavering attention stayed on him, her presence a quiet assurance as he continued.

"I can stay as I am—one of the Fallen—and keep the distance between us. That way, you'd have a chance to live free of this chaos, far from the shadows we fight against." He paused, his throat working as he forced the words out. "Or I can... become your Soulmate. But that bond would change everything. It would tie us together in a way that... it would bring all the risks to you, too."

He lowered his focus to his hands, his demeanor shifting as if the admission took a piece of him. "I just want you to be safe, Aislinn. You deserve that. A life free of the Golden Dawn, without eternal battles... just peace."

The words hung between them, unsaid truths threading through the silence. Aislinn's heart ached as she read the vulnerability etched into his every movement, the unguarded conflict in his countenance when he looked at her again. He was offering her freedom, even though it was the last thing he wanted.

Her facade steadied, a spark of calm determination rising in her features. She let the quiet hold for a breath longer before shaking her head, a gentle but resolute smile forming on her lips.

"Rowan," she said, her tone carrying a firm resolve that left no room for doubt, "you're my normal now. Whatever this world has in store, I don't want a life that doesn't have you in it."

Reaching out, she took his hand, her fingers threading through his with an unyielding confidence. Her touch was an anchor, settling him even as his doubts pressed forward. "The risks are worth it if it means I get to stay by your side."

Her words lingered between them, unwavering in their certainty. Rowan's features softened, a fragile hope coming to life in his features, though uncertainty still clung to the edges, tethering him to his fears.

"I don't want safety," Aislinn continued, her voice low but fierce, the quiet power of her conviction unshaken. "Not if it means living without you. You're the life I choose, Rowan. You. Nothing in this world could ever change that."

She squeezed his hand, letting her determination flow through the connection, and in that instant, Rowan faltered. The importance of her words struck a chord deep within him, stirring both longing and hesitation.

"Loving you... it means wanting to protect you from everything, even from me," he murmured, his response barely carried. "But I know," he added, meeting her gaze with a rawness that stripped away his defenses, "that keeping you away would be a different kind of hurt. One I don't think either of us would recover from."

Aislinn reached up, her hand brushing along his cheek with quiet care. "Then don't keep me away," she said softly, her voice calm but unwavering. "You've seen the worst the world can throw at us, and I know you're afraid of what it might do to me. But, this isn't just your world anymore. It's ours. And I'm ready for whatever that means."

He closed his eyes briefly, her words settling into him like a balm against his doubt. The conflict within him—the desire to shield her clashing against the love that bound them—was almost tangible, but her unwavering resolve seemed to steady him.

The room seemed to shift, its atmosphere no longer fragile but imbued with an almost sacred weight. Their connection held, the space between them charged with the unspoken promise of what lay ahead. United, they were a force to be reckoned with, bound by love and a choice made with confidence.

"I can't imagine a life without you," Rowan finally admitted, his tone rough, heavy with the emotions he could no longer suppress. "Every part of me wants to keep you safe... but more than that, I want to be with you. Fully, completely with you."

Aislinn's fingers tightened around his, her touch grounding him as a gentle smile eased across her features. "Then let's be together, no matter what. I'm ready for it, Rowan. Whatever risks, whatever challenges—none of it matters as long as we're side by side."

Her steadfast faith washed over him, dissolving the last traces of his hesitation. He met her eyes, determination building, their decision becoming undeniable and unshakable. "Then we'll confront it all," he murmured, conviction fierce in his words. "If being Soulbound is the way to be with you, then that's what I want. It's always been what I want."

Aislinn's smile deepened, a warmth in her eyes that seemed to envelop him, offering solace and strength. She leaned closer, her forehead resting gently against his, her words a quiet vow. "We're unstoppable as one, Rowan. I know it. I believe it with everything I am."

The room, once steeped in uncertainty, now held an almost sacred quietness, charged with the magnitude of their shared decision. Aislinn let her fingers trail lightly along his jaw, the touch tender yet resolute. In his expression, she saw not only love but the release of fear—a willingness to embrace the risks and the unknown, knowing they would face them as one.

In an instant, she closed the distance between them, her lips finding his in a kiss that spoke every implied commitment, every truth words could never hold. It was reverent, unhurried —their love unfolding in the silent exchange. Rowan's arms wrapped around her, drawing her closer, as though she were the only anchor in the storm of his world. Their breaths mingled in the warmth of the space between them, each instant steeped in profound devotion.

Rowan's lips traveled along the line of her neck, lingering with a tenderness that etched this moment into his soul. Aislinn's hands rested on his shoulders, steadying him, binding them both as they fell into a rhythm that felt timeless, as if this decision, this intimacy, had always been destined.

Each kiss, each touch, drew them nearer, the unhurried intensity of their embrace speaking volumes. Their love flourished in the sanctuary of the room, shielded from the chaos beyond its walls. As one, they allowed themselves to savor it, letting the fragility of the exchange dissolve into a connection eternal and profound.

Rowan's hands traced the curve of her back, his touch reverent, as though committing to memory every part of her against him. Aislinn responded in kind, her movements imbued with the same deliberate care. Time seemed to blur, and they lost themselves in the quiet intimacy, the world outside slipping further away.

When at last they lay entwined, wrapped in the warmth of one another, a calmness settled over them—a peace that transcended the dangers and uncertainties ahead. The risks remained, but they no longer felt insurmountable. Together, they were whole.

After a while, Aislinn lifted her eyes to his, a tender smile curving her lips, her words a gentle whisper. "We're ready," she said, her statement imbued with certainty and love.

Rowan's fingers brushed along the curve of her face, tarrying as he returned her smile. His eyes brimmed with devotion, a silent strength in his reply. "We are."

Hand in hand, they left the secret room. The air around them carried a subtle, shift—a bond newly forged, unbreakable. They were no longer merely lovers or Soulmates. They were partners in every sense, bound by love and purpose, ready to tackle whatever waited beyond the hidden door.

***

Rowan and Aislinn stepped into Eileen's office, their footsteps softened against the hush that enveloped the room. The space was dim, illuminated only by a few candles whose warm, flickering glow danced across the walls. The silence carried a hushed reverence, as if the room itself acknowledged the gravity of what was about to unfold.

On the desk, a simple note rested, the curves of Eileen's handwriting unmistakable. Aislinn glanced at Rowan, their quiet understanding passing between them before she stepped forward. Her fingers brushed the edge of the paper as she picked it up, unfolding it with care.

She read aloud, her voice low yet clear.

"Rowan, Aislinn, I understand the importance of this choice. This ritual is meant to be a deeply personal experience, so I leave you both to complete it privately. I've left instructions for the ritual below. This space is now yours."

For a minute, Aislinn glanced over the note, her mind reflective. It felt as though her mother's presence filled the room—not physically, but in the way the words conveyed respect, understanding, and an unspoken blessing. She passed the note to Rowan, her resolve evident in the exchange between them.

As their attention moved through the room, the significance of the moment began to settle around them. Eileen's office, now transformed into a sacred space, held everything they would need for the ritual. Simple yet symbolic items lay carefully arranged—each one considered, each imbued with meaning. Symbols of the Fallen were woven subtly into the surroundings, grounding the ritual in an ancient tradition that connected them to a force far greater than themselves.

Rowan stepped closer, his focus unwavering as he took her hands in his. "The ritual," he began, his tone calm yet heavy with subdued intensity, "is more than a promise. Soulbinding creates a bond that goes beyond anything we can say. It means sharing everything—our strengths, our fears... even our pain. Once it's done, there's no undoing it."

He paused, threading his fingers through hers, his touch thoughtful and comforting. His eyes searched hers, as though seeking her certainty before continuing. "It will be... intense. But I want this, with every part of me. Because it's you."

Aislinn's chest tightened at his statement, emotion surging within her. Her smile was steady, resolute, as she met his gaze with an openness that left no room for doubt. "I want it too, Rowan. Whatever this bond brings, I want to share it with you."

She squeezed his hands, keeping them both in the present as the anticipation thickened in the air. A quiet energy began to build, a hum that seemed to arise from the blend of love and determination. This was the step that would tie their lives together in a way neither time nor fate could undo.

Rowan drew a steady breath, lifting one hand to trace a symbol in the space between them. His movements were precise, the rhythm of his fingers practiced and deliberate. As he murmured the legendary dialect of the Fallen, the sound resonated through the room like an echo from another time—timeless, powerful, and steeped in meaning.

The chant carried a magic that defied understanding, weaving an energy into the air around them. A feeble glow began to rise, ethereal and warm, as if summoned by the invocation. The air shifted, vibrating with a force that pulsed in harmony with the ritual's rhythm, each word drawing them closer to the promise it carried.

Aislinn felt warmth unfurl within her, spreading outward from deep in her chest. The sensation wasn't merely physical—it was as though her emotions, her love and trust, reached outward and intertwined with Rowan's. Their connection took on a new depth, a bond more profound than touch, more enduring than speech.

Rowan's voice softened, the cadence of his words falling to a near whisper. The final invocation left his lips, the sound resonating in the stillness like the last note of a sacred song. He looked up, his gaze meeting hers, and in that instant, everything unsaid passed between them. The tenderness in his expression revealed what he so rarely spoke aloud: love, devotion, and a vulnerability only she could draw from him.

Aislinn's heart raced as she rested her hand over Rowan's, feeling the bond take root. The connection surged through her, electrifying yet soothing, as if it had always been there, lying dormant until now. Her gaze remained locked on his, unwavering and full of purpose, as she took a steadying breath and spoke, her voice ringing with unshakable conviction.

"Leis an gceangal seo, geallaim seasamh leat. Tríd gach contúirt, gach lúcháir, agus gach triail. Roghnaím tusa, a Rowan. Go deo agus go síoraí."

The sacred tongue hung in the air, heavy with meaning that felt almost tangible. They didn't just seal her vow to Rowan—they tied their love to the timeless traditions of the Fallen, rooting it in a history far older than themselves. The melodic cadence of the Gaelic seemed to hum in harmony with the magic surrounding them, weaving seamlessly into the scene.

"With this bond, I vow to stand by you," she continued, her tone rich with love and certainty. "Through every danger, every joy, and every trial. I choose you, Rowan. Always and forever."

A trace of emotion crossed Rowan's face, his eyes alight with awe and a deeper feeling—one that had waited, quietly and patiently, for this instant. He squeezed her hand, and through the connection now forming between them, Aislinn felt the full depth of his emotions wash over her. It was rooting, powerful, and absolute, wrapping them in a bond that left no room for doubt. They were no longer just two lives—they were intertwined, two souls forever linked by a force neither could deny.

"Geallaim tú a chosaint, muinín a bheith agam asat, agus tú a ghrá le gach a bhfuil ionam. Ní hamháin gur tú mo ghrá, a Aislinn. Is tú mo neart. Le chéile, táimid doscartha."

The rhythm of Rowan's phrasing rolled off his tongue, steady and methodical, carrying the intensity of his promise. The Gaelic imbued his vow with a quiet power, each syllable carrying echoes of the past while binding them to the future. The language felt sacred, a bridge connecting them to the enduring legacy of the Fallen.

Rowan held her hands fully in his, his tone steady yet thick with emotion. "I vow to protect you, to trust you, to love you with everything I am," he said, the simplicity of his words laced with the depth of their meaning. "You're not just my love, Aislinn. You're my strength. Together, we're unbreakable."

As he spoke, the room seemed to pulse faintly, the magic surrounding them growing stronger, more vibrant. Aislinn felt his vow settle deep within her, reinforcing the connection now firmly in place. Their eyes met, and in perfect unity, they whispered the final lines of the ritual, their harmony blending into one.

The ancient language poured from their lips, its cadence a melody of sound and power that filled the room with a tangible energy. As the last syllable faded into the air, the bond surged to life. A wave of energy swelled around them, cresting in a radiant glow before settling into a steady, subdued hum. The bond was forged—unseen but unbreakable—binding them to each other in a way that transcended time.

Aislinn felt the shift instantly, a new depth of connection to Rowan that took her breath away. His presence became vivid, his emotions as clear to her as her own. She could sense his love, his fierce protectiveness, and even the lingering traces of his earlier doubts fading into the certainty that now mirrored her own.

For a minute, they stood in the soft glow of the ritual, their foreheads touching, their breaths mingling as they absorbed the enormity of what they had done. The intensity was overwhelming yet comforting—a completeness that felt profound and eternal.

Rowan wrapped his arms around her, pulling her into an embrace that spoke volumes. Aislinn rested her head against his chest, their heartbeats syncing, the rhythm calm and reassuring. They stayed like that, immersed in the peace of the connection, as though they had always been a part of each other but only now could fully feel it.

Eventually, they stepped back, their hands still joined. A newfound strength radiated between them, a readiness neither had known before. Without a word, they turned toward the door, moving forward together. Hand in hand, they left the sanctuary of Eileen's office, stepping into a world that no longer felt uncertain. They were Soulbound, partners in every sense of the word, their love a guiding force for whatever lay ahead.

The hallway greeted them with a tranquil calm as they walked side by side, their connection filling the atmosphere with an inherent oath. Each step carried meaning, a silent declaration of the bond they now shared, as they made their way through the mansion's corridors toward the courtyard doors.

The warm summer air embraced them as they stepped outside, the breeze carrying the scent of jasmine and freshly turned soil. From the pool ahead came the sounds of laughter and cheerful voices. The Fallen had gathered there, shaking off the burden of recent battles with a rare ease. Ariel's laughter rang out above the others, coaxing several to join her in the water, her playful energy rippling through the courtyard.

Rowan and Aislinn approached, their hands still clasped, the pale glow of their bond visible between them. Aislinn scanned the gathering, her eyes finding Eileen seated at the edge of the group, a contented smile on her lips. When Eileen looked their way, her brow arched slightly, her gaze skimming to their entwined hands as though silently asking, Well?

In answer, Rowan lifted their joined hands, allowing the warm glow of their Radiant Surge to shimmer briefly between them. The light pulsed gently, an undeniable affirmation of the bond they now shared. Eileen's features eased into a proud, almost maternal smile, her approval quiet but clear.

With a subtle nod, she raised her glass, drawing the group's attention. Her voice carried easily over the courtyard, warm and sure.

"To Rowan and Aislinn," she said, her words filled with reverence and pride. "To love, strength, and the bonds that carry us through even the darkest of days."

The Fallen turned, raising their glasses in unison. Cheers and laughter echoed through the summer night as Rowan and Aislinn stood together, the glow of their bond reflected in their faces. In that second, they felt not only the strength of their connection but the acceptance of the family they had found among the Fallen.

Hand in hand, they shared a glance, their love and unity a subtle yet undeniable force. Whatever came next, they would overcome it together, their bond as unshakable as the love that had forged it.

***

A gentle rustling stirred the stillness, pulling Riichi back from the depths of unconsciousness. His fingers twitched, curling slightly as sensation returned in slow, uneven waves. The dim glow of the room greeted him, shadows shifting into familiar shapes as his vision cleared. He blinked slowly, letting the quiet settle around him, his thoughts gradually catching up to the subdued light that blurred the edges of everything it touched. Then, his focus landed on the figure beside him.

Takoda.

She was close, her head resting against the edge of the mattress, her face turned just enough for him to see her clearly. One hand lay loosely in his, her fingers lightly curled as though they'd been there for a while. In sleep, her usual composure had softened, the seriousness of her steady presence momentarily eased. Shadows played gently over her features, accentuating a serene elegance he had often noticed but never allowed himself to dwell on.

For an instant, he simply observed her *She's... beautiful.* The thought struck him with a force he hadn't anticipated, and for a brief, unguarded pause, he let himself admit it. It wasn't a beauty meant to demand attention—it was subtler, more deliberate, woven into the way she carried herself, how strength and grace seemed effortless in her every movement.

He'd known it, of course. It was part of why he kept his formality so firmly in place around her. Distance, carefully measured words, and guarded behaviors were his armor. Letting her in risked exposing far too much. But now, seeing her like this, unburdened and unarmored, her presence tugged at a depth within him. A feeling he couldn't ignore.

It wasn't just relief, though he felt that too. It was the profound, startling realization that she had chosen to stay. Even when she didn't have to.

Why? The question drifted through his mind, unanswered, hovering like a faint echo.

His gaze dropped to her hand resting in his, her touch grounding in its simplicity. He could feel its warmth, the gentle reassurance of her presence reaching past the defenses he had relied on for so long. For all the times he had stood alone, it had never occurred to him what it might feel like to have someone here. Someone willing to sit in silence, without expectation, simply to ensure he wasn't left to endure it all alone.

His throat tightened briefly, the thought unsettling in its unfamiliarity. She would never know how much it meant to him—not if he had any say in it. Even now, the instinct to keep his emotions contained pressed firmly against the edges of his awareness. He wasn't the kind of man to let gratitude—or anything deeper—surface so easily. *Vulnerability invites weakness,* he reminded himself, the familiar mantra wrapping around him like armor, calming the unease that her presence stirred.

And yet, despite himself, he couldn't look away.

The sound of his shallow breath was the only noise breaking the silence, and for just a fleeting instant, he allowed himself this indulgence. A brief pause to hold onto, knowing she wouldn't see the conflict glinting in his eyes.

Takoda shifted slightly, her hand moving in his, and he stiffened instinctively, the reflex immediate and automatic. Her lashes fluttered once, then again, before her eyes opened slowly, focusing on him. The calm steadiness he had come to associate with her returned almost at once, though there was a softness in the way she blinked herself awake, as if the remnants of sleep still lingered.

"Miss Takoda," he murmured, the formality slipping from his lips as naturally as breathing. The fragile solitude of the moment dissolved as he tightened his grip on the walls he so carefully maintained. "You didn't need to trouble yourself... on my account."

Takoda's lips curved faintly, her brow arching in a way that seemed to say she'd expected nothing less. *Ever the stoic,* she thought, her amusement tinged with a complexity harder to define. She had grown used to his formality, even found a kind of comfort in it—a rhythm they had slipped into without effort or acknowledgment. Yet now, as she sat beside him, watching the rigid lines of his expression soften ever so slightly, her own resolve faltered.

"Well, someone had to make sure you didn't sleep forever, Riichi," she said, a hint of playful defiance threading through her words. Her demeanor remained light, masking the undercurrent of concern that stayed just under the veneer. She'd rather not let him see the relief coursing through her at his waking or the gravity of the worry she'd carried in his absence. Some truths, she decided, were best left unsaid. But as her gaze met his, knowing he was safe, her restraint felt a little less necessary.

Riichi caught the weak smile playing on her lips, the glint of mischief in her eyes, and the sight steadied him in an unexpected way. She was here... though she didn't have to be. The realization slipped subtly into his thoughts, almost unnoticed, yet it settled over him with a strange weight. He looked away, his mind brushing against the unfamiliar feeling without fully acknowledging it.

The silence that stretched between them carried a charged atmosphere, heavy with something unnamed. Takoda's steady presence lingered, her face unreadable, while Riichi kept his focus carefully averted, his thoughts firmly tethered. Yet neither could deny the pull between them—an unassuming connection that had gone unacknowledged but refused to fade.

After a long pause, Riichi broke the quiet, his words measured as his familiar formality returned to shield him. "Your vigilance... is appreciated," he murmured, his gaze settling somewhere beyond her. "I trust I didn't cause you undue concern."

A feeble smile tugged at the corners of Takoda's lips. Still hiding behind that formal tone. The thought carried a trace of amusement, mingled with a feeling she couldn't quite define. Her focus softened as she regarded him, her own carefully maintained composure beginning to slip.

"You don't have to be so... proper with me, you know," she said, her tone gentle yet intentional. It wasn't a challenge, but a gentle reminder that it was just the two of them now, alone in this intimate exchange.

Her comment seemed to catch him off guard. His shoulders eased, just slightly, and just for a breath, she watched his usual armor shift. A muffled sigh escaped him, unguarded, before he finally looked at her. In his eyes, she caught a spark of something rare—vulnerability, tentative but unmistakable.

"I... appreciate you being here, Takoda," he said, his tone lower now, carrying the depth of sincerity. He paused, as though carefully selecting his next response. "It means more than I know how to say."

Her features relaxed at his admission, her tone low as she leaned closer. "You don't have to thank me, Riichi. I just..." She hesitated, studying his expression as the calm she carried flickered. "I needed to be here."

His lips curved faintly, a ghost of a smile touched with quiet ruefulness. It carried a soft acknowledgment of the weight between them. "I did give you my word... that I'd be back," he murmured, his voice low and firm. The statement wasn't just reassurance—it carried the quiet conviction of a promise kept, despite everything.

At his words, the calm she had held so tightly cracked. Her breath caught, and her gaze fell as silent tears slipped down her cheeks. She turned away, unable to meet his eyes, her expression hidden. Relief poured through her, raw and overwhelming, speaking louder than anything she could say aloud. This was one of those rare moments when holding her emotions in check seemed impossible.

Riichi noticed her reaction but didn't press her. Instead, he reached out, his hand weak but steady, and gave hers a gentle squeeze. The gesture carried more than gratitude—it was a silent acknowledgment, a quiet acceptance of the bond that had always existed between them. Though undefined and unrecognized, it was there, steady and irrefutable, binding them in ways neither fully understood.

Their attention fixed on each other again, the look they shared carrying more than either was prepared to articulate. It was heavy with unexpressed emotions, a connection simmering, lying dormant. A force was there—powerful and uncharted—a story waiting to be written. But for now, they let it linger, leaving the experience unresolved.

Takoda stayed at his side, her hand still entwined with his. The silence deepened, carrying with it a subtle understanding. And as the stillness settled over the room, a question seemed to hang between them—a promise of what might come, a future both could sense but neither was ready to name.

Bridge Chapter:
The Blooming Hawthorn

The faint light of dawn seeped into the room, tracing pale streaks across the walls. The dim tranquility of the house wrapped around the space, broken only by the soft rustle of fabric as Riichi stirred. Awareness crept over him in slow waves—the dull ache radiating through his chest, the stiffness gripping his limbs, and the calm that filled the air.

His eyes opened, blinking against the dim light. The edges of the room gradually sharpened, and as his focus shifted, it landed on the figure curled in the chair beside him. Takoda sat there, her head tilted against the armrest, her breathing even, undisturbed by the morning glow.

Her features had softened in sleep, the determination she usually carried replaced by a quiet ease. A few loose strands of her hair caught the light, glinting faintly, and his attention stayed there longer than he intended.

She stayed. The thought surfaced before he could stop it, settling firmly in his mind. Even after everything, she hadn't left.

For the briefest time, he allowed himself to take in the sight of her—the serenity she carried even in rest. A faint stir of warmth rose in his chest, an unfamiliar solace that both unsettled and steadied him. It had been a long time since someone had stayed—not because they had to, but because they chose to.

A slow exhale left him as he shifted his focus to the ceiling. He tried to ground himself in the present, to push away the thoughts that threatened to overwhelm him. The quiet steadied him, but only for a minute.

Soft footsteps broke the stillness. Riichi turned his head as the door opened, revealing Eileen. Her composed expression remained as steady as ever, though a faint trace of relief softened the corners of her mouth as she stepped inside.

"Good," she said simply, her voice sharp and purposeful. "You're awake."

The sound stirred Takoda. She shifted in the chair, her brow furrowing before her eyes fluttered open, heavy with sleep. Rubbing her face, she straightened in the seat, her movements unhurried. "Eileen?" she murmured, her tone thick with drowsiness. "What's going on?"

Eileen moved further into the room, her gaze flicking briefly to Takoda before settling on Riichi. "I've made arrangements for you," she said, her tone firm and clear. "You'll continue your recovery at an Airbnb in the city. It's quieter, more private. You'll have everything you need."

Riichi's frown deepened, the faint crease between his brows reflecting his unease. "That won't be necessary," he said, his tone calm yet unyielding. "I can manage here."

Eileen's lips curved in a faint, disarming smile that left no room for argument. "It's already done," she said evenly. "And I'm not here to debate."

Her focus shifted to Takoda. "I'd like you to go with him."

Takoda blinked, caught off guard. "Me?"

Eileen nodded. "Someone needs to make sure he actually rests. From what I've observed, you're the only one he listens to."

Riichi straightened, his shoulders stiffening. "Eileen, that's—"

"No." Her tone softened, but her gaze stayed firm. "You need help, Riichi. That's not up for discussion."

His jaw flexed as he turned his head, his voice lower when he finally spoke. "It wouldn't be fair to her," he said. "I don't want to be a burden."

Takoda stepped forward, brushing her hair back in an absent motion as she closed the gap separating them. "You're not a burden," she said, her tone calm but steady. She met his eyes with confidence, her gaze unwavering. "It's fine. I'll go."

Eileen's features changed slightly, a flicker of satisfaction crossing her face. She pulled a set of keys from her pocket and handed them to Takoda. "Everything is already arranged," she said simply. "I expect you both to be there by the end of the day."

Takoda took the keys, the cool metal pressing lightly against her fingertips. She glanced at Riichi, her gaze catching his in that instant before she gave a small nod. "We'll be there," she said.

Eileen paused a moment longer, her eyes sweeping over them before she turned and exited the room, her measured footsteps fading into the hallway.

The quiet she left behind felt heavier now, thick with things unsaid. Takoda hesitated, her attention resting on Riichi as she spoke. "Are you... okay with me being there?" Her voice carried a gentler edge, tentative yet sure.

Riichi's eyes dropped to the blanket draped across his lap. A pause stretched in the silence they shared before he lifted his gaze, his nod considerate though faint. "Yes," he said, his voice low.

Takoda's shoulders relaxed, the strain melting from her frame as a faint smile softened her features. "Alright. Just making sure," she said lightly, though the impact of his response settled in the space dividing them.

Riichi didn't reply, his focus shifting to the window instead. Sunlight crept across the walls, touching every corner without dissipating the unease that rested heavily in the air. Takoda stayed a minute longer, her thoughts circling unanswered questions, before stepping away and leaving him to the gentle quiet.

***

The small Airbnb rested quietly on a shaded street, its modest exterior blending seamlessly into the calm neighborhood. A gentle breeze stirred the leaves outside, carrying the faint murmur of distant traffic. Riichi stepped inside first, his duffel bag slung neatly over his shoulder. Each step was slow, his careful movements betraying the persistent ache radiating through his chest—a muted warning not to push himself too far.

The interior was plain but functional. The compact kitchen opened into a cozy living room, and two bedroom doors waited at the end of a narrow hallway. His sharp gaze swept over the space: spotless counters, neatly folded linens perched on a chair, and furniture chosen for utility rather than comfort. It was practical, straightforward—exactly what he needed.

Riichi moved into the left bedroom and placed his bag carefully on the bed. Like the rest of the house, the room was simple yet sufficient: a small dresser, a nightstand, and crisp white bedding. He exhaled slowly, rolling his shoulder to ease the tightness that had begun to settle in his chest. Then, methodically, he began unpacking. The practiced motions steadied him, offering a moment to focus on something tangible.

The crunch of tires on gravel broke the silence. Riichi stepped to the window just as a cab pulled up to the curb. Takoda climbed out, juggling two grocery bags, a small overnight bag, and a long, narrow box tucked awkwardly under her arm. She moved with purpose, though her uneven steps hinted at the awkward weight of her load.

Riichi opened the door before she could knock. "Miss Takoda," he greeted, his tone calm and formal. "You should have called for assistance."

Takoda raised her head, a faint smile curving her lips as she met his gaze. "I had it handled," she replied lightly, though a quiet exhale slipped from her as she stepped inside. In the kitchen, she set the grocery bags on the counter and carefully leaned the long box against the wall, her attention already shifting to the next task.

Riichi hung back near the doorway, his attention briefly tracking her movements before stepping forward. "Allow me," he offered, reaching for one of the bags.

"You don't have to—" she began, but her words faltered as her eyes flicked to his frame. The tension in his shoulders and the stiffness in his movements gave her pause. She stepped forward, gently nudging his hand away. "You shouldn't be doing that," she said, her tone firm yet kind.

Riichi froze, his hand hovering in the distance dividing them before dropping to his side. "I need to help," he said quietly, his tone measured, though his expression tightened as if he had forced the words out. "I don't want to feel..." He hesitated, his voice catching before continuing, "...like I'm useless."

The confession loomed over the room like a shadow, momentarily freezing the air. Takoda stilled, her gaze softening as understanding crossed her features. After a beat, she exhaled and took a step back. "Fine," she said, her voice gentler now. "But nothing heavy. Deal?"

Riichi inclined his head, a faint flicker of relief breaking through his usual restraint. "Understood."

She handed him a smaller bag, their hands brushing briefly in the exchange. "Here," she said, a subtle smile tugging at her lips. "This one won't get you in trouble."

The two of them settled into an unspoken rhythm, the rustle of bags and the quiet sounds of items being placed on the counter filling the kitchen. Riichi moved with careful meticulousness, each motion unhurried, as though it carried a weight beyond the task itself. Takoda leaned against the counter, her gaze flicking toward him from the corner of her eye.

He wasn't just moving because the task needed to be done—there was a defiance in his determination, a tacit resolve that kept his hands busy even as his body protested. The realization sent a subtle warmth curling through Takoda's chest. She quickly dismissed it, turning her attention back to the groceries.

"Good thing I brought real food," she teased, pulling out a carton of eggs. "Otherwise, you'd probably be stuck with toast and tea."

"I've endured worse," Riichi replied evenly. A faint glimmer of amusement crossed his face, brief yet noticeable enough to draw her attention. The trace of humor in his voice coaxed a soft laugh from her.

Shaking her head, she finished unpacking the groceries. Her eyes drifted to the long box leaning against the wall, but she left it untouched. It could wait. "That's everything," she said, pressing her palms against the counter as she stepped back. "We're all set."

Riichi offered a small nod, his focus returning to the neatly arranged pantry items. The silence that settled between them now carried a lighter quality, the unease from earlier slipping into something more natural.

"I'll take the other room," Takoda said after a pause, gesturing toward the second door down the hall. She stopped temporarily, her fingers brushing the edge of the doorway. "And don't push yourself too hard, okay?"

"I'll do my best, Miss Takoda," he replied, the formality slipping effortlessly into his words.

Her lips curved in a faint smile before she disappeared into her room, the door clicking softly behind her. Riichi stayed where he was, his gaze tracing the room one more time. The stillness felt different now—no longer hollow, but steady, as though an understanding had quietly taken root.

***

The bathroom was still, save for the faint hum of the overhead fan. Ri-ichi stood shirtless in front of the mirror, his focus locked on the bandage stretched across his torso. His fingers worked carefully to peel back the edge, though the jagged scar beneath pulsed with a dull ache—a vivid reminder of just how close he had come to losing everything.

At first, his movements were controlled and with care, though the awkward angle and remaining stiffness in his body made the task increasingly frustrating. The bandage snagged on the scar's edge, pulling uncomfortably. He released a sharp exhale through his teeth, irritation flashing across his carefully composed features. Adjusting his stance, he twisted slightly to try again, only to wince as a jolt of pain spread through his torso. His jaw clenched as a low growl escaped him, the effort pushing his patience to its limit.

"Need a hand?" Takoda's voice interrupted the hushed atmosphere, calm yet tinged with concern. She leaned casually against the doorway, her observant eyes fixed on him.

"I've got it," Riichi replied curtly, keeping his gaze on the mirror. His tone came out clipped, harsher than he intended, yet he made no move to temper it.

Takoda's brow furrowed, the hint of a frown tugging at her features as she stepped further into the room. "Riichi, you're going to tear something if you keep twisting like that. Let me—"

"I said I've got it!" His response cut through the air, sharper than intended, the simmering discord in the air rippling in the wake of his outburst.

Takoda froze, her eyes widening for a heartbeat before narrowing. The outburst wasn't just unexpected—it was entirely unlike him. A new emotion drifted across her face, settling into a demeanor far more distant. "Fine," she said, her tone steady, though the sting of hurt was obvious. "Do it yourself."

She turned on her heel, her footsteps brisk as she headed for the door. Her tone struck Riichi like a physical blow, cutting through his frustration with sudden clarity. Guilt gripped him, sharp and unrelenting.

"Miss Takoda," he said quickly, his voice softer now. He reached out, his hand brushing against her arm to stop her. She stiffened under his touch but didn't pull away.

"I'm sorry," he murmured, his tone quiet yet firm. "I shouldn't have snapped at you. That was... uncalled for." He released a slow breath, his hand falling back to his side. "I'm just... frustrated. But that doesn't excuse my behavior."

Takoda turned back to him slowly, her features still guarded, though a hint of gentleness relaxed her countenance. "I understand," she said, her voice calm but deliberate. She paused briefly before continuing, "You don't have to prove anything to me, Riichi. Let me help."

He hesitated, the depth of his pride pressing against the necessity of her offer. At last, his shoulders slackened, the fight in him giving way. "Please," he said, his voice quiet but earnest.

A small, reassuring smile broke across Takoda's face. "Alright," she said gently. "Let's take care of this."

She stepped closer, her movements measured and purposeful as she retrieved the first-aid kit from the counter. Riichi stayed perfectly still, his posture rigid against the subtle graze of her arm as she passed. The fleeting contact sent an unexpected ripple of awareness through him. He kept his eyes fixed forward, refusing to let his focus waver as she began peeling back the old bandage, her fingers moving with practiced care against his skin.

It wasn't just the heat of her touch that unsettled him. It was the way she moved—so intent, so precise. Her quiet focus carried an ease that was almost disarming, her steadiness drawing his attention in a way he couldn't quite control. That unwavering determination, paired with the careful gentleness of her hands, chipped away at the control he so fiercely maintained.

She's... beautiful. The thought emerged unbidden, breaking through the carefully constructed barriers of his mind. It wasn't a striking beauty meant to command attention—it was quieter, woven into her presence and the strength she radiated. The realization struck harder than the warmth of her hands, leaving him momentarily off balance.

Her fingers brushed against him again, and the fire it sparked burned deeper this time, unfurling a heat that coiled low in his stomach and spread relentlessly through his body. His pulse thudded against his ribs, the intensity rising in waves he struggled to suppress. Desperate for control, he reached for the hand towel hanging nearby, gripping it tightly and letting it dangle loosely in front of him as a flimsy shield to hide his arousal. The rough fabric twisted in his grasp, a poor substitute for the self-control slipping from his grip. Every nerve felt alive, humming with sensations and desires that were foreign, overwhelming, and utterly inescapable.

"Did that hurt?" Takoda asked, her tone gentle, her eyes lifting to meet his.

"No," Riichi replied quickly, his voice taut, nearly strained. *Control yourself.*

Takoda's brow furrowed slightly, her gaze lingering on him as though trying to discern what lay beneath his rigid exterior. "You're really tense," she observed lightly, her hands smoothing the new bandage into place with practiced care. "Relax. It's just a bandage."

"I am fine, Miss Takoda," Riichi said hoarsely, the words clipped, forced. His grip tightened on the towel in his hands, the fabric twisting under his whitening knuckles as he clenched his jaw, struggling against the storm brewing inside him.

"There," Takoda said finally, stepping back and tucking the supplies neatly into the first-aid kit. "All done. Not bad, right?"

Riichi released a measured breath, though the unease still thrummed beneath his skin. "Thank you," he murmured, his tone maintaining its usual formality, though quieter now. Despite his effort to sound composed, the strain behind his words was evident.

Takoda studied him for a flash, her head tilting slightly as though she were about to say more. Instead, she let it drop, her lips curving into a faint smile. "Next time, try not to snap at me," she teased softly, her tone carrying a playful edge. "You're not as intimidating as you think."

Riichi gave a slight nod, his eyes still averted. "Understood," he replied, his voice low, controlled.

As the door clicked shut behind her, he let out a long, uneven breath. Leaning forward, his hand brushed absently over the bandage on his chest, the phantom warmth of her touch lingering against his skin, stubbornly vivid.

What is wrong with me? The thought cut sharply through his mind as he stared at his reflection in the mirror. His jaw remained taut, his skin flushed—a physical betrayal of the emotions he struggled to suppress. With a sharp shake of his head, he forced himself upright, shoving the thoughts aside. Yet, even as he stepped out of the bathroom, the heat remained, refusing to release its grip.

***

The two weeks of Riichi's recovery passed in relative calm, bringing fleeting connections between him and Takoda—encounters neither of them had anticipated. Each day brought subtle shifts in their dynamic, gradually dismantling the walls they had carefully maintained.

One morning, Takoda emerged from the bathroom, steam curling behind her in delicate wisps. A towel was wrapped snugly around her frame, her damp hair clinging to the curve of her neck. She had barely taken two steps into the hallway when she nearly collided with Riichi.

His hand shot out instinctively, closing around her arm to steady her as the towel slipped slightly. The contact sent an undeniable jolt through both of them, her skin still damp and warm beneath his firm grip. Their eyes met, an almost electric charge filling the air around them, heavy with unspoken emotions neither dared acknowledge.

Takoda's heart raced, a flush rising to her cheeks that had nothing to do with the humidity on her skin. She clutched the towel closer, her pulse hammering in her ears. *Why does he have to look at me like that?* The thought swirled in her mind, unwelcome yet persistent.

"Apologies, Takoda," Riichi said gruffly, his tone clipped and uneven. His hand fell away abruptly, as if burned, and he stepped back with the fixed, measured movement of someone desperate to regain control.

"It's fine," Takoda said quickly, her voice pitched higher than usual. She forced a nervous laugh and darted past him, retreating into her room. As the door clicked shut behind her, she leaned against it, her heart pounding. *Get it together,* she told herself, pressing her hands to her flushed cheeks. The memory replayed in her mind: his steady grip, the piercing intensity in his eyes. She took an unsteady breath, the ghosting sensation of his touch still vivid against her skin.

In the hallway, Riichi remained rooted in place, his jaw clenched, his hand curling into a fist at his side. The memory of her warmth clung stubbornly to his palm, her startled expression carved into his thoughts. He could still see the towel shifting as she clutched it closer, the damp strands of her hair framing her face.

This is inappropriate, he scolded himself, determined to push the image away. Yet his mind betrayed him, conjuring a vivid vision of his fingers grazing her cheek, tucking a damp lock of hair behind her ear, and leaning in to claim her lips.

The thought struck like a blow, igniting a fire low in his stomach. His breathing grew uneven, and for a fleeting instant, his carefully maintained control threatened to shatter. *Discipline yourself,* he ordered silently, his fists tightening as if he could physically force the wayward thoughts to disappear.

With a sharp shake of his head, he turned on his heel, his measured steps guiding him toward the living room. Yet, no matter the distance, her presence clung to him, vivid and unyielding, hovering in the edges of his thoughts.

***

That evening, the void that stretched out was marked by a calm neither sought to disrupt. Takoda sat cross-legged on the couch, a steaming mug of tea nestled in her hands, while Riichi occupied the armchair. His posture, as always, was upright and composed, his attention fixed somewhere far beyond her. The stifled serenity stretched until curiosity began to stir within her.

"Why are you always so formal?" she asked lightly, her tone carrying an easy sincerity.

Riichi's focus shifted to her, his shoulders stiffening slightly. He hesitated, the pause weighted with implicit meaning. When he finally spoke, his words were cautious, each one chosen with care. "It became a habit, Miss Takoda. Growing up, I learned that people often judge before they take the time to truly see you. Their assumptions... are not always kind."

His fingers trailed briefly over the armrest of the chair before his attention returned to her. "By presenting myself as flawless, I left no room for criticism. My actions, my demeanor, even my appearance—they became armor. A shield I could depend on."

Takoda tilted her head, observing him closely. His explanation was clear, but there was an unsaid weight in his expression that hinted at more. "That sounds exhausting," she said softly, her voice laced with quiet understanding.

"It was necessary," Riichi said simply, though the faint rigidity in his posture betrayed the enormity of what he'd endured.

"I get it," Takoda murmured, lowering her eyes to the tea in her hands. "People say ignorant things about Native Americans all the time, like we're invisible. They talk as if I'm not there, as if I don't exist."

Her voice faltered briefly, the crack in her tone barely audible before she steadied herself and offered a small, self-effacing smile. "Sometimes ignoring it feels like the only option, but it doesn't make it hurt any less."

Riichi leaned forward slightly, the subtle movement closing some of the divide that held them apart. "I noticed," he said, his voice quieter but resolute.

Takoda blinked, taken aback. "You noticed?"

"Yes," he replied firmly. "Your features, your presence... they reflect your heritage. It's understated, but unmistakable."

Her lips curved faintly, a smile pulling at the corners of her mouth. "You're observant."

A pause hovered like an unanswered question, the air shifting as Riichi's voice dropped lower, its usual exactness giving way to a tone softer, more sincere. "I notice... everything about you, Takoda."

The words settled between them like a pulse, leaving her momentarily breathless. Her fingers froze around the mug, her heartbeat quickening as her gaze locked onto his.

"You notice everything about me?" she asked, her voice quiet, threaded with both disbelief and a spark of curiosity.

"Yes," Riichi replied, his posture shifting subtly, as if bracing himself for her response. The usual polish in his demeanor softened, and his words carried an uncharacteristic vulnerability. The way he used her name felt deliberate, almost intimate, and lingered in the silence connecting them.

Takoda's smile widened, her head tilting slightly. "You dropped the 'Miss,'" she pointed out, her tone light and teasing.

Riichi stiffened, his fleeting openness retreating behind his usual formality. "I... apologize if that was inappropriate," he said quickly, his voice measured but tense.

"Don't apologize," Takoda said, shaking her head as a soft laugh slipped free. "I think I like it," she added, her tone playful, her words carrying a warmth that eased the tension. "You should do it more often."

In that breath, Riichi's face took on a different look—a flicker of hesitation, or perhaps something deeper, passing across his features before he inclined his head slightly. He didn't speak again, his hands settling neatly against the armrests.

The silence that followed wasn't awkward. It carried a quiet understanding, unspoken but palpable, as if an invisible thread now tied them together, fragile yet undeniable.

***

The next evening, Takoda decided to change things up. After dinner, she leaned forward across the table, her grin playful and her tone thoughtfully mischievous. "Let's play a game—favorites," she declared, her eyes sparkling with amusement. "I'll start. Favorite food?"

Riichi paused, his posture composed, though his eyes held hers briefly before he responded. "Red bean mochi," he said calmly. "And yours?"

"Frybread tacos," she answered with distinctive pride. "And yes, they're amazing."

A flicker of amusement crossed Riichi's face, so brief Takoda almost wondered if she'd imagined it. "I'll take your word for it," he said.

The game continued, each question easing the silent strain enveloping them, peeling back a little more of the barriers they had built. Favorite color. Favorite place they'd visited. Favorite music. With every answer, the conversation became lighter, the guarded edges of Riichi's demeanor softening with each exchange. By the time they finished, Takoda found herself watching him with a bit more warmth. He still spoke sparingly, but his focus stayed on her a fraction longer than it had before, and his posture felt less rigid. The walls around them hadn't disappeared, but they seemed thinner now, as if something meaningful waited just beyond reach.

***

As the ache in his torso faded, Riichi returned to his morning Aikido practice in the backyard. The early light of dawn stretched across the lawn, illuminating the sharp precision of his movements. Shirtless, his skin seemed to catch the glow of the soft sunlight, every motion smooth and intentional, each step imbued with purpose. From the kitchen window, Takoda paused mid-motion, her hands hovering over the counter as her attention locked onto him.

Her breath slowed, the elegance in his movements captivating her. There was a power in the way he moved, a seamless blend of discipline and control that felt almost mesmerizing. But as the seconds passed, her admiration shifted, replaced by a different kind of awareness that spread low in her stomach, warm and insistent.

What would it feel like if that control unraveled? The thought surfaced unbidden, vivid and impossible to dismiss. She imagined him stepping toward her, his hand reaching out, the warmth of his fingertips grazing her cheek as his restraint gave way. The vision deepened, filling her senses: the intensity of his presence surrounding her, the faint brush of his breath against her lips, the instant his discipline crumbled, revealing a vulnerability raw and unrestrained.

Her chest tightened, heat rushing to her face as the vividness of the thought startled her. She swallowed hard, gripping the edge of the counter as if it could steady her. *What is wrong with me?* she thought furiously, closing her eyes in a futile attempt to push the image away.

"Focus," she muttered sharply under her breath, the frustration laced in her voice. Yet, as she turned back to the stove, the image remained stubbornly—a spark she couldn't quite extinguish. Her hands trembled as she reached for the skillet, the warmth radiating through her chest refusing to dissipate.

Outside, Riichi's movements remained seamless, his focus unwavering. Each deliberate step, the curve of his arms, and the disciplined flow of his motions seemed etched into her mind, vivid and inescapable. Takoda tore her gaze away, curling her hands into fists at her sides as she fought to reclaim control over her thoughts.

Get a grip, she scolded herself silently, forcing her attention back to breakfast. But even as she stirred the eggs on the stove, her thoughts betrayed her again. *What would it feel like if he let go, even briefly?* The question burned through her, unsettling and persistent.

***

Later that evening, Takoda surprised Riichi with a plate of red bean mochi she had prepared earlier in the day. She placed it on the counter in front of him, watching as a hint of another emotion appeared in his gaze—just enough to reveal a rare break in his composed exterior.

"You didn't have to do this," Riichi said, his voice even, though an undercurrent of weight tinged his tone.

"I know," Takoda replied lightly, shrugging to mask the effort it had taken. Yet, the way his eyes shifted from the plate to her—brief but evident —sent a quiet thrill coursing through her. Turning back to the counter, she busied herself with tidying up, though her movements were slower than usual, her thoughts drifting.

The silence between them stretched, though it didn't feel empty. As they worked side by side, Takoda couldn't ignore how the stretch that kept them apart seemed to shrink, the air warmer, charged with an energy neither of them acknowledged aloud.

***

Another day, determined to keep himself active, Riichi ventured out for a walk around the neighborhood. When he returned, the late afternoon sun poured across the street in a golden glow, framing the small bouquet of sunflowers in his hand. Their vivid petals, so bright and unapologetically alive, stood out against the muted tones of the surrounding houses.

Takoda opened the door just as he reached the porch, her brows arching in surprise as her attention landed on the flowers. "You remembered?" she asked, her tone colored with a mix of disbelief and curiosity.

"You said they were your favorite," Riichi said simply, extending the bouquet toward her.

Her fingers brushed his as she accepted the flowers, the brief contact catching her off guard. "Thank you," she said softly, the words quieter than she'd intended.

For a beat, she stood in the doorway, her gaze lingering on the sunflowers. The thoughtfulness of his gesture settled over her, warm and unshakable. She looked back at him, her lips parting as though to speak, but the words refused to form. Instead, she caught his eyes for a fleeting second before he stepped past her into the house, his presence carrying a quiet gravity despite the near-silent sound of his footsteps.

That evening, Takoda arranged the sunflowers in a vase, their golden petals glowing softly under the lamplight and adding a warmth to the room that hadn't been there before. She paused, her fingers gliding over the smooth rim of the vase as she let herself take in the simple beauty of the scene. The gesture lingered in her thoughts, its quiet sincerity carrying a depth she wasn't ready to fully acknowledge.

Her attention drifted toward the living room, where Riichi sat reading, his posture as composed as ever. Yet, paired with the vibrant sunflowers, his presence seemed altered—heavier, though she couldn't pinpoint the reason. A faint smile curved her lips, unbidden, as she turned back toward the kitchen, her thoughts circling softly, resisting clarity she wasn't ready to face.

***

The evening air hung heavy in the Airbnb, the stillness broken only by the soft hum of the refrigerator and the quiet rustle of pages as Takoda flipped them on the couch. Riichi stood near the window, his focus locked on the muted glow of streetlights filtering through the trees outside. Their dim light reflected faintly on the glass, casting shifting shapes that danced across the room.

The sudden buzz of his phone cut through the calm, abrupt and jarring against the subdued atmosphere. Glancing at the screen, Riichi saw Eileen's name flash across it. Promptly, he answered. "Eileen," he said with composure, though his stance adjusted subtly, instinctively more alert.

"Riichi." Her words carried their usual steadiness, but a trace of urgency threaded through, immediately pulling his full attention. "I've been monitoring the situation in Washington. There are reports of unusual weather patterns—storms forming too quickly, winds changing direction without explanation."

Riichi's grip on the phone tightened slightly as his brows furrowed, a flicker of concern breaking through his composed demeanor. "Golden Dawn?" he asked.

"Most likely," she replied, her tone firm and measured. "Their activities are often tied to unnatural environmental shifts. This matches the patterns we've observed before." She paused, the magnitude of her statement echoed faintly in the air. "We haven't confirmed their presence yet, but these signs are concerning. You'll need to prepare to leave soon."

"Understood," Riichi said, his response composed, though a faint thread of unease ran beneath his words.

"I'll keep you updated as we gather more information," Eileen continued. "For now, concentrate on your recovery. You'll need to be at full strength for what's ahead. The situation in Washington could escalate quickly."

"Yes, Eileen," he replied formally, his tone carrying a hint of quiet determination.

"Good. Stay vigilant, Riichi," she said before the call ended with a soft click, leaving him staring at the faint reflection of himself in the darkened window.

Riichi stood motionless for a few seconds, his fingers curling briefly around the phone before sliding it into his pocket. The weight of the impending mission settled over him, familiar and grounding—another task, another challenge. It should have felt routine.

Yet tonight, his focus wavered. Takoda sat on the couch, her attention fixed on the book in her lap. The crease in her brow deepened slightly as she turned a page, her quiet presence pulling at his awareness in ways he couldn't explain.

The usual anticipation before a mission—the readiness to leave without hesitation—was absent. Instead, an unfamiliar apprehension tugged at him. The thought of leaving this space, of leaving her, stirred an ache he wasn't ready to face.

Riichi exhaled slowly, straightening as he worked to pull his focus back into alignment. Whatever this feeling was, it couldn't change what needed to be done. Turning away from the window, his tone remained measured and calm as he prepared to speak.

"Everything okay?" Takoda's voice interrupted the stillness. Her book now rested beside her on the couch, her posture leaning forward slightly. The tilt of her head revealed a mix of curiosity and discomfort, though even she seemed unsure of its source.

Riichi hesitated briefly before giving a small nod. "Eileen informed me of possible Golden Dawn activity in Washington," he said evenly. "I'll need to leave soon."

Takoda's lips parted, her brow knitting in surprise before her demeanor altered slightly, concern softening her features. "Tomorrow?" she asked, her voice carrying a subdued edge.

"Probably," he replied, his tone composed, though the faintest change in his stance hinted at the discomfort he couldn't entirely suppress.

Takoda leaned back slightly, the tightness in her chest spreading as the reality of his departure pressed against her. She had always known his time here was temporary, but the finality of it struck with unexpected force. Her attention remained on him, his silhouette framed by the muted glow of the streetlights outside. Something in his posture felt different—less rigid, more weighted—and it made her pulse stumble. Pressing her palms gently against her thighs, she tried to anchor herself.

Why does this bother me so much? she wondered, frustration simmering at the edges of her thoughts. For the past two weeks, she had grown accustomed to his presence—the quiet rhythm of him moving through the house, the steady sense of clarity he brought to her restless energy. Now, the thought of him leaving felt like losing a connection she hadn't even realized she depended on.

She swallowed hard, her gaze dropping as her fingers toyed absently with the corner of her book. "I see," she said quietly, her tone carefully even, though it lacked its usual ease.

Neither of them spoke again, but the air around them seemed denser, layered with emotions they both refused to acknowledge. The silence stretched on, charged and unresolved, like a threshold neither was ready to step across.

***

The night settled deeper, the quiet in the Airbnb thick with a tension that hadn't been there before. The reality of Riichi's impending departure pulsed in the charged silence, unspoken but unavoidable. Takoda sat perched on the edge of her bed, her attention locked on the long, narrow box propped against the wall. She had been weighing this decision all evening, teetering on the brink of action. At last, she stood, releasing a slow breath as she lifted the box and carried it into the living room.

Crossing her legs as she settled on the couch, she carefully placed the box across her lap. Her focus shifted briefly to Riichi, who occupied the armchair, his posture upright and unwavering. Clearing her throat, she leaned forward slightly, breaking the heavy quiet. "I've been meaning to give you this," she said, her voice firm, though the faint tremor in her hands as they rested on the box betrayed her nerves.

Riichi's attention dropped to the box, his brow furrowing slightly as curiosity flickered across his features. Takoda motioned for him to join her on the couch. Unflinchingly, he rose and crossed the room with his characteristic fastidiousness. The couch shifted under his weight as he sat beside her, the closeness sending a ripple of awareness through her senses. She pushed it aside, anchoring her focus on the box she extended toward him.

"Here," she said, nodding at it. "Open it."

Riichi accepted the box with care, his fingers skimming the edges with a reverence she hadn't expected. As he removed the lid, the katana's sheath came into view. The dark leather wrapping on the handle was adorned with intricate detailing, a testament to its craftsmanship and the thought behind it. Even without drawing the blade, the weapon exuded precision and intent.

Takoda cleared her throat, her hands clasping together in her lap as her gaze darted away briefly. "I asked Rowan to help me choose it," she said, her voice softer now. "I thought… you might need it."

Riichi's fingers brushed along the hilt, tracing its contours as though committing every inch to memory. He drew the blade partially from its sheath, the quiet rasp of steel against leather breaking the silence. The polished metal reflected the dim light, its edge gleaming with an almost otherworldly sharpness. For a few seconds, he simply observed it, his expression impossible to read. Then, with care, he returned the blade to its sheath and placed the box carefully on the table in front of them.

When his eyes returned to hers, his voice was quieter than she'd ever heard it, layered with a sincerity that made her chest clench. "This… means more than I can express," he said. "Thank you."

Takoda gave a small shrug, though the nervous curve of her smile revealed her struggle to appear nonchalant. "It's nothing," she murmured, her gaze drifting away. "I just thought it would suit you."

The silence between them shifted, no longer awkward but heavy with undeclared depth. Riichi's typically guarded expression softened, and when his eyes held hers, the intensity in his look made her heart stutter. The space separating them felt narrower, as though the room itself had subtly drawn them closer together.

Riichi leaned forward slightly, his movements deliberate and measured. Takoda's breath caught as it became clear she wasn't the only one closing the distance. Her pulse raced, the warmth of his presence enveloping her senses, blurring everything else. She could feel the faint heat of his breath as her eyes lowered, drawn to his lips.

For one electrifying heartbeat, the gap separating them ceased to exist.

Then, as if jolted by the same realization, they both stopped. Riichi was the first to retreat, his jaw clenching briefly as he turned his attention to the katana resting on the table. Takoda leaned back as well, her hands pressing into her lap as if to steady herself. Her heart hammered in her chest, a flush creeping up her neck as she scrambled to find anything to say. Riichi cleared his throat softly, the sound breaking the charged silence and tethering them both in the moment's awkwardness.

"I—" she began, her voice barely audible. She hesitated, her fingers twisting the fabric of her pants. "I didn't mean to make things... complicated."

Riichi's head lifted sharply, his gaze locking onto hers. "You didn't," he said firmly, his voice low but resolute. "It's not... one-sided."

The admission hung in the air between them, igniting emotions neither had been ready to face. Takoda's lips parted, her breath catching as his words sank in. "It's not?" she asked softly, her voice carrying a mix of hesitation and curiosity.

"No," Riichi replied, his tone steady but quieter now, each word considered. "It's not."

Her pulse quickened at the certainty in his response, a mix of relief and tension rippling through her. Just for a second, she couldn't find the words. Her attention dipped briefly to her lap as she tucked a stray strand of hair behind her ear. "Okay," she murmured, a faint, nervous smile tugging at her lips. "Good."

Riichi leaned back against the couch, though the guarded edge to his expression remained. His eyes shifted to the katana on the table before returning to her. "Thank you for this," he said, his voice quiet but sincere. "And... for everything else."

"You're welcome," Takoda replied, her voice soft yet genuine. She stood, smoothing her hands against her thighs. "I should get some sleep," she added, taking a step toward her room. "Big day tomorrow."

"Yes," Riichi said, his tone measured, though his gaze stayed on her as she walked away. "Goodnight, Takoda."

She paused briefly at her door, glancing back over her shoulder. "Goodnight, Riichi."

As the door clicked shut behind her, the quiet returned, heavier than before. Riichi leaned forward, his elbows resting on his knees as his fingers traced the hilt of the katana. His jaw tensed briefly before he released a slow breath, his thoughts churning around the significance of what he had admitted—and the uncertainty of where it would lead.

***

The morning air carried a fragile stillness, amplifying even the faintest sounds. Riichi stood by the doorway, his duffel bag slung over one shoulder, the katana box balanced in his other hand. Takoda stood a few steps away, her arms loosely folded, her expression composed though her eyes hinted at an emotion she didn't voice. The reality of his departure sat uncomfortably in the tension, heavy and undeniable.

"Well," Takoda said, breaking the silence, "looks like you're ready to go."

Riichi inclined his head, his focus steady but touched with an unusual pause. "Yes," he replied, adjusting the strap of the bag on his shoulder. His lips parted as though he were about to say more, his jaw clenching briefly before he continued. "I wanted to thank you. Not just for the katana, but for... everything you've done these past two weeks. I won't forget it."

"You don't have to thank me, Riichi," she replied, her smile faint but genuine. She paused, her attention dropping briefly to the floor before she looked up to meet his eyes again. "I'm just glad I could do something that mattered."

Riichi gave a slight nod, his eyes growing warmer as his focus held hers for a few seconds longer. "You've done more than you realize," he said, his voice quieter now, the sincerity in his words unmistakable.

Her chest tightened at the depth of his words, and she shifted subtly, her fingers trailing along her arms as though to steady herself. "Safe travels," she murmured, her voice composed despite the ache blooming within her.

"And you," Riichi replied, his attention holding hers for a heartbeat longer than she anticipated. "Take care of yourself, Takoda."

The way he spoke her name, with understated warmth, sent a quiet ripple through her, but she maintained her composure, offering him a small nod. She remained rooted in the doorway as he turned toward the exit, his steps measured as he moved outside into the crisp morning air.

Takoda stayed where she was, her arms falling loosely to her sides as she watched him descend the steps. The distance dividing them widened with every step, yet her focus stayed unwavering. Her chest tightened further, as though an invisible thread between them stretched taut with his departure. Riichi, too, felt the gravity of the parting pressing against his resolve, a restlessness chipping at his usual discipline.

At the sidewalk, he paused. His grip firmed briefly on the strap of his bag as the past two weeks played through his thoughts—the shared silences, her calming presence, and the unintentional way she had shaken the control he depended on. He exhaled quietly, the realization crystallizing. *This is the right time.*

Turning back, he retraced his steps, his movements purposeful but unhurried. Takoda straightened instinctively as he approached, her pulse quickening, though she couldn't pinpoint why. When he stopped just in front of her, he set the katana box and duffel bag down carefully, his full attention now fixed on her.

For a beat, he simply looked at her, his expression gentler than she'd ever seen it. Then, stepping forward, he pulled her into an embrace. His arms settled around her securely yet without hesitation, the heat of his presence grounding her even as it sent her heart racing.

"There's something here," he said quietly, his voice low but resolute near her ear. "Even if I don't know what it is yet."

Takoda's breath hitched at his words, her chest constricting as her hands rose hesitantly to rest against his back. "I feel it too," she murmured, her voice barely audible.

Riichi pulled back just enough to meet her eyes, his dark gaze unguarded, searching hers for a fleeting heartbeat. Then, leaning closer, he pressed a light kiss to her cheek. The touch was brief but intentional, and it left her breathless, the sensation lingering long after he stepped away.

"Until next time," he said softly, his tone carrying the intensity of unspoken promises.

Takoda's lips parted, a tentative smile curving as she met his eyes. "Until next time," she replied, her voice quiet but certain.

Riichi stepped back, retrieved his bag and katana box, and turned toward the street. Takoda stayed rooted in the doorway, her fingers trailing lightly against her cheek where his lips had landed. Her chest felt heavy, yet warmth unfurled within her, steady and undeniable.

As she watched him disappear down the street, she exhaled slowly, her lips curving into a faint smile. *See you again,* she thought, the words offering comfort as the morning light spilled across the pavement. At last, she stepped back inside, closing the door gently behind her, the memory burned into her mind like an unshakable warmth.

Acknowledgements

To my amazing daughter, your love, encouragement, and belief in me mean more than words could ever express. This book exists because of you.

To my incredible friends who have cheered me on every step of the way—thank you for your unwavering support, kind words, and for believing in me even when the journey felt uncertain. Your encouragement gave me the strength to keep going.

To my amazing ARC team, thank you for your dedication, feedback, and support in bringing this book into the world. A special thank you to Barb S., Mike D., Cassidy B., and Jessica F.—your insights and encouragement have been invaluable.

And to my readers—thank you for opening your hearts to my stories. Your enthusiasm inspires me to continue writing, dreaming, and creating.

This book is for all of you.

About the Author

Jayne Anderson is an author and storyteller inspired by books, music, movies, and the timeless tales of world cultures, mythology, and religions. A former social studies and reading teacher, Jayne channels her creativity into crafting meaningful stories that celebrate individuality and imagination. Now a mother, entrepreneur, and writer, she lives in Pennsylvania with her daughter, who inspires her daily with her boundless curiosity.

To learn more, join the Sin & Salvation series community:
https://www.facebook.com/groups/paranormalromancesinandsalvation

The Fallen's

Holly
Scotland
1691-1715
Rowan
Ireland
1819-1847
Alder
Germany
1917-1944
Reed
France
1766-1794
Vine
Massachusetts
1668-1712
Birch
Arizona
1657-1685
Ash
Portugal
1729-1755
Oak
Roman Empire
47 C.E.-79 C.E.
Ivy
Peru
1520-1546
N
W
E
S

Roots

Every Fallen's journey begins long before their transformation. This map traces the origins of the Fallen across the globe, revealing the diverse heritages, cultures, and lives they left behind. Like the roots of a mighty tree, their pasts ground them, shaping their identities and their paths toward redemption.